FRAGMENTS OF A LIFE STORY

THE COLLECTED SHORT WRITINGS OF DENTON WELCH

Maurice Denton Welch trained at the Goldsmith School of Art, for his first ambition was to be a painter. However, his training was cut short at the age of twenty when he was knocked off his bicycle. The accident, from which he never fully recovered, drove him in upon the resources of his imagination, and in 1942 a new, literary career was launched with the publication in *Horizon* of an account of a meeting six years previously with Walter Sickert.

Between 1942 and his death in 1948, at the age of thirty-three, in addition to producing paintings of startling originality and beauty he went on to write three novels, 200,000 words of *Journals*, some sixty short stories and fragments and a large number of poems. His astonishing achievement was summed up a year after his death by John Lehmann, when he wrote in *The Penguin New Writing*, 'Denton Welch was lucky in finding the success he needed to develop his great gifts with the publication of his first book; but unlucky in meeting with an accident that not only eventually killed him but kept his experience within certain narrow limits. The danger in his case is that an often repeated pattern underlying his stories should come to be considered as his essential territory and contribution; let us remember, rather, the astonishing feeling for words, the incredibly sensitive response to atmosphere, the rapidly growing subtlety of characterization which, under other circumstances, with normal opportunities, might have brought within his power a range of achievement as great and diverse as any mature master of this century.'

Two of Denton Welch's novels, *Maiden Voyage* and *A Voice Through a Cloud*, together with *The Journals of Denton Welch* and the biography *Denton Welch: The Making of a Writer* by Michael De-la-Noy are all published in Penguin.

Michael De-la-Noy was born in Hessle, Yorkshire, and educated at Bedford School. He spent some years as a reporter and feature writer, and in 1983 published his first biography, *Elgar: The Man*. This was followed in 1984, to wide critical acclaim, by *Denton Welch: The Making of a Writer* (Viking and Penguin). He is also the editor of *The Journals of Denton Welch*. He contributes reviews to *Books & Bookmen* and the *Spectator*. His most recent book is *The Honours System*.

DENTON WELCH

FRAGMENTS OF A LIFE STORY

The Collected Short Writings
of Denton Welch

EDITED WITH AN INTRODUCTION BY
MICHAEL DE-LA-NOY

A KING PENGUIN
PUBLISHED BY PENGUIN BOOKS

Penguin Books Ltd, Harmondsworth, Middlesex, England
Viking Penguin Inc., 40 West 23rd Street, New York, New York 10010, U.S.A.
Penguin Books Australia Ltd, Ringwood, Victoria, Australia
Penguin Books Canada Limited, 2801 John Street, Markham, Ontario, Canada L3R 1B4
Penguin Books (N.Z.) Ltd, 182–190 Wairau Road, Auckland 10, New Zealand

This collection first published 1987
This collection © University of Texas, 1987
Introduction and notes copyright © Michael De-la-Noy, 1987

The stories contained in this collection were first published as follows: 'Sickert at St Peter's', *Horizon*, 1942; 'The Barn', *New Writing and Daylight*, 1943–4; 'At Sea', *English Story*, 1944; 'When I was Thirteen', *Horizon*, 1944; 'The Judas Tree', *The Penguin New Writing*, 1945; 'Strange Discoveries', *Vogue*, 1945; 'The Coffin on the Hill', *Life and Letters Today*, 1946; 'The Trout Stream', *Cornhill*, 1948; 'The Diamond Badge' (first part), *The Penguin New Writing*, 1949; 'Evergreen Seaton-Leverett, *Orpheus 2*, 1949; 'A Fragment of a Life Story', *Horizon*, 1949; 'Brave and Cruel', 'The Fire in the Wood', 'Leaves from a Young Person's Notebook' and 'Narcissus Bay', *Brave and Cruel and Other Stories*, Hamish Hamilton, 1949; 'The Diamond Badge' (complete), 'The Earth's Crust', 'Ghosts', 'The Hateful Word', 'Memories of a Vanished Period', 'A Novel Fragment', 'A Party' and 'A Picture in the Snow', *A Last Sheaf*, John Lehmann, 1951; 'Touchett's Party', *Chance*, 1953; 'At Sir Moorcalm Lalli's', *Contemporary Review*, 1974. All remaining stories first published in this collection, 1987.

Made and printed in Great Britain by
Richard Clay, Ltd, Bungay, Suffolk

Filmset in Monophoto Sabon

Except in the United States of America,
this book is sold subject to the condition
that it shall not, by way of trade or otherwise,
be lent, re-sold, hired out, or otherwise circulated
without the publisher's prior consent in any form of
binding or cover other than that in which it is
published and without a similar condition
including this condition being imposed
on the subsequent purchaser

CONTENTS

Introduction	9
Editor's Note	13
I Can Remember	15
In the Vast House	69
Narcissus Bay	74
At Sea	80
The Happiest Time	96
The Coffin on the Hill	98
I First Began to Write	109
The Barn	111
The Trout Stream	119
Mr Clarke	147
At Sir Moorcalm Lalli's	149
Mrs Hockey	155
A Child Meets Church and State and Poetry in Strange Places: Lady Astor	158
An Afternoon with Jeanne	162
When I was Thirteen	169
John Trevor	185
Ghosts	193

THREE FRAGMENTS:

When I Lie Awake	197
In the Autumn Weather	199
The Secret Life	201

Roger Saw the Man	202
The Earth's Crust	205
The Youth Rang the Bell	213
A Novel Fragment	218
A Party	284
Full Circle	297
The Judas Tree	304
In Brixham Harbour	313
Strange Discoveries	317
Sickert at St Peter's	322
A Picture in the Snow	329
A Fragment of a Life Story	340
Alex Fairburn	353
Evergreen Seaton-Leverett	362
Leaves from a Young Person's Notebook	373

THREE FRAGMENTS:

Faces at the Stage Door	383
Fat Woman Sleeping in a Wood	384
Cupids from a Wedgwood Jar from a Bartolozzi Print from a Drawing by Lady Di Beauclerk	385

Touchett's Party	387
The War Breaks Out	398
Velvet	400
A Dream of Vestals	405
The Fire in the Wood	407
Fear	443
Man in a Garden	446

CONTENTS

A Morning with the Versatile Peer, Lord Berners, in the 'Ancient Seat of Learning'	448
A Mews Flat in the Country	451
The Cottage after Dark	454
Brave and Cruel	456
Anna Dillon	519
Memories of a Vanished Period	529
Roger Lay on the Cliff	541
Constance, Lady Willet	543
The Diamond Badge	551
The Hateful Word	572

THREE FRAGMENTS:

Weekend	585
Amy Lechworth	589
Lady Gertrude	592
A Postscript	593
Bibliography	595

INTRODUCTION

DENTON WELCH WAS TWENTY-FIVE WHEN HE FIRST decided to write his autobiography. 'Through the months of 1940 I plugged at it,' he wrote in his *Journals*. 'Then it suddenly died on me.' But at the end of that year, inspired by reading J. R. Ackerley's *Hindoo Holiday*, he again picked up his pencil and school exercise-book and began his first autobiographical novel, *Maiden Voyage*. The abandoned autobiography, describing his early childhood in China and England, has survived and constitutes the first chapter in this miscellany of stories, memoirs and articles.

The extent to which most or even all these pieces should be regarded as autobiographical is open to debate; the line between fact and fiction in his work is often as narrow as any writer could have drawn it. Some of the pieces, such as the accounts of his memorable meetings with Lady Astor and Lord Berners, are so obviously journalistic that their autobiographical status is beyond dispute. Others, demonstrably based on his own experience, are dramatic reconstructions of real events in fictional form. 'A Fragment of a Life Story', for example, describes an emotional visit to his doctor's house one day in 1940; in reality there were many such scenes, spread over several months in 1937.

If strictly factual records such as 'I Can Remember' and *I Left My Grandfather's House* are compared with 'The Coffin on the Hill' and 'The Barn', students of the creative process can see how Denton Welch used childhood incidents, dwelt on for many years, to produce works of fiction. When recounting the river trip in 'I Can Remember', he recalls that he dropped his doll overboard by accident. However, in the fictionalized account, 'The Coffin on the Hill', he dramatizes the event: the narrator drops his doll into the river intentionally, as a kind of sacrifice. In 'I Can Remember' he writes of the time he stayed in the Oxfordshire village of Benson, and encountered a young tramp who asked to spend the night in the barn. That evening the tramp slept alone. Later, when using the same incident as a basis for 'The Barn', for psychosexual effect he has his young narrator curl up in the straw with the stranger.

Another tramp, this time an unattractive one, entered his imagination ten years after he had written a clearly factual account in his *Journals* of a walking tour in the West Country (published separately in 1958 as *I Left My Grandfather's House*). On the walking tour, he spent a night in an outhouse, hoping to be kept company by the farmer's sixteen-year-old son, who eventually went home to bed. But in his story 'Full Circle' he has the youth cuddle down beside him, only to find in the morning that his companion has been transformed into a strange old man, 'grey and seamed and filthy'. Having been rejected by the boy in real life, Denton Welch himself rejects the boy by turning him into an unappealing figure in his fiction. The theme of rejection is a recurring one in his work, as it was in his life. Although he shaped and refined the ingredients of his fiction, he remained always faithful to the facts of his childhood and youth; no writer has mirrored his life in his work so transparently, nor left us such poignant evidence of this integral connection.

The most cursory examination of Denton Welch's manuscripts reveals the amazing fluency with which he wrote. Often he would first jot down a draft of a story in order to capture an idea, and later expand the germ into a full-length treatment; 'A Fragment of a Life Story', for instance, was first drafted in the *Journals*. A few of the stories, such as 'The Barn' and 'The Fire in the Wood', were rewritten and entirely reshaped, sometimes several times. But the majority of his prose went straight down on the page, with only the very occasional substitution of a word.

The reason why a number of his pieces are unfinished must remain a matter of guesswork; these fragments are often full of interesting and perceptive writing. (Several of the *Journal* entries are also unfinished and float off in mid-sentence.) In the space of just eight years he wrote practically everything published here, as well as 200,000 words of the *Journals* and three novels, a truly astonishing achievement when considered in conjunction with his output as a painter and his precarious state of health. He was undoubtedly racing against time. Added to the natural tendency of his mind to flit from one subject or project to another, he also seems to have been unsure at times whether to record the literal facts of his life that fascinated him, especially those of his childhood, or whether to fictionalize these facts; torn between conflicting ideas of what he was trying to achieve, he often seems simply to have given up.

The two previous collections of Denton Welch's short stories, comprising twenty-one pieces in this volume, have both been out of print for many years. The first, *Brave and Cruel*, was passed for press by him not long before he died on 30 December 1948. It was published on 7 January 1949. The second, *A Last Sheaf*, was published by John Lehmann in 1951. In the present collection a conscious decision has been made to include all unpublished and out-of-print prose, irrespective of intrinsic merit, including those pieces which, for one reason or another, were left unfinished.

To attempt to explain in an introduction the genesis of nearly sixty pieces of writing, several the length of a novella, would place a pointless burden on the reader's memory; instead, at the beginning of each story, I have contributed a brief note identifying, when possible, the characters, the location and the period of Denton Welch's life to which it relates. And rather than place the stories in order of composition, I have arranged them in autobiographical sequence. It is a measure of the extent to which he was an autobiographical writer that the task of matching the incidents described with documentary evidence has been a relatively easy one. Since a number of people he knew well crop up in several stories – Eric Oliver, who lived with him for the last four years of his life, Evelyn Sinclair, whom he knew for sixteen years, first as his landlady and later as his housekeeper, and Francis Streeten, one of his most eccentric friends – I have identified them fully only on their first appearance, rather than weary the reader with repetition.

A brief word about Denton Welch's life and career may perhaps be useful for those readers new to his work. He was born on 29 March 1915 in Shanghai, of an English father and an American mother. From the age of nine until he was fourteen he was educated at a school in London and at St Michael's, Uckfield. He was then sent to Repton in Derbyshire where his two brothers, Bill (born in 1908) and Paul (born in 1913), also went to school. In 1935, when he was twenty, he was knocked off his bicycle by a car and suffered appalling injuries as a result of which, thirteen years later, he died. He published his first novel, *Maiden Voyage*, in 1943; his second, *In Youth is Pleasure*, followed in 1945; and *A Voice Through a Cloud*, which was unfinished when he died, was published in 1950. The novels, together with *The Journals of Denton Welch* and *I Left My Grandfather's House*, have all recently been reissued, and the publication of his collected short writings now ensures that his complete prose works are in print for the first time.

Michael De-la-Noy

EDITOR'S NOTE

THIS EDITION CONTAINS ALL OF DENTON WELCH'S known shorter writings and fragments. Those published in his lifetime and in *Brave and Cruel* were revised by him and edited by his publishers. Those published after his death, some of which he had revised, were similarly edited by their respective publishers. The remainder exist in unrevised manuscript and contain numerous misspellings and ambiguities in punctuation which he would certainly have corrected had he had the opportunity. In preparing this edition my aim has been to present a text which is intelligible and consistent with the first of these categories.

Titles of stories passed for press by Denton Welch are his own. Except where otherwise stated, titles of the other stories have been devised either by myself or by former editors. Details of previous publication, if any, are given at the head of each story. Further bibliographical information can be found at the end of the book.

M.D.

I CAN REMEMBER

I

I WAS BORN IN CHINA BUT I AM NOT CHINESE. MY FATHER was English and my mother American; her family had been early settlers in Massachusetts and we had old glass and silver and china of theirs and some lovely christening robes, quite yellow, with lace like spun milk. There was also the great tablecloth we used at Christmas, covered with sheaves of arrows and eagles and peacocks and palm trees, inscribed with the names of four generations.

I think that one of the first things I remember is the summer we spent in the Diamond Mountains in Korea. There was a lake with petrified logs in it and amber and the whole ground was littered with sparkling quartz. I have never forgotten the thrill of finding this lovely crystal. I treasured most the spikes of treacle black.

I can remember the strange hats the Koreans wore and the terror I felt when in a car we crossed a stream on two planks.

One day, when I ran down to breakfast, my eldest brother was excitedly telling how a bear had been seen on the road through the forest above the house. I hardly dared venture out that day for fear of being hugged to death.

My two brothers would bathe naked in the rock pools. They looked beautiful against the trees and sky, but at three I had a strong sense of shame and was too self-conscious to join them – besides, I loved to wander alone in search of precious crystal and amber.

The next spring we came to England. This was not long after the end of the First War and I shall never forget my astonishment at seeing England intact and undamaged. I had known there was a war between England and Germany and could not understand why my parents wanted to go back to a country that must surely be nothing but a mass of gaunt and smoking ruins.

First we went to Frinton and stayed in a house on the front

which had been lent to us. There were crackled green tiles in the hall. I could never understand how the crackle was done. Upstairs in the nursery was a tiny toy butcher's shop, which fascinated me; there were beautifully carved joints of meat laid out on a marble slab, a curious subject for a child's toy.

Our nurse gave us cod liver oil and malt after lunch and supper, and in this way stopped us from having the two sweets we were allowed a day. She said the malt was just as good.

I can remember finding myself at the bottom of my bed under the clothes and screaming terribly because I could not find the way out. I thought I should die, but my nurse came; she seemed an angel of goodness for once.

The wind whistled like a ghost round the four corners of this house and I can see myself sitting amongst the cushions in the dark drawing-room and feeling terrible mournfulness.

Soon a friend of my mother's came to stay with us, bringing her daughter who was, I suppose, about sixteen. The friend's name was Phyl. I hated her and called her Fidgety Phyl, as I had been told that this was a very evil person. Whenever she saw me downstairs she would send me up to the nursery, and I can never forgive the time she sent me to have tea with the nurse when I had permission to come down. Everyone seemed to obey Phyl.

Her daughter was quite different. I loved and admired her for her talent. She painted a wonderful picture of pansies on a vase and put real silver paint on the vase. She made a handkerchief box for her mother which I thought far too lovely for such a woman. It was covered in pink taffeta and lace, and had marvellous cherries and leaves in velvet and satin all stuffed and raised up in three dimensions.

One night the grown-ups and older children had a fancy-dress party. I was allowed down in my pyjamas and saw my eldest brother, who must have been about eleven, dressed as a cave man in a leopard-skin, carrying a big club with which he hit my mother hard. There was also another boy, dressed as a girl, with curls painted in black on his forehead and cheeks. I thought he looked very depraved.

My brothers used to ride on ponies while we were here and I would follow at a distance with my mother. She had a mustard-yellow hat and scarf which I thought utterly spoiled her beauty. I implored her not to wear the dirty colour, but she persisted and now it is one of my own favourite colours.

One day our nurse took my second brother Paul and myself to the police station to inquire about a lapis lazuli carving my mother had lost. I was terrified, I thought that I was being taken there to prison because they believed I had hidden it. I was amazed at their barbarity in taking me off without even asking me privately at home. I could not believe that my mother meant me to go, but the nurse insisted and teased me all the way there. She was a wicked woman.

On the beach there was a great round mine, left from the war. I was told that the fuse had been taken out, but I felt that it still might explode and was in a fever when my brother used to go up and hit it with his spade.

We found little miniature flat fish and crabs on the beach, which I loved. Unlike most fishermen I tried to catch the smallest, not the largest.

At Christmas we went to my grandfather, who lived in Sussex. The house was strange; it had had many additions and alterations. There was a miniature grand staircase, as there is on ships from the deck to the saloon. I thought the furniture very ugly, but I loved the coloured window at the top of the stairs; every pane was a different colour and one looked through each one in turn at a garden transformed.

This last was trim and intimate, with lawns and roses and a wonderful tree called Black Jack's apple tree after a famous local smuggler. It was hung with mistletoe and my mother told me that this was the Druids' sacred plant, and how they cut it with their golden sickles. Then there was the hot-house for the early grapes and the greenhouse for the grapes and peaches. How I loved the hot scented steam that passed for air in these houses.

In the bath one night my face flannel went down the waste hole. I thought it had sailed out to sea to vanish for ever. The next morning I saw, – lying in the grating at the bottom of the drainpipe – my flannel. I rushed up to my mother with it, expecting her to be delighted, but she said it was dirty and must be thrown away – I thought this very wanton.

On another day I had my first introduction to paper money. Paul and I were building little houses out of twigs and mud and leaves, for caterpillars to live in, and when I found a piece of paper on the grass, light and crisp, I thought it would make an excellent roof. Just then my grandfather passed and, stooping down, saw what I had used. He picked the pound note up and spoilt my house. He asked me where I'd found it and when I told him he said he must have dropped it. I could not believe that it was really money. I thought money had to be precious like gold or silver.

My aunt had a new kitten at this time and I loved it and I racked my brains for the most lovely name there was. At last I decided on Yellow Rose Bud; pink roses, I felt, were prettier, but something told me that yellow ones were rarer and more sublime and I knew that my mother, when she picked roses, only liked the buds. My aunt, with great kindness I now realize, for ever afterwards called her cat Yellow Rose Bud.

We stayed with my grandfather until late spring; it was then that I went to my first fair.

Our nurse made Paul and myself kneel down at our beds to say our prayers in the early afternoon, so that when we came back from the fair we could get straight into bed. I thought it very unnatural and hated doing it. When it was over she led us to the common, where the merry-go-round was in full swing. I hated it all and carried nothing away but the impression of grotesque squalor which haunts me even now in circuses and fairs. I can remember too the first time I was taken to a musical comedy – how the rows of kicking girls appeared so sinister to me.

When my mother had finally settled my eldest brother at school, we left my grandfather for Canada, where we spent the summer on a ranch as the guests of some friends. There were great maple trees everywhere and a herd of Jersey cows whose cream was wonderful. Every morning we started breakfast in the cold dining-room with oranges cut in half and sugared. I loved this particular way of eating them for some reason. Then for lunch there would often be the wonderful lemon pie topped with white of egg and rich cream which my brother and I were so seldom allowed to touch. We would watch with terrible envy our nurse eating it while we toyed discontentedly with our rice pudding. In the drawing-room there was a copy of the Venus de Milo. I thought it very ugly and asked my mother if she knew what the arms had been like. She said, 'Perhaps Venus was holding up a mirror.' I thought that she ought, if anything, to be holding up her dress.

We used to go for long walks with our nurse, who was always whistling and murmuring, 'I'm for ever blowing bubbles, pretty bubbles in the air.' She said she thought it was the cleverest song in the world. She used to take us to the dairy on the ranch where the woman made the most delicious cakes. They were dark and rich with chocolate and iced with Hypolite or marshmallow. Then there was angel food, pure white like bread.

She had a daughter called Sally who taught my brother and myself American or Canadian slang. This made my mother laugh. Every day we had maple syrup too and hard sandy chunks of maple sugar. There was a lake to bathe in, with a boat house that I longed to live in always. If you wandered up the hill, pushing through the bushes, you came to the ruins of a house that had been burnt. I found a lump of melted glass, quite purple, like an amethyst.

II

We left Canada. By 1921 we were back in Shanghai again, in our house with its long, heavy arched verandas aflame with Virginia creeper. Inside it was cool and lofty, the floors smelt of polish and the drawing-room was scattered with baskets of flowers that friends had sent to welcome my mother on her return.

Now settled in a time of living almost entirely in myself, the last stage of infancy, a quiet time of playing with my brother in the garden, building houses in the bushes and hiding in the branches of the camphor tree. We would ask the cook for eggs and sugar, then would rush out with them to the summer house and whip them together into a honey-coloured froth. This we would then eat with outward relish, but I did not like it really, it revolted me a little. We had a swing shaped like a boat; it would fly up at one end into the scented bushes, and one was lost for a second in the pink froth, to be torn out again like a rushing wind.

At the bottom of the garden were the coach-house and stables, over which the mafoo, or coachman, lived, for at this time my father still kept a most antique carriage which had belonged to my grandmother; it used to stand next to the cars, one open and one closed, looking like a broken-down aristocrat trying to keep pace with two smart parvenus.

I adored the carriage; it was our special vehicle. My brother and I looked on it as almost our own. One day when a mouse ran out from under the seat I was almost mad with excitement. The leather was so cracked with sun and weather and so polished that it seemed to resemble some ancient lacquer.

Oh the joy of starting out for the afternoon with the old mafoo in his green braided coat with many capes, and his little conical hat. Girlie, the white horse of twenty-three, would be between the shafts and our nurse would be sitting in the middle of the back seat, the aromatic and fusty mole-skin rug over her knees, keeping a nervous eye on Paul and myself as we stood upon the steps on each side pretending to be firemen. For this purpose we always would insist on taking our topees with us, winter or summer, so that we should have something which vaguely resembled a fireman's helmet. And it was lucky that we did, for one day, in a frenzy of excitement, my brother fell off the step, while we were in motion, and landed on his head; he was not hurt a bit, and after the first shock I thoroughly appreciated this artistic touch to our fireman act.

It was about this time that another accident happened which I remember well. Paul and I had our coats on and were waiting in the hall for nurse to take us out for our walk. We were playing with a walking-stick of my father's; it was made of flexible steel and bound with polished leather. After a little while there was an argument and, still no nurse appearing, we each gripped one end of the stick and pulled, trying to gain possession of the whole stick. I somehow mounted the stairs step by step, pulling hard; then there seemed to be a deadlock and, suspecting that my brother meant suddenly to let go, I leant forward so that he should not have the satisfaction of seeing me fall over backwards.

He let go, I overbalanced and fell headlong downstairs on to a corner of the iron radiator.

There was blood, great oozing drops of it seeping into the terracotta carpet – I lay half stunned, a great cut on my forehead. My brother screamed and nurse came rushing down, enveloped me and carried me, still dripping, up the stairs, my brother running at her side shrieking, 'Will he die? Will he die?' It did not hurt; my mind was like a clear pale page on which these happenings were written.

Nurse laid me on the sofa in my mother's bedroom and rang for basins and hot water; the doctor was fetched. Soon I lay still and peaceful, my head a satisfying mass of bandages. I felt most pale and interesting. My chastened brother hung about the sofa and nurse seemed almost human for once. Soon I heard the wheels of the car on the drive. There was the opening of the front door and a noise of voices – then, swiftly, I heard my mother running up the stairs. She kissed me many times and laughed and smiled and brought me all her jewels and trinkets to play with; she knew that I loved these winking bright things better than anything else and trusted me implicitly to take care of them.

Soon after this I had strange dreams – I floated slowly down the stairs, I skimmed their surface. They were built round three sides of the hall, and at the second flight I saw my mother. She lay by the telephone, in a heap, her hair over her face and she was crying. I could not stop; I glided by into the horror of the dark hall.

The banisters of these stairs seemed built for sliding down. They were large and ample; turning the corners was horribly exciting. At the bottom, fixed to the pedestal, was a sort of pagoda of bells, of all sizes and tones, used for calling us to meals. The fun of striking this on landing was tremendous.

In the well of the stairs hung a full-length portrait of my mother, at a desk with flowers and pictures on a wall behind her. She sat there for ever with a long string of ivory beads round her neck.

Another part of the house that I loved was the attic. This was large and divided into four rooms, two large and two small. In the first large room my eldest brother had at one time had boxing lessons with some other friends. It was not kept locked and so was comparatively commonplace. We used sometimes to try sliding down the stairs on a tray and I always remember the time I tried to pick myself up by sitting on the tray and pulling at the two handles on either side of me.

It was the other three rooms that were so exciting. They were always kept locked except when my mother went into them for some reason. Sometimes I would hear her in there and would rush up so that I could be let in too. One passed first through a little dark room in which was kept an old dressing-case filled with Victorian jewellery which had belonged to my grandmother.

There were strange, thick, gold bracelets, a great ring with a fleur-de-lys on it in fire-opal, a mourning brooch of jet and pearls, a long necklace of white sapphires fitted into a chain; scent bottles, chatelaines, vinaigrettes and belts of cast silver. The whole case seemed filled with treasure to me, and I never tired of undoing the little leather boxes and unwrapping the faint-mauve cotton wool.

Also in this room were the white elephants, the wedding presents that my mother did not like: grotesque carved blackwood tables and chests.

Through this was the other big room. Trunks were ranged all round the walls. In these were stored all the small relics of the past that I loved so: the yellowed christening robes, a flowered waistcoat of grey satin, little wax dolls, a card case of cut velvet and another of tortoiseshell and gold, a strange old cribbage set in ivory and satinwood, the picture cards all having feet instead of the two heads of today. There were the old tablecloths and shawls, the fans, the lace, the miniatures, the wonderful book of flower pictures meticulously painted by my great-grandmother.

The farthest room was a cul-de-sac; in it slumbered a baby's cot and the remnants of a lacquer screen, with curtain rods hung with great wooden rings.

The storeroom downstairs next to the pantry was another locked room and another source of delight. Here were kept rows of earthenware and glass jars, filled with jellies, jams, chutneys and pickles. The tea was in painted boxes lined with silver, and the coffee-grinding machine reared its strange head at the corner of the table.

China and glass were stored here too – I can see now the harlequin set of glasses, one red, one blue, one yellow, one purple, one white, each wreathed with vine leaves, that must have once graced Victorian tennis parties.

At meals my brother and I each had our own utensils, without which we would not eat. They were our christening presents. Each had a silver mug and porringer, a silver knife, fork and spoon. When I went back to China for a year after I had left school, I found my place at table laid with my spoon, my knife and fork – our old cook had told the boy that I would eat with no other.

III

Soon after this I went to my first school. It was a small kindergarten. I shuddered when I heard the sentence and implored my mother not to send me, but she said she was sure I would like it and it would be so nice to learn something. So one morning I was taken with my brother into the Jaws of Hell.

There I was left with some other children and a woman with pale hair. They horrified me. I was given a little desk and the woman with pale hair wrote strange signs in my new book; she said that they were numbers up to nine and would I copy them very nicely underneath? I began laboriously to copy, my heart swelling with the feeling of captivity. When I had got to five I noticed the little dash at the top and, feeling sure that she had made a mistake, I carefully copied it out several times leaving the stroke out. The teacher came up a little later and put them all in, but I hardly believed it to be correct even then.

The next thing we did was to begin making a little church out of match-boxes and coloured paper. This was much more to my taste and I began soon to be thoroughly interested. This lovely church grew in the succeeding days and I will always remember the day that I put the coloured transparent paper in the windows.

I soon began to get fond of Miss W., and from her I learnt many things. Of course there were unhappy times too. There was the terrible day when I came to school with golden sailor buttons on my shirt. One of them became loose and, in the way that children have, I began to push it up one nostril and to gently blow it out again.

Suddenly I sniffed inwards instead of blowing out. The button stuck, I tried to blow, it wouldn't move. I let out a terrible wail, Miss W. rushed up. I told her what had happened and she took me quickly to a room and told me to lie down on the table (I don't know why to this day). Then she must have telephoned my mother for, through my tears and despair, I heard her footsteps and her voice and soon we were both sitting in the car going to the doctor to have the button removed. The situation had improved enormously the moment my mother had appeared. I felt I could bear the fact of having a button in my nose for life if she was with me; now in the car I was almost calm and my mother said, 'Now, darling, let's try once more to blow it down,' but it was no good. So we went to the doctor and I sat in front of the window, and with his little forceps he jerked the button sharply out. Oh the flood of relief, the laughing and tears! I loved the button now and wanted to keep it, but when it had been pulled out the doctor had thrown the little golden ball far out of the high window over the tree tops into the street.

There was another horrible occasion when some of the little girls at the kindergarten were dressed up as gnomes for some play. I arrived late and, seeing these little apparitions, thought that some of my schoolmates had been transformed by a wicked fairy. To make matters worse, these children, seeing how superstitious I was, began to lay strange spells on me. These I did not quite believe, but it was enough to make the day a failure – to feel that at any moment I might – just might – become a toad.

I believed so many things at this time. I believed my toy wristwatch really ticked. I believed the terrible story a friend told me of some children who played truant from school and were stolen by gypsies to be used in a circus. They were skinned, and wolves' hides sewn on instead. She said the nuns had told her this as a warning not to stray from home or play truant from school. I believed that babies were born out of breasts and that just the miracle of being married made them appear.

This summer we went to Wei-hai-wei, which is by the sea. We had taken a house in Half Moon Bay, on the cliffs, with a great apricot tree overshadowing the front. The baths in the house were enormous earthenware kongs, or jars, decorated with patterns of birds in yellow and brown glaze. We had had to leave our nurse behind in Shanghai, as she had fallen in love with a man and wanted to marry him. He afterwards turned out to be married already and my mother told me that our nurse was very unhappy and she had died. I suppose now that she killed herself.

Every day we would take a picnic and our bathing-suits to the beach below and spend the day there. To get to this bay one either walked across the promontory or went round it in the rowing boat. When the sea was rough, I found the passage in the boat very terrifying and would insist on walking by myself through the fields where the peanuts and maize grew, down the deep-cut path with the little rock plants growing between the stones.

Arriving on the beach, I would see the boat rising and falling as they tried to beach it and would feel glad I was not in it. We had a little house of matting made on the beach and in this we would undress and keep our things. After our bathes we would be given two ginger biscuits each – I loved these, and the Huntley & Palmer tin gives pleasure to me even now.

My brother and I had a passion for the shells that we found. We laid them out in wooden boxes on cotton wool. Fan shells were the most rare; they varied from white and pink to deep coral. Sometimes the coral ones were tiny, like a lacquered fingernail.

We would make expeditions to other parts of the coast, sailing and then walking over miles of cushioned thyme and tufted grass. Perhaps we would eat by a wayside shrine, the little painted gods and painted walls washed and faded by the weather.

Once we were taken to a Chinese play. The theatre had been hastily constructed on the beach, near the Chinese town, and as we walked towards it in the evening we passed the salted shark which was lying out to dry in the sun. When it was ready it would be eaten. The play was an exciting pandemonium: terrifying warriors, wonderfully dressed, were standing on tables piled on top of each other; soon one threw himself off and lay as if dead. Another was riding on a fantastic hobby-horse. There was strange, nasal singing and hot scented towels were distributed for the audience to steam their faces in. Here was something old and so conventionalized as to be almost like a religious ceremonial.

The British warships in China would spend much time at Wei-hai-wei, and one day we woke up to see the long grey ships lying in the harbour by the island. My brother was wildly excited and at length persuaded Lara, the handsome Italian boy whom my brother adored and whose parents had a nearby house, to sail out with him to the nearest of the ships. Lara was about seventeen and so much older than Paul. He sailed a boat and rather enjoyed having Paul as a willing slave. They set out secretly the next day, early in the morning. We knew nothing of it until Paul returned at lunch, flushed and happy. By great good luck they had reached the warship safely and the officers had taken them on board and entertained them.

One night we had a most exciting party out of doors. All the grown-ups were to dress as children and the older children as grown-ups. I was only allowed just to go and see the beginning before I went to bed.

The party was being held on an old tennis-court behind the beach. Lanterns were lit on poles all round and there were trestles covered with white cloths and heaped with what I imagined to be delicious food. I tiptoed up to look and to my horror discovered that the food was an elaborate mixture of horrible things. There were great jellyfish on silver platters. Heaps of queer seaweed and sand, decorated with sea urchins, bloated deep-sea fish and a sinister collection of animals in shells. Then there was every sort of berry one had been told not to eat, and fantastic-looking fungus and toadstools heaped in a cake-basket.

This was Lara's grotesque joke. All the real food was hidden under the trestles.

The air was purple and the moon was beginning to shine on the sea. Lara was playing on his flute and I was crying with disappointment that I had to go to bed. I lay in the dark under my mosquito net and looked at the shadow of my toy junk which had red-brown sails and was varnished bright yellow.

I had a strange habit at this time of asking my mother for her signet ring, which I would thread in a lock of my hair, tying it firmly with another. Then I would run along the beach looking for shells or exploring, and as I ran I would feel it bang and bob against my head. My hair was very curly, like my mother's, and I could knot it easily, but one day I lost the ring while I was on the beach. I hunted everywhere. I waited until the tide went out, but I never saw it again. My mother was not very angry, but I missed this toy very much. It was my fetish and talisman.

I would like to smarm my hair down after we had been bathing so that I made a glossy cap. I thought it looked very smart and grown-up like this.

Sometimes when we went out in the hired carriage on the bumpy roads I would pretend to be a very bad-tempered woman called Lady de Courcy. Nothing was ever right for her. I would sit on the step issuing strange orders and finding fault with everyone and everything. I can always remember the abuse this imaginary lady heaped on Americans – because they wore their hats crooked!

During this time in Wei-hai-wei I was painfully learning to swim. I had a life-belt made of kapok which I always wore, but nothing would induce me to jump in out of my depth. One day in the boat my mother wickedly pushed me in. I gasped and gurgled and thought she had got tired of me and was going to drown me. I could not forgive her for days afterwards.

IV

In 1922 we came to England again, this time to leave my second brother Paul at school. He was only eight, but still it was decided that he should be left. Our great-aunt Blanche had suggested that we should take a house near her at Birchington and consequently we soon found ourselves at St Anthony's.

It was squat and urban, with a sun-lounge. In the garden was a miniature building with one room which we were to call the Wendy House, at the sentimental prompting of Wooly, the governess that was soon to come to us.

Before her we had Miss T., who took us to see her friends who lived in what she called the Smuggler's Cottage. There were horrible snakes and centipedes in bottles of spirit on shelves in the bathroom of this house, and I could hardly wait to escape.

Miss T. was very artistic and, as I already showed signs of a certain aptitude, she thought she would teach me to draw. She set up some drapery and gave me a piece of charcoal. I laboured and smudged and rebelled, I ran with my charcoal into the garden. I can see now the impatient whisk of her skirt as she turned her back on me and went into the house, clutching the board and the paper.

Soon after this she left and I was allowed to go on with my childish drawing.

Hilda, a friend of my mother's who was staying with us at this time, has told me since that one day she found me drawing a conventional sun, but instead of the straight rays I had made waving, sinuous ones. Asking me why I did this, I thought for a minute and then said, 'It's the sun with the wind in its hair.'

Auntie Blanche's house was reached by a footpath through a waving field of corn. In her hall were Chinese pictures on rice paper of horrible tortures. Bright and delicate, they horrified, yet held my eyes. There was a round turret at one corner of the house. I hated it. It seemed so imitation.

I was desolate the day my brother went to school. I wandered in the garden and went to look at the underground house we had made for worms the day before. The worms had all escaped through the earth and only the little cardboard lids and strange food we had laid out remained. I found a bit of string that we had played with and I thought I should never get over my loneliness.

On my depression burst a new bomb. This was Wooly. She wore pince-nez and had two wings of hair that left her ears exposed. She took Kruschen salts, and I always remember the queer feeling I had on that first night when she bathed me.

She was energetic and full of anecdotes, always about herself and her past. She managed me very much more than I had ever been managed before. With Wooly, the ginger pudding always had to be eaten to the very last crumb, even if it choked one and the sullen tears were streaming down one's cheeks.

My life became defined. There were special ways of drying oneself, eating, sleeping, brushing one's hair, folding one's clothes, and these rules must not be broken.

But in spite of all this, I liked her. We would walk along the cliffs or go into the town to do some shopping, and always I would be holding on to her elbow and playing with it by rubbing the loose skin over the hard bone. It gave me a curious sensation which I have never forgotten. Wooly's arms were white and heavy. Only this protruding bone was without the cushion of flesh; there was only the loose supple skin that I would roll backwards and forwards over it. Later I can remember rubbing the cheeks of my dog in just such a way when his jaws were taut and rounded by holding a ball.

There were funny little darts in one shop that we went to. They had bright coloured fluff for a tail and tiny needle points. I liked the red and yellow ones best and Wooly would call me 'red and yaller', as if it were a term of abuse.

She would tell me on these walks of her past life: of the enormity of her sister who took the Crown Derby tea-set when their mother died, whereas it should really have come to Wooly; of her life in Africa with her late husband, when all the natives would come to her saying they were dying and all they really needed was a little castor oil which she would give them, after which they were her willing slaves and eternally grateful.

She would tell me of the terrible whips the Boers used and how they would rub salt afterwards into the wounds they had inflicted on the natives.

There was the story of her industrious childhood too: how she would apply herself to any problem that she did not understand until she had mastered it, how she never liked to be beaten by anything. Sometimes, after these intense bouts of application, she would go to bed and lie staring at the wallpaper until the roses wove themselves into the pattern of her dreams and ran riot, taking strange forms, opening and shutting their mouths.

'This child,' her parents said, 'will certainly have brain fever, if we do not stop her working.'

And she was made to sit quietly in the old garden. I imagined her, at the time, in the frilly trousers and hooped skirt of the thirties and forties of the last century, bowling a hoop, thus unconsciously placing her birth quite sixty years too early.

It is strange that I had these bright mental pictures of Wooly's childhood. She must have thrown an unreal air of romance over it all that attracted me.

Wooly had a jewel-box, in which were many interesting things. There was the Queen Anne threepenny-bit, and the George II florin that had been enamelled in different colours on one side and made into a brooch.

One day a friend of my eldest brother's came over for the day on his bicycle. He told us that he collected coins. Wooly came down after lunch with the threepenny-bit and gave it to him. I felt stiff and thick inside with jealousy and envy – to give it to a complete stranger when I had coveted it for months!

Wooly was the first person to tell me of the beauty of wild flowers, of cowslips and primroses. I secretly knew that they were not nearly so beautiful as roses and lilies, until she took me one day to picnic in the bluebell wood. One could not walk for crushing them. I did not know what to do until Wooly said that it couldn't be helped and plumped firmly down on her coat in the midst of them.

At St Anthony's I slept in a room which was on the ground floor. She told me that I must not be frightened and then repeated a terrible story about a girl she knew whose hair had gone white in a night because a burglar had pressed himself against the window and made frightful faces at her.

In the morning I would rush into my mother's room and watch her having early-morning tea. Sometimes she would still be lying asleep and I would have the faint feeling of not quite wanting to kiss her until she was fresh and alive and not still half asleep. By the basin was a bottle of glycerine, honey and cucumber hand-lotion. I could never believe that it was really made from honey and cucumber; I would ask my mother about it and pour some on my hands to smell it and to feel its stickiness.

Wooly would read to me sometimes in the Wendy House. She had a book of stories which elaborated the nursery rhymes and I was told not to interrupt; I would listen, taking it all in, but still half watching the many earwigs which would crawl in from outside. My eldest brother, when he came back for the holidays, would put these earwigs on pennies and then would pass electric shocks through them and kill them.

One day of the holidays my eldest brother said he wanted to go to the films. He had a friend with him and after lunch they both got ready to go. Paul implored my mother to let him go too, but neither of us was allowed to. He began to cry and shout, and at last he climbed on to the roof of the Wendy House and said that he would swear at everyone if he was not allowed to go. I had a superstitious terror of what might happen. I waited and waited. Paul cried and shouted still. Then, disappointed past all endurance, he shrieked, 'Damn fool, damn fool, damn fool!' I did not know what would happen, I was overawed at this boldness and wickedness.

The outburst seemed, however, to have relieved the situation and he soon came down quite quietly and smarmed his hair with water. Tea was very quiet that afternoon and my brother and his friend had the decency not to mention the film they had seen.

This friend, who was at Uppingham at the time, had brought with him his violin. I never heard him play it, but he would take it out from under the bed and hold it under his chin with the little velvet cushion wedged against him.

One night he made a booby-trap for Wooly. It was a pillow and some shoes placed over her door so that they fell on her when she went in.

Wooly told me what terrible things she would do to him. She sewed up his pyjamas, she made an apple-pie bed, she stuffed his socks with holly. To no avail – he never blinked or said a word.

My mother had difficulty with the servants at that time. The cook ran out one day into the garden, saying, 'It's no good, I've beaten until my arm aches and it won't go right.' She was referring to the mayonnaise which my mother had asked her to make. I think she imagined the request to be the height of unreasonableness, when all most people did was to go and buy a bottle of salad cream.

After she left I went into the kitchen with my mother, and right on top of the dresser we found fragments of sauce-boats and dishes and cups she had broken and hidden there. We could not get anyone to replace her straight away, and so our food was sent from a hotel in a sort of covered cart. I remember the miracle of it being hot and its typical hotel taste. I liked the excitement, but my mother thought it very nasty.

I was taken soon after this to Canterbury and saw St Augustine's throne. I wanted to sit on it – I wanted to sit on a real throne – but no one would let me. I was secretly very disappointed that it was not studded with precious stones and never had been.

We went to Reculver as well and I can remember the tombs in the ruined nave and the feeling I had that the sea might at any moment come in and engulf it all.

The love for old things had been growing in me ever since I could remember and now I wanted to know about everything old. Wooly filled this need a little.

One day we went to visit my Aunt Dos's mother who lived at Broadstairs. It was hot and I had on my white sailor-suit with the long trousers. It was cut exactly like a real sailor's and I was very proud in it, but I would never wear the cap. I refused to wear a hat all my childhood, on account of the terror of having to take it off to strange ladies and the feeling I had that hats were like the collars round dogs' necks – a mark of servitude.

We had lunch first in a restaurant in Broadstairs; there was salmon and salad, and I felt afterwards the tightness of my sailor trousers round the waist as we walked along the hot street. My mother was very pretty in cool linen, and she had just bought me some miniature tumblers and a decanter on a glass tray; they had black and red lines round them.

We arrived at the door and were led down the long glassed-in corridor that joined the garden gate to the house. It was dark and cool, with early-nineteenth-century Gothic windows. We were taken out into the garden, with its wide lawns and great ilex trees. In one corner was a concrete staircase leading right into the ground.

We were taken down to the locked iron door and, when it was opened, torches were turned on and an empty concrete room was laid bare. This had been made, deep under the ground, because of the air-raids of the last war and, whenever the warning sounded, my aunt's mother would send round for all who could take refuge in the shelter.

When we got outside again, she showed a strange bent bit of metal and said it was one of the things that had dropped in the garden.

The Pekinese did not like me at all, and I thought, as I have often thought since, how very deformed they looked.

When I got home I washed my tiny glasses and jug, and then began using them by pouring the water from the jug into the glasses. They were like thimbles filled with rain.

Wooly, that night, when I was having my bath, held the sponge filled with water high above her head and squeezed it, so that the deluge fell on the drum of my stomach and splattered off like raindrops on a pavement. This gave me a strange and delicious sensation and I implored her to do it again, but she suddenly thought better of her joke and would do it no more.

V

We went up to London for a little, before going back to China. I was taken to the Tower of London and was wildly excited. I feasted my eyes upon the jewels. I wanted to know which was the queen's crown and which was the king's. I was so used to the plain circlets of the fairy-tale pictures that I did not at all like the arches and plush caps of the crowns in the Tower. I felt that they were vulgar.

Disappointment waited for me in the room the little princes were supposed to have inhabited on the night they were murdered. I had expected a bed, an elaborate one with hangings and everything else as they had left it; all that I saw was the gaunt, bare squalid little room.

I screamed, 'Mummy, where's the bed, where's the bed?' and everyone laughed.

When we got to the prison where Guy Fawkes had been kept, I wanted to know what sanitary arrangements were made for him. My mother suggested that perhaps something was brought in and taken out again, but I wasn't really satisfied. I seemed to be very practical and literal that day.

This time we went back to China via the Suez Canal. We had had to book Wooly's passage later than our own and so she had to go second class, which seemed to offend her very much, although she spent most of the day with us. However, going second class had its compensations, for I soon began to be told of the charms of a certain gentleman who was a rubber planter; how he had offered to take her ashore at the next port and how in Ceylon he had tried to buy a star-ruby ring for her. I asked Wooly why she had refused and she said that she couldn't accept anything like that. I could not quite understand this, and thought that I should certainly accept a ruby ring if anyone offered me one.

Soon they were almost enagaged and Wooly kept putting strange, rhetorical questions to me, such as, 'Shall I accept him?' She told me how well off he was, how good, how kind, how clever; and yet, through all her praise, I felt he must be fat and a little bald, with a well-developed taste for gin-slings. At Singapore he disappeared, after having asked Wooly to marry him. She had reluctantly refused, as my mother had strongly urged her to find out a little more about him before taking the plunge.

Wooly was unhappy, but somehow seemed to bear up. She would do lessons with me in the morning on deck. I was stubborn and found the multiplication tables very difficult. At eleven I was allowed lime squash with ice in it. Sometimes Wooly would stop it if she thought I was worse than usual. I thought she was a demon.

One day she went down to do something with my mother and left me in charge of the friend who had brought up the message. This woman was plump and smart, with high-heels and pearl earrings. She was a chicken and knew less than I did about the multiplication tables. She waited with an anxious eye for Wooly's return, telling me the while that my sums were right when I knew they were quite, quite wrong. I thought, 'I'm not such a disgrace if this grown-up fat lady can't do it either.'

The children on board the ship had to have their meals before the grown-ups and I can remember the whirring fans and the endless succession of days on which we had buttered eggs and chicken and rice. The chicken always had a horrid, bitter taste which I have never known since.

There was an American woman on board called the Princess de Bourbon. My mother got to know her quite well and I often found them sitting together. She was a rather faded-looking woman who repaired the damage with make-up. Her teeth were always pink from her lipstick. She must have eaten lots of it. One day the stewardess brought us some of her handkerchiefs by mistake. They were embroidered with little coronets in the corner, which I thought very romantic.

One day Wooly told me that someone was very ill in the second-class part of the ship. The next day she told me with solemn relish that she was dead. I always imagine that I saw the service on deck and then the coffin shrouded in black slowly lowered over the side into the water, but this may only have been a graphic description of Wooly's.

When we got back to Shanghai my lessons began in earnest for the first time. After breakfast I would be allowed a little free time and would speed out to my tiny garden near the stables. I did it all myself, which included making the little bamboo fence round it and laying the brick path. At one end was a big plane tree, round which my path wound to a miniature stool under its shade. Rambler roses, from cuttings, had gradually covered the fencing and I had an earthenware stoop as a bird-bath. The flower I think I loved the best was my salvia, and when the winter came I dug up the plant and put it in the greenhouse, in an effort to keep it alive.

I took the little watering-can with the rose and watered it all lovingly; then I would hear the hateful call, 'Denton, lessons.' And I would have to go towards the house, rubbing the mud off my hands and then washing them in the cold, dark lavatory downstairs. Reluctantly I would walk up the stairs and then settle myself, with my books, at the nursery table.

Wooly has told me since that it was almost impossible to teach me sometimes; I would just sit, weeping sullenly until my face was red and swollen. Only, when my sums went right, everything was changed and I felt a quiet delight.

Then there was practising on the piano. Wooly would sit with me until my fingers would turn into stubborn sticks – this in spite of the fact that I had implored my mother to let me learn to play. 'Little Boy Blue' was one of the pieces that I had to play, meanwhile singing the words. It was an American version and instead of 'haystack' was written 'hayrick'. I had learnt 'haystack', and with the stolid pedantry of childhood I considered everything else wrong. I would never sing 'hayrick', in spite of the insistence of Wooly and the many bitter words we had about it.

One day she told me to stand in the corner until I was sorry for my behaviour. I stood and looked at the electric-light plug which was there. I put my two fingers on the two points and sprang back, having received a shock. I thought Wooly had engineered it and could not conceive of anyone being so devilish.

I went out every week to dancing classes at Miss Sharp's. Miss Sharp looked like a Lautrec drawing come to life: grey hair piled high on her head, an eagle nose with the piercing, bright eyes of a bird, and always wearing the black stockings and short pleated skirt which somehow gave her a cadaverous and depraved look.

Bone thin and agile as a cat, she must have been at least sixty. Her tongue was terrible, her energy untiring; when the children were at their last gasp and the Russian refugee who played the piano had at last rebelled, Miss Sharp would quickly take her place on the music stool and play fiercely while she drove us through the dance with shouts and biting sarcasm.

How often I have seen the Russian driven almost to distraction. She would come in, smiling nervously and smelling heavily of *chypre*. She would sit down, after having moved the seat about a lot, and then take off her aged fur and the many rings she wore. These jingled in a little tarnished heap as the piano vibrated. Her hands, the colour of Standard Bread, rose, curled and fell with terrible precision.

I was very romantic about her and felt that she'd left her heart in the steppes; and that the terrible trek across Siberia had broken her and only her shell was playing these metallic dances for us, as her soul was dead. My mother had evidently told me of the tragedy of these refugees and I had elaborated on the theme.

I learnt to distinguish left from right at Miss Sharp's and ever afterwards, whenever I'm in doubt, I see the room again with the window and fretwork shelf-bracket on my right and the dance floor on my left.

Once I fell down with the little girl who was my partner. We thought this a huge joke and were laughing together when Miss Sharp came up like a cloud of thunder. She gave us to understand that we were gauche, ignorant, vulgar animals and of course I was chiefly to blame for not leading my partner properly. I was never quite allowed to live this down.

The sword dance and Christmas dance were utterly delightful. Miss Sharp countenanced no waltz but the 'round and round' of her youth and, to end, there was always the polka and gallop. I thus received a dancing education of perhaps the seventies and eighties of last century.

We all had to appear in white. Two friends always used to come from their car to the entrance jumping in woollen flea-bags, like rabbits. This was because their parents thought that they would get cold on account of their bare legs.

Then there were the terrifying riding lessons. I had a demon of a pony called Whiskers and every week I would go with him to the riding school which was run by Cossacks. There I would solemnly ride round the covered ring, first trotting and gradually going faster and faster, trying all the time to do everything correctly.

Wooly would sit, watching critically and telling me not to be a jelly.

The Russians had a terrible habit of suddenly hitting one's horse if they considered it was being lazy. Whiskers would shy viciously and I would often be flung off into the soft brown dirt. My puttees that I had done up so laboriously would unravel themselves and my hair become matted like a swallow's nest.

What a relief it was to come out of the dark, horse-smelling arena into the daylight and to feel, at last, that one was walking on one's own feet.

The Cossacks were young and sinewy and fierce; they punished the horses as if they were stubborn human beings.

Only once did I ever begin to like Whiskers and that was when he went wild one day, got out of his stable and danced all over the flower-beds and lawns like a mad thing. He looked so dashing, his yellow eyes glinting as he raced through the roses and reduced them to ruin.

My father and mother had decided to make a trip to Java when the summer came, and so it was decided that Wooly and I should go to Mo-kan-shan to stay with some friends called Allen who had a house up there. The two Miss Allens were maiden ladies whose parents had been missionaries many years ago. They were American and their house in Shanghai was filled with furniture which dated from 1850 to 1860.

I am not sure how one goes to Mo-kan-shan, but what I remember is a long train journey, then stopping the night with a Dutch consul somewhere. He was tall and rather fleshy. He wore a monocle and collected beetles. There were whole trays of them in his library, brilliantly coloured, varnished, iridescent. He asked me to collect for him while I was at Mo-kan-shan and gave me a horrible lethal bottle.

I took it, feeling rather flattered, and went up to bed. Wooly left me and put out the light. Then I began to hear noises. They were faintly like the chattering of sparrows, but I knew they were human. There were silences and thuds and little furtive rustles. My heart was so thick, I felt it must press against my lungs and stifle me. I ran on to the landing. I screamed for Wooly. She came, much too slowly I thought, and went to the windows. I expected her to be clubbed by an unseen hand, but all she found was that the balcony of the servants' quarter almost touched the windows and that they were sitting there in the cool of the evening.

The next day we set out in a motor-boat up the interminable canals. The sun was hot and the engine smoked and chugged; we passed under beautiful ruinous bridges, exaggeratedly arched, their masonry joined without mortar and all hinging on the wonderfully carved keystones. The houses and hovels along the bank were terraced. One was of cut stone, like a jigsaw puzzle.

The evil green water fell away from us and spread out like a plume behind. I looked at the person who was sitting next to me on the dirty velvet cushion. It was a Eurasian girl with black hair and cream face. I looked down at her hands, at her turquoise ring. On one hand she had a little thumb sprouting out of the normal one. I saw it with a shock and felt sick. I looked away and then returned to it. I hated her, I wanted to have her done away with, blotted out.

We left the motor-boat and got into sedan-chairs. They were carried on heavy bamboo poles by garlic-smelling coolies glistening with sweat. They grunted and sang, as slowly we swung up into the mountains. We left the watery rice fields, the pools between the rocks, and passed by the neglected tea terraces. The path was steep and narrow, the efforts of the coolies were agonizing; the sedans swung from side to side and I was terrified. I thought I was much too heavy for them and that they would lose their balance and throw me down a gully.

The light was fading now and the great bamboos were waving in the evening air. What I have since realized to be Offenbach's 'Barcarolle' was humming through my head. Wooly must have been singing it. I hummed it out loud to stem my fear.

Far above us I saw little points of light. I shouted to Wooly, and the coolies began to sing more lustily; it seemed to echo across the mountains, through the air which was heavy with night smells and the sound of rushing water.

The Miss Allens had heard our coolies and were at the door, silhouetted against the warm light. They paid the coolies and dismissed them in a masterful way, speaking Chinese. The fact that they could speak Chinese impressed me very much. They led us into the living-room, which had a lot of varnished wood in it and basket-chairs. Miss Ethel went to the kitchen and brought back a laden tray. There was tomato soup with a blob of cream floating in it, and pumpkin pie, which I had never tasted before.

Soon after this I was taken to bed and when the light was turned out I went to the window and saw the great bed of mist which lay in the valley between the mountains.

VI

The next morning I was up early. I saw that we were right on the mountainside and that the garden was in terraces. Everywhere were bamboo groves, luxuriant ferns and tiny rock-plants. Everything was broken and woven together with streams. The springs bubbled straight up through rocks and sand. There were bamboo pipes leading from some of these. I followed one line down terraces through the bamboos and suddenly I was in a little clearing with a swimming-pool before me. The pipes were steadily filling it. I knelt down and put in my hand. It was stingingly cold.

Then I remembered my lethal bottle and my promise about catching beetles. I rushed back to the house to get it, but I was caught. I was to have breakfast, and then there were lessons and a weird system, invented by Wooly, of fingering and practising without a piano. That afternoon I went for a solitary walk with my bottle. I found strange things and popped them in without looking, but I soon got used to killing and did not mind. I kept wondering if I had found anything very rare and what the Dutch consul would say.

After tea we went down to bathe. The pool was now full of the bright, bitter spring water. By this time I had learnt to swim and I felt proud as I did my energetic breast-stroke.

In the days that followed I would rush down early to the pool in my black cotton bathing-suit and let the water slowly envelop me. I would swim and turn and feel the hot sun burning on me. Wooly always made me wet my hair.

The Allens took us for wonderful walks. They bought me a long carved staff, brightly painted. I would run and pole-jump with it as they walked. My staff was a sort of talisman and I wanted it always with me. I loved its gnarled end, with the face of the old man and the peaches and bats.

They also gave me an umbrella of oiled skin, covered all over with flowers and symbols. I would sit under it in the mountain rain and let the trickles seep into the moss all round me. There was a strange smell from it, of linseed and paint and dirty human hair.

When the mists came down, the house lay there, a little lump on the mountainside; damp streamed from the windows and Ethel would serve tomato soup with the sickly rich lumps of cream in it.

Our bedroom was dark and Wooly would sit in the shadows, taking Kruschen salts or rummaging in her trunk.

The Allens taught us to play mah-jong, and on these long wet days we would sit above the chattering blocks, shuffling them together on the green baize table.

Wooly also taught me to knit. I could never cast on or off, but would do rows of purl and plain with delight. I became absorbed. I did not even want to leave it when the sun came and an expedition had been planned to the valley.

On these occasions there would be much preparation, much mixing of salt and pepper into a sort of pale pumice-powder, and much wrinkling of greaseproof paper.

If it was a long way, we would start out down the mountain in sedan-chairs. Whenever I got into one, the Offenbach 'Barcarolle' would sound again in my ears. To this tune, rocks, pools, bamboos would pass by. I would sway from side to side and feel the straining of the coolies as they bore the chair. We always moved in a cloud of garlic. The blue of their faded cotton trousers was always before me.

When they set us down, we would walk a little further to a river bank or pool; then we would undress and stand in the water, our toes curling round the smoothed pebbles. Miss Allen's head, in a rubber cap, would emerge and her face would shine, a dull purple under the coating of talcum powder which she must have used. Her nose was big and the pores were large. There were many snowy mountains and craters.

Ethel would be on the shore, spreading the lunch, unwrapping the drumsticks and taking the lid off the Russian salad.

Then we would all rise out of the water like wet seals and lie on the rocks which were hot, like hearth-stones.

We all dressed before lunch, in the nooks our modesty had discovered. Wooly would tell me to rub myself hard with the towel.

After our meal we would wander in search of interesting things. Once we found a monastery, set about with ancient ginkgo or maidenhair fern trees. There was a ruined well, with an elaborate stone balustrade in front, and we saw the yellow-robed monks, their shaved heads shining, pass in and out of the arched gates.

Miss Allen asked one about the well and he told her some strange heroic story which I cannot remember properly – only that some martyr died there for his religion. Then he took us all into the guest-hall, which was dark and heavy with old smells. The courtyard through which we passed was paved with flat stones, between which long shoots of grass waved like feathers. The coloured tiles were slipping from the roofs.

Another time, when we had not gone so far, we came on a European house which had been deserted. This was much higher up the mountain, and looking down from the broken windows I saw the paddy fields like a glistening draught-board below me.

The roof had fallen in and all the glass had gone from the windows, but there were the sagging iron beds, the crockery and the books, each standing dreamy sentinel, until they finally decayed.

The scene roused an echo of Miss Allen's parents' missionary zeal, and she exclaimed, 'How honest the peasants must be to leave it all here!'

'How honest!' I copied fervently as I fingered a frying-pan which seemed to reek of the greasy living of the cities.

We once went too to the empty house of a friend of Miss Allen's. We had with us a girl of about twenty. Everyone thought her very pretty and clever. She wore her hair in two curled-up discs over her ears. I was told I had to take off my sun helmet to her when we first met; I grudged doing it very much.

She was supposed to be very good at bridge and I thought of her, unaccountably, as I would now think, in the abstract, of the head of a women's college at a university.

The house we went to was in a wood and the swimming-pool in which we bathed was dank and dark with rotting leaves. It was ghostly and horrible and exciting.

Miss Allen had started a conversation about what she would do if she were very rich, and everyone was joining in. Nobody but myself mentioned jewels, lapis lazuli baths and gold taps. Everyone was being extremely puritanical and saying that they would give most of it away and live on the rest in a Tudor cottage in Sussex with their spaniels.

All the way home I argued, with myself, the senselessness of taking one's hat off to strange women who played bridge and wore their hair in rolled-up plaits.

I was soon to have my revenge, for one day I was to hear with wild excitement that my mother had returned from Java and was coming to Mo-kan-shan in a few days. I waited with terrible impatience, until one evening, as we were sitting on the terrace and the valley was filling with mist, we heard the strange sing-song of the coolies and saw the twinkling lights they were carrying.

Nearer and nearer they came, winding up the mountain; I wanted to go and meet them, but was not allowed in case I should get lost.

At last the chairs were at the door and I was kissing my mother frantically. Her luggage was being unloaded from the other chair and we all trooped into the hall, which smelt of the oil lamp which flickered in the draught from the open door.

I rushed upstairs with my mother and she took off her hat. I held her hand all the time, only letting go when she knelt down and undid her dressing-case. She took out several parcels and put them on the bed in front of me.

'They're for you,' she said.

I stared at the tissue-paper and then undid them wildly. There was a pig made out of a coconut, with red eyes and sharp, pointed, coconut ears. It was a money-box with a slit in the back. Then there was a bird made out of a polished buffalo-horn. Its beak was a long, sharp point and it was streamlined, like water poured from a funnel. The last parcel was flat and I could not think what it might contain. As I unwrapped it, the joints of it wriggled and I saw that it was a marionette in two dimensions. It was made of thick parchment and mounted on a horn stick. It was a terrible Javanese dancer with a red mouth and black pointed eyes. The jointed arms were painted with great bracelets. I made it dance and it seemed like a devil.

There was tomato soup and pumpkin pie again that night. They were Ethel's favourites and she made them perfectly.

The next day we moved my mother's things up to the hotel, as there was really no room for her to sleep at the Allens'. That night we had a typhoon. I knew nothing about it until I was told. I quickly went up to see my mother. I met her on the doorstep and she told us all with laughing eyes how the plaster on her wall had suddenly decided to leave its moorings in the middle of the night and how she had woken up with her mouth full of dust and the bed smothered in bits like icing sugar. She fled just before the rest of the plaster fell.

Even on this exciting morning Wooly made me do my lessons and I felt that nothing could be more cruel than keeping a son from his mother.

That night the Allens had planned a moonlight picnic by the pool. The little lawn was hung with lanterns and I was allowed to stay up.

After the lovely chocolate ice-cream, we talked and sang, and my mother told us about Java. Then gradually we rose to our feet, one by one, and went to the edge of the terrace and watched the moon rising. Soon we were holding hands and dancing slowly and rhythmically round the pool. My mother was next to me and on her other side was the girl with the earphones. Suddenly my mother gave her a wicked little push. I gasped – there was all that cleverness and bridge playing, those curled plaits and that proudness; there it all was, floundering in the water. This was the thing I had to take my hat off to. The water made the thin dress stick to her and she looked like a naked bird whose skin sticks to its bones. I was horrified at my mother's behaviour; I did not know how she could have been so wicked.

The girl's head appeared, gurgling and smiling self-consciously. She did a graceful side-stroke across the pool, got out and then went on dancing in her wet dress, like some schoolteacher doing a revived Greek dance in classical folds.

My mother was a little red and shamefaced at her foolishness, but the girl, I think, enjoyed it all.

The next morning I got up early to bathe. My mother came with me and I danced about with nothing on – Wooly would never allow me to do this – I rolled in the water, feeling it hug me closer without the cotton suit between. It was glorious freedom.

Then we heard a rustle in the bamboos and the hateful girl appeared, her earpieces guarded by green rubber. All my shame fell on me like a coat and I crouched, clutching my knees, looking fiercely nonchalant. My mother brought my bathrobe and I slipped up through the bamboos, hating the awful girl more than ever for seeing me naked.

After breakfast I saw her sitting on the terrace, her thick, reddish hair covering her face and shoulders. She was drying it in the sun.

My mother only stayed a few weeks with us and then returned to Shanghai. We were to follow later. The day she went, I sat in the bedroom looking at the coconut pig and longing to go back too. The holiday was never quite the same again. I wandered disconsolately in search of beetles and dug little ferns up and planted them in other places. I dammed the streams with mud and stones and watched small lakes forming.

A woman called Auntie Mary came to stay. She was nobody's aunt that I knew of, but she was always called this.

She was fairly young, with a flat face and very restless eyes. She would lie in bed late and take aspirin, although she was a Christian Scientist. In her house in Shanghai she would jump off the opium couch on which she had been sprawling and run to the piano, where she would rattle the keys in a frenzy as she sang 'Three o'Clock in the Morning'. Just as she got to 'Nothing to do', she would fling her hands down with a hopeless gesture and slouch on the stool, looking far away, with a sort of twisted mouth. One never quite knew if her behaviour was genuine or theatrical.

At the Allens' she was given the best room, in which all the furniture was green bamboo. She would make fun of it and the

Allens too when I went in to see her in the morning, and I would join in and enjoy this malicious gossip with a grown-up.

I was joyful on the day that we left. I wanted to get back to my garden, my mother and my treasures, as I called my collection of curios.

I left the beetles with the Dutch consul and anxiously watched his face to see it light up when he discovered the very rare one which I felt that I must have found. But he was only very polite and jovial.

When we were nearing Shanghai, Wooly told me that in about ten minutes we should be there. I knew that if you counted to sixty, a minute had passed, so I laboriously started to count the seconds. Then I had a brainwave: the time would pass far quicker if I counted in fives!

I began this labour-saving method. Five, ten, fifteen, twenty – the minutes flew. Soon the whole ten were done. I rushed from the corridor into the compartment where Wooly was, to ask her why the train hadn't stopped.

VII

My mother was in the cool, dark drawing-room when we arrived. It was early autumn and the Venetian blinds were half down. She was dressed in a strange tea-gown of cherry-satin ribbons and white-dotted muslin. It was split up the sides and there was a tunic top. She held out both her arms and I ran into them. There were other friends there and we all began talking while my mother showed things from Java: the tawny sarongs that looked as if they had been embroidered with silver and gold and then dyed in stale blood; a wonderful beaded belt that was thick and constricting as a corset; a set of brass utensils for chewing betel-nut; and more marionnettes, stranger and fiercer.

As soon as I could, I ran toward the stables, to see what my garden was like. There were weeds, the bird-bath was dry, with cracked slime at the bottom. Everything was choked and neglected.

Something went stiff inside me and I hated everybody for not caring about my garden and not looking after it. I was down on my knees. I weeded and watered furiously. I fetched the little rock-plants that I had brought from the mountains. They looked like the dried bottoms of artichokes.

When I had finished I went into the house and up to the nursery, where I opened the drawers of the little chest in which I kept my treasures. I rubbed and fingered the painted snuff-bottle, I made the facets of the rock-crystal lumps shine in the light. I played with the filigree box inlaid with kingfishers' feathers. I rubbed my amber bead so that it picked up paper, and pretended that the small ivory netsuke was really alive. My father called these things junk and the very thought of this insult made me turn red.

Lessons were getting increasingly difficult with Wooly and one day, after a secret conference, I was surprised and horrified by being told that I was to go to school. Again I cried and implored my mother not to send me, but the next day found me setting out on Whiskers with the old mafoo walking by my side. We were going to Mrs Paul's house, where she had a school for small children. The schoolroom was at the top of the house and on a wide low table were letters of the alphabet on squares of cardboard. We all sat round, as if we were gambling at a casino. Mrs Paul would say a word and there would immediately be a mad scramble of fingers, ferreting for the right letters to spell the word. Whoever got it right first, won. Mrs Paul always gave me the impression that she had been cooking in front of a kitchen range, or that she had just had a hot bath and dressed in the steamy bathroom, or else been sitting on a terrace in the sun gulping down cups of hot coffee. She had that fatigued, pale damp look, with tails of greying hair that had strayed from their place.

One day she asked me to lunch with her own little boy; we sat in the drawing-room at a small table by the window which, although we were on the first floor, reached to the carpet. This gave a strange, romantic, perilous look to the room, as if the windows were oubliettes, through which one could suddenly push one's guest after having eaten and drunk with him exquisitely. He would be standing there, watching the moonlight on the rubber leaves of the laurel bushes, the smoke from his fat cigarette circling like apple peel thrown over a shoulder. Then there would be a push and a thud on those same laurels.

For lunch we had curry; the rice was dry and almost brittle and the curry itself was greenish-yellow. We piled peanuts, desiccated coconut and chutney on top. I did not like it because it was not like the curry we had at home.

Mrs Paul was preoccupied and said, 'Yes, dear,' to everything.

I only saw Wooly now in the afternoons and early mornings. It made a difference, not having lessons with her, although she still ruled all the rest of my life.

As Christmas drew near she would take me out to parties. I remember one well. It was at the house of a friend of my mother's whom I had not met. She had just come back from Switzerland with her small daughter who had been at a school there, where they wore no clothes and rolled in the snow. I was shown a picture of her sliding down a chute into it.

We started with a Punch and Judy show. I had never seen one before and thought Punch the most disgusting, criminal type. When he began hitting the baby with hard wooden thuds, I felt its skull crack and knew that none of us were safe while grown-ups thought that this sort of thing was funny. When tea-time came we all trooped into the dining-room and sat round the large oval table. I noticed that there were two cakes: one was big and the other very big. I began to eat some jelly out of a decorated orange-skin, then I noticed that the French governess was fiddling with the biggest cake; she seemed to be cutting it and at the same time pulling something.

Suddenly the cake fell open into evenly divided quarters. Its centre was a mass of little white bodies. They began to dart all over the table. I saw that they were white mice with pink eyes. There was an uproar and screams of delight. Governesses and Chinese servants were deftly catching them as they jumped off the table and putting them into little cages in pairs. The cages had wire wheels in them and, as the noise subsided, I heard a thin whirring as the small mice pedalled frantically round.

I looked at the cake again and saw that it was made of wood. All the quarters met in the middle and when a string was pulled they fell apart. The outside was iced with real sugar. I immediately thought of the 'four and twenty blackbirds baked in a pie'. I held my mice very close, in their cage, and smelt them. I sat quietly with them until the end of the party, when I could take them home. I gave them bread and water and cotton wool to sleep in. The next morning the bread that was left was hard and dry, and my mice smelt stronger. I cleaned their house and watched them lovingly as they pedalled or slept on the cotton wool.

Just before Christmas Miss Sharp was giving an exhibition at the Town Hall. I was to dance in an Irish jig. I had to have brown knee-breeches, a red waistcoat with brass buttons and a bottle-green coat. My hair was brushed forward.

I remembered the picture of the man with the pig, called 'The Last Match'. I didn't want to look like that. The rehearsals were exciting. The Town Hall was almost disused and still held the very spirit of the mid nineteenth century in its cast iron and palms and in the folds of the beef-blood curtains, trimmed with fantastic braid.

Miss Sharp's voice would echo in the great hall as she told us that our thumpings would bring down the enormous pine rafters.

'Lightly,' she shouted, 'like a fairy.'

The exhibition day was a delicious nightmare. There were the rows of mothers and visitors all round the edge of the room, while under the sickly yellow lights we danced and turned in our romantic clothes.

Up in the roof, the rafters soared into blackness, while down below the lights shone on us as they do on the ring at a boxing match. My Irish jig was a terrible combination of pride, self-consciousness and concentration. Afterwards we all joined in the Christmas dance, where you clap your hands and shuffle your feet as the partners work up and down. Miss Sharp had nothing good to say for us, although I think she was proud. As I rushed down the dirty stone stairs that must have been built for elephants, a Catholic girl buttonholed me and told me how she was going to be christened. I was horrified. She was eight years old and I told her it should have been done when she was born. She only smirked and looked knowing and told me about her white clothes. The Catholic religion gave me the same feeling as those white porcelain flowers under glass globes which I saw in cemeteries – something old and depraved and florid and fly-blown.

Strangely enough, some of the Jews in Shanghai gave children's Christmas parties and one to which I was asked at this time was an eighteenth-century party. I went in a blue suit with knee-breeches and powdered hair. There was noise and light when the door was opened and my hostess appeared, rounded and benign, with her small son who was in lemon-coloured satin with an elaborate silky wig on his head. I immediately felt that my get-up was very homemade. My powdered hair was not nearly up to the standard of this curled wig. I was led to the long narrow tables which were glittering with candles. There was cream in everything. Cream horns, cream stuffed into brandy-snaps, éclairs squirted when you bit them. I felt almost sick and longed for jelly and sorbets. After this we were taken to the drawing-room where a Christmas tree that reached the ceiling was blazing. It was fiery and barbaric and a fitting background for our hostess, who stood in front in her black velvet and pearls. Her grown-up nephew fished the presents off with a long stick and she graciously gave them to us. I had a richly bound book of Greek myths. I turned the pages idly, for I could not yet read, until my eyes fell on a picture of Prometheus chained to the rock, a vulture hovering over him. He was nearly naked, his athlete's chest and arms pinned to the rock, his powerful legs straddled apart, his perfect features contorted with pain. It gave me the same feeling that crucifixes did. I felt shame and admiration. I shut the book quickly. I did not want anyone to see me looking at the picture.

The grown-up nephew was now doing conjuring tricks. He had taken off his coat and rolled up his sleeves. His arms were thick and muscular with light hairs on them in spite of his dark chin. He was young and full of horse-play. He put eggs in his mouth and made them disappear. He drew them out of other people's ears, then made to throw them against the wall, but they always vanished in time.

At last Wooly said that it was time to go home and I was soon undressing in the nursery and looking at the other pictures in my new book.

We were going to spend Christmas on a house-boat, up the river. I had never been on one before and was thrilled by the little saloon, the still smaller cabin that I had and the shining paint and glistening brass. Soon we had left Shanghai and were sailing upstream. The servants were chattering and cooking in the galley, and little green curtains in the saloon were fluttering in the wind from the minute portholes. I went to look at my cabin again. All the woodwork was dark old mahogany. There was a glistening, metal tip-up basin and two bunks, one on top of the other.

I climbed up to the top one and lay down on my back, feeling the gentle motion of the boat and holding over my head the strange toy I had brought with me. I should really have outgrown it by now; it was a curious home-made cross between a gollywog and a doll. It was made of green velvet and had a white face which I was always touching up with my paints. Its eyes and lips grew ever blacker and redder. I leant with my toy out of the porthole. I held it negligently and it fell. Its white face faded into the green water. I was horrified, as I would have been if a human being had fallen overboard. I rushed up on deck for a pole. One of the hands tried fishing with a hook. It was useless, my toy was drowned. Its painted face would all be washed away. I moaned and wept for it of course, and my mother was very silent. Knowing that I liked to taste strange things, she slipped away and came back with two glass jars.

We sat there in the stern of the boat, eating the pearly little onions and the green tomato chutney with our fingers, watching the grey clouds and the grey water go swirling by. The strange harsh tastes bit into my tongue and pleased me.

My mother was so clever. The next day when I woke I was almost happy without my toy. We spent most of the day on shore. The house-boat was moored at the side of the river in front of the ruins of a temple. There were only a few, spiky columns rising out of the weeds and a huge, broken incense-burner, carved out of granite. My mother coveted it and wanted to take it back to our garden and put it so that it could be seen and to fill it with water for the birds. We went in search of someone to ask about it. We found some priests in their ramshackle, flimsy monastery.

I thought they would tell my mother that it was sacrilege to remove the incense-burner and that they would be angry with us; but their eyes were rapacious and their lips smiled smoothly as they bargained for dollars with my mother. When it was settled, they sent us coolies with long poles, and the incense-burner, settled stiff in the earth and weeds, was slowly prised up and lashed with rope to the poles. Then began the procession, bearing it to the ship. The poles were bent like a crescent moon and the coolies' faces shone with sweat. They gave theatrical groans and sang higher and higher in their strange falsettos as they strained to get it on board. The stern sank noticeably as at last it was secured to the deck. We waved to the priests and were off. They smiled and turned their backs. I saw their discoloured black gowns and shaven heads disappearing into the jungle of dead weeds and broken columns.

The next day was Christmas and there was lots to eat, but my presents had been left behind and so I had to wait for those. After lunch we went on shore and walked up into the hills. It was cold and grey and the wool of my scarf rubbed my ears and neck. The hills were honeycombs, the cells of which were tombs. There were mounds of earth and small shrines with top-heavy roofs. Many were excavated in the shape of a horseshoe, with an altar in the middle. Here the families would come to worship their ancestors. The ground was littered with gold and silver paper money which had been offered as a sacrifice.

I wandered off by myself and went round the ridge of a hill.

The dry grass grated and rattled about my bare knees. I saw a ruined grave and went up to it. Its side had broken open and I saw the rotting coffin and a faded piece of blue cotton. I went nearer and saw a skull, the reddish hair and livid flesh still clinging to it in strips. I was covered with fear which held me tight inside. I ran round the ridge, scratching my legs, but never stopping till I found my mother and father. I did not tell them what I had seen; it was too horrible and fascinating. That night in my bunk I lay on my back and thought of the skull. The red hair was the detail that horrified me most. All Chinese have black hair. They never dig a hole for the dead; they raise a mound or build a little brick house over them.

We arrived home a few days after Christmas and I rushed upstairs and looked at all the parcels that were waiting for me.

School began again and everything settled down monotonously until the spring, when there was general turmoil as we gradually packed and got ready to sail for England again to see my brothers. All my childhood was spent in travelling backwards and forwards from China to England and England to China. In this way my mother divided her time equally between my father and my brothers.

VIII

The year 1924 saw us in England, looking for a house to spend the summer in. A friend in Oxfordshire found us one near her and we spent the time before we moved in touring. I loved this, although the car made me feel a little sick. My father had come with us this time and he drove while my mother sat next to him and I was alone in the back. The car was new and needed breaking-in, so we climbed and descended the hills very gently.

We went to all the places that Americans and strangers go to. We stayed at the Lygon Arms and I was spellbound as a pretty American told me, while we were sitting in front of an enormous fireplace, that she had Cromwell's room. She said that it was the only one which hadn't been fitted with electric light, as this might have spoilt its atmosphere.

We stayed at the Peacock Inn at Naseby and my father and mother had the room with Queen Victoria's bed in it. I seem to remember that it was heavy mahogany with a patchwork quilt on it. My own room was on the top storey, with a little dormer window that looked on to the garden and the rushing stream.

My father had bought me a little Wedgwood plaque that must have once ornamented some clock or candlestick. Hope with an anchor was pictured on it. I would wash it lovingly with my father's shaving soap and then lie on my bed staring at it and listening to the rushing water.

We visited Haddon Hall from there. It had not then been reinhabited and was almost empty of furniture. The Manners had deserted it for more than a hundred years, and our guide pointed out where the raindrops had sunk into the huge wooden tables in the hall.

The gardens were wonderful, in terraces, falling into the woods, lost in the early summer haze. I was enchanted. I had never seen a great, historic house before and could think of nothing else.

My parents, seeing how interested I was, took me to Chatsworth and to Hardwick, and I wandered through the lovely, tarnished rooms believing every word the garrulous guide said.

From Naseby we went to Repton, where my eldest brother was at school. We stayed at Burton and went over to see him each day. The hotel was Georgian and they still had much of their old china and plate which they kept in a cabinet. This was a new period to me. So far we had only stayed in Tudor places. My mother told me what she knew about the eighteenth century and I became absorbed. Something inside me told me that this sort of architecture was greater than all the beamed cottages put together, which I had had such a mania for.

I wandered with my mother down the soiled streets of Burton looking for 'Georginical' houses, as I called them. The air was heavy with the smell of beer. I had never been in a manufacturing town before. My mother bought me a small book about a family of rabbits, and I always associate this sentimental, domestic story with the dirty gutters and greasy dust of Burton.

At Repton there was more history for me. The old priory was being drastically restored and battered Norman columns in the undercroft were being displayed. My brother told me how a whole set of medieval tiles had just been unearthed and how they had been stolen almost the next day. I worried over this and carried about with me a real sense of loss.

The first day we arrived was Speech Day and I loved the salmon mayonnaise and claret cup we had in the huge marquee. I only was allowed to sip the claret cup, but I loved the very thought of it – to drink real wine, and such strange wine, with grapes and strawberries and cucumber in it. Cucumber has always seemed exotic to me – ever since I saw my mother's glycerine, honey and cucumber hand-lotion at Birchington.

The cricket and speeches I found monotonous, but otherwise I was enjoying my day. The art school, in the old priory ox stables, I thought very romantic, especially the plaster casts. All through my childhood I had very reverent feelings for Greek and Roman sculpture, ever since my mother had showed me the collection of photographs she had made when she was at school in the convent at Florence.

Before we left, my father climbed with me up the tower of the parish church. We went round till we were dizzy and every now and then I caught a glimpse of the green land through the narrow lancets which were like the slots of a money-box. The stone spiral wound itself out at last and we were on the parapet, wind blowing and sun shining. I dared not look over the edge till my father took me. Then I felt I was in an aeroplane. All the stairs I had climbed didn't count any more. I was suspended and swaying in the air.

On the way down we stopped to look at the bells. I remembered the terrible story of a girl who had clung to a bell to muffle its sound with her body. I was in a fever to get away before someone should start ringing them downstairs.

When we left Repton we went to stay with the friend who had found the house we were about to move into. The first night we were there I had a scene with my mother. We were in the bathroom and I was being unbearable. Suddenly she picked up the ivory hairbrush and began to smack me with it; I began to hit her behind with my hand and we went round in a circle of whirling hands and brushes. The situation was rapidly developing into farce, but although we were both almost laughing, neither of us would admit it, and after the exercise had calmed us down we both separated and went to bed quite quietly.

I slept in the next room to Mrs Hayes's small girls and before I got into bed I went in to say goodnight. They were cleaning their teeth, the nurse standing over them. The toothpowder they used was kept in a glass salt-pot with a china lid with a hole in it, such as you see in hotels; it even had a monogram on it. I wanted to know where they had got it. The girls, with great glee, told me that their nurse had stolen it when last they had stayed in a hotel in London.

I was very surprised and felt she ought immediately to be taken to prison. Nevertheless, I thought her very bold and daring, and have never been able to look at a hotel cruet since without thinking of her.

The next day, down in the drawing-room, Katherine, the eldest girl, showed me an old blue and white doll's tea-set, kept reverently in a cabinet. As we fingered and touched the pieces, she said very carefully but casually that it was several generations old. I knew about centuries but I could not imagine what generations were. I carried the word about with me all day, and by the end of that time had placed the date of the tea-set quite five hundred years back.

In the afternoon we set off to see the house we had taken at Benson. The car was full and we children were getting more and more unruly. By the time we got to the house, I felt as if I had never lived in anything but a bear garden.

I looked up and saw the new hedge and the red-tile-hung house. It had a very repressed unmarried look. I screamed, 'It's much too tidy for us!' Dreadful frowns and grimaces were made at me and I was silenced. We walked up the brick steps and opened the gate into what once was a very precise formal garden.

It was not precise now. The little box-hedges were ragged and there was much long grass where no grass of any sort should have been.

The gnarled little fruit trees, trained against the walls, hung in a crucified way, as if the nails were supporting them, not restraining them.

The appearance of the house from the road was deceiving. Nevertheless there was a certain decayed charm about it. We rang the bell and waited at the open front-door. I could see through the cracks between my elders a picture of a man on a white horse and above it two crossed swords. At last a fat woman appeared and Mrs Hayes introduced us to her. She talked a lot and her eyes looked vaguely and shrewdly into the distance. Her dress was white and tousled. She showed us all over the house. It had been added to at various times and the rooms had low ceilings and were interesting shapes. They were dark and cool and heavy with the undisturbed atmosphere which only comes through years of neglect. Everything had been arranged, so we could not have refused to have it, even if we had wished to. I could see my mother looking and planning in her mind.

After we had seen everything the fat lady told us that her daughter was out in the paddock, helping to make the hay, and took us out there so that we could play in it too. The fat lady's daughter was several years older than we were and rather imperious. I thought she looked very like a gypsy, with her pouting lips and hair matted with hay.

When we came back to the house, Colonel S., the fat lady's husband, had arrived and after some more talk we left.

The next week we moved in. My mother was convinced that the whole house had to be spring-cleaned. Soon the place was in chaos. A huge machine from a vacuum-cleaning company was chugging on the lawn and dragging as much dust out of the carpets as it could. They lay flat on the lawn, pale and exhausted after their ordeal.

The sun glinted on the polished Regency and Victorian furniture which was waiting to go back into the rooms.

Inside, the naked squares of white floor and the stained surrounds were being scrubbed. Often when a bit of furniture was moved, it was found that the distemper on the wall only stretched to its edge – then was a different colour behind. The walls had been repainted with the furniture in place!

I took several of the old dark paintings off the walls, including the man on the white horse which I had first seen, and ran upstairs with them. With a nailbrush and my father's shaving soap I began to scrub them. I was delighted; the water acted as a varnish and made everything look richer and brighter. I got lots of dust off and then I dried them. They looked dull now, and I was disappointed, but I waited for a little, and then polished them with Adam's furniture polish. I thought they looked lovely and took them down proudly to show them to my mother. She was horrified at my drastic treatment of them, but had to admit that they looked nice. I hung them up again and turned my attention to the dining-room table. It was round and early Victorian, with a very elaborate walnut veneer all over it. I looked at the lovely grain and then began polishing furiously.

I was obsessed with the idea of cleaning and polishing, and went round the house, looking for things to do.

Much of the house was covered with thick creepers, and in the long, narrow room which I had chosen for my own the light seeped in greenly, as into an aquarium. The clustered leaves were slowly narrowing down the windows.

The drawing-room downstairs was the only room that the S.s had kept in any sort of order. The floor was parquet and on it was laid an old Brussels carpet of cabbage leaves and cabbage roses.

Instead of the dark oil paintings there were faded watercolours in this room and the walls were covered with a striped paper which resembled watered-silk.

There were three steps down into my mother's and father's room, which was very large. The whole time we were there it had a bare look, as my mother said that the carpet was too old and dirty for even the vacuum cleaner to be able to do anything with, and so she had the floor scrubbed and the white centre and the stained surround left bare. The bed was twisted mahogany placed on a raised platform and the old swinging cheval-glass gave one a grey, dream-like appearance when it was gazed into.

The S.s and their family had lived in this house for many years, gradually getting poorer and poorer. The war was the last blow; from then on they must have lived in cheerful and unpretending squalor.

By the time the house was again in some sort of order my brothers had returned for the holidays and I suddenly lost my interest in polishing everything and began to bicycle, with Paul as my teacher. He would guide me over the little paths in the garden and round the tennis-court. At the entrance to the court there was a terrible obstacle in the shape of a crab-apple tree which scattered its bright little hard fruit all over the path. I would strike one with my front wheel and would be off in a moment, lying on the humid earth, laughing rather anxiously; then I would finger one of the little red balls and bite into its crisp, acid heart. I would feel the juice skinning my teeth, roughening my tongue, as a cat's is rough. I thought all cleanness lived in crab-apples.

My brother, with male vanity, would show off in front of me, rushing at a grass bank and, as he was upon it, skidding so that the flat lawn showed the brown, fan-shaped scar his wheels had made.

The first day he took me on the road we went along the quiet lanes and my confidence grew; then suddenly I heard a car. It was in front of me – I saw its nose appearing round the corner – the whirr of its engines was in my ears and my courage failed me. I slipped off into the ditch and felt the cool cowparsley closing over me. The wheels of my bicycle were revolving aimlessly, as a chicken walks about when its head has been cut off. My brother rode up, furious with his pupil. He called me coward, funk and clumsy lout.

As I picked myself out of the ditch, shamefaced and casual, I saw the car slowly backing towards us. It was filled with an open-faced family party who stared and smiled nervously. There were more explanations and more contempt was poured on me by my brother. At last they drove off, satisfied that they were not responsible for my mishap, and we returned into the stable-yard. We found my father doing something to the car. When he saw us he turned to my brother and asked him to take a message to Mrs S., who, when she left the house we were living in, had returned to an Army hut, with her Colonel and her grown-up children. Paul was very shy with strangers and he made weak explanations of why he could not go and then darted into the house. I was left to take the message, and proudly conscious of my ability to talk to strangers even if my bicycle riding was not up to Paul's standard, I went towards the hut. I was not prepared for the sight that met my eyes when the door was opened. If I had been told beforehand, I should never have gone.

Being a child, my voice was high pitched, and I can only imagine that Mrs S. thought by it that I was one of her daughters.

I had knocked on the door and waited until I heard someone ask, 'Who is there?' Egotistically, I had answered, 'It's me.' The door was opened, disclosing Mrs S. in her elaborate, soiled corsets, the suspenders dangling about her heavy, blue-veined legs, her hair like a slovenly rook's nest. With an impatient, outraged exclamation she turned about, displaying her huge buttocks, like dirty blancmanges, and fled into her bedroom. From there she carried on a ladylike and furious conversation, either with herself or with me – I could not tell – emerging at last in the ruin of a feathered peignoir in that shade of off-white which nature reserves for soiled articles.

She was queen-like and austere, almost making me feel that *I* had appeared naked and in an obscene attitude before *her*. I went back to the house rather shaken, with a horror of corsets firmly fixed in my mind, which has never left me.

The next day it rained and I was disconsolate. I went out of the back door into the stable-yard and pattered through the puddles to the disused barn. I entered by the huge, crazy door and shut it behind me. I was in darkness with the smell of dust and mice and hay in my nostrils. The light came in through the cracks in the doors and the walls. I climbed up on to some boxes and hung on to a beam, pretending I was a monkey. I took my raincoat off and jersey, to be freer. I gnashed my teeth and made contorted faces, I gibbered and tried to hang on with one hand as I scratched myself with the other. I pretended to eat imaginary peanuts and to crack the shells with my teeth. When I grew tired of this, I sat down on the boxes and thought how miserable I was. Suddenly, it flashed through my mind that I should pretend to be a slave who had to live in the barn and sweat and labour all day. I remembered the pictures of Greek slaves I had seen and, with a tremendous sense of daring, I pulled my shirt over my head and saw myself white, in the cracks of light. It was a much easier matter to take off my trousers, as I had always felt *much* more self-conscious about exposing my chest than the lower part of my body. I stood naked in the dark barn. The excitement was bubbling from my heart into my throat. I felt I was an ancient Greek, free and fierce and like a clever animal. I wanted to appear naked in public. I looked out of the barn and saw the rain and the blank windows of the house. I thought I would feel the rain spitting on me, so I glided into it and began to dance, concentrating fiercely on my movements. I bent my wrist and elbow joints sharply and began to feel very religious.

I wanted to belong to a sect who did devil dances all night round a bonfire on a wild moor.

Suddenly my brother appeared, but he seemed to show hardly any surprise and followed me into the barn, where I began to swing like a monkey again from the beams. Soon he had no clothes on too and we were dancing and swinging like mad mice. We sang and shrieked, we were so excited and then as suddenly we subsided and began to put our clothes on again. I thought it all the greatest fun, especially as I felt that the grown-ups would be horrified. Suddenly, desperately, I thought I would tell my mother. I was so vain about my wickedness.

She laughed and smiled and I saw she had a far-seeing, inward look.

IX

One day I saw one of the Miss S.s coming up to the door, so I ran to open it before she could ring. She had come to ask us to go to a pageant in which she and her sisters were taking part. An aunt was staying with us at the time and the next day we all got ready to go. I was excited as I was told that I should see Queen Elizabeth riding on a horse with her foot in the original stirrup which had been kept in a nearby country house ever since her visit.

The day was hot and thunderous and we wandered in the lovely garden in which the pageant was to be held, waiting for it to begin. My aunt, who was fat and tired, sat on the grass and spoilt her dress which I admired very much; it was thick white Chinese silk with a charming pattern woven in it. When she got up, there were the great green and brown smears where her big thighs had crushed the grass. I felt that she ought never to be trusted with nice clothes.

By this time the pageant was nearly in sight; it was winding slowly round the great garden. At last I saw the red wig and false pearls of Queen Elizabeth's head. I could see very little else until I was lifted up; then I saw the famous stirrup. It was very large and heavy, like a boat. Miss S. was a page in green velvet. She looked rather outsize for a page, but I suddenly realized that male clothes suited her much better than female clothes. Her eyes were dark and flashing and she had that heavy brick-red colour which is so masculine.

I was a little disappointed in the pageant. I felt that nobody had taken it quite seriously enough.

The Thames was very near us at Benson and we would go down to swim or boat nearly every day; we often would take tea out in a punt and I loved trailing my hand in the water and watching the weeds at the bottom being torn and driven by the current. My father once fell in, which excited me very much. The boat began to leave the shore when he had only one foot in it. He began to do the splits and, as he wasn't a ballet dancer, he couldn't conclude the operation. It shook my belief in the infallibility of adults.

There was much lemon and orange squash drunk at home. I always remember a thick orange grenadine which I liked to drink neat, pretending that it was a liqueur.

We often would go over to the vicarage at Ewelme. It was a severe Georgian house, tall, with some blocked-in windows. The vicar's wife would say, 'If the blocked-up windows were unblocked, there'd be no walls to put furniture against!' In the hall were old prints and there was a red, blue and gold Derby tea-set in the drawing-room. I loved the stately house and its contents and would get the vicar to tell me about it and also about the church. He said that his predecessor had taken all the eighteenth-century pews out of the church and had put in pine ones instead.

Everyone at this time was talking about appendicitis and this had so frightened the vicar and his wife that they had just had their daughter operated on, in spite of the fact that she had shown no signs of poisoning at all.

They explained their reason by saying, 'What should we do, out there in the country, if Maisie should develop appendicitis? It was much better to have it out before the trouble began.' I always wondered why they didn't have themselves operated on too. I suppose the reason is that one always fears for the people one loves, but feels that God will not allow anything like that to happen to oneself.

The vicar's wife would often complain of Maisie's cousin who had come to stay for a few days. She was a modern girl and used lipstick; she had her hair permanently waved and was very restless. The vicar's wife had given her a trowel to do some gardening with, but Maisie's cousin could never stick at anything. In half an hour she would be in the house again, standing about and saying that she'd go mad with boredom. My mother tried to suggest that perhaps she would get over this restlessness, but the vicar's wife felt that the whole modern generation was damned and only hoped that she would be able to preserve Maisie from its influence.

Some other friends of ours were staying in a hotel nearby which had once been a country house. The Thames flowed at the bottom of the garden and two swans always sailed there.

Sometimes my father would take us in to the small town of Warborough, which was quite near. Once he took us into the jeweller's shop to fetch his watch which had been repaired and while we were there the old jeweller showed us some filigree work out of the backs of old watches. My father bought us each one of these watch backs. Mine had ostrich feathers and an urn on it and Paul's had a classical mask and foliage. I soon persuaded Paul to give me his too. I also discovered an early-Victorian fourpenny piece, or groat, which I carried away with me.

When we first went to Oxford I was terribly excited, but I can remember very little except that the twisted pillars in front of the church in the high street amazed me, and when I saw the Martyrs' Memorial I thought of all the martyrs shrieking and screaming while dense smoke and flames were blown about all round them.

My father bought me an old print of Christ Church staircase, which I took home very carefully between its sheets of cardboard. I put it with my other treasures in the tiny room which opened off my bedroom. I would sit in this small cupboard and polish my things by the hour, and as I polished my thoughts would flow easily and I would have strange ideas and imaginings about the past.

My brother had got an airgun by this time and we would put old bottles in the stable-yard and try to shoot them. We tied them to a tree too, so that they swung, which made it even more difficult. I never hit anything at all.

One rainy night a tramp arrived at the back door and asked if he could spend the night in the barn. My mother said that he could and early next morning I got up and saw him go. He was grey and unwashed and quite young.

My mother had discovered a very good cook in the village; she made delicious spaghetti and knew many recipes for savouries. I think she liked devils on horseback best and I remember eating the strange combination often.

Suddenly my father began to look ill, and before I knew what had happened I saw him being carried into an ambulance and then disappearing down the drive. I learnt afterwards that he had had to be operated on for appendicitis and I remembered what the vicar's wife had said about it. I did not go to see my father in the nursing home, but I can remember when he came back, rather pale and thin. He went back to China at the end of the summer, and when my brothers had left for school I learnt with horror that I was also to go to school until Christmas, when we should all be going to Switzerland together.

The school was in Queen's Gate and I was to board with some people whose daughter also went there until my mother should come to London to join me.

I can remember the terrible day she took me to the door of their house. I was crying bitterly and the horror of the long row of coloured brick houses almost overcame me. I had never lived amongst such dreariness and did not know what I should do.

Mrs Spencer, whom neither of us knew, came to the door and let us in. She was small with a sweet face and was very kind. I looked at the varnished paper in the hall and didn't know what to do. I trusted my mother passionately not to leave me here and yet I couldn't trust her, as I knew she would. When she finally abandoned me I thought I should burst. Mrs Spencer tried to comfort me, and when I was quieter she went to the kitchen and made me some custard. I watched her and was interested. I had never really watched cooking before.

When it was ready I tried to eat it, but did not like it, as I had seen it being made. She asked me about China and travelling, and I told her about the boat called the *Empress of Scotland*. She said, 'But there isn't an Empress of Scotland.' She of course meant a person, but I thought she meant a ship and so went on trying to persuade her that there was, as I had travelled on it.

When her daughter came in I made friends with her too and she took me up to bed. I undressed and cleaned my teeth and looked out of the window at the fading chimney-pots and backyards.

I did not know how to bear it and I went to bed crying again.

In the morning Gwen, the daughter, took me to school after a hurried breakfast in the grey little dining-room at the back of the house. We caught buses and tubes, and once Gwen told me to get up, as a lady wanted to sit down. I could not bear doing this; I hated showing what I considered exaggerated respect to women just because they were women. It made me feel debased and ashamed. I always felt that chivalry was just a game that titillated the sexual feelings of both parties, and when a French governess said to me once, '*Les gentilhommes sont toujours galants*', I went red with shame.

When we arrived at South Kensington tube station we walked past the starched chalky bulk of the Natural History Museum and turned into Queen's Gate. Inside the door of the school was a subdued buzzing of girls' voices and the insistent smell of turpentine and beeswax. This was a girls' school where a few small boys were also taken. In the clean-smelling darkness of the hall I saw all these girls with their soft brown hair, and one in particular caught my eye. She must have been about sixteen. She was quite olive coloured, as smooth as rubber, with big animal's eyes and tight curled hair as dark and shining as black treacle. She was quite beautiful and very arresting. Later on I was to be at another school with her brother.

Gwen, who was much older than I was, left me in the hall and soon I found myself with the other small girls and boys in the tall Victorian drawing-room on the first floor. Our mistress was a charming woman, tall, fair and kind. I admired her and felt completely safe. I was bad at everything except handwork and drawing.

This was the only school I ever really enjoyed. Everything seemed to be done for the interest of doing it. Perhaps it was because it was a girls' school and so more or less civilized.

There were such charming interludes as being read to after lunch, lying on the floor with cushions underneath our heads. We sang round songs and made strange bags in very big cross-stitch. Although I was nine I could not read, and I hated this lesson almost as much as mathematics. There was the poetry lesson when our mistress asked a small boy why he looked so sulky and he said because poetry was sloppy, and I remember her answering that all the best poetry was written by men. I cannot understand why he thought it was sloppy, because what we were learning was 'A Wet Sheet and a Flowing Sail'.

There was the thrilling moment every day when the bell went at the end of the morning's work, and we who stayed to lunch had that half hour with our mistress, alone in the upstairs room, when she would read us the most exciting book about a boy and a girl who by chance discovered some caves under a ruined church in which many strange things were going on. To me it was not hackneyed and still does not seem to be.

This little private reading was quite different to the after-lunch reading, which was listened to by the whole of the school.

In the evening I would go back with Gwen. By the time we got to the rows of little houses it would be dark and Mrs Spencer would let us in with brightness and rather sad gaiety.

After the custard or tapioca pudding made on the gas-ring in the dining-room, I would go up to the back bedroom which was mine and, after cleaning my teeth, would get into bed. Gwen and her fat friend would often come in and talk and laugh before I went to sleep. I used to offer fantastic remedies to the fat friend, as she was always talking about slimming.

We laughed and laughed, then I would fall asleep wondering how everything could be so squalid and frightening and yet bearable.

In the morning the sun would sometimes still be red and, as I looked at myself in the mirror by the window, it would light up my face and hair so that I looked dipped in red.

One morning Gwen stopped at South Kensington to buy fruit. We were all going to take some fruit to school that day so that it could be given to a hospital. Gwen bought apples, then turned to me and asked me what I would like to buy for the hospital. I bought grapes and felt very self-conscious and ashamed, as I always have of charitable actions. I was very glad when I got rid of them at school.

Lunch in what must once have been the billiard-room was always gay at school. The light from the cast-iron and glass dome broke on our heads and gave the room a sad, hopeless look, like an aquarium or prison, but from the long tables rose the streams and clouds of talk like the argument of sparrows in a tree. At Mademoiselle's table only French could be spoken and at this table I was silent except for '*Oui*' and '*Non*' and '*Merci*'. I was glad when the next week came and I could move on to another table. Shepherd's pie was born every few days in the kitchen and eaten with relish by us. There seemed no monotony in its constant reappearance.

Twice a week we would go to some fields in a train and play hockey. I hated it and was very careful about my behaviour. I would watch what the big girls did and would imitate if need be. I was always put in some unimportant place at the back of the field and would have plenty of time to study the ribs of my brown corduroy trousers and the curved grain of my pearl-coloured hockey-stick.

Every Sunday I would be collected from Mrs Spencer's by two friends of my mother's. One was a painter and we would often have tea in her studio, where the smell of paint intoxicated me. The size of her paint tubes thrilled me too. They were as large as my toothpaste tube.

I was taken for many expeditions on these Sundays. Once we drove to Windsor and finished up at a restaurant in Eton where we decided to have lunch. It was dark with beams and orange curtains, and we were the only people there until the door burst open and three Eton boys came in holding their cruelly used top hats. They talked loudly and ordered a great deal to eat. When they had gone our waitress told us that they had gone back to their lunch. My friends turned to me and said that I would have to eat as much when I went to public school. I was horrified – I loved food, but I could not bear to be stuffed. I really believed them. It worried me for the rest of the day.

Soon after this my mother came to London and we went to see the hotel where she had booked rooms. We looked at the drawing-room – it was red and white with a loud-speaker like an enormous ear-trumpet – and our bedroom too was very depressing. I could see that my mother could hardly bear it. The manageress was talking in a soothing, confident voice, as if we were new lions to be coaxed into our cages. We returned her smiles and when she had left we quickly shut the bedroom door and kissed each other. We felt cleaner soon and made up our minds to leave at once. We walked to another hotel we remembered and booked rooms there, then we went back to beard the manageress. She was terribly upset. She said that she had never had any trouble before. I felt very sorry for her and wished she would get annoyed so that I need not feel sorry any more.

The new hotel seemed quite like a haven and I arranged the small things I most cared for on a corner of the dressing-table and watched my mother unpack. My father had gone back to China and she was unhappy in those first few days, so she took me to Harrods and bought me a fairy-cycle so that I at least should be happy. The present made me delirious and I rode it all over the huge pavement outside the Victoria and Albert Museum, utterly delighted. I bumped into an old lady, but would not wait to apologize, and I heard my mother trying vainly to excuse my extreme rudeness.

Our hotel was so near the school that I was surprised when I was told that I should still stay at school for lunch instead of having it with my mother, and I was even more resentful when I found that a friend who needed a job was going to sit and read to me or take me out when school was over so that my mother could be free.

I did not realize that the illness which killed my mother was just beginning to show itself. She, who had been so young and full of life, was just beginning to die, and the change must have been terrible for her. Once I found her resting on the bed and it made me cry. My mother never used to rest. She looked the same, with her wonderful gold-brown curls and the brick-dust colour of her cheeks, as if they were wind-whipped; but when the curtains were drawn at night, she would feel stifled and ask for them to be drawn back again, and going up steep stairs she would be tired and wait a little on the landings. It made me harsh and cruel and I would tell her not to be silly, not recognizing in this the mother who danced, played games and swam and pushed me under if I would not swim too.

I was lonely, seeing so little of my mother, but I still enjoyed school, and Molly, the friend, would read to me and try to amuse me conscientiously. I enjoyed sitting by the fire while she read. It was generally a rather grown-up school story *Stalky & Co.* I would follow the stories of the boys who seemed as decisive as men and wondered if I should ever be like them.

At the weekends we would go into the country, if we had been invited. Once we were going to Guildford and were late for the train. We ran stolidly, desperately, and when we were in the compartment my mother nearly fainted. I could hardly believe it and was very callous as the man next to her grew more serious.

At Guildford we were met and taken to the big, ugly villa where out friend lived. I can remember now the long drive through the dripping rhododendrons and the gleam of the great plate-glass windows as the tyres crunched the gravel underneath them.

The servants were all silent Indians with white coats and crimson turbans, and the house was ugly with tiger skins and Japanese carved-ivory.

Our friend was an invalid in a wheelchair and his housekeeper–companion was Eurasian. Her magnolia skin and Chinese eyes were sinister in the smart Western clothes, and her competence and metallic cheerfulness were disturbing. The invalid seemed to me a charming old man and his gold snuff-box with the diamond initials on it entranced me. He is the only person whom I have ever seen taking snuff. He knew someone who was an expert jeweller and silversmith at one of the London art schools and had got him to make many precious things such as this wonderful snuff-box, which lately I have been told cost £2,000. The whole house showed the riot of wealth without taste, even conventional taste, which was perhaps its saving grace.

IN THE
VAST HOUSE

The following fragment is probably based on Denton Welch's recollections of the house in Shanghai that belonged to his maternal grandmother, Katherine Denton, which as a small boy he would certainly have visited, though he never actually lived there.

WHEN I WAS SMALL I LIVED WITH MY GRANDMOTHER — all alone except for the servants — in a big house. All around was the spreading park which shut out the world. Everything was very still in the house; there were only the voices of the servants which could sometimes be heard through the closed doors and the singing of my grandmother's canary. It was a green bird in a wonderful Chinese cage of silver gilt set with coral and lapis lazuli.

My grandmother was very old and queer; she always wore the old-fashioned cravat and tail-coat of a man. Below the waist I do not think she ever wore any outdoor clothes, as she always sat in a wheelchair with a rug tucked around her legs. Her hair was yellow-grey, brushed forward into romantic wisps about her ears, to which were fastened two black pearls. She would sit all day long by the French window in the library, looking out across the park. Sometimes she would grunt and swear to herself.

She did not really like me very much and I was either left alone to do as I wished or else put in the charge of Will, the footman.

He was tall and broad and I loved him dearly. If I were playing on the floor while he was serving my grandmother at her table by the window, I would creep up and kiss his strong legs. He would shift his feet slightly to show that I tickled, whereupon I would do it again until my grandmother, hearing my heavy breath and my giggles, would shout, 'Geoffrey, come out from under the table and stop teasing Will.' Then she would turn to Will and say, 'Take him away, Will, and give him a good flogging if you think he needs it.' She always spoke of any sort of corporal punishment, however mild, as flogging.

Will, with a shamefaced, repressed grin, would then bend down and say, 'You come along with me, Master Geoffrey.' I would feel his dry hands groping for me under the table and the scratch of their hard palms as they brushed my face and legs. Then I would be borne up by those arms, which always seemed to me like an iron crane, and held against his warm hard chest. I would feel the regular hammer against me and, like this, we would leave the room, myself an anxious but willing prisoner. When the library door was shut and we were in the wide, portrait-hung corridor, Will's nature would expand and he would lift me on to his shoulders and walk with a swaggering step, sometimes running and lunging. I was delighted and terrified and would tighten the grip of my legs around his neck, so that the short hair at the back of his head would prick my flesh and he would shout out that I was choking him and would bring his chin down on to my knees and expand his neck muscles. I would relax my grip and he would hold my hands up and would pretend to be a dancing bear with a monkey on his back.

If it were after lunch and the time when I should rest, he would often take me to his room, which was in the dome, and so of course at the top of the house; he would climb, with me still on his shoulders, up the narrow servants' stairs, and at last would throw me down on his narrow, white-counterpaned bed. His face would often be shining with sweat after so much horse-play and the veins would stand out on his large hands which were covered with the red-gold hairs which I liked so much. I used to think that his hands looked as if they were dusted with powdered gold, when the sun shone and made the fine hairs glint.

When he had made me settle myself to rest on the bed, he would take off his coat and, sitting down by the window, he would begin to stuff his pipe and to find the sporting news in the paper.

I would watch him through the slits of my half-closed eyes, my eyelashes knitting together and making a veil through which he appeared.

I would see the slight furrow, as his eyebrows were brought up and down by his concentration on the scores. The white sleeves of his shirt would be rolled up and the blur of gold hair would lie like a bloom over the flesh of his arms. They were as thick as my thighs and I exulted in their hugeness and strength.

My eyes would pass from him to the dressing-table where the swing-glass would be hanging drunkenly, and where the photographs of Will's sweetheart and his sailor brother would stare back at me. Will's sweetheart had soft hair, like a mouse's nest, and eyes that focused on a future of which she seemed terrified.

His brother was in a gym vest and sailor's trousers, sitting on a cardboard rock with arms akimbo. His eyes seemed to say, 'What next, what next? I've done all that's expected of me so far.'

I would watch a fly sitting on one of Will's studs and then hear it buzz as it threw itself against the mirror trying to fly through it.

Perhaps at last I would doze off, and when I awoke with a slight feeling of sickness I would see that Will's chair was empty and that his pipe, with the ashes still in it, was on the windowsill.

I would steal across to the window in my stockinged feet and pick up his pipe. I would wipe the mouth-piece and then put it in my mouth, pretending to be Will. The taste of the burnt tobacco would sting my tongue and fill me with nausea and strange pleasure.

If he had left any clothes lying about, I would slip them on furtively and feel my warmth releasing the pleasant smell of Will's body, so that I seemed to be lapped and enveloped in him.

If I heard him approaching, I would hurriedly wriggle out of his garments and pretend to be putting on my shoes. When he came in he would help me and then bend my face up to him and draw his strong fingers through my hair like a comb. He would take me down to the varnished room, where tea was laid every afternoon, and leave me there alone until he fetched my grandmother in her wheelchair. I would sit by the hissing fire and look round at the room, which never ceased to amaze me. It had been decorated for an ancestress in the eighteenth century and everything was painted or lacquered in it. The ceilings and walls were panelled in wood and painted with strange, erotic scenes from the classics. The doorway and wainscot, window frames and chimney-piece, were green-and-red marbleized wood and there were columns and architectural ornaments with wreaths of flowers. The varnish with which all this painting was covered had mellowed to deep amber and the whole room, ceiling and walls, was polished once a month with beeswax so that it glinted and glistened from sunlight and firelight. The furniture was mostly Venetian, gilded and painted and decorated with old engravings, mixed with Chinese cabinets covered with thick lacquer on which were incised faded peonies and flying birds. There were Chinese jars filled with dried rose leaves, so that when Will took the lids off before my grandmother appeared, the breath of a hundred summers rose faintly from them. Every year another handful of petals was put in and the jars were so large it would seem that they would never be filled.

On the mantelpiece and on the top of the tallest cabinet were octagonal silver vases, swelling in the middle, which held faded ostrich plumes, dyed yellow, crimson, green and blue, darkened with dust and age. From the centre of the room hung the great chandelier of Venetian glass decorated with coloured flowers and leaves and bristling with wax candles.

While I was staring at all these things, the door would open slowly and my grandmother would be pushed in by Will. The corners of her mouth would be pulled down so that it would look like the sagging slit in a pillarbox. Her eyes would go straight to the tray by the fire, where the silver kettle and the spirit-lamp with the honey jar shaped like a Grecian urn and all the other tea things were laid out. Then, when her chair had been wheeled up to the fire, Will would leave us and we would settle down silently to eat the soft floury scones, the toast, the sandwiches and the cakes. I was only allowed one piece of cake and would nearly always choose the rich, black plum-cake which was made with molasses.

My grandmother would eat greedily, with great concentration, and when she had finished she would lie back in the wheelchair and restlessly turn the rings on her fingers and pluck at her cravat pin, running her hand endlessly up and down the lapels and seams of her coat. Sometimes she would take a book from her lap and read to me, but she would never finish the story and always left me in a terrible state of suspense. Once, while she was reading one of *The Ingoldsby Legends*, I noticed that her voice was thickening and faltering. I grinned and squirmed on my chair. I did not know what was going to happen. At last she stopped reading, letting the book fall into her lap and flattening her hands out on it with a smack as it fell. She threw her head back against the chair, looking up at the ceiling, and cried out in a voice heavy with grief, 'Emma used to love this one, the ghosts always frightened her so.' She was crying bitterly by now and I sat, as still as a mouse, thinking of what I knew of Aunt Emma, as I called her.

When my grandmother had married she had told my grandfather that Emma must come to live with them too. He was ready to agree to anything at that time and so Emma had come, and thenceforward my grandmother and Emma had lived a vital life almost totally excluding my grandfather. While they were fishing or riding or boating on the lake, he would be left to wander morosely in the park or to read alone and unwanted in the library.

At last, worn out with boredom and disappointment, he had died. His loss was hardly noticed, except that Emma and my grandmother now hardly even bothered to disguise their passion. They shared the same room and were inseparable in everything. When Emma suddenly died, my grandmother completely withdrew from everyone, living alone in the vast house until, when my parents died, I joined her.

NARCISSUS BAY

This story, which was first published by Peter Quennell in the Cornhill *magazine (July, 1945) and reprinted in* Brave and Cruel, *refers to a time when Denton Welch was about seven years old.*

ONE SUMMER, WHEN I WAS STAYING WITH MY MOTHER at Wei-hai-wei in China, I remember seeing four men and one woman coming down through the woods from the mountain. Two of the men had their hands tied behind their backs; their chests were naked, and they had thick ropes round their necks. The other two held these ropes, which they made to curl and ripple as they drove their prisoners on. The woman walked behind. Her dusty black hair was torn down over her face and shoulders. Blood oozed from cuts on her scalp; a patch of oiled paper had been stuck over one gash, and her lips were swollen and bruised. White cotton puffed out of the sharp tears all over her quilted clothes. She was crying and shaking her head exaggeratedly. In her hands she carried a thick stick broken in two. Where the bark had peeled off, I saw blood on the white, silky wood.

I stood dumbfounded, watching them pass out of the lemon-coloured light under the leaves into the biting sunshine. The woman as she passed me held out the broken stick in pantomime. She ran her cries together, making them into a sort of whining song. The two men holding the ropes jerked the necks of their victims, swore at them, spat on their yellow-brown backs. Then the little procession moved on down the rocky path to the town.

I watched until they disappeared round a bend. My fascinated eyes came back to the cool leafy place where I was, and I could hardly believe what I had seen. I pictured it all to myself again, and the story was unfolded. I saw the men beating the woman outside a thatched hut, close to a smouldering fire. She had exasperated them in some way and they both set on her. But her screams at last roused the village policemen, who came running to help her. They threw ropes round the necks of her attackers, and tied their hands behind their backs.

Now they were all going down to the court house in the town, where the woman would show the blood-stained stick and tell her story. She was nursing her tears – just as I had done myself – because she wanted the judge to be sorry for her.

This all came very vividly to me. Perhaps the woman's expressive dumb-show had made it easy for me to reconstruct the whole story.

I thought again of the blood seen through her matted hair. It was the most barbarous sight I had yet seen and I held it to me with all the violence of new possession. I could not have rid my mind of it if I had tried.

Gradually the picture so overwhelmed me that I began to hate the glade where I had first seen the sight. I darted away, down towards the beach, and did not stop running till I felt the sand under my feet.

On the beach I found two girls I knew, playing outside their bamboo-matting bathing-hut. They were both older than I was; they had reddish down on their thick arms and legs, and their lips were full and well shaped. They treated their Belgian governess with the utmost harshness.

Now, as I approached, they called out and said that they had decided to eat nothing for the whole day. They would touch no meat, no sweet, no wheat, no beet; no fruit, no root; no nut, no gut; — . They rhymed until they had nothing but nonsense words left; then, to fill a gap, I said, 'Where is your mademoiselle?'

'*Elle est grosse et grasse*,' chanted the elder girl, taking no notice of my question, pleased only to have an opportunity of abusing her governess. She repeated her sentence several times in a very loud voice and curved her hands in and out in imitation of the repulsive lines of Mademoiselle's body.

I knew then that their governess was quite near, though hidden. I guessed that they had driven her into retreat behind some rock, where she was knitting. They would go on insulting her until they were tired of the game.

I wondered whether to tell the girls about my extraordinary

experience or not. I really wanted to keep it to myself, but I had not the control. I wanted too to describe the horror to them and the unreal, magic atmosphere.

I began to tell them about the ropes, the wounds, the blood and the broken stick. They listened contemptuously, sometimes throwing out their arms and legs, or twitching their nostrils in disbelief. But I knew that I had stirred them.

'What a liar!' the younger one said when I had finished. She said it mildly, as if she'd known me to be one for a long time.

'Which way did they go?' the other asked with heavy sarcasm; but her eyes were watching sharply.

'Towards the town,' I said. And immediately they were away, over the sand and the rough tufted grass. They were running down the white road and Mademoiselle had risen up from behind her rock and was screaming to them to come back.

'Mary! Rosalie!' she cried, but they never turned their heads. Hopelessly she started to run after them. The town was forbidden and she did not know what she was going to say to their mother.

I watched her fatness jellying for a little; then I turned away and searched for fan shells along the beach. Once or twice I had found softest pink ones and ones of coral scarlet, but now I found nothing. I wondered whether to go home or to go on to the end of the bay and have tea with Adam Grant and his mother.

I decided to visit Adam. I was still restless. My thoughts were seething and my body tingled. I would arrive a little early and perhaps a little dirty, but I hoped Mrs Grant would not mind.

I walked slowly over the wet sand, close to the waves; but I soon reached the stone steps and the rock pools. I idled on the steps, leaning on the iron rail and staring into the depths of the pools from above. At last I climbed up to the terrace and found Adam lying there in a wicker chair. He looked up and told me importantly that he wasn't very well, he wasn't allowed to bathe, and his mother had pinned a flannel band round his stomach because she thought he had a chill there.

This struck me as ridiculous and rather disgusting in hot weather, and I said, 'But what good will that do?'

'Of course it's the thing to put on for a chill in your stomach,' Adam replied pompously; then he pretended to go on reading his book.

I stared at him. He was rather a fat boy with hair like coconut matting. I laughed to think of the flannel band round his stomach. Still he kept his eyes on his book; but I smiled, knowing that I could make him drop his show of indifference.

'Today I saw two men with ropes round their necks, and a woman who'd been beaten all over,' I said flatly, without any colour, to give my words their greatest effect.

Adam's head jerked up.

'Where? When did you see it?'

He seemed about to run out to look for the sight as the girls had done.

'Oh, it was a long time ago, up on the edge of the wood,' I said languidly.

Adam poured out questions and I answered them with maddening slowness and vagueness. The story filled him with excitement, but at the end he remembered to say, 'How awful for two men to beat a woman like that!'

He was still showing horror at the brutality, when his mother called out in a boisterous sing-song voice, 'Tea's ready!' and we both got up to go into the cool shaded dining-room.

There we found Mrs Grant and another, younger boy, who, with his nurse, was also staying in the house. We sat down at the long narrow table and Mrs Grant began to pour out. While Adam passed the bread and butter, I watched her. She was a soldier's wife, and I had the idea that she was very superstitious. Perhaps I exaggerated, but I imagined that her religion was made up of patent medicines, charms and unmeaning rites – such as the pinning of the flannel round Adam's stomach. I felt sorry for her – she was so very benighted and unaware of real things.

The other boy was silent. He was nervous and puzzled because he believed nearly everything that was said to him.

I looked at the tea and saw that it was good: peanutbutter, brown bread, chocolate biscuits and sponge cake. At first I was pleased; then I began to feel out of sympathy with everyone, and I longed to get away and be alone.

We played in the garden after tea, hiding behind the huge hollyhocks, springing out at one another.

Adam told the younger boy to eat one of the dead flower heads, then to drink some slimy green water in an earthenware crock. He shouted at him, 'If you sit on the lavatory seat too long a swordfish will come up and bite you.'

I saw Derek's face jump. He really believed it, and the thought was going to frighten him for ever.

Adam followed up his success with other horror stories.

'If you swim into a jelly-fish and it stings your face, it'll blind you; and if even a baby octopus gets hold of you it can suck the life out of you. A shark too can bite a leg off as easy as anything. Once they brought a man in with no arms or legs left.'

Derek put his arm across his mouth and bit the flesh. His eyes were terrified. He wanted someone to deny the stories, but I was too lazy and uninterested to do so, and his nurse was far away, gossiping to Mrs Grant on the veranda.

Adam made a lunge at him with a pole and when he flinched said, 'What's the matter? I was only pretending that I was harpooning a whale.'

To get away from us Derek ran into one of the bathrooms and locked the door. Adam climbed up to the window and made terrible faces through the glass; then he said, 'You won't sit on the seat, will you, because of that swordfish.'

At this Derek burst into tears and wailed so noisily that his nurse came and reprimanded us all, not sparing Derek. I could see his eyes still puzzled, terrified, longing to find protection somewhere. I turned away, ashamed for myself and ashamed for him. His nurse began to undress him for bed. I heard the bathwater splashing.

Adam followed me out on to the rocks below the terrace. I disliked his stomach band, his fleshiness, his superstitious mother, and wished he would leave me. I wanted to be alone to watch the orange sun sink down into the sea.

To get away from him I moved from rock to rock until I was on a level with the pools. Still Adam followed me. I remembered that he was not supposed to bathe, and, lying down on the edge of a pool, I dipped my arm in and said, 'How lovely the water feels this evening!'

'But you know I'm not allowed to bathe,' he said accusingly.

'Aren't you?' – and I rolled into the delicious water with my shirt and shorts and sandals on. I beat about with my hands and shouted out my delight.

Adam went stiff with envy and resentment, but I took no notice of his venomous remarks until I had played and splashed enough; then I climbed out and said, 'Lend me a lantern, I'm going home.'

It was not really dark enough for a lantern, but I wanted to carry a lighted one along the beach.

Adam grudgingly found me his, and I lit the candle; then, after asking him to say goodbye to his mother for me, I set out along the ribbed sand.

The oiled cotton of the lantern was painted with large scarlet and black characters. I danced and jumped about, making the light bob up and down and throw shadows like ghosts. Showers of drops fell from my soaking clothes. Far out in the bay the phosphorus was beginning to fringe the wavelets.

The scene of the early afternoon came back to me with sudden violence. I saw again the woman and the four men winding down through the trees; and for some reason my thoughts jumped to the shrine which I knew was on the mountain above them. My mother and I had once climbed up to it and eaten our picnic on the thymy grass in front. With my fingers I had picked out the little rock-plants, like the flat round bottoms of artichokes.

The walls of the shrine were covered with peeling vermilion plaster and under the black curling roof were gods with little plates of food set before them, and joss-sticks, and gold and silver paper money scattered everywhere.

The clouds came down so low that they turned into veils of rainbow mist when the sun shone through them.

I thought of the utterly still, deserted place and I thought of the baked mud gods, all painted bright and gilded, gazing down, unmoving, caught in a trance, just watching everything, holding up their fingers, flashing their eyes and teeth for ever.

AT SEA

In this story 'Robert' is the author himself. It was first published by Woodrow Wyatt in English Story *(fifth series, 1944) and reprinted in* Brave and Cruel.

ROBERT SAT ON THE DECK HOLDING A BOOK IN FRONT OF his eyes and wearing a very preoccupied and intellectual expression. He was pretending to read. He mouthed words silently, smiled as if amused, then looked grave and serious. Every now and then he glanced about him, to see if anyone was noticing him. The stewardess came up with a cup of hot soup. She bent over him and said, 'What! You reading to yourself! Clever lad. Here's your soup and your mother wants you when you've finished it.'

Robert smiled at the stewardess and took the soup proudly. He felt rather ashamed of deceiving her over the reading, but decided that the deception was worth it, if it gave him this comfortable, proud feeling.

He began to drink the hot peppered soup and to crumble the hard water-biscuits. He could never understand why biscuits of this extreme dullness were made. 'Even grown-ups can't really like them,' he thought, although he knew how perverse and disgusting their taste in food could be sometimes.

When he had finished the soup and made sucking noises against the lip of the cup in imitation of some voracious animal, he went down to the cabin. He was always annoyed when Americans called cabins 'staterooms'. It reminded him of palaces, of death, of politics, of candles round a coffin in a cathedral. It was showing-off and pretence. Rooms on boats were cabins.

His and his mother's cabin on 'A' deck had really been designed as a drawing-room to a suite, but it had been partitioned off for this particular trip across the Atlantic and two beds had been put in. The walls were covered with dull panels of grey and rose tapestry. There were canework and gilt chairs and nothing much else, except a rather smelly little washstand which had been hurriedly installed. The mixture of commercial luxury and improvisation was surprising. Robert was both impressed and depressed by this particular cabin, different to any he had shared with his mother before. She, as an American with her older sons at school in England, was always travelling backwards and forwards; and wherever she went she took Robert.

There she lay on the bed, still in her nightdress. She did not feel very well and had decided not to get up till lunchtime. She was reading *Science and Health, with Key to the Scriptures* by Mary Baker Eddy, but when she saw Robert, she raised her head and smiled. Robert thought, for the thousandth time, 'My mother is young and pretty, most people's mothers look old and ugly.' Always he felt this when he looked at her; especially if, as now, she were a little bedraggled and unwell. When in the morning she asked him to kiss her before she was absolutely awake, when her eyes were still heavy and she felt almost damp from the warmth of the bed, he would have the curious proud feeling mixed with distaste. And sometimes he would not kiss her until she was quite awake and smiling, with her curly, fried-bread-crumb-coloured hair fluffed out and pretty.

'Darling,' she said now, 'which dress shall I wear? You choose and put it out with nice stockings and shoes.'

Robert thought swiftly and methodically. He knew his mother's clothes well; not her underclothes – he did not understand them and did not want to, they seemed too fragmentary and bitty – but her day dresses, her coats and skirts and especially her evening clothes interested him deeply. He would often tell her that something did not suit her. He had even used violence on things of his mother's that he did not like. Once he had pulled off and mauled a mustard-yellow hat with a velvet bow which he could not bear.

This being the period of the late 1920s, the dress which Robert chose for his mother to wear at lunch was extremely short. It was of light soft beige wool and had a very broad shiny black belt that looked as if it were made of creased American cloth. He put out cobweb-thin flesh-coloured stockings and a pair of snub-nosed snake-skin shoes with very high heels.

His mother looked at what he had laid out.

'Darling, do you think snake-skin goes with that wool?' she asked tentatively.

'Yes, why not? It's just right,' he answered with matter-of-fact emphasis.

'Oh well – if you think it looks nice. Tell me, what have you been doing on deck all morning?'

There was a slight pause, then Robert said rather desperately, 'I – I've been reading.' His voice grew bolder, more brutal towards the end, as if he were daring his mother to gainsay him.

'Reading!' she echoed incredulously. 'You reading! Why, Miss Hawethorne told me that she could only get you to spell the simplest words out; and whenever I've tried to get you interested, you've always become sulky or implored me to read to you myself. Darling, you mustn't pretend you can read when you can't; and you *must* learn to read so that you needn't pretend. It's terrible; you're really quite old now. Perhaps it's my fault for taking you about so much, but you really must try to get hold of it, then you'll love sitting all alone and reading the most wonderful things; Shakespeare and the Bible and *Science and Health*, and *Alice in Wonderland* and Michael Arlen.'

'I *can* read,' said Robert obstinately, his cheeks burning with shame. 'The stewardess thought I could anyhow,' he added. It was a poor little spark of defiance and bravado.

'You are not to pretend and you're not to lie. You can't read and you know it and you're ashamed of it. Don't let Mortal Mind get hold of you and keep you back; know that as God's child nothing can stop you from learning.'

'I *can* read!' Robert almost screamed at his mother. He was on the verge of tears. She leant forward in the bed and smacked his face hard.

'You are not to lie. No gentleman lies,' she said with icy contempt. This change from the religious to the social field was startling and disconcerting. The hardness in her voice frightened Robert. It was so much more difficult to follow her now that she was not talking about realities. God was real. Wickedness was real (in spite of what his mother and Mrs Eddy said), but gentlemen didn't seem real at all. He knew that gentlemen lied; the very fact that they called themselves 'gentlemen' was a lie.

He looked down on his mother on the bed. He had not cried when she smacked his face, although her hand had stung, and he had been shocked and startled. If he had cried, she would have been more victorious. He wondered what to do to regain his integrity and pride. He thought of smacking his mother's face in return, but he didn't quite dare do so, for the heat was leaving him. He thought of discomforting her by pulling back the bedclothes or by some hurting remark, but suddenly another idea came to him and he quietly went over to the clothes he had laid out and began to put them away again.

'Robert, don't put them away; I'm just going to get up and bath,' his mother called, but he took no notice. When he had shut the huge wardrobe-trunk again, he left the cabin, without another word.

He wandered about the deck, then went into the writing-room and began an imaginary letter on the elaborately hideous ship's notepaper. The letter was to begin in English, but there were to be long passages in French and Italian, and there was even to be a snippet of Russian. He had it all planned. He began legibly enough, 'Dear Friend, Here I am at sea,' but as his small stock of real words gave out, he began to invent ones, and when he came to the sections which were to be in foreign languages, he twirled and twisted and jabbed with the pen until he had made an extraordinary pattern on the paper.

'That ought to do,' he said to himself at last, having covered several pages. He looked at the elaborate scribble carefully, as if he were reading an important document through and checking it; then he took an envelope and licked it portentously. He sealed it down and wrote a most imposing address. The flourishes and capital letters were grand enough for a royal proclamation.

He took this letter out with him on deck again; and when he thought no one was looking, he posted it in one of the enormous open-mouthed ventilators. He threw it up in the air. He saw it hover, then disappear down the black throat. He wondered where it would go. He associated the bowels of the ship with the bowels of the earth, and thought of ugly black demons seizing on his scholarly letter and reading it with interest and delight.

The gong for lunch sounded. Robert went to wash his hands. He smeared down his hair with his wet hands, as this always proved to his mother that he had washed. He wondered again why it was considered so despicable not to wash before meals.

He went into the dining-saloon and saw his mother already at their table. She had on the dress he had chosen, the stockings and the shoes. She was smiling and talking to a friend over her shoulder. She looked well and happy. There would be no more talk of gentlemen and lies.

'Darling,' she said, 'you *were* naughty to put all my clothes away again, but now don't sulk any more. Come and have minced chicken and rice. You know you love minced chicken and rice.'

Robert did not smile, but was immediately submissive to his mother, at least in spirit if not in words.

'Can't I have curry and all those things to put on top?' he asked with very little hope.

'Darling, the chicken and rice will be so much nicer. They don't really know how to make curry well on this ship.'

Robert allowed his mother to order the whole meal with no more resistance. He looked about him and saw the woman at a nearby table whose looks he so admired. She was utterly different from his mother; cold-coloured, not warm; tall, not small and childish; graceful and studied and rigid, not gay and spontaneous and completely unselfconscious. She held her back so straight when she bent forward. The effect was overpoweringly impressive to Robert. It was like a marble goddess leaning down from a cloud. When she put her elbow on the table and turned and twisted her wrist, the poised utterly careful mannerism bewitched Robert. He found himself imitating her, both consciously and unconsciously. He tried leaning towards his mother in the same rigid way. He held up his napkin with the drooping, fallen-bird posture of the left hand. He wiped his mouth as if it were made of precious porcelain.

He did not love this woman at all. Something about her was even repellent to him; but his admiration for her knew no bounds. The ceremoniousness of her disciplined Diana-like body fascinated him. She was with a handsome young Jewish man, who morning and evening showed a great deal of cuff and the most beautiful emerald and diamond links. She spoke to him slowly, graciously, coldly smiling now and then with her archaic Greek-sculpture smile.

'Darling, stop staring and eat your chicken,' his mother said, recalling him.

After lunch they went out into the vestibule and sat down in deep chairs and had coffee. Robert poured out and passed a cup silently to his mother; then he saw his mother's new friend Mr Barron approaching. He turned his back a little more and pretended to be occupied with the coffee-pots. He opened the lids and looked inside, even pretending that the skin off the boiled milk had stuck in the spout. Mr Barron, so delicate and spectacled and poor and gentlemanly looking, clapped him on the back heartily and said, 'Aha, looking after your mother well? I like to see a chap looking after his mother.'

Mr Barron smiled as broadly as he could, but, owing to the refinement of his features, he only managed to look like a skeleton.

Robert's mother smiled back at him gaily and said, 'Come and sit down and have coffee with us. Robert will pour you some out and get another cup for himself.'

Robert looked at Mr Barron and said, 'I wasn't looking after my mother, I was only pouring out because I like playing.'

There was a slight pause. Robert's seemed such an unnecessary childish contradiction, yet it held in it a deep antagonism. Mr Barron was embarrassed and so grew even more unnaturally hearty.

'Come, come,' he said boisterously, 'this'll never do. We all know that you'd do *anything* for your mother. And quite right too. I don't think any fellow could wish for a more charming one.' Here he made an awkward, deeply sincere bow towards Robert's mother, and immediately grew red at this foreign gallantry.

Robert watched the pantomime with cynical, taunting eyes; then he said something preposterous to shock and terrify Mr Barron into retreat for ever.

'I wouldn't let them put a red-hot poker into my behind, as they did to King Edward II; so you see I wouldn't do *anything* in the world for her.'

'Darling!' his mother said in shocked and laughing surprise. 'Whoever told you of such a thing?'

'Miss Hawethorne,' said Robert flatly. 'I asked her what they did to him in the dungeon and she told me. She doesn't think people should beat about the bush, and she says I'm old enough to know the truth.'

'Yes, Robert, but if you're old enough to know the truth, you're old enough to know when to mention things and when not to mention things. It's not right to say things like that just to be surprising. Talk about them seriously, not in a silly way.'

Mr Barron was now so nonplussed by Robert's dislike that he was pressing cigarettes on Robert's mother when he knew that she did not smoke because she was a Christian Scientist. He looked at her with deep admiration and respect.

'I've asked a few people to tea in my cabin, won't you come too and dance to the gramophone afterwards?' he asked at last, still gazing at her rather too reverently. Robert was not conscious of feeling jealous of Mr Barron, he only wished that his mother would not waste time in his company. There was so much for them to do together. His mother was teaching him how to do her petit-point, and now he had nearly done all the left ear of the squirrel in her beautiful embroidery. He was getting so good that they could silently work at each end of the canvas. Only sometimes did he have to ask her to match wool or thread the needle when the wool came unravelled. It was a joyful time, doing the embroidery with his mother.

His mother was half accepting, half refusing the invitation.

'We were going to do some more work together and I was going to paint you one of those weeny little pictures you liked, and you said I had to learn to read properly,' Robert burst out in a torrent.

'Yes, darling, but we've got plenty of time to do all that. It's very nice of Mr Barron to ask me and I'd like to go.'

'What am *I* going to do then!' Robert screamed, betrayed. '*I* can't sit eating too many little cakes. *I* can't go dancing! And afterwards you'll drink cocktails. They'll make you drink cocktails, and you know what Mrs Eddy says. She says Scientists don't need such false stimulants; she even thinks tea and coffee are wrong.'

Robert looked at his mother in a broken-hearted way.

'Mummy,' he burst out in a sudden strangled melodramatic voice; 'don't go dancing in his stuffy cabin and drinking cocktails. It's Error trying to get hold of you.'

Mr Barron's extreme discomfort made him lift himself on his hands and waggle from side to side uneasily.

'I think I – er – ' he began.

Robert's mother was furious with her child for being so uncontrolled and primitive.

'Robert, stop talking nonsense and go away, if you can't be civilized. Leave Mr Barron and myself alone; you've bored us quite long enough with your pretentiousness and your tantrums.'

She turned towards Mr Barron with the most engaging of smiles and seemed to snuggle down to a long cosy talk.

Robert got up. He was torn with horrible pangs of shame and frustration.

As he passed Mr Barron he made the vulgar whorish gesture of lifting his foot and displaying the whole sole in contempt, at the same time looking over his shoulder with a sneer on his face. He had seen two schoolgirls doing this in America and it had impressed him. The showy insolence of the unsuitable gesture comforted him for a moment.

He saw Mr Barron's skeleton, hearty, terrified smile grow from ear to ear.

'Please overlook his impossible behaviour,' he heard his mother say. 'He must be left alone at the moment, but when he recovers I shall see that he apologizes to you. Where on earth did he learn that disgusting trick!' Then she laughed, quite genuinely amused through her anger. And this was the worst thing of all, her refusal to take his protest seriously.

He went up to the 'winter garden' which was always more or less deserted until tea-time. Here the large palms stood about between panels of elaborate Edwardian latticework. Trellis roses were painted dimly and delicately on the lattice. There were large gloomy mirrors.

In one corner he saw smoke rising from behind a canework chair. He went up and found the woman he and his mother privately called Princess Bonbon. She was reading and smoking a fat Egyptian cigarette. She was indeed some Bourbon princess, but was of English birth. She seemed to have no husband, at least not on the boat. When Robert's mother first told him who she was, he was thrilled. He knew all about Marie Antoinette from Miss Hawethorne and was always longing to ask the Princess Bonbon how her husband's ancestors linked up with this fascinating queen, but he never dared. He knew it was wrong to appear even to notice that she was a princess. But he felt that she must be different. You couldn't be ordinary with Marie Antoinette tacked on somewhere behind.

He looked at the Princess Bonbon carefully once again. Again he saw a smear on her teeth of the cerise lipstick which she always wore. He had never seen her without this rather frightening ornamentation. It was as if the teeth had become delicately bloodshot. She was an awkward, lanky, very English woman, whose clothes were too brightly coloured and artistic to be smart. Her face was plain and flat, as if the bone structure had fallen in slightly. The bright cerise lipstick made her pale skin look grey-white and uneven in pigmentation, almost blotched. In spite of magenta chiffon scarf, diamond clip, peacock and mustard jerkin and bag, she looked colourless and effaced, tired, angry, wasted.

'Hullo, Robert,' she said; 'come and talk to me. I'm all alone here.'

He went directly up to her and stood very straight with his head bowed respectfully. At that moment his manners were perfect. He was ready to treat any woman, but his mother, with the most extreme chivalry. He waited for the Princess to ask him to sit down. She patted the stool where she had put up her feet and he sat down beside her not very attractive shoes. She had chocolates in her lap and she held out a big pistachio nut one and he, although he did not care for this sort, opened his mouth dutifully and let her thrust it a little too far in. He munched, making as little noise as possible. He became awkward and uneasy, not knowing what to talk about after the tumultuous scene with his mother and Mr Barron.

'Would you like to come and see Joey?' asked the Princess suddenly. Joey was her liver and white spaniel which was kept in a special kennel at the farthest end of the boat deck. She was always talking of Joey, bemoaning the fact that he would have to be left in quarantine for six months as soon as they reached Southampton.

'Yes, let's,' said Robert, pleased and relieved at the suggestion. He stood up and held the Princess's chocolates and book, while she put a little more lipstick on her mouth. She saw in the mirror the pink stain on her teeth, and rubbed them in a workmanlike fashion with her thin handkerchief. Robert thought how foreign it looked, with its profusion of embroidered flowers, its large coronet and rococo initials. 'It's French or Italian,' he thought. His mother's handkerchiefs were plain, smooth, delicate, lovely.

The Princess Bonbon led the way and Robert followed a few paces behind, like her page or squire.

They climbed up to the boat deck where the biting wind struck them. The Atlantic, unbelievably monotonous and real, came as a shock too. It was an endless carpet, bulging and yielding, because of the draught along the floorboards beneath it.

Joey rushed at them, madly straining on his chain. The Princess, having brought nothing for him, gave him chocolate after chocolate out of her box. Joey swallowed them as if they'd been flies.

'It's no good,' said Robert. 'He's too greedy even to taste them!'

'Oh, the darling, darling, darling,' said the Princess, dropping on her knees and clutching the scrambling Joey to her. He licked her face, mauled her chiffon scarf, bit the checked bag. Then he tore away to the extent of his chain, as if suggesting a ten-mile walk.

They marched him up and down the deck for about twenty minutes. They talked very little between themselves but a great deal to Joey.

'Oh pet, petkin, petskin,' cried the Princess, 'I can't bear to think I'll be parted from you for six months in a few days' time.'

At last they grew so cold without overcoats that they had to leave him. He whined dismally, danced on his chain, implored. The Princess's heart was wrung. She turned quickly away and said, 'Mr Barron's asked me to his cabin for tea and drinks and dancing; come with me, Robert, and give me moral support.'

'That's where my mother's gone,' he said, suddenly remembering the whole ugly scene in the vestibule.

'Do you like that Mr Barron, Princess?' he asked, on impulse. He had never called her 'Princess' before. Now he seemed to warm to her and long for her to say something spiteful about Mr Barron.

'I think he's a very nice man, don't you? So clever and quiet, and yet quite gay at the same time.'

'Why does he smile like that?'

'Like what, Robert?'

'Sort of like a dead man.'

'I think he's rather nervous, like so many sensitive people.'

'He offers my mother cigarettes and cocktails and he knows she thinks they're wrong.'

'He only wants her to have a good time. I think he admires your mother very much, and quite naturally. She is very attractive.'

'Do you think so?' Robert was delighted; the annoyance of Mr Barron was quite forgotten.

They reached the door of Mr Barron's cabin and heard noises of amusement and gaiety. The gramophone was playing 'My Cutie's due at two-to-two on a big chu-chu.'

Robert pushed the door open for the Princess and stood back as he had seen grown-up men do. The room was very smoky. People were sitting on the bed and others had overflowed into Mr Barron's private bathroom. He himself was mixing drinks while Robert's mother was sitting childishly hunched up in a chair, pouring out tea as if she'd been hostess. She held out cups for anyone to take. She was like a charming eighteenth-century street hawker. The cups were her wares; her mouth, a little open, seemed to be singing their goodness.

There was a slight stir when the Princess came in with Robert. They brought a completely different, unconvivial atmosphere with them. Mr Barron hurried up, still holding the shaker, and in his nervousness offering it to the Princess to drink out of. She smiled her flat, plain smile. Nothing seemed to matter. She could not be happy. People began to chaff Robert and offer him sips from their various drinks; until one managing soul thrust her tea into his hand and forbade him to sip another cocktail or to eat another alcohol-soaked cherry. Robert refused even to look at his mother; but he knew that she had left the tea and had accepted an Old-fashioned cocktail. Then he knew that she was dancing with Mr Barron and that others were dancing too. All the couples could do was to circle on the small patch of bare carpet, but their activity set up a rhythm and vibration through the whole, fairly spacious cabin.

Robert lay down on the bed and shut his eyes. He felt a little sick from the cherries and the sips and the Princess's pistachio chocolates. Someone tried to make him eat bread and butter, but he would not.

Fat tears squeezed out of his eyes. He tried to hold them in by shutting his eyes still tighter, but they always managed to wriggle out. He dashed them on to the eiderdown where they made little dark splashes.

The Princess Bonbon came and leant over him and saw that he was crying.

She said, 'What is wrong, Robert dear?' Then, feeling ineffectual, she went over to his mother and touched her shoulder as she danced with Mr Barron.

'I think Robert's rather overtired or feeling ill; shall I take him back to your cabin?' she asked.

Robert's mother immediately left Mr Barron's arms and went up to the bed.

'What is wrong?' she asked rather coldly, bending down.

'Go away, pig,' he screamed, then turned over on his face and buried it in the eiderdown.

He felt his mother's hands on his shoulders and her warm breath on his neck. He wriggled his shoulders violently and kicked back his legs. He knew that he was about to make the most terrible scene. He had the sudden fear that his nervous excitement would make him lose control of his bladder. The shame, if this happened, would be terrible, but he also thought with detachment that it would be funny to wee-wee on Mr Barron's soft bed.

'Don't be troublesome, Robert,' his mother said briskly. 'It is so bad to make scenes in public. People never do it. They think it very ugly and in very bad taste.'

This mention of good taste, correct behaviour and public opinion struck Robert as extraordinarily frivolous and wicked.

'I don't care what anyone thinks,' he shouted into the thickness of the eiderdown; then he sprang up and ran into the centre of the cabin. The two or three dancing couples stared at him. He felt with horror the sudden warmth on the inside of his leg. His mouth fell open. He screamed some abuse at his mother, then with tears pouring down his face he ran from the cabin, slamming the door behind him.

He made straight for his own cabin; there he snatched up his towel and flannel and rushed to the bathroom. He locked himself in and gave himself up to a fit of weeping; then suddenly his heart went quite hard and he felt ashamed of himself. He got on to a stool and, crouching over, dipped his head deep into a basin of cold water. Afterwards he washed his clothes methodically and efficiently and pressed them against the hot-water towel-rail until they steamed and gradually grew dry. He dressed himself again and left, quite emptied, chastened, apart; a hundred miles from the world, the ship, his mother, everything.

He got ready for bed early and waited until the stewardess brought his hot milk and biscuits. She had also managed to filch a striped ice-cream for him from the dinner menu. She always brought him some delicacy, apart from the plain milk and biscuits. Robert thanked her and then, after she had made her few nice gossipy remarks and left, he went over to one of the portholes and threw the ice-cream as far out to sea as possible. Striped ice-cream of this sort made him feel sick, but he would never have told the stewardess this.

After he had cleaned his teeth as his mother had taught him (up and down, not across) he lay down on the bed and shut his eyes, still leaving the light on. He felt that he wanted to cry again, but the hardness in him poured contempt upon his other self and instead he began swearing at his mother with the worst oaths he could invent. The only real swear words he knew were 'damn' and 'bloody', and so he twisted and elaborated these with fanciful beginnings, endings, middles.

Suddenly the door opened and he knew that his mother was about to enter. He shut his eyes even tighter and began to breathe deeply. He tried to make snoring noises. She came over to him and touched him. He took no notice. He knew she was bending low over him. He showed no sign and tried to imagine himself turned to granite. His mother shaded the light away from him and started to change for dinner. He heard the tinkling of rings and other things on the glass-topped table, and the soft plop of garments being shed. He made his eyes into narrow slits and watched her impatiently doing up her dress at the side. He saw her leaning forward to the mirror and making up her face in a slap-dash way; a dart of lipstick, a slash of black pencil, the cream rouge in two little balls on her cheeks smudged in and in until they almost disappeared. He was anxious to see the whole effect of her before she went in to dinner. He could tell how unhappy and out of patience she was. She would go in to dinner, ready to shock and surprise, to appear startling. She had put on her bizarre black dress with tulips made of dyed feathers dangling from one shoulder almost to her hips. The dress showed her knees in front and swept down in a curve behind like a half-moon.

She got up and snapped the light off with a vicious flip.

Robert gradually floated further and further into sleep . . .

When he next woke the light was on again and he saw his mother in the middle of the cabin; she looked lost, unhappy and unwell. He knew that it was late. He knew that she had been dancing and that she was very tired. He wondered if she had drunk cocktails or champagne or any other intoxicating drink.

She came over to him gently, and he smelt the tobacco smoke which had soaked into her clothes from the choking air of the ballroom. It came out in waves, mixed with her scent.

When she saw that he still pretended to be asleep, she turned away to undress; then, as if too ill and exhausted to go on, she fell down on her bed and began to say fanatically but softly, 'There is no life, truth, intelligence or substance in matter. All is Infinite Mind and its infinite manifestation.'

Robert knew how ill she must be feeling. She lay still holding on to the eiderdown, waiting in a trance to feel better.

He opened his eyes and looked at her; he could not go over to her or touch her, but he longed to help her. He formed his face and mouth carefully into the right shape and then began to sing very gently:

> What is thy birthright, man,
> Child of the perfect One;
> What is thy Father's plan
> For His beloved son?

He waited a moment to gather breath and to remember the second verse correctly:

> Thou art Truth's honest child,
> Of pure and sinless heart;
> Thou treadest undefiled –

He had forgotten what came next. He was overcome with the beauty and sadness of his own singing. He was going to cry because his mother was ill on the bed. He wasn't going to help her. He was going to cry.

He jumped angrily out of bed and crouched by her on the floor. He held her hand and arm fiercely. They neither of them said anything, but his mother was breathing deeply, trying to master her illness and pain.

'Sing, darling,' she said after a pause. 'It's lovely when you sing for me.'

He still held her arm tightly and untenderly, as if it were the spar of a ship and he a man in the water. He knew so many hymns, but only the first verses of them. He wanted to sing something so consummate and wonderful that his mother would turn over and smile and be happy for ever; but he knew that she was dying and that she could not save herself. He only knew this sometimes in a flash. At other times he would be completely hypnotized by her gaiety and liveliness into believing that she was not ill at all and that she would live for ever.

Now he decided to sing,

> Eternal Mind the Potter is
> And thought the eternal clay;
> The hand that fashions is divine,
> His works pass not away.

His mother was growing less tense; she sighed, turned towards him and smiled.

'Don't cry, darling,' she said humorously, for the tears were now streaming down his face, 'don't cry, I feel so much better.' But he could not stop, they poured down and he made no sound, only stared at his mother, his eyes boring deep down into her. He could not sing any more, he could do nothing, only watch his mother and let the tears stream down bitterly.

THE HAPPIEST TIME

In Denton Welch's second novel, In Youth is Pleasure, *his father, 'Mr Pym', nicknames him 'Microbe' or 'Maggot'. In the following fragment, again set in his maternal grandmother's house, he becomes 'Flea', and his father 'John Markham'.*

YES, IT WAS ONE OF THE HAPPY TIMES OF HIS LIFE, perhaps the happiest; but he was not to know this, sitting there on the low stool in front of the fire, eating his supper of bread and butter and hot milk, while his father read to him.

They were in the library, not a very large room but a lofty one, with a snug cushioned seat on top of the radiator in the wide bay-window. The long windows were curtained now in smoky purple velvet. The carpet was purple too; the pool, made by his father's lamp, showed brilliant plummy violet. The rest, in shadow, seemed almost black in its consuming warmth. Round the walls were low bookcases with glass doors, and, above these, many old engravings of Peking's Forbidden City made by a Jesuit missionary in the seventeenth century.

It could not have been called a beautiful room; the proportions were too clumsy and the furnishings too haphazard. But to the child, very much aware of his surroundings, it was beyond criticism. Was it not part of the house that had been built for his grandmother, the house that had harboured him all his long, crowded, eight years of life?

A stranger, seeing the room for the first time, would have found it almost impossible to tell where he was on the earth's surface. England he might have guessed first, because there was an undeniable flavour of the later Victorian club about the heavy mouldings, the lofty ceilings, the windows and doors just a little larger than life, so that a man felt puny in opening and shutting them.

But it was England with a twist. Where in England would one

see quite such a lampshade – all exquisitely patterned gauze stretched over silk, trimmed with elaborate knots and tassels? Where would one find a long, shallow porcelain trough, filled with water and red-veined marble pebbles, in which strange bulbs grew, not quite like our narcissus? Their scent spread out secretly on the warm air in the room; it was the scent of a far country, strange, pure, delicious, unforgettable.

One was in China, of course; that is, if the cosmopolitan city of Shanghai can really be considered part of that country.*

'Don't stop reading, Daddy,' said the child, holding out a piece of bread and butter to the flames, so that the butter should melt and friz, and the bread become delicately smoked. 'But I want another cocktail, Flea,' protested his father with comic querulousness. John Markham always called his only child Flea, because the child was small for his age, and because John Markham secretly considered the name Timothy affected, although he had allowed his son to be christened thus willingly enough, simply to please the passing whim of his wife, Rosa. He was pleased when he found that, as soon as the child was out of the grotesque rubbed-brick cathedral, no one ever thought of calling it anything but Tim. That at least was bearable; but for himself he would stick to Flea.

'Didn't you make enough, or did you drink too quickly?' Tim asked, looking at the large empty cocktail glass.

'I only made a thimbleful. Finish your milk quickly and we'll go and mix some more.'

Tim gulped down the last drops obediently, then stood up in his pyjamas and padded woollen kimono. The Japanese designer had made a pattern of sparrows quarrelling and communing in and out and round about a flimsy latticework. When Tim turned his back, showing the whole of the design, there seemed to be an angry flurry of little birds.

Father and son went into the pillared hall, passed under the ponderous arches and entered the dining-room.

---

* Both grandfathers of the child had come to the still raw settlement in the sixties of the last century. They had prospered, one in shipping, one in tea, and helped to make the city what it had become. Their great houses of grey and red rubbed-brick still stood to give a notion of their wealth, their love of comfort and show. [*Denton Welch's footnote.*]

THE COFFIN
ON THE HILL

'The Coffin on the Hill' was first published by Robert Herring in Life and Letters Today *in June 1946 and reprinted in* Brave and Cruel.

PERHAPS I WAS EIGHT WHEN MY PARENTS TOOK ME AT Easter time up the river in a house-boat. I shall explain here that in China a house-boat is not a terraced barge, all plate-glass windows, white balustrading, frothy pink geraniums and ferns. It is a compact little motor-launch fitted with saloon, tiny cabins, bathroom and galley. In it one can explore the canals and waterways.

Part of the fascination of that journey must be put down to the fact that I don't know where we went. I only know that it was up the river Yangtze from Shanghai.

For days beforehand my mother superintended packing of food, clothes, rugs, bed-linen and drinks for my father.

Boy, Cook and Coolie were coming with us. When I went to visit them in the kitchen, they gathered round me and teased me, telling me not to fall in, or the drowned people would pull me down and keep me under. Although I took it as a joke, I shuddered too, seeing arms like water-weeds or octopus tentacles stretched up to grasp my kicking legs, dragging me down, not demonishly, but with a horrible, greedy sort of love, as though they wanted to keep me and gloat on me for ever. I thought of the dead faces; the eyes, the nose, the mouth, eaten away by fishes. But they were still able to weep from the holes where their eyes had been, and cries locked in bubbles escaped from the shapeless mouths.

When I told my father about these drowned men, he said that

the Chinese in old times described in this way the dangerous current, which was supposed to drag people down if they struggled.

I think he saw how much I had been dwelling on the subject, for he laughed at me and made me feel excessive and unreasonable.

At last everything was ready and we drove down in the afternoon to the bund. The great mass of shipping on the river before Shanghai alarmed me. I felt that a small house-boat could never thread its way between all the steamers, junks and sampans; but as soon as we were on board, I was so enchanted that I forgot everything but the little world of the boat. I wanted to explore the whole of it at once, and so, to begin with, I did nothing but run up and down the deck in a mad, excited way. When I was a little calmer, I dived down the miniature companion-way and found myself in the saloon; but my mother was there, unpacking the silver, and I was afraid she might ask me to arrange the pepper and salt and mustard pots neatly in one of the little mahogany cupboards, so I darted past her and came to the first cabin.

I tipped down the shining metal basin, pressed the hot- and cold-water buttons – quite new to me and so far more delightful than clumsy taps – then I tucked myself up in the bottom bunk and pretended to be asleep in mid ocean; but the restraint was too much. I had to jump up, put the toy ladder into position, and climb into the top bunk where I watched the light from the water jigging and flashing on the ceiling.

By now we had begun to chug gently up the river. The city was left behind and I could see green banks through the porthole. I heard Boy talking in the galley; being still too restless to settle, I thought I would go and see what he was doing.

I found him preparing tea, while Cook and Coolie squatted on their haunches and played a game with little round discs. Boy was singing to himself in his high cracked voice. It was something intricate and tricksy as yodelling, and I longed to be able to copy him when he produced his piercing little trills and grace notes. They were sad and keen and sweet, like some fruit vinegar.

When he had finished the egg sandwiches, I helped him take the tea to the bows, where my father and mother were sitting, with rugs over their knees, for it was still cold.

My father watched and smoked and drank many cups of tea,

while my mother and I ate the sandwiches, Cook's crusted sponge cake and the American cookies. As we sat there, perched up in our wicker chairs, like three figureheads, I felt that we were part of some marvellous, rich procession, and an important part too – grotesque and strange perhaps, but significant. The touch of nightmare was there because the little boat, so perfectly compact and self-sufficing, was all at variance with the flat land, the little frog-green ponds and the clusters of curling grey roofs half hidden in the bamboo groves.

Sometimes mangy dogs came out of the villages to bark, and once we passed a squeaking wheelbarrow, loaded with people sitting back to back, and looking in their quilted clothes like so many rolls of bedding. How they chattered amongst themselves, and how extravagantly the wheelbarrow-man groaned and grunted and chanted! He was half-naked, and the wind was biting; yet the sweat poured off him. Some of the people pointed at us and were clearly being witty at our expense, finding us very ridiculous and amusing.

Before it was really dark, my mother suggested that I should go to bed, hinting that I would then be able to get up very early in the morning. I hated the thought of sleep, but I knew I had to go, so I said goodnight to my father without kissing him and went down alone. My mother would come later to see me in my bunk.

The pale eyes of the portholes gleamed on each side of the saloon and there was a faint glimmer over the surface of the lockers. The sound of the engine came to me and the lapping of the water. The air seemed weighed down and given some deep dreaming meaning by the scent from lovely bulbs, which I think must have been China New Year flowers; or were they hyacinths?

I touched them, and I touched the delightful green pom-poms on the minute curtains. Leaning forward and putting out my tongue I licked the brass rim of one of the portholes, in order to realize the ship with all my senses. Then I curled up in a corner of the fitted seat and felt like a mole, or some other perfectly happy blind animal, burrowing deeper and deeper, coming at last to its true home.

My mother found me there and chased me into the bathroom and stood over me until I had cleaned my teeth and done everything else in her own approved way; then she saw me into a top bunk in one of the cabins and put beside me the curious doll which I insisted on keeping; though some grown-ups told me that I was too old to play with it – to say nothing of being quite the wrong sex.

Leaning over the side of the bunk and clutching the doll, I began to tease my mother, pretending that she was getting me to bed early, so that she could drink cocktails with my father – for whenever my mother drank a toast or took a sip from my father's glass, just to please him, I would officiously remind her of her principles.

After we had kissed and hugged and she had left me, I began to talk to the doll, whose name was Lymph Est. I have had to invent that spelling, because the name has never been written before, and I cannot, of course, explain what the words mean. They just came to me one day, and I repeated them over and over again, until they turned into an incantation.

The doll was neither masculine nor feminine, but a sexless being, like an angel. It was broad and squat, and it wore a kind of convict's outfit – meagre trousers, jacket and cap of bottle-green corduroy. Its white silk face was painted with black eyes, the shape of greatly enlarged fleas, and it had a scarlet mouth, like the slot of some rococo pillarbox. Two red dots did for nostrils. It possessed no hair or ears.

I used to talk to it, not because I believed it was alive, but because I needed an audience for my hopes and plans – an image that would not answer.

'Do you like this ship?' I now asked Lymph Est. And then I began to tell over all its delights and beauties, until the cataloguing of them sent me to sleep.

❖

I woke to find long grasses poking through the porthole. We were moored close to the bank and I could smell the earth. Leaving Lymph Est on the pillow, I ran up on deck in my dressing-gown. Everything was hidden in a soft mist, but the sun was gradually melting a way through. I longed to go on shore to explore the unknown land, but Cook was already making the breakfast, while Boy laid the table and Coolie pretended to dust with a bunch of cock's feathers on a long bamboo; just as if we were in a palace antechamber, twenty feet high, instead of in a miniature saloon, where even I could touch the ceiling by standing on the lockers.

I remember smell of coffee and smell of oatmeal porridge on that morning, and then my mother making scrambled eggs with butter and cream in the chafing-dish. I watched the eggs curdle and thicken, saw my father's portion put on a piece of anchovy toast, but mine on a plain piece. As I ate, the mouthfuls seemed to stick half-way, still leaving the void of excitement underneath.

Soon after breakfast the last shreds of mist evaporated, and then we saw in the distance, on the left bank, a group of buildings shining in the sun. Boy said they might be part of a monastery, and this made my mother want to visit them at once; so the engine was started and we moved on. My mother kept looking through my father's field-glasses and telling us what she could see.

'There are ruinous pavilions round a courtyard,' she said, 'and a sort of paved way leading down to the river.'

She passed the glasses to me, but I was not good at adjusting the lenses and only produced a milling, curving blur. But in a little time we were before the monastery and I could see it all for myself.

Stone carvings of lions and horses guarded the paved way, and through a thick brown mat of ancient grass pierced this year's acid blades, hiding the bases of the statues and the steps up to the broken pavilions. Directly in front of us bulged a granite incense-burner, rather like a witches' cauldron. The lip was broken, and I did not think it very beautiful or interesting, but for some reason my mother fell in love with it. As soon as the little gangplank had been put out, she ran on shore and started to stroke the harsh surface with her hand.

For a few moments we were unnoticed; then the monks came down to us in a little group. I stood still and watched, never before having seen shaven heads or thick dusty black robes or clacking wooden rosaries. The monks were very young, with faces as smooth as mushrooms, and they were smiling shyly and secretly and had their hands hidden in their sleeves. When they were within a few feet, I caught a curious smell both animal and aromatic, and it filled me with uneasiness.

My mother smiled at them and bowed, and my father nodded

THE COFFIN ON THE HILL

more awkwardly, but neither could speak Chinese, so Boy was called hurriedly to act as interpreter.

Boy told us that the monks were pleased to see us, but we must not expect any entertainment, for they were very poor and their monastery was falling into decay. Boy waved his hand rather contemptuously in the direction of the collapsing buildings. Altogether he seemed to treat the monks with very little respect.

It was now quite clear that we were being asked for money, and my father began to fiddle with coins in his pocket, wondering, I suppose, how best to make a present to the monks. At last he thrust two or three silver dollars into the hand of the spokesman, muttering as he did so, 'And they'll only gamble it away or spend it on opium, I expect.'

To give jokingly and ungraciously was with him a convention that meant nothing at all, but I was afraid that the monks would understand his words and resent them.

Of course they did not. They were all smiles and charm and urbanity. They asked Boy if there was anything that the lady would like, and when he translated this, my mother's eyes went straight to the incense-burner.

They gave it to her at once, smiling at her for wanting the broken thing, telling her that all this side of the monastery had been abandoned, only one wing at the back being kept in repair.

Although my parents had often condemned rich Americans for carrying off Spanish cloisters and black and white Cheshire manor houses to their own country, they neither of them seemed to hesitate over the incense-burner. Perhaps it was not important enough to trouble them; in any case it was soon being carried to our boat by several of the strongest monks. My father walked in front to show where it should go on the deck.

When it had been lashed to the rail at the top of the companion-way, my father gave the monks cigarettes, which they smoked ceremoniously as they watched us glide into midstream. We waved to them and they waved back. Their faces had all gone sad and thoughtful, and I felt that they were prisoners chained to their ruin, but longing to go exploring with us. I had the idea that a monk's life was nothing but a waste of idleness, and I decided that they would all go mad in the end.

Soon they were out of sight and I could wave to them no more; then I turned to the incense-burner and started to examine it with my mother. Under the mud in the bowl we found the burnt marks of the joss-sticks. These made me think of sacrifices in the Bible, and I imagined white lambs and new-born babies being slaughtered and then roasted in the bowl by a High Priest with a knife as long and curving as a scythe. The more he slaughtered, the more holy he felt. I could almost smell the meat sizzling. What had begun as an alarming fancy ended up by merely making me hungry.

Without saying anything to my mother, I went to get the green tomato chutney and two forks. Pickles were for me the symbol of the free, grown-up life, and I pretended that I liked them better than sweets.

My mother smiled when she saw what I brought for a mid-morning titbit, but she took up a translucent green fragment on her fork, and sat with it poised before her. She was looking at the low hills far away, and I wondered what she was thinking about, she was so still and smiling. I watched her, while the tang of the chutney roughened my tongue and dried up my mouth . . .

Once we passed a pagoda with fairy-like grass growing on its many roofs; and then there was a beautiful little white marble bridge over a canal. I remember too somewhere logs floating in the water. I was sure that they were dangerous to our small boat, having heard stories of icebergs and steamers; but although I waited for the tearing, crunching sound, nothing happened and we sailed on smoothly.

When we stopped again, it was at the foot of a hill which stretched back from the river in a long arm. My mother suggested having our picnic at the top of the ridge, gazing out over the land; so my father took up the picnic-case and I a little basket, and we started to climb up through broken terraces and tangled bushes.

It was not long before I saw that the whole hill was a huge graveyard. Walls that had looked like curved garden terraces were really horsehoe graves, and there were simpler ones, where the coffins had not been buried, but little windowless, doorless brick houses had been built round them.

It did not seem strange to us to take our picnic to the top of this dead city and eat it there, surrounded by ten thousand hidden skeletons. In China there are graves everywhere.

My mother chose a bank where the grass was blown flat by the wind. Below us the land stretched away endlessly; and I could just pick out our little boat on the curling white river. My father said the position was too exposed, but he acquiesced with mock resignation, and made a business of taking off his coat to shield the spirit-lamp.

The leather picnic-case was old. Plated flasks and sandwich-cases fitted round a square kettle, which appealed to me strongly because of the delicate cap and chain on the spout. Apostle teaspoons and knives with yellowed ivory handles were arranged in a fan shape in the stained green satin lining of the lid.

My mother began to open the cases and take out chicken bones, Russian salad, chocolate cake and oranges, while my father poured himself out a drink from the wrong flask and grimaced when the babyish white trickle appeared. He made coffee for my mother by throwing spoonfuls into the boiling kettle. She said that the drink was not a success, but I was delighted when she allowed me to colour my milk with it.

I gnawed my drumstick and ate little pieces of piquant stuffing. There was roasted brown skin to crunch, messy salad to be played with, and then the cake, black and rich as leaf mould. The pieces of orange at the end seemed to tingle all through my mouth, cleaning away all other tastes that had ever been.

When my father was lying on his back with a cigarette between his lips, and my mother was motionless, lost in the view, I got up and ran away from them without a word. I went to explore the graves, hoping to find some ancient coin or ornament hidden under a stone, or just lying on the ground, undiscovered, but for all to see.

I jumped down from terrace to terrace, clambered under bushes, lifted stones, but found only beetles and insects. I was wondering what to do next, when I saw at the end of the ridge one of the simpler brick graves which seemed to be broken open. I hurried towards it, feeling a little afraid, but hoping for great things.

The whole of one corner had collapsed. I could see the coffin quite plainly and when, trembling with excitement, I bent even closer, the coarse weaving of a piece of cloth jumped out at me from a crack in the rotting wood.

These things were so exactly as I had expected them to be that I saw through the coffin and the shroud to the skull, the loose teeth, the clots of hair and the white bone. No need to pry any further. My dreadful pictures had come true. The imprisoned, concealed smell of the monks had been bad, but there was a worse, more evil smell here – a smell that was forcing me to know what happened in the end. Rotting wood and cloth and human bone were changed now. They were dead.

I knew that I must never say a word, that I must just walk away as if nothing had happened; but when I turned to the place where I had left my father and mother, they were no longer there. I saw only the picnic things spread out on the grass.

I started to run; and every now and then I called out to my mother in a very even plain voice that perfectly expressed my fright. There was a hollow sound in the curved arm of the hill, but no human answer.

I came upon my mother just when I had begun to feel that I might never see her again. I turned the corner of a peeling stucco wall, and there she was, framed in one of those charming completely round Chinese doorways. She smiled at me slumberously and serenely. It was clear that she had wandered away to meditate in that forgotten tomb garden.

I ran up to her and stood, breathing hard, but not touching her or saying anything. She seemed the very opposite of all that the coffin held, but this only made my confusion worse, for I knew that she would come to it at last; and that knowledge was unbearable.

I would have liked to say, 'Up there you can see a rotten coffin with some rotten cloth poking through a crack, and under the cloth . . . there's a rotten man,' but I knew that it was forbidden, that if I did so she would frown and gaze into me to discover what had been left at the back of my eyes. Then she would turn away and say with careful casualness, 'Darling, you oughtn't to have looked,' and I would be made to feel peering and a little indecent.

So I said nothing, but took her hand and walked back with her to the picnic place, where my father, back from the bushes, was now packing up the case and scattering crumbs for the birds.

THE COFFIN ON THE HILL

We said very little as we climbed down again to the boat. The clouds were gathering and pressing lower, and soon after we had settled ourselves in the saloon I heard rain pattering down on the deck. The surface of the river began to hiss and boil, and such a delicious feeling of snugness was created that tremors ran through me and I pressed Lymph Est hard against the cushions of the seat under the portholes where I was lying. My father took up the book that he had been reading to me at home, and my mother started to work on her neglected piece of petit-point. She had not touched it for months, but now she sorted the wools with quiet pleasure and began to put stitches into the conventional acanthus leaf. Her hand rose and fell like a sparrow snatching crumbs from the canvas.

I listened with one part of my mind to my father. He was reading something about the ancient rivalry between Genoa and Venice. The heroine's name was Maria. I remember, because my father *would* pronounce it in the English way, although my mother insisted that the *i* should be *e* as in Italian.

The other part of me talked to Lymph Est. I got a sort of mournful, gruesome pleasure out of saying over and over again, 'Tomorrow we go back.'

♣

We were amongst the ships again in the thick of the river traffic, with hooters droning and the shouts of bargemen ringing out, making me believe that something terrible was about to happen.

Boy, Cook, Coolie, my father and mother, were all packing and tidying, preparing to leave.

I lay in my top bunk with Lymph Est held above my head. I was trying to pretend that the journey had only just begun, but I knew it was over and that we were back in the hateful confusion of the city.

I suddenly remembered the drowned people, and I saw again the piece of shroud poking through the coffin on the hillside. An extraordinary impulse seized me, making me hold Lymph Est out of the porthole above the water.

For a moment I hesitated, afraid, yet longing for the pain and the sight I would never forget; then, as if absent-mindedly, I relaxed my grip of my fingers and shut my eyes.

When I opened them again, I saw Lymph Est's squat limbs, silk face, whorish black eyes and scarlet mouth all framed in the mud-green water. No dead men dragged it down. The kapok stuffing kept it floating perfectly. Lymph Est was unmolested and serene and doomed.

And as I watched it sailing away, I was pierced by my own wantonness, and I started to call out for help.

Coolie ran along the deck with a boat-hook and tried to fish Lymph out for me, but it was beyond his reach. I watched it disappear between the coal barges; and as I looked for the last time on that extraordinary face, my feelings were so interwoven and twisted that I felt mad.

Boy, Cook, Coolie, all comforted me so gently. What was I to do? Was I to take everything to myself, hypocritically, pretending that it had been an accident? Even if I dared to explain, what could I say?

Had I sacrificed Lymph Est just to cause a sensation, to fix people's interest on myself? The knowledge of what I had done was not clearly revealed to me; but now I know that I gave Lymph Est to the river because of the corpses at the bottom, and because of the thing wrapped in cloth on the hill.

I FIRST BEGAN
TO WRITE

The brother mentioned in this fragment was Paul, with whom Denton Welch went to school at Repton in Derbyshire and later sailed to China to live with their father.

I FIRST BEGAN TO WRITE WHEN I WAS NINE. I REMEMBER it was a Gothic poem and my mother asked me when I showed it to her why I wrote on dead things. We were in Switzerland, and I looked out of the hotel windows and knew that I should never show her anything again. I did not want to write about anything that I did; only about the dead and past.

I felt my poem might be silly; it was almost consciously silly behind the cardboard chivalry.

I did not write again until one day at school when I was fourteen. We had been told to write the chapter of a ghost story. I knew this one lesson was for me. I wrote about the silver sconces on the walls and the high bed crowned with ostrich feathers, the red damask of the curtains and the lovely dress the graceful spectre wore.

I was used to no praise, so when the master said that this was a picture seen, I felt a little intoxicated.

The next time that I wrote was in the Red Sea. I was sixteen and was going to China with my brother. Suddenly from the deck we saw the hot rust-coloured mountains sweeping down into the sea as if they were crumbling heaps of sand, and I knew that I must write a poem. I had my drawing-book with me and I ran to the rail and leaned against it, writing and smiling.

When I got to China I saw some lotus leaves in a pond, and I seemed to feel their flesh and veins and stems. I was in a public park, lying on the grass, and I was suddenly happy when I found that I had brought my stub of pencil and an old envelope.

I wrote with excitement. It was longer than anything I had written before and I wondered if it was good.

After this I met a soldier whom I admired and I wrote many poems. I knew that they were bad, but I liked writing them very much. When I showed the nature poems to my brother, he frowned a little and said that they were rather unformed. I lay back in bed rather hurt but feeling that he did not really know. Oh those summer nights in that penthouse in Shanghai. How the streams of light twinkled that lit the roads eight storeys below. The heat and the mosquitoes did not seem to come so high, and I sat thinking of my poems and whether they were good.

None of the stories I wrote got beyond the first page. I never wanted to tell a story; only to write how I felt.

Back in England again the next year, I was at an art school. I was not happy. I lay in a field, neglecting drawing from the Antique, trying to write my school story. I knew how difficult it was; I had no perseverance.

Then I was very ill and I wrote in bed for over a year. It was in the night that I wrote and the very early mornings – sometimes poetry and sometimes just what I felt. I was very interested in the last doctor I had and I wrote many unfinished stories about him. I felt I wanted to die and everything I wrote ended with death. This thought was with me so much that one day I felt that I must leave nothing behind me.

I found all my old notebooks and the scraps of paper I had used. I read everything, longing to want to keep some of it; but I never wanted anyone to read it, so I gradually cut more and more out of the books until there was a heap of loose leaves and the empty covers lying on the floor. Then I burnt the leaves in the fire – all my adolescent writing, keeping only in my head some of the lines which I could not forget.

I kept the covers for painting boards and that very day began to write again in a new notebook.

THE BARN

The setting of this story is the house in Benson, Oxfordshire, which the Welch family rented over the summer of 1924 when Denton Welch was nine. The story was first published by John Lehmann in New Writing and Daylight *(Winter, 1943–4) and was reprinted in* Brave and Cruel.

I TURNED AND SKIDDED OBEDIENTLY ON THE LITTLE patch of lawn at the side of the house. My brother was teaching me this accomplishment and he was an exacting master. I looked over my shoulder at the last brown wound on the grass. It was meagre, not bold and fierce like the gashes my brother made.

'Don't be such a funk, Denton!' he yelled from his position under the crab-apple tree. 'You can't skid properly unless you turn and jam your brakes on as hard as you can.'

He snatched the bicycle from me, threw his leg over it, pedalled furiously for a few moments, so that I felt he must certainly end in the hedge, then turned violently, making a superb chocolate fan on the emerald grass.

I was lost in admiration. He was so ruthless and competent.

'Now do it again!' he ordered, severely.

I mounted on the gravel path, tore on to the little lawn as wildly as I dared, overshot the appointed skidding-place by a few feet, and tried desperately to turn where all the scattered crab-apples lay. Of course my wheel caught on one of the bright, hard little fruits, and I suddenly lay sprawling beside the madly revolving pedals of my bicycle.

I was hurt and dazed, but I dared not show it; so I laughed and smiled anxiously, and then, in desperation, picked up one of the little red balls and bit into its crisp white acid heart. I felt the juice skinning my teeth, roughening my tongue, making it feel like a cat's tongue.

I made no attempt to get up, but lay there indolently, thinking of the cleanness of the apple, smiling slackly. I knew that this behaviour would disgust my brother, but I had to wait until I had recovered a little self-respect. I could not jump up straight away, still shaken, looking flustered and foolish.

Paul turned from me contemptuously and was about to walk into the house when my father appeared at the French window with a note in his hand. He held it out to Paul, saying, 'Take this to Mrs Singleton for me, will you?'

My brother jerked his head away sullenly. He hated encountering other people.

'Can't Denton take it, Daddy?' he asked.

'Why should he when I've asked you?' was the reply.

'Because he doesn't mind. He likes old ladies!'

And with this last shouted jeer, my brother darted down the path and was away into the fields, no one knew where.

'I expect he'll have a guilty conscience about that later,' said my father comfortably; then, turning to me, 'Will you take it, Denton, since he's so silly?'

I felt proud. This was something I could do easily. I was not nervous of people, unless they were other children or rude old men. I hated the very thought of an old man. It spelt dirt and bad temper to me. With women it was different. I felt that, whatever they were like, some part of them was human and could be reached.

I took the note and, leaving the bicycle still lying on the grass, walked out of the garden, between the tiny box-hedges, into the lane.

Mrs Singleton was our landlady. When my parents had rented her house for the summer, she had moved out with her Colonel, her dogs and her grown-up daughters to the Army hut which had been re-erected on the edge of their land, at the far end of the lane.

I walked down the lane, keeping close to the brook and looking down into its depths. Hosts of tiny minnows flapped their fins to hold their position against the current. I loved the brook. The house was called after the brook, but Brook House somehow did not sound romantic; it sounded dull.

As I got nearer to the Army hut I composed my face and took the letter from my pocket. I had a deep snobbish pity for Mrs Singleton, because we had turned her out of her dignified house, where her family had lived for a hundred years, into this squalid little Army hut.

The front door was open, and some soiled gym shoes lay beside it. I gave a quiet, well-bred, rather furtive knock, and the door swung with an unpleasant creak.

'Who's there?' shouted Mrs Singleton, peremptorily. Her voice came from the room on the right of the hall. It sounded so hard and questioning that I became uneasy.

'It's me,' I said childishly.

I can only imagine that, from this, Mrs Singleton imagined me to be one of her daughters, for the next moment she appeared before me in all the glory of soiled and elaborate corsets, which reached from her bosom to her pale grey thighs. She wore no stockings, and the suspenders dangled uselessly against her heavy blue-veined legs. Her hair was like a nest made by some very slovenly rook.

With an exasperated, outraged exclamation, she turned about – displaying her huge, grey blancmange buttocks – and fled into her bedroom.

From there she carried on a ladylike and furious conversation either with me or with herself. I could not tell which, for I was too frighted to listen or to distinguish the words.

She emerged at last in the ruin of a feathered peignoir.

With a queenly and austere gesture, she held out her hand, making me feel that it was *I* who had appeared before *her* in a semi-naked and disgusting condition. She took the note in silence and shut the door. I too felt that it was no time for small-talk.

Rather shaken by the horror, I walked slowly back to Brook House, wondering what to do with myself. My brother, I knew, had disappeared for the rest of the day. As I walked drops of rain began to fall. They hissed into the brook and spat against my face.

I entered by the stable-yard gate, and walked over the cobbles. The puddles were growing between the big curved stones. Outside the disused barn I stopped, and pulled at the huge, crazy door. It opened creakingly. I went in and shut it after me.

I was in darkness which smelt of dust and mice and hay. Chinks and cracks in the walls shot beams of light into the blackness.

I climbed on some boxes, then caught hold of a beam and swung there, like a monkey. I gnashed my teeth and contorted my face. I gibbered and hung on with one hand as I scratched under my arm with the other.

I grew hot, swinging in the darkness, and my arms began to feel the strain. I broke my last imaginary peanut between my teeth and spat as disgustingly and coarsely as I could on the invisible floor; then I sank down on the boxes and thought that I was miserable and lonely indeed.

And as I lay there I decided to be a slave who had to sweat and labour in the barn all day. But slaves had to be naked. I put my hand inside my flannel shirt and felt the flesh on my chest. Slowly I leant forward and began to pull the shirt over my head. It was straining work, for I was sitting on the tails. When my body was free of the shirt and my arms were imprisoned in it above my head, I looked down at the vague whiteness of my skin. I thought of the men I had seen, with tufts of strong hair on their chests and under their arms. It was ugly and beautiful at once, I thought.

I caught hold of the beam again and swung about fiercely, hurting my arms, straining the muscles as I pulled myself up. I swore not to stop pulling until I had rested my chin on the top of the beam. At last, with a shudder of pain and pleasure, I brought it to rest there on the rough, beetle-eaten oak. The harsh wood grazed the soft skin on my throat.

Then slowly and gently I felt my trousers slipping. They slid caressingly over my hips and fell with a soft plop to my ankles, where they caught in bunched-up folds. I still hung there, supported by my chin and my tingling arms. Soft draughts of air blew deliciously against my complete nakedness.

'Now I am a criminal whose feet have been tied together, and whose body has been stripped by the hangman,' I told myself. 'I shall be swinging here till late at night, when my friends will come to cut me down.'

I hung there not moving, living passionately my idea of a criminal on a gibbet; while the rain beat against the great barn door, and drops fell from the roof.

Gradually, as my strength gave out, I sank nearer to the ground, until my arms were stretched out agonizingly. There were still some feet to fall to reach the ground. I decided to drop, although I knew that my feet were trapped in the trousers. I fell in a crumpled mass, and lay on the barn floor with the short pieces of hay pricking me. I felt the smooth, satiny mounds of bird-droppings against my flesh. Slowly and wearily I put on my shirt, pulled up my trousers, ran my fingers through my hair, and went in to tea.

✤

Towards evening, as I sat in my little room, polishing my favourite possessions – an ugly Japanese ivory, a Chinese agate chicken and a painted tear-bottle (how many times had I tried, without success, to catch my own tears in it!) – I heard the cook go into the library and begin talking to my father. This was unusual, and I stopped polishing and waited to hear any of her words.

As she opened the door, about to leave the room, this remark floated up the staircase well: 'He wants to know if he can put up in the barn for tonight, sir.'

I heard my father say, 'I'll come and see him.' Then he followed Cook into the back of the house.

I waited excitedly. Who wanted to put up in the barn for the night? I looked on it as my barn, where I did secret things. When my father came back I ran down to him.

'What's happened, Daddy?' I asked.

'Nothing. A tramp only asked Cook if he could sleep in the barn because it's raining so hard, and I said of course he could.' My father made a gruesome horrific face and added, 'I hope he won't murder us all in our beds tonight!'

I was fascinated and frightened.

'May I go and see him?' I asked urgently.

'Certainly not. He doesn't want to be stared at. Cook has given him something to eat, and then he wants to go to sleep in the hay. He's very tired.'

I shut the door and went upstairs again, tingling with excitement. I decided to visit the tramp in the middle of the night, when everyone else was asleep.

I got ready a bundle of blankets to take out to him, and a bottle of sweets I had been given.

Impatiently I waited for supper to be over and 'goodnights' to be said. I lay in bed with all my clothes on, and my mother came and kissed me and put out the light.

'If only she knew!' I thought. 'If only she knew –!'

She went downstairs again, and I heard her talking to my father. At last I could wait no longer for them to go to bed. I snatched up the bundle of bedclothes and the bottle of sweets, and ran down the back stairs out into the dripping stable-yard. Then I ran back again to get my torch.

I crouched over the blankets to keep them dry. The huge door swung open easily and I turned my torch on and shone it in all the corners and into the thickness of the hay.

At first I could see nothing, then I saw him lying full length in a deep nest of hay which billowed in soft, high walls all round him. He was asleep, and as I stood still I heard the heavy rhythm of his breathing.

I tiptoed up to him, and, too curious to be considerate, shone the torch full on his face. For a moment the face remained still and grey and smooth as marble, except for the crisp stubble on his chin. There was no expression. He looked beautiful. Then, as he suddenly woke, his face broke into a cobweb of connecting lines. His eyes and his mouth fell open in fear, and he shouted out hoarsely, 'What's that? Who's that?'

I was frightened at the change I had brought about.

'I've only come from the house,' I whispered urgently, 'to bring you some blankets and some sweets.'

'Let's have a look at you, mate,' he said. 'Shine the torch on your face.' I obeyed, delighting in the word 'mate'.

'How old are you?' he asked.

'You'd better guess,' I said, playing for time, wondering how many years I could add to my age without appearing too absurd.

'Oh, I see –' His voice tailed off and I was afraid he was going to fall asleep again; I snatched at the first thing and asked, 'And how old are you?'

'What do you want to know for?'

Then he relented and added, 'I'm twenty-four, if that's any good to you.'

It was clear that I amused him. This upset me.

'Do you like sleeping in this barn?' I questioned him almost severely.

'It's not a bad old place. Better than being under a hedge on a night like this.'

'I'd like to do what you do,' I said earnestly, looking at him. 'I'd like to walk miles every day, and sleep in a different place every night, and get my own food.'

'Oh, no you wouldn't, mate; you'd be much too soft. You'd be half dead after a day of it,' he jeered.

I handed him the sweets, feeling deeply hurt; although it was comforting that he still called me 'mate' after seeing my face. I looked up at the beam above our heads and said abruptly, 'I do exercises in this barn on most afternoons.'

'Getting your muscles up?' he jeered again.

Since he would not take me seriously, I fell silent. I pointed the torch so that the beam lay on the length of his figure in the hay. He had the sort of body that I wanted to have when I grew up. It was not tall, but solid and compact, and rounded. Through a rent in his trousers I could see his hard thigh. I thought how different his flesh was from Mrs Singleton's. And at the thought of her, hot blood rushed up into my cheeks.

'I'm going to sleep in the hay too!' I said.

'What for? Ain't you got a bed?' he asked coldly.

'I want to try it,' I said.

'You'll cop it if your ma finds out,' he warned me humiliatingly.

I looked at his body again. I could smell it now in the warm hay. I had a hard, quite callous feeling that the blankets were too clean to be put over him.

'Are you warm enough?' I asked. He did not answer. The next moment I heard his deep rich intakes of breath. Wrapping myself in the blankets, to stop the hay from pricking, I lowered myself gently beside him. Deep, deep, into the hay I sank, until we were in one nest. He did not wake again, but stirred a little in his sleep, turning towards me. I drew as close as I dared to him and lay, my head close to his chest, so that I could feel the rhythm of its rising and falling.

All night we lay together there. Towards dawn I woke up to find that he now lay face downwards and that he had thrown an arm over me. I waited, not being able to sleep any more, hoping that he too would wake up.

When he did, he looked straight into my eyes from a few inches away and smiled. He was not teasing me any more; he had accepted me.

Slowly he raised himself in the hay and jerked his clothes this way and that, readjusting them. This was his morning toilet. He ran his hand over his face, rubbing his eyes roughly, and crackling the stubble on his chin.

'Well, I must be getting along,' he said.

'I'm coming too,' I announced.

'Don't be bloody daft,' was his answer. I took no notice, but began to roll up the blankets. I wondered whether to take them with me, but decided that they would be too heavy. I hoped that he would unpack some of the food Cook had given him, but he didn't; he just went on hitching his knapsack up and ignoring me.

We went out into the weak sunlight in the slippery cobbled yard. He took no notice of me, but trudged on out of the yard into the lane, past the twinkling brook through the village, and out on to the heath-like stretch beyond. There he sat down and I sat too. In perfect silence he offered me a piece of cake and cheese. We munched together and he drank cold tea from his tin.

At last he stood up, and looking at me harshly, compellingly, he said, 'Now go back, you silly little sod.'

THE TROUT STREAM

The 'Mr Mellon' in this story was Mr Wattie, the retired senior partner in Arthur Welch's firm in Shanghai. Denton Welch was nine at the time of the first visit to his house.

The story was first published in the Cornhill *magazine (Spring, 1948) and reprinted in* Brave and Cruel.

I

HOW WELL I REMEMBER THAT FIRST VISIT TO MR MELLON! My mother and I had been asked to spend the weekend at his great villa near Tunbridge Wells. He was an old friend of my father's, and since my father was abroad at this time, I think he imagined that we were lonely, sitting in our Kensington hotel, looking out at the fossilized trees in the gardens of the Natural History Museum.

We set out on a dark rather foggy afternoon in early autumn. The light under the dirty glass dome of the station was thick and yellow. The train was just about to start and we had to run down the platform to reach a coach. As I skipped along by my mother, I suspected nothing. I was excited by the hurry, rather pleased that we had to scramble in this way; but when the door of the first coach had been wrenched open and my mother's suitcase tossed on to the rack, I saw that there was something strange about her. She stood, swaying a little, a sort of smile on her face, her bag still open, although the porter had been tipped. I thought that she was about to move her hands and head in rhythm, perhaps even to hum a song. Then the middle-aged man opposite had jumped to his feet, had taken hold of her, was touching *my* mother! Between the little white tufts of hair above each ear, his chunky lips were working up and down in agitation. He was saying, 'Oh, is there anything I can do, madam? Lean on me. Shall I get a doctor?'

He seemed impossibly fussy and protective. He was turning my mother into one of those fainting, delicate women I had heard about in stories, when really she was the strongest, most capable mother anyone could want. Why, running was nothing to her; she could dance and swim and ride and play all sorts of games. No one in the carriage would know this now, because of the man. They would all think her a weak woman who had to be held up, fanned with newspapers and given smelling-salts.

I looked up in amazement and said, 'What is happening, Mummy?' Then I pulled at her to make her sit down, for she was still standing, with her head almost against the man's shoulder. Slowly the train began to move out of the station. My glance darted up to the vast glass roof, so far away and threatening; it returned to my mother fearfully. But she was recovering. Her smile lost its sleep-walking quality before my eyes. She looked up at the man and thanked him charmingly for his attention, explaining that she had only felt faint for a moment; then she sat down beside me and took my arm.

We said nothing at first, each, I suppose, feeling relieved and yet shy. I was impatient with her too, for giving the wrong impression to the people in the carriage; I had always been proud of her youthfulness and vigour. I was not to know that this was one of the first signs of the illness that was to separate us soon.

When we were near the end of our journey, my mother told me not to say anything to Mr Mellon or his housekeeper about her faintness, since she wanted no sort of to-do now that she was well again. So it was in a rather strained and careful mood that I left the train and went towards the long black car that was waiting for us. Already we were coming within the influence of Mr Mellon and I must let no word slip. The car itself, with its high old-fashioned body and glittering carriage lamps, already lighted, was a disappointment. I had expected a man of Mr Mellon's wealth to have a Rolls-Royce, and here was something that I could not even give a name to. Still, it was good to have darkness outside, but to be in the warm padded box with my mother, to be smelling the slightly aromatic dried-up air and playing with the scent bottles, matchboxes and engagement tablets of old cracked ivory – the cracks were black, like my nails when I was sent to scrub them.

On the outskirts of the town we left the wide avenue and turned in between large clumsy gates. The car lamps glistened on the fresh paint, showing the branches of monkey-puzzles and rhododendrons beyond. There was a little lodge of grey and red rubbed-brick. Everything was hard and ugly and beautifully kept. It reminded me of public parks or cemeteries; and this effect, together with the shock of my mother's passing illness, and her wish that nothing should be mentioned, all helped to oppress me, so that I dreaded coming to the end of the long curling drive, where Mr Mellon and his housekeeper would be waiting for us.

I suppose it was this wish to shut the world away from me that has made me forget almost all the details of our arrival. Just the sight of three huge plate-glass windows, curtained and lighted from within, remains. We were approaching them quickly; then there was the crunch as the wheels braked on the gravel under the granite porch.

✤

It is the next morning that is still so clear. It must have been the hour before lunch. I know that my mother took me into the room where Mr Mellon always sat, the one with the three long windows.

It overlooked the gravel, the starfish flower-beds and the whole stretch of lawn in front of the house. The sun was pouring in, draining the fire of colour, making the invisible flames seem rather overpowering. I had been told that Mr Mellon was an invalid, so his wheelchair did not surprise me. Only the plaid rug across his knees made me wonder fearfully what the legs could be like underneath. Were they all withered away? Were they like drumsticks when the chicken has been eaten? The face beamed at me. I thought it looked like a very large, scrubbed, kind potato. There were only little mounds and valleys, all colourless and smooth with no wrinkles. Mr Mellon held out his hand and I went up to his chair. He held me against his side. He seemed extraordinarily fond of children, I thought; too fond to be quite comfortable, for I was conscious of his big body so close, the hardness of the wheelchair and the heat of the fire. Then the door opened and Mrs Slade the housekeeper came in.

Mrs Slade was the smiling, confident hostess, and yet somehow it was clear that she was no unpaid wife, friend or relation; perhaps her very competence set her apart. My mother had explained to me that she was half-Javanese, but I could not quite accept her appearance and kept gazing at her whenever I thought that it would not be rude. I did not like her very soft, creamy skin, or the almost freckled duskiness round her long eyes, but their strangeness held me. I thought the grey seemed out of place in her black hair, for her body was flat and supple, like a young person's, and she was very small.

She began to ask my mother how she had slept, whether she had been brought exactly what she liked for breakfast; then she went over to the fire and wheeled Mr Mellon back a little, as if she knew, better than he did himself, what was comfortable for him.

'It's nearly time for drinks,' she said brightly and, turning to me so that I too should be included in her attention, she added, 'My daughter Phyllis will be down in a moment; she is just washing her hands. It is so nice for her to have someone of her own age to play with.'

I was a little alarmed by Mrs Slade's efficiency, afraid of that smiling hardness. She seemed not to be aware of my nature or my mother's. Her mind was always occupied with the arrangements of the day; and the comforts and pleasures she planned for us were made to sound like duties. She was like the harsh little lodge, the monkey-puzzles and the sharp-edged drive.

The drinks were brought in by one of the tall Indian servants in his red turban and long white coat. As soon as he had left, Mrs Slade turned to my mother and said, 'The Indians are new since you were here last, aren't they?'

'Yes, where did you get them?' asked my mother.

They were indeed remarkable; all tall and silent in their red and white uniform. Ever since we had arrived I had been wanting to know why they were in this English villa. I knew that Mr Mellon had made his fortune in the East, but it had been the Far East, not India.

Mrs Slade was explaining.

'We had so much trouble with English servants that at last we thought we would try these Indians; they work as a team. A friend of Mr Mellon's told us of them.'

'They seem very good,' my mother said.

'Yes, I think they do their work well on the whole, and the cook makes excellent curries. You will see; we are to have one today.'

This was delightful news to me, since curry was almost my favourite dish.

All this time Mr Mellon had been beaming at me, at my mother and at Mrs Slade, sometimes saying a word, but usually leaving the conversation to Mrs Slade. Now he took from his pocket a little gold box and I was suddenly excited to see the lid blaze with large initials in diamonds. The initials were too big for the box, making it seem crusted and clumsy. I was still more excited when he opened the box and took snuff. Noticing my fascination he held out the box to me. I went up to him again and took it, but did not dare to smell the snuff, imagining that I would sneeze or choke at once. I just held the box and drank in its great value and the beauty of the diamonds.

'I thought only old people, people in history, took snuff,' I said uncertainly, thinking of wigs and swords and other things my mother had told me of.

'I take it because I mustn't smoke, you see,' Mr Mellon said, then added, 'You like my box?'

For one intoxicating moment I thought he was going to give it to me. What would it feel like to possess a diamond-studded snuff-box? But he was only amused by my reverent interest. I felt he was almost laughing at me.

'I've another one here,' he said. 'I wonder if you'll like it better.'

He fished in his other pocket and brought out a box with a little urn of flowers on it. The urn, the flowers and ribbons were in every colour of precious stone. I tried to name them: ruby, sapphire, emerald, pearl – I knew no more.

'Oh, yes!' I said with a sigh of wonder and amazement. Could I be really holding such boxes? What would happen to them when Mr Mellon died? They seemed more desirable to me than anything else I had known.

Suddenly Mr Mellon took the boxes back from me, slipped them carelessly in his pockets and said with complete irrelevance, 'One day when my legs are better, you and I will go out in the woods behind the house and climb up to where the white elephant lives. I'd like to show him to you.'

I was nonplussed. I knew that Mr Mellon was paralysed and could never walk again. I knew that there were no white elephants – certainly not in England. Was this a game of make-believe? I was painfully embarrassed.

Mr Mellon saw it and laughed. I turned to my mother for help and guidance.

'Ah! Here is Phyllis at last,' broke in Mrs Slade. 'How long you've been!'

I guessed that Phyllis had been keeping away on purpose, for she was a dark heavy girl with nothing at all to say. Her eyebrows met in the middle and already she had black hairs on her arms. She stood against the wall, utterly impassive and confident. I could not help thinking her very ugly, and it was a shock to my self-satisfaction when Mr Mellon showed even more delight in her arrival than he had shown in mine. He asked her to bring him one of the little cocktail titbits, then when she stood by him, he put his arm round her shoulders and said, 'Phyllis is a good old sort, isn't she! I've been talking about our white elephant, saying we must visit him when I'm up and about again.'

Phyllis's response to this was a sort of grunt that seemed both sullen and lazily good natured. It was as if she knew his nonsense of old, but was ready to put up with more of it, since he was good to her.

At lunch I was surprised to see so many Indians; there seemed to be one for each of us, and they came and went with such silent smoothness. Sometimes there was the lowest murmur behind a screen, sometimes Mrs Slade made a sign with her hand; and her eyes followed them constantly. I felt the strain of her watchfulness and saw that she ate in quick abstracted snatches, hardly looking at her plate.

But the curry was what really occupied my attention. There was rice bright gold with saffron, chicken in its glistening brown sauce; then came innumerable little dishes of condiments. I suppose we had chutneys, Bombay duck, chopped coconut, egg, parsley, peanuts and many other stranger things I still cannot name. I know that I piled them up until I had a little mound, then dug into it joyfully with my spoon.

As soon as I had satisfied my greediness a little, I began to look about the room: at the walls covered with a heavily embossed gilt paper in imitation of Spanish leather, at the sticky landscapes and still-lifes in plaster frames almost a foot deep. Out of the windows I could only see lawns, laurel hedges and the corner of a white conservatory, all cast-iron spikes, silvered poppy-heads and Gothic tracery. A sense of the deadness of things began to oppress me. I thought that all Mr Mellon's possessions looked as if no one had ever wanted to use them or enjoy them. I wondered why he had them and kept them in such perfect condition.

Mr Mellon's long head now seemed to me to be like a peeled satiny log. Phyllis next to him was like some coarse little fair negress, unaware of anything but food. Her mother's much more delicate Eurasian face with its smile and its strain filled me with uneasiness. I looked at my mother with relief, kept my eyes on what always pleased me. Here was the only object that did not seem strange or ugly or inauspicious to me.

Mrs Slade must have planned that our first lunch should have an Eastern flavour throughout, for we finished with tinned mangoes. The long spoon-shaped slices swimming in syrup disappointed me, because the preserving had made them taste more like peaches than anything else; but I had a second helping, since Mrs Slade seemed to expect it.

Afterwards Phyllis took me into the paddock to show me her pony. A groom brought it out, but then left us alone together. I was feeling at a disadvantage, because Phyllis had changed into riding-breeches and looked even tougher and more self-sufficient than before. I thought too that I would probably be expected to ride as I was, in shorts, which would mean two raw patches on the insides of my legs. And what if I should fall off, or show any sort of fear? Phyllis would just look away, hardly even bothering to be scornful. The visit to the paddock was an ordeal.

Phyllis stood for some time with her arm on her pony's saddle, doing nothing. The running together of her thick eyebrows gave an effect of frowning, but I think she was really looking at me with no expression at all. At last she said, 'Are you fond of riding?' She might have been asking if I liked cleaning my teeth or performing some other irksome duty.

'Yes, last year I rode every week,' I explained. 'But now we are living in London.'

At this Phyllis gave my bare knees a glance and remarked, 'But you haven't got any breeches'; then she swung herself on to the pony and trotted briskly to the other end of the field. I watched her go, wondering how soon I could leave without seeming rude. I wanted to explore the grounds by myself.

As she returned, I tried to show some interest, but Phyllis passed without a word. Her face was set; she might have been all alone. I felt that my welcoming smile must look silly indeed.

Several times she rode round the field, solemnly, without taking any notice of me; I was only saved from the growing awkwardness of my position by the sudden appearance of Mr Mellon and Mrs Slade. My eyes had wandered towards the house rather longingly; and then I had seen what looked to me like the strangest of little horseless carriages. It was approaching down one of the winding yellow paths, threading in and out of the trees very rapidly and smoothly.

Soon I could see that it held Mr Mellon with Mrs Slade sitting at his feet. Mr Mellon waved his hand, as if beckoning, so I ran to the gate of the paddock and let myself out.

They had stopped in the protection of a bank of shrubs with mottled leaves, and against this bright yellow and green background their faces looked very pale. I saw that the little carriage was an elaborate motor or electric bathchair. Mr Mellon's head was framed in the folds of the calash hood, while Mrs Slade squatted cross-legged on the tiny space left on the platform in front of his feet. Seen thus, sitting before him like a little Buddha, she was stranger than ever to me; but I also thought her smile seemed happier and more spontaneous, as if she really enjoyed fitting herself so ingeniously into the bathchair and racing down the garden paths with Mr Mellon. She suggested that I might like to try riding in her position and rose from the platform like a dancer, hardly using her hands, and with her legs still crossed. Mr Mellon said, 'Yes, you just see if you can fit in as neatly as Mrs Slade, and then we'll go for a fine ride.'

I crouched on the platform uncomfortably, afraid to lean back for fear of hurting Mr Mellon's legs, or of feeling them against me. I imagined terrible skeleton legs that could not bear even the lightest touch. Mr Mellon turned the chair round and we began to glide almost silently towards the house. We passed Phyllis, still riding round the paddock. Mr Mellon waved; she gave us a glance, seemed to take in the fact that I was sitting at his feet, and returned one wooden gesture.

'I expect you and Phyllis get on like a house on fire,' Mr Mellon said: 'she's as good as any boy at riding and playing games. You should see her throw a cricket ball!'

Again I wondered that Mr Mellon could show such fondness for Phyllis; she seemed so very unenticing to me.

We were now passing the house and reaching the wooded ground behind. As soon as the path began to rise a little Mr Mellon said, 'I know I told you about the white elephant that lives at the top, but we'd better not go to see him today. It's not very good for the chair to pull two uphill, and I expect Mrs Slade's wondering where we've got to.'

I was only too pleased to drop the subject of the white elephant and agreed that we ought to go back at once; but when we were near the front door Mr Mellon suggested leaving me, so that he could go back to Mrs Slade and bring her up to the house in the chair.

As I wandered into the hall, I thought dimly that Mr Mellon also enjoyed riding in the chair with Mrs Slade. It might be one of their chief pleasures. I knew he admired her for being so small and supple that she could fit on to the footboard where no one was supposed to sit. I wondered if they ever went out of the grounds in the chair, taking a picnic perhaps and a book; and if they did go out, did people stare to find her sitting there at his feet like an Eastern idol?

How quiet the house was! I guessed that my mother had gone upstairs to write letters or to read on her bed. I began to want to know about the other rooms leading off the hall. I had only seen Mr Mellon's room and the dining-room. Very gently I opened one of the heavy mahogany doors and found myself in what must have been the drawing-room. The first thing that caught my interest was a cabinet filled with Japanese and Chinese ivories, some too large to have been made out of only one tusk. There was a smiling woodman with a basket of sticks on his back; a woman in fantastic ceremonial dress; then I saw it – a man crouching down, holding out one hand beseechingly. He must have been a beggar; he was naked except for a few rags and so wasted that there seemed to be no more than a film between me and his tiny skeleton. It was a moment before I realized that the little creatures running over him were rats and that they were gnawing his flesh. The carver had shown the tears in the skin, the rats' minute beady eyes, the teeth of the agonized man. Looking deeper into the open mouth, I saw even a tongue curling back convulsively.

What a horrible thing this delicate ivory was to me! How could anyone carve such hideousness so lovingly? How could another human being be found to possess it? And yet the little figure fascinated me; I had to turn it over in my hands until every detail had been taken in; then I shut it back into the cabinet and left the room tingling.

Tea was being laid out on small tables in Mr Mellon's room; I went in and found my mother already there. I wanted to tell her about the little starving man, to take her into the drawing-room and show it to her quickly before the others returned; but something held me back. It was as if the sight were indecent and I did not dare to share it with her.

Soon we were all eating scones and guava jelly, sandwiches of several different sorts, and little cakes brightly decorated with silver balls, crystallized violets, rose petals and little spikes of angelica. Mr Mellon said to me, 'You'll want to be with Phyllis again after tea; grown-ups aren't nearly so much fun, are they?'

I wriggled, trying to think of something to say that would not slight Phyllis, yet would show that I preferred the company of the grown-ups.

When tea was over, I managed somehow to get out of the room alone. Perhaps I put on the grave air that children assume when they want to be 'excused'. Once free, I waited in my room until I felt that Phyllis had settled to some amusement without me; then I stole downstairs again and let myself into another of the unknown rooms.

This one was a sort of study, or perhaps, because of its size, it might have been called the library, although books were not the most important part of its furnishing. A huge roll-top desk stood in the middle of the room and round this were spread all types of wild animal skins: lions, tigers, leopards, polar bears, brown bears. All their heads were mounted, with fierce glass eyes staring, and pink plaster tongues, rough as sandpaper, hungry for the taste of blood. These roaring mouths seemed just to have loomed up through the floor, so that I could imagine the flat skins gradually filling and taking shape after them, until I would be surrounded by living wild beasts.

'But how can Mr Mellon wheel his chair in here with so many heads on the floor?' I thought; then I began to notice how unused every object in the room looked. The books were all shut away behind glass in the rather small bookcases. There were no magazines lying about. The ashtrays glistened. Even the blotting-paper on the desk was almost without ink stains.

I sat down on the polar bear and had began to ponder again on the peculiar deadness of all Mr Mellon's possessions, when the door opened softly and my mother looked in.

'Darling, don't prowl so,' she said, coming across to me, still rather quietly; 'they might not understand how fond you are of things. They might think you were being too inquisitive.'

'I expect they think I'm playing with Phyllis,' I answered.

'Well, anyhow, let's say goodnight and go upstairs now; it is nearly your bath-time.'

'But Mummy, have you ever seen so many animals with stuffed heads in one room before?' I asked, to keep her for a few more minutes from taking me to bed.

Should I try to hold her interest by telling her about the little rat-eaten ivory beggar? But once more I put the idea from me.

❖

When I was bathed and in pyjamas and dressing-gown, by the imitation logs that glowed so rosily on the hearth in my room, I said, 'Mummy, who will have Mr Mellon's snuff-boxes when he dies?'

My mother frowned a little.

'We don't want to think about people dying.'

'But I want to know,' I persisted.

My mother seemed to be wondering whether to tell me something or not.

'Has Phyllis explained that Mr Mellon is going to adopt her?' she asked, lifting her eyebrows.

'No, Phyllis hardly says anything at all.' Then the full meaning of my mother's words came to me and I added excitedly, 'Will *she* have the snuff-boxes and everything then?'

'I expect so, darling, but it won't be for a long time, so don't talk about it or think about it any more.'

But once in bed, with the lights out, I thought of nothing else. It seemed to me the greatest waste that Phyllis should have anything more than the necessities of life; then my imagination was caught by the wonderful change in her fortunes; for, without having heard a word on the subject, I pictured Mrs Slade and Phyllis in very difficult circumstances before they had come to Mr Mellon.

I must have been asleep for some hours when I was woken by soft bumping sounds and the murmur of voices. The noises frightened me and even after I had recognized one of the voices as Mrs Slade's, I felt anxious. What could be happening? There was another gentle bump. Mrs Slade said, 'There we are! Up at last!' and I heard a sort of comfortable grunt from Mr Mellon.

I realized that she was wheeling him to bed. Could she have pulled him up the stairs alone? The stairs were shallow, but Mr Mellon would be very heavy and awkward in his wheelchair. It did not seem possible for so small a woman. Perhaps the Indians had helped, and now she was only manœuvring some odd steps on the landing. They passed my door, still talking in undertones. Mrs Slade's sing-song voice was murmuring comforting things, as if she were talking to a child; Mr Mellon just grunted, or replied in monosyllables.

Their intimacy surprised me, for even while riding in the bathchair together there had been some formality; and, before that, I had thought them quite cut off, in spite of Mr Mellon's jolliness and Mrs Slade's metallic smiles. Now they were like two old friends who no longer had to be very polite. It is true that Mrs Slade still sounded dutiful, for I remember thinking, 'She hasn't finished yet!'

but it was the dutifulness rather of an old nurse than of a professional hostess.

Long after all sound of them had ceased, I felt haunted. My mother's sudden giddiness in the train had fixed my mind on pain and illness, so that I had been made specially conscious of Mr Mellon's useless legs; then I had crept into the drawing-room and seen that terrible starving man gnawed by rats. The fearful feelings awakened in me, together with what I thought of as the great ugliness and deadness of Mr Mellon's surroundings, made me long for tomorrow when we would go back to London. Everybody had been kind, even Phyllis had meant no harm, and yet I wanted to draw away from all of them.

Only the jewelled boxes and the wonderful curry were truly happy memories.

II

I did not see Mr Mellon again for about six years. During this time he had moved to a house of his own building, a few miles from his old villa. My mother was no longer alive, and I paid this second visit with my father on a hot summer's day.

The approach to the house had lately been planted with all kinds of ornamental shrubs and trees, ranging from green through yellow to pink and greyish-blue. I found myself contrasting their gay feathery leaves with the dark glistening toughness of the monkey-puzzles and rhododendrons at the villa. The drive was so thickly planted that I could see nothing of the rest of the garden, nor did the house come into view until we were almost upon it.

It was long and low, only one storey high, built of a light pinkish-fawn brick, with metal casements; apart from its squatness, the sort of house that any prosperous businessman might build. When the door was opened by an English servant, I grew even more disappointed. What had happened to the Indians? Was nothing strange left? I began even to regret the ugliness which had disquieted me as a child. I would have found it stimulating now.

My eyes brightened when we were taken into the room where

Mr Mellon sat, for it was octagonal and the floor was an inlay of rubber in baby blue and pink and yellow; it reminded me of nothing so much as the top of some gigantic cake prettily decorated with soft icing.

As I walked forward to shake hands with Mr Mellon, I felt its slight resilience.

Three sides of the octagon were of glass, and Mr Mellon's chair stood so that he had the whole of the garden before him. While he was welcoming my father boisterously I stood looking out of the window in some wonder. It was a complete surprise to find the house built almost on the edge of a small ravine. The garden fell away at once in narrow terraces, held back by large flat rocks. More pointed rocks thrust out of the ground, and a path with stone steps wound in and out of these until it reached smooth lawns and a stream at the bottom. A small rustic bridge led to the other heavily wooded bank, where the ground sloped away more gently.

'Not bad, eh?' said Mr Mellon, suddenly taking notice of my interest; 'you'd never think we had anything like this here, would you? I must say the landscape gardener has made a good job of it – really a very clever chap.'

My father went to the window to admire the scene, so that both our backs were turned when Mrs Slade came in with Phyllis. I was the first to hear their footsteps. Mrs Slade, like Mr Mellon, seemed hardly to have changed at all, but Phyllis had grown into 'a breasted woman', as I put it to myself. Her arms and legs were beefier than ever, and she was much taller than myself. But the full bosom gave me the greatest shock. I thought of her as the mother of fat twins. And was that *lipstick* on her mouth? Were girls who were not yet sixteen ever allowed to wear lipstick? Apart from this sudden redness, her face was much as I had remembered it. True, the eyebrows had become even thicker, leaving no sign that the long fat caterpillar had ever been two smaller ones affectionately rubbing noses. The expression too had strengthened; the sullenness was now almost formidable; but I was quick to see again that it was misleading, that it arose from her eyebrows and from her quite unmalicious indifference to other people.

As soon as Mrs Slade had greeted us with many smiles and

bright remarks, and Phyllis had nodded her head and held out her thick hand, Mr Mellon suggested that we should be shown the house and garden.

'Oh, yes,' said Mrs Slade to my father, 'you've never been to this house before, have you? We like it so much now that it is finished at last. It is much more convenient than the old one; there are no stairs, you see; Mr Mellon can wheel himself wherever he likes without having to call anyone. All the floors are rubber to make things as quiet and comfortable as possible; I wouldn't have anything else now; they are so bright and so easy for the maids to keep clean.'

Still chattering, Mrs Slade led us into the garden first, to give us an appetite for tea, as she explained. She knew very little about the flowers and rock-plants, but she kept drawing our attention to things by saying, 'Aren't those pretty?' or 'Mr Mellon's very fond of that,' or again, 'I think this is rather rare, but there's nothing much to show for it, is there?'

My father was walking with Mrs Slade and I with Phyllis, but since Phyllis said so little, I found myself listening chiefly to the other conversation. I heard Mrs Slade tell my father about the number of men it had taken to move some of the rocks into position.

'But weren't they already here?' my father asked in surprise.

'Oh no, nothing was here – only the banks and the stream.'

Mrs Slade's voice was very high and fluting; she seemed to be amused by my father's simplicity on the subject of gardens.

'Of course,' she went on, 'this is not a very good garden for Mr Mellon, most parts are so steep; but he took a great fancy to the site and *would* have the house here.'

'Do you like school?' Phyllis suddenly asked, bringing me back to her with a jerk.

'Yes,' I said hurriedly and quite untruthfully; 'do you like yours?'

'It's all right; some of the mistresses are a bit dim. I needn't stay after next term though, if I don't want to. Mello says I can go to a finishing school abroad – I can choose where.'

'So she calls him Mello,' I thought; 'and they're going to let her go to one of those schools where the girls just do what they like!'

This further proof that Phyllis was being treated almost as a grown-up filled me with envy. How I longed to have some attention paid to my own private wishes!

We had now reached the bottom of the cliff garden; Mrs Slade led us across the strip of lawn to the rustic bridge. I leant on the gnarled balustrade and looked down into the water. It seemed quite shallow.

'Oh, do you know what Mr Mellon has had done?' she asked, as if here were a topic, of especial interest to men, that had been almost overlooked. 'He has had the stream stocked with trout. There are gratings underneath the water at the boundaries of Mr Mellon's land so they can't swim away. We are hoping they will settle down and have lots of families.'

I now caught a glimpse of a dark shape fanning the water with its silky tail. It held its position under the far bank, then darted away in a flash, leaving me to search for others. I thought of their bodies, soft as mole-skin and with a sort of filmy shimmer over them, perhaps a little like the bloom on untouched plums. I knew very little of trout and probably confused them with my memories of lovely prune-coloured carp.

But I was not allowed to gaze into the water for long; Mrs Slade told me to cross over and look up at the terraced garden and the house.

'It is rather a good view,' she said; 'someone told Mr Mellon it was like the hanging gardens of Babylon, but I don't know how he knew.' She gave her little tinkling laugh.

Far away I could see Mr Mellon in his great bow-window; he looked like a captain on the bridge, I thought – a captain who had sat down and given up worrying about his ship.

After a moment he saw me too and waved. He was smiling broadly, as if I had done something to amuse him. I waved back; he took out his handkerchief and pretended to be a boy scout signalling. I wondered how long I ought to keep my eyes on him.

'We'd better not go any further now,' Mrs Slade was saying to me; 'there is much more to show you, but it's rather a stiff climb back and you'll be wanting tea; perhaps your father will be able to bring you over again quite soon.'

Crossing the stream rather reluctantly, I started to walk beside Phyllis again. In spite of my envy, I felt warmer towards her since our slight talk; we had never exchanged so many words before. I tried to begin another subject.

'Can you bathe in the stream?' I asked.

'Not now the trout are in it.'

Her tone made me feel I ought never to have asked such a question.

'Mello says they mustn't be disturbed.'

'Does Mr Mellon ever fish for them?'

'Oh, no, he never goes down there.'

'Who does fish then?'

'Nobody's allowed to until the fish have had babies; they've got to settle down.'

'Well, who *will* be allowed to fish?' I persisted, rather hopelessly.

'Oh, I don't know, people who come, friends of Mello's, I suppose. He might let you, if you come next year.'

Phyllis paused after this last kind remark; I realized suddenly that she was about to tell me a secret.

'As a matter of fact I *do* sometimes bathe, if you'd really like to know,' she said, grandly; 'there's a place where the trees lean over the water; I take off all my clothes and go in there – with nothing on,' she added, to make sure that I understood her fully.

She was looking at me, trying, I think, to find out the effect of her words. Did she want me to be confused and red? Or was she hoping for a lively interest in her nakedness? Perhaps she only wanted me to admire her devil-may-care attitude towards Mr Mellon, the carefully nursed trout, and the curiosity of the gardeners.

It was difficult to return the gaze of those sulky eyes. The thick red lips were set as though carved out of wood and painted. The whole face had the relentless quality of some Polynesian image or African ju-ju. I felt that the only protection was for me to make my face as mask-like as her own. I tried to do this, and when she saw that I had nothing to say, she began speaking again herself.

'Of course, it's not much fun, you can't really swim, it's too shallow; I just splash about.'

'Aren't you afraid of being seen?' I asked, as colourlessly and casually as possible.

'Oh, the trees make it quite private, but I wouldn't care much if one of the gardeners did come along. He wouldn't tell. Even if he did, Mello would only be a bit angry at first about his fish. I could get round him; he lets me do what I like.'

This was spoken as we climbed the last few steps to the house. I was afraid that Mr Mellon might hear through the open window, but Phyllis did not even trouble to lower her voice.

My father and Mrs Slade had sunk down on one of the stone seats on the terrace, and when Mr Mellon saw how hot my father was from the climb, he called out, 'You'll want something instead of tea, I can guess!'

My father laughed and shook his head; but I think he was very pleased to see whisky and soda appear with the tea-tray.

As soon as everything had been brought and we were left to ourselves once more, I turned to Mrs Slade and asked what had happened to the Indians.

A bright stare came into her eyes, she held her neck so stiffly that barely perceptible tremors ran up to her head.

'Oh, we had to get rid of them,' she said, with careful smiling unconcern; 'they were good at first, but we found that the cook was awfully extravagant – then we had trouble with one of the others.'

There was a sudden gleam of fierceness in the soft brown eyes, as if some memory had stung her; the next moment it was drowned in smiles which asked me to believe that the Indians had been nothing but an amusing trivial episode. I wondered why the thought of the Indians should have excited Mrs Slade; I guessed that she had been worsted in some scene with one of them, and that her Eurasian blood still felt the outrage. I had never seen her angry before; there had been a sort of quenched anxiety and a preoccupation with the details of the day, but her attitude to other people had seemed unchanging. In public at least she treated her daughter and Mr Mellon with the same brittle sociability that she accorded to little-known guests. I remembered how as a child I had been disquieted both by her Eastern appearance and her mechanical smiles, and now a little of the uneasiness returned. I saw her as a woman who hid so much that when a spark of feeling did escape, it flashed with all the rage of the fire within. This rather sensational picture of her made me want to turn away from the long oily eyes, and the creamy cheeks that were too soft. I wanted the reassurance of my father's sleepy good nature; even Mr Mellon's embarrassing heartiness and Phyllis's silences were refreshing.

We sat long over tea – my father and Mr Mellon had begun to talk about the past; and so little time was left for our inspection of the house. I felt disappointed as we hurried down a wide gallery, glancing into room after room almost without pausing.

I remember chiefly the various patterned rubber floors, the monotonous primrose and chromium of every fitting in the kitchen, and the fantastic decoration of the bedroom which Mrs Slade laughingly said should be mine when I came to stay, since I was fond of 'artistic' things.

The modern four-post bed had a pagoda roof with little wooden bells under the curling eaves; it was painted in dull blue, pale meat-red and yellow ochre, and all the mouldings were picked out in gold. On the dusty mauve walls large dragons coiled towards each other ferociously; their claws and teeth and scales were also gilded. The chairs had elaborate latticework backs. Everything was so new, so matt, so European in spite of all Chinese hankerings, that I was reminded at once of some painted backcloth for *Aladdin* which I must have seen as a child; the furniture and walls had the same powdery distemper bloom, and the designs the same coarseness as the bold scene-painting.

Here, as in every other room, I looked for the little ivory carving of the starving man that had so horrified me on my first visit to Mr Mellon, but it was nowhere to be seen. I doubt if it could have been found, even if I had not been so hurried; for everything was changed in this new house. Nearly all the floors, walls and hangings were in the pale shades associated with babies, powder-puffs and sugared almonds, just as the shrubs in the drive had the light feathery leaves that I had never seen at the villa. There everything had been rigid and glistening and tough; here all was downy, almost scented – even the fantastic things were in pastel colours. But in spite of all changes, something of the villa's atmosphere remained. As we walked back to the octagon room to say goodbye to Mr Mellon, I tried without success to define what spirit it was that still lingered under the soft prettiness.

Mr Mellon was gazing out of his huge window and taking snuff; I saw him for a moment through the crack of the door before he was aware of us. His face was quite blank and empty, more than ever like a peeled trunk of wood. The welcoming smile that suddenly puckered all the features gave me a stab of discomfort, so that I wished I had not caught him as he was alone.

'Seen most things?' he called out with rowdy boyishness.

There was a flash of light as he put his jewelled box away.

'Pity you hadn't more time. All the more reason why you must come again.'

He put his hand up to my shoulder to say goodbye; then, perhaps because he could no longer treat me as a child and hug me, he stretched out his other arm and caught Phyllis, who was moving towards the terrace. She allowed herself to be drawn to him with her usual seeming ill grace; he encircled her waist, swung her gently on her feet and gave her stomach a loving pat or two.

'We'll want to see him again very soon, won't we, Phyl?' he said.

Phyllis grunted.

I was becoming more and more uncomfortable, when the opening of the door created just the slight diversion necessary for a not too unnatural escape. As soon as the heavy hand was taken from my shoulder, I turned, to see a new face hovering in the doorway.

'Yes, what is it, Bob?' asked Mrs Slade, brightly.

'Oh, excuse me, madam, I came to see if Mr Mellon was ready for his massage; it's his time.'

'In a minute, Bob, in a minute,' Mr Mellon called from the other end of the room.

'Yes, sir,' Bob said, and shut the door.

There had just been time for me to take note of Bob's curling fair hair, pink-brown colouring, and pursy cheeks. These last gave to his face the cast of an earlier century. His eyes seemed to stare a little, as though the lids were not quite full enough to cover them. He was near enough to my own age to make me conscious of his body under the white coat and dark trousers. It was as if I were asking myself, 'Will I look anything like that in four or five years' time? Will I have thick legs, thick arms, deep chest? Will I look so well fed and strong?'

He appeared to be a favourite of Mrs Slade's, for she turned to me and said, 'You've not seen Bob before, have you? He's a very nice boy; he first came only as a valet; then we had him trained as a masseur, and now, although he's only nineteen, he does everything for Mr Mellon. It is an excellent arrangement.'

Mrs Slade might have been talking to herself, or to an intimate woman companion, instead of to a young boy; I realized that my appreciation of Bob would not satisfy. She wanted real enthusiasm.

Mr Mellon held Phyllis till the last moment; then, as we were leaving the room, he released her with a playful spank, saying, 'Off you go, Phylly, to wave goodbye.'

But Phyllis did not run forward to escort us to the car; she ambled along, some way behind her mother.

My last picture was of her leaning against the open door, while, in the hall behind, Bob hurried back to the octagon room to begin his master's massage as soon as possible. Mrs Slade was showering us with busy smiles and hand-wavings. The car started, we turned and were quickly lost in the feathery trees.

III

Once more Mr Mellon, Mrs Slade and Phyllis disappeared from my life; I did not even hear of them, or if I heard, I quickly forgot the slight mention of some unimportant detail. But when I was nineteen, a new friend at the art school asked me to his parents' home for Easter, and I accepted impulsively.

So one grey evening I found myself in a little Sussex village, standing on an unknown doorstep, feeling very reluctant about ringing the bell.

I need not have been anxious about my visit, for the house was comfortable and my friend's mother seemed really pleased to see me.

She had just returned from Egypt; it was clear that her husband and son had not listened to her experiences with nearly enough interest; she was delighted to be able to pour all her stories into a new ear, to have a listener who paid attention and seemed to want to know more.

When asking me to stay, my friend had said rather brutally, 'My mother's an awful fool, you know.' Perhaps she did show more capriciousness and wilfulness than is quite acceptable; but in spite of these slight signs of childish whining or petty tyranny, we were soon on very good terms, even going off together to explore churches and a ruined abbey, while the others stayed at home.

When we came back from these expeditions, my friend would look at me as if he were wondering how I could have borne his mother's company for a whole morning, or afternoon. I imagined that the father also flashed glances at me sometimes; he seemed to be looking for signs of weariness or irritation, and because he could not find them, he was grateful, more polite than ever, yet somehow less friendly. It was as if he were relieved to see my easiness with his wife, but felt cut off from real communication with me just because of it. I had the vague notion, perhaps quite fanciful, that both father and son would have preferred it if I had appeared to enjoy myself less.

On the fourth or fifth day of my visit, John's mother announced at breakfast that there was to be a tea-party in the afternoon. Extravagant groans came from John and his father, and once more they made me feel that I too ought to be pulling some sort of disapproving face instead of wearing the ridiculous smile of the perfect guest, pleased at any suggestion, however inane.

Both John and his father had threatened to go out; but as the time for the guests to arrive drew near, I noticed that they were looking trim and fresh, as though their faces had been dipped in cold water, their hair brushed vigorously and their ties straightened.

Tea for so many people had been laid on the long dining-room table, and I was placed next to my hostess.

'Come and sit near me and help me with the teacups,' she had called in her soft screech; 'John is no use, he only thinks about his own stomach.'

At first I had little time to listen to conversation because I was walking round the table with cups of tea and plates of buttered toast and scones; but when I came back to my place, the fluting, warbling tones of the woman on the other side of John's mother caught my attention. There was the faintest suggestion of the electric guitar about her voice.

'But, my dear,' she was saying, 'you should have been there; it was fantastic, but quite fantastic! In all our eighteen months of house-hunting we've never come across anything like it. All the floors were rubber; I had the awful feeling that I was trapped in a gigantic lavatory; it was terrifying. One room was fitted up as a sort of tea-house in Chinatown, another was sexagonal, I think, if there is such a word, and it doesn't sound too rude; anyhow, all these six or more walls seemed to close in on one, and there was an enormous window which just screamed out for one of those horrible dentist's chairs.'

At first her words floated in a void, but as the description grew, they seemed to link up with something in my own experience; I began to listen intently.

She was talking of the garden now.

'Darling, even the plants were weird, and there were *the* most enormous rocks – rather marvellous really, if they hadn't seemed so completely out of place. The money that must have been poured into that garden!'

Surely there could be no more doubt? It was Mr Mellon's house and garden that were being so cruelly described. I realized for the first time that, since we were so close to the border, Mr Mellon's place in Kent could only be five or six miles away at the most. Feeling angry with this unknown woman for laughing at tastes that I myself had always thought strange, I decided to go over to see Mr Mellon as soon as possible; then it came back to me with a shock that she had been talking of a house that was to let or for sale, an empty house, whose key, decorated with a large label, must hang on one of the local house-agent's hooks.

Where had Mr Mellon gone? Was he at this moment building another house somewhere else? I suddenly wanted to know all that had happened since I last saw him.

While the woman was describing the house and garden, John's mother had not spoken, but her eyes had danced. Now the words came pouring out.

'But Dulcie, didn't you know? Didn't anyone tell you about that house?'

'Oh no, *do* tell me, I haven't heard a word. Is it haunted by some horribly unclean spirit? Or has *the* most atrocious murder been committed there? I can believe anything, *anything*.'

'No, it wasn't a murder, but the place is quite possibly haunted by now,' said John's mother with satisfaction, her eyes dancing more than ever. A faint flush had come into her cheeks.

She was in no hurry to reach the climax of her story; she seemed to wish to savour both her own excitement and the suspense of her audience.

'Perhaps you wouldn't have heard of it,' she mused; 'perhaps it *is* rather a local tragedy.'

'Darling, stop maundering! I'm mad to know what happened.'

'Well, you remember the rock garden?'

'Yes.'

'And the path leading down to the stream?'

'Yes, yes, pet, don't be so ponderous, I remember it all perfectly.'

'Well, one day the housekeeper ran down the path, jumped into the stream and drowned herself.'

The words seemed to tumble over each other, as if John's mother had suddenly grown tired of trying to unfold her story skilfully. For a moment I could not grasp their full meaning, then the exclamation, 'It's Mrs Slade, she means Mrs Slade!' kept ringing in my head like some battle-cry or line from a famous poem.

'But why did she drown herself?' the woman was asking. 'We must know *everything*.'

John's mother beamed gratefully.

'Of course I didn't know them myself, but I've heard little bits from people who did; they've all said that it was the queerest household. The man was an invalid. He seems to have been very good indeed to this housekeeper, who was half-Japanese or something of that sort; he had even adopted her daughter.'

The woman called Dulcie raised her bald-looking eyebrows.

'Yes, I thought that rather an interesting point too,' said John's mother, 'but anyhow, when this daughter suddenly eloped with the chauffeur, the mother was so upset that she just flung herself into the stream; and I'm told it's only quite shallow. One of the gardeners found her later.'

Something had mounted from my stomach to my heart, to my head. Perhaps I had turned very red. I looked at my hostess's bright chirpy smile and understood why her son thought her so silly. Now that she had told her story she was like a bird waiting for crumbs. Her head was cocked a little to one side; she seemed to be contemplating her own winsomeness, to be modestly disclaiming any credit for the suicide which had interested us so much.

Through the surge and tingle in my head, I found myself asking her if she was sure that the daughter had run away with a chauffeur.

'Someone like that,' she said, a little piqued to have her story questioned; 'actually, now you ask me, I believe I did hear later that he was more the personal servant of the old man, the sort of valet–nurse.'

'Was he called Bob?' I asked, unable to stop myself.

'How should I know?'

John's mother was staring at me curiously. She was about to ask if I knew the family. I picked up a plate of little cakes and started to pass them round the table. When the question came, I pretended not to hear, but I answered it under my breath, to myself, 'Yes, I knew them, but not very well. She wasn't half-Japanese, she was half-Javanese – I expect it was Bob who ran away with Phyllis; I only saw him once for a moment, but I can imagine it so easily with him. It must have been Bob.'

People were already beginning to leave the table, to wander into the other room or talk in groups near the windows. I decided to put down my cakes on a side-table and escape into the hall.

I was out, and nobody had called my name or appeared to notice me. I could hear the chatter and smell the cigarette smoke creeping under the door. It was still quite light outside; I opened the front door and let myself into the garden.

I walked behind hedges until I came to the old stables; there I found John's bicycle and began to pump the tyres. I tried the lamp and saw that the battery was fairly new. That was good. I would need it.

By great good fortune I found my way without a mistake to the village nearest Mr Mellon's house; after that my progress was more difficult. But at last someone directed me down the right lane; I came upon his drive, and had almost passed it before something told me to look again. Yes, that was the drive; the trees and bushes were bigger, but I could recognize them.

It was dusk now; objects were beginning to lose their colour and sink into each other, like lead soldiers melting on the nursery fire. I saw an orange square of light somewhere through the trees and wondered if a caretaker lived there. I was suddenly afraid of being discovered in Mr Mellon's grounds. What explanation of my prowling could I give? I remembered my mother saying, 'Darling, don't prowl so.'

Pushing my bicycle into the shrubs, I walked swiftly down the drive till I came to the point where it turned and one saw the long squat house. I stood still, shocked by the blankness of the windows; they were oblong eyes over which a terrible fungus of nothingness was growing. And the porch was a great black mouth, the jaws of the whale that swallowed Jonah, the gates of Hell in an ancient wall-painting. I could not walk into the yawning cadaverous blackness under that plain brick arch; I could not even look through those neat metal casements, now that they had been turned into horrible eyes filmed with cataract. I stood back from the house, staring through its walls, picturing Phyllis and Bob as they prepared for flight. Phyllis would be packing everything of value into a small soft suitcase, while Bob waited rather desperately by the door. She would put in all the jewels and trinkets Mr Mellon had ever given her. She would be methodical, heavy, placid; but Bob would be pulling at his collar and jerking down his sleeves. His large eyes would roll from her to the door and back again. She would take no notice of his longing to be off, until the last object had been fitted in.

Because I knew nothing of them as they were today, because I did not even know for certain that it was Bob who had gone with Phyllis, my picture seemed squalid and meaningless and dead. It was the counterfeit of a counterfeit. The bare fact that Phyllis had run away with a lover was in itself papery and unreal. I had been given no reason, only told that it was so; therefore my mind kept teasing and plucking at ideas.

At last I made myself turn from them and from the house; I would strain no more after reasons, just let thoughts float through my head, while I wandered in the garden.

It was a relief to plunge into the bushes. Somehow they were not fearful, as they might well have been at nightfall; they seemed to offer warmth, a protection against the balefulness of the house. I pushed and threaded my way blindly, till I came out on a ridge of the ravine, some way from the house. To the left I could see the great window of the octagon room gleaming palely against the sky. There was no proper path here, only a sort of gardener's track along the ridge. I walked to the end, then began climbing down from terrace to terrace, avoiding the plants by standing on the rocks. The garden was still being tended; I could see patches of softly crumbled, weedless earth. Birds were scudding across the sky, calling forlornly, as though the coming of night were some sort of catastrophe for them. When I reached the foot of the ravine, I was hot and tired; sweat had begun to sting in the scratches I had received from the shrubs and trees. I sat down on a rock enjoying the cold moistness that was already coming from it. The stream flowed near me, industriously, secretly, like some man who, thinking he is alone, sings and mutters and swears at his work.

I sat listening for some moments, then stood up and walked towards the bridge. From the other bank I looked up the tortuous path. All at once I thought of Mrs Slade as she must have been when she ran down to drown herself. I saw her crying, crying, stumbling over the artfully uneven stone steps, chattering madly all the time. Nothing could stop her; if she fell, she was on her feet again in a moment, stockings torn, knees bleeding. She was like a wingless bat, wrapped round in a little whirlwind. Her greying hair flared out in a tangle wilder than Beethoven's, and her eyes had grown into pools of boiling tar. They were still growing; suddenly I was caught up in them, so that I plunged into the stream with her and heard them sizzle as we struck the water ...

I was standing now on the very brink of the stream, looking straight down into the black water. The night wind ruffled the surface into little fish scales. One of the birds kept up its perplexed lost flying and calling. Darkness was gathering in the branches of the trees behind me, thickening under the rocks, turning them into grotesques and derelicts standing in puddles of ink. One was a man with an elephant's trunk which he clutched to himself desperately. Another had huge monkey ears; all the rest of him had sunk into a belly like a giant's teapot. The biggest was an ancient pugilist who had given up hope and died at last by the side of the road. He was a vast lump of sagging muscles and despair.

High up above them the dark bow of Mr Mellon's window jutted out. I thought of him sitting there, taking snuff, staring blankly, waiting for Bob or Phyllis or Mrs Slade to come. I saw him as a great sick bird, a turkey wrapped in flannel. How long was it before he realized that he had been deserted by all three of them? Did he watch the gardeners bringing the body up the twisting path? Where was he now? Had he found other people to look after him?

Then I remembered how fond he was of the stream, how he had stocked it with trout and told Phyllis not to bathe there.

And all the way up the cliff, back to my bicycle in the drive, I kept wondering if the fish had been very disturbed when Mrs Slade plunged in and drowned herself.

MR CLARKE

Despite the opening sentence of the following fragment, it was almost certainly not written at the time of the visit described. 'Mr Clarke' is clearly the same character as Mr Wattie ('Mr Mellon' in 'The Trout Stream').

LAST WEEK I AND MY MOTHER WENT TO STAY WITH Mr Clarke. He lives in a big house at Guildford and we ran so hard to catch the train in London that my mother nearly fainted. She is very pretty, with fat pink cheeks and fair curls; she looked awful lying on the cushions, nearly fainting. I pretended it was not her at all until she was all right. She is really very thin, all made of small bones, and it is only her cheeks that are fat. She does not put on rouge because they are quite pink anyhow. She has plenty of very pretty clothes and my father doesn't mind when she buys more, because he says women are no good if they don't look pretty. Sometimes he gives her very nice diamonds, but she says to me afterwards, 'Don't tell Daddy, but his taste isn't quite the same as mine, as I should like to swop this thing for something else.' She doesn't like the dangling sort of earrings and he has given her three pairs now. She wants to swop them for a bracelet. I say wait until he gives you one pair more and then you can get a better bracelet with bigger diamonds.

We were very lonely in London because my father had gone back to America and so we were very pleased when Mr Clarke asked us to stay. He was one of my father's business friends until his legs got paralysed.

When we got out at Guildford, there was a black man waiting for us and he drove us to Mr Clarke's house. It is called Aurora, and when you go in at the gate it is all thick bushes and dripping leaves. The drive is very long and the tyres crunched a lot on the gravel, but as it was night I couldn't see very much.

When we got to the front door the black man rang the bell, and somebody inside switched on the porch light and then let us in. It was another black man, only this one was wearing a red turban and white coat. Behind him was Mrs Wallis, who is Mr Clarke's Eurasian housekeeper–companion. She has black hair and Chinese eyes and wears very proper English clothes.

She smiled a lot when she saw us and said to my mother, 'The Indian servants are new since you came last. Mr Clarke was so tired of trying to find good English ones that he thought he'd try these as an experiment.'

My mother said that she thought they looked romantic, and then we went into the small room where Mr Clarke was. He was sitting in his wheelchair by the fire with a rug over his legs and he looked wedged in, as if he couldn't get out, because he is rather fat. He has fairly white hair and says he likes boys and girls very much. He was very pleased to see us and laughed and talked a lot while he was shaking our hands; then we all sat down and my mother took off her gloves and I looked at the room. It was quite small with a very big window which had pale curtains.

AT SIR
MOORCALM LALLI'S

'Sir Moorcalm Lalli' was in reality Sir Eliezer Saleh Kadoorie (1867–1944), an immensely wealthy philanthropist who made his fortune in Hong Kong and Shanghai and was benefactor of schools and hospitals all over the world. Sir Elly, as he was known in England, lived at 6 Prince's Gate in Kensington, London, close by the school in Queen's Gate which Denton Welch attended from 1924 to 1926.

This fragment was first published in Contemporary Review *in March 1974.*

HERE, IN MY WARM BED, ON THIS GUSTY BLEAK EVENING, it amuses me to recall that day, twenty years ago at least now, when, as a little boy, I was taken to lunch with the old Levantine in his grotesque Prince's Gate house. It is just a twinkling little experience that lives and lives and lives and will not die, although for months, even a year or two, it may be leathery and vapid, like chewed meat on the tongue, a tasteless, pointless thing, just one of a thousand past experiences that almost irritate because nothing seems to be left but a sort of unmeaning poignancy.

His own name was fantastic enough to English ears, but since it would be incorrect to use it here, I must try to think of something of my own; so I shall call him Sir Moorcalm Lalli. This is, no doubt, an impossible name for anyone of any ancestry, but since Sir Moorcalm's was so mixed and I never had any true idea of what the mixture consisted, it will do well enough. My father, who had a great respect for him, would nevertheless talk laughingly of Baghdad, Cyprus, Jerusalem and Constantinople. Clearly it was vain to look to him for accurate information. He had only met Sir

Moorcalm in the course of business in the East, and he was not the man to probe or be inquiring.

Sir Moorcalm had only lately settled in London, to contribute to party funds and so, in due course, to receive his knighthood. Now that everything was accomplished, it seemed likely that he would soon be returning to a warmer country and one more to his taste. He met us in a little room at the end of the long dark hall. At first I was so amazed by the decoration of the room that I could not fix my attention on him properly, but I saw that he was very small and at once approved this littleness; I suppose, because I myself was small for my age. My next thought was, 'That man in the hall shouldn't have taken away my red coat. I would have matched perfectly in here,' for all the furniture, and there was a great deal of it, was of scarlet buhl. It bulged and glittered and looked cruel and hard. The ormolu mounts of naked breasted women struck me as both ugly and improper. I was not to know then that in this sort of work tortoiseshell is laid over a ground of red paint, so I took it that the cabinets and tables were all manufactured from some garish imitation. The objects in the cabinets, the bronzes, the ivories and porcelain figures, both horrified me and lured me on. I wanted to inspect everything, but knew that I must sit still and not appear inquisitive. Sir Moorcalm had taken my mother to a ridiculously dancing French chair – I felt that at any moment it might begin to bounce about, carrying her with it. He was saying to her, 'But my dear lady, abroad I have a palace compared to this.' He waved his hand contemptuously at the room, the house, the whole of Prince's Gate. 'It is incredible, the expense in London; and what do you get for your money? A house in a row, looking on to Kensington Gardens.' I was immediately aware of the humiliation of such reduced circumstances. Sir Moorcalm was speaking again: 'Abroad my house is all white stone, marble you know. All along the front is a great closed-in terrace, and every pane is bevelled plate-glass.'

Sir Moorcalm almost waited for my mother to gape. I was aware that this was 'boasting', but never having known it before in grownups, I felt that perhaps *they* were allowed to do it. Besides, I rather enjoyed it. I wanted too to be told of greater magnificence, wilder extravagance. If he were not discouraged, he might go one better than bevelled plate-glass in all the windows. My eyes left the room and I began to watch Sir Moorcalm. I noticed that, although he called my mother 'dear lady', he leant towards her with a hard, eager, unhappy expression, as though he were chiefly interested in keeping her pinned down to her chair. He seemed afraid that her attention might wander or that she might jump up and walk about the room capriciously. He would glance anxiously at my father too. I was the only one who was not expected to listen to his complaints. I was relieved, but also a little hurt, that he should dismiss me as too young to be treated seriously. My parents listened to him with polite and careful sympathy, but he seemed to refuse their understanding, as though he were not to be cheated out of his dissatisfaction by a kind word or two. I began to take in the details of his face and form. The little hooded eyes, the hooked nose and nutcracker chin, the slightly bowed back all reminded me of a witch. I had a picture of him dressed in witch's clothes, carrying a very new broomstick; but I could not see him with a cat. He would be as indifferent to a cat as he was to me.

The door opened and a footman came in with drinks and emerald-green pistachio nuts in little silver bowls. I had only seen these nuts before on chocolates, where the isolated little patches of green had been taken for granted; but here, in this scarlet room, the colour sang out, fixing my attention, making me aware of the strangeness of such food instead of the usual roasted peanuts or almonds. I nibbled one after another, savouring their flavour and peculiar hard–soft consistency. Titbits of vivid green were just what to expect in some story of enchantment and witches. I let my imagination play round the nuts, pretending that they were poisoned.

Outside, the grey day pressed against the window. Sir Moorcalm began to apologize for the lateness of his sons. As he was speaking, they appeared, smiling in the doorway, rubbing their hands vigorously. They were both very much alike, both tall, well covered, with glowing faces and rather large teeth. They wore striped double-breasted suits. Their robustness made their father seem frailer, more witch-like than ever. Their manner was embarrassingly optimistic and boisterous, especially to me. Sir Moorcalm's querulousness retreated into the corners of the room. He appeared to look on his sons with a sort of grudging pride, as if they had no right to be so tall and young and glistening, and yet he would not have tolerated them otherwise. The rather mechanical liveliness that they brought with them, as soon as it was switched from me back to my parents, left me with a feeling of greater freedom. I was satisfied somehow that the grown-ups were now fully occupied, would notice me less and less. I could stare to my heart's content, perhaps even pick things up and examine them. My eyes had been caught by a marble portrait bust in a dark corner. It was of a woman with Edwardian 'cow-pat' hair and a lot of lace at the throat. I marvelled at the carving of the lace, but it was some moments before I gave any thought to the sitter. Then it came to me suddenly that here was the likeness of Sir Moorcalm's long lost wife. I had once heard her story from my father and it had caught hold of me. Years ago there had been a terrible fire in Sir Moorcalm's house. His wife had had a favourite parrot. She had insisted on returning to her burning bedroom to rescue it. She did rescue it, but lost her own life in doing so. This bald little story had turned the unknown Sir Moorcalm's wife into an abstract heroine. She was the woman who had given her life for her pet. She had braved the flames. Small wonder that a bust had been made of her! I sat and gazed at it, taking in her rather heavy features, trying to read kindness and courage into every line. I wished Sir Moorcalm could be made to talk about her, but I guessed that her name was never even mentioned in his presence. I must contemplate her effigy in silence. I longed to know if my father or mother had recognized her. Were they too thinking about the heroic rescue? The remembrance of it had brought the whole room to life for me.

All through lunch, in spite of the frightful solemnity of the footman behind my chair, in spite of confusingly elaborate food, I felt her there in the back room on her pedestal. She wasn't smiling, she wasn't taking any interest; but she was there in her heavy marble folds, the frozen waterfall of lace gushing from her throat. Perhaps my concentration in some way influenced my mother, for she unexpectedly began to talk of the danger of fire. It was only some passing remark, but it was enough to make my father glance up at her anxiously. Sir Moorcalm was silent. It was impossible to

AT SIR MOORCALM LALLI'S

tell how much he noticed. His chief concern seemed to be with the food and his guests' enjoyment of it. He would recommend things lugubriously, as though the words were wrung from him and he would really have preferred to criticize. Once or twice he did make a faint complaint. I expected that the utterly inexpressive footmen behind our chairs would at last show some sign; but nothing changed, they might have been deaf and dumb. Their immobility began to weigh on me, so that I longed for lunch to end. The two sons kept up their Stock Exchange jokes and lively patter, but even my inexperienced ear could detect the effort behind the brightness. We were, I suppose, a very ill-assorted group, with my father as only the frailest sort of link.

After lunch the sons excused themselves with hearty smiles and handshakes; there was business to be attended to. Although they smiled, one knew that business really only called forth solemn, almost sacred feelings in them. It was not to be trifled with, not to be set aside for a slight prolonging of the luncheon hour. The door shutting behind them brought a slight sense of relief. I felt more at home alone with old Sir Moorcalm. He took us upstairs to have coffee and to show us his collection of Persian rugs. They were everywhere. As we entered the lofty drawing-room, with its heavy cornice and long windows, a sort of breath of rugs came to meet us. They were on the walls, on the chairs, on the floor. Rugs were laid over carpets, silk rugs over woollen ones, until one had a suffocating feeling of cosiness. Sir Moorcalm stroked them, lifted them, turned them over, told us their different names. He leant over a sofa with my mother, showing her his favourite silk rug. She balanced her tiny cup precariously. I wondered what Sir Moorcalm would say if she spilt any of the treacly coffee on his rugs. I had never been allowed Turkish coffee before. I drank mine very slowly, pretending that I liked the cloudy, almost muddy liquid. The feeling of the padded cell increased. The layers of rugs seemed to grow thicker and thicker. I was growing very hot. I wished I could touch the marble bust on her marble pillar; then I remembered that the real woman had gone back into a burning building, had climbed up burning stairs. I saw the flames licking round fallen beams, the smoke belching out through cracks in the wall. She struggled on, searching blindly for the parrot's cage. It was a nightmare of heat and agony that I had conjured up. The picture stayed with me, hung about me stranglingly. I could not bear to think of the poor charred body, and yet I had to.

I stood very still, hoping that no one would notice my face. If I did not even move an eyelid, perhaps I would grow calmer and be able to endure the stifling snugness of the drawing-room for a little longer. I prayed for my mother to be quick. 'Be quick, be quick, be quick,' I said, staring out of the window, with my eyes so wide open that they felt they would never shut again. At last my mother noticed me. She could see in an instant that something was wrong. She was at my side, asking me in a low voice if I felt unwell. I could only glance away without answering. She had turned to Sir Moorcalm now and was saying, 'I think we ought to take him back. You gave us such a splendid lunch; he may have had too much to eat!' She was trying to pass the situation off lightly by pretending that I had been greedy. I did not mind; I only wanted her to get me out of the house.

Sir Moorcalm looked at me mournfully, with very little love. 'Poor boy,' he said, using an ancient, oriental, humbugging tone; 'we must send him back in the car.'

My mother began to protest.

'No, no,' Sir Moorcalm held up his hand like a prophet; 'I won't hear of a refusal. The man can be round at the front door in five minutes.' He went to the wall and pulled the richly painted Victorian china bell. As he did so, he tried to smile at me benignly, but his pale lips seemed to find it easier to form themselves into a sort of snarl or sneer.

I let myself be led from the room, still holding my head very stiffly. No one had said anything, but I felt vaguely that I had not been a credit to my parents. If I had been iller, I might not have felt so guilty. It seemed to me that my enormous lunch and the Turkish coffee . . .

MRS HOCKEY

When Denton Welch was eleven he was sent to St Michael's Preparatory School in Uckfield, Sussex, the setting of this fragment. The headmaster was an Anglican clergyman, the Reverend Harold Hibbert Herbert Hockey, and Wilmshurst was the butler.

I WENT OUT OF THE SCHOOL DOOR AND RAN DOWN THE drive to meet my mother. She turned to pay the taxi and then saw that she had no small change in her bag. So we carried her suitcase into the headmaster's porch and opened it there to find her other bag.

She had just come back from Paris and I saw her beautiful pale-green underclothes lying on the top. I pulled one towards me to look at the silk and lace more carefully, and my mother, suddenly remembering the respectabilities, said, 'Don't pull it out, darling, the taxi-driver might see.' But I did not let it go because I loved to feel it – one side rough, crystallized crêpe de Chine and the other liquid-smooth satin.

Suddenly I saw the two little boxes of chocolates nestling in the corner of the suitcase, one of rosebuds and one of *langues de chats*. I knew they were for me. I thought of the delicious French coffee-chocolate taste. Then Wilmshurst silently opened the front door and waited for us to go in. As I passed him I smelt that lardy smell which seems to hang round even the most senior school servants. I pictured him getting butter on his black cuffs, smearing his waistcoat with grease from the joint. I thought, as I had thought many times before, how nice it would be to be able to draw one's nostrils together as one did one's lips and yet still be able to go on breathing.

Mrs Hockey met us at the foot of the stairs. She had just come down in a new dress. It was brilliantly patterned and coloured, and she carried an eighteenth-century quizzing glass with an enormously thick lens through which she peered. The legend in the school was that she was so blind that she had given the prize for the best boy's garden to a quite neglected one almost completely overgrown with huge dandelions. I wondered how much her eyes hurt her and whether she would ever go quite blind.

As she saw the blur of my mother and myself approaching, the slightly bewildered look left her face and she held out her hand with a charming yet patronizing grace. Her scarlet scarf fluttered with her movement. I sensed in a minute that my mother was quite equal to her. It gave me delight to think that she was mistress of the situation.

'I hope my brat's been good,' she said playfully.

All the patronage and some of the charm evaporated. Mrs Hockey was not used to mothers who were playful and called their children brats.

'I expect that you'll want to be alone with him so that you can have a good long talk,' she said.

'How clever of you to guess!' my mother exclaimed; and even I could not tell if she were being ironical or not.

'Would you like to take him out for a walk or would you rather sit here in the lounge?'

At the word 'lounge' I pinched my mother's arm, which I was holding. I knew how she hated it. She said that it ought always to be pronounced with an Australian accent to give it its full flavour. I was so pleased that Mrs Hockey had used it, yet sorry for her too, because she did not know my mother's feelings.

'I think we'll go out for a walk,' my mother said.

'Then Harold will see you when you come back,' Mrs Hockey announced with importance.

'Yes, there'll be plenty of time then,' my mother answered lightly, with a sweet smile.

I tugged at her arm to get her through the baize door, into the boys' quarters and so out of the hateful building.

'Darling, are you happy?' she asked urgently, as we walked over the asphalt to the cricket fields.

'Oh, it's miles better than I thought it would be,' I said; but then no one knew what depths of misery I had imagined for myself. I knew that we must not talk about school. It was a closed subject – taboo in some curious way.

I danced along, holding tightly to her hand, flaunting my lovely mother and protector. Today I was safe and I did not care what questions and jeerings I saved up for myself tomorrow. But my mother did, for she said, 'Darling, don't let's hold hands till we get out of the playing fields,' in the same voice as she had said, 'Darling, don't pull them out, the taxi-driver might see.'

'But Mummy, it doesn't matter what they think,' I shrieked joyfully.

We walked down by the 'gardens', each one a square bed filled with browning autumn flowers and surrounded by little hard mud paths. Being a new boy I had not been allotted one yet.

I took my mother to the gap in the hedge which I had already discovered, then we were out of the school grounds, on free soil at last.

I danced and swung on my mother's arm. People seeing me would have thought that I was eight, not eleven.

'Mummy,' I said, 'the last few days I've been wanting to "go" all the time. Why do you think it is?'

My mother saw that I was interested from a scientific point of view.

'I expect it's the sudden change to cold weather, darling. Also, you've probably been frightfully excited about all the new things you're doing.'

We were climbing the hill now. I let go of her hand and pushed into the bracken, and she waited while I 'went'.

A CHILD MEETS CHURCH AND STATE AND POETRY IN STRANGE PLACES: LADY ASTOR

This fragment describes one of many theatrical entertainments produced at St Michael's, Uckfield. The title is Denton Welch's.

BEFORE THE PLAY BEGAN WE SAT ON THE LOCKERS round the edge of the playroom, scraping our feet in nervousness on the parquet, so worn and roughened into hillocks and splintery parts by the roller-skaters. We had our *Mikado* clothes on and were made up wondrously. My blue eyelids and slanting brows gave me intense pleasure. I paid unnecessary visits to the lavatory to see myself in the great sinister, filmy, changing-room glass.

I was one of the Three Little Maids from School, Peep-Bo, the least important. Michael Astor was Pitti-Sing and the heroine was an atavistic monkey-faced boy called Bell.

I held my script tightly in my hand, mouthing my few precious lines half to myself, half out loud. 'I must be perfect,' I thought, 'quite perfect.'

During this concentration I noticed a shuffling of feet. I vaguely wondered what it meant, but took no notice, as people had been twitchy with nervousness in all corners of the room. Then suddenly, with the strange and unusual swish of their flowered kimonos, everyone stood up and I saw that a thin tailor-made woman with steely hair and no hat, carrying a large box under one arm, had come in. She was at the far end of the long room, alone, with no master accompanying her. I thought that she was some strayed

A CHILD MEETS CHURCH AND STATE

parent and felt sorry for her, and annoyed that she should disturb our feverish concentration. I felt that she must be very embarrassed to see us all standing there before her sheepishly.

But as she advanced with sharp, bird-like steps I saw that there was no mistake and that she was not in the least embarrassed. Each one of her movements was intended and challenging.

'Sit down all of you!' she called, again, I thought, like a sharp bird.

We subsided obediently into crumpled, coloured bundles on the lockers. I resented our docility. It was so slavish to sit down because a stranger told us to!

The woman put down her cardboard box, took off the lid; then, holding the uncovered box in both her hands, she came towards us.

'Choose!' she ordered, presenting it to the first boy of the long row on the lockers. He ducked his humble head, dived with his hand into the box and brought out a most rich-looking chocolate, utterly delicious with red cherry and pistachio nut.

'But our lipstick!' I thought. 'What are we going to do? We've all got lipstick on!'

The box was rapidly coming down the line. With each chocolate went a bright, metallic injunction, not to be greedy, not to be slow, not to smear our make-up or forget our parts; all half serious, severe, poking fun at us.

Then, when each boy had his chocolate, came the questions, mostly answered by herself, for we were all too shy to do more than smile and giggle. Even her son wore an uneasy, anxious smile.

I began to think how full of bounce and fun she was, how 'showing-off', and I admired her. 'Not many people would dare to behave like that, would dare to tease and persecute and amuse sixty or seventy boys all at once. Does she do it in Parliament?' I wondered.

A master came in to tell the chorus to get ready for the stage. They shuffled out and I buried myself in my script again, picking out the tiny lines I had to memorize.

'Soon, soon,' I thought, 'the Little Maids will have to trip from the back of the stage to the audience, singing their stupid song.'

I could feel the sweat pricking in tiny pin-points through my heavy paint.

When at last we did stand at the head of the three steps, there was a slight mishap; Bell clumsily made them rock in some way, and we in all our heavy black wigs and paint and artificial flowers rocked with them.

There was an unfeeling, quite animal titter from the audience of parents which amazed and frightened me. I could not believe that they were laughing at us after all these months of rehearsal and effort. We, who looked so thoroughly beautiful and romantic. Even Bell's monkey face was transformed, and I had heard someone raving over Michael Astor. I remembered again how furious I had been, because I was vain as only boys can be vain and knew that I was the pick of the bunch.

Now as we stood there, tremulous from the accident and their coarse giggle, I wondered what would happen. I wondered if we should begin our song properly or not. Bell gently mouthed 'Three . . .' a second before Astor and myself, then we broke in unison into the dance song. Even then I thought it was horrible for so-called schoolgirls to be so arch – as depraved as prostitutes in gym tunics with golden pigtails down their backs.

The opera gradually unwound itself until another mishap brought a sweep and gulp of sound from the bestial audience. Nanki-Poo, in throwing the rope when he attempts to hang himself, pulled his wig awry so that his own bright hair showed. I watched this in terror from the wings.

Now the play was spoilt indeed. Two such pieces of unintentional comic relief were too much to bear, especially as the audience had shown such amazing and disgusting appreciation.

After it was all over, the finale, the encores, the curtains, I crept into the big schoolroom, heavy with disappointed pride. A staring-eyed boy called Cochran, looking exactly like the picture of Queen Caroline in my history book, from the brick-dust grease-paint all over his face, tried to attract my attention by pinching my behind. I took no notice, but walked on to the High Desk, which was the Three Little Maids' appointed changing-place. Bell had just left, taking his clothes with him, but Astor was there being helped by his mother out of his wig and kimono. Lady Astor gave me an unmasked, penetrating stare, as if she were trying to read who and why I was, and what I might become. For one moment she

A CHILD MEETS CHURCH AND STATE

seemed to me like a not very well-informed fortune-teller bent on solving a riddle and preserving her reputation. There was a little scorn too and a feeling of scant consideration.

'Come here and turn round and I'll undo you too,' she said briskly.

Her clever fingers explored my kimono, making me acutely self-conscious. She found the pins, drew them out and clicked them together with the neatest gesture; but there was no love or giving about her actions, only efficiency and the sort of impatience which inhabits someone who gets outside herself to lead back in an inexorable circle to herself.

AN AFTERNOON
WITH JEANNE

Of the manuscript of this story, set when Denton Welch was twelve, two pages (indicated by ellipses) have not survived.

... I WAS ALREADY DESIGNING DRESSES FOR MY mother. True, she never had any of the designs carried out – they were always much too daring and 'suggestive'. I had that passion for exaggeration which finally does away with the shoulder-straps and which splits the skirt almost to the very bust. The one thing I would never uncover in my drawings was the bosom. My favourite idea was a sort of Egyptian effect, with the arms and shoulders left completely bare and the rest of the dress gathered into a heavy collar which rose high up on the neck and encircled it.

From this description you will gather what sort of little boy I was and how I am able to remember this particular 'get-up' so well.

As I have already said, I shrank back into the bushes and watched with all my eyes. I wondered how I was going to be able to pluck up enough courage to enter the house for lunch. My eldest brother was a known evil, but how was I going to manage this terrifying vision added to him?

I must explain here that my brother was, at this time, still at Oxford; in fact, he had only just gone up the term before. We only saw him on these occasions when he suddenly appeared in his fuming, roaring car, with its exhaust like a vacuum cleaner and its swollen bonnet held down with thick leather straps.

My father, home from the East, had taken this house for the summer, and a friend, with her little daughter, had offered to keep house for him, as my mother had died the year before. Mrs Sparks, the friend, did not particularly care for me. I first realized this clearly when I overheard her trying to persuade my father to put my name down for boxing lessons for my next term at school. This was a diabolical way of getting her own back, I thought. I knew how vindictive she was, because she went on saying, 'It will do him so much good!'

I have always had a rather furtive taste for 'scenes'. Something in me is ashamed of it, but something else tells me that it would be cowardly and weak minded not to be open, blatant, extravagant and astonishing at the last moment.

In this particular case I pushed open the study door noisily and stood there, saying nothing for a moment. Then I burst out with excitable phrases like, 'Why haven't I been asked about this?', 'What's it do with you?' – this to Mrs Sparks with as much fierceness as I could muster.

The result was, of course, that I was in disgrace for the rest of the day and, in a lesser degree, for the rest of the holidays. How my elders hated me for not wanting to learn to box, for not wanting to be taken down a peg by some other manly little boy.

It is wickedly easy to make a child feel degenerate. Now that my mother was dead, both at home and at school I was made to feel lazy, unnatural, vain. The word 'unwholesome' rather describes the character they tried to pin on to me. I enjoyed eating sweets too much. I brushed my hair too much, enjoyed my clothes too much, tried to be 'highbrow'. (This accusation was brought because I was fond of reading *Oliver Twist*! Foreigners have no idea to what lengths English children go to conceal the fact that they like reading 'classics'.) Because I had not yet learnt the absolute necessity for secretiveness, I was open at all points to attack.

Rapidly, in one horrible year after my mother died, I learnt that 'no one must pretend to be anything but ordinary'. 'No one must show that he is enjoying anything unless it be something that no human being could possibly enjoy; then he must make believe that he quite enjoys being beaten at school or being blown up with bombs.' 'Never say anything that is not a cliché, for it will be considered affected and stupid. If you expect any signs of affection or love you will only get looks of disgust. And if you show even the faintest spark of intelligence or pleasure in your appearance...

♣

... At last I drove myself into the house. They had already sat down. The girl was next to my father. She was talking animatedly and the crystal necklace reminded me of enormous drops of sweat trickling down her neck.

Mrs Sparks was watching the servant anxiously as he passed the dishes. He had only come to us the day before and his previous experience had been in a school at Eastbourne. Consequently the dark clothes were greasy, the fingers black and generally firmly grasping the dish unpleasantly near the food.

I looked at the lank hair flopping over his eyes and saw that he was nervous too. Mrs Lemon, the weird cook, had found him for us. If you went into the kitchen suddenly you would find her smoking. Sometimes she would put the cigarette behind her back, but with me she had given up even this gesture.

Once, when the others were out, she had laid up my place in the servants' hall of the kitchen. So we all sat down together and ate shepherd's pie. I was secretly horrified and rather pleased at the same time.

Now, as I came into the dining-room, I apologized for being late and sat down hurriedly. Mrs Sparks looked at me, but said nothing for some moments; then she criticized my hair, saying jokingly that I would soon have a long bob. I waited in horror for the witticism, 'Why don't you have an Eton crop like Jane?' But it did not come.

I took lots of egg sauce with my fish and tried to comfort myself.

After lunch we all dispersed. My father and Mrs Sparks had their coffee in the study, where the owner of the house had spread a long range of bound *Pink 'Uns* and Dickens. My eldest brother took Jane into the drawing-room, which was stuffed with late-Dresden, very lacy figures.

I went through the garden, into the paddock, where behind some bushes was the cesspool. I lifted off one of the heavy lids and looked at the elephant-hide of filth below me. It moved about and swayed. I contemplated it for some time, even stirred it with a long stick; then I pushed back the lid, and wandered away.

Jeanne, Mrs Sparks's little girl, saw me across the lawn and came towards me. We walked together round the garden, ending up in the black-currant bushes behind the hard tennis-court. I suddenly had the impulse to shock her. I pulled open all the buttons of my shirt and spat, two things that did not come naturally to me at all. As I have already said, breasts, male or female, had to be covered in my eyes. Spitting too was a forbidden act, altogether filthy.

Jeanne did not even seem to notice. She just went on eating the black fruit and smearing the purple juice over her hands until they looked horribly bruised.

'Look at that!' she said, holding up her hands in glee. 'They're covered in aristocrats' blue blood. I've been guillotining hundreds of aristocrats this morning.'

She smacked her lips and licked her chops, rubbing the stained hands together, as if in joyful anticipation of more bloodshed.

At other times, of course, she would be on the other side. She would be the female Scarlet Pimpernel stealing all his thunder, or the beautiful Marquise de Bumfranche rescued at the last moment. (Jeanne always invented French names with an improper or risqué English sound embedded in them.)

I looked at Jeanne. I disliked her because I envied her. She was a girl and was treated with politeness and humanity. However naughty she was at school, nobody would think of beating her.

As I say, I looked at Jeanne and made an awful face; then I hit her hard. For one moment she looked blank and shocked and otherworldly, like a revenant; then her mouth broke into a yell, her eyes twisted and creased up, spurting tears brimmed over the lids, and with a whirl of arms she tore and scratched at my face viciously.

Then we fought and tussled under the black-currant bushes, banging and bruising each other, biting and pinching. I could feel Jeanne's breath on my face and I had hold of her knickers. I yanked at them until the elastic broke. Jeanne screamed and ripped my shirt from shoulder to waist at the back. We felt each other's warm humid flesh; I her thigh and she my back. The terrible damage to our clothes sobered us. We each began to search desperately for suitable excuses to tell our elders. And the soft unprotected feeling of each other's skin suddenly made us kind. We wanted no more violence.

'Sorry, Jeanne,' I said impulsively; 'I'll help you join the elastic, I know how to sew.'

Jeanne held my hand tightly, dramatically, like a desperate aristocrat in the French Revolution.

'I'll mend your shirt, nobody need know. You can say the laundry did it and sent it back mended. I'll put red criss-cross thread to mark it like they do.'

We looked at each other's faces. They showed the scars of battle.

'We fell off our bikes into those brambles on the edge of the footpath just coming out of the wood. It's very narrow and overgrown there, and we were going too fast and crashed. I went in first and you couldn't stop and landed on top,' I said decisively. We told each other this little story for some time to memorize it.

We left the black-currant bushes arm in arm. This was a little self-conscious, but it was comfortable. We wandered towards the kitchen door. The servants were amusing themselves rather doubtfully. The new houseboy had taken off his black coat and was hugging himself to demonstrate the passionate embraces of the lovers on the beach at Eastbourne under the moon. His eyes were thrown up to the ceiling in ecstasy. Mrs Lemon and the two young maids were screaming with unfeigned delight.

None of them stopped as we appeared at the door. We were not worth bothering about. Jeanne and I both assumed an outwardly haughty air, but we were both, I think, seething with curiosity and longing for Arthur to go one step further in his demonstrations.

'We want an egg, some sugar and a little lemon juice,' I said to Mrs Lemon in a lordly way. A lordly way means bored, grand, drawling, half asleep.

We took these ingredients out in a little bowl, beat them with a fork and then ate the frothy cream.

'Delicious!' we said, trying not to taste the rawness of the egg through the lemon and the sugar.

Suddenly I had another idea. I said, 'Let's go back into the house and have a bath in Lux; it's marvellous – piles and piles of frothy lather like white-of-egg mountains.' Quickly I added, at Jeanne's anxious expression, 'You can't see anything but pink faces coming out of white-of-egg mountains.'

Very quietly we went back into the house, through the servants' quarters and up the back stairs. Everything seemed very still. Evidently my eldest brother had taken the girl Jane away somewhere to drink or dance. I thought again of her enormous crystal beads, and hoped that she had left.

We made our way to the bathroom which was least used; it was at the end of a passage. I took the Lux out of a cupboard under the basin and emptied the complete contents into the bath; then I ran the water and watched the froth forming and the steam rising. We stirred with one of the scrubbing brushes with a long handle.

When the time had come that the bath was completely filled with foam, Jeanne and I looked at each other awkwardly. Neither of us cared to undress in front of the other.

'We'll both turn our backs, then keep our eyes shut till we're sitting down in the water,' I said desperately and firmly.

Ceremoniously Jeanne turned her back and I mine. Then, when we were undressed, we felt our way towards the bath and got in. At one point I nearly opened my eyes, because I thought that I had lost my direction; but I knew that if I did I would have terrible feelings of self-condemnation, so I didn't.

When I felt Jeanne's toes against my thigh I opened my eyes. We were both enveloped in a wonderfully mountainous sea of froth. The millions of bubbles were continually bursting into a thousand pieces. And as we stirred and beat with our back and legs they re-formed to such an extent that we thought they would overflow on to the floor.

Our faces were radiant with delight in the new situation.

'Isn't it marvellous!' I said.

Jeanne nodded. We rubbed our bodies all over with our hands and played and wriggled in the foam for a long time. Very gradually the suds began to subside. I looked at Jeanne anxiously.

'We'd better get out, don't you think?' I said.

Again we shut our eyes, after having measured the distance to our towels and clothes. We silently rubbed ourselves and got dressed. Then we turned round and decided with one accord to climb up on to the roof and sit away from everyone.

We clambered out of the landing window and along the ridge outside three small bedrooms. After this was a dangerous place which I hated to cross. It seemed much easier now and we both did it gracefully, with no hesitating. We climbed up to the gable-point above Mrs Sparks's bedroom and nestled down on the other side, in the charming nook made by the fanciful chimney-stack. Here was a secret place from all the world where we could sit in peace for hours. Far away down below, we heard the servants' laughter – my father calling Mrs Sparks's Christian name 'Molly' and then their quiet talking as they walked up and down, up and down, in the rose garden.

Jeanne and I said unmentionable, malicious things about our nearest and dearest. I said that I thought my father smoked opium and she said that her mother had a lover. We knew they were lies, but we loved to bring our reading into our lives. It was the deepest tragedy, we both felt, that we could not link life to books, or books to life. We did our best. By the time we had finished, we had made my eldest brother and Jane into a pair of most unscrupulous villains. He had evidently taken certain frightful but unstated liberties with her person, which she allowed only because she was able, in this close proximity, to rifle his pockets and even steal the cufflinks out of his shirt.

Suddenly we tired of these lurid stories. We talked of tortures for a little, but that too palled. We sat silent; then Jeanne began to sing very softly:

> *Frère Jacques, frère Jacques,*
> *Dormez-vous, dormez-vous?*
> *Sonnez les matines, sonnez les matines,*
> *Din, din, don,*
> *Din, din, don!*

I joined in a bar behind. We tried to keep the parts as clear as possible. We rose to a crescendo on the ringing of the bell. It was nice and clever to be singing French – really cultured and haughty and beautiful and grand. It was noble to be singing French high up on the roof in the afternoon sunlight. We were above and beyond and on top of everyone. And at that moment I loved Jeanne and she loved me because in no other way could we go down and face subjection again.

WHEN I WAS THIRTEEN

This story was first published by Cyril Connolly in Horizon *in April 1944 and reprinted in* Brave and Cruel.

WHEN I WAS THIRTEEN, I WENT TO SWITZERLAND FOR the Christmas holidays in the charge of an elder brother, who was at that time still up at Oxford.

In the hotel we found another undergraduate whom my brother knew. His name was Archer. They were not at the same college, but they had met and evidently had not agreed with each other. At first my brother would say nothing about Archer; then one day, in answer to a question of mine, he said, 'He's not very much liked; although he's a very good swimmer.' As he spoke, my brother held his lips in a very firm, almost pursed line which was most damaging to Archer.

After this I began to look at Archer with more interest. He had broad shoulders, but was not tall. He had a look of strength and solidity which I admired and envied. He had rather a nice pug face with insignificant nose and broad cheeks. Sometimes, when he was animated, a tassel of fair, almost colourless hair would fall across his forehead, half covering one eye. He had a thick beautiful neck, rather meaty barbarian hands, and a skin as smooth and evenly coloured as a pink fondant.

His whole body appeared to be suffused with this gentle pink colour. He never wore proper skiing clothes of water-proof material like the rest of us. Usually he came out in nothing but a pair of grey flannels and a white cotton shirt with all the buttons left undone. When the sun grew very hot, he would even discard this thin shirt, and ski up and down the slopes behind the hotel in nothing but his trousers. I had often seen him fall down in this half-naked state and get buried in snow. The next moment he would jerk himself to his feet again, laughing and swearing.

After my brother's curt nod to him on our first evening at the hotel, we had hardly exchanged any remarks. We sometimes passed on the way to the basement to get our skis in the morning, and often we found ourselves sitting near one another on the glassed-in terrace; but some Oxford snobbery I knew nothing of, or some more profound reason, always made my brother throw off waves of hostility. Archer never showed any signs of wishing to approach. He was content to look at me sometimes with a mild inoffensive curiosity, but he seemed to ignore my brother completely. This pleased me more than I would have admitted at that time. I was so used to being passed over myself by all my brother's friends that it was pleasant when someone who knew him seemed to take a sort of interest, however slight and amused, in me.

My brother was often away from the hotel for days and nights together, going for expeditions with guides and other friends. He would never take me because he said I was too young and had not enough stamina. He said that I would fall down a crevasse or get my nose frost-bitten, or hang up the party by lagging behind.

In consequence I was often alone at the hotel; but I did not mind this; I enjoyed it. I was slightly afraid of my brother and found life very much easier and less exacting when he was not there. I think other people in the hotel thought that I looked lonely. Strangers would often come up and talk to me and smile, and once a nice absurd Belgian woman, dressed from head to foot in a babyish suit of fluffy orange knitted wool, held out a bright five-franc piece to me and told me to go and buy chocolate caramels with it. I think she must have taken me for a much younger child.

On one of these afternoons when I had come in from the Nursery Slopes and was sitting alone over my tea on the sun-terrace, I noticed that Archer was sitting in the corner huddled over a book, munching greedily and absent-mindedly.

I too was reading a book, while I ate delicious rum-babas and little tarts filled with worm-castles of chestnut purée topped with caps of whipped cream. I have called the meal tea, but what I was drinking was not tea but chocolate. When I poured out, I held the pot high in the air, so that my cup, when filled, should be covered in a rich froth of bubbles.

The book I was reading was Tolstoy's *Resurrection*. Although I did not quite understand some parts of it, it gave me intense pleasure to read it while I ate the rich cakes and drank the frothy chocolate. I thought it a noble and terrible story, but I was worried and mystified by the words 'illegitimate child' which had occurred several times lately. What sort of child could this be? Clearly a child that brought trouble and difficulty. Could it have some terrible disease, or was it a special sort of imbecile? I looked up from my book, still wondering about this phrase 'illegitimate child', and saw that Archer had turned in his creaking wicker chair and was gazing blankly in my direction. The orchestra was playing 'The Birth of the Blues' in a rather remarkable Swiss arrangement, and it was clear that Archer had been distracted from his book by the music, only to be lulled into a daydream, as he gazed into space.

Suddenly his eyes lost their blank look and focused on my face. 'Your brother off up to the Jungfrau Joch again, or somewhere?' he called out.

I nodded my head, saying nothing, becoming slightly confused.

Archer grinned. He seemed to find me amusing.

'What are you reading?' he asked.

'This,' I said, taking my book over to him. I did not want to call out either the word 'Resurrection' or 'Tolstoy'. But Archer did not make fun of me for reading a 'classic', as most of my brother's friends would have done. He only said, 'I should think it's rather good. Mine's frightful; it's called *The Story of My Life*, by Queen Marie of Rumania.' He held the book up and I saw an extraordinary photograph of a lady who looked like a snake-charmer in full regalia. The head-dress seemed to be made of white satin, embroidered with beads, stretched over cardboard. There were tassels and trailing things hanging down everywhere.

I laughed at the amusing picture and Archer went on, 'I always read books like this when I can get them. Last week I had Lady Oxford's autobiography, and before that I found a perfectly wonderful book called *Flaming Sex*. It was by a French woman who married an English knight and then went back to France to shoot a French doctor. She didn't kill him, of course, but she was sent to prison, where she had a very interesting time with the nuns who looked after her in the hospital. I also lately found an old book by a Crown Princess of Saxony who ended up picnicking on a haystack with a simple Italian gentleman in a straw-hat. I love these "real life" stories, don't you?'

I again nodded my head, not altogether daring to venture on a spoken answer. I wondered whether to go back to my own table or whether to pluck up courage and ask Archer what an 'illegitimate child' was. He solved the problem by saying 'Sit down' rather abruptly.

I subsided next to him with 'Tolstoy' on my knee. I waited for a moment and then plunged.

'What exactly does "illegitimate child" mean?' I asked rather breathlessly.

'Outside the law – when two people have a child although they're not married.'

'Oh.' I went bright pink. I thought Archer must be wrong. I still believed that it was quite impossible to have a child unless one was married. The very fact of being married produced the child. I had a vague idea that some particularly reckless people attempted, without being married, to have children in places called 'nightclubs', but they were always unsuccessful, and this made them drink, and plunge into the most hectic gaiety.

I did not tell Archer that I thought he had made a mistake, for I did not want to hurt his feelings. I went on sitting at his table and, although he turned his eyes back to his book and went on reading, I knew that he was friendly.

After some time he looked up again and said, 'Would you like to come out with me tomorrow? We could take our lunch, go up the mountain and then ski down in the afternoon.'

I was delighted at the suggestion, but also a little alarmed at my own shortcomings. I thought it my duty to explain that I was not a very good skier, only a moderate one, and that I could only do stem turns. I hated the thought of being a drag on Archer.

'I expect you're much better than I am. I'm always falling down or crashing into something,' he answered.

It was all arranged. We were to meet early, soon after six, as Archer wanted to go to the highest station on the mountain railway and then climb on skis to a nearby peak which had a small rest-house of logs.

I went to bed very excited, thankful that my brother was away on a long expedition. I lay under my enormous featherbed eiderdown, felt the freezing mountain air on my face, and saw the stars sparkling through the open window.

I got up very early in the morning and put on my most sober ski socks and woollen shirt, for I felt that Archer disliked any suspicion of bright colours or dressing-up. I made my appearance as workmanlike as possible, and then went down to breakfast.

I ate several crackly rolls, which I spread thickly with dewy slivers of butter and gobbets of rich blackcherry jam; then I drank my last cup of coffee and went to wax my skis. As I passed through the hall I picked up my picnic lunch in its neat grease-proof paper packet.

The nails in my boots slid and then caught on the snow, trodden hard down to the basement door. I found my skis in their rack, took them down and then heated the iron and the wax. I loved spreading the hot black wax smoothly on the white wood. Soon they were both done beautifully.

I will go like a bird, I thought.

I looked up and saw Archer standing in the doorway.

'I hope you haven't put too much on, else you'll be sitting on your arse all day,' he said gaily.

How fresh and pink he looked! I was excited.

He started to wax his own skis. When they were finished, we went outside and strapped them on. Archer carried a rucksack and he told me to put my lunch and my spare sweater into it.

We started off down the gentle slopes to the station. The sun was shining prickingly. The lovely snow had rainbow colours in it. I was so happy I swung my sticks with their steel points and basket ends. I even tried to show off, and jumped a little terrace which I knew well. Nevertheless it nearly brought me down. I just regained my balance in time. I would have hated at that moment to have fallen down in front of Archer.

When we got to the station we found a compartment to ourselves. It was still early. Gently we were pulled up the mountain, past the water station stop and the other three halts.

We got out at the very top where the railway ended. A huge unused snow-plough stood by the side of the track, with its vicious shark's nose pointed at me. We ran to the van to get out our skis. Archer found mine as well as his own and slung both pairs across his shoulders. He looked like a very tough Jesus carrying two crosses, I thought.

We stood by the old snow-plough and clipped on our skis; then we began to climb laboriously up the ridge to the wooden rest-house. We hardly talked at all, for we needed all our breath, and also I was still shy of Archer. Sometimes he helped me, telling me where to place my skis, and, if I slipped backwards, hauling on the rope which he had half playfully tied round my waist.

In spite of growing tired, I enjoyed the grim plodding. It gave me a sense of work and purpose. When Archer looked round to smile at me, his pink face was slippery with sweat. His white shirt above the small rucksack was plastered to his shoulder-blades. On my own face I could feel the drops of sweat just being held back by my eyebrows. I would wipe my hand across my upper-lip and break all the tiny beads that had formed there.

Every now and then Archer would stop. We would put our skis sideways on the track and rest, leaning forward on our sticks. The sun struck down on our necks with a steady seeping heat and the light striking up from the snow was as bright as the fiery dazzle of a mirror. From the ridge we could see down into two valleys; and standing all round us were the other peaks, black rock and white snow, tangling and mixing until the mountains looked like vast teeth which had begun to decay.

I was so tired when we reached the long gentle incline to the rest-house that I was afraid of falling down. The rope was still round my waist, and so the slightest lagging would have been perceptible to Archer. I think he must have slackened his pace for my benefit, for I somehow managed to reach the iron seats in front of the hut. I sank down, still with my skis on. I half shut my eyes. From walking so long with my feet turned out, my ankles felt almost broken.

The next thing I knew was that Archer had disappeared into the rest-house. He came out carrying a steaming cup.

'You must drink this,' he said, holding out black coffee, which I hated. He unwrapped four lumps of sugar and dropped them in the cup.

'I don't like it black,' I said.

'Never mind,' he answered sharply, 'drink it.'

Rather surprised, I began to drink the syrupy coffee. 'The sugar and the strong coffee will be good for you,' said Archer. He went back into the rest-house and brought out a glass of what looked like hot water with a piece of lemon floating in it. The mountain of sugar at the bottom was melting into thin Arabian Nights wreaths and spirals, smoke-rings of syrup.

'What else has it got in it?' I asked, with an attempt at worldliness.

'Rum!' said Archer.

We sat there on the terrace and unwrapped our picnic lunches. We both had two rolls, one with tongue in it, and one with ham, a hard-boiled egg, sweet biscuits, and a bar of delicious bitter chocolate; tangerine oranges were our dessert.

We began to take huge bites out of our rolls. We could not talk for some time. The food brought out a thousand times more clearly the beauty of the mountain peaks and sun. My tiredness made me thrillingly conscious of delight and satisfaction. I wanted to sit there with Archer for a long time.

At the end of the meal Archer gave me a piece of his own bar of chocolate, and then began to skin pigs of tangerine very skilfully and hand them to me on his outstretched palm, as one offers a lump of sugar to a horse. I thought for one moment of bending down my head and licking the pigs up in imitation of a horse; then I saw how mad it would look.

We threw the brilliant tangerine peel into the snow, which immediately seemed to dim and darken its colour.

Archer felt in his hip-pocket and brought out black, cheap Swiss cigarettes, wrapped in leaf. They were out of a slot machine. He put one between my lips and lighted it. I felt extremely conscious of the thing jutting out from my lips. I wondered if I would betray my ignorance by not breathing the smoke in and out correctly. I turned my head a little away from Archer and experimented. It seemed easy if one did not breathe too deeply. It was wonderful to be really smoking with Archer. He treated me just like a man.

'Come on, let's get cracking,' he said, 'or, if anything happens, we'll be out all night.'

I scrambled to my feet at once and snapped the clips of the skis round my boot heels. Archer was in high spirits from the rum. He ran on his skis along the flat ridge in front of the rest-house and then fell down.

'Serves me right,' he said. He shook the snow off and we started properly. In five minutes we had swooped down the ridge we had climbed so painfully all morning. The snow was perfect; new and dry with no crust. We followed a new way which Archer had discovered. The ground was uneven with dips and curves. Often we were out of sight of each other. When we came to the icy path through a wood, my courage failed me.

'Stem like hell and don't get out of control,' Archer yelled back at me. I pointed my skis together, praying that they would not cross. I leant on my sticks, digging their metal points into the compressed snow. Twice I fell, though not badly.

'Well done, well done!' shouted Archer, as I shot past him and out of the wood into a thick snowdrift. He hauled me out of the snow and stood me on my feet, beating me all over to get off the snow, then we began the descent of a field called the 'Bumps'. Little hillocks, if manœuvred successfully, gave one that thrilling sinking and rising feeling experienced on a scenic railway at a fun fair.

Archer went before me, dipping and rising, shouting and yelling in his exuberance. I followed more sedately. We both fell several times, but in that not unpleasant, bouncing way which brings you to your feet again almost at once.

Archer was roaring now and trying to yodel in an absurd, rich contralto.

I had never enjoyed myself quite so much before. I thought him the most wonderful companion, not a bit intimidating, in spite of being rather a hero.

When at last we swooped down to the village street, it was nearly evening. Early orange lights were shining in the shop windows. We planked our skis down on the hard, iced road, trying not to slip.

I looked in at the pâtisserie, confiserie window, where all the electric bulbs had fluffy pink shades like powder-puffs. Archer saw my look.

'Let's go in,' he said. He ordered me hot chocolate with whipped cream, and croissant rolls. Afterwards we both went up to the little counter and chose cakes. I had one shaped like a little log. It was made of soft chocolate, and had green moss trimmings made in pistachio nut. When Archer went to pay the bill he bought me some chocolate caramels, in a little bird's-eye maple box, and a bar labelled *'Chocolat Polychrome'*. Each finger was a different-coloured cream: mauve, pink, green, yellow, orange, brown, white, even blue.

We went out into the village street and began to climb up the path to the hotel. About half-way up Archer stopped outside a little wooden chalet and said, 'This is where I hang out.'

'But you're staying at the hotel,' I said incredulously.

'Oh yes, I have all my meals there, but I sleep here. It's a sort of little annexe when there aren't any rooms left in the hotel. It's only got two rooms; I've paid just a bit more and got it all to myself. Someone comes every morning and makes the bed and stokes the boiler and the stove. Come in and see it.'

I followed Archer up the outside wooden staircase and stood with him on the little landing outside the two rooms. The place seemed wonderfully warm and dry. The walls were unpainted wood; there were double windows. There was a gentle creaking in all the joints of the wood when one moved. Archer pushed open one of the doors and ushered me in. I saw in one corner a huge white porcelain stove, the sort I had only before seen in pictures. Some of Archer's skiing gloves and socks were drying round it on a ledge. Against another wall were two beds, like wooden troughs built into the wall. The balloon-like quilts bulged up above the wood.

'I hardly use the other room,' said Archer. 'I just throw my muck into it and leave my trunks there.' He opened the connecting door and I saw a smaller room with dirty clothes strewn on the floor; white shirts, hard evening collars, some very short pants, and many pairs of thick grey socks. The room smelt mildly of Archer's old sweat. I didn't mind at all.

Archer shut the door and said, 'I'm going to run the bath.'

'Have you a bathroom too – all your own?' I exclaimed enviously. 'Every time anyone has a bath at the hotel, he has to pay two francs fifty to the fräulein before she unlocks the door. I've only had two proper baths since I've been here. I don't think it matters though. It seems almost impossible to get really dirty in Switzerland, and you can always wash all over in your bedroom basin.'

'Why don't you have a bath here after me? The water's lovely and hot, although there's not much of it. If you went back first and got your evening clothes, you could change straight into them.'

I looked at Archer a little uncertainly. I longed to soak in hot water after my wonderful but gruelling day.

'Could I really bath here?' I asked.

'If you don't mind using my water. I'll promise not to pee in it. I'm not really filthy, you know.'

Archer laughed and chuckled, because he saw me turning red at his coarseness. He lit another of his peasant cigarettes and began to unlace his boots. He got me to pull them off. I knelt down, bowed my head and pulled. When the ski boot suddenly flew off, my nose dipped forward and I smelt Archer's foot in its woolly, hairy, humid casing of sock.

'Would you just rub my foot and leg?' Archer said urgently, a look of pain suddenly shooting across his face. 'I've got cramp. It often comes on at the end of the day.'

He shot his leg out rigidly and told me where to rub and massage. I felt each of his curled toes separately and the hard tendons in his leg. His calf was like a firm sponge ball. His thigh, swelling out, amazed me. I likened it in my mind to the trumpet of some musical instrument. I went on rubbing methodically. I was able to feel his pain melting away.

When the tense look had quite left his face, he said, 'Thanks,' and stood up. He unbuttoned his trousers, let them fall to the ground, and pulled his shirt up. Speaking to me with his head imprisoned in it, he said, 'You go and get your clothes and I'll begin bathing.'

I left him and hurried up to the hotel, carrying my skis on my shoulder. I ran up to my room and pulled my evening clothes out of the wardrobe. The dinner jacket and trousers had belonged to my brother six years before, when he was my age. I was secretly ashamed of this fact, and had taken my brother's name from the inside of the breast-pocket and had written my own in elaborate lettering.

I took my comb, face flannel and soap, and, getting out my toboggan, slid back to Archer's chalet in a few minutes. I let myself in and heard Archer splashing. The little hall was full of steam and I saw Archer's shoulders and arms like a pink smudge through the open bathroom door.

'Come and scrub my back,' he yelled; 'it gives me a lovely feeling.' He thrust a large stiff nailbrush into my hands and told me to scrub as hard as I could.

I ran it up and down his back until I'd made harsh red tramlines. Delicious tremors seemed to be passing through Archer.

'Ah! Go on!' said Archer in a dream, like a purring cat. 'When I'm rich I'll have a special back-scratcher slave.' I went on industriously scrubbing his back till I was afraid that I would rub the skin off. I liked to give him pleasure.

At last he stood up all dripping and said, 'Now it's your turn.'

I undressed and got into Archer's opaque, soapy water. I lay back and wallowed. Archer poured some very smelly salts on to my stomach. One crystal stuck in my navel and tickled and grated against me.

'This whiff ought to cover up all remaining traces of me!' Archer laughed.

'What's the smell supposed to be?' I asked, brushing the crystals off my stomach into the water, and playing with the one that lodged so snugly in my navel.

'Russian pine,' said Archer, shutting his eyes ecstatically and making inbreathing dreamy noises. He rubbed himself roughly with the towel and made his hair stand up on end.

I wanted to soak in the bath for hours, but it was already getting late, and so I had to hurry.

Archer saw what difficulty I had in tying my tie. He came up to me and said, 'Let me do it.' I turned round relieved but slightly ashamed of being incompetent.

I kept very still, and he tied it tightly and rapidly with his ham-like hands. He gave the bows a little expert jerk and pat. His eyes had a very concentrated, almost crossed look and I felt him breathing down on my face. All down the front our bodies touched featherily; little points of warmth came together. The hard-boiled shirts were like slightly warmed dinner-plates.

When I had brushed my hair, we left the chalet and began to walk up the path to the hotel. The beaten snow was so slippery, now that we were shod only in patent-leather slippers, that we kept sliding backwards. I threw out my arms, laughing, and shouting to Archer to rescue me; then, when he grabbed me and started to haul me to him, he too would begin to slip. It was a still, Prussian-blue night with rather weak stars. Our laughter seemed to ring across the valley, to hit the mountains and then to travel on and on and on.

We reached the hotel a little the worse for wear. The soles of my patent-leather shoes had become soaked, and there was snow on my trousers. Through bending forward, the studs in Archer's shirt had burst undone, and the slab of hair hung over one of his eyes. We went into the cloakroom to readjust ourselves before entering the dining-room.

'Come and sit at my table,' Archer said; then he added, 'No, we'll sit at yours; there are two places there already.'

We sat down and began to eat Roman gnocchi. (The proprietor of the hotel was Italian–Swiss.) I did not like mine very much and was glad when I could go on to *œufs au beurre noir*. Now that my brother was away I could pick and choose in this way, leaving out the meat course, if I chose to, without causing any comment.

Archer drank Pilsner and suggested that I should too. Not wanting to disagree with him, I nodded my head, although I hated the pale, yellow, bitter water.

After the meal Archer ordered me *crème de menthe* with my coffee; I had seen a nearby lady drinking this pretty liquid and asked him about it. To be ordered a liqueur in all seriousness was a thrilling moment for me. I sipped the fumy peppermint, which left such an artificial heat in my throat and chest, and thought that apart from my mother, who was dead, I had never liked anyone so much as I liked Archer. He didn't try to interfere with me at all. He just took me as I was and yet seemed to like me.

Archer was now smoking a proper cigar, not the leaf-rolled cigarettes we had had at lunch-time. He offered me one too, but I had the sense to realize that he did not mean me to take one and smoke it there before the eyes of all the hotel. I knew also that it would have made me sick, for my father had given me a cigar when I was eleven, in an attempt to put me off smoking for ever.

I always associated cigars with middle-aged men, and I watched Archer interestedly, thinking how funny the stiff fat thing looked sticking out of his young mouth.

We were sitting on the uncurtained sun-terrace, looking out on to the snow in the night; the moon was just beginning to rise. It made the snow glitter suddenly, like fish scales. Behind us people were dancing in the salon and adjoining rooms. The music came to us in angry snatches, some notes distorted, others quite obliterated. Archer did not seem to want to dance. He seemed content to sit with me in silence.

Near me on a what-not stand stood a high-heeled slipper made of china. I took it down and slipped my hand into it. How hideously ugly the china pom-poms were down the front! The painted centipede climbing up the red heel wore a knowing, human expression. I moved my fingers in the china shoe, pretending they were toes.

'I love monstrosities too,' said Archer, as I put the shoe back beside the fern in its crinkly paper-covered pot.

Later we wandered to the buffet bar and stood there drinking many glasses of the *limonade* which was made with white wine. I took the tinkly pieces of ice into my mouth and sucked them, trying to cool myself a little. Blood seemed to rise in my face; my head buzzed.

Suddenly I felt full of *limonade* and lager. I left Archer to go to the cloakroom, but he followed and stood beside me in the next china niche, while the water flushed and gushed importantly in the polished copper tubes, and an interesting, curious smell came from the wire basket which held some strange disinfectant crystals. Archer stood so quietly and guardingly beside me there that I had to say, 'Do I look queer?'

'No, you don't look queer; you look nice,' he said simply.

A rush of surprise and pleasure made me hotter still. We clanked over the tiles and left the cloakroom.

In the hall, I remembered that I had left all my skiing clothes at the chalet.

'I shall need them in the morning,' I said to Archer.

'Let's go down there now, then I can make cocoa on my spirit-lamp, and you can bring the clothes back with you.'

We set out in the moonlight; Archer soon took my arm, for he saw that I was drunk, and the path was more slippery than ever. Archer sang 'Silent Night' in German, and I began to cry. I could not stop myself. It was such a delight to cry in the moonlight with Archer singing my favourite song; and my brother far away up the mountain.

Suddenly we both sat down on our behinds with a thump. There was a jarring pain at the bottom of my spine, but I began to laugh wildly; so did Archer. We lay there laughing, the snow melting under us and soaking through the seats of our trousers and the shoulders of our jackets.

Archer pulled me to my feet and dusted me down with hard slaps. My teeth grated together each time he slapped me. He saw that I was becoming more and more drunk in the freezing air. He propelled me along to the chalet, more or less frog-marching me in an expert fashion. I was quite content to leave myself in his hands.

When he got me upstairs, he put me into one of the bunks and told me to rest. The feathers ballooned out round me. I sank down deliciously. I felt as if I were floating down some magic staircase for ever.

Archer got his little meta-stove out and made coffee – not cocoa as he had said. He brought me over a strong cup and held it to my lips. I drank it unthinkingly and not tasting it, doing it only because he told me to.

When he took the cup away, my head fell back on the pillow, and I felt myself sinking and floating away again. I was on skis this time, but they were liquid skis, made of melted glass, and the snow was glass too, but a sort of glass that was springy, like gelatine, and flowing like water.

I felt a change in the light, and knew that Archer was bending over me. Very quietly he took off my shoes, undid my tie, loosened the collar and unbuttoned my braces in front. I remember thinking, before I finally fell asleep, how clever he was to know about undoing the braces; they had begun to feel so tight pulling down on my shoulders and dragging the trousers up between my legs. Archer covered me with several blankets and another quilt.

When I woke in the morning, Archer was already up. He had made me some tea and had put it on the stove to keep warm. He brought it over to me and I sat up. I felt ill, rather sick. I remembered what a glorious day yesterday had been, and thought how extraordinary it was that I had not slept in my own bed at the hotel, but in Archer's room, in my clothes.

I looked at him shamefacedly. 'What happened last night? I felt peculiar,' I said.

'The lager and the lemonade, and the *crème de menthe* made you a bit tight, I'm afraid,' Archer said, laughing. 'Do you feel better now? We'll go up to the hotel and have breakfast soon.'

I got up and washed and changed into my skiing clothes. I still felt rather sick. I made my evening clothes into a neat bundle and tied them on to my toboggan. I had the sweets Archer had given me in my pocket.

We went up to the hotel, dragging the toboggan behind us.

And there on the doorstep we met my brother with one of the guides. They had had to return early, because someone in the party had broken a ski.

He was in a temper. He looked at us and then said to me, 'What have you been doing?'

I was at a loss to know what to answer. The very sight of him had so troubled me that this added difficulty of explaining my actions was too much for me.

I looked at him miserably and mouthed something about going in to have breakfast.

My brother turned to Archer fiercely, but said nothing.

Archer explained: 'Your brother's just been down to my place. We went skiing together yesterday and he left some clothes at the chalet.'

'It's very early,' was all my brother said; then he swept me on in into the hotel before him, without another word to the guide or to Archer.

He went with me up to my room and saw that the bed had not been slept in.

I said clumsily, 'The maid must have been in and done my room early.' I could not bear to explain to him about my wonderful day, or why I had slept at the chalet.

My brother was so furious that he took no more notice of my weak explanations and lies.

When I suddenly said in desperation, 'I feel sick,' he seized me, took me to the basin, forced his fingers down my throat and struck me on the back till a yellow cascade of vomit gushed out of my mouth. My eyes were filled with stinging water; I was trembling. I ran the water in the basin madly, to wash away this sign of shame.

Gradually I grew a little more composed. I felt better, after being sick, and my brother had stopped swearing at me. I filled the basin with freezing water and dipped my face into it. The icy feel seemed to bite round my eye-sockets and make the flesh round my nose firm again. I waited, holding my breath for as long as possible.

Suddenly my head was pushed down and held. I felt my brother's hard fingers digging into my neck. He was hitting me now with a slipper, beating my buttocks and my back with slashing strokes, hitting a different place each time, as he had been taught when a prefect at school, so that the flesh should not be numbed from a previous blow.

I felt that I was going to choke. I could not breathe under the water, and realized that I would die. I was seized with such a panic that I wrenched myself free and darted round the room, with him after me. Water dripped on the bed, the carpet, the chest of drawers. Splashes of it spat against the mirror in the wardrobe door. My brother aimed vicious blows at me until he had driven me into a corner. There he beat against my uplifted arms, yelling in a hoarse, mad, religious voice, 'Bastard, Devil, Harlot, Sod!'

As I cowered under his blows, I remember thinking that my brother had suddenly become a lunatic and was talking gibberish in his madness, for, of the words he was using, I had not heard any before, except 'Devil'.

JOHN TREVOR

This story was inspired by visits Denton Welch made while at school at Repton to nearby Chatsworth House, home of the Dukes of Devonshire. In 'John Trevor' he is clearly recognizable, and the character of 'Jim' may be based on his friend Eric Oliver, with whom he lived at the end of his life and who was renowned for his drinking. The manuscript of this story survives incomplete by two consecutive pages (indicated by ellipses).

JOHN TREVOR LOOKED OUT OF ONE OF THE GREAT plate-glass windows of Shipley. The gardens were grey in the early afternoon light. He was wandering alone through the staterooms, not knowing what to do with himself.

He was the laundryboy turned painter, befriended by the Duke, who gave him his lodging and one hundred a year.

Most of the time he was alone in the great house, except for the servants and the librarian. The librarian had begun it all; he had brought him to the notice of the Duke – and John did not know whether to bless him or to curse him.

Painting had seemed so much more worthwhile before it had been made an obligation. He looked at the picture he was carrying. It was of the Palladian bridge in the grounds. He was doing it with elaborate underpaintings of blue and brown, and how he hated it! The calmness, the beauty, the precision of his drawing, now meant nothing and they had meant everything when he worked at the laundry.

Occasionally, when the Duke was down to stay, he would ask to see some work and would say nice things about it, and sometimes there would be a picture in a London exhibition; but, apart from the librarian, no one saw his work or cared about it.

Of course, he had always known indifference, but it had not

been so bad before he was receiving the Duke's patronage. Now he felt on the edge of great things which would never happen.

As he stared unhappily out of the window, he saw a small party of boys in straw-hats, obviously led by a master, crossing the wide courtyard, and he remembered what the librarian had said at breakfast: that some boys from the nearby public school were coming to see the furniture and pictures that afternoon. The art master was a friend of the librarian and so it had been arranged.

As John looked down on them dreamily, he wondered what they would be like. If he stayed in the staterooms he would soon find out; so, going to the little closet at the top of the stairs where he kept his things, he got out the picture he had begun of the oval drawing-room and, taking it in there, found his old position and began to work . . .

✢

. . . Then he began talking about the furniture and unlocking the cabinets. When the party moved on, John followed. He loved the house when he was not utterly alone in it, and did not tire of looking at its treasures. They passed through the staterooms, which opened one into the other with no passageway, and came into the long library with all its early-Victorian fittings. The librarian mounted the little, cast-iron, spiral staircase which led to the gallery and brought down some of the illuminated manuscripts.

Everyone remarked on the wonder of the gold, and the librarian shortly answered, 'There's nothing to go wrong with the gold, it's the colours that are the wonder.'

He moved towards an easel on which was a picture, covered with a piece of velvet. He took it off, saying imperturbably, 'And this is our Memling.' The boys crowded round looking at the sparkling little triptych. 'If there were a fire, the picture would be put into a specially constructed box which could then be thrown out of the window.' The boys gaped intelligently, and John looked at the lovely bronze head that was near. It was covered with a green patina and he could see the little holes where real hair had been inserted. The carved eyelids hooded the places where no eyes were.

They were shown the little private dining-room, which was

reached through one of the doors covered with dummy books. The boys were more fascinated by the delicate wax pictures than they had been by the Memling and John noticed one intently looking at the empty medicine bottle on the sideboard, reading the label: 'To be taken three times a day. His Grace the Duke of B—'

In one of the long galleries the librarian turned to him and said, 'Now Trevor, tell us the difference between this Van Dyck and this Keller. Why is one infinitely better than the other?'

Now I must perform, John thought bitterly. Now I must tell the well-brought-up boys what I know about painting. He turned to them and said, 'For one thing, the stockings in the Van Dyck have much more luminosity.' He lingered over the word, drawing it out with an open mouth. He thought what he said had sounded silly and he wanted to make it sound sillier still. The librarian smiled, not noticing or pretending not to notice, and led them all down the grand staircase. He was talking fussily to the art master and John caught snatches: 'Of course the Duchess wants to put those Chinese Chippendale chairs you've just seen in a better place, but it's so difficult to know where they should go.'

'You're Chinese Chippendale yourself,' John wanted to scream. 'You're old and quirky and utterly debased.'

They had left the house now and were walking in the grounds. They were mounting the steep white steps on each side of the cascade. The water dripped from carved shell to carved shell and emptied at last into the blue basin below.

In the little pavilion above, John knew they would be shown the weeping willow made out of lead, under which the unwary visitor sat, to be soaked by hidden jets of water in its branches and twigs. This eighteenth-century practical joke summed up, for John, all the luxury which he loved and hated so much. It was so wanton, so useless, and yet somehow graceful.

The boys were all laughing at the joke and wanted to see it work. The librarian told everyone to stand back, then he went to the wall and turned a little tap. Immediately the air was filled with fine rain. It poured from the delicate twigs and the floor was soon awash. The boys stood back against the wall, giggling in a manly way.

John, standing in the doorway, saw a young gardener pass. He looked in and, smirking slightly, touched his cap and passed on. John saw his white shirt with the brown marks of the soil on it, twisting between the trees. He followed slowly and caught up with him at the little potting-shed. He sat down on an old crate and watched the gardener work, then he offered him a cigarette and began to smoke himself. They did not talk, until the gardener suddenly said, 'You fed up?' John nodded dully. 'Well, why don't you come down to the pub tonight? I'm goin'. I'll give you a lift on my motor-bike.'

John was surprised and said quickly, 'Thank you very much, but –'

'Why,' the other broke in, 'you haven't got anything else to do, have you?'

'No.'

'Well then, you meet me outside the gates at 'alf past eight and we'll shift.'

John's mood suddenly changed. 'All right, I'll be there.' He waved his hand and disappeared through the trees. He was just in time to see the boys getting into the van they had come in. It was painted khaki and generally used when the school had an OTC field day.

There was much laughing and talking, and he saw that each boy now held a paper bag. One had taken out a heavy-looking doughnut and he imagined them all stopping outside the gates and eating their picnic tea.

The art master's red little lips were moving as he said goodbye, looking down on to the librarian's sagging face. Then with waves and polite shouts they were off.

John turned into the house, past the footman's draught-chair with the great side wings and up the wide low-stepping stairs.

He did not go to the librarian's room, where he knew that tea would be laid. He climbed till he came to his own small room and, when he shut the door, fell down on the bed. His face was deep in the pillow and he breathed out of one nostril only. The soft firmness of the bed, pressing against his chest and stomach, comforted him. He lay still and soon he was asleep.

One of the maids, Kathleen, woke him. She was bending over slightly, pulling his shoulder, and saying, 'Dinner ready, Mr

Trevor. Mr Rose sent me to tell you.' She was looking at him anxiously, as if he were ill, and John saw the tenderness in her face, which annoyed him. He sat up, feeling sick, and said, 'All right, I'll be down.' Then he waited, scowling, until she should leave.

She turned slowly at the door and asked, 'You're quite all right, sir?'

'Yes, quite.'

He was overcome with impatience. He quickly pulled off his clothes and put on his blue suit, smearing his face with the wet flannel and combing his hair.

The librarian did not put on evening dress for dinner when alone, but nevertheless he always changed into a dark suit and liked Trevor to do likewise. He was trying to educate him.

Dinner was depressing; there was empty talk about the boys' visit and tiring questions were asked about the progress of his work. Kathleen waited alone. They always dined at the little fireside table in the librarian's sitting-room. He liked it so. There was claret to drink, but John only had one glass. He had never really got to like the taste of alcohol.

While they had their coffee, sitting in the armchairs, he looked up at the little ormolu clock on the mantelpiece and thought, 'I shall be late. Shall I go or not?'

Then the strange new feeling came over him again and he found himself rising from his chair clumsily and saying, 'I think I'll go up to my room and finish off that letter I began.' Weak and silly to explain he was going. He could see the swift working of the librarian's mind and the little upward jerk of his eyebrows, but there was no comment; he only lifted his head and said, 'Well, if I don't see you again, goodnight.'

John pushed swiftly down the dim passage and let himself out finally into the night air. The stones of the gravel pressed up into the soft crêpe rubber of his soles and he sensed them with the balls of his feet. They crunched damply beneath him. He could see at the end of the long avenue the light of the young gardener's motor-bicycle.

He became as hearty as he could when they met and soon he was holding on tightly as they drove through the low layers of mist which lay on the fields surrounding the sheep like cotton wool round Easter eggs.

They made their way from the dark inn-yard into the bar. There were not many people there; it was not very gay. The painted china levers stood on the bar like fixed ninepins, and John stared at their intricate patterned marbling. 'These are very pretty,' he said to the elderly woman who was serving.

'Yes, they are quite unique, like. A lot of people admire those.'

The young gardener said, 'Come on, what are you going to have?'

John thought quickly and said, 'A bitter.' He felt this was right.

What a curious taste beer had, he thought – so unappealing; and how curiously slow were its workings. Anyone could tell that wine or spirits would intoxicate, but beer – it was like some dark medicinal tea. He drank his down quickly and ordered two more.

There was talking beyond the chenille curtain at one end of the bar and soon two adolescent girls emerged. The elderly woman told them that they should be in bed.

'Oh, Mrs Bradman, let them stay up a bit longer,' the gardener broke in.

'Yes, Auntie, do let us,' added the smaller one. She must have been about fifteen years old.

They were laughing and talking with the gardener, whom they called Jim. John was introduced, and suddenly said to them, 'What are you going to have?'

'They're not allowed to have anything.' Mrs Bradman was definite.

'It's Gwenda's birthday tomorrow, Auntie. Can't we have an egg-nog?' the little one pleaded again.

Mrs Bradman looked at John questioningly and, seeing his nod, she stretched up heavily and took down the pale, opaque bottle from the shelf. She poured out two little glasses of the thick liquid and the girls took them and laughed, holding them up to their eyes.

The thick bar separated the girls from the men, who were now drinking barley wine. The small pale drinks stood opposite the tall dark ones on the wet board.

John had began to talk a lot and the girls were giggling at him.

Mrs Bradman was unbending. She saw that he did not mind spending money.

The gardener was mixing drinks very curiously. He now decided that they should drink whisky.

Suddenly he disappeared, but no one thought anything of it. They thought he would be back directly.

John went on talking to the girls and his voice grew louder. Other occupants of the bar began to take notice of him. The things he said made them laugh. So one from the other room put his head round the door and asked if he would like to play darts. John answered that he was afraid he did not know how. The other scowled and said softly, 'Oh, I see, you're only a drunk.' A little spasm of anger shot through John and he drew himself up to look at the other man, but he had already disappeared behind the door.

It was some time since Jim had disappeared and an old labourer leant forward from his bench and touched John's elbow, saying, 'Hadn't you better go and look for your mate?'

John moved as certainly as he could to the door. He said a quick goodnight with hardly a smile and was gone.

The cold freshness of the night accentuated his drunkenness. He felt soiled. He could see the chromium of the motor-bike glinting in the darkness, and by it, half lying, half sitting, was Jim. He had been sick and seemed to be dozing.

John sat down by him on the wet grass and took his arm. 'We'd better get home now, Jim.' He looked at the motor-bike and added, 'We'll walk, you can fetch your bike tomorrow.'

Jim nodded obediently and lay back, pulling John with him. They lay there a little together, gathering for their walk.

When they rose, they linked their arms systematically and began the long walk to Shipley. They did not talk. Jim's greater weight was half supported by John, who was much steadier.

Once they stumbled and fell, lying in the long grass at the side of the road for some time. They lay very close for the warmth and Jim was asleep in a moment, snoring lightly. John watched the still eyelids and open mouth and felt the strong body relaxed warmly against his own. It was pleasant out of doors like this – he felt sober now. Jim was steadier too when he awoke, and they moved on.

At the gates of Shipley they said goodbye and Jim went quietly to the back door of the lodge, where he lived with his parents.

The long drive was terrible to John, with nothing to think about but his own return. He felt sick, and from far off he could see the light burning in the librarian's room. The rest of the great façade was noble and black.

On the gravelled court his footsteps seemed louder than bells ringing.

He did not have to wonder how he would get in. The librarian was soon there, unbolting the great door.

'Really, Trevor, what are you doing out at this time of night? The servants have all gone to bed and I've had to wait up for you.' Then: 'Good Lord, you're drunk. If this sort of thing happens again I shall have to tell the Duke.'

'I wish you would,' John almost shouted, as he pushed by him into the hall and lurched, half running, up the stairs.

'I wish you would,' he yelled again from the top. But as he made his way down the long corridors, he knew that the librarian would never tell the Duke what had happened. He knew that he was caught for ever.

GHOSTS

Writing in his Journal *on 8 October 1944, Denton Welch remarked that he was struggling to write 'a "feature" for* Vogue, *on "Ghosts and Dreams"'. The piece does not seem to have appeared, but from that commission may have resulted this story (first published in* A Last Sheaf) *or one of the three fragments that follow.*

THE FIRST STORY I EVER WROTE WAS A GHOST STORY. I wrote it at school for the last English lesson of the term. I remember the tremor of excitement that ran through me when I heard the master, so like a rather strong-smelling black retriever, giving out the announcement for preparation.

As I had been taken to see Knole in the holidays, my mind immediately turned to those wonderful rooms for material. I stole the ostrich plumes off James I's bed, the silver sconces off the walls, the brass locks presented by William III to the Cartoon Gallery, and the eighteenth-century proportions of the Venetian Ambassador's bedroom.

I panelled my imaginary room in pine and finished it with a heavy cornice. From a cracked punch-bowl came the faint scent of mildewed rose leaves, and a hissing fire of green branches spat and danced on the scratched marble hearth. The hangings of the fantastically high bed were of rose madder damask, faded in parts to tawny, dried-blood colour, and they were so rotten that they had to be held together on a new foundation by countless lines of cross-sewing. It gave me great pleasure to describe all these remembered details.

In this grand bed I put myself to sleep, after having blown out the eight candles in the four sconces. As I wrote, I became more and more involved in my own story.

Suddenly, in the middle of the night, I awoke and found myself staring up into the dome of the terrifying bed. I lay sweating, wondering what was going to happen.

I remembered a line, perhaps from Ecclesiastes or the Psalms, 'the hair of my flesh stood up', and it seemed such a perfect description of my feeling that I put it down word for word.

Gradually, from the depths of the room beyond the bed, a lighted figure emerged. It was no ordinary ghost, rattling bones and chains, but a beautiful woman, tall and sweeping and not young – ageless, like the queens in fairy-tales.

She glided up to the bed and stood there, twisting her rings and mouthing painfully. She wanted to tell me something and she was dumb!

I can't remember how I ended my story, but I suspect that I left it dangling in the air, as most true ghost stories are left.

I liked my story too well not to feel alarm when the time came for it to be read out by the black retriever. What if he should maul it and make it appear ridiculous!

I sat near the back of the class, and he took several other stories first. One he refused to read in its entirety because a great parade had been made of visiting nightclubs and 'coming home with the milk'.

I looked at the 'unwholesome' boy who had so successfully added to his reputation for wickedness by writing in this way, and was amazed to see how calm he kept under the master's contemptuous glance.

With an exasperated crackling of pages the black retriever spat, 'I can't read out any more of this appalling stuff!'

Such scorn would have withered me for days, but the boy who specialized in vice just wore a bored expression; 'blasé' I think he would have called it.

When at last my story was reached, I stopped breathing and waited for some dreadful pronouncements; therefore I was astonished when I heard the master say, 'Now this at least has something good about it. The writer has tried to create a romantic atmosphere, and whatever he has described he has first seen very clearly in his mind.'

This was intoxicating enough from the black retriever, who, I thought, disliked me. To be called 'the writer'! But when he began to read my story soberly, as though it were 'real literature', my heart was filled with gratitude. I listened to my own sentences with only a bearable amount of embarrassment, and knew in a moment that I wanted to be a writer.

All went well until 'the hairs of my flesh' was read out. Instantly laughter broke out all over the room and voices called out, 'Oh, I say, Welch, do they really stand up?' 'Oh Welch!'

Unwisely rushing to my own defence as a writer by referring them to my august source, I protested, 'But it's in the Bible! You can read it there.'

This started a second storm of laughter, groans and mockeries. I thought, 'Let them laugh. Everything is ridiculous if you like to make it so.' I even began to laugh myself . . .

Then I forgot all about this story, until some time later when I had left school and was staying at a friend's house near the sea in Sussex. Besides myself there was one other guest, and as we sat on the sunlit lawn, shelling peas for supper, she started to tell me of this true experience.

She had gone up to stay at a large old house, I think in the Midlands. Her room was in the eighteenth-century part, with walls panelled to the ceiling, and heavy sash windows.

Immediately my mind flew back to my own story, and although she told me that her bed was modern, uncanopied and very comfortable, I still saw her in my ancient plumed bed with the crimson curtains moving in the draught like furtive animals.

She read a little as she lay in bed, then she switched off the lamp and went to sleep.

In the middle of the night she was woken, just as I had been in my story; although it was not a beautiful woman that she saw, but a huge filmy egg, made out of mucous membrane and lighted from within. It floated slowly through the darkness until it was above her in the bed. She saw with horror then that the egg-shaped glow encased the face and shoulders of a man. The shoulders were naked and just below them the body dissolved into stringy, phosphorescent mucus. Round his head was a squirming halo of the same. The flesh was of an extraordinary ruddiness, and exaggeratedly tight, as if the image had been blown up with a bicycle-pump.

The young man was grinning at her, showing his white, animal teeth. On his forehead were hot brown curls and the needle points of his eyes bored into her.

Fascinated, she watched the face until it disappeared on the other side of the bed, then she lay still, wondering what it could be, until, most surprisingly, she fell asleep again.

In the morning her host and hostess told her that the image appeared in various parts of the house, not only in that room. Sometimes it sailed down the passages. The face and shoulders were all that could ever be seen. They had no explanation to give for the appearance of the image, except a rather unconvincing tradition about a young man, a villain and an ancestor of theirs.

For a moment after the end of the story we went on shelling peas in silence. The pods, as they were ripped open, made a sucking noise, like mouths gasping for air. My mind was busy comparing the true experience with my invented one. I could think of nothing but ghosts; I was filled with the idea of them.

And jumping up restlessly, I left my companion, and the peas in the china basin, and the empty pods on the lawn; and I wandered a long way until I came to a black pool almost surrounded by tangled thickets. I knelt down and dipped my hand in the still water. My fingers were magnified into fat, curling grubs. Baring my arm, I stretched down till I felt rotting branches and twigs soft as horses' noses. I pulled, and a mossy, peeling antler rose dripping from the pond. Delving still deeper I came to a pie of excrement and leaves, layer on layer, and limp and black as chow dogs' tongues.

It was evening now, with the sun setting. I looked up at the turquoise sky, then down at the stirred-up water where black motes like pepper starred the pinkness of my tingling arm. From across the pool a dull blind window suddenly flashed back the dying fire of the sun, and a rush of birds streamed out above me. I saw the woodman's ruined shelter of branches tied together, and his pile of bark peelings turned now into a mass of dead mottled snakes.

Everything at that moment held a secret. Everything was haunted. But human eyes were not the right eyes, and my ears would never hear.

Three Fragments

The setting of these three fragments on 'ghosts and dreams' is the area surrounding the house in Kent, Pitt's Folly Cottage near Hadlow, where Denton Welch lived from 1942 to 1946. Oxon Hoath was one of his favourite picnic spots.

WHEN I LIE AWAKE

WHEN I LIE AWAKE AT NIGHT, THE DREAMS THAT I HAVE just had always lead my thoughts to ghosts, and my spirit flies out of the Gothic-revival window, over Kent, across the mist-wrapped fields, to a black pool on the edge of a dripping wood. I dip down deep into the black water and feel the rotting layers of leaves.

Then back away from the medieval dwelling and the red-brick Georgian farm-house, up the narrow lane to the corner where gypsies have lived in their caravan for several months, close to the bald patch in the orchard where a flying bomb landed. They seem lost in the dream too: boys with their feet flung out, half in the ditch, half out; women with the most untrusting eyes on earth; children whose faces are like dinner-plates after dinner has been eaten; the modern clothes torn, twisted, arrayed into some quite other pattern.

Past these to the brow on Gover Hill, close to the house that the romantic have named Rats Castle, where two stone images guard the door; then down the newish avenue of trees, through the park to Oxon Hoath. To the west of the house is the Cedar Walk, spreading flat layers of green, like huge ancient fingers underneath grass, delicate and fine as towelling.

Push open the heavy cast-iron gate, the stone gate-pillar broken and knocked about by the soldiers, and then walk till you come to the edge of the barnyard which is a corruption of the word 'bagnio'.

On this shallow lake swans are swimming and the fish jump all the time, but so quickly that one can never see their heads or tails. A huge elm has fallen into the barnyard and cannot be lifted; in its fall it crushed the boathouse, so that now a twist of wood and corrugated iron is all that remains. The cows in summer love this ruined spot to hide in from the sun and it smells of them the whole year round. There is a humped stone bridge with a stile at the bottom, with PRIVATE inscribed in an alarming red on one of the bars.

Climb up to the top of that bridge, where the boys have wantonly been knocking the stone ledging into the water, and from there look across the rushes and the water, up the curving meadows, where the cows are still browsing, to the old house all stone and early-nineteenth-century mansard roofing, with windows in the central domed piece.

The moon is rising now and the clouds that are near it, or scud across it, all have white haloes and cores of central smoky black.

Then the old house winks its windows wickedly, blind eyes yet flashing. And in the rooms so still hang mirrors that have reflected two hundred years of faces. Think of them: child faces in a screaming fit, black with passion; young-girl faces wondering and dreaming like unwritten books; worn faces, taut and brooding; and ambitious faces all aglow yet afraid, waiting, hoping, planning. Thus face wipes out face, year after year, in the heart of the glass, until they form a terrifying clash. What can the glass think of all those faces, no respite from them, all filled with life, then fading?

Back away across the park, down the Alphabetical Avenue, each meagre unhealthy-looking tree's name beginning with a different letter, until one sees the curved shape of the window, in again at it, shut it tight, draw the curtains, turn on the gas-fire and sit by it.

IN THE AUTUMN WEATHER

IN THE AUTUMN WEATHER I THINK OF GHOSTS. WHEN I walk by the edge of a black pool in a wood in Kent and look across to the tall ochre-coloured house with blind windows on the other side, I see the ghosts in those empty wainscoted rooms and I see the ghosts too under the black waters, lying on the layered bed of rotted leaves and antlered twigs.

In the violent-coloured wood too are presences, in every tree and hollow. And one's treading feet on the crackling leaves seem almost an enormity, with so many listening on every side.

I pass the Georgian farm-house which is joined to the medieval chapel, now used as a store and barn; and then the ghost voices become so insistent that I have to look up above through those stone walls to the interior, which once was all paint and glass and woodwork with iron and needlework. Now nothing, only the wind in the roof, the rows of silent apples on their newspapers, the mouse droppings and the ears of last year's corn left here and there amongst the mass of straw.

And in the mushroom fields outside there is a brooding melancholy that seems to spring up through the grass. The horses look at you and the cows too, not with eyes, but bottomless wells of sorrow, cynicism and acceptance. No joy or pain, only a remembering of all the countless years before the other cows and other horses gave to make these here in the field in Kent.

And in the apples too is stored a waiting knowledge, a resigned ghost-haunted dream, a trance state before the rotting, the slicing, the eating, the extermination.

All over the countryside is the ghost-web flung, each tiniest object soaked and saturated in its atmosphere.

Deep in your heart you know that the bar between the living and the ghost world is death, and that stored in each living thing from the moment of its birth are these remembrances and echoes somehow of the death before they were born as well as the death to come.

Go home through the fading light and sit by the fire in your tiny cottage, with tea and books and the world outside destroyed, demolished, locked from you. But there, even there in the flame light, you will hear the voices between the leaves of your book, know the silent waiting of the rosewood worktable, feel the presence behind the ticking of the clock, see the figures in the picture move. For dead things are alive, with a loving all their own, and human beings know with every twist and turn what centuries and centuries close round them like swaddling clothes and what illimitable actions stretch out into the future, even now working out their faint and wild foundations.

THE SECRET LIFE

THE SECRET LIFE THAT COMES WITH LONELINESS TENDS all to dreams and ghosts. I go for a walk in Kent and inevitably my footsteps lead me down a forgotten narrow valley to the edge of a black pool hemmed round with tangled thickets. The pool is black through the rotting of many thousands of leaves in it. If you should dip your hands into Swanton Pool you would see the tiny motes like pepper starring all the water against the pinkness of your flesh, and if you should delve deeper, sinking down your arm, you would come to sable twigs, supple as leather and yielding as the velvet of horses' noses, and then to a sort of pie and excrement of leaves, as limp and black as chow dogs' tongues, layer on layer, like a well-made omelette.

Beside the pool is a house masked in ochre stucco, with high-pitched roof and sash windows that flash back the light as blindly as do the spectacles on a face in the firelight. Too close to the house is a cedar tree whose great brooding arms spread out in a gesture, both threatening and protecting, which is disquieting. The door of this house is open, but no one is seen going in or coming out.

Then, leaving the pool behind you and walking on through the wide spreading woods, you would come to clearings where faggots and poles have been chopped and piled, and the bark in long peelings lies piled together like a mound of headless unmoving snakes with mottled skins. You see there the woodman's little ruined shelter of leaves and the frame on which he cut. There is nothing in the woods but the drop of water from the branches, the memory of past fires and toadstools under the yew tree.

ROGER SAW THE MAN

This unfinished story, in which Denton Welch uses one of his favourite pseudonyms, 'Roger', is his only known attempt to describe a sexual encounter with a woman.

ROGER SAW THE MAN WALKING WITH SOME OTHER labourers down the wide street of the little country town. He could not fail to notice him, his clothes were so picturesque. He wore old-fashioned corduroys, cut with a flap at the top, like sailor's trousers, a shirt and waistcoat and a red and yellow handkerchief knotted round his neck. On his head was a cap and he wore sidewhiskers. His hair was like orange sand. The whole effect was gypsified, yet English. He was a short man but well made.

Roger at sixteen stared and anything strange held his eyes. The man left his mates at a corner and, turning round, saw Roger staring at him. He did not seem a bit nonplussed, but asked Roger for a cigarette. He did not leave when he discovered that Roger had none, but walked at the side of Roger's bicycle until they were on the outskirts of the little town. He told how he and his family were down for the fruit picking and how they lived in a caravan. Then he told Roger about his time in the Army and what life was like in the East.

'What do you think of that?' he suddenly said, and Roger, looking round, saw that he had pulled open his shirt, exposing the whiteness of his chest and the portraits of the King and Queen with many flags and flowers tattooed on it. 'That's what I had done in Hong Kong,' he added. Roger got off his bicycle to examine the elaborate markings more closely. The strange blue and red faces loomed through the ginger hairs on the man's chest and the fairness of the skin on which they were tattooed changed sharply at the neck to dull copper.

'Did it hurt very much – having it done?' he asked.

'Not much, but it isn't finished yet. I don't expect I'll ever have it done now.'

They went on walking together, past fields and orchards, until they came to a cart track. 'My caravan's up here,' said the man, jerking his head. 'Come up and have a look at my missus.'

Roger did not know what to do. 'I think I'd better go home,' he said.

'Nao, come on,' the man urged and so he found himself saying, 'All right,' and following over the rough field until they came to the far corner, where a caravan was half hidden amongst some trees by the edge of a stream. Three children were scrambling on the stream's bank and screaming loudly to each other. They looked up, their dark eyes round in their dirty faces. The door of the caravan was open and someone was moving about inside, scraping dishes and cooking-pots together.

The man shouted, 'Annie, come out and see the gentleman.' She came to the door and looked out. She was young and sulky, with fair hair and sluttish clothes. She did not say anything, but gave Roger a piercing look. He dropped his eyes and blushed.

'What's for supper, Annie?' the man shouted again.

'Nothing, didn't you bring nothing back with you?'

'No, I found I hadn't nothing on me.'

'Well there ain't any money 'ere either, so you'll have to go 'ungry.'

There was a pause and then Roger suddenly said, 'I could buy something if you like.'

They both looked at him keenly, then the man said, 'Thanks mate, very much, half a crack'll do.'

Roger gave him a half-crown and saw him go back towards the village shop. He was left alone now with the screaming children and the woman.

'Would you like to come in and see our caravan?' she said.

He mounted the step-ladder and looked at the stove and the benches that turned into beds at night. Many things were hung from the ceiling and walls, and the air was stale although the door was open. He was very near the woman in this narrow box and he could smell her whenever she moved.

'I'll be gettin' on with the supper. You sit down and make yerself at 'ome,' she said.

His eyes followed her as she unhooked things. She often would stretch over him to reach things. He sat very still, wondering when he could escape. She was nearer than ever now, laying plates and knives on the flap she had pulled out from the wall. He could hear her breathing and whenever he looked up her eyes were fastened on him.

Suddenly she sat down beside him and said, 'I think I've done all I can till 'e brings in the food. Like a cigarette?'

She opened the greasy tin and held it out to him.

'No thank you,' he said, 'I don't smoke.'

'Have a try.'

He shook his head, but she took one up and pushed it against his lips. He felt the roughness of the tobacco at its end and opened his lips slightly to receive it.

When she had lit hers she blew out the match and, pushing her face near to him, told him to put the unlighted point of his cigarette to the glowing end of hers and then to draw his breath in. She put her hands on his shoulders to steady herself and, as he breathed in and choked, she laughed. She got up and hit him on the back, which made the coughing worse. When it had subsided she said, 'Feelin' better now? You'll soon get used to it.'

Then she lay back in her corner and stared at him. 'I like you.' He went deeply red and looked towards the door. She leant forward, against him, pushing him back; then she stretched up her long neck and kissed his cheek with her sticky lips. He moved his head, but she was half lying on him and he could not get up. He lay there dully submitting to her kisses while her hands explored his body. She thrust one under his cotton shirt, stroking the flesh on his chest. Then she felt the hard roundness of his stomach under his belt . . .

THE EARTH'S CRUST

Denton Welch was seventeen when he enrolled as a student at the Goldsmith School of Art in New Cross, London. Adam Street has since been renamed Robert Adam Street, and the house in which he lived has been demolished. 'The Earth's Crust' was first published in A Last Sheaf.

WHEN I FIRST WENT TO AN ART SCHOOL, IT WAS DECIDED that I should live with my eldest brother in Adam Street, off Portman Square. His two rooms were at the top of the little Georgian house and my bedroom was on the ground floor. Between us we had a woman with a tightly held mouth and contemptuous eyes, and a curate viscount who ran up the stairs and usually carried a music-case stuffed with papers. In the basement lived the owner of the house and her children. She had a harsh dry cough which tickled the back of my throat whenever I heard it.

In houses where people live behind closed doors, unknown to one another, some emanation broods in the passages and especially on the stairs. Perhaps it is just vague, diffused suspicion. This house had it in particular. The embittered woman, going to the bathroom with her sponge, moved almost furtively, as if afraid of eyes staring down from the top landing; and the curate, as he bustled past me with his papers, seemed to be escaping from someone or something. Even the landlady appeared to be affected by the atmosphere. She climbed up from her basement with a look of deep anxiety and secretiveness on her face. One had the impression that she had something to hide which gave her a great deal of trouble. Yet it was all illusion, for she was a conscientious woman who kept good rooms and gave excellent breakfasts.

These were brought to our rooms on trays. I would have mine before I bathed or dressed. I usually began with iced grapefruit already sugared, then went on to scrambled eggs, toast, coffee, and marmalade. And all the time I would be reading a book with the lamp on, because my old room had only one window and was dark. Although it was dark, it could have been a charming room, for it still possessed its high wainscot and old L-shaped hinges on the door; but the landlady's stained oak Cromwellian furniture and cretonne curtains had almost completely overlaid its original character.

At the last moment I would run out of the house to catch my bus, without even going upstairs to see my brother. The art school that had been chosen for me was in the south-eastern suburbs. It had been chosen by my aunt, because she had once bought a print from the man who taught wood engraving there. The journey out to it was long. The bus crossed the river, passed under thundering Vauxhall railway bridge and came to Kennington, where the blackened acanthus railings of the Regency church were covered with yellow and red placards, asking for money. I would be sitting on top of the bus, right in front in order to see everything. On the other side of the road was a park with screaming children standing in the paddling pond and splashing one another. The girls had their dresses bunched up above their thighs or tucked into their bloomers. Little boys, clad only in braces and trousers, ran amok, shooting off water pistols. Girls screamed more piercingly than birds, lolled out their tongues and rolled their eyes like epileptics. There was madness in the air.

When the children had been left behind, my eyes turned to the small factory, which advertised for women to work sewing machines.

I pictured the sweat shops: the scores of pedalling feet, the darting needles, snapping thread. I saw the girls' bent heads, their hair cascading down. I smelt the sweat, the strain, the powder, the knitting, and the buns in paper bags.

Then there were the butchers' shops with pink lamps on all day to make the meat look rosy and good. I saw pigs' faces with bunches of parsley in the scalded mouths.

Along the pavements thronged the people, like bottles walking, their heads as inexpressive as round stoppers. What if some god or giant should bend down and take several of the stoppers out, I thought. Inside there would be black churning depths like bile or bitter medicine.

So many of the people still carried sleep in their faces. Grey skin, bleary eyes, rough hair, seemed to show that they had been forced from their beds and were only waiting for the day's work to be done, when they would throw themselves down again.

The lunatic asylum at Peckham, so remote in its old building behind high walls, cut off from trams and buses and crowds and posters, was dreaming of another age and time. I peopled it with lunatics who knew that they were great historic figures. Queen Victoria was there with a tray of silver paper medals, which she graciously bestowed on the nurses and doctors who pleased her. Napoleon brooded; and Joan of Arc smiled in ecstasy as the flames licked up.

I always hoped to see a face appear at one of the top windows – just the glimpse of a face looking up at the clouds; but there was no sign of life.

I next tried to penetrate the walls of a great warehouse. There was furniture that had been stored there for fifty years, I told myself. Mice ran between the legs of the tables and nibbled at the doors of the huge sideboards, misled by a ghostly smell of cheese and biscuits. Moths silently munched through green baize and damask wool. The tickless clocks kept watch. The chairs held out their arms. The rolled Turkey carpets were like giant cocoons, waiting to burst open. Everything had life, but it was muffled, furtive, secret.

The Marquis of Granby was my stop. I would get off the bus, cross the road and enter a large building which had dusty evergreen bushes round the door. The main part was devoted to the training of schoolteachers, so I would run down a long, dark passage till I reached the stairs which led to the art school. I would climb up as quietly as possible, for I was usually late, get my drawing-board and pencil, and glide silently into the Antique Room. Students already astride their 'donkeys' would glance up at me, then down again. They seemed both curious and uninterested. I was too new to have any friends. I thought that they would talk *about* me, but not *to* me. Sometimes there were only two or three girls in the room, and then they would talk about men, as if I were just another plaster cast. I was left to get down on my paper something that looked a little like the Hermes of Praxiteles.

The master, when he appeared, would perhaps say, 'This is just fun – you are amusing yourself.' He would say it mildly, even tolerantly, but my cheeks would tingle, and I would crouch over my drawing, as if to conceal and protect it. I had not yet learnt to enjoy an art school. I would long for the end of the morning.

At lunch-time most of the students ran down to the refectory on the ground floor and had a large lunch with the schoolteachers-to-be, but I had found a shop which sold crisp rolls and butter and slices of good liver sausage. Further down the street a baker kept strange fig biscuits that I liked. With this food I used to walk down a side street of early-Victorian houses – one with plaster eagles on each side of the door – until I came to a later, stone church that blocked the end. Plane trees and small patches of grass surrounded it. I had discovered that if I sat on the steps of the great west door, which was never opened, I could be in the sun and yet hidden from the road. In front of me was a trim garden and a house. I would crunch my roll and biscuits as I gazed at the beds of tortoiseshell wallflowers or at the railway line beyond, and for a few moments would feel happy and content; even the curiously rude Victorian contractor's gargoyle nearest to me would add to my pleasure. But then the isolated feeling and the useless feeling and the imprisoned feeling would sweep back over me and I would know that I was alone on a stone step with no idea of how my life was to be lived.

One day, while I was sitting there, a youngish man in a dog-collar came hurrying round the north buttress, which partly hid me. He opened the garden gate, and when he turned to latch it again he saw me. I was afraid that he was going to turn me out and reprimand me for irreverence, but instead he smiled as if quite used to seeing me there and as if he approved. He said that he had often noticed me from the vicarage windows and he was glad that I enjoyed the peace and quiet and the sun; then, just when he seemed about to lean on the gate and talk, his manner changed. He had evidently remembered that he had no time to spare. With one more smile he turned and walked quickly towards the house.

I was left with an empty feeling, as though something nice had been taken away from me capriciously. He had so obviously wished me well; I began to wonder if some shyness or stiffness in me had driven him away. I was filled with regret. He might have been a friend instead of a stranger. I could hear the clanging trains in the New Cross high street, and the dust and filth seemed to be trying to invade my retreat. I got up to go back to the school.

I walked a different way, along a footpath between fences, to delay my return for as long as possible. The class that afternoon was 'book illustration', and the master who taught was so nervous that he either praised extravagantly or spat out some demolishing remark and then glided away, seemingly dismayed by his own excessiveness.

I sat on a high stool, trying to design a frontispiece for *The Way of All Flesh*, which I had chosen as my book; but it seemed hopeless. No ideas took form, and the extraordinary perversity of my materials conquered me. No one was there to help me technically or to give me the confidence which would have made my thoughts run clear. I toyed with my brushes and paints and longed for the end of the afternoon.

At last it came and I was free to get away from the school. I left the other students laughing and shouting and washing their brushes in the lavatory basins. I seemed to have no connection with them. They belonged to another world. I ran down the tunnel-like passages and let myself out into the open air.

I was filled with a sort of exultation. What should I do? Should I wander in the drab streets around me? Past the eel shop, where the writhing black things were slowly dying on zinc trays; there was a bicycle shop which blared music against the noise of the trams, and beyond that was a junk shop where I had noticed some little prints in old oval frames. They were sepia coloured by Bartolozzi, the sort I had read about. I went to bargain with the man, who turned out to be likeable and understanding, but he would not sell me the smallest one for five shillings – he wanted eight. We talked a little and I turned the pictures over and saw that one had the charming old framemaker's label still on it. I wanted that one particularly, but it was even more expensive. The man was busy. There was no place for me. I said goodbye and walked away, unsatisfied.

I walked in the direction of 'home'. I would catch a bus later, when I was tired. I stared at the people's faces, looking for something that I had known a long time ago or had perhaps dreamt about. But the faces told me nothing; they were set and oblivious, like slices of pallid cheese wrapped in grey muslin. So many people, yet nobody for me.

I jumped on to a bus and let the scene merge and blur and melt. The motion soothed me into a waking sleep. I sailed high above noise and dirt and danger.

At Park Lane I got off and walked into the park. There were lovers there lying in the grass, and I thought how flimsy they looked, like trash washed up on a beach, or corpses in an old war photograph. But what were their thoughts? I wondered. Were their minds filled with extraordinary things which only came to flower when they lay down? Had they forgotten all about the world outside, or did the eyes of other people give an added excitement? Would some of them be lovers for years after this day's beginning?

My questions multiplied and grew more fantastic. I think something ancient in me really condemned them as whores and lechers, but I ignored this deeper feeling and invented for them strange situations and romances.

I could not stay in the park all the evening, and I hated to go back to Adam Street alone, so I decided to have tea and ice-cream at Fuller's. But when I sat down at the small round table and had the chocolate-fudge sundae in front of me, my malaise increased rather than diminished. People at the other tables leant towards one another and talked in low contented voices. Outside the traffic roared and grated. I hurried through what I had meant to enjoy, then turned into the street again.

I began to walk very slowly towards Portman Square, letting the crowd push me this way and that. Outside the house I found my brother and a friend just about to set off for the evening. They asked me perfunctorily to join them, but I looked at the friend's rolled umbrella, at my brother's smartness, and I felt tousled and callow. Their age, their sleekness and assurance made them inhuman. I said hurriedly that I had to visit an old friend of my mother's. They talked and joked with me for a moment, then walked off down the road, the friend swinging his umbrella a little.

Having said that I was going to see my middle-aged friend, I decided that I would. But when I had climbed up the stone steps to

THE EARTH'S CRUST

her old-fashioned flat, there was no one at home. The bell buzzed through the empty rooms. I bent down and looked through the letter-box. The hall was fawn colour and dead. It seemed possible that ghosts were haunting the flat while she was away. I listened for sinister movements and voices, then turned away almost in despair. To find the door locked at that moment was a catastrophe.

I trudged back across the bridge, feeling sick and empty. It was almost dark now and the lights were lit. Near the Marble Arch I noticed a group of people not moving but standing still on the pavement outside a fun fair. As I passed them I heard blues music, the ping of balls and wire springs, tinkle of money, and over everything the snarling voices of two people in the doorway. A young woman in black with fair, parched-looking hair confronted a man, whose tie had blown over his shoulder. A belt with a nickel buckle was pulled tightly in round his stomach. He was lifting his lip, sneering at the girl's stream of abuse, hunching his broad shoulders as he pushed his hands deep into his pockets. Then, as she paused for breath, he began. He poured contempt on her clothes, her body, her age, her voice, her class, her sex. He seemed to be trampling on everything they'd ever known or done together. I stood quite still on the edge of the crowd, too horrified and fascinated to break away. I could picture them just the night before, close to each other in the dark, or kissing like the people in the grass. Now they were murderous, searching for the worst poison and the sharpest pain.

The woman began to move away. She seemed to be broken and conquered by the man's brutal words; but all at once she darted back and slashed him in the face with her handbag. It was as if he had at last said the unbearable thing.

There was blood. The metal clasp had caught his cheek, and as he put his hand up to it, the woman burst into a storm of tears. He made as if to rush at her and smash her face in, but people in the crowd caught his arms behind him. Seeing him powerless, the woman with a strange movement jerked her head up and her tongue flashed out like a serpent's. For one moment she was quite spiritualized and transformed with hate; then she slipped through the crowd and I saw her running, half crouching, along the pavement.

She was sobbing again violently. Hate was over, and only misery left.

The man turned and tried to fight the men who were holding him. The little crowd swayed. I broke away and started to run too.

In my dismay it seemed to me as if the earth's crust had cracked and I had looked through and seen reality at last.

THE YOUTH RANG
THE BELL

Denton Welch was eighteen when he decided to leave Adam Street, partly to escape his brother Bill and partly to be closer to the art school. His search for lodgings eventually led him to a house in Croom's Hill, situated not in a 'quiet blind alley' but directly facing Greenwich Park. His landlady, recognizable in 'Miss Green', was Miss Evelyn Sinclair.

THE YOUTH RANG THE BELL OF THE HOUSE IN THE crescent on Blackheath, then waited very anxiously.

The door was opened almost at once by a large woman with tight dark eyebrows and waved hair. She was frowning and the youth hated to think of the fighting tautness of the great bosom under the tired stretching cardigan.

'Who is it? What do you want? There is no "governor" in this house so it's no good asking for him.'

She was about to shut the door in his face, but he must have looked so innocently affronted and bemused that she stopped, waiting for him to say something.

'The lady at the Christian Science reading room told me that you took paying guests,' he said carefully, using the words 'lady' and 'paying guest' to please her, but hating her at the same time with all his heart for her crude barbarian manner.

A curious change came over the large woman. She went quite blank. It was as if the curtain had come down so that the scene could be changed. This pause was necessary for the readjustment of voice, manner, pose and movement. She was still a little truculent, feeling that she had been tricked into the wrong behaviour by the unexpectedness of his appearance and by the strange blend of determination and anxiety in his face.

'Oh,' she said, giving a well-bred little laugh, as though she were delicately amused at her own impetuosity. 'Come in. We can talk in the drawing-room.'

She led Martin into a fine room the width of the house, with slender sash windows at each end. But the atmosphere was degraded and polluted by her treasured possessions. The sepia photographs of soldiers, and one of a woman with feathers in her hair and a train, the ferns and cactus plants, the coloured cushions, Christian Science periodicals and gardening magazines, seemed to spread a slime over everything.

Martin felt that it would not do for him, that he could not live there. He was trying not to hear the pretension in Mrs Sedley-Morgan's voice, trying not to notice the repeated gurgle of amusement as she displayed her house *so* carelessly; but he was being swamped by her rapacious eyes, the bird-like will to force that streamed out of her.

She took him to the top of the charming severe staircase and threw open a door.

'Of course, this is my best room,' she said; 'isn't it lucky that it's just become empty! I usually have such amusing young people in the house – students mostly. You are a student?'

'I've just begun at an art school,' Martin said, hating to answer her, but compelled by the fierce eyes.

'Oh, what fun! Isn't the view exciting across the heath to the pond? And the sun streams in, just streams in. I charge three and a half guineas.'

The sudden mention of money was a breath of truth blown on the trash so unexpectedly that it jarred and startled, and seemed for a moment even uglier than the lies.

Martin looked at the green coiling wallpaper, perhaps a pattern adapted and perverted from a Jacobean embroidered bed-hanging.

Is it worth three and a half guineas, he thought soberly, to live with that, and with the sun that streams in, the view of the duck pond, Mrs Sedley-Morgan's mountain breasts and those eyes inexorable and alcoholic as corkscrews? What sort of people would like it? There must be a sort.

He had thought her eyes alcoholic, partly because they corkscrewed into him, and partly because they frightened him, just as alcohol did. They were demons ready to seize on him and force him to their will.

'Yes, it's very nice,' he said; 'but may I let you know? I must talk it over with my people.' He had no people, except the elder brother from whom he was about to break away. He mentioned 'people', feeling that Mrs Sedley-Morgan would then be less inclined to stampede him into a decision there and then.

'Oh, well, if you'd rather they made up your mind for you . . .' Again the little *mondaine* gurgle and this time a flutter of the hand to accentuate it.

She sailed down the stairs in front of him. She had a presence, there was no denying it. That was the most horrible thing about her. All those soldiering years in India were behind her.

In the hall she did a curious thing, to underline her amateur standing, it would seem, or perhaps merely to insult.

'If you'd like anything cheaper, I know a little Miss Green who comes to the church. She's starting a house on the other side of the heath. I said I'd tell people about it. I'll go and get you her address.'

Martin heard her rummaging in her sordidly untidy bureau. She came back with the address scrawled on an old envelope. He took it, thanked her and turned abruptly away, as if he could bear no more of her. He was down the stone steps and out of the crescent in a few moments.

How clean it was on the heath! How easing, how relieving. The tightness was going from his muscles, the constriction of his breathing, his seeing, his thinking. 'Bitch of a woman, bitch of a woman, bitch,' he kept saying under his breath. But soon he was singing the words out loud, almost hoping that he would be heard by the children playing round the pond or the passing bicyclists.

He wondered whether he could stand another interview or not, and decided in the end to force himself to go to Miss Green's.

After a short search he found the house in a quiet blind alley off the heath. It had plane trees in front of it, and its eighty-year-old flat stucco face was reassuring. Again he rang the bell and waited.

This time a younger woman, a woman of perhaps thirty-eight or thirty-nine, opened the door. Her hair was bobbed in the fashion of the 1920s. She wore a white knitted jersey, so long that it was almost a tunic dress, and one of the dark brown eyes had a slight cast in it, so that she seemed to be looking away shyly and engagingly as she confronted him.

He looked beyond her at the clean quiet hall and knew at once that Mrs Sedley-Morgan had done her good turn for the day. How annoyed she would be, if she could see his satisfaction in this other house, his calm acceptance of Miss Green's disjointed manner and far-away eyes!

She took him upstairs, turning to him at the bend and saying quietly, almost as if she were talking to herself, 'This house has character. We haven't been here long. You should have seen the dirt! It made me feel quite hopeless for about the first week.'

The first room she showed Martin, he decided to have. It looked on to the trees, was small, had a grey carpet, grey walls, a large grey cupboard built out from the wall and a new raw-looking basin with hot and cold taps. The extreme freshness and characterless quality of the room were just what he was needing. He wanted to submerge himself in the quiet greyness, to be left alone there at once. But Miss Green would have it that he should see the other rooms before deciding. She took him all over the house, telling him simply that she had no other guests yet. Every room was in the same subdued, utterly safe taste. The monotony of it filled Martin with gratitude. He had craved just this soft greyness, as of the interior of a brain, this absence of all exuberance and invention.

'May I bring my luggage and come back tonight?' he asked.

The pain and discomfort of answering a question directly, of making any decision, were showing clearly on Miss Green's face. Martin thought, 'She is floating in grey clouds all the time.'

'Yes, I think so,' she said at last, 'I think that would be all right.'

Martin nodded jerkily, then hurried away to collect his things from his brother's dark little mews flat behind Chester Square.

When he got back Miss Green had prepared supper for him alone in a small front sitting-room under his own bedroom. He sat there reading a book and drinking her tomato soup, which he guessed had been blended cleverly from vegetable stock, milk and tomato crystals. The rest of the meal was equally frugal and acceptable.

He went to bed that night relieved of a great weight of homelessness and the horrible exacerbation of his brother's presence.

A NOVEL FRAGMENT

'A Novel Fragment', published in A Last Sheaf, *describes Denton Welch's life at art school, where he was from 1932 to 1935. Here he becomes 'Robert' and Evelyn Sinclair, his landlady, 'Miss Middlesborough'. 'Gerard Hope' was his art-school friend Gerald.*

I

ROBERT AT LAST JERKED OPEN THE DOOR OF THE LIFE Room and stood on the threshold, not daring to look at the model. Out of the corner of his eye he could just see the edge of the dais where a piece of squalid green baize hung in folds. Clutching his drawing-board even tighter, he made straight for a vacant 'donkey' and straddled it. He busied himself with pencil and rubber and penknife. Then, angry, at last, with his cowardice, he stared straight in front, truculently.

The shock was as great as he had supposed it would be. The sight of all that mauvish flesh with the hank of dark hair sent a tingle of horror right through his body. Madame David, with her elaborate arrangement of pulleys, had slung herself from the ceiling in one of her poses from the old masters. One arm and one leg were supported in nooses while she reclined on the dais, cupping her chin in her other hand – it was contortionist – and through his panic, Robert wondered if she was supposed to be Venus floating on a cloud. Madame David looked up and smiled broadly at him. She seemed to be cracking nuts between her teeth. He felt the furious wave of red spreading over his face. In desperation he bent over his board and began to try to draw the amazing figure. Those heavy tubes which were her arms and legs – how was he to relate them to that swelling stomach and torso? The breasts, curved and globular as the breakfast-cups on the LMS Railway, seemed impossibly difficult, with their nightmarishly large purple-pink nipples. He felt dimly that there must be something wrong with the nipples, that they must be swollen; he was even afraid that before the end of the lesson they would have spread a little further up the smooth white globes of flesh.

Busily he fell to drawing the head, the only part at all familiar to him. He had just outlined the dark untidy mass of square-cut hair and was beginning on Madame David's softening and ageing cheeks and lips when the half hour struck. Two jangling notes sounded from the school clock.

Madame David unhitched her arm and leg so that they fell against her with a soft thud.

'I think a little rest, eh?' she said, smiling to include the whole class, and still munching her nuts. Then she drew herself up slowly, stretching out her arms and tautening her whole body, so that a tremor went over her wide surfaces of flesh. She reminded him of a dog who suddenly becomes rigid and taut in the presence of another.

The students put down their pencils or brushes and relaxed. Some hunched their shoulders and lolled against the walls, others gathered round the stove where they carried on an animated conversation with Madame David. She was now dressed in a feathered peignoir, very much the worse for wear. Sections of mauve flesh could be seen through the rents in the dingy silk. She wore it impressively, allowing it to slip from her shoulders, and only gathering it together with one hand on her bosom. She held her head well back and laughed and smiled, making her mouth into that hard, very square shape which is used by trained singers. The plucked eyebrows danced up and down; there was much eye-work and she told the story of how she once looked after a little boy and taught him to box.

'I made an athlete of him!' she chanted gaily, throwing back her hair. She pronounced the *th* in 'athlete' as *t*. What was her curious accent? Was it French or Polish or Jewish or all three? Robert could not decide.

He was listening to her carefully now; gradually he edged nearer and nearer to her circle. Although he had been at the art school for a month he was still rather nervous of the other students. Some of them showed surprise to see him in the Life Class so soon, but they were kind to him, only joking and chaffing in a friendly way, as they made a little more room round the stove. It was habit that drove people to the stove. The room was much too hot already for people in their clothes.

Madame David looked at him rather disconcertingly as she finished her story. There was no pretence about her stare; she was assessing him physically. Her gaze rested finally on his small feet with their high arches. She would see the whole shape clearly, for he wore sandals which only consisted of straps and soles.

'You ought to be a ballet dancer,' she said emphatically. 'You could do springs like Nijinsky.'

Terrified of showing any pleasure at this remark, he turned his head away and muttered something gruffly.

'How old are you?' Madame David demanded.

'Eighteen.'

'Ah, perhaps a little old, but you might do something if you worked hard.'

Obeying a sudden impulse, she let the peignoir fall to the ground; then she began vigorously to slap her biceps and thighs. The soft middle-aged flesh trembled at her brutality, but she did not care, she was demonstrating the exercises for a ballet dancer and a boxer. She swung her legs and arms, swivelling her torso in a miraculous curve at the same time. The stomach undulated, the breasts rose and fell. She was triumphant and magnificent.

The students watched in admiration; even the ones who were tempted to laugh seemed impressed at the same time, and their amusement died away as their interest grew. It was impossible to tell what Madame David would do next.

At last, laughing and panting, she threw herself down on the cushioned dais.

'And this is supposed to be a rest!' she gasped out between breaths.

She lay there for a few moments, then she looked up at the clock and became businesslike.

'Time's up!' she cried girlishly, as she sprang to her feet.

'Now for some naughty ones for the fashion designers!' She winked so extravagantly that Robert almost expected her heavily mascaraed eyelashes to become entangled and stuck together. He wondered what she was going to do. She dived into the models' cubicle, and came out wearing nothing but a suspender-belt. Pulling the elastic away, she let it snap back against her flesh with a resounding smack. She laughed loudly at this result, and the whole class laughed with her.

'Short poses,' she announced, taking up a position. 'Next time I put on my stockings, then something else – you know what – I forget the name. Strip-tease, only the other way round!' She ended with another enormous wink.

Robert turned his paper over and tried to get something down. He knew that he would have to be very quick. The realization of the shortness of the pose made him uneasy and flustered. He found himself concentrating stupidly on the fastenings which dangled round Madame David's thighs. Then the door opened and Mr Bridgeman came in.

He stopped by each 'donkey', or easel, for a moment, sometimes drawing a little diagram, sometimes only muttering a few words and passing on. Robert waited for him in sweating anxiety. He was horribly ashamed of his drawing and he tried blindly to hide it from the master by leaning forward and almost crouching over it.

'Let me see what you've been doing,' Mr Bridgeman said, mildly enough. Robert sat back and smiled shamefacedly. He could say nothing and waited for the master to speak.

'This is just fun,' Mr Bridgeman said at last. 'I don't mind your having fun, but it isn't the way to learn drawing.'

He took the pencil from Robert's hand and sat down on the donkey. Robert stood over him, watching uneasily.

'In drawing you must learn to construct, not just to depict surfaces.' Mr Bridgeman started to draw in a corner of Robert's paper. Madame David was soon turned into a series of tubes which exaggerated and brought out her volume and stance. Mr Bridgeman suddenly got up the middle of his drawing and passed on, saying no more.

Just as Robert was about to begin again, the pose came to an end and Madame David disappeared once more into her little box. The heat in the room was becoming stupefying. It made Robert's head buzz. The dust-laden atmosphere, thick with the smell of the stove and the students, seemed to coat the inside of his nostrils.

Madame David danced out in her black silk stockings, looking depraved and jolly. She seemed an impossible mixture – a benevolent Beardsley woman – a good-natured vixen. She held her hands coquettishly and pointed one toe in a graceful, dainty pose most unsuitable to her. Robert thought that she would now be good to paint, for the black stockings brought out the pearly, nacrous quality of her flesh and made the mauve tint acceptable.

He fumbled through the rest of the lesson, trying to get some sort of scribble down each time, before Madame David put on yet another garment. In the days in the Life Room that were to follow he was to learn that Madame David was almost the only model who was alive and human. Many of the others seemed drugged, apathetic, enveloped in a mist.

The class broke up noisily, there was a sudden surge of animal life in the students. They banged their boards noisily as they put them away. Girls pushed back their hair and reddened their mouths and men tap-danced clumsily and sang. Billings, the good-looking lame boy with the aggressive chin, sang 'Trees' with passion. He always did.

Robert made his way down to the lavatories, where rows of people were washing their brushes in the basins. The soap was being thrown along the line with much swearing and laughing. Each man ran his brushes round the hollow which had been made in the soap, then he rubbed the brush vigorously on the palm of his hand, making various coloured foams, one after the other.

Robert did not wait to wash the black lead off his hands; he went down to the refectory dirty as he was and bought 'milk with a dash' and two huge shortbread biscuits. One or two North Country students seemed to consider these biscuits an extravagant luxury. They twitted him now, as he sat down at the long table, on his liking for them.

'Twopence for a biscuit!' one said. 'I wouldn't pay twopence for a biscuit when they give you a whole plate of soup for that!'

'But you don't want soup at tea-time,' Robert suggested.

'Why not?' the other asked, and he managed to put into this question the intimation that he thought Robert impossibly affected and refined in not considering soup for tea.

There was little more conversation. The North Country students continued to talk amongst themselves – such a mixture of bawdiness, housewifely gossip on substantial meals and good lodgings, and their progress in their art-teachers' course – the urns hissed and the waitresses joked or were rude as the students streamed up to the counter to buy.

Robert left early. Going down the long passage, he pushed open the swing doors and stood amongst the sooty bushes. It was already dark outside; lights winked and glittered and the trams sent out electric sparks. He passed through the entrance gates and walked to the bus stop. Other people were gathered there in an unhappy knot. All their faces seemed worn down with pain and ugliness. He could not bear to look. He felt the wave of gloom and despair sweeping over him. He jerked his feet about to stop it and threw out his hands, turning his head from side to side, as if to shake off his trouble.

When the bus drew up he climbed the stairs and sat right in front. He watched the people on the pavements and the shopkeepers in their lighted windows. It was nearly closing-time; there was a final bustle before the shutters went up. He noticed again those unpleasant pink lights with which the butchers illuminated their meat. The warm boudoir-pink glow made the raw pieces of dead animal even more horrible.

He got off the bus at the Green Man and started to walk over the heath. In the distance he could just see the last glimmering of the Ranger's House and the gates of Greenwich Park. It was windy on the heath, and far away, as if in a deep valley, seemed to lie the whole of London. In the air above hung that puce glow which always gave Robert a slight sense of wonder. He thought it one of the most extraordinary colours in the world, and often tried to define it, saying that it was like the curious purple of a burnt-out fire-grate.

In Chesterfield Walk the lovers had already congregated. Each bend was occupied, sometimes with two couples; and under the heavy, ancient trees, which now afforded no extra shadow, men and girls still leant against the painful, corrugated bark as they had done in the summer.

Robert walked over the gravel behind the seats. If ever he learned how to draw he wanted to make a picture of the lovers under the trees in the dark. The problem of the night setting never ceased to tease him. He could see in his mind's eye the grouping of the lovers – the darkness fusing them into pyramids, two-headed ghosts and strange pagodas – but how was he to re-create the actual darkness?

He walked down Croom's Hill, passed the Catholic church and came to his lodging. His room was in a Queen Anne house which had been altered and refitted in the later eighteenth century, in the Regency, and again towards the end of Queen Victoria's reign. Now it was a guest-house, with hot and cold water in the bedrooms. The basin in Robert's room cut into the high wainscot brutally. He hated to look at the fine thick wood gouged and cut out to make a passage for the snake-like pipes. Around the rest of the wainscot he had balanced his old green and gold plates and, close to his bed, a whole row of brilliant oranges. Sometimes in the early morning he would fall on these oranges greedily, eating them one after another or squeezing the delicious juice from three or four of them into his toothglass. Then he would bring back more oranges the next evening to replenish his line along the wainscot.

The chief glory of Robert's room, and the object which had decided him in coming to the house, was the Adams mantelpiece which stood across one corner. The extreme refinement of its detail made one think that it was moulded in composition and not carved in wood. It looked a thoroughly commercial product of the late eighteenth century, but how attractive it was! How 'elegant' and 'chaste'! That there were probably ten thousand other mantelpieces with bas-reliefs of rams' heads, swags, husks and quivers of arrows made from the same moulds did not matter in the least.

A squat little gas-fire stood on the old, cracked marble hearth. All the rest of the room, including the high wainscot, had been repainted a thick pinkish-grey, but the mantelpiece had been reverently left shabby, with half a dozen different coats of paint showing on the most worn and polished surfaces.

The only window, which looked out on to the park, was charming. It was really a triptych – the largest light with semi-circular head in the middle, flanked on each side by little slits only three panes high and one across. Miss Middlesborough, who owned the house, said that the little slits had been blocked up when she bought the house; they had only been discovered when her architect brother went round methodically, knocking all the walls with his stick. He heard the hollow sound, tore away the wallpaper and the canvas on which it was stretched, and there were the little openings stuffed with old rubbish and newspaper but still complete with their thick wooden sash frames and old glass. Outside the house the stucco covering had to be taken away; then the old curved glass let through the light again, after perhaps a hundred years.

As Robert lay in bed in the morning he delighted to look through this distorting, mauvish glass. It twisted the trees in the park into shaky, watery shapes and made any birds which flew across look jagged or worm-like.

Little wheeled traffic passed up and down Croom's Hill; the chief noise was the ringing of feet on the pavement and voices talking. Until far into the night couples or groups of people seemed to be going up to the heath or coming down from it.

Now, as Robert entered his room, he pushed the window up at the top to shut out the sound; then he washed his hands and brushed his hair in preparation for supper.

As he went downstairs to the dining-room he heard a faint twanging and knew that Miss Middlesborough's old father was playing his great golden harp in the basement. He played entirely according to his own whim and fancy, never having learnt to read music. The strains were unrecognizable as European melodies, but old Mr Middlesborough would have it that they were hymns and sacred airs. Sometimes he would sing in high, goatish falsetto; then the whole effect was almost overwhelmingly bizarre and strange, especially if he could be seen as well as heard; for it would be discovered that he dressed for his harp-playing in an old corded dressing-gown and curious woollen cap which, together with his little square beard, lent him a strikingly Jewish and Old Testament appearance.

Robert was the first down; he sat by the fire and waited. The dining-room was the least altered part of the house. The plain, thick-moulded, early-eighteenth-century mantel, with its grey marble surround, held an art nouveau grate, but apart from this, and the window which had been added perhaps in the Regency, the room was as it had been planned. A heavy, indented cornice joined the ceiling to the walls richly; there were shutters and a seat to the original window and the door was very wide with huge L-shaped hinges. So many coats of paint covered the woodwork that in some places the carving and moulding were almost lost sight of.

Elsie, the maid, came in with the soup. She was a beautiful girl who managed to work for Miss Middlesborough and also to act as usherette in a cinema. Robert never understood how she did it. Tall, delicately thin and brittle looking, she always wore her cheap, brilliant clothes charmingly. Now, as she came in with the soup, she had a vermilion jersey with glass buttons, and a silly little sprigged apron tied over her navy-blue skirt. Her lovely transparent face, so very well painted and enriched, turned towards Robert as she put the plates down on the table.

'Good evening,' she said guardedly, with only the beginning of a smile.

Steps were heard crossing the hall; the door opened and the curate of St Saviour's came in. He was a pale, flat-faced man of twenty-eight or twenty-nine, who smoked many cigarettes and spoke of himself as the 'Reverend Parker' in telephone conversations. He came from an industrial town on the borders of England and Wales and always wore the very light-grey flannel trousers which had been fashionable there in his early youth.

He gave Elsie an extravagantly bold look and said, 'Hello, Beautiful!' She bridled, and turned towards him in spite of herself. She seemed genuinely to despise him, yet she could not help taking notice of him.

'Who are you talking to?' she asked, turning an elaborately blank stare on him.

'Who do you think, my dear? Him?' he added, pointing at Robert with his nicotined finger, and chortling at his own display of wickedness and perversity.

Robert squirmed in his armchair and turned his face abruptly to the fire. The vulgarity of the 'Reverend Parker' was insufferable. He remembered the one horrible occasion when he had gone into the lovely Hawksmoor church and found this creature mouthing and aping, his unpleasant voice made far more repulsive by a top-dressing of ecclesiastical refinement.

It was in vain that Robert told himself not to be bourgeois and reactionary; nothing could reconcile him to beings of this type. It was not snobbishness that made him hate them; it was their snobbishness that he hated; their pitiful little shams: their cloak of what they grandly imagined to be aristocratic wickedness and daring; their appalling assumption that they were as good as he was, if not better.

Robert laughed to himself as this last thought passed through his head. His conceit always tickled him. But he still found it good not to dislike the 'Reverend Parker' for any reason but that of his insensitive stupidity and pretentiousness.

Parker was now twitting Elsie on her lack of response to his gay salutation.

'I don't know why you say things like that, Mr Parker,' she answered flatly.

'Why shouldn't I say good evening to a pretty girl?' Parker gave an exaggerated leer.

'Why don't you just be yourself?' asked Elsie with detachment, as she left the room.

'Funny girl, that!' said Parker to Robert. 'Can't take a bit of fun as it's meant. When she brings my breakfast up in the morning her face never changes if I say something bright; she just puts the tray down, says "Good morning" and leaves the room.' He mused for a moment, then added, 'I suppose she's nervous at me taking notice of her.'

This suggestion was so outrageous that Robert felt relieved when he found that he need not answer, for Miss Calthrop entered at this moment and Parker immediately began to talk to her.

'Good evening, your ladyship; and how are your patients?' he said. Miss Calthrop was the Lady Almoner in a hospital, which always seemed to amuse him.

'They're as well as can be expected; and how are your parishioners, Mr Parker, if I may ask?'

'Oh, I suppose they get along as best they can. I never see anyone but old women in church – and a few young ones,' he added after a pause, as if he owed it to himself not to underrate his powers of attraction. 'The Vicar got all high and mighty this morning after early service because he could see my flannel bags below my cassock – said it wasn't reverent and I must get something dark – damned if I will!'

They sat down now at the table, for Miss Calthrop said that her two friends, who also had rooms in the house, were out to dinner.

The food was well cooked and appetizing. Elsie served them in perfect silence and Parker talked loudly about his fiancée.

'Every time I see her she tells me she's got something more for our future home. It's frightful, Miss Calthrop; a man feels tied hand and foot when his fiancée keeps collecting more and more stuff together. I'm quite weighed down under all her wardrobes and carpets and toast-racks.'

'You're a very lucky man,' said Miss Calthrop, heavily defending her sex. 'And you ought to be extremely grateful that you have such a provident girl for your future wife.'

'Oh, I'm grateful all right,' said Parker, with mock resignation. Robert knew in a moment why he could not bear him – it was because he was always approximating himself to some character in cheap fiction – now he was the long-suffering, hen-pecked male. It was really too disgusting. Robert remembered the wonderful phrase in *Lord Chesterfield's Advice to His Son* – the bit about hating fools so profoundly because in their company he always felt himself a fool.

Robert felt utterly humiliated at having to eat with such a creature. With what thankfulness he saw him go out of the room after Miss Calthrop! He sat down again by the fire, blissfully alone once more. Miss Middlesborough came in with a cup of coffee for him. He thanked her and then burst out, 'That Mr Parker is really too appalling!'

'He is a little bumptious, isn't he?' agreed Miss Middlesborough. 'But he isn't a nuisance in the house, and he's quite kind to people in his way.'

Miss Middlesborough went out of the room again and Robert leant towards the bookcase to read the titles. A Greek lexicon, some early bound *Chambers's Journal*, Thackeray's *The Virginians*, several obscure novels and *The Essays of Elia* stood closely packed together. Robert chose the Lamb, and started to read about the wonderful old house in which the child used to roam. It was exactly what he loved to read about, so he quite forgot his surroundings until the front-door bell rang. It was very loud, and he could not help noticing it, but he did not imagine it had anything to do with him, until the dining-room door opened and Gerard Hope stood in front of him.

He jumped up from his chair, looking a little too surprised for absolute politeness. He had only been spoken to by Hope on the day before, when they had both found themselves alone in the Antique Room. It had been towards the end of the day and Robert was the only one still trying to draw the Clapping Faun. Hope, a senior student, had come in to arrange a still-life group for one of the evening classes, for to act as pupil-teacher was part of his course.

He looked across at Robert and saw *De Profundis* lying on the donkey in front of him.

'What d'you think of that?' he asked smiling.

'Not very much; I bought it off a stall at lunch-time; I've read somewhere that it was all cut about before it was published. That's what's wrong with it, I expect – most of it's left out!'

They both laughed and went on talking about Oscar Wilde. Neither of them knew very much and there were pauses.

'What do you do in the evenings?' Hope asked at last.

A little taken aback by the direct question, Robert answered hurriedly, 'Oh, I don't know; I read and go for walks over the heath.'

'That sounds rather gloomy. Don't you ever get depressed?'

'Sometimes – but I don't think it's what I do that makes me depressed.'

'What is it, then?' asked Hope rather sharply. Robert could not answer, and again there was a slight pause.

'I have to spend most of my evenings going round to my various friends and cheering them up,' said Hope, showing a little too much gaiety and brightness.

It was clear to Robert that Hope wished also to come and cheer him up one evening, so he was prepared for the next question: 'Whereabouts do you live?'

'I have a room in an old house in Croom's Hill. Do you know it? Opposite Greenwich Park.'

'Oh, I know it quite well; I live fairly near there myself. How far up or down the hill are you? What is the number of the house?'

Robert told him with that slight feeling of reluctance which comes when another has been working hard for information. He got up, put away his drawing-board and said goodnight rather more abruptly then he would ordinarily have done.

Now here was Hope in the doorway waiting to be welcomed.

'I just thought I'd look in to see if you were at home, since I was out in this direction,' he said breezily as he took off his gloves.

Robert held out his hands to take Hope's coat and then pulled another chair up to the fire. Hope sat down and held his hands to the flames; Robert noticed that his nails were very clean and very carefully filed. This surprised him, for art students generally had nails black with pencil dust or gruesomely coloured with Slizanne crimson or some other staining colour. Hope's hands too were very smooth and white, with only a very few dark hairs on them; and this also was surprising, for his small round head was covered with almost black hair, and although he could be no more than twenty his jowl and upper-lip were already swarthy, and rough with shaving.

He suddenly looked up at Robert, and Robert was able to notice that his eyes were of a quite clear blue-grey. They held a curious glittering expression which was too bird-like or lizard-like to be comfortable.

'I've just had some coffee,' said Robert, looking at his empty cup. 'Wouldn't you like a cup too? I'll go and ask Miss Middlesborough.' But as he got up to go to the door Miss Middlesborough came in bearing a tray with coffee-pot and milk and biscuits on it.

'I thought your friend might like something hot, and I don't suppose you'd say no to another cup either!' she said, smiling at Robert.

They both thanked her warmly, as people do when their wishes have been granted with no effort on their part. Robert enjoyed pouring out the coffee. He passed the biscuits to Hope, and they settled down to talk. Hope seemed determined to interest and amuse his new acquaintance. He started on the topic of the public schools – always so fertile a field for anecdotes of the ridiculous and the sexy. From this he jumped in some way to the supernatural, and Robert suddenly found himself listening intently to an experience which had befallen Hope. The scene (at least in Robert's mind) was an ancient schoolyard with a church on one side and the ruins of a priory on the other. Hope was there with a countryman and two dogs. They seemed to be waiting for something. Soon a shape, eddying and swirling and menacing, appears through the broken arches of the priory. The dogs bristle and bare their teeth. The countryman runs forward with a heavy stick and Hope closely follows him – only to find that the menacing shape is made by the smoke from a smouldering fire left by some gypsies who have encamped amongst the ruins.

At the end of the story Hope smiled and Robert tried to hide his disappointment at the anticlimax; for at the beginning of the story his interest had been gripped.

'It didn't really happen to me at all, you know!' Hope said complacently. 'I wrote it for a Somerset magazine and they printed it last month.'

Angry and confused at having shown so clearly his belief in the fiction, Robert turned red and said, 'You completely took me in.' Then, before he realized what he was doing, he held his wrist out and looked at his watch. It was well past midnight, and he suddenly knew that he had enjoyed Hope's visit, for otherwise the hours would not have melted away thus rapidly.

'It's frightfully late,' he said gaily. 'Do you think you've lost your last bus or tram or train or whatever you travel by?'

He was yet to learn that Hope never missed buses or trains – unless he had planned to.

'Oh no, there are several more yet,' Hope answered calmly; 'anyhow, I can always walk if I do miss the last one.'

They both got up and Robert helped Hope into his coat. Softly he drew the huge bolts of the front door and undid the unwieldy chain. The whole house was sleeping.

He walked down the steps with Hope and their feet went ringing over the pavements together, for a little way; they said goodbye at the corner, and Hope asked Robert to come to his house for their next meeting.

Robert ran back, thinking of how stimulating this new friend was. 'He actually tries to be interesting and amusing to other people!' he said to himself in wonder. He as yet only saw this as a virtue.

II

After that night Robert saw a lot of Hope – not at the school, but in the evenings, after work. He went to Hope's house for a meal. He did not want to go, for he was afraid that he would have to eat food he did not like, but when he arrived at the house in Queen's Grove, somewhere down a road leading to the river, he found that Mrs Hope was out and that they had the house to themselves. Hope had laid the meal in a little room leading off the kitchen. Two candle flames sailed and swam in the air above the table, the rest of the room was in darkness. Hope took a casserole from the hob-grate and held it in a folded napkin. When he dug the cold spoon into the spaghetti, the rich pink sauce spat and bubbled, it was so hot.

'Did you make this yourself?' said Robert with a new respect, as he tasted the delicious dish.

'Of course; we have no slaves. We're so poor we have to live in a slum, as you've already noticed.'

He turned his eyes straight on to Robert and gave him a metallic smile. Robert was thrown into confusion, fearing that his face had betrayed him on entering the house.

Someone ran boisterously up the stairs, taking two or three at a time, it would seem.

'Who's that?' asked Robert, surprised. 'I thought you said that you only lived with your mother and that she was out.'

'Oh, that's my eldest brother. He has a separate flat on the top floor with his wife. We have nothing to do with them; they only use the stairs.'

'What does he do?' asked Robert, not having learnt yet that this is not a good social gambit.

'He's a chemist,' said Hope, adding hurriedly, 'not the sort that keeps a shop, you know, but the research sort.'

They both laughed nervously and fell to eating. Robert noticed how thoughtfully the table was laid. Under the glasses were little painted discs from a German beer-garden. Gothic scripts, brilliantly enamelled flowers and animals spotted the wood. An arrangement of gaudy dyed feathers and crisp paper flowers frothed out of a Victorian white china boot.

'You have made the table pretty,' Robert said appreciatively.

'Oh, do you like it?' asked Hope as carelessly as possible; and from this Robert could tell how much time and thought had been given to the little meal. He felt pleased and flattered and wanted to do justice to it all.

Hope poured out more cider and took away the spaghetti plates. He lifted another dish from the hob, this time a glass one, and said, 'This is a sort of special apple charlotte that someone told me of. You put treacle and lemon juice and other things in it too.'

'How lovely it sounds!' Robert exclaimed. 'You really ought to be a chef, not waste your time painting!'

'Shall we clear away and wash up now?' asked Robert, with a little too much eagerness, at the end of the meal. Hope was clearly offended and shocked.

'Good God, no! My mother will do that when she comes in. We haven't had our coffee yet. Let's take it into the other room.'

He stooped down and picked up the brown French earthenware pots, asking Robert to carry the absurd little cups and the sugar.

Nothing has been left to the last moment, thought Robert. Even the coffee is hot and ready on the hob, so that all we have to do is to drink it!

They went down the narrow passage, Hope leading the way and turning up the gas with a soft plop, as they entered the sitting-room.

'You see how primitive we are!' he said, grinning at the bracket. 'Doesn't it give you an effect of Gissing and Constantin Guys and Ernest Dowson?'

'My grandfather will never have anything else,' Robert said hurriedly. 'He thinks the light is much kinder to the eyes.' 'How queer this sounds,' he thought; 'the gas has made me stilted and Victorian.'

'Sit on the corner of the sofa near the fire,' ordered Hope.

Robert let his eyes travel round the room. Above the mantelpiece was a large picture by Hope. It was a still-life of an unrolled map, on which lay a coiled rope, a shell, a globe and an elaborate gilt bird-cage in which was imprisoned the plaster cast of an eye of heroic size. The painting was meticulous and plain, with no tricks of surface or texture. This plainness and approximation to the actual objects reinforced the obvious symbolism. Robert knew that the huge eye in the cage was Hope surveying all the countries of the world from the house in Queen's Grove.

'That's awfully good!' said Robert, much impressed. 'How on earth did you do the bird-cage with the eye in it? – all those bars and then the ones behind them – I would have got terribly confused.'

'My mother thinks it's frightful,' said Hope. 'And someone else who saw it said that I was obviously trying to be a surrealist, but I just did it for my still-life subject last term. I didn't even know what a surrealist was then.'

'What a good thing! It wouldn't have been nearly so good if you had known – don't you think I'm right?'

'Yes, perhaps you are. If I'd seen more surrealist pictures I might have spoilt my own by putting in some entrails, and one of those sticky, sluggish streams which might be milk, or blood, or ink, or all three mixed together!'

'Why do they copy so?' asked Robert, with a worried look. 'Or is everyone's subconscious stuffed with the same images? I can't believe that.'

'It's all fashion. You'll see; it will change from broken-nosed statues and ferns and entrails and giblets and web-footed babies into something quite different in a year or two,' said Hope. 'I like it, don't you, in spite of so many shams? Art needed it badly, I think. All those apples on plates and bits of newspaper under fish – oh, and the violins and guitars – they were getting dreadfully boring, weren't they?'

'They were – those people who shrieked "literary!", as an insult, were also getting terribly boring. Of course, they're shrieking it more than ever now, but happily the surrealists have made people understand that it isn't an adjective only to be applied to the criminal classes in painting.'

The conversation was becoming a little stilted; for it is not usual for students to talk much of their work, unless in heated argument.

Hope picked up a book and sat down next to Robert on the sofa. 'Do you like looking at old photographs?' he asked.

'Love it,' said Robert. 'I can never really have too much. Snapshots are best – when people have their hair down, or are caught in their bathing-slips, looking absurd, or perhaps much better than in their clothes. Then there is the sad part too. Don't you feel terribly sad when you look at the pictures five years, ten years old? When you see yourself as you were and when you remember everything that has been caught in the snapshot, the minute twigs on the bush, the flowers and the corner of the garden-seat or wheelbarrow?'

'These are snapshots,' said Hope. 'So I hope you'll find them absurd and sad enough.'

He opened the book, resting one of the boards on Robert's knee and drawing himself closer, so that the book should not fall between them.

'This is me at three years old with my father,' he pointed out.

Robert saw a little boy in a white fur cap, holding the hand of a large ungainly man with a spade.

'He was always digging in the garden,' Hope explained. 'That's how he killed himself in the end. He saw an enormous weed and pulled at it with all his might. Of course, it had a root yards long, and the next thing we knew was that my father had fallen down dead. You see, he was over seventy-five. I've got a sister of fifty – isn't it amazing?'

'What did they say when you appeared?' asked Robert in mock surprise.

'I hardly like to think,' answered Hope in the same vein, with mock primness.

Wedged close to the fire, Robert began to feel very hot. He could not move away because Hope was sitting so near him on the other side. The stiff pages were turned, one by one, very slowly. Hope put one arm along the back of the sofa behind Robert's neck; then, when a particularly funny picture was discovered and they were both shaking with laughter, he placed his other hand over Robert's, under the book as if to steady him.

Robert finished his laugh carefully; then, with a jerk, he jumped to his feet, saying with unnatural heartiness, 'Christ, I'm hot! Sitting so close to the fire and all that laughing have made me sweat like anything!'

He made as if to wipe his face with something from his pocket, then found it to be the remains of the bright paper napkin he had had at supper.

'Look what I'm trying to do!' he said, gaily throwing the ragged paper on to the flames with a flourish.

Hope watched him with a show of detached amusement. His head was well back on the cushions of the sofa and he had thrown his feet up, so that he lay full length. Robert noticed for the first time how hollow his cheeks were for so young a man. He also saw in a flash that the curious glittering of Hope's eyes was due to nothing so much as to his habit of puckering the skin all round them when he looked at things or people. It was as if his face contracted in tingling excitement as he fixed his gaze.

Now he looked at Robert almost contemptuously, as if to say, 'What are you gesticulating and jumping about out there for? Why do you get covered with confusion for no reason at all? You're hysterical.'

'Play something for me,' said Robert, looking towards the black cottage piano hurriedly.

Hope lazily got to his feet and asked, 'What would you like?'

'Anything,' said Robert. 'You play and I'll dance a gay fandango, or a stately pavane, or a sprightly jig, or whatever it may be.'

Hope broke into 'Shepherd's Hey' with syncopated variations of his own. He really played extremely competently, with a rather attractive touch of vulgarity.

Robert threw his arms and legs out with wild abandon, since nobody was there to watch. Sweat trickled down his face and ran into his eyes, but he said, 'Go on! Go on!' when Hope made as if to leave the piano stool. The piece, and with it the mood, changed; Hope played something of Schumann's and, after it, 'The Merry, Merry Pipes of Pan'.

Robert rushed at him excitedly. 'Stop that appalling tune,' he shrieked through the noise. Hope let his hands fall from the keyboard and looked up in surprise. He did not enjoy being interrupted.

'Don't you hate it yourself?' asked Robert in amazement. 'I hate it more than – than Kipling's "If",' he finished with spluttering emphasis.

'Why should you dislike it more than any other light tune of that period?' asked Hope coldly.

'I don't know, I can't think. It's just repulsive to me.'

Hope would play no more after this, and Robert was exhausted, so they both sat down in silence and waited.

'Would you like to see my own room?' Hope asked at last, not knowing what to say.

'Yes, do show it to me. But after that I really must go. It's so late.'

Robert followed Hope up the linoleum-lined stairs. The turned banisters looked Edwardian and mean. Hope turned the gas up in his room, and the first thing Robert saw was a line of boots: a huge pair of wellingtons, some wooden clogs and a pair of fur-lined snowboots.

'I love boots,' said Hope, rather pleased to explain his idiosyncrasy.

'Do you ever go out in your wooden clogs?' asked Robert, to be amusing.

Hope took him quite seriously. 'Of course not. I hate making myself conspicuous.' He turned his gaze on to Robert's rather extravagant clothes and let it stay there for a moment.

Robert lifted his eyes hastily and took in the rest of the room. Hope had arranged a rope in loops all round the cornice, and the panels of the door were painted with harsh Greek honeysuckle and key patterns. On the desk two very gaudy Russian dolls sprawled drunkenly, and the mantelpiece was decorated with a long line of those frightfully painted German discs, two of which had been used under the glasses on the table at supper. More of Hope's paintings stood with their faces to the wall and a riding-crop was nailed up over the bed.

'I'm not sporting or sadistic or masochistic,' said Hope laconically, noticing the direction of Robert's gaze. 'I found it in a field near Dorking and brought it home as a souvenir. It's got M.E.R. on the silver band. What do you think it can stand for? Marcus Edward Rawlins, I always tell myself.'

They both laughed at the nasty name, and Robert said, 'Wouldn't it be awful if you scourged yourself with the hunting-crop every night before you went to sleep? I can imagine you as a holy man being proud of the drops of blood that trickled down the white wall.'

'Can you?' asked Hope interestedly. He really seemed flattered that he could be imagined in this character. 'I'm afraid I'm not a very holy man, though. Religion doesn't mean anything to me and it never has. I know that your sort often adores going to church for the smells and the sights and the pretty bells; but it just seems utterly silly to me and I get irritated and come out.'

'What do you mean by "my sort"?' Robert asked suspiciously, a little fiercely.

'Oh, you know, the romantic, airy-fairy sort that loves to be titillated; that gets carried away.'

'It sounds as if I was the sort of person who loves to be tickled all over with feathers; and who was that Roman emperor who buried his boys in rose leaves and then picked the petals off one by one in his mouth? I suppose you think I'm like that. What peculiar impressions we give other people!'

'Are you sure you've got the story right?' asked Hope with interest, ignoring the last part of the sentence. 'I think I must read about the Roman emperors. They seem to have left no stone unturned where sensations are concerned.'

'Who wants to be titillated now?' asked Robert in triumph.

'I must go,' he said, moving to the door. 'I shan't get enough sleep unless I do.'

'Do you think of things like that?' asked Hope incredulously.

'Yes, don't you?' was Robert's simple reply. 'I suppose we all have our own fads, however old or young we are – yours may be that you must get enough exercise, or that you must be "regular", as the advertisements put it.'

'But I am "regular"!' said Hope almost angrily. And Robert knew that that was *his* fad.

Hope turned the gas low in his room and saw Robert down the dark stairs to the front door.

'Goodbye, I have enjoyed myself,' said Robert. 'You're a fine cook!'

'Shall we go for a long walk in the country one weekend?' asked Hope rather rapidly and disconnectedly, as if he were afraid that the suggestion would not be liked.

'Yes, let's!' said Robert, taken aback, but not unpleased. 'We could both take sandwiches and chocolate and fruit, or find a not too Tudor tea-house, if it were too cold to sit out of doors.'

'Good, we'll fix it up soon, then.'

The door clicked sharply and Robert heard Hope walking down the passage. He was to learn that at meetings or partings Hope was always abrupt and brusque – like a schoolboy aggressively self-contained with his parents on Speech Day.

III

It was the very earliest spring – all mud and puddles and winter aconites with petals unpleasantly like the stiff wings torn off poor beetles. The shell-like shape and brittleness were so exactly alike. The patches of blue seemed to be racing as well as the clouds in the sky. Robert had brought his silver-knobbed stick and Hope his umbrella. Each regarded the emblem of the other with disfavour.

'Where on earth did you get that from?' asked Hope, pointing to the cane.

'In a junk shop. It cost five and six. Isn't it nice? Have you seen all the little Chinese people on the silver knob, and isn't the Malacca fine?'

'Don't you think it's rather stagy?' suggested Hope.

'Perhaps I like the stage,' said Robert, adding as sweetly as possible, 'Haven't you ever learnt to roll an umbrella?'

'What's the good of rolling an umbrella when one has to use it every other moment?'

'Don't you think it looks just a tiny bit drab blowing about and flapping in the wind? They always remind me of meat-teas or funerals or the "smell of a congregation on a wet Sunday afternoon", as Aldous Huxley has put it.'

'I'm afraid I don't a bit mind being taken for a member of the middle classes, if that's what you mean; and are you quite sure that you've got that quotation absolutely right?'

They trudged on in silence, disgruntled with each other. Hope had arranged the whole day. He had suggested that they should take the train down to Dorking and walk to a charming cottage he knew of, where they could have tea. Robert had agreed to everything, finding the plan already laid so carefully.

They passed a long line of trees which dipped down into a

hollow and then rose, leading the eye to a little church on the top of the hill.

'The vicar of that church used to be a great friend of ours when we were small,' said Hope, pointing with his umbrella; 'he was so fond of my brother that he wanted to adopt him. I can't think why, for my brother was a fiendish child. He invented a terrible game called Operations. For this, I had to strip myself naked and lie down on the table, which had already been covered with a sheet. Then my brother, dressed in another sheet, with a handkerchief tied across his mouth and nose, would approach me, a devilish look in his eyes. Sometimes he would produce an enormous jack-knife and scrape it across my shivering flesh; but worse, far worse, were the times when he passed electric shocks through me. You can guess what part of me he chose for these experiments. The pleasure, the pain, the excitement and the shame are vivid to me still. One day the vicar silently opened our bedroom door, just as the operation was coming to an end. He must have seen my brother's intent, gloating face and my own agonized one. He must have seen my naked, twitching limbs, the electric battery, and what was being done to me, but he said nothing. For a second I saw his glasses glittering as he watched us, seemingly fascinated, then he brushed his hand roughly across his mouth and shut the door with a click. My brother only came to with the sound of the door. His head jerked up and he looked about him rather wildly. I told him that the vicar had seen; he rushed at me with my shirt and pulled it over my head, telling me to dress myself at once. The sheets were folded up and put away and the batteries hidden. We waited, not daring to go downstairs. Through my fear and horror I hoped that this would stop my brother from ever practising on me again. It did; for although the vicar never said anything about it to our mother and father, we lived in terror that he would. He never even mentioned it to us, or hinted that he had seen. Don't you think that was curious?'

'Yes,' said Robert, 'unless one imagines that the poor parson was much too ashamed and horrified ever to think of your brother's wickedness again. But, tell me, did it change his attitude to your brother?'

'Not a bit; he seemed to be more affectionate towards him than ever!'

Robert laughed loudly and Hope joined in. The walk was much more enjoyable now that they were swinging along in a rhythm of mind and body. There were no more arguments about sticks or umbrellas, and although they were not in any way marching in step, a sort of coherence had been established between their movements which helped both of them along.

'Walking with someone else is much easier, isn't it?' said Robert.

'Sometimes,' Hope answered carefully.

The cottage, lost in the fields, with only the narrowest lane leading to it, came into view.

'How do they ever get enough customers?' asked Robert. 'Nobody would know that it existed, unless they were told.'

'Well, I suppose people do tell, then,' said Hope. 'You see, it's a sort of guest-house as well; you can have rooms there.'

They pushed open the little wooden gate and walked up the brick path, which was mossy and treacherously slimy.

'This is where we fracture our thighs and remain in bed for life,' Robert called out gaily as his muddy shoes slipped.

Hope knocked on the door; it was opened to them by an elderly woman in glasses, whose white hair had that curious nicotine-stained tint at the sides. It was dressed in what Robert always thought of as the cow-pat manner, that is, puffed out at the sides and flattened on the top. She seemed genteel and therefore uninviting. Robert was about to regret being brought to the cottage, but then she left them and he felt contented again.

Two people were already in the living-room, sitting close to the huge fire and talking in whispers. They were very much in earnest about something, for they filled their mouths with scones and jam and cream and then leant over their steaming teacups, nearly touching noses in their eagerness.

'Are they in love?' whispered Robert.

'I don't think so. I think they're discussing the supernatural. Astral bodies and ectoplasm and all that stuff.'

'You don't think anything will happen, do you?' asked Robert in mock alarm. 'I should hate it if an incubus or succubus or something came along and started doing things!' He turned in his chair and saw the two cats on the other side of the fire.

'Just look at those huge, enormous capon-cats!' he cried out in surprise.

'I thought you'd like them.' Hope smiled complacently. 'Have you ever seen such animals? They just sit there all day licking their fur and drinking milk.'

'But their faces! – they're so conceited they can only blink.'

'Wouldn't you be conceited with fur like that?'

'But think of the price they've had to pay! That ought to have knocked some of the stuffing out of them.'

'No doubt it has,' said Hope with an elaborately wry smile.

'Stop it, stop it; the spiritualists will hear,' hissed Robert.

The tea arrived and they started to spread their scones with jam and cream.

'I'll be hostess,' piped Robert in falsetto, seizing the teapot and arching his neck gracefully. 'How do you like your tea, Mrs Hope? Milk in first and two lumps?'

He smiled at Hope roguishly and crooked his little finger, as he held the sugar tongs over the bowl.

Hope immediately became a restraining influence. 'Do be careful,' he said, 'or they'll send for the police and have you taken away, you're so convincing.'

They stuffed their mouths with scone and talked quietly, until the intent couple got up to go. Then they smiled at each other and relaxed and went to sit in the chimney-seat, where they sprawled out their legs to the fire. Robert, as he lay back, played with one of the huge cats. It bore with it for a little and seemed almost about to purr, when it suddenly changed its mind and gave one of his fingers a little darting bite. The shock made Robert sit up. He held out his finger, but no blood came. He felt disappointed.

'That'll teach you not to take liberties!' Hope said with glee. 'Would *you* care for it if a perfect stranger began to tickle *your* ears?'

They asked for the bill and divided it scrupulously. The white-haired woman gave them a coldly curious look through her spectacles, and they wondered about a tip.

'She is too genteel,' said Robert firmly, as she moved away.

The walk back to the station was long and dreary. They began to quarrel almost as soon as they left the cottage. Robert wanted to cut across some fields and Hope told him bluntly that he did not know the way. Their strides did not coincide; one was always in front of the other, or behind.

The twinkling lights of the station were a relief to them both. They sat back in the carriage and sighed. Other people clambered in and wedged tightly against them. Robert shut his eyes and pretended to go to sleep.

IV

At the art school Robert was gradually being accepted by the other students. Some of them called out to him now as he arrived in the morning, and the lame boy, Billings, told him dirty jokes or sang to him while he washed his brushes in the lavatory.

The two sisters, who worked with him in the Antique Room, suddenly became communicative. They called him 'Sonny Boy' in friendly derision and told him, in a roundabout way, of their budding love affairs. Nothing seemed to have happened yet, and Robert suspected that they had only met the young men once or twice, when other people were present. To be perverse, the dark, almost swarthy, younger one would say, 'I like an oldish man – grey at the temples and friendly wrinkles round the eyes and all that – they're so experienced!'

'Jane, why will you bring out all that novel muck?' her sister would ask exasperatedly. 'You know you'd hate a sugar-daddy more than anything else on earth.'

Robert wondered why they talked like this in front of him. He felt in some dim way he gave them encouragement. He never asked them deep questions, but he found himself showing more sympathy and understanding than he felt.

Sometimes they would suddenly switch from love to poetry. Being almost straight from their convent school at Ramsgate, they still thought of Rupert Brooke as a poet of today. Indeed, he was the latest one that they knew anything about.

'How marvellously handsome he was!' said Jane. And once she

brought a book to school with his portrait in the front. The photographer had taken him with naked shoulders and with his head thrown back, so that his glistening hair swept away in a wing.

'Do you think he took off his shirt in the photographer's studio, or did he just pull it down?' asked Robert. He was always repelled and fascinated and curious about these naked-shoulder photographs. Theirs seemed such a peculiar brand of vulgarity.

'What a ridiculous question to ask!' shrilled Jane indignantly. 'Why should it matter what he did, so long as the photograph was made?'

The taking off of shirts reminded Robert of the sculpture model.

'Have you seen the new sculpture model?' he asked innocently – adding after a moment, 'He's an all-in wrestler.'

The girls jumped to their feet.

'Let's go and see him,' they said together. 'Sonny Boy, you're to show us the way and chaperon us.'

Robert led them up the stairs and into the smaller modelling-room, where wire armatures and clay figures, wrapped in damp rags, gave the room a macabre and beggarly aspect. The half-pulled-down green blind bathed the ceiling of the room in a wicked, deep-sea light. Through the open door which led into the larger room they could see the students grouped round the model, busy at their stands. The model stood above them on the dais in a pose of arrested action. His tawny body was magnificent – everything coarse and blunt and strong.

'He must have a sun-ray lamp,' whispered Robert. 'He couldn't still be that colour from last summer.'

'Shut up!' said Jane sharply. She turned to her sister. 'Oh, Madge, isn't he marvellous!'

They all three began to move into the other room as quietly as possible; the master was not there. They stood at the foot of the dais and gazed up at the model. He truly was a fine-looking man, and it is so unusual for a model to be this that they did not trouble to hide their admiration – or not all of it.

Jane was the most open; her eyes glistened quite simply with reverence and lust, and her breath came in short, very gentle gasps. It was clear that she wanted to be his slave.

Madge just stared and smiled and looked rather pale. Robert

seemed more analytical; he wanted to study the excellence of the body. He envied it almost painfully – the hard thighs and stomach, the pectorals, Greek in their square-cut shape, the over-developed arms and legs with thin biceps and calves like hard rubber balls. And the wonderful brown stain on the skin with the red glow behind it – seen against the universal grey of the room, where everything was coated with clay dust – this colour seemed almost to vibrate and tingle.

One of the students called out, 'Rest.' The others laid down their tools, and the model, seeing Robert so close, put a hand on his shoulder and jumped down from the dais. As he jumped, his arm just brushed one of Robert's cheeks. Robert felt the hair on the forearm tickle, like spider's legs. A shiver went through him; he looked up and smiled at the model.

'Don't you get tired of holding that pose with your arms out?' he asked.

'Oh, I'm used to it now. It was different at the beginning. I used to think it harder work than wrestling.' He grinned at Robert and showed that one of his teeth had been chipped; but the effect was not unpleasant, for the tooth was still white, and all the rest of the face had a rough unfinished effect which blended. Robert saw how tough the skin was from sun and exposure. The coarse pores and stiff hairs reminded Robert of Gulliver in the bosom of the giant.

'Have you given up wrestling now?' asked Robert.

'Oh no. I do both. I'm having a rest from it now, though, as I hurt my arm.' The model straddled his feet apart and put his two thumbs under the string of his bright scarlet 'triangle'.

'Do they do all sorts of queer things and try to gouge your eyes out?' Robert asked, wanting to draw him.

'Some of them are dirty,' said the model; 'they try sticking their fingers up your nose. I always bite them if I can. Another chap always tries tweaking hair – scalp, chest, under your arms, anywhere – I've seen him tear out handfuls. God! It's painful! You wouldn't think it was so bad, but it is.'

Robert was pleased that the stories were getting horrific. He encouraged the model, until suddenly he found himself being used for a demonstration. 'I'll show you a trick or two,' the model said, comfortably and slickly. 'Just let yourself go loose and I'll do the rest.' He caught hold of Robert purposefully and twisted him round so that he fell on the floor; then, before he had had time to collect himself, the model had got him into some impossible position between his legs. Next, Robert found himself hanging over the model's back, being held by one leg.

The rest of the students began to laugh. 'Look at Sonny Boy being treated rough!' shrieked Madge and Jane gleefully. The model began to march up and down the room with Robert, like some trophy, still hanging down his back.

Robert was crimson in the face from laughing and struggling and being upside down. Learning a lesson from the model, he tweaked the hairs on his legs, as he hung down, and said, 'Let me up, let me up; I'm going to burst!'

The model was pretending to put him head-first into the clammy zinc-lined clay-bin, when the master who taught sculpture came in. He smiled at the scene and said, 'Work-time now; no more horse-play.'

The students went back to their stands. Robert adjusted his clothes and his hair as best he could, and moved to the door with Madge and Jane.

They settled down in the Antique Room once again. The plaster casts seemed even more unsympathetic than usual, and their drawings more inept. They waited for the lunch-hour restlessly and then ran out to the lorry-drivers' 'Good Pull In', which was nearby. To go to this place was entirely Madge's and Jane's idea. Robert was dragged there unwillingly. They made it difficult for him to refuse by saying that they could not go if he would not go with them. Both the girls ordered huge Cornish pasties, but Robert insisted on having only a plate of peas and a cup of coffee. The peas were shedding their semitransparent skins, as snakes do, and the coffee had little coins of fat floating on the surface.

'Don't be so fussy,' said Madge, noticing Robert's face. They ate more or less in silence. The workmen and drivers, every now and then, would look at them rather suspiciously. All three of them still wore their overalls, which made them difficult to place, for an outsider.

One of the drivers spat on the floor and was reprimanded by the proprietress. He looked shamefaced and said, 'Sorry', wiping the back of his hand across his mouth, as if to rub out the memory.

Madge and Jane and Robert got up and paid their tiny bills. They went out into the street and pushed through the crowds, insisting, as fiercely as they could, on walking three abreast.

The prospect of settling down again in front of the plaster casts was uninviting. They dawdled on the stairs, talking and fooling. Jane pirouetted and twirled so that her skirts flew out like a Spanish dancer's.

'You'll break your neck if you lose your balance,' Robert said.

'Oh, but you'd catch me, wouldn't you, Sonny Boy?'

The headmaster came up and passed them without saying anything; but they immediately looked purposeful and set their faces in the direction of the Antique Room. They sat down on their donkeys and idled with pencil and rubber. Robert, in desperation, began a new drawing; and, as he concentrated, minute little scenes from early childhood and recent schooldays floated in and out of his mind, mixing and overlapping and sometimes obliterating each other. Jane's voice, singing a heart-breaking cowboy song, made a solid background for his thoughts.

Towards the end of the afternoon Billings passed through the room. He was wearing shorts and a red and white striped football vest, and he carried a hockey-stick. Robert saw the thinness of his lame leg for the first time.

'Come and play hockey,' Billings called out as he went through the other door. 'On the top field – there are some other sticks in the corner of the still-life cupboard.'

Robert and the two girls ferreted about in the huge cupboard and at last pulled out some dilapidated sticks. They tried them on the floor, bending them to see if they had any spring or if they were too badly split.

Robert had nothing to change into, so he just took off his tie and jacket. The girls left their overalls on to save their dresses from the mud. Jane was for tucking their skirts into their bloomers as children do, but Madge did not take her seriously.

There was a bustle in the art school. People ran about with very little on; and soon a thin line of students was seen going to the top field.

Sides were chosen by a squat little Welshman and Billings. Robert found himself on Billings's side. The game was curious and fluid. There seemed to be no definite boundaries. When the ball had been chased too outrageously far afield, voices would cry, 'Bring it back, bring it back.'

Robert decided that, as he was so bad at the game, he must hit the ball hard and follow it up relentlessly. He became quite vicious, pushing and bustling and chasing after the ball in a menacing way. He was delighted to see that people were frightened of him. The Welshman seemed furious. 'Can't you control yourself?' he asked in his sing-song voice. 'What's the point of charging about like a bloody bull?'

Madge and Jane were far more expert at the game than most of the others. The nuns had taught them well. 'Don't bungle so, Sonny Boy!' they shrieked, as Robert missed the ball and hit a poor Lancashire girl's ankles.

The light was fading and turning to a hot rosy glow, as the sun sank down behind the elephant-grey clouds. For a few moments the beauty of the scene was arresting. The grotesquely dressed figures, waving their sticks and shouting, seemed to be dancing some strange ballet against a wonderful backcloth. The smoke and the dull thunder of London were all around.

Robert forgot the game and just stood and watched until the Welshman threw his stick up in the air, caught it again and shouted, 'We can't see any more; we'd better stop.'

The teams crowded to the edge of the field and pulled on coats or sweaters. Robert forgot Madge and Jane altogether and wandered back to the building alone. In the twilight it looked majestic, like the garden-front at Hampton Court; the round arch swallowed him up. He went to get his coat and left the school still dreaming.

At the corner, by the bus stop, he went into the lavatory of the nearby pub. Someone was already in there. He could just see the dark shape against the glistening, discoloured tiles and the pink polished-copper pipes. The man turned his face towards Robert as he stood near, and said pleasantly, 'Evenings are drawing out a bit now, thank God, aren't they? Let's say goodbye to bloody winter.'

Robert agreed and said no more. The face of the other, when turned towards him, had been like a white moon, with all the features lost in the half-light. Now, as they went out of the door together and stood waiting for the bus under the street-lamp, Robert saw that the man was very little older than himself. His face was lean and he had too long an upper-lip, but his colouring was of that fresh brick-dust shade and he wore no hat on his curling brown hair.

'We both go the same way, then, I see,' the man said jauntily.

'I get off at Blackheath; do you?' asked Robert.

'Well, I can get off there or ride on a bit further. Sometimes I walk, sometimes I ride.'

Tonight he had evidently decided to walk, for he took a ticket to the Green Man, as Robert did. He started to talk about himself as soon as the conductor left them; cocking his legs on the window-ledge, for they were sitting in the front seat on the top of the bus, he began.

'I've just come out of the Army,' he said.

'How have you done that?' said Robert. 'I thought one had to sign on for years and years.'

'Oh yes – my time wasn't nearly up.' He paused for a moment, then went on. 'I had had a sort of nervous breakdown, you see – and my mother said she had to have someone to help her in the business. Taking both together, they let me out.'

'Did you like it at all, or couldn't you stick it?' Robert asked.

'Oh, it was all right in some ways – it was different for me – you see, I was in the band and was getting a lot of musical training. Do you like music? I was learning to play the cor anglais. I don't know why I went off the deep-end. Everything seemed to get just a bit too much for me. Bloody silly – I used to weep for no reason at all.'

He had gone very red as he talked rapidly, and now he looked at Robert with a shamefaced smile, as if he hoped to be understood and excused. Robert saw that his eyes were a bright, hard blue and that the tiny veins at the corners were slightly inflamed. The bright blue and this faintest pink mist at the edges of the whites made his eyes staring and arresting. The rest of the face was good looking but contradictory; for it was placid, perhaps rather animally inert.

The lips were soft and fruit-like and the teeth white but uneven and a little projecting.

'I can understand that all right,' said Robert with emphasis, masking his concentrated gaze as the other looked back. 'Don't we all get dragged down, and don't we all want to scream our heads off half the time?'

'Oh, it's so good to hear someone say that,' said the other. 'My mother's so horribly sensible and everyone else in the Army makes me feel like a BF. I'm perfectly fit now – it was just that ghastly routine of spit and polish and don't answer back. The Army psychologist said I had anxiety neurosis, and wasn't he right. I was so anxious I couldn't even decide which bootlace to do up first without worrying myself silly!'

He laughed with special heartiness and loudness and they climbed down the stairs and jumped off the bus. Robert began to wonder when and where his companion would branch off. They started to walk across the heath, against the wind.

'I haven't told you my name,' the man said suddenly; 'it's Russell, John Russell. What's yours, may I ask?'

Robert told him and they walked on in silence until, to make conversation, Robert asked, 'What are you thinking of doing now that you're out of the Army?'

'As I said before, my mother wants me to help her in the business – it's a drapery shop. Doesn't sound very glamorous, does it?' He stopped talking, as if he were waiting to gauge the effect of this last remark on Robert. Robert said nothing, so he went on, 'I might do this or I might try to get some more musical training and then get a job in an orchestra. I don't know what I'm going to do; I'm just feeling my way about at the moment.'

Again the talking dropped. The wind beat the tails of Russell's raincoat about. Suddenly he turned to Robert and said, 'Will you go to a concert at the Queen's Hall with me next week? I have an old friend who has given me two tickets.'

'I've never been,' said Robert stupidly, as if this were an excuse for not going; then he pulled himself together and added, 'Yes, I should like to go very much, thank you.'

Russell seemed delighted. 'Oh, good!' he said. 'I thought I'd have to go on my own.' They arranged to meet at the bus stop. 'Don't fail me now,' said Russell anxiously. They came to a road which led down the hill. Russell stopped and turned to Robert; he seemed to be peering as hard as he could through the darkness.

'Here's where I have to leave you,' he said hurriedly.

'Oh.' Robert held out his hand. 'Goodbye, then; we'll meet next week.'

Russell took the hand and held it for a moment, then, with a lightning movement, his head swooped down and he kissed it. For a second he knelt before Robert in such a posture of mixed clumsiness, melodrama and sincerity that a cry of protest sprang to Robert's lips. He choked it; but he could not restrain the stiffening of his body. His hand went dead; then it was free and he saw Russell disappear in the darkness, running hell for leather down the hill.

'He's not mad,' thought Robert. 'Only lonely and stagy. That's why he tried picking me up. I'll go to the concert next week.'

He had to admit that the little bit of homage, mawkish as it was, had undoubtedly appealed to his vanity, in spite of making him feel a fool. 'He must be awfully pleased that I was friendly,' he said to himself.

Robert walked on across the heath and down Croom's Hill. He wanted to relax and think alone in his room. He was looking forward to it. He put his key in the door and then climbed up the stairs. There was a crack of light under his door; he pushed it open, feeling exasperated. Hope was lying on the bed, reading. His trilby and umbrella lay by him as if they were a parody of helmet and sword. He looked up at Robert with special indolence and languor.

'Well, what have *you* been up to?' he asked with a rather untrustworthy smile of indulgence.

'I've just been walking across the heath from the Green Man,' said Robert; he looked at Hope not very invitingly and added, 'I didn't know you were coming round; have you been here long?'

Hope gave a huge yawn and said, 'Oh, hours and hours!' Then he sat up, his whole manner changed and he said with relish, 'As a matter of fact I was on the same bus and only got here first by running all the way.'

He watched the effect of his words on Robert. Robert became

confused by the stare. 'Where were you sitting? I never saw you. Why didn't you call out?'

'You seemed very well occupied as it was, and your friend appeared to have a lot to say.'

'Hardly a friend,' interrupted Robert. 'I'd only just met him in the public lavatory the moment before.'

'He looked more like an escaped lunatic, I must admit; he seemed awfully vehement about something.'

'He was telling me about his time in the Army and how he had a nervous breakdown. I'm going to a concert with him next week.'

'Do be careful,' said Hope, with mock anxiety. 'You don't want to be dismembered and left in various suitcases in all the station cloakrooms in London just yet, do you?'

'Don't be absurd; he's not a bit mad. He only gets worked up. He lives with his mother who keeps a draper's shop, and he's really interested in music, so it's all very sordid and drab for him.'

'Now for Christ's sake don't start welfare work. You're not a bit cut out for it and you'll land yourself in a God Almighty mess.'

'What on earth do you mean? I'm not doing any welfare work. I *want* to go to the concert.'

'That's what I thought.' Hope got lazily to his feet. The smirk on his face was so insulting that Robert ran at him.

'Get out of my room,' he shouted. 'Can't I ever be left alone? How I loathed finding you here when I came in from the heath.'

The shock of these words made Hope quite serious for a moment. He was so wounded that his face lost all expression.

'I'm sorry,' he said. 'I didn't know I was such a bore.' Then in a flash he twisted it all and, as he did up his raincoat-belt, he added light phrases to hide the reality. 'You might have told me that you found me so repulsive! How was I to know? I thought you were lonely in the evenings.' He smiled at Robert sweetly. 'Don't come down, will you! I can easily let myself out.'

He shut the door softly and Robert felt a pang of pain and anger. Acting! 'Everyone I meet or know is always acting!' he thought. That Russell person on the heath, bobbing about and giving himself a nice thrilly feeling of self-abasement; and now Hope pretending to be so humble and mild and whimsically amused and misunderstood. But even as he thought these things he felt guilty, for he knew that everybody's acting, including his own, was only the dress of the reality – and even if it was a fancy dress or disguise, yet this in itself gave the clue to that reality.

He lay down on the bed where Hope had been. He hated to feel the slight warmth that was still there.

V

Russell was already waiting when Robert came up to the bus stop. Dressed in a blue suit with a rolled score tucked under his arm and a thick white scarf wound round his neck, he looked a combination of oarsman, bank clerk and musician.

He smiled at Robert, then pulled out a handkerchief and blew his nose. They were both a little nervous of each other.

'I'm so glad you've turned up,' Russell said.

'Didn't you expect me to, then?' asked Robert.

'Oh yes – but you never know – you might have been stopped, or you might have changed your mind.'

They climbed on top of the bus and sat, again, right in the front. The journey down the Old Kent Road began.

'Isn't it lovely?' said Robert, when they saw the gleaming river with the strings of lights reflected in it. 'Wouldn't it be awful to dive into the black water now and swim about amongst the stone piers? Do you think they've got barnacles on them? Or do they only live in the sea? Think of the black mud too, at the bottom and at the edges – yards deep so that you sank right up to your neck!'

'Why think of it if it's so nasty?' asked Russell.

'I don't know; I always do when I cross the river at night. If I'm walking, I often imagine that a person just in front of me is going to jump on to the parapet, stand there on the fat stone balusters just for a moment and then fall outwards, rigidly, like a ruler. I imagine the splash coming sickeningly late after the fall. I wonder what I would do in such a case, whether I could ever pluck up courage to jump in after the would-be suicide. Then I imagine that I have done this and that the person is clutching at me frantically and drowning me as well.'

'You're like a kid frightening itself on the way upstairs to bed at night,' said Russell.

They walked up to the hall and joined the end of the long queue.

'When we get in we might find my old friend who gave me the tickets,' Russell said. 'He told me he'd try to come; he may be late though.'

They sat down in their two-shilling seats, and when the music began Russell unrolled the long score on his knees and drew Robert's attention to the line of notes being played, by following it with his square-tipped fingers. Robert leant forward and politely kept his eyes on the score. He did not follow the music for long, but found himself gazing at the pink finger. He noticed the black crescent of dirt under the nail. It was not particularly revolting; it seemed to suit Russell's hands well. He was one of those people who would always seem fresh, although they were never scrupulously clean.

Robert found this bending forward and arching of his neck tedious. He sat back and shut his eyes to listen properly. The music flooded over him in a lovely wave. He kept as still as ice, knowing that the feeling would only last a moment.

Before the moment died, a nudge from Russell broke and splintered it to bits. He drew Robert's attention to the score severely. Robert was so angry that he turned his head away and muttered, 'Leave me alone. I don't want to look at your bloody score!'

Russell twitched his lips and withdrew into himself completely. There was a sort of vicious jutting out of his chin, and a no-expression in his eyes.

In the interval they did not look at each other at once; then both evidently decided to pretend that nothing had happened.

'Do you think your friend's here?' asked Robert, smiling.

'I don't know; I can't see him. Shall we go and get some coffee? We might find him there.'

They walked round the curving passage where people leant against the wall, laughing and chattering.

The first person they saw in the crowded room was Russell's friend.

He pushed towards them, smiling and showing the gold in his teeth. The short paunchy body and the fish-shaped head, covered with silvery bristles, repelled Robert. He hated the worn pin-striped suit, the watch-chain with the spade guinea and the boy scout's fleur-de-lys in the button-hole. He remembered being told now that this person had been Russell's scout master.

'Introduce me to your friend, John,' said the man, smiling ingratiatingly and reassuringly at Robert.

'It was very good of you to give us these tickets for the concert,' said Robert after they had shaken hands.

'Oh, I always give John tickets. He must hear good music, you know.'

There was a pause; the man slipped away and came back bearing two cups of coffee. He opened his arms dramatically and held out the cups to Robert and John.

'Oh, you lucky young things!' he said, with fervour. 'What wouldn't I give to be right at the beginning of life again, with all youth's glorious chances and friendships before me!'

This outburst immediately embarrassed both Robert and John. They took the cups and looked down at their feet with confused smiles. Robert gulped the hot drink too quickly and felt the pain wriggling down his body like some knotted rope.

The warning sounded. People began to crowd out of the room. Robert put his cup down thankfully and turned to say goodbye. The man caught Robert and John by the hand, linking both of them to him at the same time.

'Well, this is where we have to part,' he said; 'enjoy yourselves, my children, and – be good!' As he stressed the two last words he dropped their hands and gave them each a lightning pat on the shoulder. Then he chortled and slipped out of the door to go back to his more expensive seat. For so dumpy a man he moved rapidly.

'He's all right,' said Russell, as soon as they were alone. It was almost as if Robert had offered some criticism.

'He seems very kind,' said Robert guardedly.

'He's always talking about being young, that's why he likes young people so,' Russell explained.

They went back to their seats, and this time Russell did not produce a score. They sat without moving until the final insanely prolonged burst of clapping.

'Will they never stop?' shouted Robert through the din.

Russell looked pained and clapped and thumped all the louder.

They streamed out into the cold dark street and started to walk to the station, for they had decided to go back by train. Knots of laughing, talking people passed them. Robert felt sorry that he was only with Russell. He wanted to belong to one of the parties – to be going somewhere to eat and drink. He leant on his stick heavily, giving his gait almost the appearance of a limp. He did not know why he did this, but he enjoyed tottering awkwardly.

'Why are you doing that? Have you hurt your leg?' Russell asked. He jerked his foot out at the stick and sent it spinning over the pavement.

Robert ran after it, not a bit annoyed. 'Don't maltreat my stick, it's valuable,' he said gaily.

'Why did you bring the bloody thing?'

'Because I like it.'

'Looks bloody silly to me. You know, you ought to be careful, or you'll be making yourself conspicuous.'

'But what *I* can never understand is why nearly everyone wants to appear *inconspicuous*. It seems such a queer ambition.'

'Then you must be a bloody exhibitionist and that's what I bloody well think you are.'

'Have you no other adjective? That one gets a little monotonous. Can't you think of something worse?'

Robert was getting angry. He hated this sort of animal truculence more than anything else, and could not bear intolerant criticism of his clothes or appearance.

They got into an empty carriage and waited in silence. Their dislike of each other was brewing. When the train started to move, Russell got up and pulled all the blinds down capriciously; then he sat in his corner and stared across at Robert. His gaze was so intolerant that Robert became uneasy; he felt that there might be some outburst – perhaps weeping and more self-abasement.

'Don't sit there staring at me like a stuffed pig,' he said, hoping by rudeness and cheerfulness to shake Russell out of the mood.

'I'll do what I bloody like,' said Russell, leaving his mouth open after finishing the words.

'Well, all I can say is, then, don't be so *bloody*-minded.' Robert turned away, pulled up the blind and looked at the lights out of the window.

The next thing he knew was that Russell was sitting very near him on the seat and that he had caught hold of him by the shoulders and was shaking him playfully.

'None of your side now,' Russell said with a warning smile.

Robert shook his shoulders roughly, then stood up and faced Russell.

The next moment they were fighting, rolling over and over on the filthy floor and falling against the seats. In a flash Robert remembered Hope's mock warning; and he was still able to laugh at it, although he was being swiftly overpowered. Russell was by far the stronger; he had also some knowledge and training.

'Now I've got you where I want you,' he said at last, pushing Robert's face still further into the dirty upholstery as he jerked his arms backwards with a brutal tweak.

Robert gave a harsh smothered grunt of pain and his body twitched, but he could not move. Russell held him down firmly and knelt on his back.

'Now who's won?' asked Russell triumphantly.

Robert was clearly gasping for breath; he was blowing bubbles of saliva into the seat. Russell held him down for one more moment, then raised him up by the shoulder and let him fall back against the cushions.

Robert lay with half-closed eyes, swallowing great intakes of breath. The sweat was trickling off his face, and his hair looked warm and damp.

Russell stared at him for a moment in dismay, then started busily and fussily, like a nurse, to repair the damage. He fastened the button at Robert's throat and put the tie straight; then, pulling out his handkerchief, he started to wipe Robert's face gently.

'I only hope he doesn't lick it and rub, when he comes to a dirty place – as nurses do,' thought Robert stupidly. But he was past all resistance and docilely allowed Russell to minister to him.

'That's better,' said Russell when he had put most things to rights. 'I'm afraid your shirt's torn a bit,' he added nervously and humbly.

'That's all right,' Robert answered absently. He was still feeling exhausted.

When they arrived at Blackheath, Russell linked arms with him and led him down the platform. At the station door, when the fresh wind hit them, he let go of his arm and said, 'Well, goodbye; I hope you didn't mind me getting rough.'

'Oh, not a bit – why should I? And thank you for taking me to the concert.'

They parted on this blank note. Russell gave him one more hang-dog look, shook his head roughly and then swung round and strode away. Robert could see his clumsy white scarf after the rest of him had been swallowed in darkness.

'How queer!' he said aloud, and went on saying it several times as he started to walk across the heath. As he dipped down into a hollow he remembered that neither of them knew the other's address.

'All the better,' he said; and he went on repeating this too.

VI

Hope, of course, had not been to see Robert since the night of the scene. At the school they passed each other in the corridors, or worked together in the Life Room, without speaking. Each tried to look natural and not sulky if their eyes met; but the constraint between them was becoming tiresome.

Robert broke it at last, because he had received a curious letter from his aunt. She had written, 'Would you like to ask your friend, Hope, to spend a few days with you in the Easter holidays?'

Robert never remembered her doing anything like this before. All the years of his schooling she had never suggested that he should have a friend to stay. And as he had not wanted to have anyone, this had seemed quite natural.

He wondered what to do – whether to suppress the message or give it. One part of him did not particularly want to have Hope to stay; he had also the suspicion that the headmaster had told his aunt that Hope's was a good influence towards hard work and industry. He knew that his aunt had written to the headmaster about his progress – a strange thing to do at an art school – and he resented this invitation which smelt of interference. But he knew how pleased Hope would be, and so felt mean in concealing it.

Seeing Hope alone, in front of the big composition he was doing for his examination, Robert decided suddenly to go straight up and tell him.

'My aunt wants to know if you'd like to spend a few days with us down at my grandfather's, at Easter.'

Hope gave the slightest glance out of the corner of his eye and went on dabbing at a clergyman's trousers.

'That's very nice of her,' he said, 'but how does she know I exist?'

'Oh, I expect I've told her about you in a letter, and I think Clive has too, for she seems to think you a prize-pupil.'

They both laughed, and naturalness was more or less restored.

'As a matter of fact,' Hope said, 'Clive spoke to me the other day and said he thought you were promising, but that you didn't work hard enough, so would I keep an eye on you and give you a bit of encouragement. He said your aunt was worried about you and had written to him.'

'I knew it, I knew it!' shrieked Robert. 'What busybodies they all are!' There was a pause, then he added, 'But will you come, or have you something better to do?'

'Of course I haven't, and of course I'd like to come. Will you tell her, or shall I write?'

'Oh no, I'll tell her when I answer her letter – it'll be rather dull, you know – nothing but my grandfather, a white Persian cat, my aunt and her wire-haired terrier and me.'

'That sounds infinitely more exciting than Queen's Grove and my mother, which is the alternative,' said Hope dryly. He was still busily touching his painting here and there with darting, bird-like dabs. The scene was of a circus making its triumphant entrance into a country town. The bright procession of clowns, dwarfs, men on stilts and animals was being watched by the whole gaping population. A sinister clergyman (looking curiously like Hope) raised black-gloved hands. Children danced and crowed delightedly. Some drunkard was reeling out of the nearby pub and holding his head in astonishment, not able to believe his eyes.

'Won't they think it against the Church and in praise of

drunkenness?' asked Robert. 'You know what examiners are like. I don't expect they'll look at it as a picture at all.'

'Oh no, you're quite wrong; they love a rather bold subject, so that they can show how broadminded they are. They're still under the spell of the problem pictures that used to be hung in the Academy.'

'How clever you are! But don't overdo it and put in dogs lifting their legs or other rude things, will you?'

'You might give in to your childish fancy and do that sort of thing, but you know I'm never likely to now, don't you?'

Robert had to nod his head. He had never met anyone quite so reasoning as Hope.

'Are you coming to the end-of-term dance?' Hope asked. 'And if so, what are you going to wear?'

'I don't know; I shall have to make something. Do people take a lot of trouble with their get-ups?'

'Some do – others go to the other extreme and dispense with almost everything.'

'Which do you do?'

'Wait and see! . . . And do thank your aunt from me and tell her that I shall be delighted to come, won't you?'

Robert went down the stairs and left the building; he was glad that he had spoken to Hope and cleared the air. He even thought he might enjoy his company at Easter.

At the entrance gates someone pushing a bicycle emerged from behind the black bushes. It was Russell. He waited diffidently for Robert to speak first; then, as nothing happened, he twiddled the handle of his bell, looked down and said, 'I was just passing and I knew it was your time for coming out, so I thought I'd wait a tick or two.'

He walked on the pavement beside Robert, pushing the bicycle in the road. 'I was going to the church at the top of your hill – it's Ash Wednesday,' he explained.

Robert looked at him with new interest. 'Are you a Catholic?' he asked.

'Yes; are you? I was going to ask if you'd like to come too.'

'I'm not a Catholic. I've only been to a service once before in my life, so I'd like to come. I've always been curious, but I've been afraid that I wouldn't know what to do – when to bob and when to bow and when to make crosses on my breast – but now I'm with you and you can show me.'

They walked along together. Robert was thinking that the day was full of reconciliations and that it was stupid to think that Russell could not get in touch with him again just because he had not the Croom's Hill address. There was always the school. Russell could catch him every day there, if he chose.

Russell put his bicycle into the laurels that screened the central-heating boiler-room, and they both entered the Gothic-revival porch – all rusticated stone and squalid notices pinned to green baize with rusting drawing-pins.

The church inside was warm and pretty. Most of the congregation were already there, kneeling. The candles and lamps twinkled; there was no other light, and they could not see to read the prayers or chants.

Russell genuflected and Robert aped him rather successfully. He copied Russell in everything and enjoyed himself.

Until the last moment he had not realized that the culmination of the ceremony was the marking of crosses in ash on the foreheads of the congregation.

As the long line passed up to the altar steps, he heard Russell whisper, 'Are you going up? I am. Do you want to?'

Robert gulped nervously. The whole affair was causing him anxiety. Any ceremony unknown to him was liable to throw him into confusion.

'All right,' he said desperately.

He followed Russell up and knelt down on the step. The priest passed along the line muttering something for each person. At last he stood in front of them. Robert saw the hand outstretched; then he shut his eyes and felt the soft touch of ashes on his forehead. Their feel was like dry worm-castles, he thought. He followed the tracing of the tiny cross on his skin and suddenly became possessed with an excitement that was almost sexual. He trembled hungrily and felt an upsurge of heat. He knew that it was nothing to do with religion in the accepted sense of the word – it was the solemnity, the intimacy, the touch of the curious stuff on his skin, that had caused it.

He went back to his seat still elated and hungry. Russell looked at him, but seemed to notice nothing. With one more genuflection they left the church and went to pull the bicycle out of the laurels.

'Let's go for a walk over the heath. I don't want to go in just yet; do you?' said Robert.

Russell looked at him with a certain amount of pleasure.

'Your ash-cross suits you,' he said, 'I don't know why.'

'God! I'd forgotten about it!' Robert cried, putting his hand up to wipe his forehead. Russell caught it and threw it down.

'Leave it,' he ordered; 'don't wipe it off.' Robert smiled weakly.

'I think we must look like two Hindoos,' he said; 'they always seem to walk about with spots of different-coloured earths and paints on their faces.'

They walked swiftly over the dark heath. Their shoes cut through the harsh dirty grass. They linked arms and started to sing. Russell was full of directions and orders.

'Don't slur the notes,' he would say, or, 'You sing alto, I'll sing bass,' then when Robert tried his part, 'That's not alto but the most peculiar sort of castrato I've ever heard!'

They laughed and reeled from side to side until Robert tripped over the bicycle and lay on the ground, helpless.

Russell jerked him up, dusted him down with hard slaps on the back and behind, and said, 'Don't jelly. Pull yourself together!'

'Come back to supper,' Robert suggested; 'I expect Miss Middlesborough will have enough.'

Russell became uneasy.

'No, I don't think I'd better come in,' he said.

'Why on earth not? What's wrong?' Robert asked.

'Oh, I don't know; she may not like it, and, besides, my mother will be expecting me.'

'Don't be absurd; of course you'll come back.'

Robert led the way down the hill and got out his key to open the front door. As they stood on the doorstep Russell seemed to get really uneasy. He held his handlebars restlessly, as though about to spring on to the bicycle and disappear.

'I'd better come another day when I'm expected,' he said, looking about him almost wildly.

'What is wrong with you?' asked Robert. 'Do you expect to be eaten alive as soon as the front door's opened?'

'No, it's not that, but she may not like your bringing a complete stranger into the house.'

'What do you mean? You are hardly a complete stranger to me now; and, anyhow, how is Miss Middlesborough to know that we have not been friends since childhood, and, even if she did know, is it her business to inquire into her lodger's friends and acquaintances? What a peculiar guilt feeling you've got about everything.'

'Oh, I have, I have – I can't help it. I can't bear meeting strangers. I always think they'll be suspicious of me.'

'Then how did you pluck up enough courage to talk to me?' Robert asked abruptly.

'I get mad moments when I have to say something to someone and I just thought you seemed approachable.'

'But it was dark and you could hardly see me.'

'Oh, that didn't matter – I just felt it.'

Robert pushed open the door and went into the kitchen to tell Miss Middlesborough about Russell.

Supper had already begun, and when they went into the dining-room the curate was already sitting at the table with the three women.

His eyes went straight to the crosses on their foreheads. Then he looked down and pretended to notice nothing. Robert was again about to sweep his off with the back of his hand, but he suddenly felt this to be cowardly and mean. He sat through the rest of the meal, acutely conscious of the sign on his face.

Russell hardly spoke all through the meal. When the others left the room he looked across at Robert with relieved dog-like eyes.

'Let's go upstairs and drink our coffee in my room,' said Robert. He picked up the cups and led the way.

They both lay outstretched on the bed and only raised their heads to drink.

'You've got your room up rather nicely,' Russell conceded, 'but don't you think you need a chair or two, for state occasions? It's all right for us to lie on the bed, but you can't be on the bed with everyone, now can you?'

'Well, you see, I asked Miss Middlesborough to let me have my own furniture in my room and I'm gradually collecting it. I go to all the junk shops I can find. One day I'll come back with the most beautiful chairs you've ever seen; until then everyone must be content to lie on the bed – even Queen Mary and the Pope – I don't mean together, of course.'

Russell took something out of his breast-pocket and held it above his head.

'What's that?' asked Robert.

'It's a picture of me as a soldier-boy.'

'Let me see,' said Robert interestedly, holding out his hand.

Russell jerked the picture out of reach, then changed his mind and handed it to Robert.

'Don't I look odd!' he said shamefacedly.

Robert saw a stolid-looking Russell wearing his inert, animal expression. The skin over his face seemed very shiny and tight and glowing. He wore riding-breeches; his legs were encased in puttees; a little spur caught the light at the heel of the clumsy boot. His outstretched hand clutched the rim of a pot of ferns and all his buttons glistened against the ancient photographer's background of painted balustrade and distant hills.

'Where did you have it taken? The décor's absolutely period perfect. But for you, it might be a carte-de-visite of 1870,' Robert said.

'It was a queer little shop in Chatham of all places,' Russell told him; 'they had the most amazing fancy pictures of sailors saying goodbye to their sweethearts – the sailors seemed to be hugging them to death, like grizzly bears.'

'You look very smart in those breeches, but didn't you even get one stripe? I can't see anything in the picture.'

'No, I was no good at all,' Russell said hurriedly.

'But what made you join the Army in the first place?' asked Robert.

'That scout master we met at the Queen's Hall really did it. He said that it was a fine manly life and that I would get my musical training at the same time; but it didn't work, it didn't work. It was hopeless.' Russell turned over restlessly and buried his face on the tattered old Indian shawl which had once been worn by Robert's great-grandmother.

After a little he looked up, his face red and sticky.

'Would you like the bloody silly photograph? I don't want it,' he jerked out, anxiously looking into Robert's face.

'Of course I would; I'd love it. I'll stick it up on the Adam's mantelpiece and it'll give just the necessary note of vulgarity,' Robert said gaily, without thinking, then he suddenly had qualms and added, 'I mean the whole scheme of the ferns and the marble balustrade is so lovely and common, isn't it?'

Russell did not understand and was quite evidently hurt. He got up and tried to snatch the photograph back, but Robert cried out and told him not to begin brawling again, so he went to the door in dejection and Robert heard him run all the way down the stairs and slam the front door.

'Now I've done it,' thought Robert. 'What a fool to give offence by being flippant and brainless!'

He took the photograph up and looked at it again minutely. It suddenly struck him as almost unbearably sad and touching. The feeling did not seem to emanate from poor Russell alone. It seemed to hover round the porcelain jardinière and the cracked painted canvas as well.

Very carefully he put it in the corner of his Victorian rosewood worktable and shut the drawer.

VII

Robert saw the alderman's robe in one of the junk shops he visited. It was hanging on a rusty hook with some beaded loincloths and a soldier's felt-covered water-bottle.

'How much is this?' he asked, fingering the crimson damask and the brilliant violet satin lining.

'Fifteen shillings to you, son,' said the pleasant-mannered Irishman. 'My partner's out or he'd charge you more.'

'The gold braid's rather tarnished, isn't it?' said Robert disparagingly.

'Why, all you needs is a drop of petrol and your old toothbrush and that'll come up fine,' the man said.

'May I try it on?' Robert asked. 'I want something for a fancy-dress ball.'

'This is the very thing, the very thing for you.' The man unhooked the dusty garment and put it as it was over Robert's shoulders. The gilded epaulettes hung some way down his arms. They both laughed.

'It's for a fat old man, full of turtle soup,' the dealer said, 'but it'll suit you fine if you take the epaulettes off and wear it as a long robe to your ankles.'

Robert beat him down to twelve-and-six and went off with the brilliant bundle under his arm. He shook it out at home and brushed it well. It had hardly been worn at all. Taking his nail-scissors he cut the threads that held the epaulettes; then he put the robe on and fastened a heavy belt round his waist.

'It's obviously medieval,' he thought, 'but what am I going to wear on my head?' He went down the stairs, still in his robe, and opened the kitchen door. Miss Middlesborough started back in surprise and he asked her if she had anything that might look like a medieval hat. She ferreted in an old cabin-trunk in the cellar and brought out a black and white fur cap.

'That's it, that'll be marvellous,' Robert cried, taking the cap excitedly.

'And what about these old feathers – would you like those, too?' Miss Middlesborough asked, holding out two black ostrich plumes and one purple.

'What a wonderful head-gear I shall have!' laughed Robert.

He went back to his room and fastened the feathers on to the front of the cap so that they swept back over his ear. He looked at his face in the glass and wondered what it was he lacked. 'I know,' he said at last, 'it's a beard – I need a purple beard.'

He hurried out to the nearby barber's where the theatrical things were sold. He bought a plaited tail of violet hair and some spirit-gum.

As he opened the front door again he heard Hope's voice. He was in the kitchen, talking to Miss Middlesborough.

'Ah, here he is,' Miss Middlesborough said when she saw him. 'I was just telling Mr Hope that I thought you'd gone out.'

'Come and help me with my clothes,' said Robert. 'I'm sure you're an excellent needleman.'

Miss Middlesborough held up a sparkling ribbon of diamanté and gold. 'Is this any good to you as well? If so, you may have it with pleasure.'

Robert could not resist it, although he did not know how he would use it.

'I know,' Hope said after a pause; 'a jewelled dagger! We'll make one out of wood and stick the diamanté on. Oh, won't you be romantic!'

'Lovely, lovely,' shrieked Robert. 'Come upstairs at once and get going on the dagger. You *are* going to be useful.'

All that afternoon they worked. Hope carved the dagger out of an old ruler and then encased it in silver paper, tying the diamanté down the front as the final touch to the jewelled scabbard. Robert was delighted. He ran about the room half naked, asking Hope what he thought should be worn underneath the robe.

'Being split to the navel, it's rather revealing, especially when one sits down,' he said doubtfully.

Hope looked round the room and saw the black and white dressing-gown on the back of the door.

'Wear that,' he said decisively, 'then you'll have double sleeves and double skirts. The effect will be much richer, the black and white will peep out through the crimson, and you'll be perfectly safe too. Of course, if you still feel nervous you could wear shorts under the whole thing – perhaps you'd better, people do get rather rough sometimes.'

'You don't mean that they tear the clothes off one's back, do you?' asked Robert in alarm.

'They don't exactly debag people, but they sometimes seem to think that a sweet disorder in the dress is rather attractive.'

'No one shall touch me,' said Robert with more firmness than he felt. He went to the cupboard and pulled out a pair of khaki shorts. Pulling them on, he buttoned them up and belted them securely.

'That's right, get your armour-plating on!' Hope called out derisively.

Robert sat down in front of the glass and started to put on the violet beard. He dabbed his jaw delicately with the spirit-gum and stuck on the fluffed-out strands one by one.

'Build it up slowly, as you would a clay model,' Hope said with approval.

When the beard was fixed, Hope trimmed it to a square, almost Assyrian shape with the nail-scissors.

'You've no idea how grotesque you look in nothing but a purple beard and khaki shorts,' he said. He got up and moved towards the door. 'Now I must go, for I've got to put my own clothes on – see you at the dance.'

Robert finished his dressing and looked at himself in the glass. The unnatural purple, the crimson, the fur, the plumes, the sparkling dagger, excited him. His cheeks were red.

The supper-bell rang and he went downstairs. As he opened the dining-room door the three women gave little gasps and cries of astonishment, but the curate remained very pointedly silent. He seemed to notice no difference at all in Robert's appearance; in fact he did not find him worth looking at at all.

Robert escaped as soon as possible, and, muffling himself in an old voluminous raincoat, he hurried to the bus stop, determined to ignore all cat-calls and rude noises from the passers-by.

Nothing happened; he reached the top of the bus with only the conductor's 'Coo! Purple Christ!' ringing after him. The lavatory at the art school was full of people changing or readjusting their clothes. Billings was entirely naked except for a tiny loincloth of imitation leopard-skin. With his jutting-out chin, straight nose, wide-apart eyes and delicately thin, withered leg, he looked like a mixture of Narcissus, from an old painting, and one of those photographs of emaciated children, from a patent-food advertisement. He was singing, as ever, hissing the words through his white, clenched teeth. The little Welshman was also in a state of undress, but he was about to don a French sailor's jacket and a cap with the red pom-pom on top.

They all groaned and exclaimed when Robert fully displayed himself in his elborate get-up.

'Why purple, Sonny?' someone asked. (This hateful name had spread.)

'Purple for perversity and passion, of course,' said the little Welshman. 'Oh, doesn't he look wicked!'

Billings tweaked the feathers and stroked them, quoting Rabelais's 'First I Wiped Me with a Feather' in a high falsetto.

'Don't you dare do anything of the sort,' said Robert fiercely, and everyone burst out laughing.

At that moment Hope entered, dressed as a sinister harlequin, with his black hair drawn back under a skullcap and his body encased in a skin-tight covering of coloured lozenges. He was heavily made-up, so that the rough skin, where he shaved, looked pitted. The white deadness of the face and the crimson mouth made Robert think of eighteenth-century actresses who poisoned themselves with their white-lead cosmetic.

There was a silence for a moment in the lavatory. People seemed to be surprised, almost shocked, by Hope's appearance. Indeed there was something macabre and Edgar-Allan-Poeish about him.

'Darling,' someone cried out at last in imitation female voice, 'you shouldn't have chosen that maquillage; Arden's "Summer Bloom" would have suited you so much better!'

Hope smiled mechanically; he was clearly annoyed. Robert hurried to join him.

'Aren't they appalling?' he said. 'They've got no imagination. They've been trying to wipe themselves with my feathers too.'

Rude guffaws, exaggeratedly hearty, echoed after them as they made their way down to the hall.

Billings and some other students had decorated the place with red and white striped awnings and huge cartoons, strongly reminiscent of pictures like Picasso's *Guernica*; so that the whole effect was of some grizzly fair ground, where half-dismembered bodies and screaming mouths met the gaze at every turn. The painting was slovenly and unmeaning; great dried cakes of the distemper sprinkled the canvas like mountains on a relief map.

Robert saw Madge and Jane sitting alone on the edge of the dance floor.

'We've just arrived, Sonny Boy,' Jane said hurriedly. Robert looked at their evening dresses.

'Why aren't you in fancy dress?' asked Robert.

'Oh, we hate dressing up; besides, you've more than made up for us, with all your purple whiskers and crimson damask!'

'How dreary and Kensington to come in evening dresses when you're supposed to dress up!' He looked at them with distaste.

Jane jumped to her feet. 'You shall pay for that by dancing with me,' she said. She whirled Robert off, making his robe fly out in a bell shape. Hope was left looking at Madge. She was no friend of his, and he hated dancing. He turned away rudely and abruptly and walked up to the band, where he asked if he could play the piano when the pianist was tired.

Jane was soon tired of dancing with Robert. He wanted to dance energetically and perhaps somewhat grotesquely, whereas she wanted to be squeezed lovingly by some great man. Robert understood her needs, and they made him feel uneasy. She was not the right partner.

'Sonny, I can't follow your steps and you're treading my silver shoes into powder; let's sit down,' she said at last.

'It was entirely your own idea that we should dance,' he said unpleasantly. He led her to one of the wooden chairs and left her without another word.

The hall was filling up. Parties of strangers were arriving and blinking their eyes rather dazedly at the decorations. 'What's it supposed to be?' he heard one ask.

'Don't know, mate,' came the merry Cockney answer; 'looks to me like as if the young students had got it up to look like a cannibal butcher's shop.'

'It's modern art,' someone else said repressively and knowingly.

Robert looked up and found the Cockney speaker staring at him.

'Couldn't you get her to do your fancy steps?' the man asked sympathizingly. It was clear from his easy gay manner that he had been drinking.

'Oh no, she didn't want to dance with me,' said Robert meaningfully.

'Come here and I'll show you a thing or two I learnt out East and in the States.' The man caught hold of Robert and started to bend him about and kick his feet into various positions.

'I've just come off a ship,' he explained, 'and you learn a lot of steps in all those foreign dives.'

Finding Robert an apt pupil, he pulled him to him, clapped their bellies together and started to prance and sway in the most extravagant but masterly way. Alarmed at this unorthodox behaviour, Robert looked about him wildly; but by this time the dancing had become rather original in all corners of the room, threes and fours dancing in rings, holding hands, like fairies or children; sedate couples of thoughtful-looking women gave a sense of stability; and frolicsome men and boys reminded one of dogs and puppies leashed together.

'You're not bad at following,' said the man as they swayed and shimmied through the crowd. 'If you want your partner to know what you're going to do next, you must hold her as tight against you as you can; then she can feel every little twitch of your body all the way down,' he added solemnly.

'That might be rather awkward,' said Robert absently; then he pulled himself up and smiled at the man. Their steps were becoming more and more intricate and flamboyant. Robert sweated as the man manipulated him with such vigour. 'This is how people ought to dance,' he thought, 'with all of their bodies and souls – they shouldn't just shuffle and wriggle.'

At last they almost collapsed on to the hard wooden seats. The man brought out the most extraordinary handkerchief with playing-cards and ladies' legs on. He mopped his glistening face and said, 'Ever seen a bit of nonsense like this before? I got it in Yokohama. Don't those Japs go in for some queer manufactures? Why, I've even heard they make life-sized rubber women what you can blow up and take on long journeys, when you feel lonely!'

The man's gaze drifted towards a model who had just come in. She wore only a straw-skirt, and two plaited discs over her breasts. Her black coarse hair hung down her back, and artificial daisies and poppies were caught in it here and there as if by chance. Turning her back to them, she perched on the edge of a table and swung her legs. The hollow in her back wriggled and changed its shape with her movements. A crowd of people were soon talking to her.

'Coo, look at that!' the man said in awe. 'Who's the hula-hula, and when does the policeman arrive to wrap her in his cape and take her to the station?'

'She's a model,' Robert explained carelessly; 'we see them every day completely naked, so there can't be any trouble when they come in skirts and saucepan lids.'

'D'you think she'd dance with me if I asked her?' the man said jokingly, but with underlying seriousness.

'Oh no, I don't expect she'll dance with anyone. She just likes to sit and talk to all those people. She'd shed all that straw if she started moving about.'

Robert really knew nothing about the model, but he wanted to dissuade the man from making any advances, for he feared that the crowd round the model would be insolent. He was right. A moment later a man in ragged trousers and khaki shirt came up to the group and pushed his way through to the model. He put his arms round her, lovingly, evidently under the impression that they should become a pair, as they were both so suitably dressed for the South Seas. The model wriggled out of his grasp and the group of people round her surged forward angrily. Although he was a heavy thick young man with pig-pink skin and broad neck, yet in a moment they had torn his shirt to rags and cuffed and slapped his pink face to an angry red. One weak-looking youth wrenched at his forelock of blond hair venomously. This made the man so angry that for one moment he extricated himself from the others and landed a smashing slap on the cheek of the youth. The youth fell to the ground and the uproar grew. The last thing Robert saw as he hurriedly left the hall was the heavy young man looking about him bewilderedly – rather like a bear attacked by terriers from all sides.

Robert realized as soon as he was in the entrance lobby how horrible the air had become in the dance-hall. Already his throat and eyes felt sore. The only other people in the lobby were an American girl, dressed all in scarlet – as a female demon, Robert supposed – and her importunate lover. They sat on the concrete steps, the man restlessly caressing the girl. He was obviously quite drunk, with drink and lust. The girl had all her wits about her.

'Darling, you can't come home with me,' she said over and over again, as the man implored and wheedled. Her thoughts were clearly somewhere else. 'You just stay right here and have a good time,' she said soothingly and absently. 'It's a pity I've got to go back home so early, but it just can't be helped.' She moved to the door eagerly; her whole attitude seemed to tell Robert that she had another appointment to keep. The man held her hand, dragging her back over the step. He kissed her in a clumsy drunken way, not knowing or caring whether his lips met hers, or her face, or neck, or breast. Everything about him seemed slurred and oafish.

The girl was now in a fever to get away. She looked at him with distaste, but still called him darling. Jerking her wrist up to look at her watch, she slipped from under the man's arm and made a dash for the door. It slammed behind her and the man looked blankly round at Robert. He didn't seem to think of chasing her. His arms hung down forlornly, and suddenly his shoulders heaved and tears began to trickle down his face.

'Don't cry, don't cry,' Robert said, almost involuntarily. The man swore at him and stumbled up the stairs blindly. Nothing could cure his misery, for his joy had been taken away.

Robert decided to leave. He looked for the last time into the hall. The uproar had subsided round the model; but the rowdier had linked arms and were now charging round the room, uttering warcries and bearing down on all before them. Near the door stood someone whom Robert had not seen before. He wore a heavy mauve satin shirt and tight mulberry velvet breeches. On his plump white hands were two enormous rings, one diamond and one pearl. His podgy face wore an expression of outraged decency.

'Yahoos,' he drawled out, turning to Robert and fluttering the hand with the enormous diamond on it. 'They never used to behave like this.' Then he lapsed again into his stolid, disapproving silence.

As Robert let himself out into the cold air he understood how dreary the whole evening had been. Even the strange clothes had only been the thinnest cloak over ordinariness and drabness; there had been no joy, no love, no pleasure, no delight and no cohesion. Each little body had rushed about distractedly, alone. Only for a moment, when he was dancing whole-heartedly with the sailor, had he had any real contact with another human being. Now he knew why the very thought of ordinary 'pleasure' filled him with despair.

He walked along the pavement, not caring whether people stared at him or not. Soon there were quick footsteps behind him and someone caught him up.

'Not a bad dance, was it?' the stranger said affably. 'How far have you got to go? We won't get any buses tonight.' Robert saw the neck of a Russian blouse sticking up above the other's collar. He remembered seeing the man in the hall.

'Are you an art student?' the stranger asked.

'Yes, are you?' Robert replied.

'No.' The man paused with mock diffidence. 'I try to write.'

Robert was suddenly filled with a sense of frustration and rage and despair, the culmination of the stupid evening.

'Well, go on trying!' he spat out derisively, before he knew quite what he was saying; then he was out and away down a wide turning, before the bewildered man could either show pain or displeasure at his uncalled-for rudeness.

VIII

The next day Hope and Robert set out for the country. Robert's throat was still sore, but he talked a lot, explaining the countryside to Hope with pleasure.

They crunched over the gravel and Robert's aunt met them in the hall. Hope's manner with her was good. He was polite, not too talkative. She led them both into the drawing-room, where Robert's grandfather was reading as usual by the fire. He looked up over his steel-rimmed glasses and said something correct and punctilious but not warmly welcoming. Hope immediately became even more correct and called him 'Sir'. This came as a shock to Robert. It struck him that Hope perhaps made too many concessions to the opinions, upbringing and period of other people. He knew how Hope despised and disliked in his heart even the common courtesy of taking off his hat. This 'Sirring' even of a very old man was almost too much out of character.

They settled down to a quiet tea. Hope passed the scones beautifully and even brought himself to pat the wire-haired terrier, although Robert knew that he considered all pets dirty nuisances.

After tea Robert took Hope up to his room; then they wandered round the garden in the evening light, ending up by the ancient apple tree.

'It's called Black Jack's apple tree,' Robert said, as they both stared up into the branches, which were rapidly melting into the darkness of the sky. 'It has bunches of mistletoe on it, and it's supposed to have been named after a well-known smuggler, but I always feel that that sort of local legend has been manufactured by some romance-loving lady, don't you? The smuggler is said to have lived in a cottage where the house now stands.'

Hope gave a grunt.

'But it's a lovely tree, isn't it?' Robert went on. 'And the mistletoe makes it romantic enough without any legend. When I was small I once took all my clothes off and climbed up into its branches, swathed only in a blanket. I sat up there jabbering and chattering nonsense for half the afternoon. I can't think why I did it now, but it meant something very exciting and serious at the time.'

The thought flashed into Robert's mind that Hope was bored. He led him down the narrow path between the thick-leafed shrubs. They were both swallowed up in terrifying, floating blackness until they reached the slimy bricks of the stable-yard. The huge coach-house door had lately been painted ochre. It could still be seen, glimmering pale and fresh; but Robert knew that the whole building was deserted and empty, except for his aunt's car, the mowing-machine, the garden furniture; and upstairs in the loft, three trunks of tousled fancy dress for a pageant, and rows and rows of shrivelling pears and apples, looking like tiny human heads.

'I've always thought it would be nice to make a little house or flat out of the stable,' Robert said to Hope with animation. 'I wish I had the money to do it with and my grandfather would let me. You could have two lovely rooms on the ground floor and then there's all the loft above.'

They went out into the road, still talking about the converting of the stables. Between them they planned something wonderfully attractive and luxurious.

'It's no good exploring the village now,' said Robert, looking down the dark road.

'Oh, let's walk for a bit; I want to stretch my legs,' Hope suggested.

Robert led him towards the common. 'You seem to be able to manage my aunt and grandfather well,' Robert said.

'Oh, I'm always able to make myself pleasant to people,' Hope answered complacently. 'I don't understand why there's all this trouble in some families – everybody squabbling with everybody else.'

'Don't you think you might overdo it unless you're careful? If you're too fluid and malleable, people may get suspicious and think you're playing with them.'

'D'you think so?' Hope asked interestedly.

'Yes, I think they end up by hating you when they see that you're only saying a thing to please them.'

'Not everybody's a suspicious devil like you,' Hope said with heat. 'You don't trust anyone, let alone me.'

They walked on in rather boorish silence, until Robert said at last, rather gruffly, 'Tomorrow we'll go exploring.'

✤

The day was warm and feathery with mist, so they fastened the dog's collar and decided to go for a long walk, with their lunch in their pockets.

'He must be brushed,' said Robert's aunt, looking down at her pet. 'Yes, darling must be brushed,' she repeated to the dog, putting her face down to him. The dog's wet tongue came out and licked a strand of her hair.

'Scampy, Scamp,' called Robert, patting the horsehair seat in the flower-room, so that the dog jumped up. He held it by the collar and began to brush vigorously, making endearing and hissing noises. 'Petskin stay still!' he ordered, as he combed its ears.

'How absurd you are with it,' Hope said. 'It isn't particularly strange that you should be absurd with it,' he added insultingly, 'but what I find so strange is the way forbidding-looking hearties and other almost extinct species melt and maunder over their flea-ridden pets. They're not ashamed to shower their "darlings" all over the place, and I've even heard one calling his spaniel "sweet-heart".'

'I suppose it betrays a deep-felt need for expressing tenderness,' said Robert sententiously. 'In England you can only do it on the dog.'

'Isn't it grizzly to think that people only keep these creatures as emotional outlets?'

'Don't be silly,' said Robert, clipping the leash on to the dog's collar.

They waded through the shingle which covered the drive.

'Why is it so deep?' Hope asked.

'Well, you see, my grandfather ordered an enormous cartload and had it spread about six inches thick all over, so that the weeds could never push through. Every week the gardener rakes it; then it looks wonderfully smooth, as if the tide had washed it; but it soon gets all churned up again.'

The sun was gradually melting the mist. The dog danced and pulled on the lead. As soon as they were in the fields Robert unleashed him. The dog took the end of the leash in his mouth and pranced backwards in the most absurd way. He worried the lead until his head seemed to be moving as quickly as a vibrating tuning-fork.

'Does he always behave like that?' asked Hope.

'Except when he chases things.'

'Perhaps he'll get shot one day by a farmer,' Hope suggested hopefully.

They passed through some park gates and started to walk up the mud and gravel road through the fields.

'Aren't we trespassing?' said Hope, turning to Robert.

'Oh no; the church is up here, close to the big house, but there is also an old "moated grange" which I want to show you. It must have been abandoned by the family and turned into a farm-house when they built that huge yellow-stone thing,' said Robert, pointing with his stick, as the newer house came into view.

They branched off across the fields, and soon were standing on the edge of a weedy and dark-coloured moat. The house on the enclosed square seemed to have dwindled and shrunk; for at one end was an isolated stone gate-house with a belfry and at the other the much-patched house. An overgrown neglected garden with ugly rose pergolas divided the two.

'Isn't it rather romantic and sinister? All decaying and gloomy,' Robert said with relish. 'I wish my grandfather lived in something like that instead of his ugly ivy and stucco house.'

'But it would cost an awful lot to make it really fit for human habitation, wouldn't it?' said Hope with not much interest.

They sat down under some trees and ate their lunch. Scamp kept pestering for titbits. He sat close to them, stiff and trembling, not quite daring to snatch the food from their hands. When they had finished they went back to the moat and threw fragments of bread to the two oily-looking swans that floated there. Robert watched one of the pieces of bread sinking into the slimy water.

Towards two or three o'clock the mist thickened again and had soon turned into a drizzle.

'What shall we do?' asked Robert as they stood in the middle of the wet fields.

'Let's get home damn quick,' Hope spat out. He now seemed to be quite out of temper. They yelled after the dog, which had disappeared. Scamp emerged from the mist in his own good time. He looked delighted, for he had found some deliciously fresh cow-pats and had been rolling himself in them very thoroughly.

Robert gave extravagant groans and wails. 'Oh, Scamp, you stinking and repulsive beast,' he chanted.

'Give him to me,' said Hope firmly. He hooked his umbrella handle through Scamp's collar and dragged him relentlessly to the edge of a dreary little stream.

'Tear up large handfuls of grass and be ready to wipe him down,' he ordered.

'Oh, don't push him in,' Robert cried. 'He'll catch cold and die and then my aunt will be taken off to the madhouse.'

But by this time Hope had already jerked the filthy Scamp into the shallow stream. There were yelps and mad scrambles for the bank, but before the poor dog could reach dry land Hope had very neatly pushed its head under with his foot and had totally submerged it.

Robert rushed at it with the handfuls of damp grass and rubbed it down. It shivered in a spectacular way – like a machine. Robert tore off his scarf and began to rub again. The dog seemed to love the vigorous friction. It stuck out its legs like stiff poles and seemed to be arching its back slightly.

'That's quite enough,' said Hope. 'You're exciting it. Stop rubbing.'

Robert made Hope run across the fields so that the dog should chase them and get warm. It gave delighted yelps and ran away with one of Hope's gloves in its mouth. They all three arrived back at the house hot and damp.

No one was in the drawing-room. Robert's grandfather was writing letters in the dining-room and his aunt was resting. Robert and Hope sat down by the fire and played their poetry game. Each wrote a line, turned the paper down and handed it to the other to write the next. When they had written the required number of lines they read out the composite poems with screams of laughter. They seemed amazingly suggestive and illuminating. There was naturally a great deal of indecency and private innuendo in them, so they gathered up the scraps of paper hurriedly when they heard footsteps.

'Well, did you have a nice walk?' asked Robert's aunt. 'And was Scampy a good boy?'

'Oh, quite good,' said Robert with emphasis. He wanted no mention made of the cow-pat rolling, for it would lead inevitably to the story of the ducking and that would not have been forgiven easily. 'It's a pity it came on to rain. We went to see the old house with the moat round it.'

The tea was brought in and Robert's grandfather made ponderous remarks quite charmingly.

Gradually the pleasant dull holiday was passing away. It had been a success. Robert's aunt looked pleased when she saw them both getting ready to go out with their paint-boxes slung on their backs.

'Have a good day,' she said gaily.

'I'm afraid we can't take Scamp,' Robert said. 'He'll get in the way and knock the easels over.'

'That's all right. I'll take the naughty devil out myself.' Robert's aunt, as she said this, put her face close to the ground and made a gargoyle's grimace at her animal. Scamp backed away, growling excitedly, not quite certain what was afoot.

The two let themselves out of the garden door and walked through the bushes.

'Where shall we go?' asked Robert. 'Is there anything in particular you want to paint?'

'No, you know the country, so you decide,' Hope answered.

'Let's go and do the church then. I like all the different-shaped tombstones and the Gothic arches. We might even invent people coming out of the tombs. Don't you love Stanley Spencer's *Resurrection* in the Tate?'

'If we're going to paint people coming out of tombs we might just as well stay at home instead of dragging all this paraphernalia for miles,' Hope said heavily. 'I thought we were going to have a day's sketching in the country.'

'Yes, of course,' agreed Robert hurriedly. 'I only meant that we could turn our sketches into something more elaborate afterwards, if we felt like it.' He did not want to begin an argument so early in the day.

They trudged down the road in the direction of the church. The sun began to shine. The straps on his paint-box and easel cut into Robert's shoulders.

'Perhaps the villagers think we look like Van Gogh and Gauguin going out for a day's work in the fields near Arles,' Robert suggested as they passed down the main street.

'In spite of the popularization, not to say vulgarization, of their legend by many books and the Medici Society's prints, I still think it very unlikely that the villagers have ever heard of those two gentlemen,' said Hope with too much solemnity. He was pleased with his sentence.

'This is awful,' groaned Robert.

'What is awful?'

'Our conversation,' said Robert. 'So empty and stupid. Let's talk about sex.'

So they talked about sex until this subject also seemed to become empty and stupid; then Hope repeated the curious story which a doctor friend had told him. It seems that the doctor had come to hear of a lonely young person who was in the habit of asking tramps and other needy people to come to his house, where he promised that they should have food and clothing. When he had them in his room, he gave them all they needed, including money, if only they would tie him securely to the foot of his bed.

This the tramps usually did, however bewildered they may have felt. Were they not being rewarded for it handsomely? But when the youth began to chant, 'Now, O master, I am powerless, and in thy hands. Do with me what thou wilt. I am thy slave!', the tramps usually became extremely perturbed and left in a hurry, abandoning the poor youth still strapped to the bed with dressing-gown cords and handkerchiefs.

At last the landlady had come in on one of these occasions, and, finding the youth trussed up and not understanding it at all, she had consulted the doctor.

'But it's perfectly easy to understand,' said Robert. 'When I was at school and horribly unhappy and lonely, I used to go down to the end of the field and chain myself up to the old horse-roller; then I'd pretend to be a slave dragging stones to build the Pyramids. You have to symbolize and dramatize your unhappiness in some way, then it almost gives you pleasure. I can also remember how frustrated I felt when a boisterous, rather likeable prefect let me off my first beating. I had so keyed myself up for the awful event that the reprieve came as a jarring anticlimax. I felt washed-out, grey, humiliated, nondescript, when I had expected to feel thoroughly sore and full of burning indignation. You see, the ending was wrong, inartistic, a flop; and this poor person, left to his own devices all day, must have felt the longing for guidance, direction, which he dramatized into the extreme form of wanting someone to ill treat him and use him as a slave.'

'Oh, let's stop all this amateur psychology!' yelled Hope at the end of this long speech. 'The amusing thing about the story is the gorgeously ornate prayer – "Now, O master, I am powerless" etc., don't you think? That's what I love.'

By now they had reached the churchyard; they began slowly to walk round the church, looking at it from all angles. Robert tried not to walk over any graves. He always felt constrained in a churchyard, as if every step might land him on a forbidden oblong. A nurse must have told him once never to tread on a grave and the prohibition still lived with him strongly.

They decided, at last, to pitch their easels on a gravel patch which led to the small chancel-door.

'This pinkish gravel will be nice with green grass, won't it?' said Robert.

Hope merely grunted. He was busy wriggling out fat worms of paint.

'Oh, they're lovely, aren't they! It's a pity to spoil them by messing them about on a board,' Robert exclaimed, as he watched the paints emerging from the tubes.

'Speak for yourself,' was the obvious answer which Hope made.

They worked in silence for a little. Robert concentrated on the texture of the walls, exaggerating the pattern of the stones and stressing the too ambitious Gothic-revival tracery which replaced the original in the windows. Hope's picture was far more atmospheric and, of course, more accomplished generally.

They both gazed at the other's picture and said, with mental reservations, 'Oh, yours is much better.'

'Mine might have been done by an old lady who wanted, in her youth, to be the English Berthe Morisot,' Hope added to this, and Robert capped it by saying. 'And mine's like a McKnight Kauffer poster – all black lines and over-accentuated design.'

Their modesty lasted as long as neither criticized the work of the other. When criticism was offered, modesty flew out of the churchyard, and sly little pats of mud were flung by both sides with careful aim.

'Oh, let's stop it,' said Robert wearily. 'Let's agree that they're both frightful. I can't paint from nature and you *oughtn't* to.'

Hope decided to ignore this last shot. He spread out his mackintosh so that they could both sit on the ground and eat their picnic.

'Don't get any grease on my coat, will you?' he said anxiously. 'If you do it will absolutely spoil this rubber material.'

'Is it sacrilegious to eat in the churchyard?' Robert asked.

'Do you want me to say "yes" so that you'll be able to feel wicked?' Hope suggested.

Before Robert could answer they were interrupted by a very handsome red setter which had slunk up silently and was now nosing their sandwiches and raising its head to give delicate sniffs. It held one paw off the ground in a graceful curve.

'Where on earth has this monster sprung from?' asked Hope in mock alarm, snatching the sandwiches away and putting them under his coat. The timid dog started back at his abruptness, and a young woman's voice called out gaily and rather insolently, 'I'm the mistress of the monster – Spangle, come here at once.'

Both turned to watch her as she walked up from the lych-gate.

She had auburn hair, was a little plump, and her mouth was a special red.

'I suppose neither of you would like to adopt the monster,' she said with complete assurance. 'You see, I've just got a new baby, and although I really infinitely prefer Spangle to the baby, yet I feel I shall have to get rid of her because she might split the baby's head open one day. She jumps about so when she's excited.'

Robert and Hope looked at each other, then hurriedly turned their eyes away, fearing that they had revealed too much to the woman.

'We live in London,' said Robert, 'and I'm afraid neither of us could keep a dog.' As he spoke he looked into the woman and thought, 'I wonder why she has to say she likes the dog better than the baby. I suppose she wants us to think she's hard and smart and dashing – isn't it quaint and old-fashioned?'

The woman had taken no notice of his explanation; she was now bending over their paintings with a profound expression.

'Effective things!' she said. 'But I think I'm inclined to see a little more mauve in the shadows myself.'

She left them and entered the church. Spangle followed her in and was not ejected. Later they saw the woman throw the dead flowers from the altar on to the rubbish heap and go to draw some water from the tap at the foot of the tower.

'Don't you know who she is?' asked Hope.

'No, I've never seen her before.'

'I thought that in country places everyone knew everybody else.'

'Did you?'

They started to pack their things up.

A PARTY

Appearing this time as 'Ian', Denton Welch describes another party he went to while at art school. 'Fat Bertha Swan' was his friend Betty Swanwick, later in life a Royal Academician, who also appears as 'Betsy' in A Voice Through a Cloud. *The story was first published in* A Last Sheaf.

FAT BERTHA SWAN HAD BOUNCED INTO THE STILL-LIFE Room, given her invitation and bounced out again, shouting, 'And see you damn well come in fancy undress – you won't be let in otherwise.'

Ian, painting alone in one corner, had smiled. He liked Bertha – even her exaggerated uncouthness and her absurd swearing amused him. He would certainly go to her party.

But now, as he sat on the bed in his room, he wondered what exactly fancy undress meant. He supposed it meant fig leaves, loincloths, straw-skirts, saucepan lids; but he wished he had asked some of the other students what they intended to wear. The knowledge would have given him more confidence.

Going over to the chest of drawers, he pulled out his faded mauve bathing 'trunks' and looked at them doubtfully. He remembered buying them with an unexpected postal order sent to him on his fifteenth birthday two years ago. His aunt had not thought mauve a very suitable colour for a boy, but he had liked them even more just because of her disapproval. Now moth holes stared up at him from important places; but these could be hidden. He had just been into the park to pick up some large plane leaves. He was going to sew a few on the shorts; the rest he would make into wreaths to wear round his neck and on his hair. Would they look like vine leaves? And would he look like Bacchus or was he much too skinny? Perhaps no one would guess that he was supposed to be a pagan god. He put his hand up and started to rub his scalp roughly. His hair at least was satisfactory, for it was short and curled tightly; although it was so strong and vigorous, the fear that it might one day all fall out sometimes came to Ian in his black moments. How terrible old age must be. How did one learn to bear the degradation?

He sat down again on the bed and started to sew the plane leaves on the shorts; next he made the wreaths, binding the stalks together with black cotton. He worked quickly and deftly, enjoying the task.

He stood in front of the mirror, wreathed and garlanded, his small feet bare. A little tingle of pleasure passed through him. The effect was better than he could have hoped. But how was he to travel to Catford in this state? He would have to put his leaves in a suitcase and dress – or rather undress – and rearrange himself at Bertha's. There was not much time to spare; he pulled on his grey flannels and navy-blue sweater, buckled up a pair of old sandals and ran to catch the bus.

Outside the small suburban house three cats wearing collars were fastened to a young oak tree. Ian saw that the tabby wore a blue collar, the ginger a green one, and the black Tom bright scarlet with brass studs. Bertha had often spoken of her cats' dislike of visitors; Ian supposed that she had put them here to sulk on their own. They certainly looked disgruntled.

Charming, heavy, swart Bertha, dressed all in Union Jacks, opened the door herself. A smooth round pillar of stomach divided her bunchy brassière from her frilly skirt. She screamed, jumped up and down like a pneumatic road-drill, then hustled Ian into a bedroom on the ground floor. There he found the clothes of all the other guests strewn about him carelessly. He shivered a little as he pulled on his leaves, gowned himself and hung the garland round his neck. He tried not to feel naked and horribly defenceless. He longed for one of those awe-inspiring gorilla bodies. No one would dare to laugh then. If he clutched the garland close to his chest, hiding his nipples, he might feel a little more protected. But Bertha gave him no time for further anxious brooding. She burst into the room and cried, 'Oh, but, Ian, you look sweet. What are you? A sort of little woodland sprite, or what?'

Overcome with confusion, Ian could only mutter savagely, 'I don't know. I'm nothing in particular, although I had thought of trying to come as Bacchus.'

'But you can't look nearly loose enough for that,' shrieked Bertha, taking his hand and pulling him into the living-room.

Mrs Swan lay on the sofa in the bay-window, her vast breasts and hips swelling up before her like miniature mountain ranges, one behind another. She wore black velvet trimmed with curtain lace, round her neck mauve pearls as large as sugared almonds glistened. Her face was unpainted but so heavily powdered that it looked as if it had grown a thick white fur.

'I'm always so pleased to see Bertha's friends,' she said. 'Dear young people all, I'm sure. I can't get about easily now, so it's a special treat to see new faces.'

There was something strangely mortifying in her universal indulgence. One was dismissed as Bertha's friend, a dear young person, nothing more. Ian looked about him uncomfortably, his anxious smile becoming more and more fixed. What could he do with himself? Where could he go in this crowd? Nearly all the other guests were from the art school, but their nakedness had turned them into strangers. Stocky little Bobby Davies was holding Veronica Tooth's hand as usual, but he was only wearing a strip of imitation leopard-skin and she looked like nothing so much as a large tablet of oatmeal soap tied with ribbons.

The lame youth, Treff Rowse, wore an elaborate papier-mâché codpiece which he must have modelled himself. Painted on it in bright colours was a terrifying face with staring eyes and wide-open mouth. One tape between his legs, one round his waist, held it in position. His buttocks were quite bare. For the first time Ian saw his poor withered leg. It was like the thin white stalk of a dying plant. How could he treat it so cruelly? How could he expose it to them all? But Treff seemed perfectly indifferent to it and everything else. He was in a sort of trance, crooning to himself and moving his arms and shoulders, quite lost in one of his never-ending variations and perversions of 'Dinah'.

There were a few people whom Ian did not know. He guessed that one of them must be Baby, Bertha's younger sister. She had transgressed all the rules and come in a boy's jacket and trousers, with a rather dirty scarf wound round her neck. Ian had been told that Baby had a passion for collecting books, which she hardly read, and that she pretended to enjoy smoking a foul little pipe made out of some soft pithy root with a surface like a lizard-skin. Ian felt in sympathy with Baby because she too was younger than the others and clearly very shy. She was so shy that he was afraid even to catch her eye.

But who could that other heavily dressed person be? That nun with white bands swathed round her face? Her clothes must be authentic; she had everything – even the heavy crucifix dangling from her girdle. Perhaps she was a real nun; but could a real nun be persuaded to come to a party, and such an undressed party? At that moment the young nun thrust her hands down and straddled her legs. She seemed to be searching vainly for pockets. Her pleasant broad face puckered and she gave a deep laugh. Ian knew then for certain that 'she' was a man.

People were gathering round the nun to examine her clothes and ask questions. They stroked the rich folds of her habit and one even picked up the crucifix shamefacedly and held it close to his face. Ian heard a girl say, 'Nuns never look at their bodies; they bath in cotton shifts that come right up to their ears. It must be so difficult chasing the soap under the wet folds.'

'I've got the hang of it at last,' replied the nun and everybody laughed.

Ian, finding himself near the door, felt that it was a good moment to slip out.

There was nothing in the hall but a great coarse needlework hanging done by Bertha. Fat golden lions with rosy tongues lolled under giant arum lilies. The hanging went strangely with the corrupt, genteel wallpaper frieze of autumn leaves. Ian stood admiring it for some moments; he had always felt that Bertha was one of the most talented people at the school. The thought of her talent made him depressed with himself. He passed on into the dining-room, not thinking of what he was doing. Here the food was already laid out on the long table. It was childish and appetizing. There were jellies and trifles, sardines and stuffed eggs and chocolate biscuits. On the sideboard stood carafes of lemonade, something which looked like raspberry syrup, and bottles of cider.

All round the walls Baby's books reached from floor to ceiling. Starting in one corner with *The Treasures of Peru*, Ian glanced quickly along the lines until he came to *The Proceedings of the Sexual Reform Congress* by the door.

Bertha, leading the other guests in to eat and finding him there, immediately accused him of gluttony.

'What are you doing in here?' she demanded. 'Have you been picking the decorations off the trifle? I can soon tell how many sandwiches or biscuits have gone.'

'I haven't touched anything, Bertha,' Ian protested, made to feel thoroughly guilty by her mock indignation. 'I was just looking at Baby's books. Hasn't she got a lot?'

'Yes, haven't I?' said Baby, suddenly emboldened and coming forward to his rescue. 'Do you like books?' She spoke as if they were avocado pears, or some other food for which a taste has to be acquired. There was no question here of weakness or excellence of different volumes. Books were books – things to be hoarded and treasured and touched.

Ignoring the food on the table altogether, Baby led Ian round the room again, sometimes crouching to pull out a large book, sometimes climbing to find a small one. Behind his polite exclamations Ian's thoughts kept turning to sardine toast and trifle and lemonade. All at once Baby awoke to her duties as hostess. She shovelled several things on to two plates and returned to their corner.

'I'm afraid you must be hungry,' she said, offering him the things that he would not have chosen himself. They ate leaning back against the shelves. A greedy clatter of knives and forks arose from the table. Mrs Swan had dragged herself up from the couch and was moving weightily round the room, suggesting a cucumber sandwich here, a stuffed egg there, a glass of grenadine or a cheese straw. Ian noticed that parts of her mauve pearls, having lost their nacreous surface, had come to look like fungus puff-balls or snakes' eggs. Spoons were already being dug into the bowls of decorated trifle. Some people were eating their little silver balls and some were not. Ian wondered for the thousandth time how they were made. He had wanted to know since his first infant party. Could it be that they were silvered with mercury? And mercury was poison – it made all your teeth drop out.

A PARTY

The din was subsiding a little. Bare arms were thrown out contentedly along the backs of chairs. Smoke rings and spirals floated up. Pink tongues flickered round the last drops of sour-sweet cider in the glass-bottomed tankards. Out of the window the sluttish back gardens and sheds were fading into each other. The room was filling with shadows, so that the rows of books seemed to be closing in on the seated guests. Bertha struck a match and lit the scarlet candles in their curious makeshift holders, contrived out of raw potatoes sliced in half. From the open scullery door came the gentle dripping of a tap and the ghosts of yellow soap and cabbage water.

For a few moments the guests sat there comfortably enjoying the workings of the food inside them and the calm excitement of the gathering night. Mrs Swan had sunk into the gnarled armchair at the head of the table and was drumming on a plate with her pudgy fingers. Satisfied little rumblings and gurglings arose from her enormous body and every now and then the lowest murmur of words escaped from her lips. She seemed to be praying or chanting to herself.

Suddenly Bertha jumped up and broke the peace.

'We must all play Sardines,' she insisted, running to the window to blow out the last of the light.

'Oh, Berty-darling, let's have a little quiet,' groaned Mrs Swan. 'It never does to jig about after food. If you do, it turns on you.'

'You can't have quiet at a party, Mother,' Bertha said, blowing out the candles and disappearing. She could be heard drawing all the curtains in the other rooms.

Soon the darkness was full of whispers and stealthily moving bodies. Ian made for the scullery door and stumbled down two unexpected steps, knocking over a metal tray or a dust-pan. Someone very near him laughed nervously at the clatter and he drew his feet back, afraid that the unknown person would trample on his toes. He could smell the sink now and the tang of shoe polish. Ancient food smells came to him, but he could find no one hiding in the corners. He left the kitchen, felt his way up the two steps and passed into the hall. Opening a door, he found himself in the bathroom – a cold white glimmer came from the bottom of the bath. He touched a soggy sponge and shivered. But the bathroom too was empty.

As soon as he opened the next door he became aware of stifled giggles. He ran his hand along the wall until he grasped a bare leg. The giggle turned into a little shriek. Something touched his head, bounced away and touched it again. A handle on a chain. He was now in the lavatory and people were huddled round the pan, some even standing on the seat. A hand stretched down to help him up. He managed to wedge himself between the other bodies. They clung together there, surging and swaying and giggling. Ian's toes curled over the lip of the seat. He imagined himself as a primeval monkey standing on a branch in the chattering forest.

All at once he felt a hand exploring him. It ran tentatively down his arm, flickered over his stomach, one finger dipping for no more than an instant into the tiny cup of his navel before travelling on to his other arm. The hand had clutched his now, was kneading it excitedly in little rushes, rather as loving cats bite each other's necks. Distractedly Ian put out his free hand and touched a crucifix. The shock of the cold little metal body sent a shiver through him, starting a hot prick of sweat along his upper lip. On his ear farthest from the crucifix he could feel warm damp puffs of breath. He listened for a moment, caught a characteristic whistle and gurgle in the nose, and knew that he must have Bertha on his other side. Now he could feel her starched Union Jack skirt scratching his side.

The anxiety of not understanding exactly what was happening was rapidly undermining Ian's calm. Who could be fondling his hand so greedily? Could the nun have mistaken him for Bertha? They both had naked stomachs. Perhaps in his excitement the nun would not notice the great difference in their bulk. Had Bertha not mistaken him, but decided to tease him with these preposterous blandishments? Perhaps it was the nun who had decided to make a fool of him. This thought of maliciousness from a stranger was particularly hurting. The final confusion arose when he began to imagine that the hand belonged to someone quite unknown. There must be five or six other people standing on the seat, all within easy reach of him. Any one of them could be making a mistake in the dark. He was sure that there was some mistake or some intended cruelty. His own hand had gone stiff with discomfort and unhappiness. Yes, it was true; no one could ever love him.

He was just plucking up courage to snatch his hand away when the last person stumbled on their hiding place and the little crowd broke up, streaming out of the confined space to laugh and talk and stretch in the hall.

They played Sardines for a long time. Once Ian hunted with Baby. Under cover of darkness she had grown bold enough to smoke her little fibre pipe. When she lit the match, Ian saw her pinched face with the delicate nose and clear pink cheeks. Her pale hair, scraped behind her ears and tucked under the slouch cap, glistened for an instant. She looked remote, fanatical, consecrated in some way – but to what? To her book collecting? He kept with her because he liked the glow which quickly grew and faded whenever she sucked at the pipe. There was a dumb fellow-feeling too – not strong, but there. Ian, trying to explain it to himself, could only think of aspects of Baby that were not in themselves very winning. She had nothing to say; her mysterious preoccupation dulled her response to other people. She seemed to enjoy flouting her body. The scraped-back hair, the dirty scarf, the rough boy's clothes, gave her a secret pleasure. While she stood alone, her eyes far away, it was easy to believe that she had a contempt for 'ordinary' people, for their cocksure silliness and unreality.

Ian grew so tired of stubbing his toes on unexpected pieces of furniture, of waiting breathlessly in the dark, that at last he crept up to the French window and let himself out into the garden. The night wind blowing on his hot skin made him shiver, but he welcomed it. He went over to the cats. They were all lying down, like the lions in Trafalgar Square. The tom had made one of those amazing smells, fascinating and horrible in their pungency, their power to evoke all scenes of human squalor and misery. Ian squatted on his haunches near the cats and made sucking, cheeping noises in a forlorn effort to please them. Strangely enough the tabby roused herself and ambled up to him. She began to rub herself against his thighs. The feel of her soft fur on his bare flesh was delicious, but somehow vaguely shaming. Like some solemnly planned voluptuousness, it was too soft, too yielding, with no tang in it. Bertha was wrong about this cat, at least – she certainly showed no dislike of strangers. The tabby, trying to climb up on his knees, clutched at his chest when she found herself slipping. Ian gave a little gasp as the claws dug into his flesh. He put up his hand and felt a little trickle of blood. He licked it from his fingers, savouring the saltness on his tongue. Then he gathered up the cat in his arms and held it against his body. It was like nursing a huge silky cocoon, a baby wrapped in folds of slime, a purring seed about to burst from its velvet pod. He bent his head, cooing over the cat as if he would send her to sleep. She patted him once with her paw, ran her rough tongue over his skin, then nestled herself more snugly in his arms. The feathery brush of her fur, rising and falling, rising and falling, began to tickle just under his armpit. As a child he remembered his father tickling him there until he was unable to scream any more, until he felt he must go mad or die if the torture did not stop. The sensations came flooding back, turning the gentle tickle into something intolerable. The cat, as though she read his thoughts, turned in his arms and tried to struggle out, but perversely he held her, flattening her against him. In her alarm she gave him a savage little bite so that he loosened his grip; then she leapt away till the leash jerked on her neck, bringing her down, dejectedly. She was like a minute slave, bitter at the thoughts of her bonds. Ian stared down at her for a moment, then he turned abruptly and walked back into the house. He held the bite of his left pectoral muscle, but there was no blood this time. He knew just how it would look; there would be tiny white tooth marks, the skin abraded round the edge, as if he had been paper too much worn by indiarubber.

In the house the game had changed to Murder, but Ian was not to know this. Every room was still in darkness. Mechanically he crept about in search of the group of hiders. He was becoming more and more weighted and oppressed, and yet, at the same time, somehow hollow, as if he were a cave through which the wind was blowing. 'Morbid' was the word his aunt would have used for him. She always made the adjective sound particularly disgraceful, and Ian, against his will, gave it the same colouring.

There was a slight rustle in the darkness beside him, a little rush, then suddenly two hands were round his throat, pressing on his windpipe. He cried out in fear and his unknown attacker chuckled demonishly. He knew it was only some game, but he could not beat down his panic. If only he weren't lost in the stifling darkness! If only he could rid himself of the shock of those hands round his neck!

The lights were switched on. Bertha looked round and asked, 'Who's been murdered?'

Ian, still collecting his wits, put up his hand like a schoolboy: 'I think I have.'

'Then lie down, you fool. You're supposed to be dead.'

He lay down on the floor obediently. Bertha came up to him and saw the smear of dried blood from the scratch on his chest and shouted out gleefully, 'It's murder all right, there's real blood!'

Bending lower, she descried the tiny white punctures with their purplish centres. 'Ian, what have you been doing?' she asked ominously. 'Have you been teasing my cats?'

'Of course not. The tabby liked me very much. She wouldn't leave me alone.'

'No, I see she wouldn't. She's bitten you. Why did you upset her? I've told you they hate strangers.'

Bertha looked down at him balefully, as if she too hated him for trying to seduce her cats. They were *hers*. She would share them with no one.

The others were growing tired of this wrangle. If they were not to play Murder properly, they might as well forage in the dining-room for more food and drink before thinking of going home.

Gradually they disappeared from the room, leaving Ian still lying on the floor with Bertha standing over him. He was content to lie there; the strangeness of it rested him. If he stood up, he would have to face Bertha on her own level, contend with her ridiculously. How could she wish to possess her cats so entirely that she resented any attention paid to them? It was so absurd it saddened him. He would find it difficult still to think of Bertha as a great comic bouncing figure with something specially worthwhile and sensible deep inside. She seemed silly now, in her attempt to dramatize a trashy jealousy; she was like a girl on the pier determined to have a scene over some 'boyfriend'.

When Bertha saw that Ian would not get up, that he had insolently shut his eyes, feigning sleep, she too left the room, loudly complaining as she went, 'Bloody fool to touch my cats. Next time they'll scratch your mucking eyes out.'

Ian had to smile; Bertha's fatuous extravagance still tickled him. He sat up and saw the clock on the mantelpiece. He had missed his last bus by more than half an hour. The thought of the long journey home made his heart sink. He would be walking through miles of streets until early morning. He felt quite unequal to it, too tired to do anything else but lie down again on the floor. He wondered if Bertha would let him stay where he was for the night. He hated to ask after the trouble over the cats, but he was just about to go in search of her when he heard the swish of heavy skirts and turned his head to see the nun in the doorway. The white face bands were undone; it was clear that she was about to take off the whole head covering. In spite of knowing that she was really a man, it was a shock to Ian when she exposed cropped brown hair. The blunt, slightly freckled face underneath suddenly fell into place. Its heartiness ceased to be disquieting. One no longer felt that one was in the presence of the games mistress at some athletic convent.

'Are you sleeping there?' asked the nun, grinning to see Ian still on the floor.

'Well, I don't know yet; I'll have to ask Bertha. You see, I've lost my last bus.'

'That's easy. I can put you up if you like – better than lying there. The floor gets damned hard after a bit.'

It took a second for Ian to adjust himself to this idea, then he decided. 'That is very good of you. Are you sure you don't mind?' Perhaps this was the friend he'd been waiting for, he must wait and see, he wanted so to talk to him alone.

At last the party was breaking up, coats and hats were being dragged off the huge pile on Mrs Swan's bed, and Ian soon found himself walking along the cold pavement with the nun, habit off and trousers on.

They passed a row of little villas and the nun said, 'That's where a strange fortune-teller lives; she's got red hair and she's sixty and she always wants me to go and see her.'

They walked on until they came to a main road and saw the rows of silent shops. Up to one of these the nun led Ian. It was a barber's shop, and when the nun had found his key they went up the steep stairs into the darkness. It was so still, one felt all the people breathing quietly in the closed rooms. They made their way to the front. The nun switched on the light, and Ian saw that there was butter in a moulded glass dish and ham on a blue-ringed plate with other food laid out.

'This is my supper,' said the nun. 'Will you have some too?'

'I don't think I could,' answered Ian, then added, 'You know, I don't even know what your name is.'

'My name is Don Billings.'

'And mine is Ian Whyte.'

The meal was dreary and a little sinister – so late at night – with all the sleeping people round.

'I lodge here with the hairdresser,' said Don. 'Her hair is red too, but I think it's real. I think she's very fond of me; you see, I help her wash up sometimes. We must be quiet when we go upstairs else we'll wake her up. She's got a husband too, but he's a traveller.'

Slowly they groped their way up the stairs, Ian touching the shoulder of Don, until they came to the top floor – they passed the bubbling cistern, and Don gently opened the door of his room and shut it after Ian. They were in darkness. Ian saw the small grey square of the window, smelt the smell of bedclothes and waited until the light was switched on; then he saw the chest of drawers with white china knobs and the little picture standing on it. It was a reproduction of a landscape by Derain. A hot sandy road between dark trees with rich shadows and an eggshell sky. It was beautiful – and Derain was Ian's new discovery. He liked Don more than ever.

'My girl gave that to me,' said Don, 'because it's like somewhere we know.'

'Is that all they like it for?' thought Ian.

Don was undressing, he pulled his shirt over his head. How brown his skin was with light golden hairs. He was firmly and neatly built. Ian admired him standing, so obviously solid and strong, with his trousers resting on his hips. 'He is like a miniature navvy with all the edges polished,' he thought.

Don put on old flannel pyjamas and turned back the bedclothes.

'You get in first and I'll switch off the light.'

Ian did so and looked up at the ceiling. The night was so warm in this little attic and it was so strange to be in a different bed.

Don got in and they lay there close together, their warm bodies making the clothes seem a little damp. Don talked about his girl and many friends. Ian felt very lonely. It was nicer sleeping in bed with someone else; one wasn't so lonely.

'And yet I used to hate human contacts and always want to be on my own,' he thought. 'I wonder if I shall like it if he turns over and wakes me up?'

So gradually they dropped into sleep and the next thing Ian knew was that the sun was shining on him palely through a mist and that there was a scream of trams on the road. He looked at Don, who was still asleep. There he lay, pyjama-jacket open, his bare throat throbbing gently, with the golden hair at its base. There was a slight new stubble on his chain and upper-lip and there were freckles round his closed eyelids.

'This is a nice friend to have,' thought Ian. 'And now I must leave him and get on one of those screaming trams to go home. I must borrow a book so that I can come back to return it another day.' Looking round, he saw on the chest of drawers a book on Maya civilization.

Gently he pressed Don's arm and watched his eyes open, then slowly they both got up and took it in turn to wash in the cold water from the jug. Ian put on his trousers, rolled up the mauve bathing-suit, then, turning to the chest, said, 'Don, may I borrow this book?'

'Yes, do.'

Don was sitting on a chair, still undressed, and Ian, not waiting to be asked to breakfast, held out his hand and said, 'I must go now, as they must wonder what has happened to me at home.'

Then he ran down the stairs and let himself out into the early-morning air; clutching the book, he walked quietly towards the tram stop, saying over and over again to himself, 'You can never tell, I might never see him again.'

FULL CIRCLE

In 1933, when he was eighteen, Denton Welch went on a walking tour to the West Country, a full account of which was written in his Journal *and published separately in 1958 as* I Left My Grandfather's House. *This unfinished story was based on one of the incidents described there.*

I REMEMBER IT WELL, THAT STILL NIGHT BEFORE THE WAR, when I walked up to the entrance of the majestic house. The last glimmer from the dead sun was still hanging in the air. It lighted up the curious twisted chimney shafts and baroque gables, dramatizing them, so that it was difficult to tell whether the house were Elizabethan or Victorian.

I pulled the long shaft of the hand-bell and heard it echoing down what I imagined to be a stone passage. Soon there were footsteps and the door was opened to me by a footman with striped waistcoat.

For a moment I was surprised and rather taken aback by this uniform, never having seen it in real life before. I had imagined in a cloudy way that if people still had footmen, they dressed them like hotel waiters. Now this nineteenth-century relic delighted me. I looked at his smooth, good-looking, commonplace face and said, 'Can you tell me where I can get a bed for the night here? I'm walking along the Downs to Winchester and have lost my way.'

He looked at my rucksack with a darting, rather furtive look, as if to read my intentions from it; then said in a soft voice, 'There's nowhere, unless you choose to go back to Steyning.'

'How far is that?' I asked.

'About three or four miles.'

I saw that I would get nothing more from him. He was waiting, not too politely, to shut the door. He wanted to get back to the wireless in the servants' hall, or to his book by the fire. I felt, for some reason, that the family was away and that the servants had the house to themselves.

It was on the tip of my tongue to ask if he could not put me up somewhere in the house, but I had not the courage to listen to the weak excuse he would probably make for refusing. So I let him shut the door gently in my face.

Now I was surrounded by the night again, with nowhere to sleep, 'unless I chose to go back to Steyning'. His wording seemed ironical. As if anyone would 'choose' to walk back three or four miles after having walked twenty!

I crossed the cobbled court and stood by one of the stone urns which punctuated the balustrade. The coarse park grass on the other side lapped right up to this low wall. I heard the noise of animals chewing in the dark and to the right I thought I caught the glimmer from some crack between the curtains of a window. I wondered if the dark mass could be a cottage. I decided to climb over the balustrade and walk across the park to see. As I passed, sheep coughed, rose jerkily to their feet, and ran away to lean against the trees in fright. Sometimes I would see them with their rumps in the air, their front legs still bent under them in an involuntary attitude of prayer. They seemed unable to move; then suddenly their legs would flick straight.

As I drew nearer I saw that the light was moving. A man was carrying a lantern out to his beasts. I felt glad that I would not have to knock again at a strange door.

'May I shelter in one of your outhouses?' I asked, hoping that my voice would not startle him.

He turned round abruptly, then came towards me with the lantern held high.

'Where do you come from?' he asked, shining the lantern on my face.

'I am on a walking tour. I have been up to the big house, but the footman said that I'd have to go back to Steyning if I wanted a bed.'

'They wouldn't help you there!' he said contemptuously. It was contempt as much for my ignorance as for the inhabitants of the house.

He stood silently for a moment, looking at me. I thought he was going to ask me into the cottage, but when he spoke, it was to say, 'Come along with me, I'll show you where there's some hay.'

He took me across the tiny farmyard and led me to a shed which joined the barn. The smell of the hay met me as I stood in the doorway. The man had gone in and was stirring it up in one of the corners.

'You ought to be all right there,' he said.

I eased my rucksack off my shoulders as I thanked him. Leaning against the wall, I realized how tired I was. I hoped that he would leave me so that I could sink into the hay.

I did not have to wait, for after one further swift glance at my face he said goodnight. I watched the lantern swinging across the farmyard and waited until it had disappeared into the cottage and the door had clicked behind him. Then I undid my belt, kicked off my shoes and, after wrapping myself in my raincoat, lay down to sleep.

I was so tired that the events of the day kept passing before my closed eyes, running and mixing together in that fantastic, restless way. Cows in their stalls nearby shook their chains or knocked against the wooden walls.

Just as I began to wonder if I should ever fall asleep, I felt the delicious sinking and fading of consciousness. I lay like this until something jerked my eyes open. I was not yet fully awake, but I knew that the dim light had changed in the shed. It was darker still. Someone was standing in the doorway.

'Who's that?' I cried out in alarm, before I realized that it must only be someone from the cottage.

'It's all right, mate,' the man said in a soft voice. He came towards me and sat on the edge of the pile of hay. I saw then that he was only a youth, two or three years younger than myself. I thought that he was probably the son of the farmer. He had a pleasant face, but his lips and eyes were sullen. He seemed almost on the point of tears.

'What's wrong?' I found myself saying against my will. I did not want him to think me curious.

There was no answer for a moment, and I thought that he had

resented my question, until he suddenly burst out, 'Would you let your father still beat you if you were eighteen?'

'Not if I could help it,' I said with a laugh, trying to make the atmosphere lighter.

'No more would I, and I haven't!' His voice reached almost to a shout on the last words. 'Just look at that,' he went on, turning his back to me for my inspection. In the dimness I could just see dark stains on the white shirt. They might have been oil, mud or blood. I said nothing, and in his impatience he pulled his shirt over his head. Then I knew what they were. On the white flesh were raw wounds and long bruises.

'He made my brother help him tie my hands to a tree, then he did that with his belt,' he said. 'But he won't do it again in a hurry; I've treated him the same way!'

'What have you done?' I asked fearfully.

'Kicked him in the belly till he was sick on the floor!' The youth laughed and leaned back till the hay pricked his wounds and he flinched.

If the man with the lantern was his father, I wondered why I had heard nothing. He had certainly not been 'kicked in the belly till he was sick on the floor' when he led me to the shed, and if the incident had happened after he left me, I surely would have heard some of the inevitable noise through my half-sleep.

However, I determined to ask no more questions. I accepted the fact that a father had beaten a son who was too old to be beaten and that the son had replied by kicking the father in the stomach.

My companion showed no desire to go back into the house; he said that he would stay with me, out in the shed till the morning. He lay on his stomach, trying to ease his back into the most comfortable position. I had ointment for blisters and scratches in my pack. I got it out and rubbed some gently on the less important wounds (I could do nothing about the others). His flesh seemed burning, and I could feel how his whole frame trembled if I hurt him.

When I had finished he groped in the dark, then found my hand and held it firmly, as if to thank me.

Almost immediately after this he fell asleep, still touching me. Moving as little as possible, I put away the ointment and lay down beside him. His smooth breathing and the warmth from his body lulled me. Soon I too must have fallen asleep, for I remember waking later at the climax of some violent dream in which my companion or someone like him, only rather older, was standing in a doorway watching a woman take a tray of cakes from the oven. She seemed quite unaware of his presence till he sprang at her, pushing her on to the kitchen range and snatching the cakes with his other hand. I awoke at the terrible scream she gave as her hands and face touched the hot-plates of the stove.

I opened my eyes. My companion still lay close to me in the hay with his hand on mine; but his breathing seemed to have grown thicker, and I thought that I smelt an unpleasant odour from his body, an unkempt, unwashed smell which had not been there before. I supposed that the warmth had drawn it out from his old clothes. I tried not to think of it and composed myself for sleep again, hoping that I would not dream.

But I did. Scene after scene of squalor and brutality passed before me. The youth was always the chief actor. In each scene he seemed to be heavier and coarser than in the last. I was always the helpless spectator, hidden in some cupboard or spying through some skylight from the roof.

In my last dream I saw him following a little girl across a common. She was pretty; she danced gaily as she went along, throwing stones into the air and skipping. I saw him steal up behind her and grasp her round the waist. She screamed, but he put his hand over her mouth and dragged her underneath the bushes. I saw him pin her hands down and kneel on her legs, spread-eagling her. Then he tore at her clothes, and I awoke with such horror that I found myself sweating, while my throat was sore with dryness. For a moment I lay there collecting myself, inexpressibly thankful that it had only been a dream. I thought I would tell my companion when he woke of the horrors I had dreamt about him. It would amuse him. I could still feel his body near me and his hand on mine. He was very still, so I did not disturb him.

Although I kept my eyes shut, I knew that it was day, because of the red glow of the light shining through the flesh of my eyelids.

As I became more conscious of my surroundings I noticed the unpleasant smell again, but there was no doubting it now. It was the smell of human dirt, despair and squalor. His hand on mine seemed strangely rough and horny, and there was a coldness pervading his whole body. I thought that he must have been chilled in only his thin shirt and trousers.

I sat up, opened my eyes and looked down on my companion. Then in a moment I had jumped to my feet and lay back against the wall, my legs and arms trembling from shock.

A strange man lay there, and his face was grey and seamed and filthy. A line of dried dirt ran round his open, grey-lipped mouth, and a dribble of saliva was caught in the stubble on his chin. The strong hair on his chest frothed out of the rents in his sweat-blackened shirt. He was utterly still. I could not understand how my convulsive jump had not wakened him.

Then I knew.

I ran to the cottage door just as I was, without my shoes. The thick mud pushed through my woollen socks and lay in little cushions between my toes. I fumbled with the buckle of my belt as I rapped on the door.

The man I had seen the night before slowly opened it. He held a towel in his hands and his arms were dripping.

'What is it?' he asked grudgingly, thinking, I suppose, that I had come to borrow something.

'Quick, there is a man in the shed. He is ill.'

I knew that my voice was much too loud, but I could not control it.

The man pushed past me, still carrying his towel. When I caught up with him he was kneeling by the man in the shed. He had torn away what remained of the other's collar and was holding his head between his hands. Then he let it fall back on the hay and stared at it.

'It's our Tom,' he said, half to himself, half to me. 'I haven't seen him for twenty years.' And in quite another voice, he added, 'Go and tell my sister Annie to come quick.'

I started to run back to the house, but a woman in a white apron met me. The strings of it were flying in the wind.

'What is it?' she asked in agitation. 'What's wrong?'

'Your brother's in the shed, he wants you,' was all I could say.

I did not go back. I left them together and waited with my stockinged feet sinking into the mud.

I heard the woman begin to weep, and through the dark opening I saw her throw her apron over her face. It seemed a curious, almost stagy gesture. 'He has come home to die, he has come home to die,' she kept on repeating.

Then I heard the man calling me. 'Young man, will you help me?' he asked.

I could not bear to touch it, but I went in and picked up the boots behind my back so that I would be able to walk without looking at it.

We laid the body on the parlour sofa. The man looked at me and said, 'He was our brother. He ran away twenty years ago because my father beat him for going out with girls. But before he left he got my father in the cow-stall and kicked him so that when we found him he was half dead. He only lived for six months after that. But Tom didn't know what he'd done!' he added passionately.

I wondered why the man had told me this terrible story, but then I realized that he had again been half talking to himself, for his voice changed, as before, when he said, 'Now I suppose I'll have to go for the police.'

It was then that I had the unreasoning fear that I might be charged with the murder of their brother.

I thought, while I waited to be questioned, of the youth who had come in the night before, and of how he slept touching me, while I saw in my dreams all the terrible acts which had made him into the tramp who lay beside me when I woke in the morning.

I wondered what instinct had brought him home at last to die after so many . . .

THE JUDAS TREE

'The Judas Tree' was first published by John Lehmann in The Penguin New Writing *in 1945 and reprinted in* Brave and Cruel.

AS I WAS WALKING HOME FROM THE ART SCHOOL ONE day, a rather plump, middle-aged man in shaggy tweeds passed me and then looked over his shoulder. He had a smooth round face with red veins on his cheeks, pepper-coloured hair and a carelessly trimmed moustache. He carried a little bunch of spring flowers – hyacinth, narcissus, daffodils – and in his other hand was a knotted walking-stick.

The first time he looked round, his face wore no expression, and it reminded me of a beefy moon or a dartboard; but when, a few yards further on, he turned again, the skin round his eyes was crinkled into a kind and sleepy smile. He slowed down, then held out the bunch to me and said, 'Like to smell?'

I was surprised, but I bent down at once and put my nose to the cold flowers. Their rich breath filled my head. A little tingle of excitement ran through me. I waited to see what would happen next.

When I raised my head I saw that the man was looking down on me with a sort of hungry benignity impossible to resist. It was as if he were saying, 'Oh, you are young and silly and unprotected, and I am old and wise and unused. If only we two could combine!'

I felt that I had to treat him with great consideration, and this feeling threw up a slight barrier of pretence. I was a little uncomfortable.

'They are lovely,' I said, referring to the flowers. I nearly asked if he'd grown them himself, but the more I hesitated, the more inquisitive and pert the question sounded. I was tongue-tied and silent.

THE JUDAS TREE

We were walking together over Blackheath now, near the church, and the pit where they light bonfires on Guy Fawkes' Night. I expected the man to say goodbye soon and branch off in some other direction, but he stayed at my side and every now and then looked down at me. He was tall.

'Where do you go to school?' he said at last, smiling again in his disarming way.

I was nettled, but also obscurely complimented. I think I felt, 'Well, I must look simple! Nobody knows what's going on in this head.'

'I am an art student,' I said trying not to sound stiff.

'Oh, that's interesting!' and his face lit up, as though an idea had come to him.

'Do you know what a Judas tree is?' He stared straight into my eyes, then added, very surprisingly, 'I've been a schoolmaster for thirty years, and I can always tell when a boy is lying.'

'I was going to say that I didn't know.' I felt repulsed at once by this flashing glimpse of another side of his character. I recognized the schoolmaster's unnecessary parade, the over-emphasis.

'Well,' he said sweetly, returning to his earlier manner, 'it is a wonderful tree that bears great rose-coloured flowers; and the amazing thing is that the flowers appear before the leaves! Judas, you know, after he had betrayed our Lord, repented and took back the thirty pieces of silver to the chief priests. But when he had told them that he had betrayed innocent blood, they gave a terrible answer; they said, "What is that to us? See thou to that." So he threw down the silver in the temple and went to hang himself. He found a bare tree, climbed up into the branches, tied the rope; then jumped. The next morning the whole tree was lighted and hung with marvellous Judas-coloured flowers. And the Judas tree, from that day to this, always bears its flowers before its leaves.'

When he he had finished this story, the man's face was rapt. He seemed transported. To take him away from the dangerous subject of the Bible, I said, rather stolidly, 'Why do you call the flowers Judas-coloured?'

'Don't you know that Judas had red hair?' he rapped out. 'I've collected every picture I can lay hands on, and nearly all the painters from the early Italians downwards have given Judas red hair.

Sometimes it's curly, sometimes it's straight, but it's almost always red.' Then he gave me the names of one or two famous painters who had *not* given Judas red hair. He blamed them for inaccuracy, saying that their Judases failed and had not nearly enough evil in them, because of the mistake.

'Don't you think I've proved now that Judas had red hair? Could so many painters be wrong? There must be something in it.' He looked at me sharply and anxiously, as though he wanted to make me agree.

I nodded and said, 'I expect you're right,' then thought this weak, so added what I really felt.

'It is all such a long time ago that nobody can really tell. Perhaps all the painters followed a tradition which was started by a man who hated red hair and so gave it to the villain in his picture.'

The man was infuriated. 'Of course Judas had red hair!' he thundered. I was able to picture him in front of a class at school, abusing the boys violently.

We walked on in silence. Still the man didn't leave me. I was about to turn to the right, pretending that I lived in that direction, when the man, with all his fierceness gone, said, 'I'm wondering if you could do something for me, since you are obviously a clever lad.' I moved about uncomfortably in my clothes, wondering what was coming.

'Could you paint me a picture of Judas hanging dead from the Judas tree, with the beautiful rose-red flowers all round him? You could do the flowers very large, and I want Judas really dead. His tongue must be hanging out, black and swollen. It would make a wonderful picture, and I've been trying to get it painted for years.'

He looked at me with intense, excited eyes. He had begun his speech cajolingly, with the remark about the clever lad, but he ended on the same vibrant note as before. It was clear that he lived for Judas and the Judas tree.

'Won't you have a shot at it?' he pleaded when I did not answer at once. 'I could give you a great deal of help over the details. I've got some enlarged photographs of the flowers, and I know exactly how a hanged man looks. His head lolls on one shoulder just like this –' Here he stopped abruptly and, drooping his head to one side, showed the whites of his eyes and the whole length of his tongue in a hideous imitation of death.

'I could sit like this for you, if you liked,' he said, still holding the pose. I wished he would stop distorting his face, so I told him how convincing he looked and moved on. He hurried after me.

'I thought at one time of having real red hair, cut from a human being, or, if that's not possible, from a red-setter, for my Judas, but my sister, who lives with me, tells me that an oil painting in which real materials are also used is in very bad taste. Do you agree?'

He seemed wistful, wanting me not to condemn his idea as fantastic.

'I think to have the whole picture in paint would be safer,' I said carefully; 'but I'm afraid I could never do it for you. It would be much too difficult. I wouldn't know how to begin on such a subject.'

We had almost crossed the heath. I should have gone along Chesterfield Walk to reach my rooms on Croom's Hill, but the man said, 'You *must* come home with me and see my reproductions of Judas; and if my sister's in she will give us tea.'

Again there was the tingle of excitement in me, the feeling that some sort of adventure might be unfolding. I had been growing a little restive, but this invitation reawakened my interest. I wanted to see his surroundings.

'Oh – thank you,' I said, 'I'd like just to look at your pictures, but I *mustn't* be late back.' I hoped in this way to make any sudden retreat seem necessary, not rude.

Somewhere behind the Green Man we turned down a long street of mid-Victorian yellow-brick houses with dog-tooth mouldings over the doors and windows.

'We live a bit further down, on the left,' the man said, then, realizing that he did not know my name, he demanded it in his schoolmaster's manner.

I told him and he seemed to weigh it in his mind, as if trying to assess its worth.

'Mine's Clinton,' he returned solemnly.

'Oh, we have a girl at the art school called Clinton,' I said. 'She comes to the fabric-printing class, and she's going to teach art.'

He frowned and looked uncertain for a moment, then he said

stiffly, 'She is no relation – no relation at all. I can trace my family back to the thirteenth century.'

The last sentence, so naked, so irrelevant and disagreeable, chilled me. I said nothing.

'If they've got any books on heraldry at your art school, you'll be able to look up quite a lot about my family,' he said smoulderingly, *willing* me to be awed.

I still said nothing and he began to boast about his family so outrageously that I wanted to laugh. Could he be serious? I had known nothing like it since early schooldays, when children vied with one another over motor-cars, the size of houses and the number of servants kept.

I was relieved when he put his key into the front door and dropped the subject of his family as abruptly as he had introduced it. We were in a dark hall now. He led me to the door of the back room, then threw it open. I saw a grand piano, a large old portfolio stand, and books in low cases, lining the walls rather meagrely. Opposite the one French window was a dilapidated brown sofa.

'Sit down, sit down,' the man said expansively. I was his guest now, no longer a chance acquaintance. He wheeled the portfolio up to me, then brought out picture after picture in which Judas appeared. Some of them were charming old prints torn from books, others were shiny 'Last Suppers' and richly glowing 'Betrayal' scenes made for Catholic children. There were dreary photographs of great masterpieces and 'details' showing every crack in the plaster or the panel. I looked again and again at evil, twisted, avaricious features, at hyacinth-curling hair, at goatee beards and at ones flowing like the little waterfalls in Japanese gardens. There was simulated love – the lips kissing while the eyes were glittering, almost radiant, with treachery. Then the torture of remorse, the last agony of realization.

But there was no picture of Judas hanged, paid out, fulfilled. For a moment I felt the lack, almost understood Mr Clinton's preoccupation with the subject.

He was sitting very close to me now, breathing on my neck as he leant over me to point with his stubby finger. I could smell juicy pipe tobacco, the animal smell of tweeds, and something between alcohol and the smell in chemist's shops. Was it the last traces of whisky, of eau de Cologne, patent antiseptic or medicated snuff? I tried to analyse it in this elaborate way to cover my growing uneasiness. Would Mr Clinton never move away to some other part of the room? Had he enticed me here for some criminal purpose? Was he perhaps going to try to string me up, so that he should at last have a living, kicking picture of Guilt and Retribution?

My thoughts grew so wild that in my nervousness I began to gather the reproductions together officiously and thrust them back into the portfolio. I felt that his eyes were burning into the back of my head. He said nothing. I wanted to get up and run.

'Did you like your school?' The flatness of the question came as a shock. Because I had expected strangeness, or even violence, I was bewildered. How did this man's mind work? Why at the climax did he always jump to some other subject, as if the first one no longer meant anything to him?

'Perhaps I liked it in bits,' I answered vaguely, 'but I couldn't have enjoyed it much, because I ran away.'

'You needn't imagine that I think any the better of you for that,' he said.

Blood rushed up into my face. Could he think that I was proud of running away from school? The pointless snub seemed unforgivable, until I remembered that he was a schoolmaster.

He began to tell me all about himself. He had been a housemaster at a school whose name I had not heard before. Nobody had ever run away from *his* house. He understood boys, and boys understood him. It was, I was made to realize, a great loss to the school when the ridiculous rules had compelled him to retire. He was not idle, though. There was all this research on Judas to be done, and he was musical. Had I not noticed the Broadwood grand piano? Did I play?'

'Only a very little,' I answered cautiously.

'And can you sing?'

'I was in the choir at school until my voice broke, but now I don't sing properly,' I said.

He looked at me expertly. 'Perhaps you had a good treble; but what have you got now, I should like to know? Maybe something – maybe nothing. Just come over to the piano and we'll see.'

I followed him in a hot state of embarrassment. Was I really to be made to sing 'ah, ah, ah, ah, ah, AH, AH, AH' in that shaming way? I began to sweat a little. But a part of me was pleased. I wanted to be able to sing well, and once my voice had broken no one had bothered with it. Was my adventure to end in free singing lessons? I hoped so. Clinton looked so competent on the piano stool. I believed in him.

I began quaveringly, afraid of too much sound and of the surprising, unnatural tone of my voice.

'Louder!' he shouted.

I grew a little bolder, ascended and descended the scale, and sang particular notes which he thumped insistently, until they sounded like tom-toms in the jungle.

His hands dropped from the keyboard and there was an impressive silence for a moment; then he looked not at me, but out of the window, and said, 'I can make something of your voice. Of course, you'll have to work. You'd better come here at least twice a week.'

'Thank you so much,' I said, really grateful, 'but can you spare the time? Wouldn't it be a nuisance?'

'Nuisance! Why nuisance? It's part of my job. I've trained hundreds of lads' voices. I hate letting them go to waste.'

At this point a woman's tired, rather petulant voice called from upstairs.

'Excuse me,' the man said, leaving the piano stool at once; 'that is my sister. I shall go up and ask her about tea.'

It was long after tea-time and I wondered what the sister would say. I heard them talking at the top of the stairs in low voices. The only clear words were the sister's irritable 'Who is it?'

I was immediately ruffled, upset, put in a false position, and I decided to leave as soon as the man returned.

I heard him running down the stairs. He burst into the room in a young way and said, between puffs, 'My sister's got one of her troublesome heads, and so I've persuaded her to stay in her room, but we can go into the kitchen and forage for ourselves.' He seemed delighted about his sister's headache. He came up to me at the piano, put his hand on my shoulder and said, 'Can you boil eggs, you scoundrel, eh? I bet you coddle 'em or make them like old leather boots, but come and try, while I make toast.' He gave me several playful punches.

I was not expecting so much heartiness and good-fellowship. His changes in personality were too much for me. I had been hurt by his sister's words. And what was the cause of this sudden gaiety? Had he a sinister reason for wishing his sister out of the way in her room? All my misgivings reawoke and I longed to get away from him. It was easy to persuade myself that he was evil.

'But I really must get back,' I said, 'or they'll wonder what has happened to me.' Even if I had stayed out all night no one would have worried; but I allowed Clinton to think that careful parents were waiting for me at home.

'Can't you just stay to tea?' he asked, quite crestfallen.

'I'm afraid not; it's getting so late.' I moved firmly towards the door and he followed me, shambling.

'You *will* try to do my picture of Judas, won't you?' he said.

He was different again – sad, deflated, almost clinging. 'And you must come here for your singing lessons.'

'Oh, thank you, I will,' I said.

We were through the dark hall and I was walking down the steps and saying goodbye over my shoulder in my haste. I smiled at him and tried to look pleased, but it was easy to see that I was escaping.

He stood under the porch disconsolately, then gave a little jerk with his hand and went in and slammed the door.

I sucked in deep breaths of air and ran up to the heath, free at last.

✣

I saw nothing of Mr Clinton for about a month after this first meeting. I did nothing about his Judas picture and avoided going anywhere near his house. I regretted the singing lessons, but would not have braved his strangeness, his unaccountable changes of mood, and the something alarming in him, even for them.

When I saw him for the second time I was with three other students. I suddenly recognized his back. He was a few feet in front of us on the pavement. He carried no posy, but he had his walking-stick.

By turning my head away and talking earnestly I hoped to brush by unnoticed; but as I passed him I heard him call out, 'Oh, so it's you, is it?'

'Hullo!' I said, stopping and trying to put surprise and pleasure into my voice.

'What are you doing, going home?' he asked suspiciously.

'No; we're having tea together somewhere first,' I said, my eyes following the other students, who were now some yards in front.

'Have you done anything about that picture?' There was accusation in his voice.

'I haven't had a moment,' I said guiltily. 'I couldn't do that sort of thing at the school, you know. I'd have to do it at home.'

He turned sharply and saw me looking at the backs of the other students.

'Well – hadn't you better go after your friends?' he said, somehow threateningly. 'Hadn't you better leave *me* and catch *them* up?'

And in this last sentence Mr Clinton seemed to put all the waste and emptiness of his life. It was so sad that I was melted and horrified. He who had once had fifty boys to bully and befriend now had no one at all. People all smiled nervously and backed away, as I had done. How old and mad and undesirable he must be feeling!

'Why don't you cut along?' he sneered. 'Why don't you join them for a jolly tea-party? You're no use here.' He darted a venomous look at me and went on jeering at my dumb, nonplussed state. I would have stayed with him, but he was driving me away with every word.

'Yes, I must go,' I said miserably, turning my shocked, startled face to him.

But as I turned he looked away and appeared to be interested in a black boy's head and a pipe in a tobacconist's window.

'Goodbye,' I said uncertainly. He never turned.

Inexplicably wounded and humbled, I ran on to join my friends.

IN BRIXHAM HARBOUR

In 1934, when he was still at art school, Denton Welch went on holiday to Brixham in Devon with some fellow students, among them Valerie White (who became an actress) and Joan Waymark.

JOAN AND I AND VALERIE WENT DOWN TO THE HARBOUR where the boats were bobbing about on the black and white slippery water. The moon was up, floating far out over the sea.

We stood on the end of the breakwater and let the wind blow our clothes flat against our bodies. It had a nice, smooth, feeling touch, like very soft hands.

Pretty, fat Valerie's spotted rain cape filled with wind and bellied out. It crinkled and glistened like the water.

Someone passed us and went sinking down the stone steps. We heard him climbing into a boat and then push off. Soon he appeared, floating on the bright moon-path. He was singing now, and suddenly Valerie joined in, high above him. We nudged and pinched her to stop, but she laughed through her singing, making more and more noise.

'Would you like to come for a row?' the man called out.

'Yes,' shrieked Valerie. She shepherded us in front of her and we waited at the bottom of the dripping stairs.

When the boat was near the man stood up, leaned forward and caught an iron ring. The boat drew up to the stone wall with a little slap and click. We jumped in and sat down quickly for fear. The boat stopped rocking as the man pulled on the oars. We were not saying anything, only waiting for what he would say.

We seemed to be heading for a square hump of a boat; like a barge cut in half.

'Come on board and have a drink,' the man suddenly said, as we drew alongside.

'What is it?' Joan asked nervously. Then she laughed a little because she felt she had been rude.

'It's a painter,' the man said. 'There are three of us on board.'

He found the rope-ladder which hung down, and helped the two girls to climb. Soon we were all standing on the deck, waiting for him to appear. He swung himself over the rail like a monkey and then led us to the cabin door. Light leaked from cracks round the windows and we could hear voices.

The two inside looked at us curiously as we stood in the doorway. One sat at a table under the oil lamp. The other lay on his back in an upper bunk. They were drinking whisky out of egg-cups.

'John, some more egg-cups,' our friend said to the one who was lying on his back.

John raised himself and felt in the mahogany cupboard at his head. We sat down at the wet-ringed table and waited. Valerie was talking a lot. She had discovered that they were midshipmen. She said that her father was in the Navy, but that he was a terrible bounder and hadn't lived with her mother for years.

If they were midshipmen, I wondered why they were all dressed in dirty grey flannels instead of uniform. And the funny junk-like boat didn't seem at all like a Naval vessel. But I was reassured when one of them said 'wizard'; for that quaint adjective had long since become obsolete in other circles.

I think that the one in the bunk was pretending to be drunk, for he would ask irrelevant questions and then break off into snatches of song.

The whisky looked very repulsive in the bright blue egg-cups. As I shut my eyes to drink I heard Valerie explaining us to the midshipmen. We were art students who had decided to go for a bicycling tour together. Every night we stayed in a different youth hostel, or youth brothel, as she naughtily put it.

'Oh, I say, but are they really like that?' our first friend asked, shocked and fascinated.

'Certainly not,' Valerie said primly. 'That's only our pet-name for them. The sheep are strictly divided from the goats at ten o'clock. But perhaps you'll tell me that's no safeguard these days!' she added knowingly, taking them all in with her eyes.

There was a moment of not understanding what she meant, then two of them blushed. I don't think they liked her for making them blush.

Valerie was well away with our first friend. She was still discussing us. I heard her say mockingly, 'I'm not exactly fascinated by him, but we get on quite well together.' I supposed that she was talking about me.

Suddenly they both stood up. There was some quick explanation about showing her something and he led her through the door. Joan and I looked at each other anxiously. We wanted to leave the painter. We had nothing to say to the other two midshipmen and they had nothing to say to us.

I looked at my watch.

'It's getting late,' I said. 'I think we ought to be getting back.'

We went on deck and heard giggling and quick words from behind a hatch. They are pretending that it's all a game, I thought. We talked loudly so that they should hear us. The midshipman disengaged himself.

'I'll row you in,' he said reluctantly.

But the boat was nowhere to be seen. He ran round the deck, peering into the black water. It had vanished. Valerie laughed and said, 'We'll have to spend the night on board.' But Joan and I sank inside.

Then across the water we heard a stupid drunken singing and the splash of oars catching crabs. Suddenly the midshipman shouted insolent commands and swear words.

'Bring that bloody boat here, you bastards.' He was showing off his male qualities for Valerie's sake. I hated to listen to it, it was degrading.

Gradually, the boat with the drunken sailors emerged from the blackness. It zigzagged across the moonlit water. We laughed to think that they were so drunk. They were making placating noises in their throats and saying, 'All right, sir,' in a rather dazed way.

They climbed clumsily up the rope-ladder and stood in front of the midshipman while he reprimanded them. They ought to knock him down, I thought.

We rowed in silence over the water. Valerie seemed to be meditating. The man caught the iron ring again and we began to prepare to jump on to the steps. At that moment Valerie rocked the boat, pushing it out slightly, then she stepped towards the stairs and, with a plushy, sloppy, bubbling sound, sank into the water. Her spotted rain cape ballooned out and she giggled. She made no attempt to climb out. The man, seeing her there, thought that she could not swim. He waded down the steps, getting wet to the waist. Holding out his arms he said anxiously, 'Catch hold of me!'

She caught hold of him, and pulled him in. They clung there in the water. I could imagine parts of their bodies touching all the way down through the wet clothes. But the man was not enjoying it. He dragged her to the steps and then broke away.

'Goodnight,' he said coldly, getting back into the boat.

'Goodnight,' we shouted, 'thank you so much for our jaunt.'

Dripping Valerie linked arms with us and we began to run so that she should keep warm.

'Well, you were well away,' I said meaningfully. 'But I am glad you gave him a ducking in the end.'

'Wasn't he a monster!' she shrieked gaily. 'The frightful way he talked to those men!'

I felt warm towards her for disliking him. Then I remembered the things she had said about us to him earlier in the evening, and the way she had been half lying on the deck with him behind the hatch, saying quick things and giggling hotly.

STRANGE DISCOVERIES

Some time after his arrival at Croom's Hill, Denton Welch moved from the first-floor room described in 'A Novel Fragment' to the 'room at the top' described in this piece. Originally titled 'Discoveries', it was published in Vogue *magazine in December 1945 under the title 'Strange Discoveries'.*

WHEN I WAS AN ART STUDENT I LIVED IN A ROOM AT THE top of an eighteenth-century house on Croom's Hill. My one small sash window looked on to Greenwich Park, where lovers lay in the grass, and dogs and children played all day under the great Spanish chestnuts. Little traffic noise came up to me, but there was always the sound of feet on the pavement, so that I had a feeling of holiday, imagining groups of people climbing up to Blackheath to go for long walks, to gather round the huge bonfire on Guy Fawkes' Night, or to swing in the painted boats when the fair came. I remember everything about this room, because I was alone in it so much and because I had never before had a place of my own to enjoy.

On each side of the window the ceiling sloped down to within three or four feet of the wide old floorboards. These had been freshly ochred, and on this unpolished, tawny floor lay the pale skin of a lioness. It belonged to the owner of the house, and the comfortable bed was hers too, but nearly everything else had been bought with my weekly pocket-money.

Every afternoon I would go searching in the junk shops of the neighbourhood. When school was over, I used to jump on a bus and then get off at any street that looked promising.

I found my dressing-table in an old stable-yard on the other side of the heath. A man kept an open-air shop there and walked up and down behind his pile of furniture, like a truculent soldier behind a hastily thrown-up barricade. He let me have the early-Victorian worktable for seventeen shillings, and I put it on my shoulder and carried it home there and then, for I was too impatient to wait for it to be delivered.

I scraped the thick dirt off the pedestal with pennies, and rubbed all the surfaces with beeswax and turpentine until the rich rosewood shone. Over the cradle-like box, which had once been covered with pleated silk, I stuck silver and black striped paper; then I stood the transformed table under a long plain mirror and put my brushes on top and my handkerchiefs and socks in the drawer.

Next to the dressing-table I placed my chest. It was really the bottom half of a Chippendale tallboy, but I covered the rough pine top with a piece of worn Chinese brocade, and pulled off the clumsy wooden knobs which had been fixed on the drawers. As I had no brass handles to match the beautiful key scutcheons, I used to open the drawers by fitting my forefingers into the holes where the knobs had been.

In one rather dark corner glowed a little Flemish cabinet which I had bought for ten shillings in the New Cross Road. It was seventeenth-century ebony and tortoiseshell work. A vermilion ground showed through the translucent parts of the tortoiseshell, and there was a thread of ivory inlay round each black panel. When I found it, the drawers were filled with nuts and bolts, and thick black grease smothered the surface. I think some mechanic must have been using it for years in his workroom.

In this same New Cross shop, kept by an easy-going man and his Irish friend, I also bought an alderman's robe, which I had cleaned and mended, so that I could use it as a dressing-gown. It was made of thick crimson damask, lined with violet satin. The hanging sleeves and the hem were heavy with gold braid, and to wear it made me feel old and grand and unreal, so that I would put it on when I wanted to escape from my true self for a little.

My only chair was found, one weekend, in a country shop. It had little out-sweeping feet and a Greek spoon back, and so I suppose would be called Regency. The back was painted in white and terracotta, with the classic honeysuckle pattern surrounding a Gothic cusp and trefoil. The mixture of styles made it strange and,

STRANGE DISCOVERIES

to me, very attractive. I found too, when I sat in it, that the curved back fitted round my own like a shell.

The bed I covered with my great-grandmother's cashmere shawl. There were huge holes in it, but I ignored these, and saw only the amazing tree pattern which crept over the surface and seemed to gather to it all the lovely colour clashes and harmonies that there are.

Just above the bed, so that I could gaze into it in the morning, hung a little Rajput hunting scene, which I had found one day by running uninvited up the dark stairs at the back of my favourite shop. I had waited for some time in the show-room, and no one had appeared; so, armed with the excuse that I was looking for the owner, I broke into his private apartments.

I found him industriously repainting the clouds in a seascape. He was so good natured that he didn't even show surprise at my sudden intrusion. He let me look at everything, and it was while I was exploring the derelict room next to his own that I discovered the Indian miniature. Tiny huntsmen on horseback moved between rocks and trees, while their women bathed in a lotus pond. I thought for one moment that it was a shiny reproduction cut out of the *Burlington Magazine* and put behind dirty glass in a blistered maplewood frame; but when I took it to the light, I knew that I was wrong.

I think the man let me have it for eight shillings; and on my first free day, I took it to the British Museum, where someone in the Print Room told me that it was of the early eighteenth century.

'It is the sort of thing we would like here,' he added, but although his hint delighted me, I pretended not to notice, and took my drawing away, hugging it to me under my arm.

Later I was to make an even more exciting discovery, which should really be a story in itself, but I must just outline it here. One morning I was hurrying to the art school, when I saw in the old-clothes shop at the end of Croom's Hill the glint of a gold background between the rudely gaping trousers and jackets, and the sad polka-dot beach-pyjamas. I was looking at one of the smaller panels of a medieval altar-piece, but the sight was too extraordinary to be believed; and as I was already half an hour late, I ran on, telling myself that it could only be a late Russian icon.

All day the picture haunted me; so after work I went straight back to the shop.

The picture had gone from the window. A moulded glass butter-dish and a jug full of steel hat-pins stood there instead. I was afraid that it had been sold and that I would never see it again, but I went into the shop and after hard work discovered that the picture had been taken upstairs to be kept for a dealer.

Although I had only ten shillings in my pocket, I persuaded the man that I was able to pay the ten pounds he was asking, and he at last brought it down and held it out to me reluctantly.

I saw Mary and Joseph and the ox and the ass on each side of a baby whose little old man's body was prickly with gold rays; and in the thick gold sky swam an angel, bearing a scroll on which I could just read the words *'Gloria in excelsis'*.

I knew that I must have the picture, and I bargained until the man came down to four pounds, then I stopped, not daring to press him any further. I left the ten shillings and ran back to the house to borrow the rest from my landlady.

When, a few days afterwards, I showed the picture to Professor Constable of the Metropolitan Museum, New York, he told me that it was Italian work of the late fourteenth or early fifteenth century, probably from some country place near Siena.

This knowledge enchanted me for weeks. Sitting alone in my room, gazing at the picture, I would try to remember his exact words and the way he looked as he passed judgement.

Then my eyes would wander to all the other things that I had collected. A few, like the picture, were rare and valuable; others, like the rosewood worktable, were quite ordinary; but they all brought something to me, gave me their usefulness, their beauty or their strangeness.

I would sit there musing, until perhaps Miss S., my landlady, came to ask me down to tea with her father, when I would go into the garden and find them under the fig tree which could never bring its fruit to ripeness, but always dropped it in a hard green shower. We would eat apricot jam on soft bread and butter; and afterwards the father would wander away, saying vague, polite things.

Soon a strange discordant music might come from the house;

STRANGE DISCOVERIES

then I would know that he was playing his harp in the lovely old flagged kitchen.

I had seen him once in his woollen dressing-gown and skullcap, sitting in front of the huge golden instrument, plucking at the wires with his hands, while his eyes seemed fixed on the golden woman's torso at the top. And as he played, he sang a stern hymn in a goaty falsetto, for he was a Plymouth Brother; but not, I believe, any longer of the 'closed' order.

SICKERT AT
ST PETER'S

It was while he was convalescing after his accident in 1935 that Denton Welch made his celebrated visit to Walter Sickert, accompanied by Gerald, the art-school friend portrayed in 'A Novel Fragment'. This account was to be his first published work, appearing in Horizon *in August 1942. It was reprinted in* A Last Sheaf.

I HAD BEEN IN BROADSTAIRS FOR MONTHS, TRYING TO recover some sort of health after a serious road accident.

My doctor, knowing that I was an art student, tried to persuade Sickert to come and see me, but he wouldn't. I was told that he stormed off down the street, saying, 'I have no time for district visiting!'

That was while I was still in bed. When at last I got up, someone engineered an invitation to tea on Saturday afternoon. So he did not escape me after all.

Just as I was about to leave the nursing home for St Peter's, Sister sailed into my room, closely followed by Gerald, an art-school friend. He had evidently come all the way from London to see me.

I controlled my face as best I could and said, 'I'm going to tea with Sickert. What are you going to do? Can you wait here till I get back?'

He gave me one rapid glance and then said firmly, 'I'll come too.'

I was horrified.

'But you haven't been asked!' I burst out.

'That doesn't matter. One more won't make any difference.'

Feeling powerless in my convalescent state against his strength of will, I let him climb up beside me in the aged taxi which bore us swayingly to 'Hauteville'.

Sickert had not lived long in the house and it was still being altered. One entered through what at one time had been the 'cloakroom'! I remember with vividness the slight shock I received on being confronted with a glistening white 'WC' as soon as the door was opened.

Mrs Sickert stood beside it, welcoming us charmingly, with great quietness. She led us into what must have been the original hall. It was now a sort of dining-room, furnished with a strange mixture of interesting and commonplace things. An early-Georgian mirror with flat bevelling and worn gilt frame hung over the art nouveau grate. Seen thus together, each looked somehow startling and new.

We left our coats and passed on into the much loftier and larger drawing-room. The first thing I noticed was that the floor was quite bare, with that stained 'surround' which makes the white boards in the middle look so naked. By the sofa stood a stringy man who was about to go bald. The pale gold hair was still there, but one could tell how thin the crop would be next year. He looked at us with piercing eyes and fidgeted with his teaspoon. Mrs Sickert only had time to tell us that her husband was still resting, but that he would be down soon, before this man engaged her again in earnest conversation. She could only show us attention by pouring out cups of tea. My cup was of that white china which is decorated with a gold trefoil in the centre of each piece. Gerald's was quite different. It was acid-blue, I think, with an unpleasant black handle and stripe; but I noticed that both our spoons were flimsy and old. I turned mine over and saw, amongst the other hallmarks, the little head of George III winking up at me.

I looked at the other things on the table, at the brown enamel teapot, the familiar red and blue Huntley & Palmer tin, and at the strange loaf which seemed neither bread nor cake. In spite of myself, I felt that at least I was seeing Bohemian life.

I was glad that the man was keeping Mrs Sickert so busy, for it gave me time to stare at everything in the room. I saw that along most of the walls ran narrow panels, almost in monochrome. They looked like bas-reliefs flattened by a steam-roller.

They were most decorative. Mixed with these, but standing on easels or resting on the floor, were some of Sickert's own paintings. Gwen Ffrangfon-Davies dressed in Elizabethan farthingale and ruff, with harsh white light on her face, looked out from a picture mostly green and red.

Toy-like, bustled ladies and Derby-hatted men, all in soft greys and pinks, skated on a country pond. Pinned to the canvas was the original *Punch* drawing from which the composition had been taken.

Near the fireplace stood the long, brown haggard picture of the miner with his swinging lamp, just come up from the pit, grasping his wife fiercely and kissing her mouth.

As I was looking at this last picture, Sickert appeared in the door. My first sight of him was rather overwhelming. Huge and bearded, he was dressed in rough clothes and from his toes to his thighs reached what I can only describe as sewer-boots.

He had seen me staring at the picture and now said directly to me, 'That picture gives you the right feeling, doesn't it? You'd kiss your wife like that if you'd just come up from the pit, wouldn't you?'

I was appalled by the dreadful heartiness of the question. I found myself blushing, and hated him for making me do so.

Sickert came right up to me and looked me all over.

'Well, you don't look very ill,' he said. 'I thought you'd be in a terrible mess. Didn't you fracture your spine or something?'

I nodded my head.

He made an amusing, whining baby's face.

'Look here, I'm very sorry I didn't come and see you, but I can't go round visiting.' He waved his hand round the room. 'You see, I have to keep painting all these pictures because I'm so poor.'

He took up a position with his back to the fireplace. Mrs Sickert got up and carried a cup of tea to her husband. The stringy man also rose and floated to the door. He was still talking to Mrs Sickert over his shoulder, and the last words I heard as he left the room were: '... couldn't pass water for six days!'

This sounded so surprising that for one moment I forgot Sickert. Then I remembered him with a jolt, for he had begun to dance on the hearth in his great sewer-boots. He lifted his cup and, waving it to and fro, burst into a German drinking song. There was an amazing theatrical and roguish look on his broad face.

I could not believe that he always drank his tea in this way, and I felt flattered, because he seemed to be doing it especially for us.

I don't know how long the dance or the song would have lasted if the front-door bell had not rung. Sickert suddenly broke off and waited, while Mrs Sickert hurried out of the room.

She returned with a Mr Raven, whom I had met once before. After giving him a cup of tea, she left him standing on the hearth beside Sickert. He sipped his tea in silence for a few moments; then he began to feel in his breast-pocket. At last he brought out a rather crumpled, shiny object, and I saw that it was a photograph.

'This is my mother,' he said, pushing it under Sickert's nose.

Sickert drew back perceptibly and gave a grunt which might have meant anything.

Mr Raven continued, unruffled. 'Interesting face, isn't it? If you'd like to do a painting of it, I'd be very pleased to lend you the photograph for as long as you liked.'

There was another grunt from Sickert.

When Mr Raven realized that this was the only answer he was going to get, he turned very red and hurriedly thrust the portrait of his mother back into his breast-pocket. He looked just as if he had been caught in the act of displaying an indecent postcard.

Gerald and I exchanged glances. I think we were both sorry for Mr Raven and yet glad that his efforts towards cheap immortality for his mother had been frustrated.

Sickert, evidently prompted by Mr Raven's action, opened a drawer in a cabinet and also produced a photograph.

'Isn't she lovely?' he said, holding it out to me.

I took the yellowing little 'carte-de-visite' between my fingers and saw that it was of some young woman of the eighties. She had her back to the camera, so that her face was seen in profile, resting on one shoulder. She appeared to me quite hideous with a costive, pouchy look about the eyes and mouth.

I wondered who she could be. Perhaps she was someone famous; or perhaps she was one of Sickert's past wives or mistresses.

I felt in a very difficult position. Thinking as I did, I hated to be sycophantic and say, 'Yes, she's beautiful.' So I compromised very clumsily by answering, 'The photograph is so tiny that I can't see very much of her; but I love the clothes of that period, don't you?'

Sickert snatched the photograph from me.

'Tiny! What do you mean by tiny?' he roared.

He held the picture up and pointed to it, as if he were demonstrating something on a blackboard; then he shouted out in ringing tones for the whole room to hear.

'Do you realize that I could paint a picture as big as this' (he stretched out his arm like an angler in a comic paper) 'from this "tiny" photograph as you call it?'

Horribly embarrassed and overcome by this outburst, I smiled weakly and cast my eyes down so that they rested on his enormous boots.

I was not thinking of his boots. I was thinking of nothing but the redness of my face. But Sickert evidently thought that I was curious, for the next moment he had opened another attack with: 'Ah, I see that you're staring at my boots! Do you know why I wear them? Well, I'll tell you. Lord Beaverbrook asked me to a party, and I was late, so I jumped into a taxi and said, "Drive as fast as you can!" Of course, we had an accident and I was thrown on to my knees and my legs were badly knocked about; so now I wear these as a protection.'

In a dazed way, I wondered if he meant that he wore the boots to protect the still bruised legs, or if he meant that he intended to wear them as a permanent safeguard, in case he should ever again have an accident as he hurried to a party of Lord Beaverbrook's. I thought of the sensation they would create amongst the patent-leather shoes.

By this time I was so exhausted that I was pleased when Sickert turned his attention to Gerald. He started to talk about politicians, and I thought it was clever of him to guess that Gerald had an enormous appetite for titbits about the famous.

As I sank down on the sofa beside Mrs Sickert, I heard them begin on Anthony Eden. Sickert was describing his good looks. He must have sensed that I was still listening, for he suddenly turned his face on me, and his eyes were twinkling with fun and malice.

'Ugly ones like us haven't a chance when there's someone like Eden about, have we?' he called out across the room.

I was so surprised at being lumped together with Sickert in ugliness, as opposed to the handsomeness of Anthony Eden (who had never struck me as anything but middle-aged), that I took him quite seriously and could answer nothing.

I hurriedly tried to compensate myself for the humiliation by telling myself that, although it might not be saying very much, I was undoubtedly by far and away the best-looking person in the room, and this in spite of my long illness.

Mrs Sickert saw that I was ruffled and very kindly started to talk about my career. She asked me if I intended to go back to an art school when I was well enough. We discussed the various objects in the room. She told me that the two glittering monstrances had come from a Russian church. We went up to them and I took one of the sparkling things in my hands. The blue and white paste lustres were backed with tinsel. They were fascinatingly gaudy and I coveted them.

We sat talking together on the sofa for a little longer. Through our words I caught snatches of what Sickert was saying. Gerald evidently had got him on to Degas and anecdotes were streaming out. Gerald was drinking them up thirstily, while Mr Raven hovered rather uncomfortably at the edge of the conversation.

At last he decided to go. Coming forward, he coughed slightly and held out his hand to Mrs Sickert. Then, as he passed Sickert on his way to the door, he felt in his pocket and with almost incredible courage brought out the crumpled little photograph again.

Putting it down on the table, he said simply, 'I'll leave this just in case . . .'

His voice tailed off as he saw the completely blank look on Sickert's face. I knew exactly what was coming and waited for it.

Sickert gave the same enigmatic grunt. It was somehow quite baffling and insulting.

Mr Raven crept unhappily to the door and Mrs Sickert followed swiftly to put salve on his wounds.

Immediately Raven was out of the room Sickert became boisterous. He started to dance again, thumping his great boots on the floor. Gerald and I caught some of his gaiety. We did not mention Raven, but I knew that we were all celebrating his defeat. It was pleasant to feel that Sickert treated us as fellow-artists.

I wondered how many people each year asked him to paint pictures for love.

As Mrs Sickert did not return, we went into the hall, where Sickert dragged on our coats as if he were dressing sacks of turnips. Then dancing and singing in front of us, he led the way through the 'cloakroom' to the front door. I half expected some remark about the shining flush-closet, but none came.

It was dark outside. We walked over the greasy cobbles. Sickert was leading us. He threw open the creaking stable-yard door and stood there with his hand on the latch. He looked gigantic.

We passed through and started to walk down the road.

'Goodbye, goodbye!' he shouted after us in great good humour. 'Come again when you can't stop quite so long!'

And at these words a strange pang went through me, for it was what my father had always said as he closed the book, when I had finished my bread and butter and milk, and it was time for me to go to bed.

A PICTURE
IN THE SNOW

'Danny Whittome' was Francis Streeten, an eccentric character whom Denton Welch first met in Tonbridge in 1937 and who appears in various guises in a number of stories. 'A Picture in the Snow' was first published in A Last Sheaf.

YESTERDAY, IN THE COLD BRIGHT SUNLIGHT, WE DROVE through the snow to our nearest town to do some household shopping and to find, if possible, a small spare part which was needed for the car.

We tried garage after garage, turning down side roads, going from one end of the town to the other, without success. We ended our search by cruising along a wide road on the outskirts, no longer with any idea of finding the spare part, but simply to enjoy the sight of the snow on the houses and gardens for a little longer before turning home.

All at once I was aware of a gap in the thick plantation of trees and shrubs on the right. I looked up the bank and saw that two new building sites had been cleared at the top, but as yet no building had been begun. There was a clear view of the great house behind.

The sudden unexpected sight of its twisted chimneys, its stone mullions, its stepped gables, the whole Edwardian solidity and comfort of it, brought back vividly another afternoon nine years ago. I found myself concerned for its fate, angry that the trees and bushes screening it from the road had been torn up so ruthlessly. It was almost as if it had been some house of my childhood, cherished in many happy memories; yet I had only seen it once before.

On impulse I asked G. to turn into the drive, feeling fairly certain that the house must be empty. If it were not, our car should arouse little interest; we would probably be taken for builders, architects or any of the other people who had to do with the two cleared sites in the garden.

Half-way up the drive we came upon three old women; they were talking together with much gesticulation. One leant towards another as if she would breathe in her face until she convinced her or made her lose consciousness; the third gave us a quick, darting look, then hooded her eyes in an attempt to make us think that she had taken no notice, that we were not impressed on her memory for days and nights to come.

I was glad when we were past the old women. I said to G., 'Let's just go to the end of the drive, turn round and come back quickly.'

As we wheeled round in front of the stone porch with its flat Tudor arch, carved coat of arms, and oriel window above, I was just able to read the word 'home' on a new bronze plaque. The old women were explained to me then; they were patients probably suffering from slight mental disturbances.

'So it has come to this,' I thought; 'Mount Lodge is now a "home", and the garden is being torn up so that two little annexes can be built for nurses and doctors.'

Once more my mind went back to the afternoon nine years ago when I first saw it and learnt something of its history.

I had been walking in the town; I think I was coming away from the public library where I had been searching for something in a reference book. I was deep in my own thoughts, with my head down, but I became aware of footsteps behind me. They seemed to be hurrying, then a shadow loomed over me and I looked up to see a very tall, very plump man of about thirty-five passing close to me on the pavement. As soon as he was a few yards in front, he seemed to slacken his pace, almost as if he were waiting for me to catch up with him. He ambled so slowly that I did indeed draw level with him in a moment. Before I knew quite what was happening he had turned, bent down towards me with a tentative smile, and was saying in a surprising baby voice, 'Oh – you look interesting; do tell me about yourself.'

I was too taken aback at first to do anything but notice that the end of his pug nose was quite brown from tobacco smoke; it looked as if it had been toasted. But how was I to answer his extraordinary remark? The little rhinoceros eyes were still upon me. I must think of something to say.

'Does "interesting" mean "peculiar"?' I asked, as unconcernedly as possible. 'Do I need a hair-cut? Or is it my clothes? Perhaps, when you passed me a moment ago, I had a far-away "doped" expression on my face.'

'Oh no!' the piping voice protested. 'But I'm sure you write or paint or do something interesting. I've seen you several times.'

I immediately felt spied upon, as if this fat man had been hiding in doorways and side alleys to catch me out in some discreditable practice.

'Well, what do *you* do?' I asked, retaliating.

'Nothing very much at the moment, I'm afraid; but I've always had a great interest in politics, psychology and literature.'

'In that order?' I asked.

Again the flickering uncertain smile.

'Yes, perhaps now; but my childhood dream was to become a writer. I had almost finished quite a novel by the age of eleven. I still have it in my bedroom; some day I must run right through it and see what my maturer judgement makes of it.'

A delicate little titter, like sparrows chattering in the eaves.

We were walking together now as if we had known each other for years. The fat man had insisted on falling into step with me; if ever the rhythm was broken by my disregard of it, or by some obstruction on the pavement, he would give an absurd little skip and come down again on his left foot in time with mine. I half expected him to begin intoning, 'Left, right, left, right, left, right,' in a sort of sleep-walking boy scout's voice.

As we marched in this military fashion, I was able to take in other aspects of my new acquaintance. His stained grey-flannel trousers flapped against his legs rather flimsily; instead of a belt, he wore an old silk tie threaded through the loops at the top. His vivid blue jacket sagged and bulged at the sides, making it clear that he was in the habit of stuffing his pockets with all manner of objects. His face was round and pale, but whenever he turned to me I noticed again that the little eyes twinkled from beds of much darker flesh. It was almost as if he had once been given two black eyes which had faded at last to these dusky circles. His lips were dark too, and full; some of their darkness was again due to tobacco stain, and the first two fingers of his right hand might have been carved out of mahogany.

When we reached the top of the town where the road divides, I slowed my pace, meaning to say goodbye and take the right branch; but my fat friend refused to let me go. He stood in the middle of the road imploring me to go back to tea with him.

'Oh, do come back,' he said; 'there is no one at home. We can have such a pleasant chat. I do hate being left on my own.'

His baby voice was so insistent, so appealing, that I found myself resisting stoutly; then some sudden spark of curiosity burnt down all my defences and I was thanking him meekly for his kind offer.

'My name is Whittome,' he said; 'but please call me Danny – all my friends do – isn't it frightful?'

I felt called upon to give my own name. There is something formal, something sobering about an exchange of names; one is made conscious of self and the lack of intimacy that exists between that self and the new companion. We walked on in silence until we came to the gates of a small late-Victorian red-brick villa called Elm Dene; the name, in fresh white letters, was painted on each solid gate pier.

'This is where we live now,' said Danny.

Was there the slightest ring of apology in his voice? I wondered about the unnecessary 'now'; it seemed significant.

He led me past the neat carpet-bedding, under the involved cast-iron porch, and into a rather dark dining-room with blue and white plates and vases on a shelf above the panelling. Tea for one was already laid on the large pale walnut table.

The maid must have heard us enter, for she came to the door already carrying the tea-tray and an extra cup and plate. She put down the silver teapot and a rather unusual hot-water jug on a stand over a spirit-lamp. Before she left I saw that she was old and that her grey-white hair was piled rather clumsily under her wide old-fashioned cap; it escaped at the back in sad little curls and wisps. She seemed to treat Danny with a weary indulgence, as if she had known him too long to be surprised at anything he did.

My eyes fixed on the delicate blue spirit-flame; the hot-water jug above seemed more fanciful, more luxurious than the other tea-table appointments. Did it belong to an earlier period in the Whittome fortunes? What sort of a house was this that I had entered? And was it going to be difficult to get away?

Danny had begun on the toast greedily, but only after a painful hesitation because both brown and white bread had been used.

'Which is nicest,' he asked anxiously, 'brown toast or white toast?'

'Both are nice,' I said prosaically, rather in the tones of a patient nanny; although he was so much older, his childish importunity, whether natural or assumed, had the effect of making me feel 'in charge' of him.

His fat dimpled hand still hovered above the toast dish. The two brown fingers looked like little chipolata sausages dancing in the air. He finally plumped for white toast, stuffing a whole finger into his mouth and champing noisily. He seemed to revolve the toast round and round, and as he did so, his body heaved from side to side, reminding me of pictures of Dr Johnson; or was he more like an enormous praying mantis?

'My father won't be back for some time,' he said, with his mouth full. 'He still goes up to the city three days a week.'

I said, 'Oh, I see,' not knowing what else to answer. Things were going very badly indeed. I wished that I had not given in to my foolish impulses and trapped myself in this dark room with its ponderous walnut furniture and coarse blue plates and jars. Danny perhaps could tell that I was eager to escape, for almost before I had finished the last morsel of my cake he was pressing a cigarette on me, as if trying to keep me with him for at least another quarter of an hour. It was clear that he preferred any company to none, that he had a hatred of being left alone.

'Come up to my bedroom and see my books,' he said, catching at another method of keeping me a little longer.

I followed him upstairs and down a narrow passage. He opened a door and I found myself in a little room where every piece of furniture, except the iron bed, was heaped with books. There were piles on the floor, even the tiny fireplace was blocked with them. Danny flopped down on the bed and began to open volumes on his knee. Sometimes he would thrust one towards me, pointing out a passage, a title page or an illustration. They were mostly fairly well-known novels of the twenties and books on psychiatry with lurid case histories printed in the appendix. There were political books too, but these I found so dull that I can remember nothing at all about them.

My eyes strayed to a small photograph above the bed. I saw a little boy of four or five, dressed in white party clothes after the fashion of the first years of the century. He looked both plump and petulant. The rich glow of his silk socks and jersey made it easy to dismiss him as the traditional 'pampered darling'; yet there was an attractive seriousness about the face, as if the child already had thoughts for his own future.

'Guess who that is,' said Danny, puckering his face gleefully.

'Too easy,' I answered. 'It's you, of course, in your party suit.'

'Did you really recognize me?' he asked, a wistful humble note creeping into his voice. 'Yes, I was a promising, pretty child; and now I've got fat and almost given up hope of ever doing anything at all.'

He was angry, not so much with himself as with Fate for playing this dirty trick on him. How dared she make him fat and take away his hope!

He bent down and pulled a suitcase from under his bed. Opening it, he began to rummage until he had gathered eight or nine faded green exercise books together.

'Shall I read you bits from my childish novel?' he suggested tremulously.

'Yes, do,' I said, feeling quite eager to listen. Surely the novel of a child of eleven would have something interesting about it!

He opened the first book, smoothed the page, then shut his eyes and exclaimed, 'No, no, I can't. I might be terribly disappointed in it; it might spoil it for me for ever. Besides, you haven't seen the setting yet. I'd like to show you where we used to live; then, if I do decide to read you bits, you will have a clear picture of the background.'

He stood up, all agog for me to follow him. We went down the back stairs and out into the garden. He was secretive, wishing to surprise me with something, so I asked no questions. We crossed the lawn behind the house and came to the vegetable garden. At the far end Danny unlatched a little gate and led me down a narrow path between thick hedges. Soon we were in the shadow of a solidly built stable and coach-house. Danny pushed through a gap in the hedge. I followed and found myself looking down into a white cucumber frame where baby chickens cheeped and fluttered round their mother. Danny bent down, grasped one rather anxiously and began to cherish it in his hand, murmuring baby language to it. Was this what I had been brought to see? The chickens were very pretty, but I had no wish to pick one up, to feel the trembling little bunch of feathers struggling in my hand.

'Aren't they sweet? Aren't they sweet?' chanted Danny with half-closed eyes; then he seemed to remember what he came out for. He put down the chicken and led on through the bushes. We passed the cobbled stable-yard and came out on an overgrown drive banked on either side with rhododendron, laurel, holly, box and other ornamental shrubs. I noticed a forlorn lamp-post with broken glass and empty bulb socket; leaves surged up to smother it. A few more years and it would be lost. The drive twisted artfully. Danny was hurrying now, as if he were impatient to confront me with what lay at the end. His excitement was rising. Under the great weight of his belly his twinkling feet seemed small and neat and extraordinarily agile. I thought of him as the Minotaur charging down the windings of the labyrinth.

We turned a corner and he stopped suddenly. 'There it is,' he almost squealed; 'that's where we used to live.'

I saw the mechanically picturesque outlines of Mount Lodge for the first time, the studied disorder of mullions, transoms, archways, spandrels, parapets, gables, dormers, crockets, finials, and diapered chimneys piling up and up, bewildering the eye so that it clung for relief to some minute detail – a carved leaf, a shield, a chip in the stone dressings, a damp patch on the brickwork.

'What a whopper!' I said, knowing that it would please Danny.

'Yes, isn't it,' he agreed, between giggles of sheer pleasure. 'My father built it in 1905. I can't think why, really, because it was always too big and mother much preferred picnicking in a little cottage she had. Still, he would insist on it; it's supposed to have cost about £17,000. Perhaps it gave him a feeling of achievement. In those days he was rather a flourishing stockbroker; but things aren't the same any more; we finally had to leave the house six years ago. It has never been let; nobody wants such a large place. The gardener still lives over the stables and keeps plants in the greenhouse. Those were his dear little chickens we saw.'

We began to walk towards the house, climbing some stone steps to a terrace before a great bay-window. I peered through the dusty glass and saw elaborate parquetry and a plaster ceiling heavy with bosses.

'That's the drawing-room,' Danny explained eagerly; 'and there's a morning-room, a library, a billiards-room and a conservatory as well. Unfortunately I can't let you in because my father hides the keys ever since I allowed a rather wild friend, who'd lost his last bus home, to sleep in the conservatory. The irritating creature amused himself by breaking panes of glass. I'd never have let him in if I'd known he was so tight.'

I was moving round the house, looking in at all the windows, while Danny pattered after me, describing the past in disjointed snatches. He had so much to tell; he could only spend a moment on each episode.

'Of course, once we went rather grand and had a page with buttons all down the front; the funny thing was that he and I belonged to the same boy scout patrol or pack or whatever it's called. We used to meet in the evening and pretend that we'd never set eyes on each other before. Then there was the time when my mother asked an Austrian count to stay. In a morose fit he locked himself in his bedroom for hours and hours, until we all felt that he must have committed suicide. He came out at last, calmly playing with the cat. Do you know what I used to say to people about this cat?'

'I can't think,' I said absently.

'I used to say, "Have you ever seen a cherry-coloured cat with rose-coloured paws?" When they shook their heads, I'd tell them that I had one and show them Tinribs with his *black* body and *white* paws. They never thought of black cherries or white roses.' Danny giggled as if somebody was tickling the soles of his feet with feathers. He saw me looking at the rough tussocky grass which swept away in an ever widening fan until it reached a curving bank rather like some primitive earthwork.

'Of course, this was such a marvellous lawn, but it hasn't been mown for years. Once we had a garden party and I dressed up in all my mother's beads and rings and brooches and sat in a darkened tent, pretending to be the gypsy fortune-teller. Nobody recognized me and I prophesied terrible things – financial disasters, and deaths, and the most peculiar love affairs.'

At the back of the house we came upon a desolate little patch fenced round with miniature palings. Danny opened the tiny gate and stood in the middle of the weeds.

'And this is *my* garden,' he announced dramatically; 'I've had it ever since I can remember.'

'You don't seem to have done much work in it lately,' I said. It was curious how Danny forced one into the position of nurse or schoolmaster. Why should *I* censure his laziness?

'Oh, I can't keep my mind on anything these days. If only I could, I'd have more important things to do than a child's garden; but I worry and worry and worry and nothing gets done – nothing!'

He was staring at me desperately; his bottom-lip looked swollen, as if it had been stung by bees. It trembled a little. I turned away and remarked brightly on the first thing that met my eyes.

'Is there a pond behind all that dry bamboo grass?'

'Yes, it's terribly overgrown and weedy now, but we used to have a tiny boat on it. One of my mother's fantasies was that we should one day sail about on it, eating chocolate creams of every imaginable colour – a white one, a pink one, a blue one, a green one, a mauve one, an orange one, a lemon one – can you think of any more colours?'

'What a quaint conceit!' I said laughingly, still trying to keep Danny from his black thoughts.

'Yes, she was like that . . .'

His voice tailed off. I imagined that his mother was dead, that he was dwelling on his memories of her.

'She used to paint quite a lot, you know,' he added. 'Would you like to see some of her pictures? A few are still stored in one of the stables, I think.'

I followed him towards the cobbled yard. We entered a stall and stood over a manger, turning back watercolours in narrow white frames. There was a still-life of anemones, jade beads and a little gilt Buddha; there were several garden scenes, bright with herbaceous borders; more ambitious landscapes of churches, rivers and autumn woods.

'Is your mother still alive?' I asked at last, shirking the difficult task of saying anything about her painting.

'Oh yes, but she's had to go away, if you understand what I mean. She has a little cottage near the sea. It's better if she only comes over occasionally to see us.'

I didn't understand, but it was clear that I could ask no more. Mother perhaps was a little mad.

Danny replaced the pictures with neurotic exactitude, easing each corner into perfect alignment with the next.

'Let's go back by those winsome little chickens again,' he said.

We started to push our way through the bushes. I heard a car in the drive and thought little of it, but Danny stopped at once.

'Who can be coming here?' he asked, exaggerating his perturbation. He turned back with a noisy crackling of dead twigs. A large black car swished by, then stopped. I could see the rounded top of a hackney-coach label. Someone was getting out, a rather beautiful, 'over-blown' woman in a sable coat thrown open carelessly. She wore no hat and the light glinted on her snugly waved, greying auburn hair.

'Darling!' she exclaimed, swaying gracefully towards Danny. 'They told me that you were probably in here; I suddenly felt I had to come over and see you both. Aren't you pleased? Now take me back and give me a lovely strong cup of kitchen tea – that's what I want.'

Danny was gazing at her open-mouthed. Mechanically he bent to kiss her. 'But we never expected you. It's one of Daddy's London days; he isn't home yet.'

'D'you ever know when to expect me?' the woman laughed. 'It doesn't matter about Daddy; I can wait.'

'Oh! But I have a friend in the bushes,' said Danny, remembering me.

'My dear, what an odd place to have him, or her! Please introduce me at once.'

The handsome woman came towards me, peering from side to side. I emerged from my hiding place and waited, smiling awkwardly.

'What must you think of Danny, leaving you to pine in there?' the woman said, holding out her hand.

Danny had followed her excitedly.

'This *is* my mother,' he explained, his voice mounting higher and higher. His excitement expressed itself in little snorts and grunts. The delight he felt in being able to show her to me seemed to crown his day.

'Has my son been showing you our old house?' she asked. 'I suppose in my heart of hearts I think of it as "a dear old place", although it was never really "me"; Ronald was the one who would insist on it. Still, I have my memories, such odd ones some of them.'

Danny's mother began to bite her pearls; she fiddled with them till she had the diamond clasp in her fingers. It flashed and winked at me like a knowing eye.

'What has this great son of mine been doing lately?' she asked, still addressing me, but never waiting for an answer. 'Anything? Or nothing at all?'

She put her hand up to Danny's shoulder as if she would shake him playfully.

'How often have I said, Danny darling, "men must work and women must weep"? But with no effect; he doesn't take the slightest notice. He's the laziest lump in all Christendom.'

She tried to give him a little push, but his great bulk nearly overbalanced her. She reeled and her face came near to mine. I saw the heavy powder on the rather uneven skin, the slightly bloodshot corners of the handsome eyes. The delicately shaped and painted lips parted. There was a sudden breath of spirits. And then I understood.

Danny was watching me closely, giggling at the consternation on my face; he seemed to be waiting for something else – for the complete exposure of his mother? I turned and walked rapidly away, afraid to listen or look back.

That last scene was printed on my mind; it had lived with me for these nine years, so that I found myself extravagantly sorry at the change in Mount Lodge and the garden. It was almost as if it had been a house of my childhood, cherished in a hundred memories.

A FRAGMENT OF
A LIFE STORY

Although set in 1940, 'A Fragment of a Life Story' describes events which occurred around 1937 when Denton Welch was living at 54 Hadlow Road, Tonbridge. The doctor was Jack Easton, whom Denton Welch had first met in 1935 when convalescing in a nursing home in Broadstairs following his accident. 'Touchett' was Francis Streeten and 'Lydia' was Evelyn Sinclair, now his housekeeper. The story was drafted in the Journals *on 2 December 1942; this final version was first published in* Horizon *in September 1949 and reprinted in* A Last Sheaf.

FOR SOME REASON I HAVE BEGUN TO THINK AGAIN OF that late January afternoon at the beginning of the war when my curious fat friend Touchett took me to the parish hall to see a religious film. The film was thirty years old, and Touchett kept telling me this, wanting me to marvel at its age.

I had gone with him to strange meetings before. Once it had been to a lecture on corporal punishment at the Baptist Hall, where he heckled the poor schoolmaster until I became very embarrassed. And another time we had left the adult school hurriedly when some of the adult scholars, not caring for the political tone of the speaker, began to throw scalding coffee and the rather solid buns which had been provided for refreshment.

I had been very ill; so I told Touchett now, when he asked me to go to yet another meeting, that I did not feel strong enough for scenes. He assured me that the parishioners would behave perfectly.

But as we took our seats at half past three on that sullen afternoon, something seemed to click inside me. I couldn't bear the smell of the parishioners' furs, or the sight of the tatty bows on their hats. I couldn't bear the smell of the raw wood chairs, or the feel of their rush seats through my trousers. I couldn't bear the blistering, disintegrating flicker of the ancient film. The silver spots and smears tore across the camels, transfixed the asses, raced down the flat-roofed buildings, and made Jesus' face into a painful jigsaw puzzle.

There is no doubt about it, I was overcome with the horror of living. It was too disgusting for any words.

I jerked myself to my feet and pushed roughly by Touchett, who quavered after me in a babyish whisper, 'What's wrong with you? Are you going to be sick?'

Still looking straight in front, I said, 'I can't bear it any more; it's awful!'

'Don't you like the film?' he asked. 'It'll get even better soon; and, as you know, it's thirty years old and has probably been preserved specially for us by Providence.'

Anyone not knowing him would have thought he was serious. There were subdued murmurs of 'Hush.' I made for the door blindly. I seemed to be almost fighting my way to it. I half fell as I caught hold of the handle.

The cold air blowing on me struck me as pleasant in some way, but I could not tell why. I did not seem able to explain anything to myself. I even wondered why the light was so weak on this winter afternoon.

I began to walk down the town. I crossed the bridge and still followed the high street until I came to the great black station-yard where the trains were shunting and snorting. On the other side of the road, outside the public library, a youth stood, whistling mournfully and hunching his shoulders. He wore no overcoat, and several buttons of his shirt were undone, so that his meagre chest could be seen. But his lips were the colour of watered milk, and the smart nickel belt-buckle quivered against his flat stomach.

Fascinated by his bravado, I stared for some moments; then he noticed me, and glared back so balefully that I let the wind sweep me on at once.

I looked up at the spire of St Stephen's Church. It appeared to me as a huge sharpened stake, put there by God for an instrument of torture. I imagined a gigantic body hurtling down from heaven and landing on this spike, pierced through the belly, the arms and legs spread-eagled and turning like windmills in their agony. I saw the long golden hair hanging down to the earth in heavy ropes and nets, enormous drops of blood caught and held between the strands. I saw the wonderful ancient British chieftain's face – like Caradoc's in an old engraving – with flaxen moustaches round a crying Greek statue's mouth. The eyes I saw as a statue's eyes too – blank and blind.

All this time, while I gazed so long at the tower, a policeman must have been watching me, for he now called out jocosely, 'Can't you tell the time yet, mate? You counting it up?'

I wanted to spit on him, to swear, to shock him, to wake him up. How I hated all policemen!

I started to run up the hill, towards the doctor's house. He had been in my mind all this time. I pushed through the dripping bushes at the gate; one of them had an aromatic smell which I shall always remember, for, as I passed, I tore off a piece and crushed it between my fingers. I ran round to the drawing-room window, concentrating on the smell of the crushed leaves, knowing that I was storing it up in my memory.

Already the curtains were drawn, but I flattened the side of my face to the pane and saw, through a chink, the corner of a cream-painted bookcase, the edge of the standard-lamp, and a few strands of dog-basket. The walnut glow of the wireless, the treacly stain on the deal boards, and the dove-grey carpet, struck me as more than ordinarily smug and complacent.

'Quiet good taste,' I murmured to myself; then, liking the silly words, I said them again quite loudly. They rang out in the stillness. I was in a terror, expecting the window to be thrown up at any moment. But nothing happened; only the little Aberdeen moved. For a moment it crossed my line of vision; and I thought that it looked exactly like an amazing little middle-aged, middle-class gentleman.

> 'O little Aberdeen,' I prayed,
> Sitting upon the floor inside,
> 'I'd, free from any thought of sin,
> Become your melancholy bride.'

A FRAGMENT OF A LIFE STORY

The idiotic rhyme struck me as so full of meaning that I remembered again with hot shame the time when, as a child, I had asked, 'Grandpa, what would happen if a man married a dog?' This too had been 'free from any thought of sin'. I had merely imagined a rococo scene with a fat spaniel, dressed in a veil and orange blossom, emerging from a Gothic-revival church on the arm of a well-groomed gentleman. But my grandfather had been too outraged and shocked to say more than, 'Don't speak of it! Don't speak of it!' And so my question had gone unanswered.

Now, as I watched the final tremble and creak of the basket's edge, as the dog settled, I felt deserted by all the world. I knew that no one anywhere would ever have pity on me again. I saw all the hard granite faces set in a long range against me. I walked up hills and down valleys between avenues of granite faces.

And suddenly I felt that I must get into the house, that I could no longer stay outside. I guessed that the French window of the study would be unlocked. I turned the handle very softly and slipped into the dark room.

I could almost smell the medical books and the rack of neglected pipes. I huddled into the heavy curtain behind the door, and for a moment felt comforted, because I was no longer outside; but at the thought of the cold garden I was so overcome with sorrow for myself that I began to cry quite uncontrollably. I made noises like an animal or a musical instrument, squeezing out my breath or hissing it in through my teeth, muttering things that finished on a little scream, like steam escaping. I nursed my crying, wishing for it never to stop.

When at last the drawing-room door opened and steps came towards me, I crouched down lower to the ground in an ecstasy of hope and fear and shame. I wanted to become smaller and smaller – to become a kitten, a rat, a mouse, crouched at someone's feet in the dark.

The light was switched on, and there was a moment while he looked round the room before seeing me behind the door.

'What are you doing in here?' he asked, assuming that tone of shocked surprise which nurses use when children wet themselves. 'You mustn't get into people's houses and hide behind doors, you know!'

He pulled me up to my feet and held me against him, to steady me, for I was trembling violently with lust and fear. For a moment I felt secure and serene. I no longer had to think for myself. I was even being held up and supported physically. Oh, it was lovely! I wanted to walk about, closely guarded like this for ever. I dug my fingers into his arm fiercely, trying to get at the bone through the flesh.

Then, very gently, I felt him withdrawing. He still held me, but there was a tiny gap between our bodies, and his arms had gone rigid. I was so enraged that I flung away from him and made for the window, cursing and swearing at him with all the filthiest words I could remember. 'You bucking feast, you ruggering bat!' I screamed.

He called my name urgently, and seemed about to follow me into the garden, but something made him change his mind; for, the moment I was outside the French window, he came forward and bolted it sharply. His face seemed almost wickedly triumphant, as he looked out at me through the greenish glass.

'Go home and go to bed,' he said sternly, before he turned away. I rushed round the corner of the house and plastered my ear again to the drawing-room window. I heard him come in and say something to his wife and her friend. One of them answered him.

'What a pity!' she said. 'He's so young. It must be terribly difficult to know what to do.'

I stood there fascinated and delighted – they were talking about me! I strained to hear every word, and was rewarded with remarks about parents, money, curious taste in clothes and undirected sex life. All the cruel words were varnished and stuck together with treacly pity. I screamed out against the appalling caricature. My screams set up a tiny, wiry vibration in the window glass. I could feel it on the tips of my fingers.

There was no answer, unless the silencing of the voices could be called an answer.

A sudden thrill and exaltation passed through me. I ran to the front door and rang the bell, hardly knowing what I did. The maid let me in just as he crossed the hall. He came towards me purposefully. I started to shout.

'What an amusing time you all must have discussing me! Do go on, I want to hear some more.' Then I sighed and laughed very stupidly.

He caught hold of my arm, and was about to put me out of the door, when I shot out my other hand and clutched the banisters. Creaked and moved as he pulled at me roughly. I was amazed; he was using force! Why, he was even hurting me, and he was a doctor! I was exhilarated. Never again would I have to believe that he was entirely good and right. He was being brutal!

My protests grew as my strength gave out. I had to let go of the banisters, and he was jerking me nearer and nearer to the door. I kept on laughing and shouting and swearing to show that I did not care, that I was not almost mad with horror at this last treachery.

With the final desperate jerks I saw the strong hairs on his arms, as his cuffs rode up. 'Very black hairs, very strong arms, and very gold cufflinks enamelled with school crest,' flashed across my brain. I knew now that he had lost his temper. It was wonderful. A sort of pure triumph of evil the moment seemed to me.

The door slammed, and I sat for a moment on the step where I had fallen. Quite suddenly I decided to go home and try to kill myself. I had the little black box of Prontosil tablets he had prescribed for me. I was sure that they were dangerous, for he always asked me anxiously how I felt after taking them.

I ran down the hill. Although my body was still weak, I was filled with a seething energy. The policeman stared at me again as I dashed past the church. This time I did spit, but not until I was several yards away from him.

I crossed the bridge and looked down for one second at the swirling water, half lost in the gathering darkness.

'If he were here to see, I'd jump straight in,' I said aloud.

I ran up the road and let myself into the garden. As I put my key into the front door, I heard someone moving in the sitting-room. I pushed open the door and saw Touchett by the fire.

'Hullo,' he said, smiling sleepily. He looked exactly like a fat 'doctored' cat; I could even imagine whiskers and a tail.

'I thought I'd come round and see what was wrong. Why did you rush off like that?' he asked. 'You *were* stupid, because you missed the crucifixion, which was marvellous. The agony!

And the thunder and lightning effects!'

This careful innocence would have enraged me at other times, but now I felt radiantly alive and able to appreciate and embrace everybody and everything.

'Ask Lydia to bring in the supper,' I said; 'I'm just going into the other room to change my shoes.'

I went into my room and sat on the bed, on the velvet-covered eiderdown which I liked so much. Automatically, I began to unlace my shoes, until I remembered that this was not at all what I had come to do.

I picked up the little black pillbox with its edging of brilliant magenta. My name, with Esquire after it spelt at full length, looked curiously pompous and important. I opened the box and pulled out the cotton wool; underneath lay the Prontosil tablets in their glowing nest. The magenta flushed their whiteness from all sides. I counted the tablets. There were sixteen.

'Surely,' I thought, 'sixteen tablets should have an appalling effect, if taken all at once.'

I filled a glass with water and sat down again on the bed. Quite methodically I put the tablets one after another into my mouth, and washed each down with a gulp from the toothglass.

'It's easy,' I thought. 'I wish I had some more.'

Looking round the room for anything else to take, I had the notion of swallowing a little pair of curved nail-scissors, or of crushing the glass tumbler between my teeth; but I dismissed these as extravagant ideas.

I stood up and heard the last little gurgle inside me, as the final pill and gulp of water chased each other down. 'I've really done something!' I thought. My gaiety mounted up into a huge exuberant wave.

I burst into the other room and saw the steaming soup on the two trays in front of the fire. Touchett was waiting for me politely. Greedy people always do wait politely.

'Have some soup, dear Touchett, some lovely steaming soothing soup,' I shouted. I snatched the decanter from the bureau and slopped a lot of sherry into both soup bowls.

'Now you've probably made it cold,' said Touchett petulantly. He bent over his bowl and took delicate little sips; then, finding it

A FRAGMENT OF A LIFE STORY

to his liking, he started to empty the spoonfuls down his throat with rude sucking noises.

'You are unbelievably disgusting,' I said, feeling quite affectionate towards him. I slopped more sherry into two glasses, but forgot to stop pouring, so that a little golden waterfall splashed from the glass to the tray, and from the tray to the carpet. My first thought was for a damp cloth; but then I realized with a shock that, in a little time, messes on the floor, far worse than this, would no longer worry me.

'I could even throw butter at the walls,' I thought, 'and it wouldn't matter.'

At the thought of butter, I spread my biscuits thickly and began to eat. I had become as hungry as a domestic pet.

'I must enjoy every moment of *my* Last Supper,' I told myself. I poured out glass after glass of sherry for myself and Touchett, until the decanter was empty.

'Now that's finished and there isn't any more,' I said. I felt unhappy.

Touchett gave me a suspicious look; he had placed two of his nicotined fingers on either side of his right eye, and seemed to be propping the lids open. It was a curious trick which I had noticed before.

'Why should you want any more sherry?' he asked. 'You usually drink nothing at all, and I can hardly ever get you into a pub.'

I felt a creeping tingling and swimming in my head. I became terrified and thrilled. Suddenly I burst out with what I had done. I wanted to shock and horrify.

'I've just swallowed sixteen Prontosil tablets,' I shrieked, 'and I'm beginning to feel very peculiar.'

Touchett gave me an utterly blank stare, like a child looking over the palings of the infant-school playground.

There was a moment of complete silence, then questions gushed out of his mouth.

'What are they? Are you all right? Why did you do it? Are they dangerous?'

He jumped to his feet and leant forward, breathing heavily. I could smell the tobacco, the beer, the sherry and the soup all mixed up.

I tried to calm him.

'Don't be stupid, don't be stupid. I only feel a little queer.'

I seized a dish and ladled roast potatoes on to his plate. He loved Lydia's roast potatoes. But Touchett was frightened. He heaved his great body about in the chair and plucked a cigarette from his pocket, not looking at the potatoes. Then he started to wolf them without any of his usual signs of enjoyment. No smacking lips or eager eyes for the next mouthful.

'Why did you do it?' he asked again, thoroughly irritated with me for spoiling his evening.

'I'm still quite all right,' I said, 'and we must finish our meal in peace.'

My head was reeling and my eyes seemed to be focusing curiously, so I shut them and saw myself as a small boy standing upon the dressing-table in red and white striped socks. I was standing on the dressing-table so that I could see my socks in the mirror. At that moment I loved the reflection of my red and white socks better than my mother, my father, than all my family put together.

I opened my eyes again and looked at Touchett I could tell from his sharp furtive glances that he was about to jump up and leave me.

'Those nicotined fingers!' I thought. 'Why, there's even a brown patch on the end of his nose! And those unspeakable teeth!'

'Touchett,' I said sharply, 'you ought to have your teeth seen to.'

He looked at me.

'You seem to be very censorious all of a sudden,' he said.

'But wouldn't you like to be dashingly handsome with a new "guinea set"?' I asked.

He drew himself up and looked very haughty and dignified.

'I'm terrified of dentists,' he said quietly. 'Don't bother to bring out all the old clap-trap about fear of dentists being linked with self-abuse. I know it all very much better than you do.'

I stretched out my hands and said, 'Don't go!' Whereupon he lurched to his feet like a frightened bullock.

'You go to bed,' he urged, 'or get the doctor.'

The drumming was rising to a crescendo in my ears. As he pushed his way clumsily to the front door, I followed, snatching up a stick in the hall. We began to walk rapidly in the direction of his house.

My legs were becoming curiously heavy, but I laughed and sang and cracked stupid jokes, saying how disgusting it was to desert someone who was dying. When we got to the fork at the Star and Garter I shouted again.

'You can't go! You can't! What's going to happen to me? I can't be abandoned like this. It's shameful. You're a monster.'

It was midnight. The lights were burning in the silence. Nothing moved.

'It's like a stage-set,' I thought; 'and I'm the chief ranter.'

'Shall I take you to the doctor's?' Touchett asked half-heartedly.

'Which one?'

He mentioned a name I did not know.

'Yes,' I said – 'if I can get there.'

Then I saw the craven, lazy light come into his eyes again, and he veered away rapidly, saying, 'Goodnight. I really must get home. Go back to bed quickly.'

I screamed oaths and blasphemy after him, still half in fun; then, alone, beginning to be frightened, I wondered what to do.

Somehow I dragged myself home; past each appalling lamp-post. The fire was still burning in the sitting-room. I told myself that there were things to burn, while I was still alive.

I took all the notebooks with my poems in them, and some letters, and threw them on the flames.

The poems crackled gracefully and disappeared, but the imitation leather book backs sizzled, fried and flamed until the chimney caught fire. Up, in the heart of the wall, I could hear the roar of the burning soot.

'Quick, quick!' I called to Lydia. 'Bring some water; the chimney's on fire.'

She ran in with two blue enamel saucepans. I snatched one from her and threw the water into the grate with delight.

When water hit flame there was some sort of explosion. I jumped back. The room was filled with grey smoke. I saw Lydia like a ghost through the smoke. A little piece of scalding ash struck my cheek.

'It's all right,' I said savagely, to stop all her exclamations.

Then I lay down on the sofa and thought that the time had really come. I was in some way losing all the salt and virtue of my senses. All was dumb, muffled and thickened disgustingly. It was as if all my thoughts were reflected in some ghastly fun-fair mirror, the sort of distorting glass which is never funny, always frightening.

I held my breath for twenty seconds, and then gabbled out the name of Touchett's doctor to Lydia. I spoke so rapidly that she could not understand me. When I repeated myself, she gave me a long look, and then went to the telephone rather unwillingly.

I swayed into the bedroom and fell down on the bed. I lay there wriggling and lashing about, not being able to stay still for a moment, because of the soaring, swelling pain in my head, and because of my fear at the approach of the new doctor.

At last he came. He stood in the middle of the room, not saying anything; then he turned me roughly towards him.

'What's all this?' he asked sternly.

'He's just like a prefect who's discovered some peculiar goings-on in the disused cricket pavilion,' I told myself. 'He looks just like one, too – square head, pink mouth, wide shoulders. Skin smooth as the back of a child, as they say at the BBC.'

I thought all this because I was very frightened of the doctor and wanted to give myself some courage and bravado; but it was no use, I had none. A terrible wave of self-consciousness made it impossible for me to look at him, but I jerked out something about the tablets, and waited for his awful words.

Suddenly his prefect's manner dropped from him.

'First of all I think we'll try to make you sick,' he said with businesslike gaiety. I laughed; the anticlimax was so funny, such a delicious relief.

He went in search of mustard, hot water and a spoon.

I drank the yellow stuff in gulps, and waited, expecting to be violently sick. I imagined a horrible bright orange cascade of vomit from my mouth. I hated to be sick in front of the doctor. But nothing happened.

'No go?' he asked, looking at me inquiringly.

'I don't think so,' I said. 'Does it matter, if I'm not sick? Will it be serious?'

'You'll have the hell of a headache for the next day or so, but that's about all,' he said with hearty malice.

I felt dashed. He was laughing at me. I was ridiculous and puerile. I did not know one drug from another. I was ignorant.

'Will you give me something for my head?' I asked, for by now it felt as if it were about to boil and crack open.

'Much better not,' he said. 'You've taken quite enough for one night!'

He laughed and joked, teasing me, making a fool of me; then he suddenly broke off and said, 'The ridiculous is sometimes very near to the sublime.'

I was startled; the remark was so sententious, so out of character. He's saying it specially for me, I thought; specially to make me feel good inside again. And I was very grateful, and tried to forget my resentment at his seeming unconcern about the Prontosil tablets.

At last he took up his hat and his case. He came forward ceremoniously, like a prefect again, only this time a nice prefect, congratulating someone on playing well in a match.

'Let's shake hands,' he said.

I sat up in bed and held mine out. We shook hands. It was not silly, although it was very artificial.

Shaking hands is much more solemn and full of meaning than kissing, I thought. You kiss your aunt, you kiss your pet cat, but you never think of shaking hands with them like this.

I cannot tell whether I slept that night. I know that I first felt a certain happiness and comfort which was soon swallowed up by the terrible pain in my head. I know that this growing, bursting pain made me open and shut my eyes. Each time I opened them I saw the white mantelpiece palely glimmering in the darkness. The mantelpiece seemed to bend and cockle and become alive. Its flatness twisted into things that were nearly arms and legs. It seemed to swell towards me, then recede. And I seemed to spring out to it and back, like a tennis ball on a piece of elastic. I sang hymns to the mantelpiece and prayed to it. It brooded there, a squat flat deity, giving off waves of evil power.

When next I became conscious, it was bright daylight. Lydia had brought my tea; it lay beside me steaming in the little terracotta Chinese pot. I felt glad and happy – I felt horribly sick and soiled.

Then both feelings, and many more, were all submerged, as wave after wave of realization broke over me. I saw that nothing was changed; either in the world or in me.

ALEX FAIRBURN

Denton Welch was twenty-three – the same age as 'Alex Fairburn' – when he wrote this story. Two years previously he had fallen in love with his doctor, Jack Easton, who had looked after him following his accident, and during that turbulent episode he had consulted a psychiatrist in Mayfair.

ALEX FAIRBURN BENT HER FAIR HEAD NEARER TO HER work and counted the stitches of her petit-point. The fire stretched and yawned at her feet and through the thick curtains she heard the bell-like trickle of the water in the drainpipes. It was seven o'clock on an autumn evening and she was alone.

She had spent most of her time alone since she had left Jack. The thought of him twisted something inside her. It was not hate or fear that she felt but just shame – to have made such a mess of their marriage – from the very start. She could not bear to think of it. They were both so stubborn, nobody but a fool would have imagined that they could live together. But at twenty-one she had been a fool and now two years later she realized just how large a one. She thought of Jack with his thin pointed eyes and mouse-soft polished hair, the smallness of his bones and the egoism of his face in repose (the sort of face Little Lord Fauntleroy might be expected to have had in the days when his goodness had begun to wear thin), the queer smell of his feet when he took off his socks and the sparkle of his nonsense at a party. Then she thought of her resistance to his will, her foolishness, the beauty of her face and the wealth that made her independent of him. 'Everyone told me not to marry him,' she thought. 'Daddy said he hadn't enough money and Mother just said don't, but I did and then made everything much worse by behaving so stupidly when I found out my mistake. As if drinking too much could ever make you forget that you had married someone so like yourself that he was unbearable.'

When Alex left her husband she had gone to a psychologist and been analysed. There had been the endless journeys to the little upstairs room in Wimpole Street and the tense sound of her own voice answering questions and saying whatever came into her head. It had all been so formless and floundering, and yet the psychologist seemed to have a pigeon-hole for everything. She left half-way through the course and then she found religion.

She went to stay with a friend in the country town where the Oxford Group had sent a mission, and one night at a friend's house she met some of the young men and women from Oxford and suddenly became very enthusiastic. She read her Bible daily, applied only the minimum of make-up to her face, and settled in a cottage near the sea.

The petit-point work was all part of a scheme and of course there was no drink in the house.

Her family thought it peculiar, but they were so encased in their wealth and the selfishness which it bred that nothing really got through to them from the outside world. They came once or twice to the country cottage and thought it 'very jolly', but wanted to know if she was not very lonely there. Alex replied that she was not, with brittle over-emphasis.

She could indeed scream with boredom at times. She had asked all the friends she could think of to come down and spend a few days with her, but had so overpowered them with her conviction of the meaning of life and had bullied them so with the confidence that this conviction had given her, that they all in turn had left before their time was up and now she was left alone, and even the Belgian maid had gone that very day.

Now that it was autumn things seemed even drearier and she did not know what she would do next.

The needle darted in and out of the canvas. Never had anyone been so savage about doing petit-point before. Alex thought of the pattern she had bought ready-painted in the shop opposite Harrods. 'It may not be creative,' she said to herself, 'but at least it's work. What would I do without it?'

The click of the garden gate broke through her concentration and she looked up, hands on the work in her lap, waiting for the bell to ring. It did not, but she heard the thud of feet walking along the wet path to the back door. Then there was a knock and she went to open it. The beads of rain were dripping from the low eaves and through their strings she saw a dripping figure, young and grey in the evening light.

'Excuse me, miss, but could I put up in your barn tonight? I'm on the road and it's that wet.'

Alex looked at the speaker again quickly. He had tow-coloured hair and a thick-set mouth. His ragged jacket and grey flannels were heavy with rain, and Alex caught the gleam of newspaper through the cracks in his squelching shoes.

'Come in,' she said hurriedly, acting on impulse. She stepped back and held the door open for him. He followed her sheepishly, hanging his head and fingering the straps of the greasy knapsack on his back. 'Won't you take off your wet coat and dry it by the fire? Of course you can stay here tonight.' Alex went over to the boiler and stoked it. It was still on, luckily. She opened the door and arranged the clothes-horse in front of it.

The young man, still tongue-tied, was easing the knapsack off his back, his eyes glazed and unmeaning.

When Alex turned from the fire, she saw him standing there by the kitchen table. He had taken off his coat and it was hanging from his lowered arms and dripping steadily on to the tiled floor.

She realized with a shock that he wore no shirt, only a dirty sweat-stained singlet such as stokers wear, and she saw the pale hair on his chest over the semicircle of its neck.

His whole attitude was so shamefaced and dejected that she hardly dared to look at him. She took the coat gently from his hands and arranged it across the horse. A thin steam rose from it, carrying the smells of the man and his tobacco with it.

'Would you like a hot bath?' she said suddenly; then, feeling she had been tactless, she added, 'You've got so wet, I should think you need warming up.' A wan smile lit his face, making it look quite weak, and he replied, 'All right, if yer like.'

'Come on then, I'll show you the way.' Alex was bristling now. She led the way up to the landing and fumbled in the dark linen-cupboard for a clean towel. Her hands fastened on its rough comfort and she drew it out. She smiled self-consciously when she saw its colour by the bathroom light. It was pale lilac and monogrammed with her initials – a part of her wedding presents. She turned on the taps and poured the Russian pine essence into the bath from the great green bottle that stood on the mirrored shelf.

The little room was filled with its scent and the clammy steam which frosted the taps and shining tiles.

Now that she had no excuse for staying longer she went to the door and, turning, said, 'Don't put your wet things on again after your bath, I'll find you something else.' He gave a half-grudging obedient nod and she shut the door.

Outside in the dry warmth and darkness of the landing, Alex's mind raced. This new Samaritan feeling had entirely seized her and she did not stop to analyse it. She felt her way to her bedroom and went in. The lamp by the bed glowed under its peach shade and in the dim light she searched in the bottom of the chest of drawers for the sailor's trousers she had bought in Gravesend and worn once or twice on the beach and in the garden.

She found them and held them up. She had had to buy them large, as otherwise her feminine hips, slight as they were, would not get in the tight top part of the trousers. She hoped he would be able to wear them. She looked among her jerseys and found the largest. It was thick, with a high polo collar, and she had worn it for riding.

When Alex had found these, she went quickly to the dressing-table, adjusted her hair and touched up her light make-up with lipstick and powder; then she went to the bathroom door and said, loudly, so that he could hear through his splashing, 'I've got some clothes here for you. Will you give me your own to dry?'

She heard him get out of the bath and walk towards the door, then the door opened slightly, and his hand and forearm with the golden hair glistening on the pink flesh were thrust forward, holding the sopping clothes and shoes. She took them with an involuntary fastidiousness and walked down the stairs. In the kitchen she put them with the coat in front of the boiler and went to the larder. The smell of cold and fat was disagreeable, but there was a dish of spaghetti that the maid had prepared that morning and also several tins of soup and fruit.

The milkman had left the regular quantity of cream she had every day and Alex felt that she had almost enough to make a meal.

She turned on the electric stove and put the spaghetti in the oven and the soup in a saucepan on the hot-plate. Then she hastily laid the table in the kitchen and poured the tinned loganberries and the cream over a sponge sandwich which she had found uncut in a tin.

She looked at the table and felt that she had done all she could. The sight of the tumblers made her realize that there was nothing in the house to drink but water. Her scruples were quite gone by now and she wished she had something to offer him. Then she remembered the bottle of whisky she had bought last month when her white Alsatian was dying and the vet had told her to feed it on whisky and white of egg. She had been so distracted at the time that she had rushed to the nearest pub and bought a whole bottle. Her dog had only lived two days after this and so there it was still, almost full.

She had put it out in the garage to get it out of the house, and now she ran out to get it. It was still there in the corner covered with a few cobwebs.

She brought it in and wiped its neck and stood it on the table. There was no soda water, so she stood the water jug next to it. She could hear him fumbling on the landing upstairs so she called out, 'There's no light up there, can you find your way down?' She could not quite hear his answer, but in a few moments she saw him standing in the doorway, still red from his bath, wearing the sailor's trousers and her jersey. He had combed his hair with his fingers and it coiled in rough order on his head. The gold stubble was still on his cheeks and chin, but the dirt had gone and, as he moved forward, she caught the glint of his bleached eyelashes as they shone in the light.

The steam from the wet clothes was filling the room and, as they sat down to eat, drifts of the warm human air blew between them. He ate gingerly at first; then gaining confidence, he applied himself with concentration and Alex ate methodically too to keep him company. She saw that his hands, which moved so steadily, were still mooned with black at the tip of each fingernail.

'Would you like some whisky?' she asked him when the soup

had been finished. 'Thank you,' he said, looking at his plate with an embarrassed grin playing round his mouth and lowering his eyelids.

He did not wait to watch what instrument she used for the spaghetti, but said, simply, 'I'm afraid I don't know which tool to use.'

Hurriedly Alex replied, 'I should use any one you like.' Then, feeling this unhelpful if polite, she added, 'I'm going to use a knife and fork.' She quickly picked up the knife she had not intended to use and began eating.

Every now and then he took drinks from the glass of whisky and when it was empty she filled it again without asking him.

She noticed that the food and drink were heating him. A light dew of sweat made his face shine. The atmosphere in the room was warm and steaming, like a laundry.

When they had finished the loganberries, she said, 'You go into the other room and make up the fire, while I heat the coffee.' She showed him the door across the landing and then went back to the electric stove. She could hear him banking up the fire and then the stillness when he had finished. The coffee and milk which she had mixed in the saucepan frothed up to the brim and she snatched it away before it should bubble over.

She placed it as it was with the cups and sugar on the tray and went with it across the landing. When she opened the sitting-room door, she saw him standing in front of the fireplace just staring at the picture above it. It was a Dutch flower piece – not stimulating – and his whole body seemed so hopeless that she guessed he was not looking at the picture but quite through it.

He turned when he heard her, but did not offer to help her, he just hung his hand.

Alex drew the little table in front of the sofa, the only really comfortable piece of furniture in the room, and then fetched the cigarettes and chocolates from the desk.

'You must be so tired; won't you sit down?' she asked, indicating the sofa.

He leaned back stiffly in one corner as she poured out the coffee. She passed it to him with the sugar. The cup slipped in the saucer and she saw his face give a start and lurch.

When they had both taken cigarettes, he quite surprisingly leaned forward and struck a match for her. The light from it gave his impassive face a false animated glow – as the rose lights in butchers' shops enhance the colour of the meat.

He breathed rather deeply after his meal and she saw that he was getting hotter than ever in the heavy sweater. Feeling that conversation was impossible, she got up and went to the wireless and turned it on softly.

As she sat down again, she noticed that his eyes had a more unfocused, less starting look. The muscles of his face were less tense and his long legs in the wide sailor's trousers seemed more relaxed.

The music was formless and unmoving, it was difficult to know who would appreciate it, but looking at him again, she realized, with sudden alarm, that his lips and nostrils were twitching and that his chin was thrust forward stubbornly. 'Oh Lord, don't let him break down,' Alex prayed swiftly to herself. 'What shall I do?' Then she sprang up and went into the kitchen to fetch the whisky. She brought it back with the tumbler of water and two glasses on a tray. She let her hand fall on his shoulder as she set the tray down. She could feel the heat and the trembling of his body through the wool. 'Cheer up, let's have a drink.' She spoke harshly and brightly, and she could see him stirring and contracting, as if he were gathering himself together. He gave a low sound of acknowledgement and nodded his head.

She moved nearer to him on the sofa so that she could pour out the whisky from the little table in front of him. She put a lot into his glass and only a little into hers. She did not like the taste. She hoped it would cheer him up. As he put the glass to his lips, she heard it ring against his teeth. He was trembling. He drank it in large gulps so that he would not have to go on holding the glass. Then he began to choke. This was too much for him. He gasped, choked and wept all at once. Alex prosaically knelt on the sofa and thumped his back. He was breathing with great sighing gulps now, his body lying open, arms thrown out and legs straddled by the paroxysm.

Something caught at Alex as she saw him stretched in the corner of the sofa. She leaned across him, her long neck arched, and bent her lips down to his cheek. He made a movement with his face away from her. She lay against him and heard his heavy heart beats, then slowly she stretched her hand out over his head and switched off the reading lamp. The light from the fire played on the ceiling and walls and shook light from every polished object that it caught. There was no noise but the rain, the hissing of the damp wood and his deep breathing.

She put her arms carefully round his chest. The weight of their two bodies together made the sofa sag. They slipped to the ground, narrowly missing the table with the whisky tray, and lay together there on the bear-skin rug in front of the fire. He put his big arms round her drowsily and she felt the heat from his body eating into hers. His face was glistening with sweat. Alex knelt up by his side and pulled the thick sweater up from his waist. At last she got it over his head and only his arms lay imprisoned in it, stretched out above him. She looked down at his face and he smiled, his eyes half closed. He drew his hands out of the sweater and, holding them up, drew her down so that her cheek was against his chest. It felt to her skin like fine grass scattered on satin. She closed her eyes and whenever she opened them she saw the light of the flames gilding the white top of his body.

They did not go to bed that night, but lay in front of the fire on the bear-skin, dozing and waking. Alex got cushions and rugs and banked up the fire.

Towards dawn she went soundly to sleep and woke two hours later to see him standing over her and looking down. He had changed into his own clothes and the straps of the knapsack were across his shoulders.

'I must be going,' he said, and shifted his feet nervously. Alex jumped up, the whole memory of last night returning to her. 'Don't go, don't go yet. You must have some breakfast.' She sped into the kitchen and found two kippers and began making toast and coffee.

He stood in the doorway, watching her and not saying a word. Sometimes he looked at the kitchen clock. They ate their meal in silence, then he got up and went to the door. 'Goodbye,' he said. Alex couldn't stop him or say anything, she could only stare. She watched him go out and heard him walking down the path and opening the gate into the road; then she came to life and ran after him. When she got to the gate he was already a little way down the road; he turned and gave her a rather clumsy, distant wave. It stopped her from going further. She slowly turned back into the house and sat down again at the breakast table, leaning her head down on it with her arms curved round. She shut her eyes and felt the smell of kippers and butter and coffee piercing through her thoughts. She lay some time like this; then, resolutely, she sat up and brushed her hair back. She looked at the congealing fat on the plates and the mahogany skin of the eaten kippers, the dregs in the coffee-cups and the smears of butter and marmalade on the small plates.

She cleaned it all into the sink and began washing up. When she had finished, she stoked the boiler, then went into the other room. The rugs and cushions lay on the floor in front of the fire, which was out, and there were her jersey and sailor's trousers which he had worn. She looked at them and did not move, then swiftly she bent forward and, gathering them up, she held them close to her face and smelt them. The smell of his body clung to them still. She folded them and put them down on the sofa, then she cleaned away the rugs and the whisky and the coffee-cups. When the room was tidy, she switched on the electric fire, as she had not remade the open one, and, fetching her Bible, she sat down to read. When she had finished her chapter, she sighed and, taking up her petit-point, made the needle dart in and out of the canvas. She worked faster and faster, trying not to think at all, but she kept on saying to herself, in endless repetition as the stitches grew, 'I didn't even give him sixpence, I didn't even give him sixpence.'

EVERGREEN
SEATON-LEVERETT

Denton Welch was introduced to 'Evergreen Seaton-Leverett', whose real name was Mrs Hayes-Jackson, in 1938 by John Hesketh ('Alec Gale'), a friend with whom he had been at prep school. The story was first published in Orpheus 2 *in 1949 and reprinted in* A Last Sheaf.

I FIRST SAW HER DRIVING DOWN THE MAIN STREET OF the old inland watering-place which I was exploring. It was impossible to miss her, since she drove in a dark-green limousine belonging to King Edward VII's reign. Beautiful brass carriage lamps glistened on either side of a chauffeur and footman, whose uniforms were also of dark green. She sat, perched up behind them in a glass box, a plump little woman, her brilliant terracotta hair topped with a sort of black satin cottage-loaf.

As the car drove by very slowly, she smiled and bowed to the people on the pavements with the greatest good nature and impartiality; she might almost have been parodying a royal personage. The round red face was crumpled and creased with so much smiling, but what was interesting was to see something in it to make me feel that a few of the smiles were for herself. She seemed to be enjoying her own preposterousness, laughing at it a little. It was as if she were saying something as simple as, 'Oh, Lordy, Lord! The dear people in the street, and me sitting up here like an old aunt sally!' The little eyes were watering with amusement and pleasure; once she dabbed at them, then looked up to heaven, and again I could imagine her exclaiming, 'Oh, Lord!' The mouth was a little open all the time. Before she was past me, I remember thinking, 'She holds her head rather stiffly. Is she afraid that it might shake? If she wore jet bugles on that hat, would they still go on trembling after the car had stopped?'

My heart bounded at the spectacle she made in her progress down the street; for the world has become so mean that we no longer expect to be given the chance to stand and gape in admiration. When it comes, we are almost shocked, made to feel guilty. There is a return of that dreadful fear that seems to hang about all true fairy-stories. Fairy godmothers, in spite of their goodness and magnificence, are sinister; golden coaches that suddenly appear may as suddenly disappear, leaving deserving girls in rags by the kitchen fire.

I thought of all this as I turned down a narrow alley leading to the common. Who could the woman be? Was she some obstinate old dowager, refusing to be jostled out of the habits of her youth? She looked too sweet natured to be anything so tight. Perhaps she was a singer, an actress from the past, who still loved to draw men's eyes. Hugging the thought of her to me, I looked up; and there she was again in reality, sailing up the road that lay between me and the gorse bushes.

At the corner of the alley I waited to watch her approach. There were few people here, so for a moment she had stopped smiling and bowing. Her eyes were down on her gloves; she seemed to be playing a sort of delicate pat-a-cake with herself, placing one chubby hand on another, stopping sometimes to pick and pluck at her sleeve. In front of her the chauffeur and the footman sat so stiffly that they reminded me of two green bottles waiting to be uncorked.

When the car had almost reached me, some peculiar spirit took possession and I found myself bowing and smiling — almost as extravagantly as she did these things herself. The moment she noticed me, her face lit up; she fluttered her hand, then turned to wave again through the oval bevelled glass at the back of the car.

What had I done? Had my excessive civility made her mistake me for a friend? Or was she interested quite simply in anyone who seemed to wish her well?

I stood staring after her until the car bowled round the corner and was lost in the trees.

I was not to find out any more about her until several months later when I was again in the town. While walking along the upper common, I suddenly came face to face with someone I had not seen since schooldays. I was sure of him because I remembered at once that he had lived in the town all his life. After our first exclamations and surprise, we sat down together near some great slabs of rock and started to smoke cigarettes. All round us children played amongst the rocks, climbing over them, squeezing between them, laughing, screaming, digging in the sand that had collected in nooks and crannies.

Soon I was asking all about the wonderful woman with tomato hair.

'Oh, but don't you know?' exclaimed my rediscovered friend. 'That's Evergreen Fanny.'

My mind at once rejected the silly name, but I waited in silence to hear more.

'She's years and years old, nobody knows quite how old; my mother says she was seventy, twenty years ago.'

Extreme age was something I had not associated with the woman in the car.

'She's an amazing ninety, then,' I said. 'She looked more like sixty when I saw her.'

'I know, that's the extraordinary thing; she never seems to change. Mother says she's looked exactly the same ever since she can remember. That's why everyone calls her Evergreen Fanny.'

'Does your mother know her personally?' I asked.

'Yes, in fact she's about the only woman Evergreen enjoys seeing. But she loves men. If you like, I'll get Mother to ring her up and ask if we can go along this evening for drinks. Are you free?'

I nodded eagerly.

'I shall always remember first seeing her,' Alec Gale continued. 'I suppose I was about five. My mother had taken me shopping, and on the way home we ran into Evergreen. We met her on the pavement in front of the hotel, only a few yards from where we're sitting at this moment. The brilliant red hair and fantastic clothes made such an impression on me that I couldn't take my eyes off her. All the time she was talking to my mother I was staring open-mouthed. At last Evergreen turned and wagged a finger at me archly. "Isn't it sweet?" she said. "I do believe the dear boy is admiring me." My mother, whose guess was a good deal nearer the truth, bundled me off before I could say anything too frightful.'

I was silent, remembering the effect of strangeness on myself as an infant. There had been a man who rode a blue bicycle and sang psalms at the top of his voice . . . But Alec was speaking again. 'Of course, it isn't real,' he said.

'What isn't?'

'Why, the hair. It's a wig. The nurse who came to look after Mother when she had pneumonia told us that Evergreen had three: best, second best and everyday. At night she keeps all three on tall stands at the foot of her bed. But I'm not going to tell you any more about her; you must see her for yourself. As soon as I go home, I'll get Mother to telephone. Come to tea with us and I'll take you along afterwards. Her house is only just around the corner.'

He gave me his address and we stood up.

'Till this afternoon, then!' he called, turning to wave to me before disappearing over a ridge. I thought I caught a glint in his eye, as though the idea of introducing me to Evergreen afforded him a wicked pleasure. Memories suddenly came back to me of the simple-minded Casanova's delight in being taken to see a real duchess, and of his extreme discomfort when his malicious friend disappeared, leaving him in the clutches of the ancient and lascivious woman.

'But why should you think of anything so absurd?' I asked myself. 'Evergreen does not appear to be in the least lascivious; and even if she were, she would probably not have the slightest inclination to be lascivious with *you*!'

❖

That evening, as Alec led me from his house to Mrs Seaton-Leverett's, I was filled with doorstep fears and anxieties. I had never before been to see someone simply out of curiosity, and it seemed to me that I was bound to be found out and punished in some way for my impertinent inquisitiveness.

We turned the corner and began to walk down a street of late-Victorian houses showing seventeenth-century Dutch influence.

Terracotta plaques, elaborate gables in steps, broken pediments and heavy cornices diversified each simple family box. We stopped in front of one where a tiny crimson windmill whirred beside a cement pool fringed with jagged, skull-like glints. Not far off, emerging from a privet bush, a little cement girl, also painted crimson, lifted her frilly skirt invitingly and rudely. Looking up, I saw that each window-box to the house was a miniature crimson fence with five-barred gate in the middle. The scarlet of the geraniums behind fought interestingly with the crimson latticework. All these commonplace garden ornaments had been given a strange grim twist by this blood-red colour.

Alec led the way up the path and rang the bell. The door was opened by the footman I had seen in the car, but how different he looked without his cap and uniform! He was young and weak, with thin damp hair, and bluish flesh about his nostrils. His suit was of dark greasy serge. He asked us rather breathlessly to wait in the dining-room while he announced our arrival to his mistress.

As we passed through the narrow hall, I just had time to look up and see that the lampshade was a Japanese paper parasol hung upside down. The bright flowers and birds looked old, dust-greasy and fly-blown. There was the faintest smell in the air of ivy, ancient meals, tom-cats, upholstery and fungus. It filled me with a strange disturbance, perhaps because it brought so vividly to mind the phrase 'a living tomb'. What did it mean? A tomb for living? A tomb that was alive? This house was both.

All the curtains were drawn in the dining-room and three electric bulbs dressed in red crêpe-paper crinolines shone down on the table, making the yellow-grey oak look pale and dirty and naked. The rest of the room glowed darkly and rosily. I heard the whirr of an electric fan and turned to find one in the corner, coloured ribbons streaming from its guard. It had the soiled gaiety of the Japanese sunshade and I was made to think of long-forgotten fancy-dress balls on battleships.

Seeing that the mirrored overmantel was stuck all over with cards, I went up to glance at some of them. They were invitations to garden parties, dinners, weddings, balls and christenings. All were yellowed, curling at the corners and thick with furry dust, so that they had an almost artificial air, as if they had been made to look old for a stage production. The few I read were all from peers. I remember best the garden-party invitations from the two marquesses whose places lay on either side of the town.

'She's kept every invitation she's ever had,' whispered Alec, sliding up to me stealthily. 'When she offers you sherry she'll tell you that it's one of the last bottles from the cellars of her grandfather's castles; she's been saying it for years. Actually she gets it round the corner where we do.'

His jaunty interruption broke up my mood. I wished I had been left alone to contemplate the rosy butcher's shop glow, the dust, so thick that it had grown spiders' legs and arms, the grandees' cards, and the writhing waterlilies on the shoddy art nouveau sideboard. How was it that Alec, after seeing this interior, could still think of Mrs Seaton-Leverett as a comic figure?

But now the ill-looking young man had returned to take us to his mistress.

'This way, please, sirs,' he said in his resigned, breathless voice. He led us up the stairs, glancing back many times as though he were afraid that we might not be following or that we had not yet learnt to climb stairs properly and might be needing his help.

Whenever his eyes were off me for a moment I turned to study the wall opposite the banisters. It was decorated with pages from a wallpaper sample book pasted haphazardly over the original dingy surface. A page of imitation brickwork followed a page of glossy marble. Purple grapes hung close to fantastic wood-graining and a square of meat-red damask. There was part of a frieze of pastel crocuses and a horny patch of Lincrusta panelling. My eyes began to rove and falter. The patterns and textures set before me were as bewildering as the profusion of dishes at a banquet.

And when we reached the drawing-room, or boudoir, if that is a fitter description, and the man withdrew, leaving us alone, my eyes skimmed with such rapidity from object to object that I felt dizzy. Everything was known, commonplace, but in such incongruous relation to the next object that it became startling. The bow-window was draped in coarse grey lace; from the middle of each opening a large Easter egg, decorated with varnished scraps and tinfoil, hung down forlornly, reminding me of pictures I had seen of bombs in readiness to drop from aeroplanes. Photographs covered the walls, and between these, especially round the fireplace, were large saucepans and frying-pans, tied back with tasselled curtain cord, sometimes stuck with a posy of artificial flowers, a bow or a tiny flag. A large Union Jack covered an occasional table on which stood flimsy glasses, a plate of candied cherries, a plate of strident pink coconut ice and a decanter with sticky dribbles from the lip. For me the room evoked extraordinarily the atmosphere of the Near-Eastern brothel. Although I had never been in one, I had always imagined just such dirty lace, such chi-chi paper flowers, such sickly wine and sticky sweets. But there was one great difference. This room was sunless and a little damp. Perhaps the chill was all the more evident because one knew that this was no spider's parlour decked to lure in stupid flies, but a parlour decked for no other purpose than the owner's quirkish humour. She was alone with her scraps and tinsel, her Easter eggs robbed of their chocolates long ago.

A door opened and footsteps sounded in the passage. She stood on the threshold looking in at us. I had not expected anyone quite so short. Her black skirt was short. The sleeves of her white silk jersey were short, revealing puffy pink arms. She again wore a black silk hat; but this one was tall and straight-sided, with the narrow brim pulled down to her eyebrows, so that only little puffs of red hair showed above each earlobe. One chubby hand poised on her breast made me feel that she might burst into song.

'Ah!' she said, moving towards Alec serenely and jerkily, rather like a toy duck on little wheels. 'Naughty boy for neglecting me so long!' Still holding one of Alec's fingers, she turned to me. 'Now tell me what his name is – I'm sure I shall like it.'

Alec introduced me.

I found myself hoping that she would approve of my combination of sounds.

'Oh, that's *very* nice. I like that.'

She said it over to herself, savouring it on her tongue as some tea-taster might sample his latest blend. A new picture jumped into my mind. I was not a person; I was just three syllables moving about and talking.

Mrs Seaton-Leverett sat down in a basket-chair near the fireplace. One hand was still on her bosom, and since her fingers played a perpetual tattoo on her breastbone, my eye was often caught by the dusty twinkle of her rings. They gripped the chubby fingers as brass bands grip the cormorant's neck; or were they more like tiny sparkling boa-constrictors forever tightening their death-hold?

I was able now to take in other details of her dress. The blue and white check, which hung down over the black skirt, was not a proper apron, but only an unhemmed piece of cloth pinned with two huge safety-pins at the waist. Other smaller safety-pins held strips of lace and ribbon in position aslant her bosom, so that she looked as if she had just returned from an investiture where some outlandish prince had decorated her with all his strangest orders. I pictured her going into shops, buying these snippets of lace and braid and ribbon, pinning them across her bosom at once to enjoy the effect.

She offered us the sticky sweets and sherry, and, sure enough, she told us that the sherry was one of the last bottles from her grandfather's cellar.

'It should be good, it should be good,' she repeated airily; 'my grandfather put it down years ago.'

A slight pang passed through me; I could have wished that Alec's prophecy had not been so perfectly fulfilled. I was all for Evergreen. I wished her to be mysterious and unaccountable, baffling to those shallow people who came to smile or laugh.

My eye was caught by the glistening surface of a large photograph.

'Oh, that is a picture of your car, isn't it?' I said, over-enthusiastically. 'I like its body very much.'

Her face lit up. 'You do like it? That is nice. But, my dears, it has been *such* a trial. It has had to have a whole new engine. It appears that they couldn't do anything more with the old one. It has been a great expense, but I'm hoping now that it will go smoothly for many years.'

For a moment she seemed to forget us; her eyes wandered to the window; she drummed on her bosom and murmured in a far-away voice, 'Yes, yes, yes, it has been a great expense, but it's a nice car. I do like a car to be a car.'

I cast about in my mind for something else to say, afraid of allowing Evergreen to sink too deeply into her daydream. Could I say anything about the decorated frying-pans on the wall or the old Easter eggs? I wanted to know their history, the reason for their preservation; but perhaps Evergreen would resent my curiosity; perhaps she would open those round little eyes wide and I would be made to feel like a pet pug who has misbehaved on the drawing-room rug.

It was Evergreen herself who broke the tension. Still in her far-away sing-song voice she began to tell us about her great-nephew who had inherited the grandfather's castle.

'He *is* a naughty boy,' she mused, shaking her head; 'he's got rid of the place to the National Trust – the whole village as well, if you please! And he never consulted any of us. He shouldn't have done it, it wasn't right.'

'But aren't you glad that it will always be preserved now?' I asked, trying to say the soothing thing.

'Yes, but that isn't the point; he shouldn't have parted with it without letting us all know.'

Evergreen was still shaking her head, but her expression had softened; she seemed to be willing to excuse her nephew's naughtiness, because, if the truth were to be told, she really admired his boldness, his decision, his high-handed behaviour.

I nibbled a piece of coconut ice, sipped my sherry. The footman came to the half-open door, then slipped in furtively, a box entirely encrusted with tiny iridescent shells in his hand.

'Excuse me, madam, the cigarettes,' he murmured, putting the box down on the Union Jack tablecloth.

'Oh, how clever of you to remember, Henry!' said Mrs Seaton-Leverett affectionately. 'I'm afraid I never think of offering them, because I don't smoke myself.'

As soon as Henry had left, she turned to us and said, 'I'm not at all happy about him. You know, he's not strong, and now, with this new Government Order, I'm so afraid they'll take him off and put him in some dreadful factory or other.'

'But surely not!' protested Alec. 'They can't do things like that yet. He's in a perfectly good job here with you.'

'Oh, do you think so? I'm so relieved. I felt that they might say that he was much more necessary somewhere else; but he ought not to do anything strenuous, he mustn't have strain, he can't stand up to it.' Evergreen's solicitude was charming.

But was this to be all? Were we only to have light gossip about her car, her nephew and her servants? Would none of the fantasy of the house get into the conversation? Every tinsel flower, every saucepan and miniature flag held a secret, some thought or feeling embalmed in it. The whole house seemed filled with tiny, unseen presences. They were all waiting for us to go; we were prying, curious people, the outside world. Evergreen fenced with us politely, kept us at bay. However long we stayed she would utter nothing but friendly platitudes.

I could see that Alec was growing restless; everything pointed to our going, yet it was very reluctantly that I rose to my feet. I wanted to stay with Evergreen alone. I wanted to hear her talking in that dreamy far-off voice, describing the ancient balls, the marriages and christenings.

'What, are you going, my dears?' she asked, suddenly taking notice of us standing before her, ready to hold out our hands. 'Now, you must come again, both of you, soon. I liked your name so much; what is it?' she added, turning to me.

Delicate Henry showed us to the door; he seemed more resigned, more patient than ever. From the top steps of the porch he smiled at us, rather as a dying man might smile a brave farewell to his wife and children.

I did not look round until we had walked a few paces down the road; then some wish, perhaps to see the crimson garden ornaments for the last time, made me turn my head. My eyes travelled to the window-boxes on the first floor; there was Evergreen, standing in the bow-window with the dirty lace curtains pulled aside. She was staring down at us with a curious look of incomprehension on her face. It was as if she did not know who we were, or what we were. She would look thus, I felt, at the woodlice and other strange insects found under a stone. She was not hostile, but on her guard, a little repelled by what she saw. Hers was a ghost face at the window in a dream; and then the glass pane turned it into a drowned face staring up from the bed of a clear river. She had taken off her hat, so that the unbelievable hair rose up from her forehead like a sulky flame. The unyielding eyes beneath were still upon us; the mouth had not yet found any reason for being pleased.

Turning away abruptly, I tried to speak to Alec, to share some fragment of my thoughts with him. I wanted to say, 'She is a prisoner in that extraordinary house; each object binds her with a spell.' But how hollow it sounded! How artificial! He would only laugh. I could not express the half of my thoughts; they were as unformed, as numerous and impossible to catch, as tadpoles in a pond.

Soon afterwards I heard of Evergreen's death. I heard too that she had divided her fortune between Henry and the chauffeur. It was difficult to imagine Henry enjoying thirty or forty thousand pounds; he had been so self-effacing, so breathless, so fragile. How would he bear the great weight of Evergreen's money? Had she dealt him a blow from another world, finally flattened him out under a pile of bank-notes?

Alec told me that the house was empty now, that all the crimson ornaments were gone and the windows blank; but I knew that the spirits of the paper flowers, the invitation cards, the coloured streamers and the frying-pans would always lurk there for me, together with the figure of Evergreen at the window, the amazing sullen lazy flame of her hair curling up into the shadows.

LEAVES FROM
A YOUNG PERSON'S
NOTEBOOK

The nursing home which is the setting of this story was Cliff Coombe, on the eastern esplanade in Broadstairs, where Denton Welch spent some months early in 1939 following a set-back in his recovery from his accident. The story first appeared in Brave and Cruel.

I AM THINKING AGAIN OF THAT TIME WHEN I SPENT THREE or four months in a nursing home on the east coast. My room was on the third floor, with a bow-window in the roof. It looked straight out to sea. When the bitter February wind blew, this jutting window shook and swayed a little. My bed was pulled right up to the glass, so I was surrounded on nearly three sides by sky and water. Down below me were some shiny-leaved bushes and part of the yellow pebbled drive; beyond stretched the blue-black tarmac of the esplanade along the cliff's edge. The isolated cast-iron lamp-posts and seats on this esplanade were piercingly sad. In my curious state of health, it was very easy for me to see them as lonely, tortured creatures rooted and anchored just out of shouting distance of one another. The loneliness of that never-ending expanse of leathery sea was horribly accentuated by those florid shapes in brittle cast-iron.

Although it terrified me, I gloated on the emptiness, the negation of everything living. The suck and mumble of the waves on the beach, licking and slithering and eating, filled me with a wry, fearful pleasure. I would make words up to their everlastingly industrious, hopeless music. My words were not worthy of the music, but I would repeat them over and over again until I had lulled myself into a kind of trance. I would say, 'Across the sullen rocks and slime I feel the washing of all time,' or 'Meanwhile let's pass the whisky round, with sucking, talking, human sound; unlike that rushing of the sea, which beats outside eternally.' I would say these things a hundred or a thousand times, until the world and my surroundings had dissolved and I was alone in a mist, borne up on some grey woolly substance like brains, or the marrow from an ox bone.

Every morning at the same time, just after Sister Howe had brought up my breakfast, a small girl would go past with her mother, or nurse, and another child. This girl always looked up to my window, and when she saw me, propped up with several pillows, right in the corner of the window, she would turn to the woman and the other child and say something which usually made the other smile or laugh. I took it that she was being funny at my expense, for her white grinning face with its narrowed eyes seemed to wear a rather malicious expression.

After her witticism to the others, the little girl would fling another glance up at me, to make certain I was looking; then, rushing to the railings at the cliff's edge, she would bang her gloved hand along them, or self-consciously bounce her rubber ball in a way that seemed to express very clearly her pose of careless insolence and hard gaiety. It was as if she were saying, 'Here am I, dancing about and bouncing my ball so beautifully and deftly, and you and all the other dull things on the earth don't mean anything at all. All that means anything is me, being clever with my ball and laughing.'

And while she performed, she would sing a special yodelling song for me. She would gargle in her throat, then shoot up to the highest treble where, by rocking between two notes, she created a grotesque and extraordinarily liquid tremolo. After this she would sink right down again and gurgle in her boots, making the noises of a large animal, an elephant or a hippopotamus in pain.

During her song she would look back at me over her shoulder and widen her mouth or roll her eyes; and before she was too far along the esplanade for me to be able to see, she would usually finish her act with the most frightening of gargoyle grimaces and a strange flutter of the hands which was not meant as a wave to me but rather as a final display of elegance.

The woman seemed to take very little notice of this girl. She generally hurried along holding the other child's hand and allowing this one to scamper about and behave as preposterously as she liked.

I was glad that she did not try to repress the small girl, for her performance was very strange and amusing and stimulating. I watched all her movements with great attention and tried not to show any emotion on my face; but sometimes I could not help smiling or looking self-conscious, and if the little girl was able to notice this through the glass, she would shout with laughter and bounce up and down in one place, like a pneumatic road-drill. To have made some visible impression on me seemed to give her the greatest delight, and she at once wanted to express the friendly derision in which she held me, because I had taken notice of her.

I always watched until this devil of a little girl had quite disappeared; then, no matter how cold it was, if the day was sunny, I would collect book, paper, pen and notebook and wait for Sister to take me up on to the roof. There she would settle me in the sunniest corner with a screen tied to the back of the deck-chair to keep off some of the wind. She would spread an eiderdown over me, bring me a tray with tea and biscuits on it, then leave me till lunch-time.

At first I would just lie with my eyes shut, the sun on my face, and my body shivering under the eiderdown; then gradually, as my skin grew accustomed to the iron touch of the wind from the sea, I would throw back the eiderdown and lie only in my striped pyjamas. I would next abandon the jacket of these and occasionally even the trousers; so that sometimes in mid-February and March I lay on a roof in Thanet naked.

It was a pleasure for me to watch my body burning to a tawny colour and the hairs on it bleaching till they all shone with a brassy glint. It compensated me slightly, for it at least gave me the appearance of good health.

Sometimes it grew so hot in my sheltered corner that I sweated. I would watch all the diamond beads forming in the shallow cross between my chest muscles; then when a sudden gust of wind caught them, I would see them dashed flat against my body, smeared and scattered. The ice of the wind suddenly striking my sweating body made curious thrills of pleasure–pain, fear and exaltation, pass through me. I thought of throwing myself from the roof and allowing the wind to carry me along, until I caught in the branches of a tree, where I would hang crucified, with my arms outstretched, until my pyjamas rotted to tatters and rags, and my bones were cleaned of all flesh by the birds. I thought of them pecking out my eyes and enjoying tremendously these delicious morsels of glutinous hazel jelly. I wondered if a large bird would succeed in tearing out my tongue whole, or whether an army of tiny birds would just peck delicately at the tip and gradually work downwards until they reached the roots.

When I grew tired of lying idle, I turned from these fantasies and went on with the drawing I was doing at the moment. One of these pen drawings was nothing but faces outside a stage door. I had written 'Stage Door' on the glass panel, so that no one could mistake it. There was a pimp's face, very young and jaunty and common looking, a bearded hermaphrodite face, rather lugubrious and distinguished, a smart woman's face with hair piled up and curling Greek lips, and one of those faces which are often associated with the early Russian Ballet – the sort that has dark straight hair parted in the middle, purple brown circles under the eyes and a pouting prude's mouth sinking down at the corners into dissatisfaction and disillusion.

I don't know why I drew any of these faces; they were none of them types that I cared for or knew anything about. They just seemed to evolve themselves as I scratched the pen over the paper. Their faces were shown quite flat, like cardboard cut-outs, and each one had some particular property or distinguishing mark attached to it. The artistic lady had megaphones attached to, and streaming from, the pupils of her blind eyes, the pimp had a little black thing like a lizard wriggling out of his mouth, and the smart woman had my name cruelly tattooed on her bosom and worked time and time again into the embroidery of her dress.

Once Sister had caught sight of this drawing as she bent over me with a tray, and she'd said, 'Good heavens, my dear boy, what a queer drawing! Do you think you ought to frighten yourself like that – or anyone else either?'

And although she said this lightly and breezily as a good nurse should, I became so nervous that without knowing quite what I did, I snatched up a chocolate from the box my aunt had sent me, and thrust it roughly into her astonished mouth. My hand was shaking and the chocolate banged on her teeth and lips, but I achieved what I had blindly intended. It silenced her.

I brooded on this scene after she left me and I decided always to carry a box of chocolates with me, so that I could shove them hastily into the mouths of all who were about to hurt and terrify me by their remarks. If the chocolates were large enough they would successfully act as temporary gags, and in extreme cases, if they were thrust with violence, they might even lodge in the throat and choke.

After lying still all day, I was allowed to dress and go down to tea in the sun-room, where I would meet any of the other patients who happened to be up.

One day I found a person of my own age there. In spite of the lard-coloured hair, through which could be seen his scalp, my heart gave a leap of pleasure, for I had spoken only to older people for a whole month.

I stared at him quite openly while I ate my scone, and waited for him to say something to me across the room, but although I caught him furtively eyeing me several times, nothing happened. I became so exasperated by his obstinacy, and my own, that I was about to jump up and kick the panels of the door as I left the room, when Sister saved the situation by coming in just at that moment and suggesting that I might like to talk to Mr Johnston before going back to bed. She led me up to him and I sat down in the basket-chair at his side. We were quickly telling each other our troubles. First he told me his, which were, I thought, on the whole unreal and hypochondriacal; then I poured mine out in a torrent. I was very conscious of the lack of restraint in all I said, but I hoped that for once this would not matter. Perhaps this could be done, I felt, in the sun-room of a nursing home to another patient who was also wishing to unburden himself.

But I was wrong. Johnston only wanted to tell me how unhappy he'd been at Cambridge, how far he liked to walk each day, and what sort of salad he had for breakfast – of all meals. He didn't want to hear about my difficulties.

And when I realized this, I made up silly stories to frighten and disgust him. I told him of pathetic drunken parties which had never been. I described how friends had taken off their trousers and danced in the street at midnight in their shirt-tails, pretending they were Highlanders at a Caledonian ball. I told him that I had stirred a hundred aspirin tablets into a saucepan of Heinz tomato soup in an attempt to kill myself.

Here I made my eyes go rather wild and staring, then fixed them on Johnston. I saw that he was beginning to be uneasy. I was pleased that at last he was showing some feeling.

Suddenly he jumped up, saying that he was going to his room to fetch a book. I was left alone. I wondered what to do. I opened the narrow French window into the garden and stepped on to the gravel path. Nobody was about. I thought I would go for a walk. If I could manage it, I would get to the town. I started out along the deserted esplanade, with the sea washing and whining below me at the foot of the cliffs.

Twice I had to sit down on the freezing public seats, but at last I reached a narrow pathway which cut through to the centre of the town.

I stood on a corner where there were two inns close together. I could hear voices, some fitful half-hearted piano music, dogs yapping and barking.

Suddenly I began to chant out loud, 'Soft slow dogs that sit upon the parlour floor, watching the feet that wander here and there. Deep hard voice, crusted with smells of all humanity. Eyes searching, forever searching for that long past lover, whose breath shall never warm you more.'

It didn't seem to mean much; it was slushy; but the words pleased me, as rigmaroles do.

I thought that the right and proper thing for someone else to do would be to go into one of the pubs and drink some gin for his great unhappiness. Everything seemed to point in that direction; and I wondered why the idea seemed so very unattractive to me. It appeared as a fault in me that I did not wish to drink anything at this particular black moment.

Then, even as I thought so coldly and sensibly, an upsurging mad desire swept over me to displease, to pain myself, to draw unfriendly eyes to my troubled state. I went up to the nearest inn and pushed open one of the doors. There were only a few men in this bar and I was aware of their eyes as I crossed the room rather unsteadily. The more I tried to walk evenly, the more I lurched; and they, who were not to know my state of health, imagined, I suppose, that I had already had a fair amount to drink, for they looked at me with that sort of tolerance which is so insulting.

I ordered some gin and lime juice and drank it almost at once to cover my confusion; then I had another and another and felt more able to look at the other men and perhaps even talk to them. But they still seemed to treat me with a wary curiosity, which made me imagine that there was something startling and distraught about my appearance. As the drink began to work on me I acted up to this belief more and more. I drummed on the bar with my fingers and rolled my eyes. I muttered and hummed under my breath, jerking my head this way and that suddenly, for no apparent reason. But I did not feel drunk. My sadness was growing instead of melting away. And this incapacity to throw off my sadness terrified me.

After my sixth gin I jumped up convulsively. Something seemed to be rising up inside me to stifle me. I ran across the room and threw myself against the door. Someone called out after me, 'Steady on; take it easy.' And that enraged me, because it was just what I could not do.

I stumbled across the inn-yard and stood in the lavatory with my head and my forearms pressed against the wall. I retched. How chastened and glorious I felt for a moment afterwards! I raised my eyes and saw written on the wall quite high up and in rough, clear capitals, GOD = GOOD = STRENGTH = POWER = LOVE. Close to it was a picture of a naked lady with a great deal of fuzzy hair scribbled on her. I put up my hand and traced with my little finger the clumsy capital letters; then, still keeping my finger on POWER, I stretched across and planted my thumb on the pencilled hair in the middle of the lady. My fingers were all splayed out and I could feel the pleasant stretch of the tendons and muscles. I heard the drip and the gush of the water down the stone wall, and because of my curious arched position over that gush of water, I began to imagine that I was a rustic bridge over a cascade in someone's ornamental water garden. And the idea was so funny, and the joining together of God's Power and the fuzzy lady's hair by my outstretched fingers was so incongruous, that I felt I had to laugh. I made great booming noises which were not my real laughter. They came from my belly; I could feel it going in and out under my belt. I liked the feeling when it came back and hit the tight belt.

When I had recovered, I felt in my pocket for my pencil. I wanted to give the lady prettier, more decorative, less realistic teats. I also wanted to regularize and classicize her features. There seemed to be altogether too much soft blowsiness about her.

I set to work and had soon turned the fuzzy lady into a peculiar sort of Russian icon madonna. She had a long thin nose, almond eyes and the most wonderful embroidered filigree pattern round each nipple. She really looked like a sacred image, I thought. The nakedness made her even more holy. I felt that I ought to offer up at least one prayer to her. So I knelt down in that dirty place and prayed.

When I got up I wanted to touch something with the tip of my tongue. I wanted to touch the creamy distemper on the wall above the cascade, then I wanted to touch the polished brass water-pipe.

I went out with the chalky dry taste of the distemper mixed in my mouth with the acid tang of the brass.

I began to walk back towards the nursing home. I was feeling happier now, as if nothing mattered, and as if I had hardly any importance, even for myself. This feeling was freeing and lightening. All sense of strain had left me. I was nothing, floating in a larger mass of nothing.

But the waves beating on the cliffs and the iron lamp-posts in their glaring but weak pools of light brought back all my true misery, and I gave up even trying to walk properly. I stumbled along, lurching from side to side and sometimes lying on the pavement for a moment to recover myself.

Once a man helped me up and dusted me down and I shouted, 'Don't dare to smack me! It's none of your business.' I said it so angrily that he left me alone at once, after apologizing for being kind.

At last I got to the nursing home and let myself in again by the French window. It was late and no one was in the sun-room; I hoped to be able to creep up the stairs without being discovered; but Matron came out of her room just as I was at the top of the first flight. She looked up at me with a worried helpless look and said, 'Oh, you shouldn't go out like this, without telling anyone! It's not right. How can you expect to get well if you won't make any effort? It's not fair to treat us like this, and it's ruining your chances.'

Because she spoke vehemently and sincerely, I hated her at once. I scowled as harshly as I could, then went on up the stairs, gripping the banisters tightly.

In my room I stood against the wall, under the light. I leant against the wall, doing nothing, allowing the drumming in my head to rise, listening through it to the shut-out smudged noise of the sea.

Sister Howe came in without knocking. She had been sent by Matron. There was a sharp feeling of disapproval and efficiency about her. She said, 'You're a bad lad to go out like that! You must get into bed at once; it's long after your time. If you don't take proper care, you'll make yourself so much worse; and that's not what you're here for, now, is it?' And because I still looked quite blank, she gave me a helpful bustling smile and took hold of my shoulder as if to help me out of my jacket.

I let her lead me to a chair, and then I let her ease the jacket off my shoulders. All this time I just looked at her smooth marshmallow face and wondered what it was for, what it meant.

And suddenly I couldn't understand what anything was for. The room seemed a riddle, the moaning of the sea, myself, my nose, my hair, my teeth, and the gin taste on my breath.

I was so frightened by this un-understanding that I leapt up and ran to the thick velveteen curtains. I tried to climb up them like a cat. I hid myself in the folds and clung to the cloth above my head. I was crying now, letting the tears splash down my face and shoot out on to the midnight-green velvet, where they sparkled for a second, like quicksilver, before soaking into the darkness and disappearing for ever.

And then Sister Howe was holding me tight, pressing me hard against her football bosom. It was like a football because of her stiff, firm uniform and her starched apron top, and because her breasts were compressed and squashed flat by my chest. I could feel the bones behind her breasts. I liked the hardness of her bones, which seemed to bite down into my own bones to support me in a scaffolding.

I was quite content to let her hug me like a grizzly bear, and I let her say, 'Poor boy, you're all unstrung; you're just all to bits.'

And as she squeezed the breath out of me and soothed me, I began sentences which always stopped in the middle with a jerk, because there was no ending. I listened to the swamped smudging rush of the sea, and I thought that people should do dirty acts and wallow in their shame and sorrow and sink down in abasement, so that all the dirt in them could rise up to the top like scum. I thought that all shameful things lost their indecency when the earth began to quake, the fire to rage, the bombs to fall. It was the same now, when I was a baby kangaroo in Sister Howe's pouch. Nothing was disgusting, not even the tears; although I could not help likening their flow to the hot meaty rush of a nose-bleed.

But when all this had been washed clean out of me by the tears, and I felt thrown up and abandoned on some desert-island shore, alive but exhausted, I wondered why Sister Howe was holding me and why I should allow it.

And I quietly went away from her and lay down flat on the bed and crossed my arms and shut my eyes and said nothing.

The tears were salt, I idly thought – and so was the wonderful, booming, wriggling skin of the sea.

Three Fragments

These three fragments are rare glimpses of Denton Welch in the process of drawing. 'Faces at the Stage Door' may be a draft of the description of a similar drawing in 'Leaves from a Young Person's Notebook'.

FACES AT THE STAGE DOOR

I LAY IN BED IN A NURSING HOME OVERLOOKING THE SEA. Only three things happened to me there and these were all animal: Eating, Going to the Bathroom and Treatment. My mind was an uneasy bog through which pushed shapes and forms that had been buried and sucked under. I could not ever read. It seemed a waste of eyesight.

Slowly, when Sister had gone and my room was too still to bear, I pulled my book of cartridge paper towards me.

My fountain pen had 'Jet Black Quink' in it, which is really the colour of Royal Mourning gone dirty.

I began a fantastic face with little Greek lips and a mask. I will have all different faces, I thought. I did next a boy whose face was much darker than the flesh on his chest, as if he had taken off his shirt after, not before, long exposure in the sun. I did him. I did all the faces. They were terribly sad. They were all waiting outside closed doors. The bluestocking woman with 'Russian' hair had grown a megaphone from each eye, she was so keen on piercing into the future. The boy with the sunburnt face had tattooed on his chest two hearts pierced by an arrow, and on the hearts was written 'Alfie and Maisie'. But that was last year and now he had nothing left but resentment against these silly marks on his white body.

They were all waiting outside the stage door. Their parts were learned, but they did not know what they meant.

FAT WOMAN SLEEPING IN A WOOD

MRS B. LYING ON HER SIDE ON THE GROUND. THIS PICTURE brings back to me a far-off picnic, just before the war, when I drove with Mrs B. and her daughter, in a small red car, to a wood. We were all painters of a sort, but we did not paint, we sat and gorged and then collapsed in heaps amongst the huge dock leaves and the worm-castles. I began to pull myself together by drawing June; but, although she was an English blonde, I succeeded in making her look mulatto. In spite of this, my pen drawing was not good. I lost interest. So I turned and saw Mrs B. lying there, an impressive long wall of flesh. Her ample arm was almost beautiful. I wondered if she were really asleep or only pretending. I began with the skyline, the rich hills and dales of her thigh, her waist, her shoulder and the curving descent of her leg. Everything must be swelling and rich, I thought, and I will make her head tiny, partly to make her limbs seem Junoesque and partly because I have not left room on the paper! But it is her body, not her face, that is interesting.

June came up and laughed at the lovely bosoms and stomach that I had given her mother. But she is rich, rich and ripe and about to drop, I thought.

CUPIDS FROM A WEDGWOOD JAR FROM A BARTOLOZZI PRINT FROM A DRAWING BY LADY DI BEAUCLERK

AS I SAT ONE EVENING AFTER SUPPER, MY EYES RESTED ON the cover of an old *Connoisseur*. On the cover was a picture of a Wedgwood jar, and on the jar were cupids from an engraving by Bartolozzi after a drawing of Lady Diana Beauclerk's.

Slowly I began to draw from the cupids with my eyes focused beyond my piece of paper. I thought of Bach catching on to a tiny phrase from someone else and making something wonderful and all his own out of it. My complacency in even thinking of drawing a parallel tickled me.

I outlined heavily with my velvet Chinese ink. The cupids were looking very vicious and mischievous now, with smudges and shadows of black on their hair and cheeks. They had lost all the delicacy given to them by Lady Di Beauclerk.

Suddenly I left the cupids and did a tiny ventriloquist's dummy of a baby, on the ground, behind them. There was blank misery on its face. It was crying. The cupids had deserted it.

Now on my piece of paper the cupids were dancing and the baby was crying in a desert.

I shut my eyes altogether and leant back for a moment in the chair. When I opened them again, I realized how dark it was getting in the room. I knew what I wanted to do now. So in the half-light I drew in the Gothic pavilion, loving to do the curve at the top of the arches and the deep blackness inside the open door. Anything might be in there, I told myself horrifically. Just anything! Those cupids are capable of anything.

And when the light had faded completely I put down my drawing as it was, not able to do any more and not wanting to.

What is the use, I thought. What is the use? It will sleep in my portfolio for the rest of its life.

TOUCHETT'S PARTY

The dinner-party given by 'Touchett' – Francis Streeten – took place in the Leicester Arms in Penshurst, near Tonbridge, in 1939 when Denton Welch was twenty-four and Streeten, rather than 'nearing forty', was thirty-three. 'Markham', another friend, is Maurice Cranston. The story was first published in Chance *in 1953 under the title 'A Short Story'.*

ON AN EVENING IN THE FIRST AUTUMN OF THE WAR THREE young men met in the Edwardian drawing-room of a house on the outskirts of a small provincial town. They had been asked to dinner by an older man, who wished to give a party because he had won fifteen pounds on a horse race.

Touchett came into the room and greeted his guests ceremoniously, in order of seniority. The first he took notice of was Wilmot, a very well-made, smallish man of about twenty-six, with film-star teeth and tiny black moustache, and the remains of a charming North Country accent. He had been the leader and organizer of the local Fascist Party, until the whole thing had disintegrated in a curious scandal.

The rumour in the town was that one night a lady member of the party had been divested of her clothes, then tied in a crucified position on the blackboard easel and painted with silver paint, until she resembled the little statuette which used to be seen on the bonnets of Rolls-Royces. There had been a peeping Tom or some busybody of a policeman – in any case, the Party had ceased to exist the year before the war began. Wilmot was now in the Army, with three stripes and only the mildest questions asked about his past. In this the authorities were perfectly right: Wilmot only wanted to belong to some harsh cast-iron organization, and the Army admirably fulfilled these wants, therefore blackshirts no longer had any attraction at all. He said that he wore his with his huge brass-buckled belt to dig the potatoes in.

Markham, the second guest, was younger – nineteen or twenty at most. He had been the sub-editor of a small local paper and was now violently pacifist, admitting quite openly that the thought of bombs and guns was too terrifying for words. He had soft, floppy, damp-looking hair, a rather pretty face with a prominent chin and good jaw-line. He sometimes fluttered his hands with a too conventional and conscious grace.

The third was myself. I had been lying naked on the roof of a nursing home at Broadstairs for four months, so I was very brown and felt extremely well and lively. I had been asked chiefly, I think, because I had a Baby Austin. We were to drive in this to the country inn where Touchett had ordered dinner.

Touchett was hugely fat and babyish and, with extremely bad teeth and rather winning ways, he would often recite rhymes about 'pusillanimous pandas' or 'two halfpenny stamps look less than a penny one/Never refer to the honourable anyone.' Then would come long lines of Swinburne or A. E. Housman.

Touchett had never done anything all his life and, though nearing forty, still lived a sort of schoolboy's life in his father's house, with consequent fears about being late for meals, not making too much noise and anxieties over pocket-money. True, the pocket-money now was spent on beer and cigarettes, not on sweets, although Touchett retained a passionate love for them when other people paid for them.

Touchett's extreme tallness took away slightly from his huge stomach, but I always marvelled slightly when I saw him squeeze into the front seat of my minute car. He would always slam the door with extreme ferocity, which exasperated me.

We stood for a few moments laughing and joking before setting out. Markham made a coarse remark and Wilmot and I guffawed rather extravagantly, already getting ourselves into the mood of the evening.

Touchett put his dimpled finger to his nicotine-stained lips and said, 'Shush, shush, my father's just coming down to dinner in the next room.'

I looked at his pursed mouth and saw that even the tip of his nose was stained brown. The stain on his lips seemed to have solidified into hard little cakes.

'Let's go quickly,' I said, 'then we can feel free.'

We left the house, shutting the door in a pantomime of furtive quietness. Immediately we'd wedged ourselves into the small red car and I had swung out of the gates, a gay babble broke out. Touchett passed his cigarettes about (this marked it as a special occasion, usually they were never offered to anyone).

Wilmot put two in his own mouth, lighted them both, then passed one over my shoulder and fitted it neatly in the corner of my mouth.

'Thank you,' I said in surprise. I remembered, as I smoked and drove, the curiously melancholy effect of the bronze chrysanthemums seen in the light which was about to fade.

As we drove along the quiet roads, the intensely green landscapes seemed dead and flattened out. The waning light, in a last fling, somehow strengthened and vivified the colour at the expense of obliterating the contours. It was at that moment just before all is lost in a scale of greys, silvers, blacks and duns.

I parked in the yard of the country inn and we bundled out. The inn was called by the name of the family who lived in the historic house nearby. The arms were everywhere displayed in freshly painted blue and red and silver.

'Azure, gules and argent,' I thought to myself, enjoying the pomposity.

We entered a hall where warming pans and two grandfather clocks vied with engravings and garden plans of the nearby house, which had been torn from old topographical books. There was also a nostalgic picture, rather good, of a lady in flowing drapery leaning on a windowsill, fluttering her hands despairingly on an empty bird-cage. Outside was the callous idyllic landscape of a dream village.

We passed through this room, after leaving coats and sticks or hats on the stand. The next room held a bar like a catafalque of gaily painted wood. Saucy cocks with huge tail feathers strutted on the glasses, the shakers, the trays, the shelves, on every place where there was room for this emblem.

The coloured bottles against mirror glass looked fascinating and medicinal, like something in the druggist's shop.

'What shall we have?' said Touchett excitedly, thrilled at having fifteen pounds to squander on his friends.

'I want lemon gin,' I said decisively. Wilmot and Touchett had whisky and Markham dry Martini.

Being a Saturday night, the place was already full. A collection of curiously clothed people passed continually through the room to get to the dining-room. There were people in evening dress, people in rough tweed, people in rather greasy pin-stripes, elegant ladies with wool beads round their necks and others with string shopping-bag snoods over doubtful blond hair.

We settled ourselves in a corner by the fireplace. Markham dragged a large armchair across the room, as there were not enough seats round the table.

Almost immediately the owner of the inn, an extremely stalwart-looking lady, came in and, after deliberately wheeling back the armchair, substituted a hard and imitation Windsor in its place.

'This won't take up so much room and people will be able to get into the dining-room, the other one blocks the way,' she said firmly and brightly and rather insolently.

We all looked at her and became rather intimidated; she had such a complete air of mastery. She wore a tweed coat and skirt of nondescript colour; her hair matched almost exactly. There was something fleshy and horsy about her, and the Eton crop and the masculine leather elbow-pads on her jacket gave a twist of depravity to her appearance.

We found ourselves making the appropriate jokes when she had taken herself off with her rather rolling yet officious stride.

The waiter who brought our drinks was extremely fat and white – fatter than Touchett and almost as tall. He seemed terribly harried and every remark was somehow a supplication and a whine.

As we sipped our various drinks, Touchett told us a horrific tale of the boiler bursting in the kitchen and deluging this fat waiter with scalding water and steam.

'Wasn't it frightful?' Touchett said with childish relish. 'When the doctor came to undress him, his skin peeled off with his clothes! They were stuck together!'

I knew that Touchett was exaggerating and embellishing this story fantastically, for although the fat waiter looked white, he did not look as if his skin had been peeled off from head to foot.

We each had one more drink, then sailed into the supper-room. We were late and so it was completely full except for our reserved table. This was in the middle of the main room. To one side a glassed-in balcony thronged with tables and people hung over the courtyard.

'We must have champagne,' Touchett said, taking the wine list and pondering. He ordered what he wanted and waited for the excitement of white napkins, pails of ice, tinfoil, wired corks and fanciful Victorian shallow glasses.

Unfortunately for Touchett, these last, the very symbol of champagne drinking, did not materialize. Apparently we were to drink our wine out of the deep bulbous standard glasses which were on every table.

'But these aren't champagne glasses!' Touchett protested with a whimper, but not so loud that the waiter might hear.

'Won't they do?' I asked anxiously, not wanting arguments or trouble.

'Nobody will know that we're drinking champagne,' he complained, laughing at himself.

'Oh yes they will, Touchett. Their eyes are all glued to the fat bottle glistening with dew.'

We tried to content him by talking in this way.

When the asparagus was brought, Wilmot, rather exaggerating his rough-diamond role, said flatly, 'How do you eat it?'

'Pick it up with what God gave you, and insert it in the right hole,' said Touchett naughtily.

'Suck them like dummy tits,' said Markham, who by now was just the slightest bit rowdy.

This unfortunate remark was said so loudly that it rang through the crowded room. One could almost hear it echoing against the walls.

Markham's face went red, his eyes glistened. We gave each other kicks and thumps and taps under the table to restore order. The fat waiter hovered round us, smiling indulgently, but still somehow being pathetic and cloying.

We were almost the last to leave the dining-room. We had eaten our roast chicken greedily and Wilmot had insisted on using the wooden toothpicks in the most ostentatious manner. The longing to *épater* was abroad; our remarks became louder and more and more doubtful.

Touchett licked up his pink and white ice-cream lovingly and swallowed my wafer in one mouthful when I offered it to him.

The champagne had made me feel full of sadness and foreboding. I thought of the war which hadn't really begun yet. I idly stared at another, much younger waiter, whose skin where he shaved looked raw and tender and maltreated. This somehow too was very sad.

We were all moving out of the dining-room now into a room which seemed to be full of divans and screens. I could tell that the waiters were pleased to get rid of us. I felt that in some way we were not quite behaving properly.

Are we talking too loud, I asked myself. Are our jokes too indecent? Are we showing off? Do we look dishevelled? Can the other diners hear the personal remarks we make about them? Are any buttons undone or ties crooked?

We settled ourselves, two on a divan and two in chairs.

'We must have lots of liqueurs,' Touchett insisted.

He ordered Grand Marnier, Benedictine and Green Chartreuse; and, because the hotel would soon not be allowed to serve any more drinks to non-residents, we each sat with two or three different-coloured little glasses before us.

The fiery extraordinary taste of the liqueurs mixed up with the coffee, the asparagus, the chicken, the ice, the champagne. This moment I'll always remember, I thought, because the taste of the liqueurs has printed it for ever on my mind. I'll see Markham sitting opposite me looking over-excited, with his hair flopping over his face, very gay with monkey eyes sparkling, such a boy, as old ladies would say. I'll see Wilmot looking nice and thug-like with flashing teeth, but tolerant and loosened-up also, such a man. I'll see Touchett rather like a naughty self-indulgent yet solicitous mother who both wants her children to enjoy themselves, yet not to be as debauched as she is herself. I'll see this for ever; yet even now it's passing and will never come back. Next year some of us will probably be dead.

The waiters were now asking us politely to leave. Other guests, no doubt residents, looked at us with curiosity and a certain amount of superciliousness. I hoped there was not going to be trouble.

'Let's go,' I said. 'They want to close up here. We can all go back and sit at my place.'

We all stood up and then made our way through the bar to the hall. The proprietress gave us a firm look and a goodnight and we were outside.

As soon as we had fitted into the car, Touchett began to sing a song called 'Balls to Mr Bangelstein'. The chorus to this song was so infectious that we were soon all shouting it. We yelled it as we shot past the grey medieval palace with its huge central hall. The front façade and one wing were completely refaced in early-nineteenth-century stone, but this could not be seen at night; only the great carcase brooded alone in the fields, dwarfing the tiny village build beside it.

We climbed the hill and passed the gates of the private lunatic asylum (only mild cases taken). I wondered if we should wake any of the lunatics with our singing. I imagined one loose in the gardens, under the great spreading evergreens. Perhaps I should see a grey face pop over the wall as the car whizzed along. My mind played with many fancies, but I could not rid it of the thought of death which brooded over everything. I hugged this thought which made the night so precious.

At the gate of my flat, which was on the ground floor of an early-Victorian house, the others all bounced out and waited for me to unlock the door. In spite of their rowdiness and singing, there was an indefinable politeness and delicacy, a sort of gentlemanliness which is especial to drunk people. It is, I suppose, the feeling of give and take, and tolerance, the milk of human kindness.

They threw themselves down on the sofa and the chairs in my room. I went to get glasses and cider and whisky, for I had not beer in the house.

When I came back, Wilmot was making remarks about the two large wooden angels I had just bought.

'But they're frightful,' he said. 'They make me think I'm in a Roman Catholic cemetery.'

'And what about that awful tapestry cartoon on the wall. Look at that horrible dirty little Cupid sticking a dart right into that poor girl's bosom – it's unfortunate that there should be a damp stain just at that place too – while Venus looks on and smiles smugly with a disgustingly knowing expression. "Sacred and profane love." Your room really is too disgusting, Denton. It's like a surrealist chapel, nothing quite what is expected or where it's expected.'

It pleased me to hear the boorish remarks. I knew that they did it to please me.

Touchett sat back in the one armchair and Markham lay on the hearth rug and leaned back against his fat cushiony legs in their dirty grey-flannel tubes.

'Stop tickling,' screamed Touchett girlishly. 'I can feel your hair tickling through my trousers. Oh, my skin is so sensitive. I shall go mad if you move your head and tickle me any more.'

Markham rubbed his head up and down on Touchett's legs as an animal rubs itself against a tree trunk.

Wilmot and I sat on the sofa; by now we felt extremely friendly towards each other. I poured out whisky for him, but refused to give him any water. He threaded his arm through mine and we clinked glasses ceremoniously in what I had always been told was the German fashion. 'Surely they can't always do this before drinking,' I said hazily. 'Think of the time it would take!'

Touchett by now had become so hysterical from the tickling that I was afraid his screams would wake the dead, to say nothing of the neighbours. 'Try to be quieter, Touchett,' I implored shakily.

Touchett got up and ran across the room, trembling delicately like a blancmange.

'Stop it, stop it, Markham, you wicked boy,' he yelled in ecstasy.

Markham leapt up to chase Touchett, but Wilmot dived from the sofa and did a low tackle, grasping Markham's legs and bringing him down. There was a struggle on the floor. My little marble-topped table went down with a crash. I saw the marble fall out of its socket and lie on the floor like a curved wet slab of fish.

'Order, order,' I screamed, 'you'll spoil my bibelots,' but no one took any notice. Markham, with straining and grunting, struggled to his feet, although Wilmot still trapped his ankles fiercely. The more he struggled to free himself, the more Wilmot tugged at his trousers, until at last something ripped and the trousers slipped over Markham's hips like a flag slipping silently down the pole at evening. They gathered in concertina folds round his ankles, half enveloping Wilmot's face.

We all let out a yell and hoot to see Markham there in his dangling shirt tails. Touchett, who had flattened himself against the wall as the struggle took place, now let out a piercing laugh and groan, and disappeared into the hall. I heard him fumbling with the latch. Wilmot in devilry let Markham go and the last we saw of them was Markham hobbling with the trousers still round his ankles, pursuing Touchett across the dark little strip of lawn outside the windows. Markham had a glass of whisky in his hand which he had snatched up as he left the room. I wondered if I should ever see the glass, intact, again.

I let the curtain fall back into place and turned to Wilmot.

He looked very smoothly and creamily pale, beautiful, I thought. He said nothing.

'I'll drive you home,' I said. He followed me out to the car, still without saying anything. Then, as he stood with his hand on the door, he leant forward and was violently sick on to the road. He made no excuses, but quietly held himself in control until the paroxysm was over. He repressed any slightest sign of weakness, pain or despair which nearly always accompanies vomiting. When he felt better, he quietly began to curse and swear at me, asking me how dared I try to get him to go home by offering to drive him, and saying that he had been taught as a Fascist to fix bastards like me and that nobody succeeded in managing him.

I felt chilled by this outpouring of hate, but I pretended to take no notice. 'Don't let's go home if you don't want to,' I said.

'No, sorry, I was only being bloody-minded,' he said, getting into the car, all smiles and ameliorations, patting my arm.

I started to drive and Wilmot talked more and more accommodatingly and more and more soberly. By the time we had reached his mother's bungalow, he was treating me as he would a distinguished stranger. I was sorry that politeness had taken the place of everything else. We went into the little matchboarded sitting-room with its brown velour curtains and brass-studded leatherette chairs. Two eighteenth-century pastel portraits of Wilmot's mother's Swiss ancestors looked down on us. It flashed through my mind that I had never thought of Swiss people having ancestors.

'My real name is Édouard, but people call me Eddy – that is, the people who are not entirely in sympathy,' Wilmot added with a smile.

'You must have something to drink,' he said. 'I know you will – there's some good sherry.'

He creaked across the passage to the dining-room. I listened to either Wilmot's mother or his sister turning over in bed. Every minute sound came through the beaverboard wall.

Wilmot and I drank the very dark sherry from thin little machine-chased glasses; then I said that I must be going.

'God knows if I'll get home, I've just remembered how low the petrol is.'

'Oh, I'll fix it, I'll suck some out of my sister's car,' said Wilmot in a very workmanlike way.

'She'll be livid,' I said.

'Oh, she probably won't notice.'

We went into the outhouse where the sister's dilapidated little car stood amongst the coops and other disused instruments of the chicken farm. Wilmot found the short narrow tube, then kneeled down on the dusty ground and began sucking up the petrol. He looked very strong and square and preoccupied. Suddenly the petrol came up and Wilmot wiped his hand across his mouth, saying, 'Christ, I nearly got a mouthful!' He let the petrol dribble into a bottle.

'That's enough, really,' I said, 'you'll empty her tank.'

Wilmot held up the bottle.

'Do you think that will be enough? It's only about half a gallon.'

I said 'yes' hastily. We poured it in. Wilmot and I shook hands warmly.

'Goodbye,' he said, 'and thank you for the fine party.'

'It wasn't my party,' I said, 'it was Touchett's. Don't you remember, he wanted to spend his winnings.'

'Good God, I'd forgotten. We none of us said anything to him because he pushed off like that with Markham after him. We'll have to thank him another day.'

I started the car and waved to Wilmot in the dim hut.

'Goodbye, goodbye,' I said.

He waved back. I could just see the little black moustache and the smudge of white teeth.

Those teeth will probably be scattered all over the place next year, I thought, and the glossy moustache will have melted quite away. I looked at the dim fields, and the sheep crouching or munching the grass. The autumn mist was hovering a few feet from the ground.

At home the fire had at last burnt out. I saw the little table, forlorn on its side, an empty frame with the marble slab some few feet off. I saw the empty glasses and the tousled chairs, the cigarette ash everywhere, the wooden angels looked down, the Cupid and Venus in the tapestry cartoon shook and eddied a little from a draught.

I left the dismal room and went out to the garden gate again. I leant against the iron bars and played about with the toe of one of my shoes in the grass. My shoe touched something hard that tinkled. I bent down and, after feeling about for a little, picked up the glass which Markham had run off with. It had been carefully put down and was still full of whisky. I held it up to my lips, but the smell made me feel sick, so I poured the liquid on to a flower-bed, where it made a gentle hissing noise.

I wondered how far down the road Markham had been able to run with his trousers round his ankles. The amusing picture could not make me smile.

Forlornly I went back into the flat, fell down on my bed and tried to sleep.

'Everything comes to this,' I kept repeating to myself mechanically.

THE WAR
BREAKS OUT

The following fragment clearly relates to September 1939. Assuming 'Robert' to be Denton Welch, 'Ellen Bagnold' would be Evelyn Sinclair.

ROBERT WAS HAVING A VERY LATE BREAKFAST IN THE sun at the back of the house. He heard Chamberlain's voice droning over someone else's wireless and it annoyed him. He hated involuntary listening. He thought he caught words to the effect that the country was at war. Something contracted into a hard little ball inside him and he sat very still, with the rays of the sun gilding his naked chest and arms with warmth, for he wore nothing but pyjama-trousers.

For some moments he sat there without moving; then all the sirens started to drone, and the air was filled with such terror by their rising and falling that he lurched out of the deck-chair and stood up gulping. The next moment he had dashed into the house and shut the French windows after him.

Ellen Bagnold, who kept house for him, tore into the room, and they stood looking at each other stupidly, with blank faces. Her lips had gone a sort of blue-white, like poor milk, and she in turn rushed to the window and started to drag the old-fashioned shutters from their cases.

Having plunged the room into complete darkness, she fled, leaving him to grope about until he found the switch by his bed. He pulled on shirt and trousers and went into the front room. Through the window he saw a woman running, pushing a perambulator madly before her. Her heel turned over, her hat slipped drunkenly. It was horrible to watch. He darted to the front door and shouted,

THE WAR BREAKS OUT

'Come in here, come in here!' but she heard nothing, she lurched on desperately.

He went back and stood in . . .

VELVET

Denton Welch was twenty-five when his childhood governess came to visit him in his 'concrete box', a house called The Hop Garden in St Mary's Platt, Kent, where he lived from January 1940 to December 1941. The piece is unfinished.

SHE HAD BEEN HIS GOVERNESS FOURTEEN OR FIFTEEN years ago, and now she was to stay for the weekend. He had not seen her since that terrible last day's shopping in London, before the preparatory-school doors shut behind him and split off for ever his childhood, so that it gleamed always for him as the only unsullied part of his early life. All the schooldays that followed had seemed smeared and blotched.

He remembered her as someone with abundant energy, and hair puffed out in the manner he later described to himself as 'cow-pat'. This had seemed, in those days when his mother and all her friends were shingled, strangely old-fashioned, and this effect was strengthened when she clipped the pince-nez on to her rather long, sensitively twitching rabbit nose. She wore blouses too, and a tight watered-silk belt with a Russian cloisonné buckle – a little silver dagger thrust through a slot.

But this appearance, so surprisingly like the descriptions of governesses of an earlier period, seemed, when he thought of her mind, almost a grotesque disguise that she had put on for devilment. How she had loved to dress up at Christmas parties and at picnics on the mountainside! Often it was as a little girl in a fluffy white dress, with her hair tied with a blue bow and hanging down her back almost to her knees.

Remembering her, before he went to the station to meet her train, he thought of her as vanity, self-will, determination, exuberance, together with many other qualities, baked into a unique cake called 'Velvet'.

The nickname came back to him, and he was amazed at it, and amazed that she should have insisted on it when, to begin with, he called her Mrs Warrington.

'I'm always called "Velvet",' she had said with threateningly gentle firmness. 'I don't know why – perhaps it's because I'm soft to stroke like a Persian puss-cat.'

On that first night of their meeting, as she rubbed him down energetically in the bathroom, he had thought that no one with so much bone, so much tightness of skin and angularity, could be like velvet or a Persian cat. Still, he had called her 'Velvet' because she demanded it – and it flooded back to him with all the power of a revelation that she had very little love in her, that in spite of all their intimacy for three years, their jokes and quarrels and enjoyments, they had both, deep down, been cold and cynical about each other, with a little core of hardness that was always fed and cherished in their hearts. His childish heartlessness had matched hers, and so they were on an equal footing in some way and understood each other well.

As the time for her arrival drew nearer, he found that his rich remembrances of her, with all their ancient flavour, began to lose substance and power. They were being wasted and drained by his dread of meeting her in the flesh again.

The war had only been waged for two years and so he was still allowed a little petrol for his car. He might have had more if he had asked for a medical certificate, but laziness and distaste stopped him from petitioning.

He passed through the dark garden and then drove the Austin Seven out of the flimsy garage and turned it into the lane. The high banks and his shrouded headlamps made him feel that he was burrowing down a long, long tunnel. He was glad when he came out at the other end and saw the few lights of the station brooding in the middle of the little Victorian country slum.

He walked up and down the platform with slow steps, leaning on his stick quite openly; then he remembered that he was about to meet someone who had only known him as a robust child with no shadow of illness or decrepitude about him, and this thought drove his head upward, his shoulders a little too much back. He held the stick half behind his back in a rather ineffectual propping position.

When the train rushed in harshly and the windows smeared past him, he felt disintegrated and confused. He had spent such long periods in bed that violent movement still jarred him, and there were so many faces at the open doors. Behind them glowed the sinister blue bulbs, making them all evil.

Holding himself in his new stiff upright way he moved up the platform. His eyes were rather desperate in their search, for he felt all the cruelty of failing to recognize her. It was like a hot pinch at his stomach.

A woman wearing tortoiseshell spectacles and a tight little London hat was hovering in a doorway and waving a pale glove at him. She was doing it rather uncertainly because of the blankness on his face. Even when he felt almost certain that this must be 'Velvet', he could hardly believe in her, hardly chance the smile and the outflow of warmth that he ought to give. Velvet had never been fashionable in this self-effacing complying way; she had always been nearer to the grotesque and remarkable. And surely, she who had been middle aged when he was eight should now look quite elderly, instead of younger.

'Oh, my dear, I recognized you, but you didn't know me,' she said, judging him at once in her old unwarm way. But he was aware now of an unfortunate tone in her voice, that his childish ears had been too inexperienced to detect. She was sharp and trivial, like a bird, and her demand for respect was bludgeoning and coarse. She seemed to be saying as she looked at him so forcefully, 'See my well-cut coat and skirt, my trim hat, the white leather camellias in my buttonhole, and my thick hide suitcase. Observe my careless control of this porter and of you. You walk at my side and I am queen.'

Because he was frozen by this pretension, afraid of letting her display too much, thus causing some deep embarrassment in himself, he talked the whole time in the car and filled all the gaps with chatter. He was so disappointed by the hollowness forced on him that he wanted to blame her out loud, tell her to be real at once.

'But Hugh, it looks just like a roadside tea-house,' she said, gazing at the glimmering shape of the 'modern' concrete box he rented. Tiny as it was, it had been designed very carefully by a well-known architect for his own use, so Hugh was always a little disappointed when visitors identified it with shop fronts, cafes or amusement parks. It was not as vulgar and stupid as they so often were, but its 'functionalism' was making it look more affected, more dated, every day.

'It's a pity it insists so, isn't it?' he said; and at once he was afraid she would take this criticism to herself.

But she was not sensitive to indirect attack, and they went in at the door, sat down by the stove, and Hugh brought out his large bottle of British sherry and poured some into the old square-based glasses. The tawny liquid had a curious pink tinge, like the rosy flush sometimes seen in blond hair that has been 'helped'. Because of this flush under the amber, Hugh kept gazing at the glasses and wondering what the wine had been coloured with – or were the grapes really that colour?

'With those nice glasses you should have a nice decanter, dear. Haven't you got one?' Velvet asked.

'No,' said Hugh.

'Let me see, your birthday is quite soon, next week, in fact, isn't it?'

Velvet gave him a triumphant glance, compelling his praise, drawing it out of him.

'How amazing of you to remember!' he said, really surprised at her memory.

'Of course I remember. Who wouldn't after all the to-do of those birthdays – being woken up at crack of dawn, being hinted to for weeks beforehand, so that I should carry the messages to your mother. How artful you were! And how you loved *things*. Sometimes it almost seemed unnatural to me in one so young.'

Hugh was pleased now that she was talking about him as a child, even though the picture she drew seemed flat and distorted. He wished that she would go on, but she returned to the present and to her scheme.

'When I'm in London, I shall go to Fortnum's and choose you a nice decanter and have it sent for your birthday. They had some nice ones a little time ago with pear-shaped stoppers and shallow cutting round the base.'

'Oh, but you mustn't, Velvet. It will cost so much. Things like that are so horribly expensive nowadays.'

He was alarmed at this new demand on his emotions. He must show gratitude now, and gratitude is difficult to express, and does not like to come when it is called. It becomes furtive and shame-faced.

'I know exactly what things cost nowadays – better than you do, I expect. But I always say, if you've got the money, why not spend it? That's what it's for. These people I'm with now are what I believe is called "stinking" by your generation; so they can afford to pay me well. If they didn't, I shouldn't be there another day.'

Velvet then went on to describe the pleasures, privileges and trials of her present position, not as governess, but as house-keeper to some ship-owners with a place in the Midlands.

'The behaviour of some of the guests is too extraordinary, Hugh,' she said with animation. He knew she was warming to some startling utterance, to something that could be called improper by the very strict. As a child she had always liked to make his eyes open wider, his mouth shape an 'Oh!' of wonder.

'The other morning, I was going my round of the rooms and I found Sandy Gregg – that's a friend of one of the sons – poking something down his basin with a stick – with a stick, if you please! The disgusting young man had been sick, because he'd drunk much too much the night before . . .'

A DREAM
OF VESTALS

Denton Welch wrote a draft of this story in the autumn of 1940, revising it some eighteen months later while living at Pond Farm in East Peckham, Kent. His first title for this revised version was 'The Vestals' Departure', which he then changed to the present title.

WHAT I DREAMT MUST BE RECORDED. I WAS ON AN ISLAND – at Hyde Park Corner, where the traffic flowed on a road so wide that it reached to Buckingham Palace.

Bullets were raining down like burning hail; they seemed to come in spatters, guttering on to the tarmac, tearing holes and flattening into lead pools. Several hit me, searing and stinging my flesh.

I crouched on the island, sensing the utter recklessness of the traffic as it surged and screamed around me.

The Victoria Memorial crumbled and fell under the corrosion of the hundred thousand bullets. The white marble was like meal.

When I looked up again I saw that the bullets had stopped showering and that the traffic had ceased to flow, so that there was an almost unimaginable expanse of grey pavement. It was almost as if a segment of the world were paved. Only part of the buildings in the distance could be seen, as they were beyond the horizon.

Then I heard singing and saw processions coming slowly towards me over the curved surface.

They were all women. I watched the first band as they passed me. They seemed short and stunted and they carried palm leaves which they waved in farewell as they sang. Their swart dark faces were sullen and their eyes were like dead coal. I fancied that I smelt their bodies and their short matted hair as they went by.

Next I heard far lovelier singing; and looking beyond the palace I saw another band approaching. Glimpses of their thin white jewelled arms appeared through the cut sleeves of their velvet robes, which were all of dust colour: blue dust, rose dust, gold dust and green.

They sang and talked amongst themselves, smiling insolent smiles. These I knew were the Vestals of Christ. No one had told me, but I knew. They were the most famous body in the world. They were the link between the modern and the ancient worlds. The 'Vestals of Christ' was not a contradiction. They had never abandoned the old when they had embraced the new.

For nearly two thousand years they had lived in their complete seclusion, tending their beauty all day long. They were idle from morning to night amidst luxury of foods and silks and jewels. Their pleasure was to talk amongst themselves and dance. They were disgusted and revolted by men.

Through the centuries they had moved their palace from capital to capital; and now, after three hundred years, they were leaving London.

They twisted their insolent swan necks and swept the air with their fluttering hands, gliding and arabesqueing in a refinement of self-conscious grace.

They were going, leaving the city and its outrages. They stepped lightly over the dead bodies, talking of quite other things.

No one knew where they would next settle. Perhaps Tokyo or New York.

I saw their proud backs disappear as, still singing and chattering, they entered the fantastic medieval ship which lay waiting for them on the lake in St James's Park.

Then the ship sailed away, disappearing in a cloud, and I thought of their beauty and insolence and pride living for ever somewhere in the world.

THE FIRE
IN THE WOOD

'The Fire in the Wood' was inspired by what Denton Welch described as 'a romantic affair' he had with a woodman named Tom, whom he first met in 1941. In the story, first published in Brave and Cruel, *Tom becomes 'Jim', Denton Welch 'Mary' and Evelyn Sinclair 'Mrs Legatt'.*

I

ON THE EDGE OF A PINE WOOD IN HAMPSHIRE THERE IS a little concrete box which dates from the time when such architecture was still fashionable and rare. It looks a little forlorn and posturing now, but inside it is comfortable enough. My story begins on a grey afternoon in April, when a young woman let herself out of this house and started to walk up the path through the trees. She was going to meet an old friend of her mother's. Mrs Tuke drove over once a month at least to see Mary and take her back to tea, but she would never come quite all the way. If she stopped at the top of the hill and waited for Mary to climb up to her, she told herself that she had been wise and not wasted her petrol.

As Mary walked over the uneven rain-washed path, she felt pleasantly tired and at ease. She had been working all morning on one of her needlework pictures. Into this one she had stitched real shells, coins, fossils, beads, buttons, sequins, fur, feathers, beetles' wings, skeleton leaves and human hair. She was always looking out for new things to use. Once she had worked in a gruesome eagle's claw off an old brooch; another time she had found some sheep's teeth in a field and taken them home for dragon's fangs. Mary often chose to do fierce beasts. This morning she had made flashing eyes for her lion out of two old steel beads – their facets caught the light and glinted hungrily – then she had worked its tongue in the glossiest, flossiest crimson silk, so that it looked almost dripping with saliva. She had finished by doing a little to the rocks and groves in the background.

The thought of romantic landscape brought Mary back from her picture to the Scots pines and rhododendrons all round her. She knew the history of this wood and always took pleasure in the artificiality that lay just under its present tangled wildness. The local great lady of early-Victorian times had designed it to surround her new stone mansion, which was to have risen from the levelled site at the top of the hill. But something had happened and the house was never even begun. So the pink serpentine paths, the artfully planted trees and shrubs encircled nothing. Every year the pines had grown taller, the rhododendrons more dense, the paths less visible. Bracken crept over the ground, and the seeds of other trees planted themselves.

In some places the rhododendrons had bulged across the paths, blocking them entirely; in others they had sprung up, then joined black, sticky witches' arms and fingers, twisting and gripping together until long tunnels were formed where all the light was green and cobwebs hung down to madden human faces. Some lone bushes had climbed twenty feet into the air, as if determined to pour down their leaves in a hard and glittering cascade.

But if the rhododendrons were gross, almost threatening in their growth, the pines that rose out of them were splendid; they were great pythons, their serpent scales all mauve, brown-pink and silky in the sun. There was no sun now, but Mary always imagined the trees glinting and iridescent, at their most beautiful. She paused for a moment, leaning her face against one of the trunks and gazing up to where the grey-blue pine needles frisked and frolicked like mad pom-poms or bottle-brushes. She felt a little drugged and swimming, as if she could never stop gazing on, on beyond the needles into the limitless grey of the sky; then she was seized with the strange conviction that the tree might suddenly collapse into itself, like a giant telescope, sucking her into the ground with it . . .

It was the smell of smoke that broke the spell. At first it came to her faintly and she thought nothing of it, it had only been enough to bring her eyes down to the earth again. She walked on quickly, anxious not to keep Mrs Tuke waiting.

Just before she reached the point where two paths crossed, she smelt the smoke again; this time it was stronger, it stung her nostrils a little, but she was still unperturbed. She thought of forest fires and put the thought away from her comfortably; she was lazy and dreamy from work and from staring into the sky. She would soon have to turn to the right down one of the green tunnels which led to the road. On her other side a thick bank of rhododendrons hid everything behind it.

Mary stood still when she came to the crossway; she had heard a snap and crackle of flames, and, above her, whales and cornucopias of white smoke were bellying out of the branches. With a sudden excitement she ignored her green tunnel and ran through the opening on the left.

She was in a little clearing; straight before her blazed a great fire, and behind it stood a man with a fork. He was young. His rough smoky hair crowded down to his eyes. He wore an old striped collarless shirt, unbuttoned and tucked in, so that a V of brown chest reached almost to his worn cord breeches. These were held up by a thick, cracked leather belt, polished with long use. The heavy brass clasp kept flashing in the light from the flames. Mary could just see that it had some device on it. Everything about the man held her, she seemed unable to take her eyes from him. His whole body was so covered with little smears of mud and charcoal, little bits of moss, twig and leaf, that she found it easy to imagine him rising out of the ground itself.

'Well,' he said at last, staring back at her through the shimmering air above the flames, 'good afternoon.'

His voice was startlingly northern. He was mocking her, mimicking a genteel politeness to shame her for staring. Under the dry tangle of hair his dark eyes glowed hot and truculent. He threw on more rhododendron branches and pine needles. The dark oily leaves, despairing and surrendering utterly, sucked up the fire in one demoniac rush. The needles spat like squibs. His image was broken by the sudden leaping of the flames. The dancing, quaking features looked even more lowering than before; the mouth was so pouting that Mary almost expected to see the wet inner side of his lip.

'Hullo!' she gulped, flashing out a vivid smile and leaning

forward, as if in her anxious friendliness she would do all she could to make it easy for him to criticize or gibe.

The man leant on his fork, hunching his shoulders so that they looked too powerful and heavy for his legs in the tight-fitting breeches. Mary thought of Sindbad carrying the Old Man of the Sea. The slender legs were Sindbad's, the shaggy head and glowering eyes belonged to the Old Man crouching on his back.

'You're burning the branches?' she ventured, aware of her own inanity, yet feeling that she must speak.

'Aye, I'm finishing up for the day, burning the rubbish.'

The vowels all changed, the singing, flowing tones were like a lullaby to Mary – she had never been to the north. But what had happened to the man? She had expected him to sneer at her obviousness. He was still withdrawn and careful, but there was no more attack in his voice. Perhaps her lack of assurance had softened him, even made him a little contemptuous of her.

'All the straight ones are coming down,' he volunteered, turning to look at the three felled pines which threaded in and out of the crushed bushes.

For the first time Mary was able to take in what lay beyond the man. The long pines lopped of all their branches made her think of primitive bronze needles, lost by some long-dead giant woman. Although to walk in the wood was one of her everyday delights, she found that she could only regret the trees dispassionately, as if their destruction were inevitable, a law of God – not her affair. She wondered why she felt no resentment against the woodman, and made herself exclaim with shocked surprise, 'Do you mean all the straight trees through all the wood?'

'Aye,' said the man, 'that's right.'

He was looking at her with a faintly puzzled amusement. She might have been a pigmy at a fair, or a grotesque little dog. Mary was about to harden herself against this affronting look, when she saw his eyes dodge away from her uncertainly, almost fearfully. He began to skewer branches on his fork, until gradually his face grew calm again. Now he was patient and far away, like a man quietly enduring the extraction of a thorn, or the dressing of a wound.

Suddenly a motor-horn blared out. It continued to blare; for Mrs Tuke was deaf and harsh sounds gave her no pain. She could never believe that gentle ones would be heard.

'Oh! I must go,' said Mary, starting guiltily, like a child caught playing truant.

The man looked up at her.

'Happen somebody's impatient-like.'

He gave an amused unconcerned little grin and turned back to his work.

In her perturbation Mary began to run.

Soon she was leaning through the car window and kissing Mrs Tuke's soft amazing cheek, all crazed with tiny lines, like the crackle on porcelain. The brown reproachful monkey eyes looked up at her.

'My dear, I thought you had forgotten.'

'I do hope I haven't kept you too long,' Mary panted; 'but I've just been talking to the man who's cutting down the trees; he says all the straight ones are to come down.'

Her voice was excited.

Mrs Tuke's eyebrows went up.

'Oh, but how dreadful!' she said. 'Aren't you terribly upset? You love the wood so much. It's no good; it doesn't do to love anything; if one does, the thing is sure to be destroyed.'

There was deep monkey melancholy in her voice, bitter, hopeless and lazy.

Mary got into the car beside Mrs Tuke. She turned to smile at the companion Miss Martin, who all this time had been sitting in the middle of the back seat, holding herself aloof, so that she could welcome Mary, uninterrupted and in her own way, after Mrs Tuke had finished.

She was much more carefully dressed than Mrs Tuke. Instead of a knitted beret, rather like an egg-cosy, she wore a correct and tasteful hat. She came from Bradford, and under the refinement in her voice Mary was pleased to catch faint echoes of the woodman's vowel sounds. She wanted Miss Martin to go on talking so that she could think of the woodman saying, 'Happen somebody's impatient-like,' or 'Aye, that's right.' She even liked to remember his gibing 'Good afternoon.'

And all the time she saw him standing there, gazing at her through the flames, his eyes smoky, sullen, questioning.

♣

It was almost dark before Mary felt that she had stayed long enough with Mrs Tuke. She had tried several times to suggest leaving, but always Mrs Tuke's sad eyes had looked out at her and stopped the words. The eyes must have changed so much less than the withered face; they were bright, quick-moving, sometimes melting into sudden sweetness, sometimes diminishing into faraway unfeeling bird's points. Now, when Mary made the darkness an excuse, the eyes showed bitterness for a moment, then resigned themselves.

'Yes, perhaps we ought to start,' said Mrs Tuke; 'you have that dark walk through the wood before you.'

This was what Mary had been longing for all through tea. She had thought of it through every subject. She wondered if her abstraction had been noticed. Miss Martin, she felt sure, noticed everything.

As soon as she had kissed Mrs Tuke once again and left her on the edge of the wood, Mary went straight to the place where the fire had been. She knew that she would find no man there, but she wanted to run her foot through the velvety ash, look into the apricot heart, so lovely, still stirring, falling, crumbling, like a dying salamander.

The wood was so still that she could follow the sound of Mrs Tuke's engine until it faded from a cat's purr into nothingness. She looked round at the torn rhododendrons and fallen pines. In the darkness white scars, where the branches had been lopped, glimmered all up the sides of the trunks. It was as if each tree had many blind eyes with marble lids.

Mary noticed how cleanly, how close to the ground the pines had been sawn. She went up to one of the low smooth bases and touched it with her finger. With a shock she felt stickiness. It was oozing its turpentine, its blood.

In that moment the scene became an execution in a dream for her. Here was the great white neck with the severed head beside it; and there were the dying embers where the instruments of torture had been heated. The bushes had been torn and trampled by the eager mob. But now they were all gone, and she had come at night to sew the poor head on to the shoulders again, to wash the mud and spittle from the lips and close the eyes . . .

Mary jumped to her feet, frightened by her own fantasy. All over the wood silence and darkness coiled under the leaves, gathered there to skulk and swell. Soon the whole countryside would be overwhelmed. Mary turned to go home, and a heavy bird flapped screaming out of a bush above her. She bowed her head, walking very delicately and quickly in the middle of the path. She would disturb no other more terrifying thing, if she could help it.

II

Mrs Legatt with the tea-tray woke her in the morning. Mary looked up through narrowed eyes and saw that, as usual, Mrs Legatt's gaze was fixed far beyond her; it was as if she were forever calculating difficult sums in her head, and so had no time for faces or scenery. She had looked after Mary for the last three or four years, indeed ever since Mary had come of age and had a house of her own. Her two aunts had not liked the thought of Mary living by herself. They told Mrs Legatt to keep a careful watch over her health and her spirits, explaining that Mary had been a very delicate child, and, in their opinion, rather a morbid one, inclined to shut herself away from companions of her own age.

Mrs Legatt had smiled and appeared to listen to the aunts, but it is doubtful if, from the first day of their meeting, she had ever looked closely at Mary, or studied anything about her. She cooked well, was not over house-proud but adequate; in the times between her work she floated in her own private dream.

When Mrs Legatt had left the sleeping-porch, Mary sat up and sipped her tea. The large doors were folded back so that the whole of one side of the porch was open to the wood. The air was cold, making the chatter of the birds seem even more piercing than it was; beyond the chatter Mary could hear other noises. Children were laughing, shouting to each other excitedly; then there was a mysterious swish and crack, and a dull tremble in the earth. She knew that the woodman was already at work.

She wanted to jump out of bed at once and run to watch him, but she made herself write in her diary until breakfast, then she bathed, dressed, collected her drawing things together, and went down the outside staircase, which jutted from the house like a clumsy flying-buttress or a swimming-bath chute.

Very soon she was under the trees, climbing up to the place where the fire had been. The children's voices came to her as if bounding and rebounding off the trunks. The whole wood seemed to be shaking with excitement. Once she heard the bright ring of metal on metal, and this made her hurry more than all the other noises.

When Mary came to the clearing of yesterday, she was amazed to see how it had changed. It was now a wide space where hard light poured down on saplings which looked too weak to bear it. Great trunks lay on the ground; everywhere were crushed and mangled rhododendrons. Children ran about, delighting in this ruin. Some had boxes on wheels in which they piled the fat white satisfying chips and smaller branches; others just laughed, tumbled, screamed or chased each other. Beyond them Mary saw the woodman, stripped of his shirt, kneeling on the ground beside an older, less powerfully built man. They were sawing through a pine so close to the ground that the blade almost skimmed the peat and pine needles. They took and gave the saw with a lovely and laborious rhythm. Mary guessed that they were father and son.

Every now and then the older man wiped his hand across his mouth and sat back on his haunches. While he rested for the few moments, there seemed a bitter patience in his kneeling, in the bowing of his head. Was he telling himself that he was a fool to do work that was now too hard? Was he grumbling against the world? The son's patience seemed perfect and unquestioning.

Before she should be noticed, Mary crouched down by a torn bush and started to draw. She contrived some sort of indication of the thighs and tucked-up legs, but when she tried to catch a position of the young man's rippling shoulders and swinging arms, she felt helpless, frustrated by her lack of skill and quickness. She found herself marvelling at the brownness of his skin so early in the year, at the curve and flow of all his muscles. Once again her eyes became fixed on the worn brass clasp winking and glinting like some great eye or jewel in his stomach.

But now the children were drawing nearer and nearer, moving up behind the protection of their handcarts and baskets. Mary scowled at them and bent lower over her drawing, but they were not to be discouraged. Soon they were all round her, peering over her shoulders, pressing against her arms. They smelt of their clothes and food and of themselves. Wood smoke and pine-needle smell had caught in their hair. Their heavy serious breathing was only broken by little sniffs, coughs and gurglings inside. The first one to speak pointed with turpentine-blackened finger at the drawing and exclaimed, 'Coo! Isn't it good?' His voice sounded artificial, self-conscious.

Mary gave up trying to draw and sat back, waiting for the tree to fall. In those waiting moments the children behind her were plain and bare, shorn of all their pretences.

At the point when the sawing became most difficult and the men most concentrated, one of the smallest children broke away from the group and started to do a sort of sleep-walking dance right under the tree. The child was dressed all in soft dirty blue – blue combination suit, blue cap tied down over its ears with a blue woollen scarf. Its tiny wax face was divided by a stream of blackened snot. It talked to itself and sang and waved its arms. Dancing there under the tall pine, it looked unnaturally minute. It might have been a goblin or dwarf.

As soon as the young woodman saw it, he called out angrily, 'Who's bloody looking after that kid? It'll get killed.'

He snatched it up in his arms and turned to the children and Mary. Nobody claimed it, so Mary felt bound to go forward and take it from him. Its arms and legs hung down like a stiff doll's. Mary put it on the ground and held one of its hands. The man's look was too full; he was recognizing her, linking her with the child and condemning her neglect.

'Is it a little boy or a little girl?' he asked. 'It's dressed so funny.'

'I don't know, it's not mine,' said Mary hurriedly; 'I just thought I'd keep it out of your way.'

'What's its name?' the man asked the children.

After a pause one of the older boys called out, 'It hasn't got a name. It lives with Mrs Wooler; and it's a little boy.' He spoke contemptuously, as if all the world should know these facts about a child who, in any case, was not worth a thought.

'Well, why don't you keep it by you?' the man demanded.

'None of us looks after it; it follered us up here,' the boy explained sulkily.

Mary led the child back, feeling burdened with it in some dim way, because it had no name. She wondered if it was an orphan put out to foster parents. She thought of all the years of neglect before it.

The man had knelt down and begun to saw again. In a few minutes there was a delicate quiver at the base of the tree. The men jumped back swiftly. For an instant the pine seemed to hold its breath with the little crowd; then it swivelled and swung down, like a huge guardsman fainting on parade. The pine needles whipped through the air, making the rushing, swishing noise. Branches cracked against other trees. When the trunk smashed on to the ground, a dumb thump ran under the earth, rising up to hurt the soles of the feet. The children jumped up and down and screamed. After the tension of waiting, all their actions were extravagant. Some let out long dramatic sighs, others made whistling noises of amazement. The quick ones darted forward to seize the best chips. There was a scramble round the men, who were already hacking off the branches with their axes.

Mary still held the nameless child's hand; but now she let go musingly. The child at once began its dance again, mouthing its own words and song notes. Was it too young to talk intelligibly? Or was it an idiot child? It blew small bubbles on its lips, utterly happy in its isolation from the other children and the world.

Mary watched until it disappeared between the saplings. The child had both attracted and repelled her, so that she was confused, more than ordinarily uncertain of herself. To forget the child and its fate, she turned quickly to see what the men were doing. They were measuring the tree. The son called out and the father wrote in a dirty red notebook, then marked the base.

The children were all quarrelling and scrambling for the chips, so Mary decided to do some quick drawings while she was free of them. She got something down, but part of her regretted the lines, wished that the paper was still blank. The lines were not interesting enough to make up for the loss of pure whiteness. She had spoilt what was there, not made something new.

While she brooded in this way, her eyes were down on the paper so that at first she was unaware of the melting away of the children. When she looked up, only a few stragglers were left. All the rest had gone back to their dinners. The men had made a little pyramid of their axes and the saw, and were pulling black dented tins and old beer bottles from the bracken. The father walked off and settled himself against a trunk, but the son stretched up and took a swig from his bottle of cold tea. His back was arched; he slapped his chest and stomach with satisfaction and said, 'Ah!'

Then he looked at Mary tucked up against her bush. She was pretending to be busy with her last drawing, afraid that he would ask her what she was doing, mock her with his mimic politeness; but he said, 'When I'm having my dinner, I'll keep still and you can do my photo lying down.'

'But won't you mind keeping still?' Mary asked, taken aback.

'I won't mind if you don't,' he said. 'You're doing the work.'

He lay down where he was and started to eat his bacon sandwich and his bread and cheese. He had propped himself on one elbow, with the bottle and the food spread out before him, making an interesting arrangement. Mary began at once to draw. She wanted to please him, to repay him for his trouble, but she was afraid that her sketch would be formless and dead. In her anxiety, her hand began to shake a little.

Suddenly the father called out, 'Is she doing yer, Jim?' as if the whole affair were a great joke. He startled Mary; his amusement made her uneasy, but perhaps she was grateful for it too. She had expected glum heaviness; now both the men seemed tolerant. What had happened to the young one's smoking eyes and the sullen mouth of yesterday? To her they had been such an important part of him that she felt this calm sleepy man posing for her was a different person. She could not yet fit the sides of his nature together; and so her mind was fixed on him. She felt a vague alarm, being uncertain of his next mood.

When the dinner hour was over, Mary made herself hold out the drawing to the two men. The father said, 'Aye, that's good! She's got yer, Jim,' but the young one just smiled and nodded. As soon as the father moved away to fetch the axes, Mary found herself speaking hurriedly and urgently.

'I'd like to do a painting, but I couldn't do it here, with all the children.'

There was a pause. Mary was afraid of the emptiness between them. Then she heard him saying smoothly, 'I could come along after work for a bit, if you like. Do you want me with my axe?'

He smiled, as if posing with his axe were rather ridiculous, but woman's whims should be indulged.

Mary darted a look at him, then bobbed her head, like a small bird eating.

'I live very near,' she said. 'I'll come to show you the way. What time?'

'Five,' he said, grinning.

She gave another little nod, then gathered up her things and hurried back to her own lunch. She wanted to get away from the man so that she could think of him more clearly. She wanted to picture his rough stiff hair, his changing eyes and tawny skin. She wanted to see him sitting for her still as stone, the burnished axe-head gleaming like white fire.

III

Mary told Mrs Legatt that the woodman was coming to sit, and asked her to prepare a good tea. Mrs Legatt looked at her as directly as she ever looked at anyone.

'It's not often you want to do portraits from the flesh,' she said in her rather strange, chanting tones; 'you like to make things up, or do those fancy needlework horrors; I can't say I'd want one in a house of mine, if I had one.'

'You'd rather I tried to paint a straightforward portrait then?' Mary asked, wanting to talk about the woodman.

'Well, that depends on what he's like; it's no good trying to make a silk purse out of a sow's ear, you know.'

Conversation with Mrs Legatt was always like this; after a plain statement, a warning, a proverb, she would slip away or lapse into silence. With her there was no continuation, no further step.

Mary turned her mind to her paints, her easel and her board. She would have everything ready, so that no time should be lost when the man came.

Just before five she went into the wood to bring him back. She found him alone at the far end of the waste; he was wiping down the axes and the saw with an oily rag.

'It's quieter now,' he said, smiling half at her, half to himself; 'all the kids gone to their tea, and my dad's just taken the motor-cycle combination. It's a good thing I came on my push-bike this morning – sometimes I do, so we can go hoam separate – I must have known you'd be doing my picture.'

Here he gave his old mocking grin, but with a subtle difference: it was tamed, and Mary felt no uneasiness. She watched him finish his job, then thrust the saw, the iron wedges and one of the axes into a clump of dead and sprouting bracken. He pulled the fronds this way and that to mask his hiding-place.

'Do you always do that?' asked Mary, recapturing a little of her childhood excitement over anything buried or hidden.

'Aye, it saves taking 'em back,' he said; 'nobody'll tamper with 'em there.'

Mary thought that she would always like listening to his voice; the north-country stress and intonation would suddenly strike her again, just when she imagined that she had grown used to it.

She saw him go towards a bush and pull out a roughly painted grass-green bicycle. Instead of the usual slim seat, it had a thick broad clumsy saddle. The effect, for some reason, was embarrassing to Mary. Did she think of the bicycle as a spare athlete burdened and humiliated by a grotesquely swollen behind? Jim noticed her quick glance away and said, 'It looks a bit funny, but it's much more cum-fort-able for long journeys like. Those little ones fair cut you in half. I got it off my dad's old motor-bike.'

He started to walk beside her, the axe on his shoulder, a greasy Army satchel swinging from his arm. With his other hand he grasped the handlebars in the middle, forcing the bicycle over the difficult ground. His size and his burdens made Mary feel rather trivial; she might have been a whippet pettishly following a too serious-minded master. Anxiety gathered to sweep over her; Jim was now her guest. She tried to think of something to say.

She felt easier when they were standing together in the little polished hall, so rigid and still after the swaying tangle of the wood. Jim looked about him with gentle inquisitiveness; he seemed to be thinking, 'So she lives in this quite different sort of house!' Perhaps he was a little bewildered, but his trustfulness eased Mary.

She took him up the shining artificial stone stairs, glancing back once in time to see him hesitate, then withdraw his hand from the polished copper rail, as if he had decided that it was too glistening to touch. At the top of the stairs they passed the open bathroom door. Jim at once asked if he could wash, and Mary went to the linen-cupboard to find him a clean towel; but he protested that he was much too dirty to use it, so she left him with her own used one. She went into her workroom and drew the little table up to the stove for tea.

When Jim came out of the bathroom, his mat of hair was sleek and wet, although tufts here and there were already breaking away from the smooth surface. His nose looked bigger and his eyes had lost some of their tarry gleam. For a moment Mary felt dashed, deprived of something; then, without effort, her idea of him broadened to accept this more commonplace indoor appearance.

Mrs Legatt, bringing in the tea-tray, gave Jim a casual sidelong glance, as if he were quite the most usual thing to find in Mary's room — and yet perhaps not quite the most usual. Mrs Legatt's filmy glances always left this doubt in the mind. Was she really only dreaming, brooding on her wrongs, counting her blessings? Or was she storing the sights and sounds around her for another day? She put down the tray without a word and Mary began at once to pour out the tea and pass toast to her guest.

It was not an easy meal. Jim leant forward in his chair and ate slowly; Mary pressed things on him and strained to find words. She was glad when she had him on a stool near the great blank panes of the window. He had rested the axe across his knees in a way that she liked. His hair was growing drier and rougher every minute. She squeezed out her colours and began.

There was silence in the workroom for some time. Mary painted intently, noticing nothing until the thick creamy mess on her board became unmanageable.

'I've put too much paint on,' she said, looking up and smiling ruefully. Then she saw that Jim was as still as a frozen man. In his broad throat a vein pulsed thickly. One flap of his open shirt trembled, as if a little wind blew only on that part of him. His grip on the axe had tightened until all his knuckles were white, like bare bones.

'Shall we rest now?' said Mary softly, afraid of the effect of her words on him.

His eyes flickered, then came back from far away, a look of awkwardness, even of pain, flashing across them; he was aware of self again.

'I've never known anyone sit quite so still,' said Mary.

Jim smiled, losing some of the tenseness that had turned him into a caricature of himself.

'Aw, it's easy work sitting still.' He leant forward a little. 'May I have a look?'

The question was shy and gentle. Mary swung the picture round, hating to show it, but feeling that he had a right to look.

'My!' he said with quiet unconsidered admiration. 'But I'm afraid it's a bit too handsome.'

'It's only a beginning; I've hardly got anything down yet,' said Mary hurriedly.

Jim laughed. 'You mean you'll make it more rough, get it more like me later?'

The blood flushed up into Mary's cheeks; she bent low over her palette and began to scrape vigorously with the knife.

Jim looked out of the window. The light was failing rapidly; already the barn and squat tower on the far hill had been changed into some mysterious Gothic-revival church shrouded in blue mists.

'I must go,' he said; 'I've got a twenty-mile bike ride in front o' me.'

Mary looked blankly at him, hating to think of this journey added to all the strain of his long hard day.

'I don't always bike it,' he reassured her; 'I told you; sometimes come in my dad's sidecar, but other times we want to be independent-like.'

'You shouldn't have sat to me for so long,' said Mary; 'I had no idea you had far to go. I thought you lived quite near.'

'It's not far; I can do it easy,' Jim said scornfully; but Mary knew that, in spite of all his strength and vigour, he wished that the ride were not before him.

She got up at once and offered him the biscuits, then she poured out two cups of cold tea; they stood by the stove, eating and gulping hurriedly. There was silence, but less awkwardness between them. Still munching a biscuit, she led the way down the flying-buttress stairs to the road.

Jim swung his leg over his bicycle, then settled himself in the ribald seat, with the toe of one foot on the ground. He turned to her: 'I'll come again tomorrow then?' The words were half a question, half a statement.

Mary nodded impatiently, longing for him to start while there was still some light. She watched him crouch over the handlebars, turn into the road, and disappear. Cocked up in the saddle, with head and shoulders down, he looked formidable and inhuman, reminding her of a piston-rod or an ancient battering-ram.

She started to walk back to the workroom, taking slow steps, thinking of the woodman speeding through the dusk, all his stiff hair blown flat. She climbed up the stairs, opened the glass door; and the first thing she saw was his axe, where he had left it, by his stool. In the half-light its diamond flash had melted to a moonstone glimmering. She knelt down, then lifted it and felt along the blade with one finger. She experienced the delicate, dangerous bite of the metal. It was almost as if her finger could not leave the magnet of the edge until it had been slit and she had tasted the sour blood. She put her cheek to the cold steel cheek; she pressed her nose flat against it, while tingling silver wires seemed to dart up to her brain. She remained for some moments in this strange kowtow. Then she shouldered the axe, took up her torch, and went back into the darkening wood.

After a little searching, she found Jim's hiding-place. The torch suddenly glinted on the ugly shark's grin of the saw. Mary laid Jim's axe to sleep with the other tools in the bracken, pulling the fronds across again as she had seen him do.

IV

Jim came the next afternoon, and the next, and the next, until Mrs Legatt grew used to making tea into a larger, more satisfying meal. She would look at Mary's picture and say, 'Yes, I think it's progressing very well; if only you don't lose that "natural" look.'

About Jim himself she said very little. Once she remarked on his quietness and politeness; another time she exclaimed, 'That's a terrible long journey after a hard day's work. What a pity he doesn't live nearer!'

It may have been on the fifth or the sixth afternoon that Jim came in later than usual and Mary saw at once from his sober look that he was really tired. Although there were still great blank spaces in their understanding, they knew some part of each other by now. Mary let him in and took him upstairs, almost without saying a word. She turned on the taps in the basin, pushing the thick dirty towel that he liked towards him. He bent to wash; then she saw that his hair was full of tiny twigs, papery fragments of burnt leaf, and little curling beards of lichen. Before she had thought clearly, she had picked up her comb and run it through his stubborn thatch. A shower of little pieces fluttered down to the blackened water in the basin. Jim looked up, his face glowing and slippery and dripping. He laughed, spluttering a little water over her.

'Quite a natural-history museum,' he said with a return to his lofty, sarcastic manner. Afraid that she had offended him, Mary offered him the comb, as if giving up a badge of office; but he had turned back to the basin and was scrubbing his face with the towel. Later he took the comb and whipped the wet clots and tails from his forehead, grooving them into the still-dry hair.

They went into the workroom and sat down by the stove. Jim had brought fat creamy chips in a sack; now he fed some to the flames, and the heat glowed on their faces.

Mrs Legatt came in carrying muffins, heavy and soggy, with something good about them. They spread them thickly with jam and sipped the steaming tea from great breakfast-cups which Mrs Legatt always used now, out of respect for Jim's sex.

When the tea was cooler and Jim drank deep, half his face seemed swallowed up in the white moon of the cup. Over the rim his eyes glowed, shifted, melted, surrendering to the comforting heat.

They lay back against the cushions. Jim filled his pipe, and began to roll a cigarette out of the same damp dark tobacco. He licked the paper delicately, then twirled it quickly down and offered the weeping cylinder to Mary.

'Hope you don't mind my spit,' he said, laughingly, apologetically; 'better tuck those ends in, if you can.'

But Mary had taken up her scissors and was snipping off the odd strands of tobacco. She wondered why she was so delighted with Jim's crumpled cigarette.

Soon smoke was wreathing out of their mouths, flowing up to make a soft octopus above their heads. It hovered there, stretching out tentacles, merging, twining, melting, vainly trying to reach into the corners of the room.

Looking down at the length of Jim's body on the sofa, Mary thought that he looked like Gulliver. His knees were higher than his head; he was pinned down by his tiredness, just as Gulliver had been trussed and strapped across with the Lilliputians' spider-thread ropes. She saw him with the eyes of a Lilliputian. He was some giant of enormous size and weight. And his skin was not skin; it was too tough, too permanent. It was the finest book calf, tanned to last for centuries.

Why was Jim always reminding her of the pictures in her nursery books? Sindbad, Gulliver, even Rip Van Winkle, when his hair was full of the woods, his hands black as peat, and his wellingtons caked with mud and grass and moss. Was it because of his clear outlines, his separation from her? Did these give him the legendary quality? He was a woodman, and woodmen were linked with charcoal burners, with bears, wild boar, Robin Hood and venison pasties.

'How brown you are!' she murmured, to explain the fixity of her gaze.

'Aw, that's because I take my shirt off,' Jim said. 'My dad doesn't hold with it; he says I look like a savage and one day I'll get sunstroke and that'll teach me. He says I ought to wear woollen vest, shirt and waistcoat same as him; but I like to feel free. What's the sense o' getting more hot an' mucky than you need?'

Jim knocked out his pipe and stood up; his sense of duty not allowing him to idle any longer. He took up the pose, waiting for Mary to go to her easel and begin.

As usual Jim sat with Spartan steadfastness. Mary tried to think only of her painting, but it was impossible for her to ignore his signs of strain for long. The vein in his throat throbbed more heavily than ever; the shirt flap trembled all the time.

'Let's stop now and go back to the stove,' she said at last; 'I've done quite a lot; besides, it's getting too dark.'

Jim put his axe down, then slowly rose to his feet, stretching arms up like a man forcing with all his might against a collapsing ceiling. Behind him the light was being sucked down under the hill, sucked all away; and gunmetal clouds were surging into boneless mountain peaks. Against this wild background Mary watched his black shape. He was lowering his arms, stretching them out level with his shoulders. Now he had become a monstrous bat, escaped from some land of terrors and ghosts.

As he walked towards her over the polished floor, his wellingtons squelched, letting out little sighing puffs of air.

'Take those things off and warm your feet; they must be quite cold and clammy after all this time.'

Mary was too anxious, too urgent, clutching at anything to ease his tiredness.

'But I've got to go at once. My! It's late. Just look how black it's getting!'

Before Mary could say anything the heavy curtain between workroom and landing was drawn back and Mrs Legatt came in for the tea-tray.

'We have the camp-bed, you know,' she said gravely, as if stressing a profound truth which Mary in her frivolity had lost sight of.

For a moment Mary was nonplussed. She did not care for Mrs Legatt's sudden passages from complete indifference to meddling. They were rare; for that reason all the more disconcerting. Was she prompted by caprice? Did she speak just for the sake of creating a little situation? But before any awkwardness could grow, Mary said, 'Yes, why bother to go home? You'll only have to pedal all the way back here tomorrow morning; and you're tired. If you stay, you'll feel fresh. All we have to do is to put the camp-bed up.'

Jim looked at Mary, at Mrs Legatt, out of the window, down at his feet. Mary wished she could know his thoughts. Perhaps he felt trapped; or was he shamefaced because he thought that some remark had been misunderstood and twisted into a hint?

'Thanks very much,' he said at last, 'but I wonder what the wife'll think.'

He spoke with the jovial guilt of the stage husband, turning 'the wife' into nothing but a music-hall joke.

'You will stay then?' asked Mary, still uncertain. Jim bowed his head and Mrs Legatt slid out of the room with the tray. They both breathed more easily. Suddenly Jim sat down on the sofa and started to pull off his wellingtons.

'Oh, good,' said Mary at this sign.

While Jim tugged at one boot, she crouched down and began to coax the other off.

'You've no call to do that,' Jim said, uncomfortably; 'you'll get all mucky.'

'I can easily wash,' said Mary, bending lower. Her long short hair fell forward, sweeping the boot. She tossed it back, at the same time jerking off the boot. She had it in her hands, close to her face; she could smell the rubber and the mud. She rocked on her tucked up legs, her mouth a little open as though crooning a lullaby.

'Eh, you look that funny with my old boot,' said Jim; 'did it come of sudden an' take you unawares?'

Mary looked at him; her eyes were laughing. She put down the boot, then tucked herself up in the other corner of the sofa.

Soon the smell of cooking vegetables came floating up the stairs, seeping round the thick edges of the padded curtain. Mary felt glad, knowing that Mrs Legatt had not waited to be told, was at this moment doing her best to provide something that would not fall too far short of her idea of a hearty meal.

As they sat there together on the sofa, Mary suddenly found that Jim was talking. When she asked a question, he did more than give his usual 'yes' or 'no'; he even began to tell her things without prompting, things she could know nothing of, because they happened long ago.

'When I was a lad in Yorkshire, me and my pal used to go

rabbiting with my dog. Once we were in the grounds of the big house and someone jumped out at us from a thicket; and, do you know, it was the lord himself!'

Jim paused, still awed by this memory of the scene.

'He was swearing and cursing, carrying on at us something crazy. All on a sudden he caught hold of my pal Dick and gave him one with his walking-stick. Dick was yelling, but the lord had him by the collar and went on basting him. I could do nothing, so I ran away.'

Jim looked full at Mary, smiling to hide the little bit of shame that still remained.

'After that, Dick wouldn't go with me nor talk to me; but what could I do? Not likely I could take on the old lord, and me only ten – besides some people said he was a bit daft-like, though not so as you could always notice.'

Mary leant forward to throw more chips and coal into the stove. The shimmering orange cave was transformed into a little volcano in eruption; the coal fumed, shooting out tiny jets of gas, the wood snapped and bubbled, and white clouds rose. Jim, looking at the wood, was reminded of his trade.

'It took me two years to learn from my dad,' he said; 'and then I messed up a lot of axes. It's a proper job to do it well; it may look easy.'

'It looks anything but easy,' Mary said. 'I've never seen any other trunks sawn off flat with the ground as you and your father do them.'

'Ah, that's how you can tell a good woodman.'

Jim enjoyed her little tribute. He paused to fill and light his pipe again; when the match flared, Mary saw his eyes shining contentedly. Except for the stove's glow, they were quite in darkness now; the wild boneless peaks had been blotted out, leaving the window nothing but an oblong of heavy, sooty blue.

'Tell me some more,' said Mary.

There was silence while Jim thought.

'Once we lived in a caravan and it hadn't any windows. It was all black, when you shut the door. There was bunks round the wall and quite a big old kitchen stove. When my mum cooked, all the smoke hung about, till you couldn't hardly breathe. We used to go from place to place, wherever we had a job; me and Dad would cut the trees, and Mum would come afterwards clearing the ground, burning the leaves and branches, like you saw me doing the first day we met. But now we've got a house, and Mum doesn't come out so much; she likes to look after the home. Sometimes she fancies a change though, then she gives a hand at the end of a job.'

Jim was looking at Mary. She could see the shape of his head turned towards her, the fire glowing on one flat cheek. He was all hollows and planes, a boulder drilled and scoured by centuries of weather.

He put out his hand a very little way towards her, then drew it back. 'But you, you — I've never known anyone like you before; you treat me more like a brother than anything else — and me only a rough chap you saw in the wood last week.'

Mary stirred uneasily in her corner. How glad she was that Jim could not see her face! His voice had changed — he was urgent and faltering, a little ashamed of putting his feeling into words. She tried to think of the right easy laughing thing to say; then it seemed so false, so trashy to hedge herself about with lightness, that she said nothing at all, only stared through the darkness at him. She could just see the soft glint of one eye and the sliding up and down of the Adam's apple in his throat. 'It's like a bobbing float on the river,' she thought. Why was Jim gulping? And why was his head held back stiffly just at that angle which is seen in sleep-walkers and blind people? He put out his hand again, increasing the impression. This time he let it hover above her shoulder, never touching her, but making her feel that at any moment the tingling flesh under his grasp might be drawn up to the waiting fingertips.

'I think I shall have to stroke you,' he said at last, as if there were no help for it, no other way out. The voice was changed again; it was a child's voice now, soft and dreamy, with that ruthless concentration that acknowledges no other interest in the world.

Very gently he lowered his hand to the sleeve of her jersey. Mary could feel his hard palm grating over the wool; sometimes a strand caught in a piece of rough skin and was snapped. Her teeth were set on edge, but she could not move; she sat becalmed, waiting for the next stroke.

Jim began to run his fingers over her hair, starting at the top of her head, descending each wave and curl until he reached the nape of the neck. There he seemed to love the projecting bone with the pads of his fingers; he smoothed it and touched it gingerly. It was as if he were playing with a very pretty cat which yet held some hint of malice in its twitching tail.

But malice was far away from Mary. She was melted by the flowing motion of Jim's hand; she was a candle guttering into a subterranean pool; above her arched the sweating cave roof, livid, veined, amazing. A little door in her throat seemed to open then shut capriciously and terrifyingly.

'I want everything about him,' she thought; 'his breath, his skin, his teeth, his bones, his hair.' So she jumped up and broke away. Jim, who had caught at her hand, had to follow to the head of the flying-buttress staircase.

'We'd better get your bed in before it's too late,' she said, every word a disc of thirsty plaster in her mouth. She licked and bit her dry lips, regardless of the colour on them. Hunger was everything, was the world, but just behind it lurked Fear, although Fear was only a grey shape, a dirty fingernail, a stream of blackened snot pouring down an orphan's waxen face.

They were between the rose trees now; against the night sky the thorny stems looked like great hairy spiders' legs hopelessly tangled.

The car in the garage was a sleeping tortoise, the folded camp-bed in the corner a giant's Swiss roll of poor quality.

'Stop making everything something else!' implored Mary; 'stop saying, stop doing, stop thinking!'

She had brought no torch; they fumbled in the dark, running their hands along ledges silky with dust, feeling the sickly cream of oil beneath their feet.

'Ay, d'you know, I've got no shoes on?' laughed Jim. At last he had the bed firmly under his arm. As he passed, he banged the projecting car mirror and swore, almost with the same breath apologizing to Mary.

They were in the open again, walking apart, like two campers who have come to the end of a long empty day and have only a long empty night to look forward to.

'We are utter strangers,' Mary thought; 'if we were not, I would not be looking at him, would not be wanting the sight and the smell and the sound of him. He would be my friend; there would be no fear – and so I should be free again to think my own thoughts. How is it that something as tiny as fear – for fear is a bee's tongue, a fly's dropping – can overshadow the world? Why do I hug my fear to myself, afraid to let fear go?'

At the foot of the stairs Mary turned to Jim, offering help with the bed. He stood still, looking up at her on the second step, saying nothing. Suddenly he dropped the bed and gripped her in his arms. He had her against the wall of the house. On the other side of the concrete, in almost exactly the same position, Mrs Legatt was busily cooking the supper. Mary clung to this thought, picturing every detail of the electric stove, the pots, the pans, the wooden spoons, the thickly winking bubbles in the soup. Perhaps as Mrs Legatt bent low to stir, one of her hairs might fall into the soup. This *had* been known to happen, although Mrs Legatt would never admit it, the very mention of a hair made her furious . . .

'Hair, hair, why am I thinking of hair? I can feel his hair on my face, hard prickly stubble hair on my cheek, mouse-soft brush of lashes near my eyes. If I could put up my hand, I could even feel the hair along his arms, at his throat, and on his head – all different; but I cannot move, my arms are pinioned and I feel his belt clasp biting into me, his bony knee against my thigh. His face is all soft with warm dew; his polished face is melting in his own soft steaming breath. It is like fine stretched rubber, like Scottish bap-cakes damp from the oven; and I have heard those cakes called 'baby's bottoms' too; the girls at school would always call them this. If I turned my head, what would I see? I would look down the devouring blackness of his throat into his very guts. In the crimson darkness I would see everything working, striving, forcing; it would be like the engine-room of a mighty ship. I would be surrounded with wild blind energy; I would be a tiny beetle amongst the towering machines.'

Mary did turn her face, and her teeth struck against his; for a moment she felt the flame-like flicker of his tongue. She made a useless little jerk away, then the imprisoned hands dropped to her sides again. Jim seemed to grip her with perfect inhumanity. She might have been a ladder he had to scale. His rough raw breathing mounted all the time.

Suddenly a little shudder seemed to pass through Jim, clutching him at the end in a moment of utter stillness. Mary felt the stillness spreading out all round them; then all at once Jim drooped, seemed almost to lie against her for support. She had the whole weight of him, not taut and springing any more, but like a sleeping man hanging about her neck. Quite dazed by his change, but feeling that she must lead now, Mary took his arms from her shoulders and made towards the staircase, shaking back her hair, rippling out her arms, slapping her skirt roughly, to rid herself of the dazed, bruised feeling. Jim still lay against the wall. He gave one sigh, full of sleep and resignation at waking and beginning all over again; then he too slapped his clothes, hitched up his breeches and rolled his shoulders under the cotton shirt. Obediently he followed her, remembering first to pick up the camp-bed from the sprouting bulbs where it had fallen.

In the lighted workroom they did not look at each other; Mrs Legatt had already brought the supper and left it by the stove. Their little earthenware pots of soup steamed patiently; tempting onion breath rose up from the wide brown mouth of the casserole.

'Do you like stew?' asked Mary with awkward jauntiness.

'Oh, aye,' said Jim, and there was silence again.

Only afterwards, when they began to put up the camp-bed and Mary thought that Jim was about to pinch his fingers, did constraint disappear. She called out a sharp warning and immediately felt easier. Jim smiled down at his hands saying, 'It'd take a lot to hurt them; they're used to all kinds of treatment.' He glanced quickly at Mary's very different ones. Later, on the sofa once again, he held out his palm, broad and flat, cut with little black rivers and streams, humped with shallow pink-brown hills. He frowned over the puzzling map. Mary put out her own palm. 'Have you ever had your fortune told?'

Jim shook his head, but brought her hand close to his, as if he would tell them together. He glanced from one to the other several times, sometimes following a line with his finger, or touching a cushion delicately; then he turned both hands over and felt the skin on Mary's and on his own. He examined carefully the white half-moons of her unbroken, unblackened nails.

'What a difference!' he whistled, putting her hand into his, so that it gleamed like a thin silvery-grey fish on a wooden platter. 'Look how dainty!'

Mary, embarrassed by the adjective, made to withdraw her hand. Jim closed his over it. 'Two or three of those could get lost easy in this leg o' mutton.'

'I often wonder,' he added musingly.

'You often wonder what?' asked Mary.

'Well – well, what it's like to be a woman.'

Slow difficult red pushed its way to the brown surface of his cheeks. 'I've never told nobody but you, because it sounds so daft-like; but when I'm lying in bed on my back, maybe can't go to sleep at night, I keep thinking – what's it like to be a woman? What's it like to have a great man messing you about? What's it like to have a baby?'

'Ah, that is something I can't tell you; you see, I haven't tried yet.'

'Course not,' said Jim, shocked into propriety by her light simplicity.

Mary wished that he had not remembered to 'respect' her, for she had never felt so close to him, so eager to meet every thought and help it to live and flow. Would the barricades go up again now? Why was the question, that might have been so silly and ordinary, valuable to her? She supposed it was because it was so unexpected, so 'out of character', as some people would insist. But Jim was talking again.

'If you could do it, change over like, just for a bit, I'd like to try, have a baby and everything.'

Mary laughed. 'You'd certainly have to change completely; there doesn't seem to be anything feminine about you as you are. With some people it's much easier to imagine a transformation – they seem to fluctuate.'

Jim looked at her as if he had not quite heard or understood her words. His eyes turned up, so that white showed under them; they looked heavy and thick and slow. Only then did Mary remember his tiredness. He must have been almost falling to sleep as he asked her what it felt like to be a woman. Perhaps that was why he came near her, touched her with his unafraid simplicity.

She jumped up quickly to leave him with the camp-bed. Jim smiled gratefully and almost before she was out of the room, he was pulling the striped shirt over his head.

Mary thought of him stripping off the socks and breeches, switching out the light, jumping into bed naked. For a long time she lay awake in her porch, staring up into the sky, watching low scudding clouds cast filmy membranes between her and the upper darkness.

She heard Mrs Legatt come up the stairs, pause on the landing as if she were listening, drinking in all she could of the situation on the other side of the curtain. She passed on to the bathroom and Mary heard her scrubbing her plate, rinsing it under the tap. Soon there was the sucking windy sound of her pneumatic hairbrush. Each rhythmic stroke was punctuated by a whistling little intake of air. The air rushed in, the air rushed out, the bristles on the rubber base rose, the bristles sank; in, out, in, out, in, out – until Mary felt that she was at last being charmed into sleep.

When she awoke later, she was puzzled then alarmed by a strange bull-frog droning. In her drowsy state she tried to explain it to herself as the sound of Mrs Legatt brushing her hair; but part of her knew that this could not be true – that she could not still be brushing, nor, even if she were, could she possibly make so much noise. Then with a sudden stab she remembered Jim, knew that he was snoring. The thought of him had assailed her too violently. She felt hopeless, a little sick, drained of all love of life. Her sense of desolation made her think of a raw white dusty ruin in a desert strewn with bones. She looked out of the ruin, through the crumbling loopholes; her jaw was bound with coarse linen grave bands. She felt stifled with cloth and dust and deadness.

Surprisingly Mrs Legatt was up at six to get the breakfast; for Jim had said that he must be in the wood early. Mary heard her moving about and, without bothering to dress properly, put on trousers and a fisherman's jersey over her pyjamas.

She stood outside the workroom curtain and asked if she could come in. Jim was sitting on the edge of the bed, pulling on his socks. The laces of his breeches were still undone, but he stuffed his legs into the wellingtons just as they were. When he looked up, his face was brownish-pale and clouded. Mary saw that the bed was scattered with pieces of leaf and twig and moss that must have clung to his skin underneath the clothes. She was reminded of yesterday, when she combed his hair. The memory was sour, and to shake it away she went over to the stove and started to push the rake in and out vigorously. She put on more coal, shut the door and waited, crouching on the floor until the little gleam began to swell and flame.

They hurried through their porridge. Mary burnt her mouth and quickly poured cold milk into her spoon. Jim swallowed his rasher of bacon between great gulps of scalding coffee. It was not the breakfast that Mary had planned. It was eaten in haste with no thought or pleasure, and their hearts and bodies were numbed. In spite of her thick jersey a little shudder ran through Mary.

'Eh, someone walking over your grave? These mornings are chilly-like.'

Jim looked down; his sleeves were already rolled up and gooseflesh covered his arms.

There was no time for cigarettes or Jim's pipe. They hurried out into the wood carrying the axe between them like a baby-chair. Mary knew that it would have been more sensible to let go of the head, so that Jim could swing it on to his shoulder; but for some reason she still grasped it. She had to trot beside him in the way that had made her feel trivial. She felt guilt too, for in spite of all their hurry they were late. Already they smelt wood smoke and heard the ring of a hammer on a metal wedge.

'Looks like my mum's come too,' said Jim; 'Dad'd never go burning the rubbish yet awhile.'

Mary wanted to turn and run; she wondered what stopped her. Why had she even come out into the wood with Jim so early? Was she afraid to lose sight of him? And how would she meet the inquisitive, burrowing eyes of his father and mother?

They reached the cleared ground, passing the motor-cycle under a clump of rhododendrons. Beyond the clump a plump woman was bending to gather up an armful of small branches for her fire. As soon as she looked up and saw them, she came forward eagerly, still hugging the branches to her bosom, so that her smiling bun face glowed through the waving leaves. She was wearing her husband's dungarees, or so Mary thought, for the square masculine garment seemed to be filled out and cushioned with jerseys and a scarf. On her head was a wool-work beret absurdly like the one Mrs Tuke so often wore; for an instant Mary was transported to that first afternoon, only a week ago, when she had come upon Jim – then she was back again, staring at his mother behind the leaves, looking for sharp suspicious eyes, but finding only a sweet smile of welcome and interest.

The woman turned to speak to Jim.

'I came with Dad to help tidy up and see if anything had happened to you; but Dad said not to worry, you'd be all right with the lady who was doing your picture.'

Here she gave Mary another shy smile.

'There's no call to worry about me, Mother; I'm old enough and ugly enough to look after myself.'

Jim turned from her churlishly and looked down at his boots.

'Well, Dad will be getting proper mad at me,' he added at last, with a rather desperate jauntiness. Suddenly lifting his eyes to Mary's face, he jerked out, 'Goodbye for now,' and stalked off through the ragged bushes.

Mary watched him go, gazing all the time at the sweaty patch between his shoulder-blades; it was like the shadow of a cloud hovering over a striped field. She heard the father call out archly, 'Where you been, lad?' She was reminded at once of the mother by her side.

'I hope you didn't worry about Jim,' she said, anxious to make up for Jim's gruffness, anxious to be liked herself; 'he came in tired, then I painted till it was almost dark, so Mrs Legatt, who keeps house for me, thought he ought to put up on the camp-bed.'

Did that sound too careful? Was Mrs Legatt dragged in clumsily, unnecessarily?

'It's that good of you to look after our Jim,' the woman was saying; 'it's too much, all that pedalling after a hard day's work.'

She paused. 'Father was telling me about the picture. Have you got it handy? I *would* like to see it – that is, if it's quite convenient.'

'Oh, yes,' said Mary, bringing her eyes back from the distance again; 'I live just on the edge of the wood. Won't you come and see it now?'

'Thank you *very* much.'

Jim's mother dropped her bundle of branches and began to bank the fire. Mary, watching her, was suddenly touched and melted by the bulging figure; the mother was so eager, so friendly; and she knew almost all there was to know of Jim. Her voice was different from his; she had lost more of her northern accent, so that her native forms of speech were made to sound more purring.

When she had finished patting and poking the fire, she wiped her hands up and down the dungarees.

'You do get in a shocking state doing this work,' she said, smiling anxiously at Mary; 'that's why I wear these things,' she held the pockets out, rather as a clown does; 'they're Dad's, of course, by rights.'

They began to walk back to the house in silence. The mother was bashful and Mary kept seeing Jim's back retreating between the trees. When they had almost reached the gate, Mary began to make excuses for her portrait, protecting it beforehand against the woman's eyes.

'I'm afraid it's not very good,' she said. 'I haven't painted many people; but you might just be able to recognize your son.'

The mother was not listening; she was gazing at the little square house through the thin trees.

'Oh, my, is this your house? Isn't it nice! I've only seen a road-house done like that before.'

'Well, I'm not very fond of it outside,' said Mary, shepherding her into the hall as quickly as she could.

The mother looked about her in silent admiration.

'My! it's lovely,' she murmured at last. She looked down at the polished floor and was painfully reminded of herself.

'I hope I'm not bringing in a lot of mess from the wood.' She lifted her feet with the shy awkwardness of a child, then stood very still, afraid of showering leaves or twigs.

In her eagerness to make the mother feel at ease, Mary began to open cupboard doors, turn back rugs, draw curtains, to show off their colour and design. She brought out everything that might give the mother pleasure. Taking her into the kitchen, she introduced her to Mrs Legatt, who was wiping over the enamel of the stove. Mrs Legatt gave Jim's mother one of her strange far-away looks and continued to wipe. The mother bobbed her head and said, 'My!' once again. She had fallen in love with the fitted kitchen cupboard and glanced back at it as Mary led her to the foot of the stairs.

In the workroom Mary moved the picture forward, hiding her head behind it so that she might miss the mother's first expression.

'It's him all right,' she heard her say with a sort of dreamy love that seemed at that moment more for the picture than the man. Mary looked round the picture and saw that the mother's eyes were glowing; her smile held up her cheeks in firm little cushions.

'I want to do a lot more yet, if Jim will come again,' Mary said, heartened by the mother's pleasure.

'But they've got to start a new job tomorrow!' the woman exclaimed. 'Dad got word of it last night. It's a big job in Wiltshire and he doesn't want to miss it; that's why I've come to help clear up.'

She looked at Mary with real concern.

'How'll you get your picture finished now?'

'But there are lots of pines still standing,' Mary said, trying to cover her dismay.

'Not good straight ones; there're only four or five of them, I should say. If Dad and Jim work hard, they'll get them done all right.'

'You don't think they'll want to come back after this new job?'

'No, Dad likes to finish things up clean and have done with them.'

Mary stopped herself from further silly questioning or hoping. She ought to have known that they were going; perhaps she really had known. Otherwise why had she come into the wood so early? Why had her eyes followed Jim's back as though she were never to see him again?

'Well, I'll have to try and finish it without him,' she said with mechanical brightness; 'it doesn't matter, even if I do spoil it.'

'You won't spoil it!' pleaded the mother. 'I like it so much I'd want to buy it now, if I had enough money and knew what you'd be asking.'

Her hand went to her pocket.

'Oh! no, you must have it,' said Mary, eager only to check her movement; 'that is,' she added more thoughtfully, 'if Jim doesn't want it himself. I suppose he ought to be asked first.'

'They haven't got a proper home yet; they're living with us.'

'Jim is married then?' said Mary, feeling rather bewildered.

'Oh, yes, didn't he tell you that?'

'Perhaps he did just mention it; I wasn't sure if he was serious.'

'He's a funny lad; sometimes he'll tell you anything, other times he's like an oyster. Yes, he's married all right; but I'm afraid she's not the right woman for him. I think he knows it too now, but he won't hardly talk to me for knowing it first, so I can't tell properly any more what's going on in his mind.'

'Why isn't she the right woman?' Mary asked.

'Because she's no good,' snapped the mother, her round sweet-natured face stiffening into ugliness. 'But what am I thinking of?' she added in her old gentle voice. 'I must get back to that fire of mine at once.'

She looked at Mary wistfully.

'I'll come with you and help,' Mary volunteered.

'Oh, would you? But you mustn't mess your clothes up helping. You just sit by the fire and talk to me. I *would* like that.'

The mother's eyes went to the picture for one last look. She gathered courage to mention it again.

'And – and you'll really let me have Jim's picture?'

'Yes, if you like it.'

'Oh, it's lovely, lovely.'

The woman made a little movement as if to take the picture with her.

'I've just got to do a little more, then when it's dry, I'll send it to you,' Mary said.

'Thank you ever so. I expect Jim told you where we live, but I've got it all written down here on an envelope from my sister in Sheffield, so shall I leave you that for safety?'

The woman pulled a dirty crumpled envelope from her pocket and passed it to Mary.

Mary took it smilingly but with unseeing eyes, not wanting to know either Jim's surname or his address. Still keeping her eyes from it, she put it in a drawer.

They went out into the wood again.

Soon after Mary was settled on a log near the fire, the woman returned to the subject of Jim's wife.

'She had another fellow before, you know; but he went overseas. That's why she married Jim. I think maybe the baby isn't Jim's at all; she had it very soon. Jim's so soft-hearted he'd never let on though.'

'Is it a boy or a girl?' asked Mary, trying to draw the woman from the mother to the child.

'Well, it's a boy, but you know, it's not right.'

'How "not right"?'

Mary waited, dreading the answer; she could see that the mother wanted to sink down and enjoy the depths of human trouble with her.

'Not right in its head. It can't even sit up properly yet; it just lies back and dribbles. And now the doctor says it won't get any better and'll never learn to talk; so she's trying to get a London place to take it. She doesn't seem to care; and I think it's all her fault. She wouldn't feed it you know, though the doctor said she should, and she had lots of milk. She had one of those pumps. She only thinks about herself, having a good time. She's no good.'

Mary, sitting on her log, not allowed to help because of her clothes, had nothing to take her mind from the hideous picture of a breast pump, a whorish wife and an idiot baby. The mother's sanity and worth counted for nothing now; they were destroyed by her hate.

The mother had stopped working and come close to her; she was bending low, looking into her eyes with painful earnestness.

'I have a little girl that isn't quite right too, you know. Did Jim tell you?'

Mary shook her head, unwilling to speak. The hurt reluctant look deepened in the mother's eyes.

'But it wasn't my fault. She has the epilepsy. Nobody can blame me.'

The mother's voice rose on the last words; she stared into the wood angrily, as though defying the trees and crumpled bushes to contradict her.

'Once a month we go to visit her. We can't have her at home

because she might cut herself bad, or fall in the fire when nobody's near. Oh, it's terrible, her poor face and arms! All little cuts and scars. You see, when the fit's on her, she just falls down anywhere; she doesn't know anything till it's over. It's a terrible thing, *terrible*.'

Mary's picture changed to a young girl falling. There she lay on the rough bricks, mad parrot screeches bursting through the spittle bubbles on her lips, her whole body shaken with violent tremors. For some reason Mary was suddenly reminded of that other scene of horror she had imagined, so long ago, last week, when she saw the glimmering white base of a pine tree and turned it into a giant's neck left to bleed in silence after the clamour of his execution.

But the mother was still looking at her intently; there was more to come. Mary made a primitive little gesture of refusal, but it passed unnoticed.

'D'you think they're good to them in those hospitals? Do they treat them all right?'

The voice was urgent, entreating, uncertain; the mother was willing to be blind if she could but be blind enough.

'I don't know about them,' Mary said palely, drained of all feeling, tired to weakness, only anxious now for some chance to get away.

'Sometimes when we go to see her she's very good, sometimes not so good. She makes a great noise; I wonder if they get angry – maybe slap her perhaps.'

'I don't know,' Mary repeated desperately. She watched the bulging padded woman heap on more branches. Sizzling, whipping flames and greedy flashes were now darting through the pile. They were like lizards made of lightning. They swallowed up the black skeleton fingers and the horny polished rhododendron scales until grey robes of smoke poured from the heart. It was as if some ragged emperor imprisoned in there had shaken out the endless mole velvet of his train.

The woman did not seem to be truly aware of the flames. She fed them with no expression on her face. The hate was gone, the shame and anxiety, even the wish to keep Mary with her. The eyes were two raisins in a smooth steamed pudding.

'I am dressed in blankness too,' Mary thought, seeing herself on the log, her hair hanging down, her mouth set, her hands in her lap. 'If I could escape now!'

She jumped to her feet, then stood, uncertain of her resolution to run away so rudely.

'Oh, you don't have to go!' the woman exclaimed. 'It's a treat for me to have someone like you to talk to. I get a bit lonely with only the men all day. I'd like to show you the letter from my sister in Sheffield. Poor thing! She's had a terrible time; her husband fell off a ladder and she's been up days and nights waiting for the worst; but –'

'I must go,' Mary broke in; 'I've left everything at home. I haven't even dressed properly.'

The matter-of-fact excuse came out grotesquely, all the words too sharp and thin. She began to walk rapidly away, confirmed in her first purpose by the appeal in the mother's eyes. She would not stay, she would not give comfort, she would not be kind and gentle; she was filled with her own trouble. She would take it into the heart of the wood where she could pour it out alone.

The mother was calling after her; she flapped her hand shamefacedly, half said goodbye and quickened her pace. She thought of the mother now as a plump Bologna sausage fitted disgustingly into a tightly quilted bag; her little woollen hat was the protruding navel at one end. 'Children call them belly-buttons,' she mused; 'that's what it is, a belly-button on a sausage.'

In her agitation she was walking nearer and nearer to Jim and his father; she looked up and saw Jim's naked back twinkling between the pink-brown trunks only a few yards away. It rose and fell as he hacked with his glittering axe. The father was bending solemnly examining the teeth of the double saw. The children scurried in all directions, fighting for Jim's flying chips.

She wanted to slip past them all without a word, but one of the children called out, and the father looked up.

'Hullo! You in a hurry?' he teased.

She never answered. She saw Jim pause and look over his shoulders; he wore the smouldering sullen look she had seen first. It was as if she had never known him. He was the stranger in the wood again. She began to run.

♣

Late that afternoon she was still in the wood, lying now where she had tripped over a root; it had seemed so much more comfortable not to get up and force on through the bushes. She had rolled into a little hollow filled with pine needles, and the sun stroked her back; she had the pine scent close to her nose. Beyond this far ridge, where few people came, the trains shunted and whistled in the little country slum that had grown up round the station. They were great crooning beasts, hissing and soothing her to sleep...

✣

A child crawled through a tunnel made by dogs and appeared in the little opening. In its journey on hands and knees it had found a dead thrush with sodden feathers. It clambered to its feet and held the bird up, showing no horror at the sight and smell of death. Slowly it began to twist and arabesque round Mary, sometimes pointing at her with the bird, sometimes sweeping it up above its head and running absurdly, breaking its own solemn rhythm. Under its breath it was muttering and singing all the time.

The blue combination suit was dirtier than ever now. There were thick cakes of mud on the knees. The child's hands were caked too, and a sort of crust had collected at the sides of its mouth where the bubbles broke.

When at last it grew tired of its dance and lulling incantation, it stood still and looked about it for a moment; then very gently it laid the dead thrush in the soft nest of Mary's outspread hair.

She found it there, when she awoke.

FEAR

This description of an aeroplane crashing was written in 1941, when Denton Welch was twenty-six.

GETTING IN, SHRAPNEL WHISTLE, EVERYONE LOOKING up, not allowed to park. Fear growing, driving faster. Seeing little hut. Stopping by the stone wall and locking car. Running to little hut and finding it made of rags and poles. Rubbing my arms together, fidgeting and turning backwards and forwards in fear. Suddenly looking out of the door of the hut and seeing above, seemingly almost caught in the great trees of the old park, a diving aeroplane of fire. Made of fire, wings, propeller, body. The noise utterly shattering. I run. I run up the hill so mad with terror that I do it in spite of knowing that it is hopeless. I am doomed. Without making a sound I scream to God who I know does not exist. Was it for this that I have been kept. I think of the martyrs and witches burnt to death as I have often done before. In a moment I shall know what it feels like. Lit up by the terror of the flames. I see my beginning and end as someone else might see them, small, unfulfilled, messy. It is a horrible moment of clear-sightedness. The ball of fire in the sky is so large it will cover all the ground where I am. It is like another planet colliding with the world. My breath is coming in sore gulps. I am tearing it in so roughly that it seems to hurt the walls of my lungs. I cannot get enough of it.

There is the most terrible crash and a soft wall of heat hits the back of my neck. I look round to see the field a mass of flame. My heart leaps. 'It's come, it's landed,' it sings. The huge enormous fiendish thing has missed me. I am safe. But the relief is only a veneer on top of my terror. It is somehow quite separate from it. The two live together.

I realize as I look back that I have only travelled a few yards from the hut. As I watch, another ball, following the larger one, falls flaming to the ground where it bursts through flames on top of flames (it is the second petrol tank, but I think it is a bomb). Then the air is filled with a frivolous, devilish crackle and dance of sparks. The machine-gun bullets going off.

I can think no more. My whole being is concentrated on getting under cover. At last I reach the top of the hill. A little boy with a stick in his hands gazes down at the flaming field. I scream at him in a voice that has risen so high that it has lost all its strength. It shocks me, but I cannot stop screaming, 'Where is there shelter? Is there no cover?'

He looks at me, snarls a little in alarmed shyness, says something inaudible and walks away trailing his stick. Fear has made me so angry that I go on shouting, although I am gasping for every mouthful of breath. I realize that I am at the gates of a golf club. An old caddy comes hurrying out of the gates. I scream at him quite uncontrollably. Something perverse in me enjoys my degradation. I only want to be looked after like a baby. He looks into me in a deep, cynical, understanding way, like a wise animal.

'You've had a shock,' he says. 'You've had a shock' he says, staring at me, doing nothing.

Rippling like torn cloth, my voice, in final exasperation and terror, whistles into impossible high weak notes.

'Can't you take me under cover?'

'Yes, all right,' he says ineffectually, 'come along with me.'

I will do anything, I only want to be led. He takes me into his tin-roofed hut where there are golf balls and old clubs. I sit on an old box and come back a little into my ordinary self.

'You sit there and rest,' he says soothingly.

I gasp more noisily and lie back. I must have human sympathy.

'Isn't it frightful? Isn't it filthy?' I babble. 'Isn't it the bloodiest, filthiest thing you've ever known? It ought to be stopped. It ought to be stopped!'

I find my voice rippling again and unable to check it. He looks at me uneasily, and saying, 'You stay there,' once again he leaves me. Left alone I realize that the roof is only tin. I run out swaying. I run across the court to the golf club. On the veranda three maids are hanging together, clinging, laughing, saying they thought their moment was come. They are in tearing spirits. Words bubble out of their mouths. I flop down in a chair and they take no notice of me. I am hurt. I have been much nearer to death than they.

MAN IN A GARDEN

The friend described here was John Nicholas, later ordained as a priest. He visited Denton Welch at Pond Farm, East Peckham, some time in the summer of 1942.

MY FRIEND CAME DOWN TO THE COUNTRY TO SPEND THE day. We sat in the orchard amongst the wild foxgloves and while I drew he read me an improving book called *How to Deal with Lads* by a welfare worker, which we had found on a bookstall. We wondered if there were a companion volume on how to deal with Lassies. We wished that we had it to compare the two treatments.

And while this nonsense was proceeding I began to draw my friend's ugly face. He had assumed a severe and prim expression and I could just see his thick creamy eyelids, like two pale fishes, glimmering faintly through the dark glasses of his sun spectacles.

He had a vulgar gorgeous tie which I exulted in and made the most of. Such a common, flaunting brocade should be immortalized, I thought.

Then there was his hair, which fitted like a black skullcap. He had told me that it was curly as a nigger's when he was a child, so I accentuated the ends maliciously, making them into five love-curls lying on the forehead.

This isn't art, I thought, this is play. Then I told myself sharply not to be puritanical or the worst would happen and I would produce something as quaint and olde worlde as a Ben Nicholson circle on a square or someone else's Two Ideas and a Navel.

'Don't be hard on your "fancy",' I shouted inside myself. '"That's why art is where it is!"

So I put in the tall waving foxglove (the devil's flower), exaggerating the veins, which for some reason always make a plant look sinister and witch-like. I put in the Penguin book on the ground as a prosaic touch; my name I lovingly inscribed, shading it all round. And as the *pièce de résistance* my friend's bottom smoothly curving the striped canvas of the deck-chair. His coat makes a lovely arabesque and cave-like tent round his archaic face.

A MORNING WITH THE VERSATILE PEER, LORD BERNERS, IN THE 'ANCIENT SEAT OF LEARNING'

Denton Welch painted his picture of Lord Berners dressed as Robinson Crusoe in 1941, and the following year arranged to meet him in the Randolph Hotel in Oxford.

I FIRST MET HIM IN A HOTEL BEDROOM. HE HAD COME TO the Randolph to see the picture I had painted from one of the photographs in his book *First Childhood*. The photograph showed a little boy dressed in shaggy goat-skin with a macaw perched on his shoulder. Round his waist hung foxes' masks and the skins of little weasels. He carried a gun and a bloodhound lay at his feet. In the background loomed a classical fountain, a leering old man spitting exuberantly into a marble basin. This was the photographer's romantic touch. One could see where the backcloth joined the floor.

He came in with a bouncing step and sank down on the bed in front of the conversation piece I had made. I thought, as he sat there, that he bore a very faint resemblance to Humpty Dumpty. He immediately produced a little gold box and began furiously to take snuff. I was not offered any; and I cannot yet decide whether this was rudeness or true politeness.

'It's perfectly charming,' he said in a sort of amused, indulgent voice.

I began to ask him questions about the clothes and his own colouring at that early age.

'My eyes are still brown, but, as you can see, most of my hair seems to have flown!' We laughed together, as if decay were all a joke.

Between pinches of snuff, little suggestions for alterations and additions were made to me. I wrote the sensible ones in a notebook.

Time went on and still Lord Berners sat in front of the picture. I felt that he had done his duty, and that now he could either leave, or ask me how much I wanted for it and then leave. I was longing for him to say that he wanted to buy it and yet I dreaded it. I need not have worried.

'You'll let me have a photograph when you've finished it, won't you?' he said earnestly, looking at me. He rose from the bed at last, after three quarters of an hour's gazing.

'Oh yes, of course,' I said gaily, feeling rather miserable.

Lord Berners's eyes roved round the room. He looked at my ivory-topped bottles and brushes and then at my squalid little face flannel. It was ringed round with roses. I had found it in the toe of my Christmas stocking seven years ago, and had used it ever since.

His eyes came to rest on the bedside table where several books lay. I had purposely hidden his *Far from the Madding War* under an old volume of Pope's pastorals which had been bought for twopence. It had seemed too fulsome to leave his book about bare and uncovered. Again I need not have bothered, for he smelt it out immediately.

'What did you think of it?' he said urgently.

'I enjoyed it awfully,' I said, quite untruthfully. I thought it a trivial little book.

'I'm so glad.' He seemed to relax after my answer. I felt rather ashamed for giving him pleasure.

'I've got more coming out before Christmas,' he added with busy pride. And I understood, for I knew how easy it was to appear childish in one's enthusiasm.

'Will you write in your book for me?' I asked.

'Yes,' he said eagerly, 'but I haven't got a pen.' I lent him my stylo. He held it too slantingly and could not make it write well.

He began in big letters, 'Denton Welch, with good wishes from Berners, Oxford 1941.' The 'Berners' was extra large, much larger than the 'Denton Welch'.

He looked at the spidery lines and, shaking his head, said, 'It's not my writing.'

We went into the passage together. It was wide and long, and as we turned a corner a door stood invitingly open. Lord Berners gave me one sidelong glance; then he looked at the shining convenience in the little room and found it irresistible.

'I wonder if I might make use of this?' he said smilingly, with the very faintest tinge of embarrassment. He hurried forward with little bustling steps and locked himself in.

As I waited for him, I thought, 'Now the perfect host would go into the other compartment' (for there were two together) 'and would there noisily pull the plug just to keep his guest company.' But I did nothing.

He came out again and we walked down the Gothic staircase to the hall.

'Isn't it an extraordinary hotel?' Lord Berners said. 'John Betjeman loves it.'

'Yes, I imagine he would,' was all I could find for an answer.

We walked about downstairs looking in all the rooms. He wanted to show me one in particular, which he remembered. Rather undressed waiters told us where the bar was and looked at us curiously, wondering why we were loose in the rooms which were closed for cleaning.

I thought that Lord Berners felt annoyed with them for not recognizing him as anyone in particular.

We went up to the swing doors and were swallowed up and separated, each in a little glass case. I stood on the stone steps and shook his hand.

'Goodbye,' he said. He put on his black hat, which accentuated the fact that he was wearing a shirt of tiny black and white checks.

I watched him trotting down the pavement. He looked like a busy, useful Easter egg setting out on its daily round. And I felt lonely.

A MEWS FLAT
IN THE COUNTRY

In December 1941 Denton Welch's house in St Mary's Platt, The Hop Garden, had been badly damaged by fire. He stayed first with his friend May Walbrand-Evans who lived in The Brown Jug in Hadlow, and then took rooms at Pond Farm in East Peckham. In June 1942 he found a permanent home in the 'mews flat' described in this fragment, Pitt's Folly Cottage in Hadlow, where he lived until 1946.

MY HOUSE WAS BURNT OUT, QUITE GUTTED. I SEARCHED IN the ashes for my mother's old silver, then I left, never wanting to see it again.

I stayed with a friend for a week until I had found rooms in a farm belonging to a couple who later turned out to be quite subhuman.

And as the days and weeks went by and there seemed no prospect of my ever finding a place of my own, I almost gave up hope. The county, like every other, was chock-full.

One day I suddenly heard a rumour that there might be a flat over a garage free. I went straight to the house and was shown what is now my home. It was tiny (but was not a lot of my own stuff destroyed by the fire?). The greatest difficulty was that it was already furnished, but after a fortnight this was stored and I was able to have the remnant of my things about me.

Oh the joy of that first evening, with all the mess and weariness and the feeling that nobody, but nobody, could approach nearer than the front door if I did not wish them to.

The front door, let me explain, paradoxically is just within the back door of the 'Big House', which is connected to the garage by a covered way.

One threads one's way past the long coke bin and then enters with charming proletarian directness straight into the kitchen.

Here a Regency cupboard does duty as a larder. The rather flamboyant yellow satin doors behind gilt grills, although they seem so incongruous, have the advantage of allowing air to enter.

Above it I have hung my poster of Hadlow Castle (a fascinating Gothic-revival building) which I did for Shell's series of architectural follies. The colour here again is yellow predominantly, with vivid green lawns in the foreground. On the other free wall hangs an abstract, chiefly brilliant blue and red, by Blair Hughes Stanton, which my more phlegmatic friends insist on calling 'the stomach picture', as that is the only part of the human anatomy that they are able to discover. I, by gazing long and living with it, have found many other and more interesting portions.

Under this is the small pedestal dining table, surrounded by cane-seated 'boudoir' stools, painted bright yellow.

The kitchen table, with severely scrubbed top and frivolous blue legs, stands under the window, and all along the other wall run the sink and gas-cooker, making all the 'ornamental' furniture look thoroughly 'out of place' and amusing. What knick-knacks grace the room are large and rather heavy. On the dining table stands a heavy white urn, filled at this time of year with all the flowers that people don't generally pick, 'Because they drop'! An Italian chemist's jar painted with a very depraved looking St Luke graces the top of the Regency 'larder', and on each side of it two rather vulgar but robust Chinese kylins, in treacle-green and mustard-yellow, paw their pedestals and gnash their teeth.

The whole effect of the room is, I think, rather charmingly chi-chi and half-caste.

The kitchen is the only room on the ground floor, so one passes the door which leads into the large garage and climbs the steep stairs. In the staircase well I have hung needlework pictures, to give a warm, frowsty feeling. One is the Last Supper worked by my grandmother in the gaudiest of Berlin wools. (One can hardly imagine how a devout person could have given each Apostle's face such an irresistible twist of caricature.) The other is far more poised and dignified. It is a firescreen worked by some lady in the reign of George IV. Framed in a gold and black key-pattern, on a background of blue and white stripes, a pampered, long-eared spaniel lies on a crimson, tasselled cushion. His whiskers, in silk, are treated with great love and care on top of the wool cross-stitch.

At the head of the stairs stands a little rosewood 'chiffonier' that falls between the two stools of 'Regency' and 'Victorian'. It starts with gilt 'Honeysuckle' border, severely chaste and classical, descends in gilt columns to marble slab and mirrored back; but as it gets closer to the floor it loses all its aspirations and ends in bulbous wooden knobs.

THE COTTAGE AFTER DARK

The location is again Pitt's Folly Cottage. There was a workhouse at Pembury, about five miles away.

THE YOUNG MAN PUT THE LAST DRIPPING PLATE IN THE rack and then cupped his pipe with his still wet hand so that the hot wood hissed and bubbled very gently. He looked out of the low cottage window. Soon it would be dark; the fields beyond the garden hedge had turned grey and blank, like a fading photograph; and he knew that the wood behind the cottage would also have lost all its hectic autumn colour. It would be dark and threatening, dripping with some mysterious moisture.

With his eye he followed the footpath which skirted the garden and then undulated over the fields. It led to the village two miles away and to the workhouse on the hill, but no one was either coming or going.

The young man drew the curtains, then went into the other room carrying a lamp. He set it out on the table and lighted it. After drawing the curtains here also, he turned to the fire and threw on two roughly hacked branches of trees. The sulky, choked fire spat and smoked over the wet wood. He sat down in the shabby armchair, took a book from the pile on the table and started to read. Now and then he made notes on an already crowded piece of paper which lay in the book.

The stillness closed about him. Each piece of furniture seemed to live its own life, as if no human being were there.

He worked like this for about an hour, sometimes stretching out for other books, so that by the end of that time a fan of open books lay round him on the floor. He lay back in his chair, shut his eyes and mused for a moment. His mind was becoming too soaked with so much material. He had half decided to go to bed when he heard the click of the latch on the gate.

He waited with a curious expectancy. No one ever came to the cottage after dark. He had no friends near by. That was why he had chosen it to work in. Villagers bringing food or fuel would never come so late.

There was a rather timid knock. He went out into the cold little square of hall between the kitchen and living-room. Opening the front door, he gazed out into the thick early darkness.

'Excuse me, sir,' said a young rather husky voice. 'I was told to take this path across the fields to the Institution, but I've lost me way. Can you put me right?'

There was more yearning and entreaty in this question than is usual in a request for guidance and Bligh knew that he was going to be asked for something more. He waited for it.

'You couldn't give me a bite of something, sir, before I go on? My belly's that empty.'

The voice had become almost wheedling. Bligh thought he was clever to use the almost archaic word 'belly'. It pleased him.

'Come in,' he said hurriedly, not giving himself too much time to think.

The figure stepped forward and stood faintly illuminated by the lamp through the half-opened sitting-room door. Bligh saw that he was no more than a youth, although he hung his head so that his face was half-hidden by his cap. The faint light glistened dully on the grease-hardened rim of its peak.

Bligh took the lamp from the sitting-room table and led the youth into the kitchen. He was still hanging his head, but now, in a sudden remembrance of 'manners', he snatched the cap from his head and stood easing the webbing of the old Army knapsack which cut into his shoulders. Bligh saw that his hair was bleached cold and white on top from the sun, but that as it got nearer to his scalp it was darker, warmer and no doubt dirtier.

BRAVE AND CRUEL

Although Denton Welch set this story 'soon after the end of the war', the events on which it is based were recorded in detail in his Journals *between 19 August and 4 September 1943. 'Julia Bellingly' was his neighbour May Walbrand-Evans; 'Katherine Warde' was another neighbour; and 'Micki Beaumont's' real name was Monte Bone. After worries about possible libel, the story was first published as the title story in* Brave and Cruel.

I

ON A LOVELY-LATE SUMMER EVENING, SOON AFTER THE end of the war, I went to return some books to a near neighbour of mine in the country. As I walked down the lane to her house, everything was very still; the fields, the trees, the hedgerows, seemed to be held in a dream. Because of this wonderful calm, I was all the more surprised to find Mrs Bellingly in a state of high excitement. I had expected her to be lying on her garden-bed under the gnarled damson trees, perhaps lazily shredding French beans for her supper, or painting her nails with thick, dull coral varnish; but she was inside the house. She came hurrying to her front door and began at once to say, 'You must, you simply *must* come to coffee tomorrow to meet really *the* most ravishing young man. I've only just met him myself. He doesn't know anyone else here, and I've said I'll do all I can to get him some friends of his own age. It is all quite extraordinary; I came home last night to find one of those sports bicycles thrust into my hedge, apparently abandoned. I didn't do anything about it at once, thinking that someone would probably turn up to claim it; but by this afternoon I had almost made up my mind to telephone the police, when who should appear but this delightful creature! My dear, a complete madman! He saw my easel in the garden and came straight up to me saying, "Oh, you're an artist, and I've been looking everywhere for someone to do my portrait!" Then he began to explain about the bicycle. He said he'd thrown it down the night before, because he was too impatient to ride it any longer. He'd thumbed a car and got home in less than half the time.'

'How unusual it all sounds!' I said.

'Oh! There's masses more to come. I asked him in to tea and he told me all about himself. His name is Beaumont, and he has been a fighter pilot. He told me the most thrilling stories. He won the DFC; then he was wounded, poor boy, and had to spend months in hospital. He was bitterly disappointed when they told him he couldn't fly any more. I don't quite know what he's been doing since he left the Air Force; but he's only just come to live in this neighbourhood, and that's why he's so keen to get to know other young people. He asked me particularly if I knew any nice girls, so I've told Katherine Warde to come in too tomorrow. I shouldn't be surprised if she falls for him at once. He's a very dark boy, almost swarthy – I suppose it must be southern French blood – then he has this glistening hair brushed back, and the most laughing, dancing expression I have ever seen. He can't keep still a moment. While he's talking, he prowls up and down and uses his whole body to accentuate his meaning. Poor boy! He must have had frightful experiences as a pilot. I expect they've helped to make him so excitable; but he's not in the least depressed, no one could be more bursting with spirits.'

As she lay back on the sofa in her long room and told me all about this new friend, Julia Bellingly herself seemed bursting with spirits. Although she was a grandmother, she often displayed all the bounce and gusto of a hearty schoolgirl. She had retained that leathery quality. She would tell preposterous jokes, poke fun or wolf her food. But she also possessed a mature handsomeness that was remarkable. She had been, as she playfully – seriously sometimes – explained, 'an Edwardian beauty'. She had sat to one of the fashionable painters of that period. Each new visitor would be taken to her bureau and shown the large brown photographs of her portrait. The original was in some public gallery.

She stretched out her hand now to the little old mahogany paintbox that held her cigarettes, and I had to try to strike a match on the worn side of a long case, decorated with brocade and a bedraggled gold tassel. When the cigarette was lighted, she went on with her story.

'If you'd come just a tiny bit earlier you would have seen him. He borrowed my torch before he left; he thought he might be out late tonight and he has no front light. I do hope he brings it back safely tomorrow – I told him to come to coffee, partly to meet Katherine and you, and partly to settle about his portrait. He is really anxious for me to do it. "I would have liked it for my fiancée," he said. But when I asked him, jokingly, if he'd want me to paint her too, he said, "Oh, good lord no! She was ugly as sin. She was a nice girl, but ugly as sin. Besides, she's dead now." Isn't he an extraordinary person! The most extraordinary young man I've ever known. He didn't seem callous, just matter-of-fact. I suppose one can't go through all the terrible experiences of modern warfare without being changed in some way.'

'No, perhaps you can't,' I said, not knowing quite what to think of Julia Bellingly's young man. I got up to go back to my supper.

'Now do please come tomorrow at eleven,' Julia urged. 'Just for once you can break your rule and come out in the morning. You can fit your writing in *any* time. I *do* want you to meet this amazing Beaumont.'

'All right, I'll come,' I said, showing rather more reluctance than I felt, since I was always being told to 'fit my writing in' as if it had been some jigsaw puzzle.

Before leaving, I slipped into the cloakroom to replace the borrowed books on their shelves. Mrs Bellingly had consigned all her books to this little closet. 'Never clutter up your house with books,' was a piece of advice she often repeated.

✤

The next morning was fine and clear, so I took a picnic lunch with me in an old schoolboy's satchel and went down to Mrs Bellingly's on my bicycle, intending to ride on and have my meal in the fields or by the river after I had met Mr Beaumont.

Mrs Bellingly's front door, as usual, was open. I knocked and called out; then walked into the hall. I heard voices in the drawing-room.

'Come in!' Mrs Bellingly shouted in her rather military voice. I could tell that she was gay. Perhaps she had begun already to tell some of her jokes.

Flat blue-grey pancakes and wisps of cigarette smoke floated across the broad bars of sunlight from the windows. Someone came towards me at once, saying, 'Oh, he's got leather pads on the elbows of his jacket! I do like that, don't you?'

As he turned to Mrs Bellingly, I was able to glance quickly from top to toe of the 'ravishing young man'. To me this was certainly not quite the right description. His face, because of swarthy skin and harsh but well-formed features, seemed saturnine in spite of animation. There was a thickness and heaviness about him altogether. Thick hair swept back from his forehead; he had rather small compact square teeth. He wore an Italian shirt of white towelling and his bare arms were criss-crossed with dark hairs. Dark hairs sprouted too through the maroon cord lacing the shirt at his throat. His trousers were of dirty blue corduroy, mended across one knee with coarse stitches. He was tall, but his waist was not quite thin enough, so that his deep chest, the basket of his ribs and the waist merged together, reminding me too much of a tree trunk. He spoke with extreme exuberance and simplicity, and some of his words had a disarming cockney charm. It was impossible for me not to respond at once to his friendliness.

'So you've written a book,' he said; 'fancy being able to do that! It's marvellous.'

He picked up Mrs Bellingly's copy, which lay on a stool near him, and began to turn the pages hurriedly, sometimes stopping to glance for a moment at one of the decorations, then hurrying on, as if in search of some particular passsage.

'Mr Beaumont writes too,' said Mrs Bellingly in the decisive tone she used when more than ordinarily vague.

'No, no, you've got it wrong!' Beaumont exclaimed boisterously; 'I said I'd *like* to write.'

There was a pause in which he seemed to be thinking. Suddenly his face lit up and he turned to me.

'I say, old boy, what about us collaborating? Isn't that an

idea! I've got the material, and you can knock it into shape.'

I smiled, because I was surprised at being called 'old boy' so suddenly; even the words themselves seemed strange to me. They had the pickled preserved flavour of a past fashion. I asked him what he wanted to write about. Did he want to describe his experiences as a fighter pilot?

'Yes, that too,' he said quickly; 'but I'd been thinking of life on the road – driving lorries up to Scotland. You see, that's what I've been doing since I came out of the RAF.' He glanced towards Mrs Bellingly, then added, 'Of course, I only did it for the experience, but I know all about it – all the swear words, all the slang, how the chaps pick up girls on the road.'

Here he wrinkled up his nose, grinned and winked.

His hair had fallen over his forehead, so he jerked it back and ran his fingers through it roughly; then he pulled a little black comb out of his pocket.

I wondered what Mrs Bellingly was thinking. Did she want to hear more about the lorry-drivers and the girls on the road? Perhaps she did not care so much for the vigorous combing; or did that too give her a sense of warmth and cosiness? It was difficult to tell from her face since, except for gaiety or gloom, it was usually inexpressive. The cloudy blue eyes were too much like children's 'agate' marbles and her complexion was too hidden under peach-pink foundation cream. I felt, though, that she was as charmed as ever by Beaumont, and only hoped that others would not carp or find fault.

I heard the garden gate groan, and looked out of the window to see Katherine Warde pushing her bicycle up the path.

Her head was bent forward a little, so that I could see the crown of her rather artfully arranged hair. The curls and ridges gleamed golden in the sun, but the rest of her hair was brown. In that glimpse she looked as silent and brooding as I had often known her to be. I wondered if Beaumont would enliven her or make her more silent than ever.

When she came into the room, I thought again how pretty the short thick nose and the clear colouring were. They made her face charming, in spite of the slight look of mulishness. Only the mass of hair with its discreetly bleached waves and ends did not entirely please me. There was so much of it, and it seemed to make her small figure almost top-heavy.

Mrs Bellingly introduced her to Beaumont; she gave him a quick dutiful smile, then composed her features again and looked about the room in the indifferent way of a confused person. I brought her a cup of coffee as a protection and we began to talk in rather low voices about life at her art school in London. She was taking the drawing and painting examinations, but hoped secretly to be able to give up teaching for theatre design; she longed for some job with a ballet company.

Beaumont was talking to Mrs Bellingly in much louder tones. He seemed to be explaining how he thought conquered nations ought to be treated; I heard the words 'honourable capitulation' several times and each time he pronounced the 'h' of 'honourable' with great harshness and vigour, as if in this way to drive the adjective deeper into Mrs Bellingly's consciousness.

Just as I was listening with one ear to their conversation, so, I noticed, was he casting us a glance every few moments. At last he stopped talking to Mrs Bellingly, dropped his hands to his sides and looked straight at us. A broad smile spread over his face, he turned his eyes up to the ceiling and said, as if to the air, 'I think Katherine is very shy of me; I wish she wouldn't be.'

Then, when Katherine looked away hurriedly, he added, this time directly to her, 'Katherine, don't be shy.'

Katherine seemed overcome. I felt that she wanted to run behind the large sofa and crouch there in hiding. Her eyes darted from object to object in Mrs Bellingly's very crowded room. Like a dealer at a sale she skimmed over the Staffordshire figures, the ruby and white Bohemian glass, the glittering Empire lustres. But it was a relief to see that Beaumont did not share her embarrassment. He had come towards us impulsively and was now describing his behaviour in air battles.

'Of course, I was very cruel,' he said; 'I *am* very cruel, you know. I can't help it; I had to give the devils all I'd got. I couldn't stop myself. I used to love to "sew" a train – just like your machine, Katherine, sewing a piece of cloth!' Here he prodded the air with his finger, then laughed gleefully.

Soon we were all asking him questions. Even Katherine had

nearly recovered from being told not to be shy. Beaumont told his stories with a great many arm and leg movements. We might almost have been in the aeroplane with him. He showed us delicate white scars on his arms and one above his right eye. He explained that they were shrapnel wounds. Sometimes the one above his eye made him feel dizzy and filled the eye with blood.

'When I get angry, it goes quite crimson,' he said.

He was now so warmed to his subject that he looked at none of us. He stared through the wall of the drawing-room, as if he saw something in the sky, far above. His hands were slightly raised, his eyes shone, and his lips seemed wet. All at once he dropped his eyes to me.

'We've *got* to write a book together,' he said; 'think of all this grand stuff going to waste! What a book we could do! It would make you famous.'

I raised my eyebrows and gave the little laugh that might have been expected. He was piqued by my lightness and frowned.

'Don't laugh, I'm serious,' he said; 'it would be good.' Then, as if the strain of being serious were too much for him, he allowed a wicked grin to spread over his face.

I looked at the ormolu and gunmetal clock and saw that it was after twelve o'clock. I knew that Mrs Bellingly would soon want to be left to prepare and enjoy her lunch alone. I too wanted to ride on and have my picnic by the river.

When I stood up, Beaumont rose too.

'Which way do you go, old boy?' he asked.

'Oh, David's always going down to the river to picnic alone, isn't it strange?' said Mrs Bellingly in a tone of mild suspicion and resentment. She disapproved of pleasures that she could not share.

'Mind if I tag along some of the way?' Beaumont asked. 'I've got an appointment with someone out in that direction.'

I was quite pleased to have Beaumont as a bicycling companion, but I wondered where he could be going, since the lane I took down to the river ended in a cornfield and there was no house near, except the lock-keeper's.

All three of us said goodbye to Mrs Bellingly together. Beaumont shook her hand up and down while he thanked her for lending him the torch and promising to paint his portrait. The first sitting was arranged for the next morning, and it was settled that Katherine should be there too, to avail herself of this fine model. Mrs Bellingly, as she made the arrangement for Katherine, seemed to intimate that Katherine should do more work in the holidays, that she, Mrs Bellingly, when a student at the Slade in the first years of the century, had covered many canvases during the long summer months.

Beaumont and I wheeled our bicycles beside Katherine till we came to her house on the corner of the main road. Here she glanced quickly at both of us, smiled, wiped the expression off her face almost at once, and said goodbye solemnly. As she turned away, she gave a little duck; she might have been trying to escape the chopper in the game Oranges and Lemons. She walked towards the house with a sort of morose unconcern. It was as though she were unknown to us, and we were making her self-conscious by shameless staring.

Beaumont and I mounted our bicycles and rode round the corner. As soon as we were out of sight, he leaned towards me and said in a low, amazed voice, 'I say, Dave, isn't Katherine shy! I wonder why she is. I didn't frighten her, did I, with all that cruel talk? I can't help it you know, I *am* cruel.'

'No, I don't think it was that,' I said; 'it is meeting people for the first time that she finds difficult. Mrs Bellingly rather overpowers her, tries to manage her too much, don't you think? But of course, she *is* a very easily embarrassed person.'

For a moment or two we rode on in silence; then Beaumont turned to me again; very suddenly: 'I'm wondering if you can keep a secret.' He was mysterious, full of his secret, smiling because he had the important thing to tell.

'I suppose I do look very indiscreet,' I said.

'If I tell you, you won't think it's silly, you won't tell anyone else?'

He raised his eyebrows, making wrinkles on his forehead. He was still smiling, with his mouth a little open; he longed to tell me, but wanted too to keep me in suspense. It seemed to be a sort of game.

'Well,' he said at last, 'I've been thinking about marriage lately, and now I've met Katherine, I think I'd like to marry her. Don't laugh, I'm dead serious.'

'But you've only seen her once,' I said, quite amazed by the unreal sound of his words.

'I know, but she's my type. What a good egg that Mrs Bellingly is to bring us together! You see, Dave, I want to settle down. I never used to; it's only come over me just lately. But now I want to marry and have a baby girl.'

'A baby girl!' I exclaimed. It was impossible to tell what this extraordinary person would say next.

'Yes, don't you like them too? I don't know what it is about them; they're sort of soft and – ' he seemed to be searching for a word – 'cuddly – I don't know. Anyhow I'd like to have a little baby girl of my own.'

'Katherine is very young, you know. I don't think she is nineteen yet,' I said, for the sake of saying something. I found that I could not treat Beaumont's marriage plans seriously.

'That's all the better; a wife should be a few years younger than the husband, don't you think? And you could take a girl like Katherine *anywhere*, couldn't you? Isn't she pretty! And I bet she'll learn to dress before she's twenty-one; to look really smart, I mean. She looks very nice now, but it's sort of in a young-girl-student way, isn't it?'

When he spoke again, it was with the same secret air that he had used before, the same smile, hesitation, drawing in of cheeks.

'You know, Dave, I haven't kept off it, I've been as bad as the next man, I've had lots of women – too many; but I've always been careful to keep myself clean. That's what matters; keep yourself clean.'

Was I about to be lectured on hygiene? Or was he talking of souls? Nothing seemed unlikely.

We had now almost reached the corner where I should have turned to the left, to go down to the river; but when I told Beaumont this, he seemed so disappointed, and he persuaded me so energetically to stay with him on the main road, that I gave up my plan. I found that he had never meant to take the turning to the river. His appointment was with someone in the nearest market town. I agreed to ride on with him until I came to the top of a hill, lined with old beech-woods. I would picnic there instead.

As soon as I had decided to do this, he said impulsively, 'I like you, Dave. You wouldn't mind going up in the air, would you? You'd be all right. You'd make a grand pilot.'

All I could do was to exaggerate the surprise in my voice as I said, 'I! Make a good pilot! What do you mean?' Was Beaumont trying to make a fool of me?

But flattery so preposterous and blundering still works some charm. Perhaps the untruth itself enriches, frees the flattered person, for a moment, from his own idea of himself.

'You know I'd be absolutely hopeless,' I said coldly. I had not used his name so far, although he had already shortened mine to Dave, and perhaps he noticed this now and wanted me to call him by some name, for he said, 'Don't call me Beaumont, it's such a mouthful, call me Micki – all my friends do; only you must remember it's spelt with an *i* not a *y*. You see it's short for Michel. I really belong to an old French family.'

'How interesting,' I said, waiting for more details.

'Yes, but you see I haven't ever lived in France, because my father went to New Orleans as a young man. My father's dead now, and so my mother has settled herself in rather a nice little flat in Chelsea.' There was a slight pause, then Micki added, 'I just know a few facts about the family. They were quite important people, you know – not exactly noble, but highest provincial gentry. The name should really be *de* Beaumont, but I don't bother with the de.'

By this time we had begun to climb the long hill leading to the beech-woods, and Micki was looking very hot. On leaving Mrs Bellingly's house he had put on the jacket which hung over his handlebars, to prevent it, I suppose, from slipping off as he rode; but now he was getting so hot that I suggested he should stuff it into my bicycle-basket on top of the brown satchel holding my picnic.

'Fine, but will it get in, old boy?' he asked.

We stopped and he pulled it off with relief. He looked at it in his hands, then said, 'It's only a bought thing, isn't it awful! Perhaps it would look better if it had leather on the elbows, like yours. The wife of my great friend, Squadron-Leader Minton, is always giving me tips on dress and *she* likes leather elbows.'

'My jacket only has leather pads because the tweed was wearing through,' I explained, not quite understanding the importance he seemed to attach to them.

Micki held out his bare arms and gazed on them. They looked very dark against the towel shirt. The short sleeves stuck out above the swarthy biceps like minute fairy wings.

'You're sunburnt,' I said.

'No, I'm not; it's the filthy Latin in me.' He clucked his tongue and shook his head musingly.

We climbed on until we reached the first bend, before the steepest part of the hill. As we turned, an orange lorry appeared round the bend higher up the hill, then rushed and rattled past us. The driver called out. I took no notice, thinking that it was only some ribaldry, but Micki dropped his bicycle at the side of the road and ran back, shouting to me over his shoulder, 'Wait a sec, will you? I know this fellow.'

I sat down on the bank and watched Micki chasing the lorry. It pulled in to the side and stopped; Micki raised his head and talked to the man in his high driver's seat. Standing there in the road, laughing, waving his arms and shaking back his hair, he seemed different to me – more lithe and slender, with a greater ease about him.

But when in a few moments he ran back, he seemed just as he had been at first.

'I used to know that chap well,' he said between deep breaths; 'he's very aristocratic – French origin too, you know. He used to wear a reddish beard.'

We began to push our bicycles again, but we had only climbed a few paces when another lorry passed us, this time going up the hill. It was heavily laden with logs, and the engine chugged painfully. When it came to the steepest part of the hill, it stopped, swayed a little, then rolled back to where we were.

'Look out!' Micki cried, although I had already jumped up on the bank in case the lorry should slide any nearer.

'You've always got to be careful of those things,' he added in the same excited voice.

I wondered what made him warn me in such an alarming, grim way. Had he seen a lorry roll back and crush someone? Or did he like to make little incidents seem more important?

The lorry had now swung into the middle of the road and stopped again. Steam belched from the radiator and rose up in a white curling, waving tree. Micki ran out to the driver and said, 'You'd better let her cool off.'

The driver just smiled at him wearily, indifferently. He asked Micki to put bricks behind the wheels and Micki ran to the bank where there was a whole pile, next to the black and white St John ambulance post.

He wedged two behind each huge front wheel, then the driver climbed down and stood in the road, still saying nothing, only smiling wanly at Micki's agitation and excitement. He looked very young, and he seemed too tired to be either particularly grateful for Micki's help or irritated by it. He seemed to be asking with his heavy eyes and faint grin, 'What's all the fuss?' And Micki, when he felt this indifference, became restless, almost shamefaced, as if he had been emptied and cast aside. He pulled up his bicycle and hurried on, until the sweat trickled through his thick eyebrows and rolled into his eyes. He paused to wipe his face, then said with all his old animation, 'Let's find a good place and rest at the top of the hill!'

At last we were there. We sat down on a green bank close to a granite drinking trough, and Micki took out his comb again. He ran it through his damp glistening hair several times, then he turned to me and said, 'Dave, do you think I speak very badly? Mrs Minton, that's the friend's wife you know, is always telling me I'm much too careless. She says I say "knaow" instead of "know". You'd tell me too if I pronounced things wrong, wouldn't you?'

I was touched and surprised and confused. In an effort to be easy, I asked laughingly, 'Is Mrs Minton herself such a "beautiful pronouncer"?'

'Well, old boy, she *thinks* she is, but I'm sometimes not so sure. I'd like you to meet her though, she's very nice; and *he* was my best pal in the RAF. They've got a daughter – only fifteen, but lovely shaped breasts and very quiet and sweet. There is a son too, but he's a little sod. He's got one of those mean natures. I thought I liked him all right at first, but when I asked to borrow something last week – he's got a special sort of engineering tool you can't buy now – he hid it and then said he couldn't find it. Funny having a mean streak with such a grand guy for a father.'

'Are you sure that he hid it?' I asked. 'It might really have been lost.'

'It wasn't lost,' said Micki scornfully; 'I was looking round the house and I found it stuffed behind a lot of his clothes in a cupboard; that was a queer place for it, wasn't it? Besides, I know he doesn't like me much. He sort of looks at me suspiciously sometimes. There isn't any reason for it; it's just his meanness.'

'Do they live near here?' I asked, feeling that Micki wanted to tell me more about his friends.

'No, not very near – just outside Brighton. They've got a lovely place there, you'd like it, Dave – sort of terraced gardens, and at the bottom a hard court, a squash court and a little bathing-pool. I can go there whenever I like; my room's always ready; but of course I don't like to make use of their offer too much. They're a grand family though, and Mrs Minton seems to take a real interest in me. She's always telling me what to wear and what to say. She agrees that it would be a good idea for me to get married, and she says she'll try and fix me up herself, if I can't find anyone I like; so, if Katherine isn't having any – !'

He gave a loud laugh and threw himself back on the bank, tucking his hands behind his head. Again I wondered if he wanted his love at first sight of Katherine to be treated seriously or as a great joke.

He stretched out his arms and started to examine them just as he had done on taking off his jacket.

'God! I wash and wash and yet my skin is just as filthy looking,' he exclaimed.

I realized now that this was one of his habitual remarks, but this time he spoke with such simplicity, *really* as if talking to himself, that I was reminded at once of the story of the blackamoor who searched everywhere for some magic potion to turn him white.

After a few more minutes' rest, Micki sat up and said, 'I haven't got much to do in the town – only see a chap who owns a big garage. You sit here and have your picnic and wait till I come back; then we can ride some of the way home together.'

'Oh, I shall go into the woods and find a good place before I eat my picnic,' I said; 'and then I might stay there reading for some time; so don't expect me to be on the road for certain when you come back, will you? I may find another way home through the woods, but if I don't, I'll try to meet you here. How long do you think you'll be?'

I wanted a rest from Micki; it had come upon me suddenly that he was an exhausting companion. Perhaps I made my feeling too clear; for he said with aggrieved conviction, 'You're not going to wait, you devil.' Then, apropos of nothing, he added, 'Of course, after Uppingham I went on to Christ's at Cambridge, you know.'

I wondered cloudily if there *were* a Christ's at Cambridge. Micki contrived somehow to make even simple facts sound improbable.

Before we parted, Micki looked down at the water in the horse-trough and said, 'Let's have a wash, Dave!'

He buried his face deep in the water, splashed it all over his arms, then pressed the button of the drinking-fountain so that a jet gushed out and hit him in the eye. He laughed up at me and the hard white teeth made his skin look almost khaki. There was the redness of his tongue too, as he flicked it round his lips to drink up the drops trickling down his face. Drops threaded themselves into necklaces along stray hairs, or dangled from the wet rat's tails above his eyes.

'You press the button, Dave, while I have a drink,' he suggested.

The button was very stiff. I pushed with both thumbs and Micki stretched his mouth wide open to receive the frothing gush. It struck against the back of his throat, choking him with its bubbles. He spluttered and swore and laughed again.

I left him, still coughing and swearing, and climbed up towards the woods. Before I disappeared, he waved to me, and my last glimpse was of him trying to dry his face and arms on a large dingy red navvy's handkerchief; then he swung his leg over his bicycle and was gone.

I went deep into the woods and, after some time, found a glade where the sun filtered through the beech leaves and fell on rich green cushions of moss and the black water of a little pool. I settled there, with my back against a tree trunk, and started to unpack my satchel. I had cheese and crispbread and a little butter, then chocolate to be eaten with a fresh sour apple, and a thermos of milky coffee.

As I ate and drank, I glanced sometimes at my book, but chiefly I gazed at prospects through the wood and thought of the strangeness of Micki Beaumont.

He seemed to fit into none of the holes he dug for himself so industriously. He was not the French near-noble, the English public schoolboy and undergraduate, the RAF pilot, or even the amateur lorry-driver. Yet I wondered too if he was not a little bit of all these things mixed together in the most unexpected way, to make a strange new pudding.

I stayed in the woods till after five o'clock, partly because it was so delightful there, and partly to make quite sure of missing Micki on my way home. I hoped to see and know more of him; but on another day.

II

We met again the next week. Mrs Bellingly asked me to tea, telling me that she had invited one or two other people to celebrate Micki's engagement to Katherine. The notice had been in that morning's paper.

I was so used to Mrs Bellingly's mistakes, extravagances and wild twistings of the truth that I only opened my mouth and eyes in a kind of goggle of mock astonishment.

'But it's true!' she insisted, picking up the paper and passing it to me. The notice was already underlined in bright crayon. I began to read, 'The engagement is announced between FO Michel de Beaumont, DFC, only son of Mrs R. J. de Beaumont of Inverness...' Here I stopped and turned to Mrs Bellingly, 'But Micki told me that his mother had a flat in Chelsea; he never mentioned Scotland. He talked of New Orleans; I can't remember anything else.'

'Yes, I didn't quite understand the Inverness part,' agreed Mrs Bellingly, 'because he only told me about the Chelsea flat; but I daresay she has a place in Scotland as well. Poor boy! He doesn't seem to get on with her very well. In spite of his fine war record, she appears to take very little interest in him. Sometimes she doesn't write for months, and she's nearly always out when he calls at the flat. I suppose she's one of those women who live just for their bridge, or their clothes, or whatever it may be.'

'She wasn't described to me,' I said; 'he only told me that she'd lived in Chelsea since his father's death.'

'Oh, he's told me *so* much. The poor boy's nerves are in a frightful state. He seems to long to make a confidante of one, and sometimes he comes out with the most astonishing things. In his confusion he contradicts himself too. Of course, the ordeal he's been through is bound to have left its mark.'

As I listened to Mrs Bellingly, I was again puzzled by the strange effect she produced when she used soft words. They came out in all the usual places, but the tone was so brassy that they were made to sound almost mockingly sentimental. And yet I knew that there was no hint of mockery in her words – either for herself or for her subject.

When the afternoon came and I had put on a suit and was tying up my shoelaces, I heard Micki calling up to my window from the lane. He had come to hurry me and take me back to the tea-party. I felt the weight of his footsteps sinking into the ground under the window. As he bounded upstairs, the little house trembled. Although he moved so quickly, there was a deadness about the weight of his body.

He began at once to admire my Donegal tweed and some brightly checked socks. He rubbed his hand over my sleeve, then looked closely at the flecks of colour in the tweed and marvelled at their variety. He himself had on a Prussian-blue shirt of a curious silky linen. His tie and hairy fawn jacket were much lighter in tone. On his feet were heavy brogues. Eyes and hair glistened, and he laughed and talked so much that there was almost always the gleam of teeth as well. I felt sure that Mrs Bellingly would consider him more ravishing than ever.

After looking carefully at some other clothes that lay about, Micki went across to the open door of my hanging cupboard and examined each suit. I wondered at this close attention; he might have been the owner of a second-hand clothes shop.

Suddenly he said, 'We had a pilot at the 'drome. He was just like you. He wouldn't stand a spot of dirt on his machine. Christ, he was fussy! We used to call him Louise, but that's only a nickname. He wore marvellous pearl-grey satin pyjamas. Hardly anybody dared to tease him, but you could, Dave; he'd let you, because you're so like him. I'll ring the 'drome and see if he's still there. "Go on, bastards! Get it clean!" he'd shout at the guys working on his machine, then he'd walk up and down flipping his hands. "Polish it, you swine!" he'd call out; but they didn't mind, they thought he was grand.'

Here Micki broke off to give me an imitation of his friend walking up and down beside his machine. He rolled his eyes, swayed his hips, and lisped most preciously.

Although the act was so old and commonplace, there was such a spirit of fun and devilry in Micki that I had to laugh.

'Louise was very brave, you know,' he said, '*and* cruel. You're very brave and cruel, Dave, aren't you?'

He seemed to want me to confirm him in his fantasy, so my impulse was to say 'No' loudly and perhaps a little rudely. I wanted to stop all further comparisons and other personal remarks.

We went out into the lane and started to walk towards Mrs Bellingly's house. When we were at the gate, I looked through the rose arch and saw people already sitting in the garden. The little group on the lawn looked very brilliant; Mrs Bellingly's garden furniture was painted canary-yellow and powder-blue. The canvas of the chairs was in broad stripes of white and yellow, and the tablecloths were candy-pink. Raucous green-ringed cups stood on these cloths, quite overpowering some older, more beautiful gold-sprigged china; but the silver teapot held its own, flashing back gleams from polished sides. It was like a little lighthouse, surrounded by dark, forbidding rocks; for all the guests looked dark against the brilliant furnishings.

Apart from Katherine, there were four others: a Mrs Talbot, perhaps seventy years old, slight and spare, dressed all in black, even down to the fine stockings on her sparrow's legs – her grandniece Pamela, who had a haughty expression and some unfortunate spots – Pamela's baby girl with palest floss-silk hair – and, last of all, a Mrs Charles in a steel-grey coat and skirt, fitted tightly over squat hips, so that she looked like a neatly packed grey-paper parcel. Only the face under the gunmetal straw-hat was different in colour. It had a tawny glow and a fullness that are not supposed to be English. On first seeing her I had been reminded of Red Indian squaws and gypsy clothes-peg makers, until the more likely explanation of Jewish blood had come to me.

All these people had been introduced to Micki before he came to fetch me, but none of them showed pleasure at his return. They fixed their attention on me as the new arrival, or talked brightly to Mrs Bellingly, offering unnecessary help with the teacups or little tables.

I wondered why Mrs Bellingly had asked such people to meet Micki; they were not even well known to Katherine, who sat amongst them silent, rather too composed, with gold daisies in her ears, and her hair swept up in a new, more becoming fashion.

Micki knelt down on the tartan rug and held out his arms to the baby girl, but she, after looking up at her mother's discouraging face, turned away from him with some complaining sound. Micki took no notice, but began to twirl his large hands over her head and make gug-gug, goo-goo noises. His long hair fell over his eyes; he took it back and called over his shoulder, 'She's shy, Dave, but isn't she grand! Can't you see now why I want a baby girl?'

I saw the look of distaste on the mother's face. Her absurd stiffness so annoyed me that I dropped down at once on the rug to give Micki all the support I could. I guessed that this might encourage him to further extravagances, but that would have to be risked. At least I should be near, and he would not have to shout his embarrassing remarks.

He began to tumble the baby girl on the rug and, in spite of wild protests, to give her grizzly-bear hugs. The floss-silk hair was tousled, the stiff little skirt pulled up, to show pink panties and a line of less pink stomach. Tears soon followed, and then at last the mother, Pamela, turned to Micki and said exasperatedly, 'Oh, *please* don't upset her too much.'

'I didn't want to upset her, poor little thing!' Micki protested; but Pamela had already turned back to the others, who were discussing their gardening problems and pleasures. I could see, beyond Pamela's head, the rigid lack of interest on Mrs Bellingly's face.

The blue eyes were two smoky pebbles, washed up by the cold sea, and the mouth had set into a dark crimson line, finishing in sharp little down-curving fishhooks. She hated gardening and left her own to become a wilderness, except for the small patch of lawn on which we were sitting. She did not want to hear about Mrs Talbot's gardener's operation, the bomb damage to the grape-house in the war, and how the best muscatel vine had died at last, the absurdities of the dog and the hedgehog in the potting-shed. She wanted to make her women guests take notice of Micki and appreciate him, and, since delicate methods had failed, I guessed that less delicate ones were about to be employed. In order to hear more, I got up off the rug and carried a plate of chocolate biscuits back to the tea-table.

The first break in the tedious garden topic was seized on by Mrs Bellingly; she turned to Mrs Charles and began at once to talk of Micki, his bravery, his interesting French descent, his vitality and fire, the special quality in his looks which made them so acceptable to a painter. She never spoke softly, and now her voice rose with her enthusiasm. I wondered if Micki could hear his praises – he would certainly have enjoyed them; but perhaps he was too busy trying to comfort the baby girl with more hugs, although hugs had caused all the tears in the first place.

Katherine, I think, heard every word. She showed no sign, unless she kept even stiller than before; but she seemed to be drinking in the remarks and storing them away. I wondered if she wished that Micki would abandon the baby girl and talk to her, or whether she preferred to be left to herself, before these disapproving women. Micki did sometimes call out to her, asking her to admire the baby girl, or telling her with much gusto that he would be wanting one of his own just like her by and by; but Mrs Bellingly was the only person who paid her marked attention as the engaged girl. She had begun to call Katherine 'dear' in her peculiar sweet-hard tone; she smiled on her much more and tried to control the impulse to give orders. The effort was not made for nothing; the smiles and discipline seemed to be making the rich peach-bloom quiver a little. The face underneath had always lived a life of its own, but sometimes signs broke through the marshmallow armour-plating.

By the end of Mrs Bellingly's praises of Micki, Mrs Charles's expression had hardened into a leathery simper that would have been most affronting to anyone just a little more aware than Mrs Bellingly; for tea-table politeness veiled disbelief so thinly that the features seemed to be saying, 'Oh, but how droll! How too amusing of you to take up this attitude! Of course, anyone can see that the man is dreadfully common and almost certainly some sort of trifling impostor, but you choose this romantic view – so original.'

Mrs Charles's smiling rejection of every word at last became clear even to Mrs Bellingly. A pause stretched itself into a silence. Mrs Bellingly turned away impatiently and asked me to fetch the cigarettes from the drawing-room.

Soon afterwards Mrs Talbot struggled up from her low deck-chair to say goodbye. Standing on those fragile black-silk legs, she looked very tottery and ancient; but there was a great lump of pride and malevolence behind her pale little eyes, and I thought that it was this lump which was her driving force. Insolent pride and ill will carried her through the day, kept her from dying, from melting into nothing. I thought that each year to come would make the little beady eyes clearer and paler, until they were nothing but two sucked acid drops. All colour would drain out of her, leaving only the pure venom.

Pamela took the child up like a bundle of sticks and followed her great-aunt. She smiled a general goodbye, then the mouth drooped too suddenly, disparagingly, as if she had dismissed from her mind everything but the child's evening meal and bath, her husband in the Army across the sea, and the problems of her own face and body. Mrs Charles lingered a little, sitting forward in her chair, so that her smooth grey rump poked out assertively, giving me the fancy that perhaps, after all, this was the most important part of her and she should be turned upside down at once.

She left, still smiling her tight smile and acting her extremely correct English lady's part, giving nothing away and yet making her dreary meaning only too clear.

When Julia Bellingly had seen the last of her stiff-necked guests to the garden gate, her breast seemed to fill, to rise up like a proud figurehead's. She returned to us impatient for the pleasure and amusement that the others had spoilt.

'Katherine, let's go on with Micki's portrait,' she said; 'and you

David can stay and do a drawing. I'll give you some nice pre-war Ingres paper and red chalk.'

We followed her into the long drawing-room, where two easels had been set up near the fireplace. Micki at once took up his position and said, 'Am I right? Do I look right? Is my head at the right angle? Is that good? Does it look good?'

He held the arms of the shabby *bergère* and tilted his chin, anxious for our spoken approval, afraid that we might withhold it through inattention or lack of generosity.

'That is fine, Micki,' Julia Bellingly said, 'just a tiny bit more to the left – nearly – nearly. Now hold it, and we can begin at once!'

I had been placed on the sofa with drawing-board, paper, chalk and art cleanser – a very large and temptingly soft indiarubber, which I pinched and kneaded and thought of dreamily as 'a miniature pound of baby's flesh'. I began with no very strong desire to draw Micki, but soon grew interested and found myself accentuating the bridge of his nose, the length and the slant and the slight bulge of his eyes, the peculiar heaviness of his jaw, and the good rich shape of the lips above. I noticed for the first time that his ears were less well formed than the rest of his features, they had a punched, ill-treated appearance and they stuck out a little; but the dark wings of hair, sweeping back, sometimes flopping over them, helped to disguise this.

Micki at first sat very still, so still that the eyes fixed in a stare; he might have been falling into a trance; but after about a quarter of an hour he grew restless, twitched his nostrils, glanced out of the corners of his eyes, and said, 'Can I see now? I want to know what they're like. Do you think any of you have got me yet? I want to move now.'

'Oh, but just a little longer!' Mrs Bellingly protested. 'You haven't sat any time yet, Micki.'

Micki took no notice and jumped up to look. I felt that he would not like mine so I leant over it and busied myself with the art cleanser. But he was not to be put off; he already knew the other two pictures and only stopped to note what progress had been made. He praised Mrs Bellingly's and told Katherine that she had not quite caught his expression yet; then he came over to me saying, 'Let's have a look, old boy; what have you been making of me?'

For a moment he looked at my drawing in silence. It was clear that he felt a little shocked by it. I began at once to explain that portraits were often very unlike the sitters, and ought never to be taken to heart. They were sometimes just exercises, where lack of skill, love of distortion, a hundred other things, overlaid the likeness.

He said, 'Oh, no, Dave, I like it all right; it's fine. I just thought at first you'd sort of made me look kind of peculiar.'

He gazed at it for a little longer, then went back to his chair, and I thought I heard him murmur something to himself.

After this, the sittings grew shorter and shorter, and the rests turned into entertainments. Micki performed and the rest of us watched. When first we came in from the garden, I had noticed Katherine's cherry-red gramophone and thought how strange it looked, sitting on the slender early piano, which Mrs Bellingly persisted in calling a harpsichord. Now Micki went over to it and put on a record of the RAF 'March Past'. He had bought it only that morning and kept telling us that it was a fine thing, and that Sir Walford Davies was the composer. As soon as he heard the music, Micki began to strut up and down the crowded room, swinging his arms stiffly. All at once he jerked his head to our side and kept it there, his eyes fixed rigidly on us, while he marked time, lifting up his knees preposterously and shooting his arms straight out until they looked as long as monkey's arms.

This moment of taking the salute was the most uncomfortable of all, far worse than Micki's tricks with the child on the rug. I glanced away, smiled, tried to look at him again, still smiling, but there was no escape for me. One thing I knew, I must not look at Katherine or Mrs Bellingly. I must not even think of their expressions.

Micki stopped drumming on the floor, the hands dropped to his sides, and the fierce solemn look melted. He smiled and said: 'Ah yes, that's how we used to do it. It was grand!'

Picking up a book off the low stool in front of the hearth, he sat down, opened the book on his knees, and began to tell us about it. It was all to do with the Air Force and he had bought it that morning, when he bought the record of the march. It was *absolutely* true to life and was by Hector Bolithiero – at least, Micki's very personal pronunciation of this name sounded a little like that. There were added syllables, making the name roll and lilt, reminding me of 'Lilliburllero'.

After the book, we were asked to admire a spotted scarf, of a pattern much favoured by pilots, Micki explained. This too had been bought in the morning. It was as though Micki had gone out to collect three symbols of his past career; and now that he was showing them to us, his excitement rose. He knotted the scarf round his neck, jumped to his feet again and waved the book.

'But you ought to put my wings in!' he exclaimed. 'Couldn't you do it in silver paint? I could show you just how they go.'

He moved towards Mrs Bellingly's canvas, as if about to scratch out wings in the wet paint with the end of one of her brushes.

'No, Micki, no! Don't touch it!' she cried. 'I'm not doing you in uniform, and it wouldn't look right at all to have your wings on an ordinary shirt or jacket – whichever I finally decide to have you in.'

'But how will anyone know I've got wings then?' he asked indignantly. '*Or* the DFC? The ribbon ought to be underneath the wings. I'll draw them out on a piece of paper and tell you the colours. You could get silver paint, couldn't you, for the wings? They ought to be silver, you know. I'd like them to flash!'

'Now, I think that's enough about *your* portrait for today,' said Julia Bellingly; 'you won't sit still any more, so we can't really get on. What I want to know is, would you like me to do a portrait of Katherine for your wedding present?'

'Just Katherine, or both of us together?' asked Micki, his voice brightening towards the end of the question.

'Katherine alone, of course; I'm already painting you.'

'Yes, but wouldn't it be grand to have one of both of us! – me sort of looking into the distance, and Katherine sort of looking at me.'

Mrs Bellingly said nothing. She may have been suppressing some tart remark on vanity, which she thought unsuitable for the engaged ears of Katherine, or she may only have been changing over to another subject in her abrupt capricious way; for when next she spoke it was to say, 'Oh, Micki, do run up and see if you can do anything to the clock in my bedroom; you promised to mend it.'

Her guests were usually asked to work.

As soon as Micki had gone upstairs, it was suggested that we should tidy the room.

'That boy turns it into such a bear-garden with all his marching and striding about – to say nothing of the mess of our own paints and easels.'

Katherine and I began to plump out the cushions on the sofa and straighten the rugs. Mrs Bellingly went over to Micki's chair and turned over the fat squab in the seat. She was patting and prodding the ragged brocade, when suddenly she screeched, 'Oh, that wretch has loosened the arm of my *bergère* again! And I glued it so thoroughly only the other day. Just look what he's done with all his lurching and wriggling. Why can't he sit still like anyone else?'

She almost ran out of the room and we heard the misleading patter of her small high-heeled shoes on the hall tiles. It was as if a delicate young doe had tripped into the house. We heard her take a rush at the steep little box-stairs, then there was the muffled rumble of voices in the room above.

They came down hand in hand, Julia Bellingly, the nurse, dragging Micki, the great naughty boy.

'Now look, you're going to be shown exactly what you've done,' she said, leading him up to the chair. She might have been the severe owner of a new puppy, about to rub the little creature's nose in its 'business'.

'You are a very bad lad; you've broken the arm of a valuable old chair, which has already been mended once very carefully by me.'

Julia Bellingly banged each word into him as if it had been a nail. Micki stood by her, eyes down in mock repentance, an embarrassed smile on his half-open lips. Very gently he began to swing the arm still held by her. Then they were holding hands, swinging them, up and down, up and down, looking into each other's eyes, smiling, laughing. Micki's hair had fallen over his face. The tassels dangled, the square teeth glistened. Julia Bellingly wrinkled up her nose, then tried to make a stand for severity.

'It's no use turning it into a joke and trying to get round me; I'm really cross.'

But her face belied her words – and they went on swinging hands.

'You know, we needed people like you to come round with the mobile canteens,' Micki said to her solemnly. 'Some of the women were terrible – all stuck up and a bit sexy. What chaps like is the *older* woman full of good sense and fun.'

The mistimed, misdirected flattery fell to the ground between them, killing the smile on Julia Bellingly's face. She seemed not to care for the part of older woman full of good sense and fun. There was a hint of outrage, as if Micki, in his calculating, scheming simplicity, had at last insulted her intelligence.

'We'd better stop now,' she said stonily; 'we'll get nothing more done today.'

She began to gather up her brushes and to wipe them on an old linen rag.

'I'll just look at the grandfather clock too,' said Micki, eager to do anything to regain favour. 'I'd like to get every clock in apple-pie order for you.'

He went over to the old clock and opened the case. Julia Bellingly did not forbid him. He kept moving the pendulum and the position of the stand on the floor, waiting there until good humour should be restored.

Katherine finished wiping her brushes, shut her paint-box, then stood up to go home. I looked at her. Here was the girl who was going to be married, but it didn't seem real at all. Could many people be married in this way? Were they just caught up in a half-hearted game of ball? Was she excited or happy? Did anything show on her face? Perhaps the tiniest spark of perplexity glinted sometimes under the heavy layers of calm.

Mrs Bellingly took her into the hall and I was left alone with Micki. Shutting the clock, he tiptoed across the room to me. He put his arm round my shoulders and muttered close to my ear, 'Everything's going fine, old boy. I like her and she likes me.'

I felt his breath on my cheek, the rather tingling grip of his fingers round my shoulder. He was secret and triumphant, wanting me only to share, to question nothing. Still cupping my shoulder with his hand, he stood away from me, as if to show me his radiant expression, or perhaps to see my answering pleasure.

'And you must be best man,' were his last eager words, before he left me abruptly to go to Mrs Bellingly, who was calling.

I myself said my goodbyes and thank-yous, then left by the side door. I wanted to be alone to think over the afternoon.

It was like some Punch and Judy show or pantomime; it had that slight touch of insanity and squalor – emphatic characters playing extraordinary parts – strangely threatening because they seemed so meaningless and unrelated.

There was the silent Katherine, Mr Punch's baby, the victim whose head would be dashed against the scenery sooner or later; then Mrs Bellingly was the strident wilful Judy, with perhaps a touch of the Widow Twankey. Mrs Talbot, Mrs Charles, Pamela and the baby girl had been a chorus of wicked ugly sisters, curiously alike in spite of all differences of age and appearance. Micki had been Punch, of course, both sad and a little sinister, with the hangman's rope somewhere very near. But what had I been? I tried to think as I pushed through the overgrown garden, then climbed over the fence into the lane.

III

Once more the days passed and I did not see Micki myself, but I heard from Mrs Bellingly that he was now living in the house with Katherine and her mother. The vicar had applied to the bishop for a licence, and all the other arrangements for the marriage were being made. An old friend of the family was to give Katherine away – 'And you are to be best man!' said Mrs Bellingly, turning to me gaily to watch my surprise.

'But it's absurd!' I exclaimed, 'I never took him seriously. He ought to ask one of his Air Force friends, someone who really knows him.'

'No, he doesn't want one of them; he's determined to have you,' she answered comfortably.

There was a pause, then I said slowly, 'I don't think anything would persuade me to go to church as best man.'

I left almost at once to go to Micki.

I found him in the living-room of the Wardes' house with mother and daughter. The room with its grim black beams and great sooty open fireplace oppressed me. Some romantic music, perhaps by Tchaikovsky, was coming from the wireless and Micki was jigging and swaying to it, while Katherine watched him from a cushion on the floor with the head of her old decrepit dog in her lap. Mrs Warde, who had come to the door to let me in, now stayed by my side, and I found myself sitting with her on the low sill of a curious window, which jutted out like a large arrowhead into the derelict vegetable patch, where once the lawn had been. In her rust-red shirt and velveteen trousers Mrs Warde looked rather plump and young and anxious. She had the embarrassed movements of Katherine with less of the imposed calm. She advanced impulsively, then grew suspicious in spite of herself, so that conversation with her was a sort of shunting in and out of a dark tunnel.

I found it difficult even to mention the marriage. All I could bring myself to say was, 'I expect you are awfully busy.'

'Yes, we are,' the words came in a rush; 'and Katherine's not much good, you know. Most of the time she's out, or upstairs with her dog and her paints, so it's left to me to arrange everything.'

'Doesn't Micki help?' I asked.

'Yes, he does try; but he's so full of ideas, he wants to do everything at once, and of course that's just the way to get nothing done at all.'

As she spoke, Mrs Warde glanced across at Micki, and I caught just a flash of that strange dazed interest, that capacity for watching and marvelling which some young parents show.

'This music's a bit like the "Warsaw" concerto,' Micki suddenly called out, perhaps because he felt that we were lost to him, in our pointed window.

'That's a grand thing, isn't it?' he added. 'We had a sergeant who played it the whole time. He threw himself all over the place.' Here Micki shook his hair over his eyes and clawed the air like a mad gorilla on a chain. 'God! The sweat *poured* off him! He thumped so hard I thought he'd break a string. The next minute he'd be off in his plane. Nothing but playing the piano and dropping bombs!'

Micki played the piano on the air for a little longer, clucking his tongue and rolling his eyes at the same time; then he came out of his frenzy and turned to me.

'You're going to be best man, Dave, aren't you? It's all fixed.'

'Oh, no, you must ask one of your *real* friends,' I said in my agitation, then tried to cover the unfortunate adjective with 'someone you've known for a long time'.

I stopped, afraid of offending Katherine and Mrs Warde with more signs of my eagerness to escape. Micki's feelings seemed less important, because less capable of being hurt. I wondered why this was so, and it came to me that, from the very first, he had appeared to expect only a light, amused response, never a deeper one. Perhaps the greatest moment of truth had been at the top of the hill, when I wanted to go into the woods to eat and read, and he wanted me to wait for his return from the town. He had known then that I would not wait, and his annoyance had given me a glimpse of something underneath all the jigging and vivacity. There had been too the moment when, breathing on my ear, holding my shoulder tight, he tried to will me to suppress my uneasiness, to accept his success without question.

But Micki was talking to me again. 'Don't get stage-fright, Dave! All *you've* got to do is not to lose the ring. Just think what *we* have to go through!'

He put his hands on Katherine's shoulders and rocked her backwards and forwards; and because she sat stiffly with her legs tucked under her, she looked like one of those little weighted dolls that cannot fall over.

I appealed to Mrs Warde.

'Micki ought to choose one of his Air Force friends, oughtn't he?'

She fluttered her eyes and was not quick, so Micki answered for her.

'No, I don't want any of them, they'd come drunk or something; I want you, you're just the ticket.'

I rebelled against being used in this way. I was not a doll to be taken out of its box on special occasions.

'I shall never be anyone's best man,' I said, jumping off the windowsill; 'they seem so – so peculiar.'

What had I done now! The faces of Mrs Warde and Katherine were quite blank, making it all the easier for me to read reproach into them. I wanted to say goodbye at once and get out of doors again.

I murmured some more correct excuses, then went quickly to the door, but Micki's voice followed me still.

'Nonsense, Dave, you'll do fine as best man – you'll see! When the day comes you'll be all agog.'

He came with me into the hall; I was afraid he would offer to accompany me home, but I contrived somehow to get out of the front door and then out of the garden gate without him. I walked down the road, enjoying the freedom and the air, determined not to hear if he should call after me. Once round the corner I felt safer.

♣

But another complication was waiting for me at home. A note had been left and the writing was unknown to me. I read it hurriedly. 'So sorry not to have found you in. There is a matter I feel I ought to discuss with you as soon as possible. Could you call at my place some time today? I shall be at home all afternoon and evening – Mildred Charles.' That was all.

The urgency, the mystery, the shortness, all reminded me of the cryptic notes I had sent and received as a child – notes tucked under stones, stuffed into tree trunks, buried in the ground, or sealed in little tins to float down the river, out to sea, to the other side of the world.

But what had possessed Mrs Charles that she should be playing this game at her age, and with me, almost a stranger, and so clearly out of tune with her?

In spite of my lack of love for Mrs Charles, my interest was pricked and I looked forward to visiting her. It was almost certain that she would talk of Micki, but just because it was not absolutely certain, room was left for the most extraordinary imaginings. Would she warn me of some secret danger to myself, some hidden threat I could not even conceive of? Would she lay before me all the difficulties of her private life, then ask for my advice? Or did she want me to read through the sixteen school exercise books of her novel in manuscript before sending it to my publisher with a glowing note? Perhaps she wanted me to paint a conversation piece of her white Pekinese playing with an embroidered ball near her goldfish pool. Perhaps in a mad whim she had left me all her money and, wishing to carry the eccentricity even further, had decided to tell me herself of my good fortune.

Because I had let my fancy roam, and because her note had reawakened in me the excitement and faint alarm of the secret messages of childhood, I felt a little dashed when I found Mrs Charles bending over one of her knife-edged flower-beds. She wore a pair of thick stained leather gloves, but otherwise her clothes were as dark and neat and unexceptionable as ever. Her strictness was somehow mortifying. One had to marvel at the inhuman gloss, even while feeling frustrated by it. She stopped digging round the plants with her trowel and led me towards the house. The path was straight and sharp like the flower-beds, the grass on either side shaved so flat that now, in the summer heat, it had begun to turn a golden brown in patches.

Once under the protection of the dark little brick porch she began.

'It's about that poor gairl that I felt I ought to see you. I knew it would be hopeless to tackle Mrs Bellingly; she's so – under the influence.'

'Under the influence!' I exclaimed.

'Well, under *his* influence then – there! I've had to say it, one can't beat about the bush in these affairs it seems.'

'You mean Mrs Bellingly is under the influence of Micki Beaumont?'

'Yes, but that, of course, is her affair. She, no doubt, is well able to take care of herself; but it's that poor gairl I'm so worried about. Something must be done to prevent this iniquitous marriage. The vicar's daughter told me this morning that everything is arranged for Monday. You realize today is Thursday!'

'Yes, the marriage is extraordinary to me too, quite unreal. I've never been able to take it seriously; but if they really mean to get married, I don't see how anyone can stop them. Mrs Warde seems to like Micki very much, and the vicar by this time has probably had the licence from the bishop.'

'But does no one realize that the man's an impostor, an out-and-out rogue?'

Mrs Charles grew duskier than ever, as if darkness and not blood had flushed up behind her skin. By now I had been led into a very white little parlour. There was the glistening paint of the broad cottage windowsills, the frozen lines of glazed chintz pouring down to the fawn carpet. The chintz had a feather design, a gold feather and a brown floating for ever down white cascades. An armchair and a very small sofa, covered in the same material, stood on each side of the fireplace. Between them was an early-Victorian rosewood table with embroidery under a glass top – a pretty wreath of flowers worked in silks and wools. Three miniatures in thick black frames spotted the far wall. That was almost all that the room held.

I wanted to look about me for a moment, not to answer Mrs Charles's question, so I found myself saying rather lukewarmly, 'You feel sure then that he's an impostor?'

'Sure! Aren't you, then? Wouldn't anyone be sure who had eyes in his head – ears – I was almost about to add a nose.'

Mrs Charles laughed delicately at her own lapse into coarseness and class hatred. I was a little fascinated by it, wondering just how far she would allow herself to go.

'I think I've explained so much away by telling myself to remember that he landed on his head,' I answered.

'I don't believe he's ever even been up in an aeroplane.'

'But I've seen a photograph of him in his uniform with the wings plainly visible.'

'What does that prove?' Mrs Charles rapped out. Her manner was becoming more and more short and sharp, as if, being unable to confront Micki, she would accuse me in his stead.

'Now you must face it,' she said, fixing me with her liquorice eyes; 'do you, or do you not feel that there is something very peculiar indeed about that young man?'

'I've always thought him strange,' I replied unhelpfully; 'he tells me a lot of lies, but so do many other people. There was a boy at school who told me that he went to a fancy-dress party as a sea-horse in a tank of water. He had another story about his grandmother. When she died, she was taken up to Scotland and left on the top of an ancient tower, so that the birds of the air could pick her bones.'

Mrs Charles was becoming impatient.

'But we are not dealing with a schoolboy's fancies! I don't think you grasp the seriousness of the situation.'

'I do think it's very serious for Katherine, and I hope that something will stop her from marrying Micki, because he seems to me to be very irresponsible, even a little mad.'

'If you think in that way, you will certainly help me to prevent the marriage.' Mrs Charles looked at me quickly to see if my expression was contradicting her words.

'But what *do* you intend to do, and how do you think I can help?' I asked.

Here tea was brought in by a large weary old woman in black to the ground. I felt that her weariness, which showed so plainly in her grey cottage-loaf cheeks, was caused by years of uneasy obedience to Mrs Charles. She arranged the things on the rosewood table with painful care. Mrs Charles pulled her lips together and waited stiffly.

When we were alone again, she leant towards me and said, 'What I intend to do is to ring up my brother-in-law.'

Mrs Charles implied that her brother-in-law was powerful indeed.

'Oh, will he be able to help?'

I hoped my voice sounded irritatingly simple.

'Certainly he will – and this is where you come in; if you can give him all the details of this Beaumont's supposed career in the Air Force, he will then be able to find out if there is a word of truth in the story or not.'

Over the teacups Mrs Charles was warming to her detective work. She began to tell me all about the importance of her brother-in-law in the Air Force; and every fact was blown away as soon as she had dragged it up. For the rest of tea, I only remember vividly the obstinate shutting of my mind to every new pretension or genteel boast.

'But why don't you ring up your brother-in-law now if you want him to inquire about Micki?' I suggested, clutching at the first idea that came to me for breaking up the conversation.

'I had hoped that you would first go back and quietly find out from him all you could, so that we had something really solid to work on.'

'I think we have quite a lot to work on already. You've heard what I know, and Mrs Bellingly must have told you other things.'

'What things?' Mrs Charles asked suspiciously.

'Oh, I only meant other facts about him.'

What had Mrs Charles thought that I meant?

She sat for a moment in silence, her hands in her lap, one foot crossing the other and pointing outwards as if poised for a playful kick.

'Perhaps I *should* ring up Ralph straight away,' she said, 'so that he can begin at once with the preliminary inquiries. I can always ring him up again later, if more facts come to light.'

She stood up, still musing, then walked quickly to the telephone in the little box entrance hall. I heard her asking for the number.

But things did not go well between her and Ralph. Because I had not listened properly to her story, I did not know where he was; he was probably at home, but I imagined him in a little hut on a vast airfield, listening to her questions, thinking them absurd, and cursing her under his breath.

Mrs Charles had begun the conversation in her usual high, singing, rather gentle tones; but as each question, each description was received with less and less sympathy or interest, her voice seemed to sink, to check itself in the middle of an utterance, so that, towards the end, I heard fragments like these – 'nothing to be done then?' – 'find out more if I can' – 'I hope I haven't –'

I hurried into the hall, to be by the front door when the conversation came to an end. She put down the receiver and smiled faintly and sadly at me.

'He says he can't do much at the moment – so busy; and he wants more details. I knew we ought to have had more facts.'

'But Micki hardly ever tells the same story twice. There are so many variations,' I said, trying to make her feel less solemn about him.

'How can *anyone* be taken in by him then?' she exclaimed in amazement. 'How can the gairl's mother allow him anywhere near her daughter?'

'Oh, she seems very fond of him herself. He has been living in the house for the last week or ten days. Don't you think romancing, lies, play-acting, often come to be excused just as a sort of amusing eccentricity?'

'Well, I for one do not think them amusing. How a mother can gamble with her daughter's happiness in this way! How Mrs Bellingly could have introduced the man, or even entertained him herself!'

Mrs Charles looked up at me as I backed out of the door. I held out my hand and said hurriedly, 'I'll certainly ask Mrs Bellingly if she has told Katherine's mother exactly what she knows or doesn't know about Micki.'

Mrs Charles, still with the sorrowful expression on her face, let my hand go, then said suddenly, 'Aren't women fools! – Such absolute fools!'

'Why women only?' I murmured mechanically, beginning to wheel my bicycle down the path. When I turned to latch the gate, Mrs Charles was still staring after me. She did not wave, she just stared as if she found the exposure of wickedness a thankless, exhausting task.

✥

That evening Micki came to see me. I had been at the Gothic-shaped upper window of the cottage when he was approaching. As he loped down the narrow lane, his feet slapped heavily and carelessly on the ground, his arms flung out and back, and he shook back his unruly hair constantly.

I wanted to escape out of the back door, but knew that I must wait for him.

I heard him climbing the stairs; then he was in the room, breathing heavily and striding about, ignoring the armchair in which I kept asking him to sit. At last he sank into it, with legs sprawled out recklessly, but hands together, finger touching finger, in the precise, ancient ecclesiastical convention. Slouched down in the chair as he was, his nose almost touched the hands; so he stuffed the first two fingers up his nostrils and began picking and probing.

He was gathering courage to say something to me; I waited, hating the passing moments, hating to have to listen.

Now he was fiddling with the thick dull metal bracelet of his watch. He had undone it and was holding out the watch, not exactly to me, but as if he would contemplate it himself. The bracelet hung and rippled like a dead snake trodden flat.

'That's a fine job of work!' Micki said admiringly, but still as if communing with himself. 'I suppose it's worth twenty pounds, at the very least, any day of the week.'

I moved about uncomfortably on the bed, then made myself look out of the window and assume an absent smile, to show, without using any words, how uninterested I was in watches.

'You wouldn't like it, Dave?' he persisted. 'It's yours for – for twelve pounds.'

'But I already have a watch,' I said.

'Oh – then I wonder if you want a typewriter. I've got a grand little one that I'd let *you* have, perhaps. It's all white in a white case. It cost a bit though, I couldn't part with it under thirty. Would you like me to bring it along to show you?' He leaned towards me eagerly.

'I don't use one. I write everything with my fountain-pen.'

I felt very cold.

Micki gave me one swift, alarmed glance.

'All right, all right, Dave,' he said, 'it doesn't matter at all. I just thought you might want a watch, or a typewriter, and I wouldn't mind selling mine now, because this marriage is going to run me in for a bit of expense, and the allowance my father left me in his will is not coming through properly. Don't you worry though, old boy, I'll get by.'

And I, who had only been worrying about my own discomfort, had a twinge of that compunction which bites all the deeper because it carries with it a determination to do nothing at all to help. I wondered how one could be left an allowance in a will. Did Micki mean that all the money had been left to his mother on condition that she made him an allowance? But of course Micki was as ignorant of his real meaning as I was; he had only intended to deceive. That is what he would always be trying to do. There was no will, no allowance, no money – and there never would be. Poor Micki was doomed to lying and contriving for the rest of his life. He would contradict his own lies a hundred times a day; and in the end all his schemes would fail. He would be given only kicks, and every word he spoke would make more trouble for him.

I saw all this, yet I only wanted to get rid of Micki. I found that I could hardly look at him or speak to him. I knew that I ought to try to talk to him about the marriage; I ought to confront him with some of his lies and contradictions and ask him why he behaved so strangely, but I just sat, sullenly waiting for him to go.

'I was in Brighton yesterday,' he said gaily.

I grunted an unwilling 'Oh.'

'There was a murder there.'

I could do no more than wrinkle up my forehead.

Micki must have seen the lack of interest and belief, but still he longed to break through them, to make me laugh and feel warm towards him. He tried once more, then accepted defeat. It was as if he had said to himself, 'It is hopeless to mention money; hardly anyone will stand for it. He's turned against me now and he'll never be the same again.'

Or was it that a new idea had come to him? Whatever the cause, he gave up trying to appease me, slapped his hands down on his knees and said, 'I'd better push off – masses to do before this wedding, and I expect you writer guys never get enough time to yourselves.'

Now that he had decided to stop trying to get money from me, he seemed lighter and less anxious, but his eyes had a questing, far-away glint, and I felt certain that he would go down to Mrs Bellingly, if he had not already been to her.

He left with the remark, 'Now don't you forget, Dave, about being best man on Monday.' But he spoke so lightly, with such lack of conviction that I did not even think it necessary to contradict him again.

At times did he too hardly believe in his marriage, I wondered. When he was out of the house the thought of him was more disquieting than his presence had been. I imagined him lurching along the lane, and I felt for the first time that he was dangerous in some way, that he held a threat. His anxiety might at this moment be turning into desperation. I saw him going into Julia Bellingly's house and frightening or cajoling her into giving him money. I thought of him struggling with her, knocking her down, then searching through all the stuffed drawers of her cabinets and chests, emptying out china, glass, silver, clothes and curtains that she herself had not disturbed for years.

I pictured these simple things, because underneath there was a deeper fear of Micki. He was like a madman, a drunkard, a ghost – some being that could never be reached.

✤

I waited until I thought he would have entered Mrs Bellingly's house, if he were going there, then I followed. I was soon outside the kitchen window, which was very close to the hedge on one side of the lane. I peered through a gap in the leaves and saw that the thick curtains had been drawn early. I listened and heard voices, a low peaceable murmur. Mrs Bellingly seemed to be moving about, touching plates and saucepans while Micki talked to her and sometimes laughed. I tried to hear what they were saying, but the window had been screwed up, because of Mrs Bellingly's fear of burglars, and only a faint sound reached me through the glass.

I stood about in the lane for some minutes, then the light went off in the kitchen. I imagined that they were carrying food or hot drinks through to the drawing-room. I could hear Mrs Bellingly giving some directions in her military voice. There seemed little need for me to wait any longer.

But as soon as I was home, I wanted to be at the other end of the lane again. I felt that I might be missing something, and I wanted to talk to Mrs Bellingly myself.

I drank some tea and read a book. When I felt that Micki must have left, I walked down once more. This time I found a crack of light at the side of one of Mrs Bellingly's bedroom windows. I called up softly. In a moment there was a stealthy movement of curtains, then I heard her whisper, 'Go round, I'll let you in.' The whisper was like the harsh loud noise a soldier makes as he breathes on the buttons he is polishing.

As I waited by the front door, voices came to me from the road. A man was chuckling and laughing and a woman made much lower, more murmuring replies. I ran round the corner of the house and stood by the coal shed, until the voices passed on down the road. When I came back to the front door, Mrs Bellingly was peering out, shining a torch into the garden.

'There you are!' she said. 'Why are you playing tricks?'

'I thought I heard Micki and Katherine in the road. I was afraid he was bringing her back here.'

'For heaven's sake come in quickly then and let me lock the door.'

'It's all right, the voices have gone down the road. I expect they were just out for a little walk with the dogs before bed.'

Julia Bellingly shut the door behind me, then, still only by the light of the torch, led me upstairs to her bedroom. She was dressed in her man's bathrobe of yellow towelling, and she had taken off her make-up. Her hair was netted; the tight little grey curls looked like baby mice cowering in terror against her scalp. After clearing a chair for me by tipping corsets, stockings, and petticoat on to the floor, she lay back in the elaborate French bed and slid her feet under the coverlet. Pink light glowed down on her head from the little dome round which the striped bed curtains were gathered. Everywhere the warm light seemed to fall on cast-off clothes. They were heaped on chairs, tables, and some were even hanging out of the drawers of the fine, dilapidated walnut tallboy. A long gilt gesso table was covered with bottles, jars, pencils for lip or eye, tweezers, brushes, sprays, scissors, powder puffs and pieces of cotton wool stained peach-pink or deeper red. I thought that Mrs Bellingly must have kept every cream and lotion she had ever tried; for some of the labels on the bottles and jars looked as if they belonged to the Russian Ballet and the Cubist period.

In this warm, quiet, dishevelled setting, we began to discuss Micki. At first Mrs Bellingly could only move her head from side to side and repeat, 'I don't know,' between exasperated sighs; then she put on her tragic voice and said, 'He's been here tonight, trying to sell me his watch.'

'I thought so,' I answered; 'he tried me first. I followed him down to see what he would do here. How did you get rid of him?'

'Oh, just gave him something to eat, then wore him down with boredom – didn't speak much, just read my book.'

'What's going to happen now?' I asked, with the sort of suppressed enjoyment that goes with that remark.

'Goodness only knows!' wailed Mrs Bellingly. 'I've told Mrs Warde that I knew nothing of him before he threw his bicycle into my hedge. I've told her about all his lies and contradictions; but the silly woman won't listen; she's quite determined to go through with the wedding. Micki has won her over completely. Apparently there are times when he grows terribly anxious and excitable. His eye goes bloodshot, his face twitches. Mrs Warde does what she can to reassure him; sometimes she sits with him because he can't sleep. On one of these occasions she tried to question him a little, but he put his head in her lap and burst out weeping. "You want to do something for the boys who saved you in the Battle of Britain, don't you? Then let me marry Katherine," he pleaded.'

Mrs Bellingly paused to raise her eyebrows and shrug her thick shoulders. 'Of course, that sort of behaviour has overcome all resistance and now Mrs Warde won't hear a word against him. She just says, "Wouldn't you do and say some rather strange things, if you had had to jump, wounded, from your blazing plane?"'

'Oh, but I haven't heard the details of that story, have you?' I broke in.

'No, but what does it matter? Micki tells so many stories. Poor boy! He has too much imagination to be satisfied with the truth. But let me go on with *my* story. When I found that I could make no impression on the Warde woman, I decided to go to the vicar. He told me that nothing could be done to prevent the marriage, if the bride's parents allowed it, and if the bride and bridegroom were not disqualified in any way from marrying. So now I don't know what to do; I feel at my wits' end.'

To express her helplessness, Mrs Bellingly dropped her hands on her stomach.

'But what has changed your attitude to the marriage?' I asked suddenly. 'You seemed so keen about it before.'

Would she answer or be frozen by my baldness?

'Oh, I don't know; I've had misgivings about his stories all along, of course, but I didn't pay much attention to them. I just thought as we all have done, that oddity was quite excusable in someone who had gone through so much; but when I heard that the licence had been granted and the wedding fixed for Monday, I suddenly felt that it was all much too hurried, that they should really get to know each other before taking such a step. I realized too that Mrs Warde still knew almost nothing about Micki's background – his family and so on. He had told us that his mother lived in Chelsea and he'd told us that she lived in Inverness, but she was not to be asked to the wedding, nor were any of his Air Force friends – why? I did think it strange; and now that he's been trying to sell things, because his allowance is not "coming through" properly, I know there's something wrong.'

'Did he tell you that he was in Brighton yesterday and that there had been a murder there?' I asked.

'No, he told me that he hadn't been to Brighton after all!'

'What can you make of it? Does he forget what he's said as soon as the words are out of his mouth?'

'I don't know what to think about his romancing, but I imagine now that he has been a boy in a garage or a workshop; he knows a lot about mechanical contrivances and is always longing to tinker at them, if they are out of order. My guess is that, because of this knowledge, he was drafted into the Air Force as a mechanic, and then his head was turned by the amazing deeds that were being performed all round him. He could not be content with the plain truth of a humdrum existence any longer, and so began telling the wild contradictory stories we all have heard. Whether he actually flew himself or was awarded the DFC, I can't say. I can't even tell whether he really was discharged on health grounds, he seems so fit. Perhaps they felt that his stories almost amounted to delusions and that the poor boy was too unstable for so arduous a life.'

Julia Bellingly stopped talking; for a moment the room was quite silent. The piles of clothes, the bottles and jars, the old furniture and cherry striped curtains all seemed to have been listening too; and now one was aware of their sullen indifference, their everlasting brooding and waiting. The silly patterns on the bottles, the rubber suspender clips, held a strange aloofness and dignity.

I got up to go, then wondered if I should first stoop down to replace the underclothes on the little gilt chair. I decided not to and moved towards the door.

'Have a biscuit,' said Julia, opening her painted bedside tin and tossing me a 'petit beurre' tomboyishly. She laughed, then lay back against her pillows as if she were ill or had been through some terrible experience. She moved her head again from side to side and sighed, just to make sure that I should not miss her unhappiness and perturbation.

It was sad really, I thought, as I clambered down the stairs in the dark and let myself out, Mrs Bellingly could never be the same with Micki again, she had found him out. There would be no more jokes about spiders and passionate kisses, skeletons and toilet rolls; no more descriptions of her first dinner-party in Carlton House Terrace when, in her agitation, she tried to hack a piece off the plaster decoration, instead of helping herself to the entrée in the dish. Now she could not tell him again about the little girl who for her birthday was given a bottle of scent and a small trumpet, but was told not to worry the vicar with them when he came to tea. She was an obedient child, so she met him at the door with these cryptic words: 'If you smell a little smell and hear a little noise, you'll know it's me.'

Julia Bellingly loved this story and I was very fond of it too, although I must have heard her tell it at least six times. There were many other stories; Micki had listened to them all and laughed. Now he wouldn't hear them any more.

Before I fell asleep that night, I kept thinking of Micki in the house with Katherine and her mother. Would he be prowling from room to room, looking for money, and objects of value he could sell, or would even Micki see the madness of stealing from his future wife in order to help with the wedding expenses? Perhaps the disappointments of the day had been too much for him and he was weeping now with his head in Mrs Warde's dressing-gowned lap. Perhaps he was telling her that his allowance was not 'coming through' and that she must not even expect him to buy the wedding ring.

Since his last visit to me, I saw him always as a lost dog, forlorn, harassed, with an unenticing hint of danger that made one wish at once to get away from him. What warned one against him before he had opened his mouth? Was it the eyes staring, then circling? The badly related hand and leg movements? The scheming that was so obvious that one had a fancy of steaming, churning thoughts bubbling up against the walls of a glass skull?

IV

I did not dream of Micki, but he was in my thoughts again almost as soon as I had woken up and begun to drink my tea. There were now only two whole days before the wedding. That which had seemed so frivolous was coming nearer and nearer, insisting every minute on being taken more seriously. But still I had the feeling of sitting in the theatre and not believing in the play. How did the situation manage to be so artificial even at this moment? Was it that Katherine's face, always so composed and guarded, had never shown more than a tinge of satisfaction or perplexity over her lover's behaviour? She and Mrs Warde were sleep-walkers; their skin was like rubber; one might prick them with pins, but they would not cry out or wake up. And Mrs Bellingly was like leather; she would cuff anyone who dared to approach *her* with a pin.

After doing a little work, I got up and dressed, then went out with my picnic to a lake in a park beyond Mrs Charles's house. I planned to call on her after lunch in case she had found out from her brother-in-law anything about Micki's life in the Air Force.

I sat down on the bank near the reeds; the big carp jumped all round the great elm, which had fallen, and lay now like a small spiky pier, reaching almost to the centre of the lake. Across the ripples, I could see the old house on the far bank, all its windows shining in the sun, brown and white cows grazing close to its grey walls. I hoped the old man who lived in it would not die for a long time; 'for if he died,' I thought, 'people would not be allowed to roam at will, fish in the lake, sit on the bank, munching and reading as I am doing. The new owner would change all such slovenly ways.'

I stayed there for more than two hours, then rode back to Mrs Charles's cottage on the edge of the estate. As soon as I had entered her garden gate and could not retreat, I regretted coming. I did not want to listen to her, pick over her titbits, or even watch the ugly expressions chasing each other across her face; so it was with relief that I heard the old cowed housekeeper say, 'I'm afraid Mrs Charles is not at home.'

It was delightful to be freed from the visit which no one had asked me to pay; I rode on light-heartedly towards home and met Mrs Bellingly at the foot of the lane. She was just about to hurry into her house.

'Oh, it is terrible, terrible,' she said in a despairing murmur; 'come in, I must talk to you. I've had to keep my door locked all day, a thing I never do.'

The head shook, the mouth twisted tragically, even the blue pebble eyes rolled up once with a baroque saint's beseeching air. I must be made to feel the horror of the situation, must not be robbed of excitement by lack of expression on her part.

We went into the kitchen and Mrs Bellingly immediately put on the kettle and opened her painted tins to take out cake and biscuits. We were to have tea with our disturbances and horrors.

'I've tried again,' she said, 'I've done all I can, but the vicar's daughter says that everything is arranged for Monday. Katherine and Mrs Warde have gone to London today to get the wedding clothes – have you ever heard of anything so rushed, how can they possibly buy a wedding dress in such a way? The licence has been paid for – by Mrs Warde of course. It seems that nothing more can be done in an *ordinary* way; but something *must* be done, and you and I are the only people to do it, even if we have to do something *extraordinary*.'

'What do you mean?' I asked, rather struck by Mrs Bellingly's determined lips. She seemed to consider for a moment before answering in her tense stage-whisper voice. The teapot hung down in her hands, over the steam from the kettle.

'I've thought it all out,' she began, 'you and I must get Katherine into a car and take her to my daughter's, so that she won't be there to marry Micki on Monday.'

'You mean kidnap her?'

'Yes, I suppose I do really. I thought we'd stop at the house tomorrow or Sunday afternoon and ask her to come with us to Nan's just for the drive. Once we had her in the car we could try our very best to persuade her not to marry Micki; if she wouldn't listen we could keep her at Nan's until after Monday.'

'You couldn't keep her against her will,' I said.

'I think we ought to do anything, even that, to stop the marriage.'

'Do you think we should go to the police?' I asked, half-heartedly.

'Oh, no,' Mrs Bellingly said. As she spoke we both saw someone go past the window that looked on to the lane.

I went out at once to see if it was anyone for me, but while I was peering through the hedge, the man in some way returned to Julia Bellingly's front gate. When I turned back to the garden, there he was in the drive, holding some papers against his dark suit and fixing me with black rolling eyes. He looked alarming, menacing, and the comedian's thick eyebrows did not lessen the effect. In my agitation I confused him with a publisher who had refused my book and then been annoyed that someone else had taken it and he could no longer do business with me. Next I tried to tell myself that the man was an unknown tradesman. But he looked exactly what he was. He came up to me quietly and swiftly and said, 'I'm a detective inspector, but there is no cause for alarm. Do you happen to know of anyone who goes by the name of Beaumont?'

Julia, who had joined us, nodded and tried to nudge me as if to say, 'It has come at last.'

'Oh, yes,' she said out loud to the inspector; 'so you have come about him! We were only just wondering what to do.'

Her voice seemed full of a sort of relief and childish awe.

'Come into the drawin'-room,' she said, 'we can discuss it there.'

The detective sat down by the window, still secretive, important, baleful. He began to feel in his pockets, then brought out a card and held it out to us.

'Do you recognize this man?' he asked.

Three hideous likenesses of Micki, taken from different angles, stared out at us. He looked much thinner; he had a sort of hanged or broken-neck appearance – the eyes, the mouth and the head all slanting to one side. An indescribable air of degradation hung about him in each picture. To look at the horrible card made me feel ashamed. No one should ever be seen in that state, I thought. It seemed brutal and mean for the inspector to be showing us the card.

'Yes, we know him,' said Julia with a little gasp; then she had the idea of proving it by showing her own portrait of Micki.

'Here he is,' she said, dragging the easel forward, anxiously looking at her work, then at the inspector.

'Oh, yes, I see,' he said solemnly, afraid of being thought unintelligent or inartistic. He wished to get away from the picture back to his questions, and Julia wanted praise and admiration for her work. The portrait was an absurd embarrassment blocking the way.

'Is he mad?' I asked, to break the spell.

At this, Julia's questions began to pour out. I was pleased that she was there to do all the talking and the answering; I could draw back and listen.

When her questions became too importunate, the detective put his hands on his knees, smiled like a cat, rolled his black eyes and said, 'I'm afraid I'm here to ask questions, not to answer them.'

'But *is* he mad?' she asked irrepressibly.

The detective said carefully, importantly, 'This man is not certified, but I think he should be.'

He paused to give his words their full effect.

'Of course, you'll appreciate the fact that we don't have photographs of people for nothing.' He turned to us both with his fat cat's smile. 'We haven't a portrait of Mrs Bellingly, or of you, sir, at the station.'

Julia and I smiled back uneasily.

'We've had trouble with this man before, but it was only by chance that we got to know of his activities here. He went to Brighton the other day and a police officer there had occasion to ask for his identity card. He did not carry it, so was told to report back to us. That started one or two inquiries and we discovered about his coming marriage, and the story of his supposed Air Force career.'

'Is that quite untrue?' Julia asked.

'Quite, I think. He has been in the Air Force, but was discharged after a few months as being quite unfit for service.'

Again there was a pause in which the detective gathered himself together for an important announcement.

'You must understand,' he said, 'that my hands are tied; I can't do anything for the moment, because a crime has not yet been committed; but I'm here to prevent *bigamy*.'

'Bigamy!' Julia mouthed and savoured the squalid word, turning it into an abomination of wickedness.

'Yes, it is believed that he already has a wife whom he visits at Brighton.'

'Oh, poor Katherine, poor Katherine,' Julia said without a trace of feeling.

The detective inspector then asked a great many questions about Micki's Air Force career. He wanted particularly to know what rank he had given himself and what decorations. At last, after more fat smiles and secret airs, he left, telling Mrs Bellingly that he would be calling again later for more information.

As soon as he had gone, Julia and I sighed, lay back in our chairs and began to smoke cigarettes. We could not stop talking about him and Micki, and repeated the same questions and exclamations many times. We marvelled at his appearance just when I had said, 'Ought we to go to the police?' We kept asking, 'But bigamy! Do you really think Micki is married already?'

I left, quite exhausted by the topic, longing to get my mind on to something else, but feeling that I could not rest until I knew what was to happen to Micki.

Later that night I went down to Julia's again and we walked to the Wardes' house together. There was a car outside; we recognized it as the village policeman's. We left, but came back later. The car was still there. There seemed no sense in waiting about; we could do nothing; so we returned to our houses to go to bed. I wondered if Micki had run away. I hoped he had. And I wondered what Katherine and Mrs Warde were feeling.

How much had they been told, and how much had their feeling changed towards Micki? Everyone would be against him now, I thought; he would have nowhere to hide.

♣

In the morning Julia Bellingly ran up my stairs and burst into the room. She began to flood me in a rush of words.

'Oh, it is awful,' she said, 'awful!'

She clasped her hands in her lap. She seemed to be clinging on to 'awfulness', squeezing the very life-blood from it. These are the facts that I pieced together from her story.

After stopping at the vicar's to pay for the licence, the Wardes had gone to London and bought the wedding dress. They came back in the evening and found Micki at the house. He had managed to buy a wedding ring and showed it to them in its little velvet box.

'Won't it be lovely, darling,' he said to Katherine, 'when we are married!'

At this moment, just when all three of them were feeling so untroubled and affectionate, there was a knock at the door. Katherine said: 'Oh, I'll go, Mummy, don't you bother, you're tired.'

Micki, who had run up the stairs to look down from a window, said urgently, 'Don't go, Katherine, don't go!'

But Katherine answered, 'Of course I must go, Micki, if someone is knocking.'

She opened the door and two plain-clothes men advanced on Micki. He threw himself on Mrs Warde imploring her to save him; then, when the policemen took hold of him, he began to hit out and scream so violently that they could do nothing with him. One of them had to run to get help from the soldiers' camp near the house.

Mrs Warde had described to Julia the horrifying change in Micki's face when he knew he was caught. He had screamed and wept and clung to her; then at last he had fallen down on the floor stark and rigid, like a person in a fit.

After they had taken him away to the station, the policeman came back and interviewed Mrs Warde. They told her that Micki's real name was Potts and that he was the son of a farm labourer who had lived in a village eight or nine miles away. His father was now dead. His mother had quite despaired of him, but she had one other very honest son in the Navy. Micki had been playing different parts and imposing on people ever since he was sixteen. For the last few years he had used the name of Beaumont. It was thought that he was already married and that he had two children, but this had not been proved. The police seemed to know more than they revealed. It appeared that he had often been in their hands. When they took him to the station, Micki broke down altogether and begged them not to put him in prison again. The scene, the policeman said, was terrible to watch.

All these jerky statements, together with many others, poured out of Julia Bellingly, chasing each other as they do on the page.

'Poor Micki,' she said; 'it's too bad. I think he is a case for the doctors.'

Then she said, 'Poor Katherine, it must have been terrible for her, when they took him away.' Finally she began to protect herself.

'But I can't be blamed for bringing them together,' she stormed; 'I told Mrs Warde I knew nothing of him before he threw his bicycle into my hedge. I told them all, but they were too foolish to listen. How can people be so unwise? Extraordinary to rush into things, to make no inquiries!'

It was interesting to watch the facts being twisted so rapidly. Julia was emerging as the wise, utterly level-headed woman, who had watched the folly of others without being able to save them from themselves. *She* had never been unaware of Micki's real character. She had known him for what he was from the first.

Everything which did not fit in with this new picture was glossed over, or ruthlessly suppressed.

'He is remanded till September the fourteenth,' she said suddenly; 'I suppose we shall all have to appear in court. Won't it be frightful! But I shall just have to stick to what I have been saying all along.'

♣

Was this to be the end of Micki, this quick, violent scene, so unexpected because so like a set, arranged ending? The police breaking in just as the ring was being shown – the fighting and the screams.

I had only Julia's word for these last scenes, and she again had heard the story from Mrs Warde; so I wondered how much had been made to fit into a traditional framework of drama.

In the days that followed Julia Bellingly would slur the clear-cut ending with new snippets of information which she had managed to pick up.

'Of course it's not true about the wife and children at Brighton,' she would say; 'it's only one of those stupid mistakes the police make. Just because he knows a woman down there with two children they jump to the conclusion that he's married to her. I doubt if they were even lovers.'

Then at another time she came out with the remark, 'You remember the scars on Micki's arms, and how his eye would sometimes go bloodshot?'

'Yes,' I said, 'he told us the scars were shrapnel wounds.'

'Well, they were nothing of the sort. He once fell off his bicycle, scraped all his arms and the side of his face. A stone must have caught the corner of his eye, and that's what causes it to be bloodshot sometimes. Aren't his stories extraordinary! Everything has been turned to account.'

Julia seemed perfectly detached about Micki now; she could mention his downfall, his lyings and contrivings without even a tremor of discomfort or pain. Only sometimes did she say, 'Poor Micki,' as if regretting something that had gone for ever; and even then one felt that she might only be regretting his grotesque lumps of flattery. She seemed to have no conception of the unpleasantness of his present condition. The idea of him in prison appeared to fill her with a sort of grim resigned humour, as if the whole affair had been a game, and this was the accepted forfeit.

'When he was at school, you know,' she said, 'he used to tell the other boys such preposterous stories that they would set on him and call him a liar; then he would run to the village policeman and tell him that he had been attacked. Extraordinary for a boy to go to the police, don't you think? It's something he certainly wouldn't do now!' Here she laughed heartily.

❖

September the fourteenth came, and Julia and the Wardes were called to give evidence. How thankful I was to have escaped the ordeal of standing up in court and talking about Micki!

Again I only have Julia Bellingly's description of the scene. It is fragmentary, and coloured by her indignation at the words of the detective inspector, who spoke of her as giving Micki 'some entertainment' at their first meeting.

'Why on earth did he use such ambiguous words?' she asked. 'They might imply *anything*. I was furious. I wanted to call out that I'd only given the wretched boy some tea, but of course I didn't dare.'

She told me little about her own evidence, beyond stressing her nervousness – I guessed that this nervousness had made her appear tougher than ever – Katherine and Mrs Warde she hardly mentioned; but when she came to Micki, she began to act the scene for me, thumping with her fists and shaking back her hair as he did.

'He was quite extraordinary,' she said; 'he began by saying that he could not help making stories up and acting them; it was in his blood. Then he said the stories ran away with him, so that he couldn't control his behaviour. He was sometimes amazed at his own inventions; but he was in their power. All this time he was gesticulating, talking very fast, just as he does when he gets excited. He went on and on, until at last he had to be stopped. The most embarrassing part was when he dragged in Katherine and asked if it wasn't natural for a man to want to marry the only girl he'd ever loved.'

'What happened though?' I asked impatiently.

'Well, the things they caught him on were the photograph of him in RAF uniform with wings and a DFC ribbon, and the engagement announcement in the paper. He was given two or three months – I'm not quite sure which – for masquerading in the King's uniform.'

'It is all over then and settled?'

'Yes, he's in prison now, I suppose. It seems a silly little thing to catch him on, when his real crime was trying to bamboozle that poor girl into marrying him, so that he could live on the family for the rest of his life.'

Julia let her shoulders sag suddenly and gave a deep sigh. She had not enjoyed appearing in court, and now she was thoroughly tired. She began to murmur again about the detective.

'That absurd man, saying that I gave the prisoner "some entertainment"! How frightful it sounds! What on earth will people think, if it's reported? They won't even know that I'm old enough to be his mother.'

V

Micki went to prison and I thought that I would hear no more about him.

The latest disturbance was caused by an anonymous letter which Julia Bellingly received one morning. It was very spiteful, very petty, very incoherent; she had no idea who could have sent it. First she thought it was a woman, then she thought it was a man. So far as it made sense at all, it seemed to be accusing her of inordinate pride and snobbery. The author appeared to triumph over her, because of her indiscreet friendship with such a character as Micki. In involved sentences she was told that, after the degrading newspaper publicity, she would no longer be able to give herself grand and conceited airs.

'Whoever heard such rubbish!' Julia cried. 'I who talk and mix with anybody, just as the spirit moves me, to be told that I have a grand and conceited air!'

It did seem a strange document – written by someone in the habit of using a pen, the letters not large and florid, or too small and neat. I pictured a rather tight-faced businessman, who resented Julia's bright clothes and bags, resented her handsome face, so protectively painted and bold, resented her fat legs which moved so fast. Perhaps he had heard her voice bawling out a welcome or a goodbye – not a tremor in it, not a doubt. He had hated the parade-ground ring, and had put her down at once as an arrogant, pretentious woman in need of humbling.

Julia Bellingly made much more of an ado about the letter than I thought she would. She showed it to the cat-faced, rolling-eyed detective, who promised to do what he could about it. She wrote to the two papers that had reported the case and told them they had no right to mention her name, thus involving her in the unpleasantness of receiving anonymous letters. By the time she had finished, it was known throughout the neighbourhood that she had had an abusive letter.

But the writer was not discovered and gradually the agitation died away. Julia spoke of the letter less and less and stopped remarking on the rudeness of the newspapers in not answering. Sometimes she would burst out again against the unknown person's absurd ideas about her, but she gave up trying to find out who he or she was, contenting herself with such expressions as 'ridiculous creature', 'pathetic individual', 'petty fool'.

With the passing of interest in the anonymous letter, even the mention of Micki's name ceased for the moment. When I went out, I never came across the Wardes, so heard nothing from them; and Julia was silent because she was feeling more than ever that she was being blamed for introducing the impostor to Katherine and then encouraging the intimacy so whole-heartedly.

One person I did meet on one of my bicycle rides was Mrs Charles.

'Oh, how lucky,' she said, 'that that dreadful affair was stopped in time!'

'Yes,' I said, 'lucky for Katherine.'

'You see Mrs Bellingly?' she asked.

'Almost every day — we live so close.'

'I am not seeing her, just for the moment.' She spoke with tight competent lip movements, as if well able to manage all difficult situations. 'She will be feeling so awkward about the whole distressing business. I shall give her a rest.'

'I don't think she is very uncomfortable; I think she has shut it out of her mind,' I said.

'Nevertheless I shall give her a rest,' she answered firmly.

And I rode away, wondering if Mrs Charles were withholding herself as a punishment, or out of a true spirit of tact.

✥

Perhaps it was a month before Micki's conviction when Julia again came to me with news of him.

'Katherine has heard from Micki in prison,' she said excitedly, 'and what do you think the extraordinary boy says?'

'I can't think,' I answered; 'tell me.'

'He says that he'll never love anybody else and that as soon as he's out of prison he wants to marry her. He says that if she's still in London, he'll join her there, get work, and then they can be married.'

'But what does Katherine say? Will she answer?'

'I don't quite know; I've only heard from Mrs Warde. Perhaps her mother will write for her. I must say Mrs Warde still seems very sympathetic towards Micki; she even talked of going to see him in prison. After what has happened you would hardly believe it, but there it is. Life is so amazingly mixed and confused, isn't it?'

'Yes, people won't stay in their appointed places, they flow about like anything,' I agreed.

'Mrs Warde is furious that Micki was treated so roughly when he was arrested. She seems to be swinging over entirely to his side,' Julia said.

'I suppose she got to know him so well when he was living in the house, that she understands the problems he has to deal with,' I suggested.

'But no one can get away from the fact that he practised the grossest deception on her and her poor daughter. When he was unmasked, the shock must have been terrible for a young girl like Katherine.'

How curiously stilted our conversation was growing! Was it that we were talking about something that, for us, was dead and done with? Micki with his protestations, his insistence on continued love – could anything be sillier, less worthy of consideration? How could he go on pretending, even in prison? And although I did not know how Katherine had been behaving lately, I reproached her too for her infuriating immobility, her acceptance of all that came to pass. No other girl I knew could have been used as she had been used by Micki.

When Julia stopped talking, I took away with me only a sort of woolly exasperation at the foolishness of the whole affair.

❖

Some weeks later Mrs Warde did go to see Micki in prison. She described to Julia the strangeness of talking to him through an iron grille; then she went on to say how contrite Micki appeared to be.

He blamed himself for everything, asked her pardon for involving her in so much trouble, and swore that he could never love anyone but Katherine. He said that he was going straight from now on, that prison taught you a lot of things, and that he needed it to sober him up.

Julia recounted this conversation quite uncritically, yet the hardness in her voice made it sound quaintly mawkish and humbugging. She increased this impression when she told me that Katherine had had another letter from Micki, even more passionate than the first. I could picture him writing it, bending low over the paper, hunching his heavy shoulders; then throwing his head back, shaking his hair, as his eyes lit up and the right worn-out phrase came to him. Those eyes would shift too from side to side, anxiously, as if he half expected someone to spring up and prevent him from finishing his love letter. But at last he would be licking the envelope, showing a great deal of broad red tongue; and he would have that sleek far-seeing almost happy look of the scheming man...

♣

Then suddenly Micki was out of prison – early because of good behaviour. I met Julia in the road, and she ran up to my bicycle, waving her painted canvas shopping bag and panting, 'I've just seen Micki! He was driving a huge yellow lorry full of milk cans.'

'Did he see you?' I asked quickly.

'I don't think so; as soon as I recognized him I turned my back and crouched against the hedge. He was going very fast.'

'So he has got work,' I said.

'It would appear so, but his mother told the police he never kept anything longer than a few weeks.'

'What happens?' I asked.

'He either does something silly and gets sacked, or just becomes restless and leaves himself.'

'Perhaps he is turning over a new leaf; he told Mrs Warde he would,' I said, then added, 'Do you think he has been to see her and Katherine yet?'

'I don't know, I must find out. I think I shall go along this afternoon.'

Julia did go along that afternoon and discovered that Micki called quite often on the Wardes, in fact so often that Mrs Warde was growing just a little anxious. He was so overwhelming, she explained, and he would not take 'no' for an answer, although Katherine had retreated quite into herself and hardly showed signs of being aware of him at all.

'But we are both so sorry for him in a way,' she told Julia. 'He can't really help his difficult nature, and he's never had a chance; everyone has turned against him.'

But it was not long before Mrs Warde herself had to turn against him. He went so often to the house, stayed so long, worried Katherine so much with his attentions, that at last Mrs Warde asked a male friend to make it quite clear to him that he must worry them no longer.

'He won't take any notice of her,' Julia said; 'he just puts his arm round her and tells her not to be an old sour-puss. What an expression! Is it American?'

'Do you mean to say he won't leave them alone?' I asked.

'Well, he will now, because this man has told him that if he goes there again, he, the man, will come round to kick him out of the house and inform the police.'

'So Mrs Warde is no longer sympathetic,' I said.

'Poor woman, she's been so plagued to death that she only wants to be rid of him.'

Ever since this day, when Julia had seen Micki in the yellow lorry, I was afraid that I too would meet him on the road. I pictured him hailing me exuberantly, stopping the huge lorry with a jerk, so that a great clatter of milk cans was set up. He would lean out of his high window, or perhaps jump down and begin pumping my hand and slapping me on the back. Then would come the flow of questions and suggestions. He might want me to write a book on prison life from the inside. He might want me to tell Katherine what an excellent husband he would make. Or perhaps he would only suggest coming round to the cottage in the evenings for talk and relaxation after work.

But I was soon to be relieved of this fear of meeting Micki. A few days after he had been forbidden the house by Mrs Warde's male friend, Julia learnt from a neighbouring farmer that he had lost his job.

'He came later and later every morning, and was so careless that the farmer had to get rid of him,' she said.

'Everyone is getting rid,' I said.

'Well, what *can* you do with someone like Micki! He is hopeless – quite, quite hopeless.'

Julia was the next one to be attacked. I was with her one evening, looking at some more Staffordshire figures she had just bought, when the telephone bell rang. She went into the hall, leaving the door open. I heard the delicate clip-clopping of her heels on the tiles, then the rather weary, supercilious, brazen 'Hullo' which she always used on the telephone. It was as if she wanted to cloak her eagerness with this hard, bored sound; for she always was eager when the telephone bell rang. She would say, 'Oh, that's only the coal man wanting to know when I'll be in.' Or, 'I expect it's for you; people are always asking me to take messages for you.' And as she ran into the hall to pick up the receiver, one knew that she was telling herself these uninteresting things to keep her hopes from running away with her. What was it that she hoped to hear over the telephone? The voice of a wonderful new friend? News of a fortune left to her? I would never know, nor, I supposed, would she.

But on this occasion her voice, after the 'Hullo' did not droop in disappointment; she said with quite a warm surprise, 'Oh, Micki, it's you, is it?' Then there was a long pause in which Micki must have been saying something earnestly, for when Julia spoke again it was in a changed, much less gay voice: 'No, Micki, I'm sorry, I can't have you here. You've already put me in one very unpleasant position; I can't risk having any more troubles and difficulties.'

Again silence, while Julia listened to Micki. 'You say you're different now,' she suddenly burst out, 'and yet I hear that you've been worrying the life out of poor Mrs Warde and Katherine. I don't call that keeping to your resolutions.'

Micki's next speech was longer than any of the others. I wondered what he could be saying to make Julia scrape her shoes on the tiles so restlessly. Then at last she was drawling in her old disdainful lazy voice, 'I'm afraid I can't listen to such stuff any longer. I don't know what you're talking about; it sounds like utter nonsense to me.'

She put down the receiver quietly and came back into the room.

'It was Micki, of course,' she said. 'I had to cut him off; otherwise he would have gone on ranting all night.'

'What was he ranting about?' I asked.

'I don't know, some dreadful stuff about friends; he only liked *real* friends, people who stood by him in a tight corner. And why hadn't I stood by him, instead of giving all those facts away in court? And why had I turned against him now? Did I like kicking a fellow when he was down? Was I afraid to have him in the house, because he'd been in prison? There was more character inside a prison than out. And he only liked real friends, people who stood by him through thick and thin. He went on and on, repeating himself like a cracked gramophone record. At last I couldn't stand it any longer.'

When Julia stopped talking, her set, moonstone eyes were staring into the distance; the faint wry smile of the invalid had come back to flicker round her mouth, just as it had done in the rosy, lighted bedroom before she had thrown the biscuit at me.

With a shake of her tight grey curls, she rid herself of the contemplative mood; the filmy blue marbles came back to me and the room, the sufferer's smile grew much broader, until her teeth showed.

'Well, that's that!' she said, smoothing her hands over her bosom and down her apron. She so often wore aprons that I had come to look on them as an important part of her in the house. They were nearly always of brightly bound coarse linen or flowered curtain chintz. They were small, gathered bunchily at the waist, and always extremely dirty. It was strange, but I had never seen her in a clean one. Round the stomach the gathers and pleats, rich as an Elizabethan's ruff, gave an outline faintly and frivolously like an expectant mother's; and the greasy dirt on the arch flowers and coloured bindings made me think of some gay tea-shop wrecked and defiled by hungry rioters, or the licentious soldiery.

'I hope he doesn't bother me any more,' she said, sitting down; 'I shan't know what to do if he turns up at the door. I shall just have to shut it in his face, I suppose.'

There was a moment in which she mused.

'This is how I see it,' she began again slowly; 'one is interested in all kinds of people, one likes to see them, however strange their behaviour; but when it comes to interviews and scenes with the police, one has to draw the line. One simply cannot be caught up in all that unpleasantness. One sympathizes, but one cannot be part of it.'

I nodded, agreeing with every word, in spite of all the 'ones' she had used. At that moment the dullest most hidebound people seemed far more desirable than those who brought after them all the squalor of detectives on the doorstep and policemen hiding in the hedge.

'I only hope he doesn't ring up any more,' Julia said again.

But he did. There were two more telephone calls, and twice Julia put the receiver down in the middle of bitter recriminations. The burden of Micki's song seemed to be, 'You are no true friend; you are a traitress who abandons her friends in their misfortunes,' and Julia would reply, 'You are a deceiver, a trickster without any backbone.'

I imagined that there might be many more of those violently cut-short conversations, but after the third call there was silence.

Sometimes the thought of Micki would come into my mind and I would wonder what he was doing and where he was. Had he some new job in another part of the country? Or had he gone back to live on the mother who had despaired of him? I remembered all Micki's stories about this mother, how neglectful and uninterested she had been, how mean about money, in spite of the house in Inverness and the flat in Chelsea. Then I thought of the real mother, the Mrs Potts, who had had to bring up her two sons on the meagre wages of a farm-hand. What must she think of Micki with his fancy new name and ancestors, his startling clothes, astonishing lies and prison sentences? Small wonder that she had given him up; what else could she do, since he had flown quite beyond her reach? How she must cleave to the sailor son! The one Julia had described simply as 'very honest'. He would be sober and sensible and pleasantly ordinary. He would give no trouble by catching himself in his own web of lies and deceits. Thinking of this brother reminded me of one of Micki's stories, one I had hardly listened to at the time; it was the story of an aeroplane that had been bought by Micki and his brother for – was it two thousand pounds? They had begun to work on it in some mysterious way, improving it so much that it had flown faster than any other plane of its class. It is strange how little impression this story made on me when Micki told it. Was I used to his extravaganzas by then? Or was it that I was so uninterested in aeroplanes, and so ignorant of them, that I could be made to believe anything?

To muse in this way on another's life is to go round and round in a white mouse's exercising-wheel. The beginning is the end, and the end the beginning; one longs more and more to travel just a little distance, to catch only a glimpse of something new, however small. It was because of this wish to know something more of Micki that I asked Katherine a very plain question the first time I saw her after his arrest.

It was almost Christmas-time before we met again. I had a friend staying with me, and, since he was fond of beer, I had taken him one evening to the Blue Anchor, the mournful little village inn. We were just about to go in when someone else appeared out of the darkness and shone a torch on the door and on us. A woman's voice said, 'Hullo'; then I leant forward and recognized Mrs Warde. I was a little surprised to see her there, never having associated her with the Blue Anchor. Her arms seemed to be full of bottles, knocking and clinking together musically.

'A party of old friends has suddenly descended,' she explained with an anxious little laugh, 'and we've absolutely nothing to give them, so I thought the only thing to do was to collect all the bottles we could and try to get them filled with beer and cider.'

My friend Ted had opened the door by now and the three of us went into the saloon bar – bottle and jug room. It was only when I was about to shut the door after us that I discovered Katherine trying to slip through the crack before it became too narrow.

'Katherine!' I exclaimed. 'We never knew you were here too.'

'I came with Mummy to help her with the bottles,' she said hurriedly; 'I've been padlocking my bicycle to the fence; thieves rush for the ones outside pubs, I'm told, and what would I do if I lost mine? I've already had my pump removed – while I was having my hair done last week. I was an idiot not to take it in with me.'

I took Katherine up to Ted and introduced him to her, but Mrs Warde was already talking to the landlord through the narrow hatch and did not notice us. Although Ted opened the door for her, she could not have realized that he was a friend of mine, for when he went up to her at the hatch and asked what she would like to drink, she turned and said stiffly, 'Nothing, thank you.'

'Oh, come on,' coaxed Ted, not to be refused. 'You must keep us company.'

'But I don't even know you,' said Mrs Warde even more stiffly.

This little misunderstanding was not amusing at the time. Mrs Warde's flushed face and hard mistrustful eyes seemed so cruel and powerful; she looked ready to eat up Ted, good nature, bewilderment and all. The thought flashed into my mind that she was angry and suspicious because of Micki and the trouble he had brought her. I went forward at once to explain Ted to her. There was laughter, an apology, embarrassment; then Mrs Warde said that she must be getting back to her guests with the drinks, but she felt sure that Katherine would like to stay with us a little longer, since the friends at home were only old people like herself.

Here Mrs Warde laughed again, and she looked very young with her face still slightly pink from her anger. Below the short fur jacket I saw that she had on the velveteen trousers she was wearing when I went to tell Micki that I could not be best man.

Before Katherine had even protested or offered to help her with the bottles, Mrs Warde said, 'I'll see you later then, darling; I can easily manage alone, once I get them into the bicycle-basket.'

Ted went out with her to carry the bottles to the bicycle, and I was left with Katherine. Our drinks were waiting for us on the hatch board, so I brought them over to the silvered cast-iron table with the marble top, and we sat down together on the long bench against the wall. Above us hung a mid-Victorian overmantel, its broad expanse of mirror speckled and smoky, the gilt blackened on its frame of trailing madonna lilies, ivy, convolvulus and periwinkle.

Katherine's eyes were on the tawny cider in her glass; she seemed to be watching the bubbles rising to the surface like tiny divers. Her lips were together firmly, she looked more restrained, more self-possessed than ever. I saw that she still wore her hair swept up as she had rearranged it on her engagement to Micki; but nothing else of that time was to be remembered, it seemed; for when I said impulsively and too suddenly, 'Have you heard anything more of Micki?' there was a discouraging silence. Of course it had been a mistake to ask in that simple, crude way, but I had felt the sudden longing for direct speech without any wary refinements or delicacy.

'But perhaps this isn't quite the place to talk about him,' I added hurriedly, anxious now to clothe my bare question.

'No, I don't think this is quite the place to talk about him,' Katherine agreed. She smiled at me with finality. I knew that I could never talk to her of Micki again.

❖

Just as Julia had been the first to see Micki, so now the last glimpse of him was to be hers also.

She came to me one evening in spring and told me that she had just returned from a shopping expedition. She showed me the blue and fawn striped jersey, the coral-red string riding-gloves, and the chipped little eighteenth-century enamel comfit box that she had bought; then, after I had admired each new possession, she said suddenly, 'And who do you think was on the bus with me?'

It was as if this, the greatest plum, had been kept till last. I tried to think, but only one unusual person came into my mind.

'Was it your mad friend?' I asked. 'The one who once sent you a parcel you were frightened to open because you thought it was a bomb, but it was really a lovely jar of ginger?'

'No, no,' said Julia impatiently, 'whatever makes you think that I should run into Thelma on a bus? She's probably miles and miles away.'

'Then who was it?' I asked, tired of the guessing game.

'Micki, of course!' she exclaimed.

I wondered why my thoughts were still supposed to be fixed on Micki after all these months.

'Yes,' she continued, 'when I got on the bus, it was already very crowded, so I had to take a seat downstairs, although, as you know, I usually like riding on top. I was looking down at my shopping list to begin with, and I didn't take much notice of any of the other passengers, until we came to the top of the hill where the bus stops. I looked up then and noticed at the front of the bus a head of hair and shoulders that I felt sure I knew. Just then the man stood up and turned; it was Micki. He was very well dressed, in clothes I don't remember seeing before. I nearly made a sign to him with my glove, but he was looking the other way. As he passed he glanced down and suddenly recognized me. I was just about to smile and say something, when he jerked his head up and walked on, ignoring me completely.

'I turned to watch him get off the bus. He hesitated for a moment on the grass at the side of the road; he had half turned his back, but I could see how new his clothes were and how well they fitted him. I could see too that he was glancing at me over his shoulder, out of the corners of his eyes. In that twisted position he looked so sly, so resentful. He seemed to be wishing me ill, like some — some wizard.'

Julia sighed, then finished her story.

'My last glimpse was of him turning to walk up the little side road. Poor boy, he looked so lonely and so charming in his new clothes, with that dark rich hair brushed back and clipped crisply round his ears and down his neck. He never turned, never gave me another glance, just walked on alone, until he was under the trees.'

'Did his jacket have slits at the back and leather elbow-pads?' I asked, rudely breaking in, I am afraid, on Julia's mood.

'Yes, I think it did,' she said a little petulantly; 'but how did you know? And why should it matter?'

'Well, at least he has that, if he has nothing else,' I murmured.

'What did you say?' Julia asked sharply.

'Oh, nothing. I just remembered that he wanted a coat like that.'

'The tweed was a sort of mixture of mustard, earth and moss colours,' she mused; 'it suited him *so* well.'

I thought of Micki pausing at the side of the road, so that Julia should see each detail of his new clothes — the clothes which gave him such a proud, armoured feeling. She should be made to see that other people had not cast him off, that he had no need of her any more. She should admire him, just as she had at first; but now she should regret as well.

Then when he turned to go into the wood, he would be torturing her, murdering her with every thought for deserting him. But perhaps later the evil mood would pass and he would remember her stories and jokes and her great liveliness. Perhaps he would remember them long after everything else was dim. He might burst out laughing, when he was in prison again, or just when he was about to make businesslike love to another girl.

Here I looked up. There was some change in the room. Julia was about to cry; I could already imagine the great crystal crocodile drops trickling down her peach-bloom cheeks. And each crocodile drop would have something so painful at its core.

In desperation my thoughts raced back wildly to one of her most outrageous riddles, the one which began, 'What is it that has twenty-two tits and a ball?'

I had not guessed, nor had Micki – nobody could ever guess; and so Julia was always able to cry out exultantly, 'Why a girls' hockey team, of course!'

Did Micki remember this one? Surely he could never forget it! The young bosoms bouncing so energetically as they chased the little ball over the grass. It was preposterous, irresistible.

And here, in spite of Julia's brimming eyes, in spite of all my efforts to be grave, a strangled sound, rather like a hog's snort, broke from me. I gave up then and let the smothered giggles out.

ANNA DILLON

'Anna Dillon' in this story is clearly Denton Welch himself, and 'Mrs Eames', Evelyn Sinclair. On 21 July 1943 he had met by the river not a squadron-leader but a Norwegian sailor, whom he had invited home for tea. A 'tomato-red air cushion' had been given to him earlier that year by his neighbour May Walbrand-Evans.

ANNA DILLON LOOKED IN HER BICYCLE-BASKET TO SEE that she had everything for her picnic: thermos of coffee, Ryvita, bread, cheese, minute parcel of butter, a little honey in an old cold-cream pot, her precious ration of chocolate, an early, brilliantly red apple. They were all there; so was her childish paint-box, her block of paper and her book.

She waved her hand to Mrs Eames, who kept house for her, and rode away from the cottage with a light heart. She was going to spend the whole afternoon by the river, in her favourite spot where the rich cornfield swept down to the magenta loosestrife and the varnished yellow daisies. There was a certain tree there, against which she knew she could lean and be at peace.

To look at Anna Dillon, one would have taken her for a girl in radiant health – the glinting, curling, toast-coloured hair, the delicate brick-dust tint of her cheeks, the clearness of her hazel eyes that sometimes were quite green – all these seemed to point in that direction. But it was not so. Anna was tubercular. Many precious months of her life had been spent in sanatoria. Now she was better and was living very quietly all alone in the country, with only Mrs Eames as companion, nurse and housekeeper. Her parents had died while she was still a child. Both had left her a little money, and now that she was twenty-one she had chosen to live away from the rest of her relations. They disapproved, but could do nothing.

They also placed perfect trust in Mrs Eames to let them know if Anna's condition in any way grew worse.

Bicycling along, Anna forgot all her troubles, including her deflated lung, until her too impetuous pedalling in the hot sun made her gasp slightly.

'Go slow, you idiot,' she told herself, 'then you'll manage perfectly well.'

When she got off the main road she even forgot the war; there was nothing to remind her of it except the jog-trot droning of the few aircraft circling overhead. They were ancient biplanes, used for instructing new pilots. Their shapes in the sky struck a curiously old-fashioned, nostalgic note.

Anna left the lane and rode down a bridle-path which led between a hop garden and a cornfield. The hops with their creeping tendrils were already draped fantastically and beautifully from the wires to the poles. The path was rough, with here and there a piece of sharp tin or glass embedded in the cinders and baked mud. Anna avoided all these bits as carefully as possible, and at last reached the river bank, feeling rather jolted. She crossed the old wooden bridge and wheeled her bicycle along the towpath until she came to her favourite place. Here the cool shade from the overhanging tree spread round her. She knew that she must not sit in the sun because of her condition.

Anna took the things from her basket, blew up her air cushion and lay back against the tree trunk. She seemed to have the whole river and the surrounding fields to herself. Nothing stirred, except fish in the river and birds in the trees. The fish sometimes leapt right out of the water, showing their silver bellies. A gust of wind came to ruffle the surface of the water and to make the rich corn stalks grate against each other dryly. Anne spread her Ryvita with butter and cheese and began to eat hungrily.

As she ate, she read her book. It was an old novel by Mrs Henry Wood. It really was very amusing. Whether the humour were intentional or not did not matter in the least.

By the time Anna had reached the chocolate and apple stage she felt utterly content. Her milky coffee comforted her, in spite of the heat. She let her hands trail through the silky blades of grass, then she felt in her bag and took out her cigarette-case. It was of engine-turned gold with a diamond clasp. She had given it to herself as a present when she thought she had some money to waste.

'You oughtn't to take a thing like that just loose in your bag when you go out in the fields or by the river,' Mrs Eames said; 'you're bound to lose it one day.'

'How should I take it then? Padlocked round my neck?' Anna asked.

'You oughtn't to take it at all.'

'But I love pretty things – I enjoy my cigarettes much more out of this case than out of a paper packet.'

'You won't talk like that when you've lost it in the river or the long grass,' Mrs Eames warned her.

Nevertheless Anna still took her cigarette-case with her, and now she opened it and fitted one of the white tubes between her lips. She lit it and puffed contentedly for some minutes, wondering what subject she would choose today for her little watercolour sketch. She was modest and light-hearted about these, admitting that she only did them for her own amusement. One day she hoped to become more serious.

She got up and, taking her block and paint-box, walked a little further along the bank to get another view. She thought that she might do two willow trees, some oast-houses, a gate, and their reflections in the water.

As she looked across at this group, she became conscious of someone lying close to her in the grass. A slight bank and the length of the thick tussocks of grass had completely hidden the outstretched form until she was almost upon it. Now she looked down into the sleeping face of an airman. He had taken off his jacket and shirt, and he lay there in the full glare of the sun in his startlingly white singlet. His arms and legs were thrown out carelessly, as if he had fallen down exhausted. Sweat glistened between the bleached hairs of his very neat moustache. His brown face shone.

Anna was startled by the beauty of his calm eyelids and his mouth washed clean of all expression. Without thinking of the heat on her back or her standing position, she bent over her board and tried to get down the significant lines of his face. She worked feverishly, afraid every moment that he would wake and see her standing over him. But she soon became so engrossed that she forgot his humanity and studied him as she would a rock or a stone.

Anna smudged with her finger impatiently, trying to get the deep shadows round the eye sockets. It was while she was riveting her gaze on this part of his face that his eyes slowly opened. He looked straight into her blankly for a moment, then a grin spread from his mouth, up his cheeks, curling and broadening his nostrils and crinkling the skin round his eyes.

'You know I charge a slight fee for this,' he said sleepily, yet at the same time just managing to cock an eyebrow.

'I *am* sorry, I really must apologize,' said Anna in great confusion. 'The fact is that I was walking along, looking for a landscape subject, when I suddenly came upon you. I could not resist trying to get something down while you slept. I do hope you are not offended.'

'Fully realizing the powers of attraction my extraordinary beauty must wield over any nice girl, I am graciously able this once to forgive and forget.' The man's face showed not the flicker of a smile. Anna arranged hers to match.

'That is extremely good of you. May the humble artist be allowed to present her modest drawing as some slight recompense for her effrontery?'

Anna held the sheet of paper out to the man, bowing her head in a ceremonious gesture. He took it, at the same time raising himself and reclining on one shoulder in a lordly way.

'But my dear, it's perfectly frightful!' he said with simulated surprise. 'I had no idea I looked like that when I was asleep. I shall be careful never to do it in public again.'

'I expect that what offends you is my ineptitude. In many ways I prefer the sleeping to the waking expression.' Anna smiled sweetly.

'Oh naughty! Don't let's go on sparring any more. Will you believe me when I say that I think your bracelet's very pretty and that I may have seen worse faces in my time?'

Anna looked down self-consciously at her big amethyst and silver bracelet, and then began calmly to sketch the man in his new position.

'Still making use of me!' he cried in mock surprise, but taking care not to move.

'That's right, keep still,' Anna said approvingly; then she lapsed into silence for some time. Only the scribble of her pencil could be heard, and the delicate lapping of tiny wavelets against the overhanging banks. The man held his position well, and although he wore a wry smile, he was very patient. At last he said, 'If smoking is permitted, will the artist put a cigarette between her model's lips? She'll find a case in the breast-pocket of the tunic.'

Anna put down her pencil abstractedly and went across to the tunic. When she turned it over and saw the wings on the pocket, a tremor ran through her. She liked to touch the cloth; it gave her great pleasure. She found the case and opened it. It was empty except for two cigarette cards and an address on a torn piece of paper.

'You've smoked them all,' she said. 'Just wait a moment and I'll go back to my bicycle and get you one of mine.'

She returned with her case. It glinted in the sunlight.

'Aha – I see I have to do with an heiress,' said the airman in a stage villain's voice. He had not moved at all. The pose was held perfectly.

'It's nothing but vulgar ostentation, I'm afraid,' said Anna. 'There's nothing behind it all.'

She fitted a cigarette neatly into his mouth and lit it for him. They puffed together silently.

'What's the time?' the airman asked after some minutes.

Anna looked at her watch.

'It's nearly four.'

There was another pause.

'It's a pity we haven't got a little kettle and a fire here, so that we could make tea,' the man said.

Anna thought for a moment and said abruptly, 'Why not come back and have tea with me? Mrs Eames would be overjoyed to get it for a real live airman.' She spoke as lightly as possible, and mentioned Mrs Eames to reassure him.

He looked at her penetratingly and then said shamefacedly, 'You know, I wasn't cadging when I said about a little kettle and a fire.'

'Of course you weren't! I only wondered if you'd like to come back and have tea with me; I live quite near.'

'I would,' he said seriously.

Anna stood up.

'I'll just get my bicycle and put the things from my picnic lunch back in the basket,' she said, walking away so that he should have time to put on his shirt and tunic.

She waited by her bicycle, until she saw him coming round the corner, looking very trim and smart now he was properly dressed. She saw that he was a squadron-leader.

Anna rode very slowly beside him. They talked quietly. There was no more bantering, although they sometimes laughed.

Anna opened the gate and called out to Mrs Eames, 'I've brought a real pilot home to show you, Mrs Eames! Can you give us tea?'

Mrs Eames looked at Anna's companion and just said, 'Oh, sir!'

Although the airman did not know it, this was a tremendous tribute. Mrs Eames had long ago given up calling anyone 'sir', considering it undemocratic.

After her first moment of admiration, she looked at Anna inquiringly.

'This gentleman very kindly sat for me while I was trying to sketch on the river bank,' Anna explained. 'We both felt thirsty so I suggested coming back and asking you to make us some nice tea.'

Mrs Eames flew into the kitchen to get things ready. Anna knew just what to say to please her. She knew also that Mrs Eames would be thrilled to get tea for the unknown airman.

Anna took him into the tiny living-room and showed him her things.

He looked along the bookshelves quietly, then said, 'How pretty and peaceful it is here.'

Anna's eyes shone. 'Do you like it?' She was delighted with his simple praise.

'Yes, the pretty striped curtains, the bright old china figures and the cups on the rack, the roses in the silver bowl and the nice polish and lavender smell.'

'Sit down and be comfortable,' Anna pressed him. He sank into a corner of the sofa and seemed quite content to gaze about him and be at peace.

Anna saw the great need he had of peace. She guessed that he had gone to the river to get away from everybody and everything. There was an almost terrifying look of strain about his eyes when he thought he was not being watched. But underneath she could see the real broad, straightforward nature, that was only waiting to come back and take possession – that now expanded in the quiet cottage room.

Mrs Eames came importantly, bearing the silver tray, the Georgian silver teapot, sugar basket and cream jug. She had unpacked them from their tissue-paper and polished them in a flash for the unexpected visitor. Anna beamed her approval. She was not quite so certain when she realized that Mrs Eames had used some of the Earl Grey tea. Men so often preferred Indian to anything else that she was afraid he might not like the flavour. But she was reassured when he said, 'I haven't tasted tea like that since the war began.'

She pressed him to eat some of the toast, a tomato sandwich, one of Mrs Eames's crisp shortbread biscuits.

Then they both sat back and smoked in silence. Anna realized that they knew nothing about each other, and she was content to leave it so. She wanted always to think of him just as the airman she found sleeping by the river. She hoped he would ask no questions and tell her nothing.

He didn't; he simply sat quietly on the sofa puffing his cigarette until it was finished. Quietly, Anna walked across to give him another. She held a match for him too, and their hands touched. She felt the slight tremble of his hand through all its strength. She saw the golden hairs glinting on it. She did not want to take her own hand away; she wanted to go on having contact with this quite other, almost ruthless vivid life, so different from her own tenuous stream.

He looked up straight into her eyes through the smoke; then his hand closed on hers and he pulled her down very gently beside him on the sofa. She sank down willingly enough, content not to think at all, only to savour this wonderful new peace and security. She lay against his side in the crook of his arm. Through the uniform, rough to her cheek, she could feel his steady heart beating. Big Ben – Rock of Ages – she thought of all things set and steadfast.

Her head rose and sank as he breathed. His large hand played through her hair. He delicately stroked the glinting strands.

'Where shall I be this time next year?' he mused in a whisper close to her ear.

Impulsively she put her hand up to touch his eyelids, to smooth and stroke the hairs on his upper-lip.

'Don't let's think of anything but now,' she said. 'I am fatally ill; you go through untold dangers almost every night, but let's think of nothing but our peace and safety now.'

He bent his head down to kiss her. She raised her lips and put her arm with a child-like gesture tightly round his neck, so that the crisp stubble at the back of his head pricked her bare arm.

'Oh darling,' they both sighed together and then laughed at their unanimity. They lay there, holding each other tightly, savouring each second, knowing that too soon they would be torn apart.

Mrs Eames, with the greatest good sense and feeling, did not come in to collect the tray. The tea grew cold in the pot, but Anna got up at last and went across to pour another cup for her unknown friend. They drank the cold tea together from the cup. She parted his lips, pushed a biscuit between his strong teeth, then nibbled the other end herself. Their noses touched, they laughed and rubbed them together lovingly, like Eskimos.

Suddenly he held her to him so tightly that she felt she could not breathe.

'Oh darling,' he gasped out, 'I shall always remember this marvellous day. You can't think what you've done for me, giving me this wonderful peaceful time. I shall have to go soon and we may never meet again, but this moment will always be crystal clear, perfect, nothing can ever change it.'

His words so pierced Anna that she felt the tears on her cheeks wet and hot. She did not bother to restrain them, but cried quite simply and freely against his shoulder.

'Oh, life is just awful,' was all she could say.

'No it isn't, darling; it's just life – no use to kick and strain – got to take it as it comes.'

He paused a moment and, still seeing that Anna wept bitterly, added, 'Let's have some music to cheer us up! Where's the wireless? I'll turn it on and see what's going.'

Very gently he undid her arms round his neck and went to switch on the wireless. He tuned in to a programme of gramophone records of the twenties. The silence of the cottage was broken by the plaintive lyric:

> Diamond bracelets
> Woolworth's doesn't sell, baby,
> Till that lucky day
> you know darn well, baby,
> I can't give you anything but love.

'Come on, dance a little, darling,' he said, holding out his hands.

'We can't in this tiny room,' Anna replied, but nevertheless she wiped her eyes and stood up. He grasped her, supporting her against him, so that she felt no weight in her body, then they swayed and moved gracefully to the old music. He guided her between the pieces of furniture, but often they stood still in one place like Eastern dancers, only moving their bodies and their arms.

'It's heaven, you really do dance all my cares away,' said Anna fervently. 'I seem to forget about the war, forget about the fact that I may be dead next year.'

'That goes for me too,' he answered, pressing his strong lips to her thin crimson ones.

She clung to him, seeming to need all his support.

'Now, darling,' he said very gently, 'I've got to go, else I shall be late.'

He held her at arm's length and looked deep into her eyes.

'Don't go,' she cried, clutching at his arm.

'I must, but I think we'll meet again. I think one day we'll see each other on the river bank again and we'll come back and have tea just like this.'

He said no more and turned to jerk down his tunic and pick up his cap.

She ran to him to help, patted a hair from his shoulder, determined not to make this parting too difficult for him. She folded his ear with her hand, kissed the side of his cheek and whispered softly, 'Goodbye, darling. I'll pray for you every night. And one day we'll meet by the river again.'

For some reason they both of them left it vague in this way, superstitiously afraid of fixing a day.

Anna watched her airman walking down the path alone. She saw him turn into the road. He walked jauntily with a determination. It was clear that he was steeling himself, keying himself into the right mood for the grim night's work.

'God, keep him safe – God, keep him safe,' Anna found herself saying over and over in a low voice.

The agony of parting pierced into her and twisted like a knife, but she did not cry.

'We've had our lovely time. We can only ask for the smallest crumbs. Never dare to ask for more. If he should be killed tonight, if I should die tomorrow, we still have that. These are the tiny things we live on, they only must suffice.'

She looked out of the window. The lane was blank now, only the waving flowers in the garden and the feathery trees. Quietly Mrs Eames came in and took away the tea things. She soon reappeared and looked at Anna solicitously.

'Shall I read that nice book to you, dearie,' she said comfortingly, 'while you go on with your pretty cross-stitch work?'

Anna nodded and smiled and pulled her work towards her.

Mrs Eames sat down and took the book in her lap.

'What a nice young gentleman that was! Did you see his decoration ribbon? I couldn't tell you what it was, but I saw it.' She went on: 'He'll be dropping in again, I wouldn't wonder, now he knows where we are. He enjoyed his tea all right,' she chatted, thinking of the empty plates.

'Yes, he'll come back, won't he?' said Anna fervently, and in her heart she tried to cover the cold stone which chilled her there.

MEMORIES OF
A VANISHED PERIOD

This story, which was first published in A Last Sheaf, *describes events which probably took place around 1943. 'Angus' was a friend called Marcus Oliver who lived in London.*

I SAW, WHEN I ENTERED THE ROOM, THAT ALL THE QUAINT accessories had been brought out, as if from glass cases or refrigerators.

Champagne spat and frothed in glasses; a tiered, armour-plated wedding cake stood foursquare on its disc of silver paper; at the bottoms of entrée dishes, on seas of doubtful lace, floated little pastry boats filled with caviare; the summit of each pyramid of sandwiches was crowned with a gallant little flag. The flags bore these legends: PÂTÉ, SMOKED SALMON, KIPPER.

Fat Levantine-looking ladies laughed and made jokes from behind their heavy barricades of maquillage. A sort of deep angry 'Summer Bloom' seemed all the rage. Being curious, I could not help discovering the line where this Red Indian cosmetic stopped. Behind the ears, down the throat, came the natural whiteness, almost as a shock. Those stones, which are called zircons, flashed on plump fingers and heaved and fell on bosoms.

In spite of their size and heaviness, there was a curious, tinselly, unreal quality about the women. I could not understand it, until I realized suddenly that they, like children or actors, were 'dressed up'. Their finery was sad and limp, perhaps a little dirty. I thought of the phrase 'a brave show', it seemed so very suitable.

The men not in uniform were even drabber, more than ever bent on appearing commonplace. Only the bride's father had put on his 'tails'. He was a round little man with a benign white tonsure of hair, and one somehow knew how far his sweet smile must have carried him in the hard-headed business world.

Everyone seemed to be making remarks about the chandelier.

'My dear, why didn't it shatter into a thousand pieces?'

'D'you mean to say the bombs merely made it swing to and fro?'

'Think of having one of those glass stalactites in your eyes!'

'Aren't you terrified of it crashing down on your heads?'

'You ought to dismember it.'

This last remark was made by a grey old man with a trembling under-lip. His wife corrected him in a shrill, dry shriek. 'You mean dismantle, Herbert, not dismember. It isn't human.'

But there the chandelier remained. Being in a rich man's house, it was, of course, a cheap reproduction – yet it had its own *réchauffé* prettiness and the same squalid gallantry as the women's clothes.

I moved into the circle round the bride's younger sister. The skin was still very young and pretty round her eyes – smooth and taut, not loose or criss-crossed like chicken's skin – and her hair might almost have been dressed with lard, it was so sleek.

'Only the back windows were blown in; wasn't it lucky?' she said.

There seemed nothing to add to this statement. I stood for a moment, trying to think of conversation, then I floated on till I came to the bride. She wore the sort of dress that has been made very quickly from a fashion paper-pattern. The pins, the crinkly paper, the blue chalk, still seemed to cling to it. Its colour was green, and the orchids pinned across it were also green but of a more 'sickly' shade; for they were pale, a little bruised, breathless-seeming, with silver paper hiding their death-wound.

The phrase 'the bound, tortured feet of Chinese women' jumped into my head.

The bride had her back half turned to me. She seemed to be gazing through all her guests, through everything, into the distant future, or the past. Out over the park her eyes were roving, and because of her self-forgetfulness she was poised, dignified and quite human.

I did not notice her mother's approach until she was near; then I witnessed a curious little scene which I shall always remember.

With a harsh, black, permanently-waved sort of frown, the

mother reached out her hand and gave her daughter's thigh a brutal pinch. 'Can't you attend to your guests?' she hissed with venom.

Shocked as if I myself had been pinched, I expected the bride to start, almost to scream – at least to swear. But she did none of these things; she only walked away quietly, her trance replaced by no vivacity.

'To be pinched on your wedding day! To be pinched on your wedding day!' I kept saying to myself. I could think of nothing else.

To shake the picture from my head I turned away and looked at the bridegroom with his two friends. That extraordinary camaraderie, which only comes fully to blossom between ordinary men when one is getting married, lit up their faces. They were holding one another's shoulders, patting one another's backs, wishing good wishes, saying goodbyes, joking and chaffing as they knew they should from the pages of *Esquire*. It was painful to watch, because you felt that they really had no love for one another at all.

Suddenly, before even the first guest had thought of departing, the hired waitresses began, quite openly, to pack up the remaining food and drink. They did it almost with ostentation, flapping napkins sharply with their bird-like hands, snatching up the plates of foie gras sandwiches and shovelling them into paper cartons. The one solitary waiter in charge of them, being too decrepit to be snapped up by the Army, the Air Force or the Navy, was also too decrepit to stop their uncomely, female haste. He just looked on, weakly scandalized.

I went in search of Angus, who had brought me to this wedding, and found him, tightly hedged round with friends, in a corner of the large room. I was pleased that he had deserted me, for I had been free to look at everything from outside, like a thief, but I pretended to be annoyed and bored, and said that I thought it was time for us to go. We said goodbye prettily all round and went to find our 'things'.

Outside, in the street, we stood for a moment watching the people pouring out of the front door into the sunlight. Here they looked even worse and more unhappy than upstairs in the drawing-room. 'Cruel, cruel Sun,' I muttered; then I turned to Angus to stop myself revolving all these words and phrases.

We walked to the bus, talking gaily about the other guests. Being quite unknown to me, I was able to build up the most elaborate fancies about them. Angus sometimes corrected these by the revelation of even more remarkable facts.

I had decided to take Angus to tea with Grace and Randal. I thought they might like one another as they did such different jobs (Randal was a painter and Angus used to work in a whisky distillery); and tea we had to have, after champagne and so many curious titbits.

We climbed up the stairs to the fourth floor and rang the bell of the tiny flatlet.

Soon we were all sitting on the bed, drinking from big steaming breakfast-cups and looking at Grace's new scrapbook. It dated from about 1800 to 1830. First came 'Gentlemen's Seats', stiff, caught in a trance, a dream of antlered deer, shaped walls, half-hidden domes of tiny temples, gazebos, ice-houses, strawberry beds. Next came 'Politicians', the older ones heavily wigged, the younger ones wearing their hair romantically brushed forward into curls and tendrils. 'Beauties' followed. As is usual in such collections, only the higher walks of life were represented; there was no 'Molly Flynn, the Prettiest Milkmaid in all Huntingdonshire' or anything of that sort.

We looked at each picture minutely, carefully, making many remarks. I forgot that Angus could only be expected to have the smallest interest. Being so well controlled, he did not fidget; but at last he jumped up, saying, 'I'm afraid I have to meet someone at six'; then, turning to me, 'Are you coming?'

Only afterwards, in the thickly carpeted, curious-smelling passage, did I realize how impatient Angus had been. 'What strange hair your friend has,' was all he said. 'It's just like an albino golliwog's.'

The person Angus was meeting at six had a bad reputation. It appeared that he asked his friends to expensive places, ordered many drinks and dishes which they did not want, then revealed the fact – wasn't it amusing – he had no money on him at all.

We jumped off the bus at the Ritz and went down below to an underground bar. I felt relieved as the minutes slipped by and no friend came. Angus and I drank gin and ate Smith's Potato

Crisps – removed from their grease-proof paper packets, of course.

The place began to fill up. A mature American film star rustled into the room, followed by a curious Air Force 'escort'. When the man sat down he twined his legs together like a little pixie on the edge of a cement bird-bath.

Something very Gothic, with rings and Central-European accent, was pouring out its soul to a sleek, diffident, nervous-breakdown type of soldier.

A young grandee leant against the bar looking sober and beautiful. His double Guards' buttons punctuated him all down the front like pairs of lovers on seats in the park. I was surprised when Angus said, 'That's the Duke of R.'

For some reason I had expected a combination of names like Etherington Todd or Alex Miller.

Angus was beginning to talk now.

'Last week some of us were in here,' he said, 'and there was the most frightful smell of cat. At last we could bear it no longer, so I asked the waiter if he knew what it could be. He leant over me and said very quietly, "Excuse me, sir, but it is the Lady Robins who is sitting at the next table. We spill drinks over her, we try to trip her up, but nothing will drive her away. I think it is the Valerian, sir."'

Angus and I had some more drinks and then someone resplendent in kilt and furry sporran came in. I recognized him as an actor in a country repertory company. He belonged to a rather tawdry, bedraggled Scots family, and, before the war, had possessed an American admirer in Paris who was always kept strictly neuter in conversation. We had once exchanged two words in the pub opposite his theatre.

Now I went over to him gaily, too gaily, and of course he did not know me. I felt insulted and depressed.

'It's the kilt that's done it,' I grumbled to Angus. 'Everything before the kilt has been obliterated from his mind.'

'And a good thing too,' Angus answered tartly. 'That child needed a spring-cleaning very badly.'

We did not speak for some moments, and I was able to notice a melting and a buzzing growing in my head. I looked at the modest strawberry leaves, the ripe glamour-girl, the pinchbeck Highlander, the pixie-legged Air Force 'ace' and all the other dreary people.

'Let's go,' I said urgently.

Without waiting for him to answer, I jumped up and made for the doorway; then I ran rather jerkily up the stairs and waited for him in the street.

It was harsh and cold in the open. The evening had only just begun and could not be cut short so suddenly.

We plodded to the Café Royal and began to eat hors-d'œuvre. A peculiar feeling came over me as I contemplated the fantastic hanging confection of jagged glass which covers the electric-light bulbs. I became almost hypnotized. I identified myself with the mouse that ran up Selfridge's clock and 'did not expect such a bizarre effect, so came tumbling down with the shock'. I knew that I had not remembered the end correctly, and this worried me. Through dreaming of the mouse and the clock I began to lose a clear-cut consciousness of my immediate surroundings. The next thing I realized was that Angus was shepherding me to Dean Street.

In Piccadilly a soldier swore at us terribly. He followed behind, pelting us with blasphemies and filth. We giggled weakly, wondering why we had been singled out for this attention. He was so alone, so drunk, so hopeless and unhappy. Hate was seething inside and had to flow out. He poured it on to us and he had all my sympathy.

The pubs in Dean Street were full to overflowing. We fought our way in, pushing through the crowd of soldiers, whores, airmen, negroes and French sailors with red pom-poms on top. All round, I could feel their chests, their thighs, their legs (with the knees a little bent) pressing on me. Close to my ear people whispered to each other earnestly, ecclesiastically. The thimblefuls of golden whisky spilt on dark cloth when elbows were jogged. Someone said playfully, 'I'm feeling hysterical.' There was warmth and dirt and love and disgust and poetry and sweat.

We stayed till closing time, then smoothly, swayingly, dancing a little sometimes, we laughed our way back to Piccadilly.

It was all so crazy, so delicious, so sad; so terribly, nobly sad; like an avalanche crashing down. 'She shall have music wherever she goes,' I sang tragically.

Years, years afterwards, I thought, I shall remember this night when I was young; when we got drunk and all London was drunk with us; when lonely soldiers shouted blasphemies through the streets.

On all sides people were streaming out of doors, making jagged sections of light, like slices of cake, each time they lifted the blackout curtains. I wished that the seething and the bubbling could go on for ever.

'Angus, my train!' I suddenly shouted. We both rocked with laughter at the idea of a train, then Angus became severe.

'Get a taxi at once!' he ordered. At last we found one, and as I stood at the door, saying goodbye, the sirens blew.

Drink had made my mind free to receive all impressions, and at this sound a sense of doom struck deep down.

'I shall be killed,' I said with conviction and relish. 'I know I shall be killed. I have been kept in London especially to be killed.'

'Shut up!' Angus shouted brutally, not allowing me to wallow in the importance of death.

'Drive quickly to Victoria,' he said to the man.

'Goodbye, goodbye for ever, Angus!' I shrieked out of the window.

He raised his hand in a noble, archaic gesture; and I could see no more.

While the taxi sped along, I began to think that nothing would happen; and I was sorry that all calamities were to be avoided. I had the sense of being cheated, which is anticlimax.

Then the guns began to go off. Livid flashes jigged about and fell over the whole city, like scarecrow fingers.

'Don't be afraid, don't be afraid,' the taxi-man said, sliding back the partition window. 'You're with the only VC taxi-driver in London. He'll see you through anything.'

We dodged a street lamp, slithered round a corner on the pavement, and soon came to rest in the great well of Victoria Station.

It was dead; no lights, no noise, no trains. The hollow was filled with doom. I could not bear its silence.

'Don't stay here!' I shouted. 'It's no good. Drive me to Notting Hill Gate, please.'

I had decided to take refuge with Grace and Randal, since I could not get back to the country.

'Don't be afraid, don't be afraid,' the taxi-man chanted automatically. I had realized by now that he also was drunk. 'You're with the only VC taxi-driver in London. He'll see you through anything.'

I sat close to the window, and as the guns flashed I talked and said mad things, asking extraordinary questions.

'Where did you get the VC? I don't believe a word of it. Are you married? Are you faithful? I can't bear long noses, can you?'

My merriment was mounting almost to delirium, trying to make an armour against the bombs about to fall.

'Don't, don't have an accident,' I implored him as we swirled and scudded along. 'Awful to die in an accident when an air-raid's going on.'

I paid him at the door of the block of flats and he said again, 'You were safe with the only VC taxi-driver, weren't you?'

Affectionately we shook hands and waved; then I entered the building. The passages were littered with people who had come from their private holes to sit on the floor against the inner walls, away from all glass. Some were reading or playing cards while others talked comfortably in little groups. There was an atmosphere almost of gaiety. Propped up with many cushions were fantastic old ladies, their hair arranged in the 'King Charles's Spaniel' or 'Matriarchal Sheep' manner. One was sucking scented cachous and making curious hollow clicks with her teeth.

No one sat outside Grace's and Randal's door. For one unpleasant moment I thought that they were out; then I heard voices; so I knocked loudly with the head of my stick. Grace's head appeared.

'You!' she called out in surprise. 'I've come as a refugee,' I faltered. She took the situation in in a moment. 'Darling, you're drunk,' she said. 'Come in at once and be soothed and sobered.'

It was wonderful to be with friends again. I felt safe – even safer than with the VC taxi-driver.

I did not notice at once that someone else was lying on the divan. 'That's Michael,' Grace explained. 'He's taken refuge as well.'

Michael looked at me with extreme suspicion, and I remembered that he was Grace's mad friend who had just been let out of a home.

'Loonies within and Nazis without,' I said to myself and immediately hated the idiotic words.

I began to talk incoherently and joyfully. I still felt that I was going to be killed.

I cannot remember how it came about, but soon the conversation turned to schools. We may have been discussing something I was trying to write. Michael, who had been silent all this while, broke in now, in a deep, resonant, mocking voice, with these words, 'Porta Vacat Culpa.'

I swung round to him.

'How did you know that motto?' I asked almost sharply.

'Wasn't I there for four years?' he asked, with a long-suffering, patient smile, as if to show that the experience had indeed been an ordeal.

I saw Grace's face lighten with a smile. She felt relieved. She knew now that Michael would accept me. He was only nervous of complete strangers.

As we were still talking about this discovered link, the first bomb dropped. The swish, swish, suckling, eating, tearing noise made us jump to our feet, as if to fight some human enemy; then we ran into the little lobby away from the glass of the windows. The thud came and the huge steel-framed building gave the slightest, tenderest shudder in answer to it.

'Does it always do that?' I asked.

'When it's near,' Grace answered flatly.

I was sober and chastened now, but with something else thrilling through me.

We shut ourselves up in the tiny box of the lobby, for bombs began to fall one after the other. At one moment, when the swooping scream was loudest, Grace uttered the clear, round words, 'I am terrified.' They had no colour, which made them very real.

'Don't be silly,' Randal said in his thin, Chinese philosopher's voice.

Michael was still discussing and remembering all sorts of school happenings: cheatings, beatings, secret meetings; runs, walks, games; masters, maids and romantic friendships.

I fed his flame and enjoyed the fire too. The night wore on; my drunkenness wore off. The others spoke of it almost as a past thing.

'D. drunk is almost Byzantine,' Grace said. And I saw the phrase as something in a copybook, to be laboriously traced by endless generations of children.

'Let's go on to the roof,' Randal suggested. Grace and Michael did not want to go, so he took me up alone.

We stood by the parapet, eight storeys above the ground, looking down on to the spire of a church. The cone at the top of the spire had been sliced off in an earlier raid, leaving a tiny platform.

The wind blew over the black city where wounds of fire were spreading and tearing contagiously. In the lulls of silence one could hear the crackling, lustful flames eating, eating – never satisfied.

'When the palace was hit,' Randal said, pointing to Kensington, 'the air was filled with a delicious smell of old wood burning.'

'That was only your imagination,' I thought, but said nothing.

Far off I heard the bells of fire-engines and ambulances. I saw pictures of bells, ringing at Mass, when every head but mine was bowed – of bells on the ragged points of a jester's cap, remembered from some children's party – of the silver-gilt bells on a coral rattle which had been bitten and sucked by many babies.

'Whizz, whizz through the streets. Get there, get there, get there!' I shouted, then felt very foolish.

I tried to imagine what it would be like down in those black, empty streets. I wanted to go down, to wander about, to see the sights, the stillness and the fear, the blackness of the corners.

'Don't be ridiculous,' Randal said coldly; 'you know you'd be terrified out of your wits.'

We left the roof and went down to the flat again. Grace had asked Michael to blow up the 'lie-low'. We arrived while he was still puffing out his crimson cheeks. When it was inflated he took it into the bathroom and lay down with his head under the fat, swelling pan. The rest of us lay in heaps on the divan and in the armchair.

Fewer bombs fell. The barks from the guns began to be more isolated. The tired, frightened city seemed to be gradually contracting after its climax. I lay quite still, waiting to be swept away on a wave of sleep.

It was late when we woke. Out of kindness and squeamishness we did not look at one another carefully, but smiled and were happy, stressing, exaggerating with words the awful night.

'Isn't it wonderful, the morning, the sun, the blue sky, breakfast, everything?' we sang.

I toasted the bread. Michael laid the tea-trolley with mad precision – each fork and knife and spoon harshly regimented.

We sat down and ate. How delightful it was to feel dirty and squalid and to be accepted like that. Nothing mattered but our liking for one another and our pleasure in life.

Grace went about with streaming hair, looking like Picasso's *La Soupe*; then she pinned it up into a careless bird's-nest, which would have made even the most slovenly rook ashamed.

We left the washing-up – all the sordid remains. We threw them down and streamed into the park and the sun.

At first we could not understand it; a sort of huge snow had fallen. Enormous flakes lay everywhere. Then we saw that it was paper, burnt and charred all round the edges. The giant confetti was caught in the trees, floating on the water, carpeting the ground.

I picked up a sheet which had been licked by the flames into the shape of a landscape gardener's lake. Strangely enough, it bore the picture of a fire. In the black wood-cut an antique fire-engine raced gloriously, with plunging horses, while a gendarme pointed the way flamboyantly.

'Look, look at this strange fluke,' I said to the others.

'Keep it for ever and ever as a souvenir,' Michael advised solemnly.

'No wonder those fires burned so brightly. They were paper-mills,' mused Grace.

Here and there we saw new bomb-holes between the ancient trees. Green, torn leaves and branches lay on the ground, looking wounded and human.

'I like your silver-knobbed stick,' Michael said crazily, turning to me. 'I never dare do things like that.'

I had never thought of my stick as particularly daring, but now I was self-conscious. We talked of all the vanities of life, of lovely clothes and food and precious stones. I was feeling hollow inside, with drumming head and sick taste in my mouth, but everything seemed new, saved, relished again after years of deprivation. The dancing boats on the water – the absurd and naughty toilets of the water-birds – our own unshaven squalor – the mad talk of philosophy – how delightful they all were.

Michael was planning the post-war world.

'Anarchism's the only thing!' he shrieked ecstatically. 'Anarchism! Anarchism!' he shouted, as we all linked arms and started to run over the grass.

ROGER LAY
ON THE CLIFF

Denton Welch ('Roger') published his first novel, Maiden Voyage, *in 1943.*

ROGER LAY ON THE CLIFF, THE HOT SUN BEATING THROUGH his shirt on to his back. He did not want to move, only to lie, his face pressed to the earth, his hands clutching the tufts of grass. The sea birds screamed and there was that queer rustle that the tide makes as it drags the shingle.

After some time he sat up resolutely, composed his face and slowly pulled his shirt over his head; the sun stung his shoulders comfortingly and lit up the gold hairs on his chest. He lay down again on his back and shut his eyes.

'This cannot last,' he thought. 'It's too strong to last. What does it matter if my first book is ignored and if those dreadful people laugh at it? It's only a beginning.' He said this over and over to himself, until he was half dazed with the words.

'I must not go back to the house until I'm calm,' he thought. 'Then I can face them. They are nothing, nothing, nothing.'

It is seldom wise to go and stay with people who have known you as a child. They are so often out of sympathy with one, especially if you have aspirations which they do not share. They are bent on belittling. Roger knew all this when he accepted the Ropers' invitation, but he went; he wanted sun and sea and he longed to know what other people thought of his book.

He lived so alone, it was sometimes nice to enter someone else's family.

He arrived on the Friday afternoon in the little red Austin, and

Mrs Roper, seeing him through the windows, came out to meet him, holding out her hands. Then they had tea. There was honey...

CONSTANCE, LADY WILLET

'Constance, Lady Willet' is a portrait of Mrs Streeten, mother of Francis Streeten ('Mark' in this story), who had indeed been to prison for refusing war work. Both were alcoholics.

CONSTANCE, LADY WILLET LOOKED AT HERSELF IN THE glass and put a little more powder on her already rather thickly coated nose. She consciously over-powdered in this way so that the effect should last for several hours. She thought of herself as a handsome woman, and she was. Thick neck, broad cheek-bones, widely set-apart brown eyes, which were only ever so slightly discoloured, and pretty reddened sullen mouth all made up a pleasing whole. She thought once more that she was really wonderfully preserved for sixty-three.

She put the puff back into the box with the Reynolds' Angel Faces on the oxidized silver lid, and then pulled her gloves on. As she looked down at her half-hoop of diamonds and her wedding ring, she thought of her husband. He had only been dead a few months. Poor Harold; he hadn't had a very happy life. She'd been a disappointment and their son Mark had been a disappointment and then business had done badly and he'd lost a lot of money, and on top of everything else to die so painfully!

Constance left her bedroom and went down the breakneck cottage stairs which opened straight into the long low sitting-room. Mark was sitting by the fire reading *Fourteen: The Diary of a Schoolboy*. He had found it on one of the shelves of the rented cottage. He looked up at his mother and then turned his face away rather furtively. He had only lately come out of prison, where he had been sent for refusing to do his non-combatant duty.

He was afraid of his mother because her attitude changed almost hourly from loving understanding to the most jingo patriotism and then back again. Having no money, his allowance having stopped at his father's death, he was forced to live with his mother. He knew that she wished to be rid of him, that she did not like his large, rather dirty presence continually about the place. She was always telling him to go to the Labour Exchange and get a job on the land; to make an appointment with the dentist; to eat less greedily; not to scatter ash on the carpet. He was nearly forty and very unhappy and worried. His wife had left him long ago.

'Are you going into Tunbridge Wells?' he asked, with an attempt at brightness.

'Yes,' said Constance, 'I've got some very necessary shopping to do. Now remember, darling,' she added firmly, 'you're to be out of the house for the whole day, as I've told Mrs Cousins to clean it from attic to cellar. I shall be extremely annoyed if you hinder her in any way. You're not to come back till I return this evening.'

Mark nodded his head, and then asked rather hurriedly for a little money so that he could buy some cigarettes and have his lunch at the Green Man across the common. His mother felt in her purse, then drew out two half-crowns and handed them to him importantly.

'Darling, do try to spend less,' she said; 'you realize, I suppose, that we're as poor as church mice now. Or perhaps you don't. As you've never done a stroke of work all your life, I suppose you still have no idea of the value of money. You've certainly romped through your own as if it were water.'

Constance stopped talking, wondering if this last metaphor were quite all it should be. Mark muttered something meek and conciliating, whereupon his mother broke out again, 'I think you're much too submissive. I wish you wouldn't always agree with me, it's so dull!'

Mark was about to frame a reply, but his mother swept out of the room with a perceptible swish, calling out, 'Now remember!'

Constance patted her soft, wool dress and straightened the charming little bunch of different-coloured wallflowers which she had pinned to her bosom. The diamond chips glinted in the brooch which had belonged to her mother. It was made in the form of her father's regimental badge. She began to walk down the village street to the bus stop. Sunlight pierced through the heavy trees and dappled the warm-coloured roofs. Constance felt happy with her shiny American-cloth shopping bag on her arm.

The bus was rather crowded, but she found a place and sat contentedly looking out of the window.

Poor darling Mark, she thought, no money, no sense, no stamina. Only a silly Edwardian baronetcy and the weakest of literary urges. Those teeth, his growing stomach and his disappearing hair! What *was* to be done? She simply couldn't have him about the place for ever, and yet if she gave him a tiny allowance and told him to go away, he would get so very much worse, and she would feel horribly pinched. For the hundredth time she added up her various sources of income and saw that the total came to no more than £325 a year. In spite of her own and Mark's extravagance, she blamed poor Harold for not managing better in some way before he died.

But Constance was clever at putting unpleasant things out of her mind, so when she alighted in Tunbridge Wells she was able to give her whole attention to the people in the streets and the objects in the shop windows. Living in the rented cottage in the tiny village had given her an excitement for the town, like that of a young girl in an eighteenth-century novel. She was content to gaze in shop windows, however meagrely stocked, and to watch the passers-by. She wondered where they came from, where they were going to. She made up stories about their journeys and destinations.

Across the road was an arts and crafts shop. Constance made straight for it and looked at all the little painted gnomes, brass door-knockers, embroidered kettle-holders and fancy window-wedges. At the back of the shop she saw the dearest tea-cosy, all made of brightly coloured felt in the shape of a brooding hen. Constance longed to waste her money on it, so she went in and asked the price.

'Ten and six, madam,' the very young girl said.

Constance thought for a moment; she had very little more than three pounds to live on till the end of the month, but she quickly brushed this thought aside and decided to have the cosy.

'Then when Mark is in late his tea will always be hot,' she assured herself comfortably.

Constance went out of the shop and wandered further up the high street. She knew that the pantiles were a snare and a delusion, that the soul of the town was no longer there. She thought it a shame that there were not delightful little luxury shops under the colonnades.

When she reached the station she decided to leave her serious shopping until after she'd had a cup of coffee and a cake at Wynn's.

'I'll feel so much fresher after that,' she thought.

She sat down at a little table and watched the chattering women all round her. She felt a little lonely. She wished she too had an amusing woman friend to laugh and gossip with. 'But then I quarrelled with all mine long ago,' she told herself stoically. She enjoyed catching snatches of conversation, some of them rather improper.

She lingered over her coffee, smoking three cigarettes, and when at last she got up to go she found that it was nearly one o'clock. All the shops would be closing for lunch. She hurried to the greengrocer and was just in time to buy a lettuce and a cooked beetroot before the door was locked.

Constance wondered what to do. She did not want to go back to the cottage without doing her shopping, yet if she stayed she would have to wait a whole hour.

'Of course in the old days I could have gone to one of the hotels and had lunch, but now I couldn't possibly afford it, especially after having bought this darling tea-cosy.' She hugged the parcel to her protectively.

She saw that the pub across the road on the corner had opened and that men were going in.

It might be rather fun to ask for bread and cheese in a place like that, she thought. She crossed over and walked slowly past the door. She caught a glimpse of the bright handles glistening and someone behind the bar, but she did not go in. She decided to walk further down the town and find a more attractive pub. She was going to enjoy her adventure. I haven't been in a pub for so long, she thought. Then she cut her memories short with a shake of her head. Something bobbed about on her hat; a part of the heavy ribbon bounced up and down. This for some reason gave her a gay irresponsible rakish feeling.

Constance passed the parish church and climbed a little way up the hill, out of the town. There she found a pub on the right-hand side of the road which satisfied her. She went in and, exercising all her charm, asked if they would give her some bread and cheese. The daughter of the house was very polite and was about to show her into a private room, when Constance suddenly said, 'No, I'll have it in the corner of the bar, if I may, it's more companionable.' She gave the girl her brightest smile.

While the girl was getting the bread and the cheese and the cucumber she had suggested herself, Constance looked round the bar. It was dark and low, but everything was clean with that humble sort of spit and polish cleanness which has no trimmings.

One *can't* enter a pub without drinking *just* a little something, Constance told herself. She thought that she would order a glass of sherry, if they still had that wine. The thought of sherry reminded her of an episode with poor Harold. She admitted that she had been naughty and difficult, but after she had pulled herself together and they had made it all up, she remembered asking Harold very sweetly if she might have some sherry before dinner.

'Of course, my dear, if you will promise me to take no more than a ladylike amount,' he had replied.

Somehow the prim words had angered her, had made her go hard inside. She had laughed metallically and said, 'Darling, what an absurd measure! What *is* a ladylike amount?'

Then she had drunk eight glasses straight off and had not appeared at dinner.

But all that was past now, she had forgotten all that unfortunate part of her life, Constance told herself. She knew now how to manage her temperament. She was peaceful.

The girl brought her bread and cheese, and Constance asked for the sherry. A glass of dark treacly liquid was placed before her. Constance put it to her lips. She smelt again the clinging alcoholic smell; she loved it and it frightened her.

This is absurd, she said, and drank the sherry down so that the image of it should not frighten her. She began to eat the bread and cheese and to cut up the cucumber. The cheese was very soapy.

Perhaps another glass of sherry will give me more appetite, she thought. She waved her empty glass gaily, and the girl came down to fill it from the bottle. Constance drank it down as she had the first, because she did not like to see it standing before her.

The bar was filling up now. Workmen, shop assistants, a few

travellers and soldiers stood about and talked in quiet undertones. Constance felt depressed by their lack of vivacity. They really are half dead, she thought. She wondered if a little whisky and soda would lighten her heavy feeling. She remembered how, in the early days of their marriage, she had liked to sip Harold's drink while they sat close together in a huge armchair in his study.

She beckoned the girl towards her and gave her new order. After that she ordered two more whiskies. They gave them to her in such tiny glasses and she could add so little soda water that they were gone in a moment.

Constance had eaten as much bread and cheese as she wanted. She decided that to make her meal complete, she must finish with a liqueur. I wonder if they have any cherry brandy, she asked herself. She went up to the bar, to look at the bottles on the racks behind. The men politely made room for her and she wedged herself in between them, feeling warm and friendly. She made some amusing remarks and the ones nearest to her turned and laughed. She opened her gold cigarette-case and offered it round. The girl behind the bar told her that they had some cherry brandy – the only liqueur they did have, as it happened.

'How lucky!' said Constance gratefully. 'It's my favourite.'

She offered the soldier on her right a glass as well. He blushed and said, 'Thank you, ma'am, I've never tasted that.'

'I'm glad then to be able to widen your experience. I always want to do everything I can for any gentleman in khaki,' replied Constance banteringly.

The soldier blushed again and held his tiny little glass of red liquid up to hers. They both drunk their thimblefuls down in one gulp and Constance immediately ordered two more. She went on ordering cherry brandies until the girl said that she must keep some in the precious bottle for other customers.

'Quite, quite,' said Constance, now sublimely sweet natured. 'I only hope we haven't had more than our fair share already.' She began to talk to the soldier about the house Harold had built for her in the first days of their marriage when rubber was doing extremely well. She told him with childish delight about the morning-room, the billiard-room, the flower-room, the grape-houses. She described the gardens vividly, the croquet lawns, the rose garden and the Japanese water garden with stepping stones and irises.

The soldier loved to listen; it was like a fairy-story to him. Constance had quite forgotten the masculinity of her audience and was now describing minutiae of her tea-gowns, the velvet-lined sleeves and amber girdles; the silver spirit-kettles, Earl Grey blend, foie gras sandwiches and anchovy toast. Then she described her pets, her Abyssinian cat Gut, and her darling white Pekinese Po who would bite everyone.

'Time gentlemen, please,' and the girl's officious collecting of all glasses broke through her stories. She lingered a moment more and then the soldier suggested that they ought to be going, the doors were about to be locked. Constance settled up her final bill and then started to walk very carefully to the door. She wished the soldier and the girl behind the bar would not watch her; of course she lurched if they made her self-conscious!

Outside the door the soldier looked at her rather anxiously, then saluted stiffly, thanked her and walked away rather too rapidly.

Constance felt horribly alone. She began to wander down the hill with black misery in her heart. She had nowhere to go and nothing to do. The girl came running after her and handed her the broody hen tea-cosy which she had forgotten. Constance thanked her and looked after her yearningly as she disappeared once more into the pub.

The wind was blowing, the sun was shining, people passed her, Army lorries hooted and dashed past dangerously. Constance's misery became so acute that she leant against some railings and began to gasp.

'You all right, mother?' someone asked insolently. She saw two other faces smile.

Constance haughtily drew herself up and continued down the hill. Walking was becoming more difficult. Unaccountable things seemed to happen, her movements were not linked together harmoniously.

Constance began to sing very gravely and softly, 'Lead Kindly Light'. The difficulty of fitting all the words into the tune always fascinated her and she also felt in her sadness very close to God.

But it was no good, the terrible black melancholy was growing on her. Outside the church, close to the traffic lights so gaily red and green and yellow, a buzzing and splintering of sparks rose to a crescendo in her head. A curtain as of some thick grey and black material fell across her eyes. Blindly she put her hand up, then leant against the old soft brickwork of King Charles the Martyr's Church and was violently sick. The stream of orange vomit gushed on to the pavement. For a moment Constance stood utterly still and rigid, her eyes turned up to heaven; then she fell, still rigid as a stick. Her body smacked smartly on the hard paving-stones, she rolled a little and lay in the gutter, close to the neat kerb.

Constance was not unconscious for long, but when she came to, a young policeman was bending over her. She hated at once his self-important expression, his stupid eyes, his brutal mouth.

'What's your name?' he said harshly.

'Constance,' she answered weakly.

The young policeman and a few loiterers tittered.

'Surname and address,' the policeman insisted implacably.

Constance tried to clear her mind.

'Oh Harold, Harold darling, thank goodness you're not here,' she thought. Then she spoke in quite an untrembling voice.

'Willet is the name. Lady Willet, Garden Cottage, Langfield.'

There was a slight stir of excitement in the small crowd. The policeman was still unbelieving.

'What did you say – *Lady* Willet?'

He seemed unwilling to write down anything so palpably untrue in his little book.

Constance nodded her head curtly and tried to sit up; she still felt horribly sick and faint, but she was not going to show it to this reptile and these loiterers. She made as if to get up. The policeman said, ''Ere be careful!' but supported her in his arms.

'Send all these idlers away, Constable,' Constance said grandly; then she nearly fell down again.

The policeman began to feel rather harassed.

'Move along there, haven't you got anything to do?' he asked the crowd. They fell back a little.

Then very slowly he manœuvred Constance across the road and on to the common. He walked her up and down there for some time. Gradually she became clearer and steadier.

THE DIAMOND BADGE

When Denton Welch was thirty-one he became friendly with an admirer named Peggy Kirkaldy who features in this story as 'Susan Innes'. 'Andrew Clifton' is Denton Welch himself and 'Tom Parkinson' is his lover, Eric Oliver. The first part of the story was published under the title 'The Visit' in The Penguin New Writing *(No. 38, 1949) and the full version was first published in* A Last Sheaf.

I

WHEN I'D COME TO THE LAST WORD ON THE LAST PAGE, I felt I had to write to him at once. There seemed an urgency about the business which I did not stop to question. I sat down at my little desk in the window and there, surrounded with leaves and the sound of the birds in the garden, began my foolish letter. I say foolish, because even as I wrote, I knew I was extravagant, strained, curiously false in the words I chose to express my gratitude and enthusiasm.

What would an author think at receiving such a letter from an unknown woman? It was quite clear to me that he would probably be contemptuously amused, a little exasperated; but there would be some pleasure in receiving such tribute, and who was I to guard my dignity and deny him the only repayment I could make? I licked the envelope, pressed it down and went out to the letter-box before I could change my mind.

As I walked back down the lane, through the evening air, I felt released, as though I had got rid of something, drink or waste food, that was burdening my body. It seemed the most wonderful thing in the world to give out all the time, things that were not wanted, expressions that no one would bother to understand, smiles they could not see, and songs they'd never hear. I went into my little kitchen and started to heat some coffee and boil an egg for my supper.

The answer came in five days' time. If he were to write at all, I had been prepared to wait, since the publisher would have first to forward my own letter. Then there might be other delays. He might be travelling or living abroad. This promptness therefore both delighted and nonplussed me. I had to steel myself for a meeting earlier than I had imagined it to myself; but I had asked for it; and now he invited me to tea on the Friday, only three days away. I began rather agitatedly to plan what I should wear. Going up to my room, I opened the cupboard doors and looked at all my clothes, hanging patiently, like so many squashed flat criminals. They were nice clothes, but I had grown a little too used to them. In the end I decided on a trim coat and skirt, a little severe for me, but becoming. With this I should wear a stiff, frilly white shirt with my one and only valuable brooch, my father's regimental badge in tiny diamonds. I was aware of the rather painful gentility of such a choice. I did not really wish to present myself as nothing but a dreary English gentlewoman, but the memory of my letter returned to disquiet me. I was determined to underline the sobriety in my character in an attempt to neutralize some of the letter's excessiveness.

He wrote from a village some thirty miles away in the next county, but the journey did not sound difficult. He gave me the name of the station, the time of the train and said that his friend, Tom Parkinson, would be there to meet me in the car. Somehow all this care and solicitude struck a slight chill into me. I felt that he must often have arranged for strangers to visit him. It was as if he made a business of never denying himself to anyone, because he so despised the pomposity of ambitious little people who tried to add to their importance by a lack of all response. Then the thought came to comfort me that he might still be genuinely pleased to see people who had enjoyed his book; for, although it had been out for a year or more, it was his first book and he could not yet be so very celebrated. I had never heard his name mentioned, only read it in one or two reviews.

Tom Parkinson was there to meet me. I knew him by his searching, rather anxious eyes. They were not the eyes of a man about to welcome wife, sweetheart or friend; they were too guarded, too ready to save the stranger from embarrassment. I liked at once his beaky nose, his tallness which was yet not overwhelming, the bank of dingy fairish hair flopping over his forehead. The sleeves of his open-neck shirt were rolled up and his beltless trousers seemed to hang on his hips rather precariously; they were slack round his ankles as if they dragged on the ground behind. I knew just what the hems would be like at his heels – caked with mud and beginning to fray.

When we shook hands, I saw that he had tiny red veins under the tight brown skin on the sides of his arched nose; they were not in the least unpleasing, and the nondescript colour of his eyes soothed me. I guessed that we were almost exactly of an age, but I hoped, rather pointlessly, that he was the elder by a year or so.

He took me out to the dilapidated Morris and we started to climb the hill into the town. It was a squalid little country place, only called into being, I should imagine, by the building of the station in the middle of the last century. The one or two older buildings looked as if they had once been solitary farm-houses.

Soon we were out of the one main street and climbing another hill through frothy orchards and bare hop gardens. The contrast between excess of blossom, thick and heavy as curdled milk, and the naked poles linked to each other by lines of tingling wire, sent some sharp feeling through me. It was as if a Rubens woman, rich in the glow of her fatness and beauty, were stripped the next moment of all her flesh, so that one had nothing but the gaunt skeleton, almost heard the little bones of hand and foot tinkling.

We came at last to a narrow lane down which Tom Parkinson turned the car. It was hardly more than a track and we bounced in our seats as the wheels mounted the ruts or sank into them again. I tried to prepare my face, to wash self-consciousness and stain right out of it. I longed to look in my mirror, but somehow, with Tom Parkinson so close beside me, the gesture seemed too calculating, too businesslike. Might not his straightforward nature jump to the conclusion that my titivating was due entirely to an imbecile wish to fascinate his friend in the first moment of our meeting? I contented myself by opening my bag and fiddling about until I had the mirror out of its pocket and could just see my nose and lips shining up from the dark interior. I bent my head a little and saw my eyes. They did not reassure me. They looked steady and hard and fierce, as frightened eyes are apt to do. I simpered at myself, then smiled genuinely to remember my mother doing this when I was a child. I had thought her so utterly ridiculous.

We were slowing down. I looked up to see a converted stone farm-building over the hedge on the right. The part which had once housed carts and rakes was now glazed in. The three great windows with their thick white bars gave the place an attractive air of comfort, even of luxury. There were no ugly creosoted beams, no leaded casements or quaint 'lanthorns' on either side of the door, just the white paint and the rough silvery stone walls. At one end the building rose to two storeys. I guessed this must once have been the stable and loft. The long loft door, with a little projecting roof over it and the wheel for a pulley, was now also glazed.

Tom took me in and I saw how bare the large ground-floor room was. It was not as I would have had it at all, but I felt soothed. On the tiled floor was thick satiny rush matting in a pattern of squares bound together. The walls seemed to be the natural oatmeal colour of undistempered plaster. Over the mantelpiece was a rich still-life of glowing fruit, peonies, dahlias, sunflowers and enormous shells; indeed, everything was larger than in life. The heavy impasto was a little distasteful to me, and I found myself repeating the old phrase 'excrement on canvas'.

The puritan room was really rather a bore, but I found myself dwelling on it and almost appreciating it because it was so unalarming; and to be calmed at that moment was all that I craved for. Tom let me look about, not hurrying me in the least; then he called up the stairs, 'Andrew, we've arrived.'

I heard an answering call, deep, rather musical, a little too social, as if the whole situation were 'tremendous fun'. In spite of this slight false note, I was attracted to the voice; I knew that it was trying to make me feel at ease.

We climbed the polished oak stairs. Once I looked down on the long sober room. From this unusual viewpoint the large chairs, with their red and white striped cushions and their loose covers of rough linen, looked extraordinarily inviting. I had the childish longing to jump over the banisters and land in the middle of the broad sofa.

Tom opened the door on the narrow landing and said, 'Here we are.'

I followed him in and felt myself holding out my hand dazedly to the little person on the bed. He was terribly deformed, his hands all twisted and his body seemingly telescoped into itself, so that he was broad but perhaps only three feet tall. He had a smooth oval face with rather delicate features. His hair was red and a little silky fringe ran right round to his jaw line, framing his face and making him look like a particularly well-groomed ill-disposed monkey. He wore no moustache, so I could watch his pink lips clearly. He licked them as his eyes lit up and he said, 'I'm not *in* bed, only *on* it; I like best to loll here in my room. Don't you like to be a little up in the air? How right they were when they made all town houses with their drawing-rooms on the first floor!'

I said, 'Yes, it's nicer to be off the ground, to be able to look out a little farther.'

Tom had brought a chair up for me and I sat down, placing my bag beside me, refusing to clutch it as I wished to do.

All this time Andrew – already I named him this in my mind – was watching me with his small bright eyes. They seemed to be brimming with expectation. I think he was waiting for me to betray some sign of horror, or pity for his condition; then, I felt the eyes would have bubbled over and he would have gloated. I wanted him to get no satisfaction from me. I wanted this to be the most prosaic tea-party that had ever taken place. Already I angrily regretted giving in to impulse and writing that letter. I resented not being warned before I broke my way into this different world where nobody wanted me in particular. Why had I not been told of Andrew's condition? I found myself childishly blaming some mysterious, unknown being who should have told me everything beforehand.

Tom reappeared with the tea-tray and I felt easier. There were some very good rock cakes which he had made himself. As I ate and drank and talked, I was able to look about me in little snatches. Andrew's room was more gargoyly and frilly than the downstairs room. There was more to offend, surprise and interest. A great pile of exercise books and typescripts balanced, seemingly in absolute confusion, on a table near his bed. There was thick dust on some of them; it was clear that he would not have them touched.

Andrew did most of the talking, shooting out questions, telling gay little anecdotes, laughing, and swivelling those bubbling eyes of his. Tom sometimes murmured a word or smiled his lazy, rather private smile, which had something very slightly irritating about it. I suppose it kept one out. He seemed determined to enjoy his joke alone.

Andrew never mentioned books, and when I felt I ought to say something about this one which had so impressed me, he scowled, turned away and said, 'Let's not talk about anything so embarrassing.'

The evening wore on, and still I made no move to go. I seemed to be fascinated, held in a house where there was no place for me. It was almost as if I were waiting for something to happen. A smell of cooking rose up the stairs, and instead of getting to my feet to say goodbye, I asked Andrew if I might go down to the kitchen to help Tom. He said, 'Oh, do. He'd love that.'

Then almost before I was out of the room, I caught a glimpse of him turning the pages of a book of old engravings of the Seats of the Nobility and Gentry! My eyes had caught the title as I sat drinking my tea, and I too had wanted to look inside.

I knocked tentatively on the kitchen door. Tom came to it frowning a little, holding a frying-pan which was still sizzling from the electric hot-plate.

'Can I help?' I asked, looking up at him anxiously. I wanted to be doing something to prove my usefulness, to clear away the impression that I was one of those people who stayed too long. I still don't know why I didn't leave politely at just the right moment after tea.

'Well, the kitchen is awfully small for two,' Tom was saying rather pointedly. It was clear that he wanted me out of the way. 'But if you'd like to lay the tray for three in that corner near the larder door, I think we won't be too much in each other's way.'

'I say, is it all right my staying to supper?' I asked in a rush.

'Oh, of course; we were expecting you to.'

Tom turned back to his frying and I set about laying the tray without more ado. I knew how irritating it was to be asked continually where things were kept, so I did my best without talking to Tom, searching in cupboards, pulling out plates and forks and knives until I had what we should need. I saw that we were to have fried fish and potatoes and some early lettuces. There didn't seem to be any fish knives and forks, so I put ordinary ones; then started to make a French dressing.

'I won't put it over the lettuce in case either of you don't like it,' I said.

'Oh, but we both do,' replied Tom rather absently, his mind still on the perfect browning of the potatoes.

I shredded the lettuce with my hands, tearing each leaf into small bits, then I poured on the dressing and tossed the fragments about till they were all covered and glistening slightly from the oil.

'I don't bother to do it nearly as well as that,' said Tom, looking down at the bowl approvingly. I felt glad and hoped that he would stop classing me as just another nuisance to be borne good naturedly.

'If you don't have to be back tonight, why not sleep here?' he said suddenly. 'It would save me having to take the car out in the dark; the lights are rotten.'

'But I haven't got pyjamas or a toothbrush or anything,' I said, quite taken aback; 'besides, what about Mr Clifton?'

'Andrew? Oh, he wouldn't mind; it's no trouble to him. All we've got to do is to make up the bed.'

Matters were left like this, till we climbed up to Andrew's room, Tom carrying the heavy tray of fish, potatoes and salad, I following with the coffee which was still dripping through the percolator.

When we had both sat down near Andrew's bed, with the trays on stools before us, Tom suddenly said, 'Oh, Susan Innes is staying the night; it's much easier than getting the car out with those hopeless lights, and she hasn't got to be back for anything. I'm letting her have my new toothbrush; it's still all done up in cellophane.'

Andrew turned to me with a metallic smile and said, 'That's fine; we won't have to hurry at all then over the meal.'

'But is it all right?' I asked miserably. 'What must you think of me coming to tea and then staying the night?'

'It will be nice,' Andrew said in his smooth bland way. 'We so seldom have anyone to use our spare room.'

All through supper I felt strained. Andrew's gaiety was brittle. His amusing maliciousness made me uneasy. What would he do with me when I had gone? He would tear me into little pieces, as I had torn the lettuce. I began to wish I had left hours ago. It is terrible to be with people who are intelligent and can understand, yet who cut themselves off with a high wall of indifference. It is far better to be with crude people who do not realize half the time what they are saying or doing. One is not so lonely or so lost.

The lack of contact between me and Andrew, even between me and Tom, made me long all the time to be doing something for them, so that at least they would look back on me as a help in a practical way, a sort of temporary housekeeper who knew her business, even if she were good for nothing more.

'What can I do?' I asked as soon as supper was over. 'Can't I do some mending? I should like that; it soothes me.'

'Do you need soothing?' Andrew asked with his bright unwarm smile.

'Don't we all?' I shot out, rather too fiercely. 'But seriously, I saw an enormous hole in the heel of Tom's sock – I may call you Tom, I hope? If you have any more like that, they ought to be done at once.'

Would they mistake my longing to be doing something for a cloying motherliness? Would they think it coy to use Tom's name, then to ask for permission? Perhaps the worst transgression in their eyes would be that I had had the impertinence to mention the hole in Tom's sock. I didn't care, I was past caring. I felt that I had floundered from the beginning and might just as well go on floundering. I was on the brink of that strange desperate wish to throw all defences down and appear utterly ridiculous in the eyes of the enemy.

'That's very good of you,' Tom was saying gravely. 'I have some socks that need doing, but there's not much wool. Will you mind using all the wrong colours?'

'Of course not,' I said, 'if you don't mind wearing the peculiar darns.'

He brought me some newly washed socks and some skeins of

what looked like embroidery wool. There was a brilliant magenta colour and some salmon pink. I started to work at once. The huge egg-shaped holes gaped at me, but I soon had some of them neatly criss-crossed with the bright wool. The darns looked strangely theatrical; they reminded me of the artistic patches on the Pied Piper's cloak, or on the breeches of a stage pedlar.

We spoke little as I worked. Andrew looked at his book of engravings and Tom puffed and sucked at his pipe. I hated the juicy bubbling it sometimes made. Gradually the light faded in the room until at last I had to put down my needle. Andrew's book lay on his chest. He seemed to be staring up at the ceiling, or were his eyes shut? I wondered how it was that I could seem so domestic and settled with them and yet be so completely cut off.

'Would you like the light?' Tom asked thoughtfully, seeing me put down the sock and lean back.

'No, I'm sure you're tired of those old socks,' broke in Andrew; 'don't do any more. Let's just sit in the gloaming, or dusk, or whatever other cosy name you wish to give it.'

We sat in silence. I could just discern the little dumpy figure of Andrew on the bed. Somehow his richly striped dressing-gown, turned now to black and pale grey, made me think of a squat cold-cream jar, or a fat tube of toothpaste with the used part neatly rolled up. I pondered on his terrible deformity, guessing that he must have been born in that condition. I remembered the girl at school, so quick at lessons, so respected by all the other children, who had been born with just such a deformity – the normal-looking head, the twisted hands, the rigid little legs and thick body. Without realizing it at once, I began to endow Andrew with the qualities we all had given her. He was the brilliant person – 'brilliant' has a special, almost magical meaning for children and simple-minded people. He was wonderfully brave, fighting all the time, refusing to be beaten by his handicap. He had a loving nature and never complained. I even remembered to tell myself that his body did not matter; it was not the *real* person. The real person one day would be freed from his shackles.

It was some moment before I realized that all these blindly held beliefs about my schoolfellow hardly fitted Andrew at all. They were all lies or deceitful half-truths. He was not 'brilliant', his book was mercifully free from that quality, and his conversation, though animated and amusing, was on a level with the conversation of a hundred other people I had known. It was almost as if he refused to give the best of himself; he needed that for a more serious purpose. Perhaps he was brave in the way that we all are forced to be brave when faced with something inevitable. But I could not believe that he had a loving nature, or that he never complained. If his attitude to me as a stranger was any guide, he was certainly not very attached to his fellow-beings. His affability was only on the surface; and I was sure that Tom often had to listen to long diatribes against people and circumstances.

The last and greatest lie was that his body did not matter. Of course it mattered, terribly, horribly. It was the thing that mattered most when one first met him, and, although I knew it would matter less as one came to know him more, indeed was already not quite so important to me, it would always be there to jolt one at unexpected moments, to keep him as a person apart, a special case.

I saw his head turned towards me now in the darkness. He seemed to be thinking about me for the first time since we'd met. I moved a little uneasily in my chair, making the wooden joints creak.

'I'm afraid you must find it dreadfully dull here,' he said at last.

I answered in the same vein of conventional politeness.

'It's not dull at all, it's very good of you to have me. I feel rather guilty about staying the night when I really only came to tea.'

Tom quietly got up from his chair and went out of the room, carrying one of the trays. I felt that I had been left to talk to Andrew alone. I was not grateful to Tom for his tact.

'It is rather wicked to play such a trick on you, to let you come here without any warning. Things must be so utterly different from what you expected.' Andrew spoke suddenly with a curious mixture of taunting and solicitude in his voice. I was completely nonplussed and could only repeat myself.

'It was very good of you to have me.' Then on a lower note I murmured, 'I see no trick. I asked myself.'

'Yes, but what did you expect to find?'

'What do you mean?' I asked repressively, because I knew only too well. I have seldom been so grateful for darkness. He could see no expression. The red mounting to my cheeks was hidden from him. Only my voice could betray me. My determination to control it made every muscle tighten.

'Oh, I see; you won't play the truth game,' he said amusingly. 'Perhaps it's just as well. It's stimulating, but it's also rather painful. The trouble is one remembers for too long afterwards.'

'I can't play any game, for I'm utterly at sea. I don't know why I wrote to you, or why I came, or why I'm staying the night when I was only asked to tea.'

Andrew seemed to consider my outburst for a moment or two; then in very gentle, almost a tender voice, he said, 'Isn't it strange, I can't think why either.'

For an instant the rebuff hung in the air. It was an outrageous little sentence that had nothing to do with me; but when it flashed down to pierce me, I was so startled that I jumped to my feet.

'I'd better go, I can't stay here,' I said. Rushes of mortification seemed to sweep over my words even as I spoke.

'Oh, please don't misunderstand me,' Andrew implored. 'I simply meant that it is often impossible to understand the reason for one's own actions. How much more impossible to interpret the reasons of others.'

Is that what he had meant? Or was it a skilful side-stepping? Had my whole attitude during the visit been one of wrongheaded suspicion? Had I read far too much into harmless words and looks? I was too confused to think anything out. I only wanted to be alone. Without saying anything more I moved towards the landing. Andrew was too careful to say goodnight, in case I should be coming back. The slippery stairs and the cool, polished rail were soothing to me. I felt the uninhibited quality of the living-room rising up to bathe me round with its peace. There was a light from the kitchen. Tom was there filling a hot-water bottle.

'I've just thrown your bed together. This is to put in it, although I think it's pretty well aired already.'

He held the bottle out to me and I took it gratefully. It seemed a symbol of his thoughtfulness.

'Thank you *so* much,' I said with too much feeling; but he did not look uncomfortable. He led me across the living-room and opened another door. I was in a little room of sprigged chintz and scrubbed oak furniture: very much the spare room, or the bedroom in some tasteful country hotel. The naked wood seemed to be declaiming, 'I'm honest – no tricks about me. I haven't even any wax on me.'

'Do you think you've got everything you want?' Tom asked. 'The bathroom's just next door. I've put the new toothbrush out.'

I thanked him again for doing so much for me and he said, 'Oh, that's nothing,' then added something silly like 'Don't let the fleas bite.'

After coming back from the bathroom, I half undressed, then snuggled into the warm bed. The moon was up in the sky, surprising me with its face, for I had noticed nothing as I sat in the dark with Andrew. Its discouraging light seeped into the floor in a hard unfeeling square. Even as I gazed at it, fascinated by its unearthly, dusty chill, I heard the nightingales quite near the house. Their song, so overlaid, so caked with human imaginings, struck me tonight quite differently. I could not read unending heartache or sad sweet unreasoning joy into it. They appeared to me as watchmen, paid to guard the house, who sang and warbled mechanically to show that they kept awake. This curious conception of them grew into a conviction. It was then that I must have fallen asleep.

I awoke to find Tom bending over me. My heart was beating very fast and through mists of half-consciousness I tried to remember what had terrified me. I was still frightened. Little cries which I did not utter kept rising in my throat, then sinking back, as if to lie in wait until my control should weaken. Tom's beaky nose was near, half a threat and half a reassurance. He loomed over me like a small thunder cloud, or a grizzly bear, all furry at the edges.

'Are you all right now? Are you awake?' he asked gently. 'You were calling out. I expect you had a nightmare.'

'Was I making an awful noise?' I asked excitedly. 'I can't think what I was dreaming of. I hardly ever call out in my sleep.'

A sudden wave of shame swept over me. This final scene was all that was needed to damn me in their eyes for ever. I saw Andrew in the future turning to Tom and saying, 'Don't you remember that ridiculous woman who began screaming in the middle of the night?'

But Tom was still looking at me anxiously.

'I came in,' he explained, 'because I thought something might have got through the window and frightened you. The trouble about sleeping on the ground floor is that cats do sometimes jump in, and hedgehogs and dogs make strange noises just outside.'

In my alarm I had sat bolt upright in bed. Now I was shivering. I clutched my bare arms and shoulders, both for warmth and to hide my half-dressed state from Tom. Without seeming to notice anything, Tom pulled up the eiderdown and settled it round my shoulders. He did not immediately remove his arms, so that they hung round me as if he had forgotten about them. Heavy and comforting, they were the arms of a sleeping friend. I was incongruously reminded of the 'Babes in the Wood'. It seemed probable that the nightingales might soon all hop into the room, carrying leaves in their beaks to make a blanket over us. In our hanging together there was a drowsy cessation of strain, a loosening of bonds. I could feel the relief of tears dammed up behind my eyes. I waited for them unconcernedly.

It was then that I heard the slight noise outside the door. There was a delicate knock, then Andrew's voice, much lighter and more fairy-like, almost whispered, 'May I come in?'

Without waiting for an answer he turned the door-handle and stood in the square of moonlight. Seen in that aluminium deadness, with the dark stripes of his dressing-gown turned into velvety sooty eels, he made one think at once of a dwarf at the Court of Spain painted by Velasquez. He had that everlasting, unmoving, expressionless quality. He watched and listened. The skirts of his dressing-gown stirred very, very slightly. This made him appear more monumental than ever.

I was pleased that Tom did not immediately remove his arms from me. It would have been such a mean and paltry gesture. In his sleepiness he gradually let them slip, then turned his head and exclaimed, 'Oh, hullo, Andrew. Susan's been having nightmares.'

'I heard her cry out and wondered if anything was wrong,' Andrew said, still standing quite still.

Tom began slapping his flanks and feeling in his pyjama-jacket pocket. It was a sort of dumb show to express his need of a cigarette. I told him to look in my bag on the table. I guessed the cigarette would be slightly scented from my powder and I knew he would not like this; but I took a sort of perverse pleasure in thinking that with each puff he would be not very favourably reminded of me.

'And *I've* got some sweets in *my* pocket,' Andrew said suddenly. He was like a child vying with his schoolfellows. He came towards my bed holding out the paper bag. I took a sort of butterscotch toffee and started to crunch it appreciatively. Meanwhile Andrew was making efforts to scramble on to the end of my bed. I knew he would hate to be helped, so I let him pull himself up laboriously. He lay back against the wall to rest.

'You don't mind us like this all round you, do you?' he asked, turning to me abruptly. He still spoke in his new light voice. He seemed to be afraid of breaking up the stillness of the night. I felt how right he was.

'Of course not,' I said, 'it would be nice to talk a little in the moonlight.'

My new ease startled me. Andrew no longer held any terrors. I was almost about to fall into the trap of treating him as a pet, a kitten or a marmoset. My only anxiety was that he would have heartburnings over finding Tom's sleepy arms around me; for I had already quite convinced myself that if he loved anyone in the world, it was Tom, and that his love would not be of the sharing kind. I tried to study each feature in the moonlight. I thought he looked a little wistful, a little far away, like a child who knows his fate is in the hands of others; but perhaps this was imagination. In my present outflowing mood I was too prepared for emotion and pathos in everyone. Tom sprawling near me, half on the low bedside table, half on the edge of the mattress, was extraordinarily comforting. He said nothing, but pulled at his cigarette and blew out the smoke with a noisy unselfconsciousness that I loved to hear. The shadow from his head and shoulders fell across my face, shrouding me protectively. I delighted to look out from my cave at the long arched shape of my body under the bedclothes. In the moonlight it was like one of those medieval coffins of silvery stone, or like a great cocoon wrapped round in its web of a thousand thousand strands. I was balanced between thoughts of death and birth in a wonderful 'now' of living. The nightingales were still singing. Once more they were transformed, this time into a bird orchestra performing chamber music while we took our light refreshments of butterscotch and cigarettes. I saw them in my mind, comic as crows, or the monkey musicians in Dresden china. They cocked their heads, swivelled their beady eyes and muttered like parrots.

Andrew held his sweets out to me again and I took two in a sort of sheer exuberance, a throwback to childish slyness and greed. We munched and crunched, making a noise of footsteps on a shingly beach. I wondered what Andrew was thinking. He had suddenly become in my eyes so much less important. I took it at first that this was entirely due to the change in my own attitude; but now the slightest of misgivings stirred for a moment. Had he become innocuous and almost childlike because, for the time being, he had retreated into himself to think and to plan? Had he pulled in his head and left his grotesque little tortoise body, hard and strong, to be patted and patronized by soft pink fingers? The thought faded almost as soon as it had awoken. Andrew sitting there on the end of my bed, his little drumstick legs stuck out straight before him, was almost as comic and endearing as the nightingale orchestra I had imagined.

Again I caught myself out in a sentimental dodging of what I really felt. He was like my fancied bird orchestra, not because he was comic or lovable, but because he, like birds performing human actions, was sinister and a little frightening.

Giving my hand an angry little pat, I sat up more in bed, wriggled my shoulders under the eiderdown and determined not to spoil the present moment by barren wonderings. It was enough that we were watching the moon through the night, happy in our sleeplessness, thinking our thoughts, as though we had to be serious about the business of living for ever.

They left me just before dawn. Andrew and I had eaten all the sweets, Tom had smoked all my cigarettes. We had talked in lazy snatches, enjoying our own and each other's truisms. They had been solemn and deep and soothing in the stillness of the night.

As I lay on my pillow, alone once more, I thought of Tom. There had been no need for anything when he had left. A word or sigh would have jarred me through and through. Even a look would have seemed horribly crude and furtive. He kept his face averted and called goodnight airily, laughing at the hour. I leaned from the bed giving all my attention to Andrew.

'I hope you'll sleep,' I said, 'I'm afraid my nightmare has ruined your night.'

'Oh, I like a vigil,' he answered quaintly; 'I mean a communal one. That's why I liked the air-raids in the war. One sat about and drank tea and felt cosy because of the danger.'

He left me with this last word which is always spelt in red capitals in my mind, I suppose because I once must have seen it as a child written thus on some mysterious electrical contrivance barred round with iron spikes.

I could not go to sleep again, but I lay there resting, smoothing out all talk from my brain until I became aware of the first cold weariness of the dawn. It seemed amazing that this watering misery, as sordid as a slum, could conquer the monotonous magic of the moon, but it grew and grew in strength, filling out the trivial anxieties of the day in front of me, until I knew that I must get up and dress. I shuddered at the anticlimax of breakfast, the embarrassment of goodbyes and thank-yous, the business of starting the car and arriving at the station in time for the train. The thought suddenly came to me that I could escape everything by leaving now, on foot, before anyone was astir.

II

I went over to the little writing-table, so smugly waiting for the guest to write his letters on a rainy afternoon. Yes, there was paper in the drawer – all nicely engraved, with envelopes to match. I sat down and wrote a hurried note to Andrew thanking him for having me and explaining that I was leaving early so as not to dislocate his morning's work – he had told me that he worked from breakfast to lunch – and because I wanted to be back at my cottage before the grocer called with my weekly provisions. Poor excuses, but they would have to do.

I was careful not to leave Tom's name out altogether but to mention my appreciation of his good cooking and his thoughtfulness in preparing my room. I hoped that they would both come one day soon to stay with me for a night or two. I ended on this rather matey, tit-for-tat note. We might have been dull old friends arranging our yearly visits to each other; but I could not be bothered with refinements of thought or word. I wanted to be off. Besides, after last night I felt a sort of comradeship that permitted most things.

Never again would I look on Andrew as a devilish little dynamo about to vibrate with terrifying inhuman power. I had the secret of him; and Tom ... I cut short the smile which was curving my lips. I would not indulge my thoughts until I was in the train.

As I finished dressing and collecting my few possessions together, the alien notion of pretending to forget something and leaving it behind came into my head. Tom would find it when he came to strip my bed. He could take it as he liked, as a symbol of my thoughts for him, or just as carelessness. In either case it would give him the excuse for writing to me. It seemed necessary to arrange such little matters. The novel excitement of even such a simple scheme possessed me. I looked about for something suitable to leave ... My handkerchief? My gloves? My powder-puff or lipstick? I should be uncomfortable without any of these; besides, wasn't there something a little too frail and human about them all? They were too animal and intimate. I had never in my life found anyone else's handkerchief without a slight distaste. Even lost gloves had a pathetic look that was almost squalid.

My eyes lighted on my brooch, genuinely forgotten until now on the little shelf above the bed. What could be better for my purpose? It was beautiful in itself and yet personal. The fact that it was valuable added to its usefulness; it would be returned to me for certain.

The little diamonds winked at me and I had a momentary pang. What if Tom should overlook it, or consider it of little value, not connect it with me, and give it to the girl who came in to clean twice a week? What if it should get lost in the post? My sudden surge of feeling for my brooch made me imagine the most unlikely catastrophes. But I left it there, letting myself out of the French window with the feeling that I was deserting an old friend.

The grass was soaking. I walked as quickly and silently as I could towards the lane. The chickens, locked in their house, heard me and clucked. I muttered to them and passed on. My shoes were not suitable for much walking. I spoilt them on that morning; but I enjoyed the cool squelch of dew between my toes. I was only sorry that the heels were not lower, for they made the walk to the station more tiring than it need have been.

I sat in the narrow ladies' waiting-room, hours too soon for the train that went in my direction. Milk cans were banged about as if they had been sacred drums in a Buddhist temple. I was told that the first passenger train would be for London, so I decided to go up, do a little shopping perhaps, then return to my cottage from Victoria. It would be better to do this than to wait for five or six hours.

♣

I did not arrive home until early afternoon. How tired I was. With the dusty heavy tiredness of sleeping in one's underclothes, of meeting new people and being jerked into new feeling. The trip to London had put the finishing touches to my exhaustion.

As I turned the key in the lock, the uncontaminated stillness of my house rushed out to welcome me. I loved it all again for the thousandth time. Treasured pieces of furniture and china stood about the room like utterly reliable custodians, deaf-mutes pledged to me for life. I went upstairs and turned the taps on in the bathroom. I was pleased that I had made the colour so raucous in this usually chaste white room. The bath, hand-basin, and pan were strawberry pink, the walls the shiny yellow of a buttercup. Curtains of vivid cerulean blue plastic material let through a preposterous light, reminding one of glaciers and mammoths and Ice Queens. The harshness of the black and white rubber floor jumped up to the eyes in a dazzle.

I put into the hot water handfuls of bath-salts almost as gaudy in scent as the fittings were in colour. Lilies of the valley, enormously, swooningly large, suddenly crowded into the steamy room, sucking up every particle of air.

I wallowed in the water, lying like a dead sheep, half on my side, only moving sometimes to steam my face with a hot flannel. And afterwards in my bedroom, lying on my bed, I opened my secret store cupboard where I kept food for just such an occasion as this. I had had no breakfast or lunch, only a cup of coffee in London, so I fell on the biscuits, the dried figs and chocolate. I made watery cocoa on my spirit-stove, then dropped in an enormous spoonful of marshmallow mixture, sent to me from America.

It melted like whipped cream, covering my cup with a thick froth. When the tepid bubbles broke against my lips, I was reminded in some confused way of 'Old Man's Beard'. I saw the hedges wreathed again with the grey skeleton flowers.

I dropped a lump of chocolate into my drink to make it even richer. The chocolate melted slowly, sticking to the spoon and the sides of the cup. I enjoyed smoothing it out and letting the smears dissolve. I was a child again, playing with mud pies.

It was dangerous to wonder why such a glow of happiness had settled on me. It might dissipate if analysed. There was the soaking in hot scented water after tiredness and dirt, the food after hunger, my own chosen refuge after the banalities of Andrew's spare room; but at the back of everything, pumping radiance into every material comfort, was the thought of Tom. Just that, no questions about him, no probings; I hardly even knew what I wanted of him, certainly not his presence at the moment. I had left so early that morning partly so that I should be able to think of him and not see him again.

Looking down I caught sight of Andrew's book on the bottom shelf of the table, the book that had started the whole *adventure*, if that was quite the right word. Now that I knew Andrew, how differently the sentences would read. I would not look at it again; I had no wish to force the readjustment of opinions. I would not jar myself in any way. I wanted to sail on for ever in my smooth contentment. I could feel sleep coming, closing round me, until I was in a tingling, buzzing, tomb chamber of mole velvet.

In the days that followed I waited for a little registered parcel with the address in an unfamiliar hand. I tried to guess how Tom would write. I thought of smallish, untidy, yet businesslike letters. There would be no scrawling, no flourishing 'o's and 'd's and 's's. Of course, it was possible that Andrew would write instead of Tom. It would not matter. I waited calmly to hear from either of the friends in the little stone house with the large white windows. That my brooch was still with them made a connection that pleased me. I almost hoped that it would be kept a little longer.

But as the days passed into weeks and I still received no parcel, I began to wonder what had happened. Had Tom overlooked it on the shelf above the bed? He would not, in all probability, be very particular about dusting. Had the girl who came in to clean found it or taken it without a word, to wear with her new evening dress at the dance at the village hall? I wondered whether I should write to Andrew. It would be easy to pretend that I had been looking everywhere for it, and had at last come to the conclusion that I must have left it in his spare room. But I was held back by the hope that one day I should go to the door and find the postman with the little parcel in his hands. Wrapped round my brooch would be a long letter from Tom. How much better to wait for this than to agitate and receive a correct little note from Andrew. I began to insist to myself that I should soon hear from Tom, that the understanding, so suddenly and mysteriously born that night, could not die away to nothing. It was growing in this fallow time, and I must not hurry it. I told myself this, but despondency was gathering. Gradually I gave up waiting for the postman's knock. A sort of dullness settled over me. I was too inert even to write for my brooch. I thought of it, as I thought of Tom, as something rather unreal that had existed for me long ago.

In my strange new sluggish state it was easy for Prudence Dawe, an old school friend, to persuade me to go and stay with her for a week. I put up almost no resistance. I could see the surprise on her face when she came to fetch me in her car. Always before I had made innumerable excuses, showing quite clearly that I preferred my solitude and my own bed.

When we arrived at her commonplace, comfortable house, I was made to wait in the drawing-room like a true guest, while she bustled about in the kitchen preparing the tea. She was singing gaily, happy, I suppose, to have me to gossip with for the next seven days. I felt almost warm towards her and because I could not look at her room with any pleasure I went up to the gate-legged table covered with magazines. Prudence read many as a sort of duty. She liked to be thought intelligent and up to date. I picked up the latest number of a literary monthly and took it to the fire. It was autumn now, and cold. Vaguely I wondered what had happened to the whole of the summer. It had drained away unused and unenjoyed. My last bright memory was of the blossom and the nightingales in spring.

I opened the magazine and saw two reproductions of pictures that seemed bad in the extreme. Their dreary affectation was horribly exposed by the camera. They were as obviously cheats as the spirits photographed at a seance. I turned over the pages, ignoring a learned article on the heart-cries people scribble on the walls of public conveniences, and two long poems by a well-known French poetess.

I came on it at the end of the magazine, just before the reviews and the advertisements. It was clearly the titbit, the delightful new short story with which to finish the feast. It was headed 'The Diamond Badge' by Andrew Clifton.

I had no need to read it; indeed, I don't think I could have brought myself to look at even the first page. I suddenly knew a lot of things – what had happened to my brooch, why Tom had never written, why Andrew had seemed so harmless and childlike all at once. He *had* retreated into himself to think and to plan; this story was the result. The tortoise head *had* been pulled in, leaving me to pat the stony shell with my silly, soft, patronizing fingers.

I thought of him prowling round my room after I had left, seeing the glitter of my brooch and climbing up on the bed to seize it. He would bear it away as a prize, cherishing it while his story developed. I never expected to see it again now – or him, or Tom. I was cut off for ever. Andrew would keep my brooch; it would be a scalp, a sort of legal confiscation.

But I was wrong. When I returned from Prudence's, I heard a little plop as I opened the door. Something had fallen from the broad ledge beneath the letter slot. A tiny parcel lay on the mat and I recognized Andrew's spiky writing on the label. I gazed at it for a moment without moving, but Prudence was behind me, waiting to come in. My mind was in a maze, all my feelings dulled and fuzzy. My only clear thought seemed to be, 'And he hasn't even registered it.' With a sort of mock indignation I said it over and over again to myself. I picked up the parcel and put it on the side-table, not having even enough interest to open it.

THE HATEFUL WORD

Harry Diedz, the German prisoner-of-war portrayed in this story, came to lunch with Denton Welch ('Flora Pinkston') and Eric Oliver ('Trevor') on Christmas Day 1946. The story was first published in A Last Sheaf.

FLORA PINKSTON NOTICED THE GERMAN PRISONER AS soon as she came out of the ironmonger's. He stood near the bus stop, wearing a too-romantic rust-brown cloak which fell to his knees in graceful points. His long hair fitted his head so sleekly that it looked like a thick gold skullcap. Its regularity repelled her a little; she wished the wind would ruffle it. She was not surprised when she saw him glance furtively in a shop window, then draw out a little blue comb and run through the shining strands.

'Poor boy,' she thought a little contemptuously; 'he is a prisoner with nothing to cherish but his golden hair.'

He was a little man, several inches shorter than herself, and probably half her age. She tried not to mind the thought of her fortieth birthday looming nearer and nearer – hadn't she been through all that time and time again? Whereas he – he could be only twenty-two or twenty-three at the very most. 'Probably even less,' she thought, taking in the simplicity of his expression, the innocent smoothness of his face. She wondered whether she liked the pointed delicacy of his nose. He held his mouth with that precision often seen in Germans. Did it make him look rather missish? A little, as if he repeated 'Prunes and prisms' several times every night before going to bed.

Where the cloak fell open in front she saw that he wore the shortest of battledress blouses above dark, full trousers.

The tight little blouse reminded her of an Eton jacket – a monkey jacket. Men called them 'bumfreezers', she mused, remembering her husband with a smile.

Had she done all her shopping? The picture cord, the hooks, the creosote and Harpic? She had them all; but was there anything she needed at the chemist's? And should she go to see what sort of fish there was, or was Trevor sick of all kinds, and all methods of cooking it?

Heavens! Although her thoughts had wandered back to her, her eyes had still been fixed on the little prisoner, and now he was smiling shamefacedly, as if he could no longer ignore her gaze. What ought she to do? Could she just smile her apologies for staring, then get into the car and drive off? Or would he be dreadfully disappointed? He looked as if he were steeling himself for an encounter, as if he expected to be addressed by her at any moment. How lonely he must be feeling standing on the pavement of this bustling little English market town. No one but herself had even stopped to stare at him. His russet cloak and burnished hair aroused no spark of interest.

Impulsively Flora took a step towards him; she moved with long, easy strides, as if lazily conscious of an elegant, well-dressed body.

'You going my way?' she asked in her casual, brassy voice. 'Can I give you a lift? Masses of room.'

She waved a hand, indicating the empty car. It was characteristic of her not to modify the superciliousness of her tone, to use a phrase like 'masses of room' which he would probably not understand.

The little prisoner was all smiles and anxiety.

'Please,' he said, bobbing his head both in acknowledgement and answer. Somewhere in the 'please' a question also lurked; he was not quite sure of the part expected of him.

'Come on, then,' Flora said, overriding his hesitation, sweeping him towards the car. He sat in the seat beside her, his arms hugging his chest. He would make himself as small as possible. He would touch nothing, lean on nothing, be as little trouble as a brown-paper parcel.

Flora wished he would relax; she hated the thought of so much tautness near her. She could feel her own muscles tightening.

'Have a cigarette?' she said, pointing to the pigeon-hole in front of him. 'Matches and everything there.'

This led to the further awkwardness of having to refuse when he immediately held out the packet to her first. She could see him taking one, putting it in his mouth, cupping his shaking hands round the flame of the match. They were clean hands, which still looked dirty because of the ingrained blackness of hard work.

What on earth were they to talk about? She knew no German at all. Surely he would ask to be put down soon.

'You like the English countryside?' she asked, waving a proprietary hand at the fields and orchards they were passing.

The little prisoner gulped, took hold of himself and said, 'Oh, I like – I like *very* much.'

There was silence again. At last in desperation Flora said, 'Just let me know when you want to be dropped?'

'Please?' the German said in gentle bewilderment.

It was only then that Flora realized that he had no journey to make, that he had got into the car simply because she had invited him.

'Lord! I've landed myself!' she thought. 'I shall have to ask him in for a drink, smile and be kind, then get rid of him quickly.'

She turned down a lane, then into an even narrower drive through a nut orchard. Soon the attractive little house came into view. Flora never ceased to enjoy its smooth cream weatherboarding, its tiny Gothic sash windows and the delicate iron porch with gracefully curving roof.

'Come in and have a drink,' she said, not looking at him, but busying herself with her parcels. He darted forward to help, grabbing packages from her feverishly. Once more she wished that he would calm himself.

In the long, low drawing-room he stood about, desperately ill at ease till she almost forced him into one of her snug French chairs. Even then he was afraid to lean back lest his hair should touch the pale apricot watered-silk.

'A bit late for tea,' Flora thought. 'Besides, it's Margaret Rose's afternoon out – much easier just to give him beer as I thought at first. Perhaps Trevor will be in soon; things may be easier then.'

She went to the rather plain Georgian doll's house and took out a bottle of beer and some tomato juice. She laughed at herself for keeping the drinks in such a place. It seemed a rather coarse and vulgar thing to do; the little house was worthy of better treatment. One day she would have it repaired carefully and try to find some old furniture for it. In the meantime it served as a bottle cupboard very well.

'My name is Flora Pinkston,' she said, pouring out the beer and passing it to him without asking if he wanted it. 'What is yours?'

'I am Harry – Harry Diedz.' The little prisoner tried to make the name sound as English as posssible, but the unfamiliar 'Harry' came out as if spelt with two 'e's at the end.

'Silly to Anglicize his Christian name,' Flora thought.

'What part of Germany do you come from?' she asked.

'Thuringia.'

'Are your people still there?'

'Oh yes; I have letters every week.'

'What did you do before you were in the army?'

'I was glass-worker, like my father.'

'Did you like that?'

'Oh yes, I like.'

The little prisoner gazed into the distance, as if reliving all the pains and pleasures of being a glass-worker.

'Do you like music?' Flora asked.

'Very much.' He gave a little hissing intake of breath.

'Which composer do you like most?'

'Mozart.'

'Who else?'

'Wagner, but not so much.'

'Do you box?' Why should she suddenly ask him this? Had the stockiness of his little body put the idle question into her head?

'Sometimes a little – I try,' he laughed, putting up his hands in mock defence. 'There is very good man at the camp; he teach me. But I like football.'

Flora heard the turning of the front-door handle. Good. Trevor was back. Conversation would be less like a dreary cross-examination. He would know what to say to the little prisoner.

But when her husband came into the room, he looked anything but conversational. He was tired from his day in London; he still clutched his neat black briefcase as if unable, even at home, to free himself from his clients' problems.

He looked at the German prisoner, then glanced away. This was another of Flora's vagaries. He could hardly control his annoyance.

'Oh, Trevor, this is Harry Diedz,' Flora was saying. 'He likes Mozart better than Wagner and football better than boxing, and before the wretched war swallowed him up he used to blow the most beautiful glass objects in Thuringia.'

Was there any need for this silly 'party' brightness of Flora's? And since, presumably, she had invited the prisoner herself, why should she go out of her way to make him look foolish? Poor little devil. He was so horribly embarrassed, standing there, scraping his boots together and half holding out his hand.

Trevor nodded perfunctorily, then sank into a chair.

'What can I get you, dear?' Flora asked with a curious unexpected meekness. 'A whisky and soda?'

She went to the doll's house again and brought a decanter and syphon. She had not offered Trevor's whisky to the German, but she showed no compunction in producing it now.

Trevor drank deeply, lugubriously. He was too dejected to talk; he longed to be left alone so that he could stretch out his legs and relax.

'Why not show your friend the garden, before it's dark?' he suggested, turning to Flora with a set look in his eyes.

Flora saw the look and understood. She led Harry out into the garden much in the same way that she would take a little dog for an airing before bed. They walked between the currant bushes, past the vegetables and out on to a little lawn under an old weeping willow. Trevor liked doing the garden himself, only sometimes having an old man to dig or clip the hedges. Now, because he had been so busy in London, the garden looked a little bedraggled. The grass was rather too long and a few weeds had sprung up in the borders.

'Do you like gardening?' Flora asked, to break the silence.

'Yes, very nice,' said Harry, with such feeling that an idea suddenly came to Flora. Why shouldn't he help Trevor sometimes in the evenings? Surely Trevor would be pleased to have someone to mow the grass, or to do some of the other less interesting jobs. She turned to Harry at once.

'My husband is so busy in London that he can't spare much time for the garden at the moment. If you're free in the evenings would you like to come in and help?'

Her abruptness made it difficult for Harry to understand at first, but when he realized that he was being asked to do something very much to his taste, for which he would probably be paid, he said, 'Yes please, very much.'

The prospect of coming to this charming house and garden delighted him. It solved the problem of his evenings; it would do away with that brooding emptiness that clapped down on him after the day's work, so that he stood on the street corner, or lay in his bunk in the iron hut, despondent.

'Thank you very much,' he said again with deep gratitude. 'I come tomorrow night?'

Flora thought quickly. She was a little taken aback by his prompt acceptance. Had she been impulsive and silly? What would Trevor think? Would he be pleased? Aloud she said, 'Yes, that will be fine.' She paused a moment, dismissing him. 'Can you find your own way back to the camp?'

'I think,' he answered, in spite of not knowing where he was.

She took him through the nut orchard, leaving him at the gate.

'You go this way,' she said, pointing up the lane; 'it can only be a mile or two, three at the outside.'

'I find all right, Missis.'

He gave his stiff little bow and turned abruptly, so that his cloak swirled out like a dancer's skirt. She left him without another glance and walked back to her husband. He was still sunk deep in the chair with his knees higher than his head. Flora thought that one could tell they were attractive knees, even through the trousers; and how large after the prisoner's compact doll-like quality.

'What a little quainty,' she said, wrinkling her nose in

amusement. 'I took him to the gate and he said goodbye and he called me Missis.'

'Why you should want to ask a German back beats me,' said Trevor truculently. 'It seems pretty sentimental. If they'd won the war, you'd be laughing on the other side of your face.'

'Darling, don't be Blimpish, it doesn't suit you; and what does that expression about laughing on the other side of one's face mean? It always sounds faintly rude to me. It may be quite illogical, but it reminds me of the ridiculous phrase we used to shout at school: "Base equals Face".'

Trevor gave a wan grin.

'Well, what was the point in asking this one back suddenly?' he asked. 'They've been here long enough and you've taken not the slightest notice of them.'

'Darling, you know how I stare if something catches my eye. I came out of Griffith's and saw the flowing cloak and gruesomely brushed golden hair – oh, so picturesque. He saw me staring and smiled back. I felt I had to do something, so I offered him a lift; then when he'd got into the car I found he wasn't going anywhere.'

'Just a straight pick-up,' said Trevor laughingly. He was recovering his natural easy warmth.

Flora thought it a good moment to mention the gardening scheme.

'Will you be pleased, I wonder? I've asked him to come in the evenings to help with the grass and other boring jobs. He leapt at the idea and is turning up tomorrow.'

'God! I expect he'll dig up the bulbs, break the mowing-machine, and water the things that shouldn't be watered. But I don't mind; I've given up bothering. You have your blond plaything.'

'Dearest, don't be crude. I did it for you. You know how tired you've been lately. The garden is really too much for you, now that you're so frightfully busy in London.'

'Well, thank God you didn't offer him my whisky,' said Trevor, pouring out another drink. 'That would have been the last straw.'

The little prisoner appeared punctually the next evening. He had barely had time to gulp a cup of tea and gobble a bun after his hard day's work in the fields; but he was satisfied. Was he not coming to this nice house where the handsome lady, though a little terrifying, was really kind underneath? Had she not given him beer and a ride in her car? No other English person had ever asked him home. He scrambled into a clean shirt, then brushed his golden hair with special carefulness.

Trevor was not yet home, so Flora took Harry to the toolshed and showed him the mower.

'Be careful with the blades,' she said; 'my husband is rather particular.'

'I know, I careful. Stones very bad.'

Harry made a little gesture as if picking up a stone and throwing it off the lawn.

By the time Trevor returned, Harry had finished the little patches of lawn and the grass paths and had begun to clip the edges and weed the borders. He had undertaken these tasks without any word from Flora. His crisp sleeves were rolled up, showing sunburnt arms. The full, dark trousers were pulled in snugly round his waist by a thick leather belt. He looked like a little model of a gardener.

Trevor, hurrying past, noted what he was doing with grudging approval and dropped some word of greeting. The little prisoner stood up and bowed punctiliously.

'How well they trained them in that army,' Trevor thought. 'Too damn well – a bit slavish all that bowing and obedience.'

The next evening Trevor arrived back earlier and went to join Harry in the vegetable garden. Flora, helping Margaret Rose with the evening meal, looked out of the kitchen window and saw the two men working – Trevor tall, powerful, leisurely; Harry neat, and quick, like a clockwork toy.

'And they'll never think it necessary to utter a single word,' she mused. 'Wonderful, that acceptance of silence, even of gruffness. If Trevor's in rather a mood, Harry won't mind; he'll just go on working peacefully.' Like many women, she had an exaggerated notion of the comradeship existing between men.

But it did seem as if some sort of understanding was quickly growing up between the two. Flora would sometimes catch Harry looking up at her husband with a sort of schoolboy admiration, and Trevor would often say contemptuous patronizing things which, nevertheless, showed quite clearly the warmer feelings they were supposed to mask.

'Poor little runt!' he would exclaim, giving the ugly word its full value. 'What a life he's had. Do you know he's hardly twenty yet?'

The words sent a pang through Flora. When she went up to her bedroom she looked in the glass for a long time. She saw the ripeness of her face. Perhaps she was handsomer than she had ever been; but she did not want to be handsome. She wanted to be fresh, even a little raw. She hated herself for this preoccupation with the outward semblance of extreme youth. 'It is pathetic,' she told herself fiercely, 'and so wrong-headed. Young people are often at their very worst. They have bad skins, neglected hair, abominable clothes, and they don't know how to manage anything. Their mouths, their eyes, their legs and arms are all over the place.'

In this way she tried to fortify herself against the years to come. She ran the lipstick over her mouth, rubbing the colour in carefully; she did not want *her* face to look like a chamber daubed with strawberry jam. Where had she read that frightful description? Was it in a novel of Joyce Cary's? She smiled at herself in the mirror and went downstairs to finish arranging the table. She liked to make it as attractive as possible for Trevor in the evening. After being immersed in the squalor and intricacy of the law all day, he needed something to make him feel civilized again. She never asked the little prisoner to stay; his gaucherie would have turned their quiet meal into an ordeal, a penance. She usually just took him out a tankard of beer, or gave it to him when he came shyly to the back door to say goodnight. She remembered again his scarlet embarrassment and pleasure when, after the first week, she offered him the money he had earned. She gave it to him very gracefully, thanking him for his whole-hearted work. It was difficult for her to keep the heartless quality out of her voice, but she did look straight at him with attractive sincerity. In spite of the awkwardness of the money transaction, she suddenly found that paying him gave her a curious, sharp pleasure.

She was melted by his blushing humility and gratitude, yet at the same instant a delicious, rather shameful sense of power tingled through her.

'Paying Margaret Rose has *never* affected me in this way,' she thought, trying to laugh herself out of an emotion that seemed somehow discreditable.

✤

One rainy afternoon, about three weeks after her meeting with Harry, Flora was looking out of her drawing-room window, watching the birds on the lawn and the drops hissing into the carp-pool. The whole garden was in the trimmest order now. To look at it soothed Flora; she had been sorting clothes and rearranging the furniture in her bedroom for most of the day, and she felt tired. Suddenly she saw a figure in a camouflaged oilskin coming down the drive. For a moment the piebald cape, with its patches of chocolate, green and khaki, perplexed her; then she realized that it was worn by Harry.

'But what is he doing here so early?' she wondered. 'It's only four o'clock.'

She went to open the door for him. He stood smiling up at her, his square little teeth looking very white and rather savage in the wet, glowing face.

'Farmer says, "Go home early – too wet," so I come to do greenhouse,' he explained. 'I clean glass inside, make walls white.' He ran an imaginary whitewash brush up and down an imaginary wall.

Later, when she had called him in for tea and they sat over the empty cups, smoking cigarettes, she remembered that the Louis Quinze commode, which was her dressing-table, had not yet been moved into its new position because it was so heavy. The weight would be nothing to Harry.

'I wonder,' she said, 'if you would help me move a piece of furniture.'

'Oh yes,' he said, standing up at once to wait for orders.

'It's in my bedroom.'

Flora led the way up the little box-stairs. She said, 'Be careful not to knock your head,' before she remembered how much shorter he was than most men.

They each took hold of a magnificent rococo ormolu handle and lifted out the first curved drawer. When the carcase was empty, they moved it easily across the room, fitting it between the windows. Flora sat down on the bed to admire the new effect and Harry went to pick up a drawer; but as he bent down his attention was caught by Flora's bright scarves and bags and by a small collection of old fans, scent-bottles, bead-work purses and early-Victorian nosegay holders. He crouched over the drawer, not moving. Flora, looking down on his back so close to her, felt prompted to say, 'You are happy to come here, Harry? You like working in the garden?'

He looked up at her with his most brilliant smile. A raindrop still glistened in the little cup at the base of his throat. The unmistakable soldier smell rose from his warm damp battledress.

'I like here like my home. Before I was very sad – nowhere to go; now I think every day, tonight I go to Mr Pinkston.'

'You like my husband?' Flora asked, barely conscious of her wish for him to say something appreciative of herself.

'Mr Pinkston *very* good man, very clever, very strong . . .' Harry left his sentence in the air, finding it impossible to put his admiration into English words. He blushed a little and looked down again at the drawer to hide his awkwardness.

'This very pretty things,' he murmured, touching a sequined fan delicately. The bristles on the back of his neck suddenly glinted gold against the darker, sunburnt skin. Flora felt an irresistible urge to treat him as a little boy. She leaned forward blindly, to put her arms round him.

She felt Harry's body suddenly stiffen. He was utterly still, a frozen man. She put her mouth to the nape of his neck. The flesh was cool and she had expected it to be warmer than her lips. Harry gulped; she felt the Adam's apple rise and fall, like a squirrel leaping to escape, but tied by the leg. She was crying now. The hot tears falling on his neck appalled Harry. He turned, straining his head towards her. There was a desperate look of pity and unhappiness in his eyes. Flora saw it and was shocked into some sort of self-possession. Her hands fell to her sides. Mechanically she looked in the long cheval-glass and saw how ugly the crying had made her. The tears had no power to smudge her make-up, but they had inflamed her eyes and lids; she had reddened sockets of a rheumy old witch. 'They don't look real,' she mused; 'I've been got up for some production of *Macbeth*.' She ran her hand over her hair, fluffing a curl, smoothing a wave. The feel of her strong, vibrant hair comforted her a little. She even tried to clear her thoughts. What had he done to her? She had thought of him as a vain, pathetic, ridiculous little person. How had he cracked her hard bright shell, so that she quivered with no protection any more? Would she ever recover from the sudden devastating glimpse of herself which he had given her?

He had scrambled to his feet and was standing awkwardly before her.

'I must go now, Mrs Pinkston; tonight I help to play music for sing-song at the camp.'

His lips worked; he was trying to add something to his sentence. The words came out in a rush of almost pidgin English.

'I am thanking you so much, Mrs Pinkston, and your very good husband, for friending me; I so lonely before. Soon I go back to Germany; I tell them there you are like, like –' He strained after the one word to express his gratitude. 'You are like mother to me – my English mother.'

He was out of the room and down the stairs, leaving the hateful word tingling in her ears.

Three Fragments

WEEKEND

GRACE LAY ON THE BED FACE DOWNWARDS, HER HAIR IN greying wisps against the pillow, her hand still clutching the little fabric suitcase. From outside came the voices of the farmer's wife and daughter.

After a time she got up, went to the small mirror over the chest of drawers and straightened her hair; then she went slowly down the dark stairs to the parlour, where tea was laid on the big rosewood table. Mrs Bulmer, hearing her come down, brought in the teapot and set it down without saying anything.

Grace went to the bookcase and looked at the titles of the books. They were old novels and bound volumes of Chambers's magazine. She chose *Delia Blanchflower* and, taking it to the table, propped it against the teapot and sat down.

She ate slowly, her eyes on the book, until it got too dark to read; then she pushed back her chair and stared into the fire, thinking of herself.

Her thoughts were flickering and uncertain, like the fire. She could hardly look at some parts of her life without wincing, but here in the stillness some of her fears seemed to evaporate and she kept repeating to herself, 'I can stay here until Sunday night.'

She got up and went to the window, which looked on to the farmyard; everything was fading and merging together, soon there would be no light left. The heap of dung steamed slightly and the cows kicked the sides of the barn and rattled their chains. A young man passed, his work finished, a satchel slung over his shoulder. The smoke from his cigarette blew in at the window and Grace caught the white gleam of his open shirt.

She shut the window, drew the curtains and sat in the firelight until Mrs Bulmer brought the lamp. It glowed and made a soft pool with Grace at the edge. She tried to read her book, but could not rest; so she went to the door and, slipping across the dark hall, let herself out as silently as possible. The cool air met her and all the night smells coming from the animals and grass and flowers. She made her way down the hill towards the village. Its lights were twinkling faintly through the trees.

She wandered into the empty street and the voices coming from the inn; she climbed the steps to the black church and saw the pale glimmer of the diamond-paned windows. She smelt the yews and the long wet grass brushing on her stockinged legs. The voices were louder now; the inn door had been opened, someone had crossed the street. Grace got up to go home. She came to the lane, grown high with cowparsley and nettles, and made her way along it over the stile and through the meadow, past the dim bulks of cows, like stranded ships, still grazing.

It was not until then that she saw the other figure. It was walking slowly and she soon was close behind. It swayed a little, then fell down. Grace ran up and, bending over, recognized the man who had passed her window at the farm.

His eyes were shut and his mouth was open. She smelt the smell of beer and knew that he was drunk.

'Shall I help you to get up?' she asked stiffly. He opened his eyes and stared at her.

'All right, if you like,' he answered. She knelt down and got his arm round her neck and tried to pull him upwards. He was too heavy and fell back.

She tried again. He slowly staggered to his feet and she held him, swaying. Her legs were like two buttresses and her arms were linked around his waist. Slowly she felt him sinking again. Each button on his shirt scraped on her arm as he sagged until she lost her balance and fell with him into the deep wet grass. Her arm was pinioned beneath him and he was lying heavily on her side. His breath was on her face and suddenly his warm hard mouth, the rigid bone beneath, was pressed hard against hers, and she felt his tongue trying to find the opening of her lips.

She pushed against his throat with her hand and felt the Adam's apple rising and falling as he gulped. She grabbed at his flesh and felt the coarse strong hair on his chest. At last he lifted his head and lay back, and she swiftly jerked her arm from underneath him and scrambled to her feet. He lay there still and in a minute began to snore.

'I can't leave him here,' she thought. 'He'll be here all night and probably be dead in the morning.'

She pushed him sharply with her foot and said loudly and clearly, 'Get up and go and put your head in the stream to sober you down.'

He mumbled, 'I'm not drunk, not bloody likely,' and rolled over on his face. Then his attitude changed, and his face seemed to lighten as he said, 'But I wouldn't mind a swim neither.'

He knelt up unsteadily and, bending down his head, put his hands over his shoulders and began pulling his shirt slowly over his head. He was like a ghost in a pillowslip, headless and lumbering; then off it came and he seemed to be a white pillar of marble growing out of the tree trunk of his trousers. He sat down and pulled off his shoes and socks, and his toes, like tight bracken fronds, seemed to uncurl.

He stood up and let his trousers fall to the ground. Even the activity seemed to have sobered him. He walked towards the stream and felt it with his toe, then slowly the two shafts of his legs sank into it and he was swallowed up to the waist. His nipples were rigid with cold and his nails were blanched. Grace saw him dive like a porpoise, his long arms thrashing the surface. He was shouting now and warbling as he lay on his back, arms outstretched, his wet hair glistening in the dark.

He ran up the bank and out into the grass, which the moon was just beginning to silver. He was combing his hair with his fingers and rubbing himself with his shirt. Grace sat by a tree trunk and watched. He came up and pulled her to him and kissed her again. She did not resist this time. His flesh was like cool, clean rubber.

He finished his dressing, putting his jacket on without his shirt. They walked towards the farm, leaning on each other, she still supporting him a little. When they got to the wicket gate into the garden he said, 'This is where I'll leave you,' and slipped round to the back out of sight.

Grace walked up the brick path, wondering if she would find the door still open. It was locked. She rang gently and the old bell went clanging through the house. There were footsteps and a grating as the door opened inwards. Mrs Bulmer looked out, her eyes like duck's eyes, evil and suspicious.

'Oh, it's you,' she said. 'I thought you'd gone upstairs, so I locked up.'

The hall was black, and Grace made her way slowly across it and up the stairs, slippery with oilcloth. The air in her room was warm, with the smell of the birds that nested in the eaves and of the wallflowers in the jam-jar heavy on it. Grace looked at herself in the glass by the light from her candle and saw her greying hair.

'Thirty-four's not very old,' she kept saying to herself, as she took off her clothes and wearily rubbed cold-cream into her face. 'Tomorrow I shall be going back to Miss Moulton's registry office for maids and mistresses and I shall be listening to the likes and dislikes of maids and mistresses and writing letters to maids and mistresses, maids and mistresses, maids and mistresses.' She said it like a parrot while she brushed her hair.

The bed was cold and the cotton sheets dragged at her flesh. She looked at the grey square of the window and felt the breeze blowing in on her face.

She woke to see Mrs Bulmer bending over her and to smell the strong tea in the cup with the gilt trefoil on it.

She heard the birds, and someone whistling in the yard. She drank her tea, then got up to see if it was him. He saw her as she came to the window, and looked away. She was cut and mortified. She dressed and went down to her lonely breakfast by the fire; the sun streamed on to the table. She sat and read while Mrs Bulmer prepared her a lunch to take out, then went upstairs to put on her outdoor shoes.

As she came out into the yard he passed in front of her, the water from the buckets he was carrying slopping out as he walked. She followed on behind and hoped that he would talk to her when they had got behind the barn, but he never turned his head and she saw the gold stubble at the back of his head glisten as the muscles of his neck moved.

He went into the barn and she heard him talking to the calves.

She had her picnic amongst the buttercups, throwing her bread crusts on to a stone for the birds to find. Then she buried the litter from her meal in a rabbit hole and walked slowly back through the fields to the farm, to pack. Mrs Bulmer was surprised when she said she was going. She said, 'I thought you was going to stay as long as you could, I thought you was going on the 9.16.'

But Grace shook her head and left for the station.

AMY LECHWORTH

AMY LECHWORTH WAS A WIDOW AND HER DRAWING-room had big Chinese lions turned into lamps and there was a little table behind the sofa with glasses and bottles of gin and French vermouth on it.

When we drove up to the house we saw her standing in the drive and her face said she didn't know who we were; so we got out and smiled and walked towards her with our hands out – and she held our hands a long time, while Max explained how he had met her at a party at Egg Forster's and how she had asked him to come and see her whenever he was near.

She suddenly said, 'Oh, I remember, it was the night when I

fell down and sprained my wrist; I was feeling a little hazy and there are so many steps at Egg Forster's.'

Then she took us into the drawing-room where there were several other young men and she left us – and they looked at us and we looked at them.

One offered us cigarettes; he was German and not very tall. Another one went to pour out the gin and vermouth; he had on a checked suit. And the third one was tall and dark and very sunburnt. He told us that he had a restaurant called the Sally Lunn, and how to make very good vegetable soup.

Soon Max and the Sally Lunn (as I called him in my mind) were talking about lying on the beach in the South of France. The talk, I thought, was getting very fashionable, so I tried to talk to the checked suit; but he would talk about lesbians and I thought this also was too fashionable, so I lapsed into silence and began looking at the Chinese lions which had very ugly faces.

Then our hostess bustled in and asked the Sally Lunn how to work the Aga cooker; she had on a sort of overall and she told Max and me that she and the three boys had come down suddenly from London and found that all the servants had gone out for the day, leaving only a young girl behind who was no good to them at all. And I asked Amy Lechworth if she was annoyed and she said, 'Not a bit, I would do the same if I was one of them.' And I thought it was very nice of her.

After this we all went into the kitchen, but we did not help her very much, because we didn't know what to do; and although the Sally Lunn knew what to do, he said he couldn't do it, because there was nothing to do it with. And he still went on talking about very good vegetable soup.

Soon Amy had peeled some potatoes and they looked very white, bobbing up and down in the saucepan, and she had put the round piece of beef in the oven. I forgot to say she had very fair hair on top and had a nice face and looked about forty.

The checked suit had brought the gin and the French vermouth bottles in, and we all sat on the kitchen table holding our glasses, and I thought about too many cooks spoiling the broth – only in this case we hadn't got any broth, as the Sally Lunn wouldn't let us make any unless it could be very good vegetable soup.

After a little while I began to make faces at Max, because we hadn't been asked to lunch and there didn't seem much for lunch anyhow; but he would go on talking to the Sally Lunn and paying no attention to my faces.

Amy Lechworth saw my faces and asked me if I liked chewing gum. I said I did. Then she went to see what else was in the larder and I went to help her and she held my hand a long time until we found a cold rice pudding.

When Max saw the cold rice pudding he began to make faces at me, but it was my turn now to pretend not to see, so I began asking the German boy if he liked sauerkraut. I knew it sounded silly, but I had to say something. He wasn't looking very well and I think my question was unwise because he got up and quickly left the room.

I began to feel rather depressed so I suddenly saw the faces which Max was still making and lifted my eyebrows to answer him. Then we both got up and collected out gloves and hats and said, 'Goodbye, we're so pleased we found you in,' to Amy Lechworth. She was rather hot by now, so she didn't shake hands, but said that we must come again.

When we got into the car, Max said, 'It is a pity perhaps that we didn't stay to lunch after all.' And I said, 'It's only because you want to talk about the South of France to the Sally Lunn. Besides, remember cold rice pudding.' And he said, 'Yes, perhaps it wouldn't have been wise; we must go again when the servants haven't all gone out for the day.'

I thought this was rather a greedy remark and I wondered if Amy thought that we had only come for what we could get. Because of course we had. Then I thought of the Chinese lions, turned into lamps, sitting there year after year and making those dreadful faces.

LADY GERTRUDE

GERTRUDE WAS DYING. SHE LAY IN THE HEAVY BED, her damp hair sticking to her.

The great room, with its silver sconces and huge panel of Mortlake tapestry, showed Gertrude's love of magnificence. High up, the canopy of her bed held up its ancient ostrich feathers. Miss Fillon, the nurse, moved over the wide old boards, and in the Empire secretaire, guarded at each corner by its sphinx heads, lay Gertrude's letters.

There were so many of them, in no sort of order. Many were love letters – from mechanics and sailors, chauffeurs and ploughboys, guardsmen and policemen, a great crowd of simple men.

Gertrude had loved nothing but simple men and they in their simplicity had been overawed by the love of Lady Gertrude. Of course, in the eyes of most people she had become disreputable, but how well I can remember her saying, 'If you want something you must go and get it and when I see something I want, I wink.'

How many times have I gone into bars and suddenly seen Gertrude there, sitting at a little iron table with her latest lover, who always seemed a little drunk. How handsome they were, always the wonderful, strapping type, that Nature somehow manages to push up through all the slime and filth of slums. How beautiful she was too in those days, dark, thin-boned, with that magnolia-petal flesh. I have never known anyone less abandoned in appearance.

A POSTSCRIPT

LEFT ALONE FOR A DAY, OR A NIGHT, OR A WEEK, OR FOR years, what do you think about? Do you think about and long for the person that is not there or do you resolutely turn your back and go about your jobs with the sort of intensity that might be called fanatical, or do you make the 'normal' your ideal and watch your behaviour as a cat watching a mouse, ready to pounce on the slightest deviation from this ideal? Do you lie for long hours in reverie, re-creating, living again your past happiness, or does that seem an almost unbearable pastime? Do you get yourself between the pages of a book, and read there of old houses, rains, ferns growing between the grotto rocks, of dark pools and stagnant tanks, of statues at the end of long avenues of cedars, whose brooding arms spread out in layers like dark fungi?

Or perhaps you read of something brilliant and that helps you. Some sparkle of glass and light and tinkling water and laughing people, with wine cooler than human blood.

Perhaps it is violence and hate and fighting and lust that help. Treachery and the worst things that humans do to each other.

Or again a woven plot of intrigue.

Do you shut yourself up with the fire and artificial light, with warming food and drink and wireless music, with sewing, knitting, drawing, or do you go out and away, into the ploughed-up fields, noticing every change in the texture of the damp almost edible-looking earth, following the laced pattern of the twigs, arranging a melody from the disconnected, disconcerting screams of the birds, watching the hugeness of the sun descending, and feeling that the moon, before the night completely falls, is almost too weak to go on existing?

Do you do any or all of these things in turn?

BIBLIOGRAPHY

Brave and Cruel and Other Stories (Hamish Hamilton, 1949)

The Denton Welch Journals, ed. Jocelyn Brooke (Hamish Hamilton, 1952)

Denton Welch: The Making of a Writer by Michael De-la-Noy (Viking, 1984; Penguin Books, 1986)

Dumb Instrument, ed. Jean Louis Chevalier (Enitharmon Press, 1976)

I Left My Grandfather's House (Lion & Unicorn Press, 1958; Allison & Busby, 1984)

In Youth is Pleasure (Routledge, 1945; Oxford University Press, 1982)

The Journals of Denton Welch, ed. Michael De-la-Noy (Allison & Busby, 1984; Penguin Books, 1987)

A Last Sheaf (John Lehmann, 1951)

Maiden Voyage (Routledge, 1943; Penguin Books, 1983)

A Voice Through a Cloud (John Lehmann, 1950; Penguin Books, 1983)

FOR THE BEST IN PAPERBACKS, LOOK FOR THE

In every corner of the world, on every subject under the sun, Penguins represent quality and variety – the very best in publishing today.

For complete information about books available from Penguin and how to order them, write to us at the appropriate address below. Please note that for copyright reasons the selection of books varies from country to country.

In the United Kingdom: For a complete list of books available from Penguin in the U.K., please write to *Dept EP, Penguin Books Ltd, Harmondsworth, Middlesex, UB7 0DA*

In the United States: For a complete list of books available from Penguin in the U.S., please write to *Dept BA, Viking Penguin, 299 Murray Hill Parkway, East Rutherford, New Jersey 07073*

In Canada: For a complete list of books available from Penguin in Canada, please write to *Penguin Books Canada Limited, 2801 John Street, Markham, Ontario L3R 1B4*

In Australia: For a complete list of books available from Penguin in Australia, please write to the *Marketing Department, Penguin Books Australia Ltd, P.O. Box 257, Ringwood, Victoria 3134*

In New Zealand: For a complete list of books available from Penguin in New Zealand, please write to the *Marketing Department, Penguin Books (N.Z.) Ltd, Private Bag, Takapuna, Auckland 9*

In India: For a complete list of books available from Penguin in India, please write to *Penguin Overseas Ltd, 706 Eros Apartments, 56 Nehru Place, New Delhi 110019*

Also by Denton Welch in Penguins
Maiden Voyage

'After I had run away from school, no one knew what to do with me'

Maiden Voyage, Denton Welch's first book in a remarkable, if brief, literary career, is a semi-novelistic portrayal of his early life. It begins with an account of his last term at public school (Repton) from which he absconded. As a result, his father asked Denton to join him in Shanghai; there he involved himself in every variety of experience and adventure.

Whether recording his impressions of the Temple of Heaven in Peking, his venture into the interior, the surreptitious antique trade, the tenacious corners of British colonialism, or the effects of internal upheaval and war, he reveals his unique gift for observation coupled with a brilliantly idiosyncratic appreciation of China's beauty and richness.

'A remarkable first book, distinguished for the economy and lucidity of Welch's prose, outstanding for his ability to encapsulate powerful images of persons and places, compulsively enthralling' – Kay Dick in *The Times*

Also by Denton Welch in Penguins
The Journals of Denton Welch
Edited by Michael De-la-Noy

'How terrifyingly observant he was, down to the smallest detail,' Vita Sackville-West wrote to Denton Welch's lover, Eric Oliver, in 1949, when she first read a manuscript draft of his Journals. 'How I wish it did not break off just where it does.'

Welch had kept his Journals from 1942 until August 1948, four months before his death, at the age of thirty-three. Often written up while Welch was suffering periods of intense pain brought on by a road accident when he was twenty, they stand, as Michael De-la-Noy writes in his Introduction, 'as part of a permanent memorial to a unique and above all intensely interesting writer who achieved, under appallingly adverse conditions, precisely and immaculately what he set out to accomplish'.

'Brilliantly edited' – Paul Binding in the *Literary Review*

'Thanks to Michael De-la-Noy, a minor genius of the Forties has re-emerged' – Ronald Blythe in the *Guardian*

FOR THE BEST IN PAPERBACKS, LOOK FOR THE 🐧

PENGUIN LITERARY BIOGRAPHIES

Sylvia Beach and the Lost Generation Noel Riley Fitch
Arnold Bennett Margaret Drabble
Elizabeth Bowen Victoria Glendinning
Joseph Conrad Jocelyn Baines
Scott Fitzgerald André Le Vot
The Young Thomas Hardy Robert Gittings
Ibsen Michael Meyer
John Keats Robert Gittings
Jack Kerouac: Memory Babe – A Critical Biography Gerald Nicosia
Ezra Pound Noel Stock
Dylan Thomas Paul Ferris
Tolstoy Henri Troyat
Evelyn Waugh Christopher Sykes
Walt Whitman Paul Zweig
Oscar Wilde Hesketh Pearson

FOR THE BEST IN PAPERBACKS, LOOK FOR THE 🐧

THE PENGUIN LIVES AND LETTERS SERIES

A series of diaries and letters, journals and memoirs

William Allingham: A Diary, 1824–1889 Introduced by John Julius Norwich
Arnold Bennett: The Journals Edited by Frank Swinnerton
Lord Byron: Selected Letters and Journals Edited by Peter Gunn
The Daughters of Karl Marx: Family Correspondence 1866–98 With a Commentary and Notes by Olga Meier
Earthly Paradise Colette
The Letters of Rachel Henning Edited by David Adams with a Foreword and Drawings by Norman Lindsay
Lord Hervey's Memoirs Edited by Romney Sedgwick
Julia: A Portrait of Julia Strachey By Herself and Frances Partridge
Memoirs of the Forties By Julian Maclaren-Ross, with a new Introduction by Alan Ross
Harold Nicolson: Diaries and Letters: 1930–64 Edited and Condensed by Stanley Olson
The Pastons: The Letter of a Family in the Wars of the Roses Edited by Richard Barber
Queen Victoria in her Letters and Journals A Selection by Christopher Hibbert
The Quest for Corvo: An Experiment in Biography By A. J. A. Symons
Saint-Simon at Versailles Selected and Translated from the Memoirs of M. le Duc de Saint-Simon by Lucy Norton
Osbert Sitwell: Left Hand, Right Hand! Abridged and Introduced by Patrick Taylor-Martin
Evelyn Waugh: Diaries Edited by Michael Davie

FOR THE BEST IN PAPERBACKS, LOOK FOR THE

A CHOICE OF PENGUINS

A Fortunate Grandchild 'Miss Read'

Grandma Read in Lewisham and Grandma Shafe in Walton on the Naze were totally different in appearance and outlook, but united in their affection for their grand-daughter – who grew up to become the much-loved and popular novelist.

The Ultimate Trivia Quiz Game Book Maureen and Alan Hiron

If you are immersed in trivia, addicted to quiz games, endlessly nosey, then this is the book for you: over 10,000 pieces of utterly dispensable information!

The Diary of Virginia Woolf
Five volumes, edited by Quentin Bell and Anne Olivier Bell

'As an account of the intellectual and cultural life of our century, Virginia Woolf's diaries are invaluable; as the record of one bruised and unquiet mind, they are unique' – Peter Ackroyd in the *Sunday Times*

Voices of the Old Sea Norman Lewis

'I will wager that *Voices of the Old Sea* will be a classic in the literature about Spain' – *Mail on Sunday*. 'Limpidly and lovingly Norman Lewis has caught the helpless, unwitting, often foolish, but always hopeful village in its dying summers, and saved the tragedy with sublime comedy' – *Observer*

The First World War A. J. P. Taylor

In this superb illustrated history, A. J. P. Taylor 'manages to say almost everything that is important for an understanding and, indeed, intellectual digestion of that vast event . . . A special text . . . a remarkable collection of photographs' – *Observer*

Ninety-Two Days Evelyn Waugh

With characteristic honesty, Evelyn Waugh here debunks the romantic notions attached to rough travelling: his journey in Guiana and Brazil is difficult, dangerous and extremely uncomfortable, and his account of it is witty and unquestionably compelling.

FOR THE BEST IN PAPERBACKS, LOOK FOR THE 🐧

A CHOICE OF PENGUINS

The Big Red Train Ride   Eric Newby

From Moscow to the Pacific on the Trans-Siberian Railway is an eight-day journey of nearly six thousand miles through seven time zones. In 1977 Eric Newby set out with his wife, an official guide and a photographer on this journey. 'The best kind of travel book' – Paul Theroux

Star Wars   Edited by E. P. Thompson

With contributions from Rip Bulkeley, John Pike, Ben Thompson and E. P. Thompson, and with a Foreward by Dorothy Hodgkin, OM, this is a major book which assesses all the arguments for Star Wars and proceeds to make a powerful – indeed unanswerable – case against it.

Selected Letters of Malcolm Lowry
Edited by Harvey Breit and Margerie Bonner Lowry

Lowry emerges from these letters not only as an extremely interesting man, but also a lovable one' – Philip Toynbee

PENGUIN CLASSICS OF WORLD ART

Each volume presents the complete paintings of the artist and includes: an introduction by a distinguished art historian, critical comments on the painter from his own time to the present day, 64 pages of full-colour plates, a chronological survey of his life and work, a basic bibliography, a fully illustrated and annotated *catalogue raisonné*.

Titles already published or in preparation

Botticelli, Bruegel, Canaletto, Caravaggio, Cézanne, Dürer, Giorgione, Giotto, Leonardo da Vinci, Manet, Mantegna, Michelangelo, Picasso, Piero della Francesca, Raphael, Rembrandt, Toulouse-Lautrec, van Eyck, Vermeer, Watteau

FOR THE BEST IN PAPERBACKS, LOOK FOR THE

A CHOICE OF PENGUINS AND PELICANS

Adieux Simone de Beauvoir

This 'farewell to Sartre' by his life-long companion is a 'true labour of love' (the *Listener*) and 'an extraordinary achievement' (*New Statesman*).

British Society 1914–45 John Stevenson

A major contribution to the Pelican Social History of Britain, which 'will undoubtedly be the standard work for students of modern Britain for many years to come' – *The Times Educational Supplement*

The Pelican History of Greek Literature Peter Levi

A remarkable survey covering all the major writers from Homer to Plutarch, with brilliant translations by the author, one of the leading poets of today.

Art and Literature Sigmund Freud

Volume 14 of the Pelican Freud Library contains Freud's major essays on Leonardo, Michelangelo and Dostoevsky, plus shorter pieces on Shakespeare, the nature of creativity and much more.

A History of the Crusades Sir Steven Runciman

This three-volume history of the events which transferred world power to Western Europe – and founded Modern History – has been universally acclaimed as a masterpiece.

A Night to Remember Walter Lord

The classic account of the sinking of the *Titanic*. 'A stunning book, incomparably the best on its subject and one of the most exciting books of this or any year' – *The New York Times*

FOR THE BEST IN PAPERBACKS, LOOK FOR THE

A CHOICE OF PENGUINS AND PELICANS

The Informed Heart   Bruno Bettelheim

Bettelheim draws on his experience in concentration camps to illuminate the dangers inherent in all mass societies in this profound and moving masterpiece.

God and the New Physics   Paul Davies

Can science, now come of age, offer a surer path to God than religion? This 'very interesting' (*New Scientist*) book suggests it can.

Modernism   Malcolm Bradbury and James McFarlane (eds.)

A brilliant collection of essays dealing with all aspects of literature and culture for the period 1890–1930 – from Apollinaire and Brecht to Yeats and Zola.

Rise to Globalism   Stephen E. Ambrose

A clear, up-to-date and well-researched history of American foreign policy since 1938, Volume 8 of the Pelican History of the United States.

The Waning of the Middle Ages   Johan Huizinga

A magnificent study of life, thought and art in 14th and 15th century France and the Netherlands, long established as a classic.

The Penguin Dictionary of Psychology   Arthur S. Reber

Over 17,000 terms from psychology, psychiatry and related fields are given clear, concise and modern definitions.

FOR THE BEST IN PAPERBACKS, LOOK FOR THE

A CHOICE OF PENGUINS AND PELICANS

The Literature of the United States   Marcus Cunliffe

The fourth edition of a masterly one-volume survey, described by D. W. Brogan in the *Guardian* as 'a very good book indeed'.

The Sceptical Feminist   Janet Radcliffe Richards

A rigorously argued but sympathetic consideration of feminist claims. 'A triumph' – *Sunday Times*

The Enlightenment   Norman Hampson

A classic survey of the age of Diderot and Voltaire, Goethe and Hume, which forms part of the Pelican History of European Thought.

Defoe to the Victorians   David Skilton

A 'Learned and stimulating' (*The Times Educational Supplement*) survey of two centuries of the English novel.

Reformation to Industrial Revolution   Christopher Hill

This 'formidable little book' (Peter Laslett in the *Guardian*) by one of our leading historians is Volume 2 of the Pelican Economic History of Britain.

The New Pelican Guide to English Literature   Boris Ford (ed.)
Volume 8: The Present

This book brings a major series up to date with important essays on Ted Hughes and Nadine Gordimer, Philip Larkin and V. S. Naipaul, and all the other leading writers of today.

FOR THE BEST IN PAPERBACKS, LOOK FOR THE

PENGUIN BESTSELLERS

Dreams of Other Days Elaine Crowley

'A magnificent and unforgettable story of love, rebellion and death. 'You will never forget Katy and the people of her place . . . a haunting story' – Maeve Binchy, author of *Light a Penny Candle*

Trade Wind M. M. Kaye

The year is 1859 and Hero Hollis, beautiful and headstrong niece of the American consul, arrives in Zanzibar. It is an earthly paradise fragrant with spices and frangipani; it is also the last and greatest outpost of the Slave Trade . . .

The Far Pavilions M. M. Kaye

The famous story of love and war in nineteenth-century India – now a sumptuous screen production. 'A *Gone With the Wind* of the North-West Frontier' – *The Times*. 'A grand, romantic adventure story' – Paul Scott

The Mission Robert Bolt

History, adventure and romance combine in the most exciting way imaginable in this compulsive new novel – now a major motion picture.

Riches and Honour Tom Hyman

The explosive saga of a dynasty founded on a terrible secret. A thriller of the first order, *Riches and Honour* captures the imagination with its brutally chilling and tantalizing plot.

The World, the Flesh and the Devil Reay Tannahill

'A bewitching blend of history and passion. A MUST' – *Daily Mail*. A superb novel in a great tradition. 'Excellent' – *The Times*

FOR THE BEST IN PAPERBACKS, LOOK FOR THE

KING PENGUIN

Bedbugs   Clive Sinclair

'Wildly erotic and weirdly plotted, the subconscious erupting violently into everyday life . . . It is not for the squeamish or the lazy. His stories work you hard; tease and torment and shock you' – *Financial Times*

The Awakening of George Darroch   Robin Jenkins

An eloquent and powerful story of personal and political upheaval, the one inextricably linked with the other, written by one of Scotland's finest novelists.

In Custody   Anita Desai

Deven, a lecturer in a small town in Northern India, is resigned to a life of mediocrity and empty dreams. When asked to interview the greatest poet of Delhi, Deven discovers a new kind of dignity, both for himself and his dreams.

Collected Poems   Geoffrey Hill

'Among our finest poets, Geoffrey Hill is at present the most European – in his Latinity, in his dramatization of the Christian condition, in his political intensity . . . The commanding note is unmistakable' – George Steiner in the *Sunday Times*

Parallel Lives   Phyllis Rose

In this study of five famous Victorian marriages, including that of John Ruskin and Effie Gray, Phyllis Rose probes our inherited myths and assumptions to make us look again at what we expect from our marriages.

Lamb   Bernard MacLaverty

In the Borstal run by Brother Benedict, boys are taught a little of God and a lot of fear. Michael Lamb, one of the brothers, runs away and takes a small boy with him. As the outside world closes in around them, Michael is forced to an uncompromising solution.